THE *devotion* SERIES

DISTORTED DEVOTION
UNDYING DEVOTION
BELOVED DEVOTION

PERSEPHONE AUTUMN

BETWEEN WORDS PUBLISHING LLC

BOOKS BY PERSEPHONE AUTUMN

<u>Lake Lavender Series</u>

Depths Awakened

One Night Forsaken

Every Thought Taken

<u>Devotion Series</u>

Distorted Devotion

Undying Devotion

Beloved Devotion

Darkest Devotion

Sweetest Devotion

<u>Bay Area Duet Series</u>

<u>Click Duet</u>

Through the Lens

Time Exposure

<u>Inked Duet</u>

Fine Line

Love Buzz

<u>Insomniac Duet</u>

Restless Night

A Love So Bright

<u>Artist Duet</u>

Blank Canvas

Abstract Passion

<u>Novellas</u>

Reese

Penny

<u>Stone Bay Series</u>

Broken Sky—Prequel

Shattered Sun

Fractured Night

<u>Standalone Romance Novels</u>

Sweet Tooth

Transcendental

<u>Poetry Collections</u>

Ink Veins

Broken Metronome

Slipping From Existence

Poisonous Heart

Beneath Wildflowers

PUBLISHED UNDER P. AUTUMN

<u>Standalone Non-Romance Novels</u>

By Dawn

PERSEPHONE AUTUMN

BETWEEN WORDS PUBLISHING LLC

Distorted Devotion

Copyright © 2019 by Persephone Autumn

www.persephoneautumn.com

All rights reserved.

No part of this book may be reproduced in any form or by any electronic or mechanical means, including photocopying, information storage and retrieval systems, without written permission from the author except for the use of brief quotations in a book review.

This book is a work of fiction. Names, characters, establishments, organizations, and incidents are either products of the author's imagination or are used fictitiously to give a sense of authenticity. Any resemblance to actual events, places, or persons, living or dead, is entirely coincidental.

If you're reading this book and did not purchase it, or it was not purchased for your use only, then it was pirated illegally. Please purchase a copy of your own and respect the hard work of this author.

ISBN: 978-1-951477-02-8 (Ebook)

ISBN: 978-1-951477-03-5 (Paperback)

Editor: Ellie McLove | My Brother's Editor

Proofreader: Rosa Sharon | My Brother's Editor

Cover Design: Persephone Autumn | Between Words Publishing LLC

For every woman who looks over her shoulder.
Who has had that gut feeling someone is watching her.
Following her.
You are not alone.

ONE

"Thank you for your time, Ms. Jacobson. If you'll bear with me a few more minutes, I need to get a few more pieces of information from you."

My fingertips typed like a madwoman on my keyboard. On a roll, I gathered information from my tenth sale this month. Out of nowhere, a pen crashed into my desk, hurtled from outside my seven-by-seven cubicle.

Continuing my task, I ignored the projectile for the time being. "All right, Ms. Jacobson. I have all the information I need from you today. In the next week, you'll be receiving a packet of paperwork with further details in the mail. It will contain instructions on what you need to do to finish the process. Do you have any more questions for me today?"

She stammered as uncertainty rang in her answer.

"If you think of anything else, please don't hesitate to call back and ask for Sarah Bradley. I'm happy to answer any questions that may arise."

Ms. Jacobson thanked me, her tone more chipper.

"It's been my pleasure, Ms. Jacobson. If there's nothing else I can assist you with today, I will let you enjoy the rest of this beautiful day. Thank you for choosing Hammond Life Insurance to protect your future, have a wonderful day."

Pressing the button on my earpiece, I disconnected the call. I finished typing a few last things before saving the new client profile. A rush soared beneath my ribcage as pride infiltrated in my veins. Two weeks into the quarter and I was on fire. This was cause for celebration.

I searched for the projectile pen which fell to the floor and rolled under my desk. A small slip of paper was taped to the barrel. As I peeled the tiny note from the pen missile, I saw a familiar scribble.

Lucky bitch! You're buying drinks tonight.

I scribbled back my response, more than happy to pay for a round or two of drinks tonight. Securing the note back onto the pen, I rose from my chair—my eyes peeking over the partition walls around me—and launched it back to the desk it originated from.

"Ow! At least I didn't hit you."

I stepped out from the confines of my second home. Not as if I lived at work, but I put in my fair share of time. Like so many others, I embellished the semi-fabric cubicle walls with décor. Various pieces of bohemian art made the space more pleasant to stare at five days a week.

I eased through the sea of cubicles. In a handful of strides, I reached the plot of desk space given to one of my favorite people—Christy. Her workspace resembled the teeny-bopper magazines from our younger years—the walls splattered with vivid colors and celebrities she crushed on.

Her back to me when I rounded the corner, I stood quietly as her fingers typed with vigor. Lost in a trance with whatever task she had been assigned, Christy was clueless that I lingered just inches from her. I reached out and touched her shoulder. Her body jumped at the contact as a soft squeal erupted from her throat.

"Sorry, sorry, sorry. I didn't mean to scare you, chicky." I resisted laughing for… three, two, one.

Face shrouded in faux disbelief, Christy spun around with her fists on her hips. "And I'm supposed to take your word on that? Right after you hurled a pen at my head."

"If my memory serves correct, you fired the first shot. So…"

"True. But I didn't hit you. I only wanted it to land on your desk," Christy muttered.

"Sorry, I didn't mean for it to hit you. I took no aim. Forgive me?" My most pathetic puppy dog eyes and pouty lips groveled for forgiveness.

She turned back to her monitor and tapped the keys. "I forgive you."

The good friend I am, I allowed her a moment to finish whatever I disrupted. While she typed, I checked my watch. The digital face lit and displayed twelve-eleven.

"Hey, you want to grab lunch when you wrap up?" I asked.

Her fingers paused a split-second. "Yeah. Give me five minutes. I'll come get you when I'm done."

"Cool. See you in a few."

Falling in line with the masses, we stood at the deli counter and waited to order lunch. Carol's Deli took up half of the first floor and was always crowded.

"Number sixty-seven!" a petite woman hollered over the crowd, her eyes scanning the sea of faces. Her dark locks in a messy bun and masked by a cotton net.

"That's me!" I wiggled between a few people and stepped up to the counter.

"What can I get for ya, doll?" She poised her pen on the green order pad and smiled. I rattled off mine and Christy's orders. Tossing my call number into a wicker basket, I waited as she finished scribbling our order down. She tore the slip from the stack and read the order back to me. "Anything else for ya, hun?"

"Nope, that's it."

She reached under the counter and grabbed a numbered, plastic tent. As she jotted the number on the order slip, she handed me the table tent. "Have a seat, darlin'. Someone will bring your food out soon."

"Thanks."

Sifting my way through the throng of people, I stepped

out of the hovering lunch crowd and found Christy. She snagged us a table by the windows—best table in the place.

"Food's ordered. Shouldn't be too long," I said as I slid into the chair across from Christy.

"Cool, thanks."

"So, I read your little note. Since I got another sale today, you think I should buy drinks tonight, huh?"

"Um, yeah. You're knocking it out of the park up there, chica. I bet you already exceeded your quota for the month. What was today? Eight or nine?"

My cheeks heat under her estimation. "Ten," I muttered.

"*Seriously?* How the hell do you find these people? Compared to you, I'm a slacker. I have four sales. Four. Soon, you'll set the bar and I'll be left in the wastelands." Her smirk a mix of jealousy and sarcasm.

"Shut your mouth. You're talking nonsense. My last three sales have all been referrals from other clients. Just doing things like usual." Christy loved harassing me, just for the hell of it.

I sat nowhere near the top of the sales list. That throne belonged to Agnes. Agnes started here before electricity was invented. Okay, slight exaggeration. In actuality, she started working for Hammond Life two years before I was born. Her twenty-eight-year tenure provided her top seniority amongst the worker bees.

If Christy thought highly of my ten sales, she would flip out when she learned Agnes's numbers. Last I heard, Agnes had already sealed the deal on twenty-two new clients. My shorter tenure with Hammond of two-and-half years was laughable—not even a tenth of Agnes' time—but I had a tiny following. Agnes had a binder full of contacts. I had four sheets.

She was an absolute legend among us.

"Well, everyone loves you. They're flocking to you in herds," Christy stated.

"Herds? That's extreme. It takes over ten to make a herd. Right?" This whole conversation is laughable. There were better things to talk about off the clock. This was our time, and I was done with the shop talk. "Enough about work and numbers. What d'ya want to do tonight? Drinks, dinner, a movie? Your call. I'll buy, seeing as I'm some master sales guru now."

"Not sure. I talked with Rick last night. He's headed out with the guys tonight, so I'm open. Maybe hang at my place? Have you talked to Liz today?"

Liz wasn't just our bestie, she also worked at Hammond. We'd all started at different times, but fell into friendship easily. Funny enough, no one ever pegged us as friends—a free-spirited hippie child, an over bubbly, never-shuts-the-hell-up girl, and a punk loving goth. But our friendship bonded us like sisters.

"Haven't seen her. She must be in her fortress, hunting for prey."

We all made cracks about cubicle life. Jokes made work more tolerable. As did decorating. No two cubicles were the same. On any given day, you'd walk past Star Wars, Star Trek (and whatever you do, don't confuse the two or you'll never hear the end of it), Harry Potter, comic book paraphernalia, holiday decor, and family photos.

Christy giggled and heads turned. Her laugh a sweet, whimsical sound. "When we're done, let's stop by her desk."

"Sounds good. I vote we stay in. We can hang at your place. Watch a movie, eat takeout, drink a little. Whatcha think?"

"Perfect. I'm sure Liz will join. Want me to grab the provisions?" Christy tucked an escaped russet curl behind her ear under her thick, black-framed glasses.

"I'll grab food. You guys figure out drinks. We can sort it out with her."

A moment later, our lunch was delivered, and all conversation went out the window. My stomach grumbled loud enough for the next table to hear. As soon as the plate hit the table, I shoved a forkful in my mouth.

"Is there anything else I can get you ladies?" I shook my head, spewing a muffled *no thanks*.

He chuckled. "Let us know if you need anything else." As fast as he appeared, he vanished.

"You're a nut! Like a damn two-year-old, talking with your mouth full." Christy's musical giggle disrupted the chitchat near us.

"You know you love me. Just shut up and eat your sandwich."

I stepped inside Christy's apartment and my two favorite people greeted me.

Christy, in all her boisterous glory, bounded toward me. "Hey, bitch!" Wrapping her arms around me, she squeezed me tight like a stress ball. Then let go and disappeared around the corner. "You bring the food?" she hollered.

I trailed behind her as she walked to the kitchen. Christy and Rick's apartment was one of a few things I envied. They lucked out and got it for a steal. It had been remodeled and had the modern appeal everyone sought out. But her kitchen… it made me want to learn how to bake. Complete apartment jealousy.

Two plastic bags dangled in my hands. The scent of onions and garlic and grease wafted in the air as I set the Chinese food on the kitchen island. "Veggie Lo Mein, tofu and string beans, Kung Pao chicken, shrimp egg foo young, veggie egg rolls, tons of rice, crunchy noodles, and fortune cookies."

"It's as if you know the way to my heart." Liz's raspy tone rang out as she walked in from the living room. Right hand over her heart, she faux-swooned.

"Hey girl! Glad you made it," I said. I hugged her tight as if we hadn't seen each other in years.

"Although my body disagrees, I can't wait to eat everything. Just have to add a few extra miles to my run tomorrow."

"Liz, no one will know you ate a crap ton of greasy, delicious, carb-loaded Chinese food. There's nothing to worry about." Drawing an X over my heart, I continued. "Your secret's safe with me."

Her hazels narrowed and her slender lips scrunched. "I'm not journaling what I eat. Just don't eat much heavy stuff anymore. My body will punish me tomorrow, but it's totally worth it."

"Awesome. Christy, what are we watching?" She messed with the remote while I grabbed plates and utensils.

"I'll find it in a minute. Some new comedy on Netflix I added to the playlist. Got it... *When We First Met.*"

She dropped the remote on the table and came back to the kitchen, grabbing a plate and piling it high. A minute later, we headed out to the living room and sat sukh asana on cushy pillows around the table on the floor.

Christy brought a few beers to the table. I raised my bottle in the air and they mimicked. "Congrats for gaining ten new clients this month. And to us, reason unnecessary."

Our bottles clinked and we took a long pull from the brown bottlenecks. I didn't need a reason to hang out with Liz and Christy. Us spending time together was the same as breathing—both were essential. Whether it be Friday or Monday, anytime with Liz and Christy was perfect. Which reminds me of Monday...

"This just crossed my mind... you guys ready for the meeting on Monday?"

"Nope. We're not doing that now." Christy barked at me like a mother hen. Her eyes narrowed as she pointed a mani-cured finger at me.

"What?"

"Talking about work. The only exception was bringing up your sales. But it ends there."

"Yes, Mom." I stuck out my tongue, cocked a brow, and crossed my eyes.

My reward... A pillow to the face.

TWO

As with every other weekend in the history of mankind, this one ended too soon.

My alarm screamed an incessant buzz-wail combo and startled me from a deep sleep. What I wouldn't give for a little more sleep. But, like a good girl, I smacked the button and rolled out of bed. Sleeping another hour would have been easy, but a little voice whispered in my ear and reminded me to get off my ass and go to the gym.

Slower than typical, I slipped on my workout gear in the dark. I grabbed my gym bag after securing my hair, foregoing any extensive grooming until after. As I walked out of my apartment, I dropped my keys in my bag and walked to the gym in the middle of my gated apartment complex.

I loved having an all-inclusive gym—one of several reasons I lived here. The rent was reasonable considering the complex sat on the outskirts of Savannah. The gym—loaded with more equipment than I would ever use—three pools, and several other great amenities sold me. The gated community the best perk. Safety was immeasurable, and I never had a worry here.

The gym's bright lights glowed in the morning darkness. It'd be another hour until the sun rose. Waking this early was worth it to miss everyone else in the complex. A shiver rippled through me as I tugged the metal door handle to the gym. A rush of warm air enveloped me and defrosted some of the early morning January air.

Moving past several muscle building contraptions, I headed for the row of treadmills, ellipticals, stationary bikes, and rowing machines. They formed a line, a break between them when it changed from one type to the next. A row of benches lined up a few feet behind them, butting against half-walled/half-windowed rooms. The rooms for yoga, Pilates, or other non-equipment classes.

After I set my bag on the bench behind the treadmill, I grabbed my towel, phone, and earbuds. My bag only held a few things—a change of clothes, water, keys, and an additional towel. Since I brought nothing I deemed important, I didn't worry about leaving it unattended. Plus, early hours in the gym equaled fewer bodies.

I stepped up and straddled the treadmill belt. After I pressed a few buttons, I started my warmup. Soon it would progress into a twenty-five-minute run. Running races for medals wasn't my thing, I only want to stay healthy.

Popping my earbuds in place, I scanned my music and hit play. I picked an upbeat playlist since I needed to wake up and motivate. Today would be busy. Besides the normal hustle and bustle, we had our quarterly staff meeting. Numbers and graphs and goals galore. If I didn't wake up now, I would fall asleep once the power point started.

"You ready?" Christy stood across from my desk, pen and paper in hand. She tapped the pen like an impatient child. Christy was always happy-go-lucky, except when it came to work and meetings. Work smudged out her light.

"We do this every quarter. Not like anything spectacular will happen." I rose from my chair and grabbed a pen and paper.

"The day we're not prepared, a huge change will be announced. Mark my words." She pointed her pen at me and puckered her lips, nodding like a lunatic. What she took seriously made me laugh.

As we walked down cubicle row, I worked to lighten her mood. At the office, Christy was more fidgety and circumspect. The second she saw the conference room, Christy sucked in a deep breath. Today's meeting was for all the associates on our floor—all twenty-seven of us—plus our supervisors. Every quarter we sat in the same room, around the same round wooden tables, and picked at the sugar-laden candy in the center. Every meeting also involved a group exercise.

Liz waved to us from the chairs she secured for us. Bob from human resources and my direct supervisor, Marco, stood at the head of the room. Smiling, I waved at them as we walked over to Liz.

"Thanks for snagging us the good seats," I said.

"Hey, if we have to sit here for the next three plus hours, I'd rather not crane my neck or spin around every time something happens."

"Right there with ya," Christy added.

Like synchronized swimmers, we rolled our chairs out and sat on the faux leather. We had another ten minutes before the meeting started, meaning most of the staff wouldn't show up for another nine.

Not like I am a poster child for proper work etiquette, but punctuality speaks volumes. Arriving early gave hope to the meeting ending sooner. But no one cared.

More people trickled in—Sandy, Roger, Betty, and a few others I hadn't met. Most of my coworkers friendly, I'd chatted them up a time or two. In meetings or downstairs in Carol's Deli. Mom taught me to be polite to new people and make them feel welcome. We all remembered what the first day of school was like… *Does my hair look okay? What about my clothes? Will people like me? Do I know anyone here?* Mom reminded me everyone thought the same things and to not let such things impede making new friends.

The conference room grew louder as more people filed in and sat down, sparking conversations. I distracted myself and doodled while Christy and Liz chatted about some new hair-care product. Beauty products weren't my cup of tea.

The garden of flowers on the top blue line of my perforated notepad grew—daisies and roses amongst a bed of lush grass—when a voice interrupted my artwork.

"Good morning, Sarah."

I peeked up from my doodle to find one of my coworkers standing too close to me. The buttons on his pale, blue dress shirt ready to burst open at his belly. "Good morning, Alan. How are you?"

"I'm good, thanks. How are you? You look nice today."

I tilted my head down, glanced at my chest, and tugged on the cream-colored fabric of my crocheted, bohemian top. "Thank you."

"Are you ready for hours of sleep-inducing speech? I didn't get enough sleep last night, so thank goodness we have this meeting today." He meant it as a joke. I knew this only because of the harsh chuckle—similar to someone who'd smoked for fifty years—exiting his throat.

To make light of his humor, I said, "Meetings... they're a necessary evil."

His laughter rang louder with exaggerated excitement. Everyone nearby noticed—a few brows furrowed. What I said wasn't laugh-worthy, but to each their own.

Something tapped my hand, and I twisted to face Liz, the end of her pen hovered over my hand. Before I asked what was up, she pointed to the front of the room. Bob ready to start the meeting.

The conference room door shut, the heads of the meeting poised and ready as everyone wrapped up their conversations. As the voices faded into silence, I swore I heard *always getting in the way* resound from the table to my right. The table where Alan sat.

"All right folks, quiet down. It's almost over and then you can head to lunch." The stir of restless voices quieted once more and allowed Marco to finish. "This year's shaping up well so far, and we're only two weeks in. For those of you who are on pace to meet your quarterly goals, I thank you. Keep up the good work."

A hand landed on my shoulder and patted, and I jumped.

"Good job, Sarah," Alan whispered too close to my ear. An uncomfortable tremor rippled through my body and my shoulders shook. With every ounce of courtesy I could muster, I responded with a thumbs up and kept my face turned away from his.

Marco's voice boomed over the slight uptick in the chitchat. "Give me one more minute, people." The room quieted one last time, allowing Marco his closing statement. "Thank you. For those below par, I don't doubt you'll meet your goals. Reach out to your previous contacts and ask for referrals. Talk to friends, family, and neighbors. There's bound to be someone. Thank you for your time this morning. Don't forget our annual luncheon is next month. Bob will get more information to you soon. Keep up the great work and let's blow this quarter out of the water! Meeting adjourned."

Like the running of the bulls, everyone bolted from their chairs and corralled out the door, eager to leave the conference room. Christy, Liz, and I hung back and waited for everyone to leave.

I thought the room had emptied. The room quiet except for our chatting about where to grab lunch, I startled when a chair rolled behind me and bumped my chair. That same awkwardness from earlier rested in my belly.

"Where you ladies going to lunch? I can't decide myself." Alan's voice next to my ear.

Christy glimpsed my face—unease rose from the pit of my stomach and highlighted my features—and answered for all of us. "We haven't decided yet. Too many options nearby."

Words escaped me as I tried to translate my nervousness. It was peculiar. Alan sat at his table, alone, for the last five minutes. I'd talked with him several times since I worked for Hammond Life and never once did I get a weird vibe from him. Today, though… Today felt different. Intrusive.

Was he eavesdropping? Our chitchat lacked substance, but spying made my stomach churn. My ass was sore from sitting so long, but I was determined to stay seated. The padded chair creaked beneath me as I redistributed my weight and waited for Alan to leave. The energy in the room was stagnant and eerie.

When he rose to stand, his body invaded my personal

space as his voice thundered above me. "Well, I'm headed down to the deli. Hope to see you there."

"Cool. Enjoy your lunch, Alan." Christy's sing-song voice dismissed him.

A clock on the wall ticked three deafening beats before he pivoted away and walked out the door. Outside the room, I watched as he eyed me between the blinds a moment. Three breaths later, he spun around and headed down the corridor. I peered at Christy and Liz, my unease fading to the background. The discomfort from a moment ago replaced with mass confusion.

"What the hell was that?" Liz asked.

"Wish I knew. The whole situation was awkward. And you know it takes a lot to get me frazzled." The last part beyond true. My open and easy-going demeanor difficult to dislodge. Many of my friendships were forged due to my loving nature.

"We damn sure *won't* be going to Carol's today," Christy said, adamant.

"I am one hundred percent okay with that." Their agreement flooded me with relief and washed away any residual unease. "That being said, where should we go?"

The lunch crowd at the old bank-turned-restaurant was a madhouse today. Meeting days allowed us to venture farther for lunch. Since we had to endure hours of monotony, the company allotted us an extended lunchtime.

The waitress walked away with our orders. Miles of sunshine illuminated our table from the wall of windows. For a restaurant, the place wasn't huge, but had great personality and awesome food.

"So, what's up with Alan today? Is it me? It all seemed a little weird," Christy stated.

"He was trying to spark conversation, I guess. Maybe he doesn't have friends in the office. Who knows," Liz said, shrugging.

"You're so nice, Liz. The whole thing was still weird. Did you guys see him touch my shoulder when Marco talked about people being on track?" I wasn't sure of their focus when the speech was delivered.

"*Um, no. Really?*" Christy asked. Aversion tugged her brow and scrunched her nose.

"Yep. Awkward moment number one. When he first walked in and talked to me, it wasn't strange. More like water cooler talk. I was just being polite. But after... he wouldn't leave." This discomfort was odd. My outgoing nature a part of me as much as my hair or eyes or limbs. My extroverted mother ingrained it in me since birth.

"I read it all over your face. That's why I played coy when he asked about lunch," Christy said.

"And for that, you're my hero." I raised my hands above my head and lowered them, bowing to her.

"Whoa, whoa, whoa. Let's not go giving Christy a big head now. Put that shit away." Liz's hands swatted mine and stopped my display of worship to our friend.

"Don't be jealous, bitch." Christy giggled. "I did us all a favor. If Sarah wants to worship me, we should allow her to do so." Her eyebrow cocked as she stuck her tongue out at Liz.

"Whatever. On to something more fun. Let's talk about my birthday party. It's a couple weeks out. Thoughts on who to invite?" Liz fidgeted like a kid high on sugar.

My circle of friends was small and I prayed Liz didn't ask me to invite people. "I'll help decide food and drinks. You guys handle the invite list."

"Sounds like a plan," Liz said, pleased one task was divvied. She was giddy we were one step closer to her big day.

"I'll talk to some people and get more names added to the invite list. How many you thinking?" Christy grabbed her phone and typed on a blank note screen.

"Only twenty-five or thirty. I don't want to piss off the neighbors. Hey..." Liz pointed at Christy. "Invite a couple of my neighbors, too. That way we're not only being nice, but we're also letting them know I'm throwing a party."

"Good idea," Christy said, not stealing a moment to peek up from her phone.

Seconds later, our conversation ended when our server

arrived with our food. We lined up our plates like a buffet. Chopsticks in hand, onlookers probably thought we were fighting to the death. But this was our normal, and I loved it. I loved how we could be ourselves around each other.

But little did I know, someone else sat nearby. Someone who would turn my world upside down.

THREE

THE REST of the work week flew by, nothing notable occurring. I got another sale under my belt, by chance, and listened to Christy's tirade of jealousy.

When we weren't selling, we had a mountain of other tasks. Email correspondence the most boring of them all. Most of them follow-ups—*thank you for choosing Hammond Life* or *I haven't heard from you in a while, how's your family doing?* or *I'm sorry for your loss*. The latter being the worst.

Reports always needed filling out. Spreadsheet after spreadsheet. Endless boxes of numbers—sales, sales, sales. How many emails have I sent? Any responses? What marketing had I done? Am I on target? Blah, blah, blah. Box after box. So many numbers they all blurred together. If I spent less time on reports, I'd have higher sales.

"Ugh," I groaned as one last page of reports popped up.

I loved marketing and connected with so many people since working here. My top priority was to not be "the sales-girl on the phone". One of my favorite parts of my job was the conversations and learning about my client's lives. What brought them happiness.

Meeting new people was my bread and butter. As a child, my mother would always tell me I was too curious for my own good—often talking to strangers and making friends. As with any personality trait, extroversion is both a positive and a negative. Positive because it is how I meet so many great people—Christy and Liz included. Negative because not everyone you meet has the best of intentions.

It had been years since I had sensed something *off* about someone. This week rekindled that unfamiliar discomfort. But I did everything in my power to cast it aside. Dwelling solved nothing.

One afternoon shortly after I started working at Hammond, I was in the break room, I sat and read during lunch when Alan walked in and sat across from me with his lunch. I continued reading my book, engrossed in the words on the pages in front of me.

"Hey," he'd said. "You're the new girl Sarah, right?"

Although I wanted to devour the words in my paperback, I didn't want to seem rude, being one of the new girls on the block. So, I'd put my book down and sparked a conversation with him.

He'd seemed peculiar but harmless during our talks, and had a sweet demeanor. So, when he talked with me before Monday's meeting, I thought nothing of it. It was the mumbling comment I'd heard, followed by the hand on my shoulder, and the inquisition about lunch after apparently eavesdropping that didn't sit well with me. Several small things tangled my perception and caused me to second guess everything. The whole situation was abnormal.

But I could leave it at work. Except for Christy and Liz—and a couple other coworkers—I was a master at separating my work life from my home life. And I was adamant about keeping it that way.

One of the best parts about the weekends was not hearing the annoying buzz of the alarm clock. I woke early, but not hearing that god-forsaken noise made the entire day better.

Dragging my hair through the last loop of my hair tie, I startled when a knock broke the silence. Both hands on my ponytail, I tugged outward and tightened the band close to my scalp. Swiveling side to side, I took one last look in the bathroom mirror and fixed the sleeve of my snug sports top.

Two sets of pearly-whites greeted me when I opened the door. Their smiles brighter than the blinding sun.

"Morning, bitch. Ready to sweat your ass off?" Sometimes I wondered if Christy's father was a trucker. Or perhaps a sailor. Bitch rolled off her tongue like melted butter, no one seeming to care.

"Hey, sunshine. I need to grab my bag and I'll be ready. Either of you need water?" I asked before grabbing my bag from the couch.

"No, thanks," Liz and Christy replied in unison, followed by a fit of giggles from Christy. I swear, that girl thought everything was hilarious. She'd laugh at the most mundane things. And she was the friend who shared an obscene number of memes on social media.

"You guys practice that on your way here?" I asked through my own bout of laughter.

"Nope, we had more important topics to discuss. My party being top priority." Liz, a little girl getting her first pet; a sparkle in her eye and the broadest smile across her face.

"Cool. Well, let's chat about it more once we're in the gym." Stuffing my water in the bag, I slung it over my shoulder and headed for the door. "If we use the machines for about thirty minutes, we can catch the yoga class and use it as our cool down."

"Good with me," Liz said as her stride kept us all on our toes.

"Me too. I've skipped the last two." Christy's cheeks reddened.

"Awesome. Let's get the ball rolling. Treadmill or bikes?" My voice muffled as I pulled on the door to the gym, the familiar rush of warm air blew over us.

"Bikes," they said in unison. Again.

"You guys are too much for me today. And unlucky me, the day's just begun."

"Okay everyone. Now let's finish out today's session in shavasana. Listen to the soft sounds of the music and transition to focus on only your breath. Close your eyes. Center yourself. Feel your prana all around you." The subtle sounds of birds chirping next to a waterfall played in the background as our yoga class ended. "Great job, everyone. Until next time" —the instructor bowed at the waist, her hands in prayer position— "Namaste and enjoy your weekend."

"Namaste," the entire class repeated.

We sat on our yoga mats facing each other and waited for the other people in the class to leave. Some people bolted upright as soon as yoga ended. We always stayed a few minutes and enjoyed the solemn, peaceful moment after.

"So, ladies, what is on the agenda today?" Christy asked.

Swallowing back a mouthful of water, I said, "Well, I'd say showers are a must. Then we should finalize Liz's party. I have a few errands, but we should grab what we can for the party today."

Liz nodded. "Let's head home and shower and meet up after. My place?"

"Good with me," I said, grabbing my bag as we headed for the door.

"Me too, bitch." How Christy always used her favorite word, as often as possible, cracked me up. If I was ever on a game show and quizzed on the word she used most, I would win.

Weaving through the weights area, we headed for the exit. I threw my hoodie on and braced for the chilly morning air. Winter in Georgia wasn't as bad as some northern states—mostly because we weren't far from the Atlantic—but it was too cold to walk the hundred yards to my apartment in just a sports bra and leggings.

As we reached the door, a man entering held it open for us. Pulling up the tail end of our small conga line, I peeked up to thank him. I opened my mouth to say the words—two simple words—but froze, speechless. He looked past me and into the gym—meeting a buddy, or girlfriend, I'm sure. No way in hell a guy that handsome was single. The black cotton fabric of his hood masked half his profile. A hint of tanned skin and short, black stubble accented his jawline.

Trying to collect myself and not appear an idiot, I remembered how to speak. "Thank you. For holding the door."

Deep blue eyes swallowed me whole. My heartbeat skyrocketed as my breath disappeared. "You're welcome."

Before I spoke another word, he turned and walked off. Inside the gym he headed toward the weights and to meet whoever. Obviously someone more important than me. I had a sudden urge to lift weights.

"Sarah!" Christy shouted, her abrupt volume made me spin and jog to where she and Liz waited some fifty feet away. "Who's the hottie?"

I shook my head out of its foggy state and mumbled, "Wish I knew…" I really wish I knew.

Liz, Christy, and I sat on fluffy pillows around Liz's coffee table. Music blared in the background, but not loud enough to drown out conversation. Papers littered the table between us with various notes scribbled on them.

"So, I was thinking maybe we do finger foods." My ideas for the party food were basic. Keep it easy. Plenty of variety. Everyone stays happy.

Besides, munchies wouldn't be the focus of the night.

"Perfect. Anything in particular?" Liz asked.

"Wings, veggie trays, small deli sandwiches, chips and dips, a small cake. Simplistic with no assembly required. I'll get the wings from Tatiana's Pub. We can keep everything in the kitchen and let people grab it when they want. Do we have a head count yet?" Liz and I glance at Christy.

Christy opened an app on her phone and scrolled a moment. "I've reached out to all the usual suspects. As of now, thirty-two. Not including us. There's still plenty to hear from."

Liz may have said only thirty people, but I could see forty plus showing up and her not caring. Her parties are all about fun. The more people, the better.

"Awesome. I'll order food based on that. I'd rather run out than have leftovers for the trash," I said.

Liz nodded, her mind somewhere else. "What about alcohol? Christy, you want to make a run with me? We can grab a handful of bottles, some beer, and mixers. Split the bill?"

"Sure thing. When d'you want to go?" Christy asked as she continued to scroll through her phone. No doubt she had a spreadsheet or party planning app.

"Tonight? This weekend is the perfect opportunity to get as much done as possible. I don't want us fumbling for shit at the last minute."

"Tonight works for me. Maybe you and I go to the liquor store while Sarah gets the food sorted out and then we chill after." Christy's statement hung like a question, but was more of a request.

Every killer party Liz had thrown came with a lot of legwork. It was a process. But worth every minute.

"I'm game. I'll place orders for the trays then grab stuff from the store. Let's meet back here, order takeout, and binge watch a TV series."

"Yes." Both of them replying in unison. Again. And that was all it took for the three of us to fall into a fit of laughter. Without a doubt, we were three peas in a pod.

The rest of my weekend passed by as it always did. Gym. Laundry. Grocery shopping. A little cleaning here and there. Chilling on my couch with my current paperback. Most of the time, I went with the flow. Some things planned. But most not.

Weeknights and weekends weren't always this laid back, but having time to myself was invaluable. Next weekend, we'd be swamped with the before, during, and after party. As amazing as it'd be, we'd be overwhelmed leading up to it. So downtime now was essential.

Most weekends, we went out to a bar or nightclub and partied. It wasn't all booze and sex. Although there was plenty happening. But most of the time, it was just friends enjoying each other's company in the center of nightlife.

Rick, Christy's boyfriend of four years, was with us often. On occasion, he'd bring a couple of his buddies. There was never the sense of obligation to pair up, but we welcomed the protection against any unwanted attention.

Eric and John—Rick's friends—had drool-worthy bodies. Muscular frames, clean cut, enough charisma to keep you coming back for more. But they weren't *my* boyfriend material. After hanging out a few times, Eric asked me out and I declined. Guilt blanketed me for days, but honesty was more important. He was attractive and sweet and had a great personality. But he wasn't my type, and he'd become more of a brotherly figure rather than a love interest.

Weeks afterward, he shied away, unsure how to act near me. But things loosened up again. We'd chatted and hung out like siblings, and he'd protect me in an instant if someone bothered or pressured me. Eric was my big brother from another mother—and father—and our bond morphed into something I shared with no one else.

It had been a few weeks since we'd all hung out, but he'd be at Liz's party. He never missed her parties. Most people didn't. Anyone invited would be a fool to not show. When Liz threw a party, people talked about it for weeks after. Liz's parties morphed into a nightclub. Alcohol always flowed freely in plastic red cups. Every inch of the house would be packed. Sweaty bodies grinding against one another. Lips tasting while everyone got lost in the music. I loved every minute. Anyone who attended knew it would be a memorable night.

Grabbing my paperback, a glass of water, and my sunglasses, I stepped out onto my tiny back porch. Settling onto the plush chaise, I reached for the blanket at the foot. The temperature warmer than expected for early February, but I draped the thick throw over my legs and settled in for four or five chapters.

Absolute heaven. I lived minutes from the city, but couldn't hear it. Not even from the edge of my first-floor porch. I'd fallen asleep reading on this lounger several times. Everything about this place is perfect.

But perfection has its flaws. Even my homey slice of heaven.

FOUR

ALTHOUGH I HAD BEEN HERE hundreds of times, I was lost.

"Where's the collapsible table?" I hollered from the garage. Boxes of random stuff stacked in small mountains in every direction. Liz's garage is a live version of Tetris, the piece falling from the top, flipping around and fitting in the empty spaces.

"It's near the washing machine, behind the Christmas decorations. Do you see it?" Liz yelled back to me, her voice closer than expected, yet nowhere in sight.

I wiggled my body through the maze. The empty trail led to what was most important—the washer and dryer, water heater, electrical panel, and a few boxes she got into more often.

"I see it. But I have to move shit to get to it. You have way too much shit out here. Time for a hoarder intervention. If not a garage sale." What really had me curious was why Liz had so much boxed-up shit in the first place.

"Move whatever you need to. We'll discuss my overabundance another day. Do you need help? Last time I wedged it in nice and tight."

"That's what she said," I belted out and Liz laughed.

I grabbed the edge of the table and jostled it side-to-side until I loosened it from its holding cell. A moment later, the table slid out of its prison. I lugged it through the maze and into the house.

"Table acquired." I drew out the words and exaggerated my breath. It may have been a joke, but anyone who stepped foot in the garage got a workout.

Liz smirked at me and slapped my arm. "It's about time. I thought maybe you died in there and I would have to call somebody." She stuck her tongue out at me and zeroed in on the tip of her nose.

"Shut up. Besides, you'd have to call a search party to find me in there." I cocked my head and smiled goofily at her. "Anything else you need before I pick up food?"

"Christy? We missing anything else? Sarah's leaving in a minute."

Christy had been so quiet for the last fifteen minutes, I'd almost forgotten she was here. "Not that I can think of." Engrossed in the living room furniture layout, Christy moved couches and chairs and tables all over the place, making more room for the future crowd.

Some of the smaller pieces would be stowed in a bedroom. The more space we had, the more bodies we'd have inside. On occasion, Liz's parties trickled outside when the crowd became too much. But we tried to control the noise and keep everyone inside.

"M'kay, I'll be back in thirty to forty-five. Message me if you think of anything," I said.

Christy shot me a thumbs up as I walked out the door.

***

Cars lined the street for blocks. Liz's front yard a makeshift parking lot. The thumping vibration bounced around you no matter where you stood in the house. Friends inched closer and talked over the music. Bodies gyrated in the center of the room and rubbed against one another. Red disposable cups of beer, wine, and mixed liquor littered every available surface.

Christy stood near the front door talking with a group of unfamiliar people, Rick's arm wrapped around her waist. Her head threw back in laughter at something a guy with short, blond hair said. Her boisterous nature detectable across the house.

I spotted Liz in the middle of the living room, sandwiched between a man and woman, their bodies synchronized to the electronic rhythm booming off the walls. Liz wanted a relationship whenever she found the right person, but having fun was her current philosophy. She had patience and believed everything happened when it was meant to. And one day she'd find her mister or misses right. When she did, they would be the luckiest person alive.

I wandered from the open kitchen and headed to the makeshift bar. I tossed my beer bottle in the trash can and grabbed a cold beer from the cooler below. Something brushed against my back—a hand maybe—but when I turned around, no one was near me.

The front door opened and more bodies piled into the house, their faces hidden amongst the tall sea of people. Weaving through the foyer, I recognized Eric and smiled. His eyes lit up the second he saw me. He jutted his chin in my direction—his version of hello—and I returned his sentiment. I yelled over the crowd and music, but no way he heard me.

A glass shattered and stole my attention. I peered back to the kitchen, a group of women laughing at the mess. A guy nearby grabbed a paper plate and started picking up the shards. After I located the broom, I helped him clean up.

The beat of the current song faded just enough to transition into the next. Thumping bass kicked off the next song and the rhythm seeped into my bones. One of my favorite songs ripped from the speakers and I started dancing.

I wove between the throng of bodies and sidled up beside Liz. A second later, Christy joined us. No matter where we were, when the three of us hit the dance floor, we were unstoppable. A ménage à trois of dancing—our hips locked together, hands groping each other, bodies moving in one fluid motion. We called ourselves close friends, but in actuality, we were the friendship version of soul mates.

"There's my ladies!" I shouted at their smiling faces.

The opinions of everyone watching never mattered. I closed my eyes—Christy at my back, Liz facing my front—as the song washed away the world around us. More times than not, we danced like this. It never bothered Rick. He owned

Christy's heart, and she owned his. We were three friends who enjoyed life and music. Plain and simple.

The beat shifted and the bass vibrated the walls and deep inside my core. Instinct took over and I clutched Liz's hips, my legs grazing hers. I thrust into her as my body swayed side-to-side and my hips circled. Sweat pricked my brow and a flush spread from my neck to my navel. Liz and I had an intimacy unlike most friends.

Her hands traced down my arms and slid along the hemline of my shorts as her thumbs tucked into the waistband. A tingle spread across my exposed skin and I inched closer to her. Anyone with clear vision probably thought Liz and I were lovers or girlfriends or whatever. I gave no fucks what anyone thought.

Liz and I were best friends. She made me happy in my own skin. Was someone I confided in. There had been conversations between us at the start of our friendship, about dating. We never classified ourselves as girlfriends or being "together," but we enjoyed each other's company. And we had fun. If either of us was lonely—neither of us dated much—we hung out.

We enjoyed ourselves in other ways when it was just us. The first time we dined out then came back to my apartment to watch a movie. Turned out the movie had more sex scenes than not. One thing led to another, and we ended up naked on my couch, our mouths and hands all over each other.

From that moment forward, we weren't only best friends, we were the occasional fuck buddy. No strings. We never set any obligations because one of us might date. In some ways, we had a pact. While single, we were fair game.

So, when Liz's mouth landed on mine, my lips separated and invited her in without hesitation. The warmth of her lips and tongue mingled with mine and lit my body on fire. Christy walked in on us kissing once, so it never fazed her when it happened. And she never asked us if we were more than friends. She loved us, regardless.

"Mmm." Liz groaned as her tongue caressed mine. Whiskey and cola and sin danced over my taste buds. But I wanted to taste more of her.

The crowd hooted as wolf whistles reverberated throughout the room. Guys danced nearby and rooted for us. Weaving through the music, people expressed their opinions on our lip lock. *Damn that's hot* or *fuck me!* or, my all-time favorite, *got room for one more in there?*

No, we didn't. When Liz and I were together, it was only us. We may not be in a legit relationship, but we were monogamous.

The song slowed and transitioned to the next. Liz broke our kiss, and I opened my eyes. A thin sheen of moisture layered her almond skin. Her hazel eyes glowed, and a lustrous smile accentuated her features. I licked my lips, already missing the taste of her. So I leaned forward and gave her one last kiss.

"I need water." My throat scratchy.

She nodded and shouted over my shoulder to Christy, "Water!"

As quick as we appeared on the dance floor, we were off and headed to the kitchen. Half my water disappeared in a flash as my body screamed for relief.

"Hey, ladies! Not sure if I've ever been privy to what I witnessed out there, but that was pretty fucking hot." Eric's voice boomed and startled us.

"Of all the times we've been out, you've never seen us dance?" Liz cocked her head as a snide smile pushed up her cheeks.

"Sorry, Lizzy. I'd definitely remember you and Sarah making out."

My face heated. His words didn't embarrass me, but they put our arrangement in the spotlight. I shifted from foot to foot. Not that I cared what people thought. But I didn't want our display to be an open invitation for something else. I may be a free spirit, eyes-closed-while-I-dance-in-a-field kind of girl, but I'm not sleazy.

I zoned out while Eric and Liz talked. Their conversation trailed off as I chugged my water. A moment later, I was mesmerized by a pair of familiar blue eyes. The same dark blues I'd glimpsed at the gym last weekend. A set of blues I thought I wouldn't see again.

"Excuse me a minute." I dismissed myself from our little group and met the blue-eyed stranger halfway. His sapphires tugged at an invisible force inside me. A volcano erupted beneath my sternum. Who was this guy? Why did my pulse go from zero to a hundred at the sight of him?

"Hey, I'm Sarah. Don't think we've met." I extended my hand and hoped he'd take it.

"Jackson. Eric's friend." His palm blistering against mine. Small callouses toughened the skin at the base of his fingers. The blend of smooth and rough textures oddly arousing.

"Nice to meet you, Jackson. I might be losing my mind, but I swear I saw you last weekend."

His lips curve up a little, displaying a lopsided smile. "You did. At FitPlex. Thought I'd never see you again. Glad that didn't turn out to be true." If possible, his smile grew infinitely bigger.

"So it was you who held the door as my friends and I left."

Something stirred in his eyes as he kept them locked on mine. "My client lives in your complex, and I was meeting him."

"Client?" God, I was mesmerized by how he watched me. As if I would disappear if he looked away. But I didn't want to look away either.

"Personal trainer. I work at one gym, but travel for some clients. Depends on their schedule. What about you? What distracts you during the week?"

It's not lost on me he stepped an inch closer. "Life insurance sales and service. Not so glamourous, but it pays the bills."

His eyes scanned the room for a beat. "This party's kinda crazy, in a good way. How often does your girlfriend throw them?"

His question innocent. No added insinuation. No crude tone. Just a simple question. That he asked without prejudice made me like him more. "We're just friends. Best friends. Tonight's for her birthday, which is days away, but people are over every couple of months. Tonight's a little crazier than the norm."

"Sorry. I didn't mean to assume. I saw you on the dance

floor with her. The kiss." I might be wrong—it's hard to see in the darkened room—but I think he's blushing. For a breath, he averted his gaze. For some reason, this plucked at my heartstrings.

"No worries. I'm sure you're not the only one with the idea floating through their head. It doesn't bother us. It's difficult to explain without a long story." He accepted this and the lines that highlighted his face a moment ago smoothed out. "What about the other guy? Is he your boyfriend?"

My eyes tightened and lips pursed. *What the hell was he talking about? What other guy?* "I'm not sure who you're referring to."

His eyebrows pinched together as he tilted his head. "There's a guy that's been your shadow since I've been here, until a few minutes ago. Older than you. Wears glasses. Couldn't see much else under his hoodie. He watched every move you made."

My stomach twisted. His description was so vague it could be anyone. But who the hell would be following me? Christy and Liz invited so many people. And I didn't know everyone on the list. More than likely, people brought other people not in our circle of friends. Tomorrow I'd ask Christy and Liz.

"Not sure who he was. Christy and Liz handled the invite list. Definitely not my boyfriend." I spewed word vomit all over him. Time to put the focus back on him. "What about you? Girlfriend?"

His cheeks plumped as the corners of his mouth perked up. The sexiest dimple popped on his right, while a dazzling flash of white lit up his face. His smile belonged in movies or advertisements. Between his set of sapphire eyes and his radiant smile, I melted into a puddle.

"No girlfriend. Can't seem to find the right girl."

How was that even possible? He was gorgeous. If gorgeous was a proper term for a sinfully delicious man. He wasn't one of those personal trainers who sat on the sidelines. His biceps Herculean—the muscles defined and straining under his black cotton t-shirt.

"Don't mind me while I stand here, baffled. How can you not have a girlfriend?"

If possible, his smile grew bigger. And I melted more. "I've seen my share of beauties, but I'm also a fan of intelligence. Any girl can make herself pretty. I like the women I can talk with and it not be all about them. They're more difficult to find than you'd think. Having a sense of humor helps, too."

"Man, you're asking a lot from us females." I held my poker face as long as possible and watched his expression morph into concern. Just when I thought he would cut ties and run, I burst out laughing. His face and shoulders sagged, relief clear in his posture.

"That wasn't funny. I just thought of a hundred awkward ways to break off our conversation." His frown vanished and his dimple reappeared. Sigh.

"I thought it was pretty damn funny." I laughed, and he shook his head.

"Ha-ha. So, Sarah, what do you like to do?"

Continual conversation. Body leaning forward. Smile on his lips for days. This guy was hitting on me. No doubt in my mind. That fact did crazy things to my insides. Flutters erupted in my belly. Perspiration covered me like a too hot blanket. And my eyes refused to leave his.

When I figured out how to speak again, my voice came out breathy. "You know, a little of this, a little of that."

"That tells me nothing," he chuckled.

"Maybe I want to be mysterious." My playful, flirty side popped up as I batted my lashes.

"Well, it's working. At least tell me something. Anything. Perhaps some of your favorites?"

"My favorites?"

"Yeah. Like movies or books, food or flowers. Anything."

It was cute how we barely knew each other, and he didn't hide his eagerness to learn more. We met ten minutes ago, but something inside me said we'd known each other a lifetime.

"Hm. Let me think a minute. It's not every day a girl gets put on the spot." I paused, pretended to wrack my brain, and dig deep for the answers. "Let's see… I love smutty, romance novels. A girl can never have too many sunflowers or daisies. I'm content getting lost in the woods. And my favorite color…" I stared into the depths of his exquisite gaze. "Without question, blue."

The music faded away and the room grew void of sound as our own little bubble sucked us in. His eyes locked onto mine. Subliminal questions floated in the air. Desire invaded the small gap living between us. I wanted to kiss him. Hard.

My gaze traveled to his throat and locked on his Adam's apple that bobbed as he swallowed back words left unsaid. He broke the silence between us after ten rapid beats of my heart.

"I'd like to get to know you better." He peeked down as he drew his phone from his pocket and unlocked it. "Can I get your number?"

Eyes glued to his brightened phone screen a moment, he shifted and met my stare. A silent prayer etched on his irises. Begging me to take his phone and enter ten numbers under the contact.

My eyes dropped to the screen as I reached out and took the phone from him. I typed my name and added a sunflower emoji before entering my phone number. I didn't know Jackson, but he intrigued me. His sapphires the bait, and I was hooked.

I handed his phone back and peeked up to study his expression. His eyes glued to the screen, a smile from ear to ear, he tapped a couple of things before locking the screen and returning the phone to his pocket. My phone vibrated in my back pocket and I checked the notification. An incoming message read *Thank you. Jackson.*

Our little happy bubble burst a second later as Eric sidled up on my right. "Hey, I see you met Jackson." Eric's eyes darted from Jackson to me and back to Jackson. "You ready to go, bro? I have to help Pops out in the morning. I'll be useless if I don't get at least four hours of sleep."

"Sure, man. It was great meeting you, Sarah. Till next time." Jackson's addictive smile reappeared.

"You, too. Bye, Eric. See you soon," I said. Eric picked me up and squeezed me as if I was choking and needed the Heimlich maneuver. I smacked his shoulders. "Put me down, dumb ass!" We definitely bantered like siblings.

He set me back on my feet, leaned in and planted a kiss on my cheek. "You know you love me. Later."

Jackson walked behind Eric, looking over his shoulder at me before he walked out the front door. His beautiful blues the last thing I saw. Again.

Is it possible to ignite into flames and melt into a puddle at the same time? Because that's exactly what my insides did.

FIVE

IT'S BEEN three uneventful days since Liz's party. Three drag-ass days since Jackson walked out of Liz's front door. Three quiet days since I gave him my number. And I haven't heard a word.

No text.

No call.

Complete radio silence.

For the umpteenth time, I unlocked my phone and stared at his text message. *Thank you. Jackson.* It's there. In its own little light gray bubble. Verification, once again, I didn't imagine the whole thing.

Why ask for my number if you don't plan to use it? Several times, I'd contemplated reaching out to him. Sparking conversation. My fingers hovered over the keyboard, eager to type something. Anything. But I stopped myself, every single time.

He asked for my number. So, he should make the first move.

That's it. Period.

"Hey, bitch. Holly told me to tell you there's a delivery for you at reception," Christy said. She walked back to her desk, but didn't sit.

"Delivery? From who?" I asked, a little too loud over the sea of cubicles.

"Don't know. I was headed back in and was told to tell you."

"Thanks, Christy."

As I walked to the elevator, I tried to recall any recent orders I placed and had shipped to work. Nothing.

A sharp ding signaled my arrival to the first floor and the elevator doors slid open. Two steps out, a turn to my right, and my feet halted in their tracks.

I hope those are not for me.

My feet ambled as I took more time than necessary to cross the reception area. With each step, I prayed I made a false assumption.

They're not for you. They're not for you.

I dropped my shoulders, inhaled deeply, and schooled my expression as I approached the counter.

"Hey, Holly. Christy told me I had a delivery."

"Hey, girl. Yep. You're looking at it." Her fingers pointed to the massive bouquet of sunflowers on the counter next to her. My stomach churned at the display. "They're beautiful. You're so lucky. Wish I had someone who sent me flowers."

"Me too," I mumbled.

Her brows pinched in concern. A second later, the concern vanished. "Maybe it's family or something. Or a secret admirer." She shrugged and glanced at the flowers with longing.

As I picked up the flowers, I inhaled their sweet fragrance. "Not sure. I'll keep ya posted."

"Talk to you later," she said as I headed toward the bank of elevators.

When was the last time I got flowers? Had I ever had flowers delivered? And who sent them? I had no clue.

Unless... No. It couldn't be. We met days ago. Knew nothing about each other. Although, he did ask about my favorite flower.

Maybe it was a test. Maybe he was just curious. Or... Would a guy who knew me for all of three minutes send me flowers? How? I never mentioned *where* I worked.

I didn't remember hearing the elevator chime, but the doors whisked open to the third floor. I clutched the flowers to my side as I beelined for my little cave.

Every set of eyes locked on me, watched me, as I walked past with a gargantuan arrangement of bold yellow flowers. Being discreet was impossible. The sunflowers gorgeous, but the attention undesirable. I didn't want an onslaught of inquiries, but knew someone was bound to ask who sent them.

Four partitions away, a scruff voice made the first comment. "Wow, Sarah! Those flowers are vibrant. What a lucky girl!"

Ugh.

Turning my head as I passed, my feet slowing a smidge. "Thanks, Stuart." That's all I said. Stuart stood and watched me. The way he stared sent a shiver down my spine and I increased my pace. Had Stuart always looked at me that way? Why did I get so many weird vibes recently? Was it me?

The flowers were beyond gorgeous, but the receipt of them strange. Awkward. And had me feeling a little unhinged.

Two more steps and I'd be in my work safe place. I set the mass of sunshine on my desk and startled at the sight of Christy and Liz.

"Holy shit, girl! Who are those from?" Christy's octave and volume loud enough for the entire third floor to hear.

"Oh, Jesus! You scared the shit out of me," I said as I clutched my chest.

"Sorry. Who sent the flowers?" Christy asked again.

"Not sure. Haven't looked at the card. Gimme a sec."

Pushing a few of the blooms aside, I retrieved a small envelope from the plastic prong. I slipped my finger beneath the flap, opened the envelope, and slid out the card tucked inside.

"Who are they from?" Liz and Christy did that whole talk in unison thing again.

My eyes scanned over the words on the card. "Uh... I'm not sure. There's no name. And the message is kinda... weird." That was putting it lightly. The message was creepy, if I was honest.

"What's it say?" Liz more inquisitive than Christy, for a change.

"It says, 'A beautiful girl deserves beautiful flowers. I love seeing your face glow like the sun, day in and day out.'"

"So... sounds like it's definitely not from the hottie you met at my party. Unless you've seen him since," Liz said.

"Nope. Been hoping he'd call or text. Haven't heard a word."

Always the optimist, Christy said, "At least you have pretty flowers to look at the rest of the week."

"I suppose."

I hated telling her I wanted them off my desk. That I was uncomfortable receiving flowers with creepy, unsigned messages. The flowers a constant reminder someone watched me. Daily. Bile rose in my throat.

We sat quiet a moment. Liz and Christy took the silence as a hint to go back to their desks. For once, I was more introspective.

Christy patted me softly on the shoulder, her eyes gentle as she got up and left. Liz hung back a moment and stared at me, intrigued.

"You sure you're okay? You look bothered."

I slumped in my chair. My thoughts scattered like glitter in the wind. Not that I didn't like the flowers. They were a burst of sunshine. The sentiment bothered me. No name or indication of where they came from bothered me. All of it just sat *wrong* with me.

The context put me on high alert. Whoever sent the flowers saw me often, perhaps daily. Only two people saw me on a regular basis. One went back to her desk, the other sat across from me.

"I'm okay. I guess it's the last line that has me thrown. Like this person sees me every day. Other than you and Christy, I don't see anyone often." Christy and Liz weren't my only friends, just my favorite.

"I'm sure it's nothing. Maybe it means something else. To them, at least."

"I guess… It still feels weird."

"Want me to take them?" For the first time in fifteen minutes, I smiled. Liz offered to do this task and I immediately sagged in my seat. I loved my best friend.

"Please. What're you doing with them?"

Liz tapped a finger on her lips. "Hm. I'll set them in the break room with a sign. *Free flowers.* They'll be gone in no time."

In seconds, the nausea vanished. A veil of discomfort

lifted. "That would be amazing. Thanks, Liz. You're more than the best."

She half-smiled and her plump bottom lip curved up. Liz peeked over my cubicle walls, scanned left and right, before snatching the tainted flowers and quickly kissing me. "Anything for you. Later."

Within a heartbeat, she left with the ominous flowers. It's crazy how the simplest thing soured my mood. Flowers should bring smiles. Today, they didn't. Instead, they left a gap. A void.

Curiosity clung like a shadow. I needed answers. Somehow. Someway. Few people knew my preference in flowers. Mom. Dad. Maybe Christy and Liz. A few guys I'd dated, but months had passed, and I can't picture any of them sending me anything, let alone flowers.

And then there was Jackson.

Sliding open my desk drawer, I retrieved my phone. Jackson and I hadn't spoken since Saturday, but asking him seemed a logical place to start.

Opening my text history, I tapped on the message he'd sent me Saturday. *Thank you. Jackson.* I'd saved his number to my phone and hoped his name would've popped up before now. But it never did. How on earth was I supposed to ask him if he sent me flowers? What would I say? *Hey, did you send flowers to my job with a super creepy message?*

Ugh. This sucked.

My fingers hovered over the screen as my brain scrambled to type something not embarrassing. Think, think, think. My fingers tapped away and typed out a message. For a second, I lingered above the send arrow.

Sarah: Just wanted to say hi.

Corny. The lamest text message in existence. But I sent it. I dangled the bait and waited for him to bite.

I set my phone down and went back to what I was working on before the flower fiasco. A vase full of unpleasantries wouldn't disrupt my day. Not today.

Knee deep in my call list, I waded my way to the end just

as my phone vibrated and Jackson's name flashed on the screen.

Jackson: Hey. How are you?
Sarah: Doing good. Working like a fiend. How are you?
Jackson: Doing good. Just finished with a client. I'm bummed you messaged first. I was planning on reaching out to you tomorrow.

Tomorrow? If he'd sent the flowers, he would've messaged me today or tonight, to see if I'd gotten them. Right? So maybe they weren't from him. But I had to be certain and ask. Time to turn the awkwardness up to high.

Sarah: I have a strange question. Please don't freak out. By chance, did you send me flowers at work?

An eternity passed as I waited for his response. Did I scare him away? God, I hoped not. He was sexy and intriguing and mysterious. I wanted to see him again, but had to ask if he'd sent them. If he did, why the strange message? My phone buzzed.

Jackson: Sorry. Wasn't me. But now I have a competitor for your attention. I may need to up my game.

I read the text three times and smiled. Relief eased my troublesome thoughts and resuscitated me. Thank god the note wasn't from him. The likelihood of things moving forward would've decreased exponentially.

But now a new concern followed me like a storm cloud. Who knew me well enough to send something so personal? The million dollar question.

Sarah: I'd like to see what's entailed in this competition. Sorry for the weird question. I got flowers with an odd message and no sender name.
Jackson: If I send you flowers, you'll know they're from me. I have another client in a couple minutes. Can we talk later?
Sarah: Definitely I'm off work at 5ish. Sweat a lot today

Jackson: Maybe later…

Maybe later? Huh? Not sure what he meant, but my mind went straight to the gutter. For the rest of my day, I thought about Jackson, his deep blue eyes, and his mysterious body… hot and sweaty. A fantastic visual for the rest of my day. And my mood shifted in seconds.

Work breezed by with no further discussion regarding the flowers. Liz, Christy, and I had lunch downstairs. I shared the flirty banter I had with Jackson and let them over-analyze the texts.

Christy was head-over-heels about a new guy in my world. She rambled on and asked questions I couldn't answer. She rattled off fairy tale stories about how she saw my future. Tons of sex. Marriage. Babies. Her scenarios laughable.

Liz was excited for me, but seemed on edge. Almost as if disappointed. Or sad, perhaps. She and I would have a *date* night soon. Just the two of us. Where we would talk openly and get everything out.

Maybe I read her wrong. Maybe something else bothered her and it chose this moment to bleed out. Assumption was the enemy. So, I vowed to learn the truth.

I loved Liz. My best friend. More so than Christy. We'd shared fun and passionate times. But we talked about them. In full detail, no holds barred. Agreed they were only fun. Agreed to no strings. But maybe, when I wasn't paying attention, it evolved. I didn't want to hurt her. Ever. No matter what happened with either of us.

When Christy got up to use the restroom, I told Liz I wanted to hang out. So, before Christy returned to the table, we planned to meet at her house tomorrow night.

Simple enough… Dinner, conversation, and TV reruns. I just hoped everything went according to plan.

SIX

PEEKING through the frosted glass like a Peeping Tom, I spotted Liz inside. A shiver danced over my skin, the cool night air not the cause. For reasons unknown, I was frazzled. I had never been nervous around Liz. More the opposite. Liz grounded me. Kept me centered.

I hesitated a moment. I glanced down at my fumbling fingers, closed my eyes, and took a few cleansing breaths. Liz was my best friend. My nervousness was ridiculous. We'd done this hundreds of times—dinner alone, enjoying the other's company.

As I opened my eyes, I centered myself. This was Liz. Nothing had changed. We were still us. Comfortable in our own skin together. Watching her blurred silhouette another second, I rapped on the blue wooden door.

"Come in!"

I opened the door and stepped inside. Liz was a force of nature as she scurried around the kitchen and focused on cooking. A pot and pan sizzled on the burners. Wooden utensils off to the side for each dish. Steam wafted throughout the room and spread delicious aromas of garlic and herbs and something sweeter. When Liz took over the kitchen, everyone prepared to be wowed.

As I stepped farther inside, I set a bottle of wine on the kitchen counter. "Smells amazing in here. What's for dinner?"

She paused her feverish stirring to glance my way, a sultry

smile lit her face. "Thanks. Grilled rosemary chicken, garlic pearled couscous, and roasted carrots."

More times than not, it baffled me why Liz worked for a life insurance company. Her skills in the kitchen blew my mind. She could take the simplest ingredients and turn them into a succulent work of art. No matter how many times I complimented her cooking and told her she should do more with it, she always told me it was something she enjoyed. And she didn't want to ruin that joy by doing it as a job.

"How much longer?"

"Maybe ten more minutes."

"Okay. I'll set the table. Want a glass of wine?" I waved the bottle in the air as if teasing a dog with a toy.

Her eyes beamed as much as her smile. "Wine would be great."

Liz and I danced around each other in synchronicity. She bounced between the sink and stove as I grabbed everything else we needed for dinner. The coffee table set, I tossed fluffy pillows on the floor. Back in the kitchen, I grabbed glasses, the wine, and Liz's snazzy wine opener. A pop echoed, and I set the wine on the counter to breathe.

"Anything I can help with?" I'd run out of tasks and saddled up beside her.

The aroma of herb roasted carrots drifted through the air. Liz gave the couscous one final stir and said, "Just grab plates. Everything's ready."

We portioned out dinner, then headed to the living room. Settling onto the pillows, Liz flipped on the television and picked a random series to binge on Netflix. I poured the pale hued wine into our glasses. An unfamiliar, awkward silence stretched between us. Did Liz feel as out of place as I did? We weren't usually like this, but things were on the verge of change. I didn't want our dynamic to change. Losing Liz wasn't an option.

Leaning over my plate, I closed my eyes and inhaled. My mouth watered instantly. Fork in hand, I was prepared to dive in, until I noticed Liz in my periphery. She nudged carrots around her plate like a toddler, trying to mask how much she hadn't eaten. Discussing the change between us was inevitable, but I never wanted us to become uncomfortable. Liz meant the world to me and I valued our friendship.

"You okay?" Two words—a simple question—slipped from my lips slow and soft.

"Yeah," she mumbled, her dinner still making circuits on her plate. "Guess I was more surprised than expected when you brought up talking with Jackson. Showing me the texts made it real. I'm not sure why this shocked me. Someone as amazing as you..."

She left her thought hanging wide open. I understood where her head was; mine was there too. "I get it. We have more than your average friendship. We don't just hang out and shoot the shit. And although we've talked about not getting too deep with things, we can't change reality. That we've been intimate."

We sat there, eyes locked and loaded with questions, and watched each other. No words exchanged. No movement. Silent and still. She searched my eyes, scanned their depths, and looked for answers neither of us had.

Her pinky brushed my hand and my pulse picked up. The soft touch thrummed in my veins. Liz's eyes said a thousand things, words we'd never spoken aloud. Her chin dropped, eyes locked on our near touch, her voice a hair above a whisper. "I can't lose you."

I pinched her chin between my thumb and forefinger and brought her line-of-sight to mine. Our lips a breath apart. "You'll never lose me. No matter what."

Her eyes glazed over from the threat of tears. "Promise?"

As my best friend—my person and someone I relied on—how could she think we'd be anything less? Even if our lives changed, she would always be a part of mine. "I promise."

She closed the gap between us. Her lips encompassed mine as her tongue swiped my lower lip. I opened up to her and she caressed and stroked her tongue against mine. In this moment—lips joined, hands hugging curves—a mile long list of questions popped into my head and asked why.

Why hadn't we taken this to the next level? Why hadn't we tried to be more? Why did we hide our intimacy from everyone? People saw us kiss. At bars or clubs and the other night at her party. But that was the extent of our exposure.

Behind closed doors, though, our level of intimacy was intense. An intensity we hid. We'd been friends two years before we evolved to where we are now. So, why?

Her hand slid under my shirt, fingertips traipsed up my abdomen and caressed my lace bra. With subtle tenderness, Liz fondled my nipples through the lace. I twisted and propped myself up on my knees and tugged my shirt over my head.

"Can't lose you," Liz mumbled when our lips reconnected.

Her hands slid down and trekked to my backside. On their ascent, Liz unfastened my bra. My arms dropped, and the lacy material fell between us, exposing my pebbled nipples.

My body burst into flames when Liz's lips abandoned mine and traveled down my neck, along my collarbone and over my breasts. Her mouth and fingers greedy as she sucked and squeezed. I was mad with hunger and yanked her cotton shirt off her body. The second her bare flesh was exposed, my desire grew tenfold. No obstructions. No extra steps. Nothing except skin and heat and passion.

When her mouth was back on mine, I sucked her lower lip. Ravenous, I licked and nipped my way across her creamy chocolate-colored flesh. Desire pooled between my thighs as my clit throbbed. My mouth traced the lines of her skin, landing on the firm peak of her breasts. I latched onto her nipple, sucking and scraping the flesh, salivating at the sweetness of her skin. A moan echoed from her chest and my core clenched.

"You won't lose me," I groaned. We might not have moments like this in the future, but only now mattered. Because right now, nothing had changed.

Liz's warm fingers ran from hip to hip and traced an invisible line along the linen fabric. A slight tug at my waist loosened the strands securing the material and Liz's fingers grazed over my lower abdominals.

My mouth explored her body and left no part untraveled. Liz's fingernails etched the sides of my spine, my back bowing and lungs gasping for breath. Lust and heat and yearning surged within me. I needed more of her. Now.

She drew my lips back to hers and devoured me as if starved her whole life. Her hand slid between my skin and the linen, and skimmed the small lace triangle, stopping when she discovered my damp folds. A low growl rumbled in her chest, the reverberation spiking the insatiable hunger in my core. Her fingers circled a slow tempo.

Breath hot on my neck, Liz panted harder with each loop. "Fuck! It drives me wild when you're wet like this." Her teeth sunk into the plump flesh at my shoulder and I arched into her touch.

Liz's hand slid from my waistband, a small cry escaping my lips at the sudden loss. She stood and extended her hand. I took it as she stood me up and dropped to her knees, grasping my pants and yanking them down.

Starting at my ankles, her fingers traced invisible lines up the outside of my calves, over the contours of my thighs and hooked into the thin lace of my panties. Hungry eyes locked on mine as the lace fell to the floor.

Liz grasped my bare ass and squeezed with authority. Her mouth hovered inches from the groomed patch between my thighs. I panted when her breath coasted over my skin and teased my clit. My pulse pounded and my skin heated. I wanted her hot tongue to run the length of my slit. Wanted it to circle my most sensitive place. To lick and lavish my clit and folds. My core ablaze, I wanted her to forgo dinner and eat me.

She peered up, hazels hooded and ignited. I framed her face with my hands, the tips of my fingers clawing her siren red hair. Liz leaned forward, inhaled deep, and licked from the junction of my thighs up. My back bowed, and I thrust my pussy into her.

The room faded away as my body landed on the plush sofa cushions, the cool fabric prickled my skin. Liz forced my legs apart and rubbed along my thighs from knees to cleft as her mouth peppered kisses.

Lips kissed. Mouth sucked. Teeth bit. She consumed every ounce of me, pausing at my core. As she hovered over the soft, pink flesh, her breath came in hot bursts and I trembled, unsure how long I could withstand her teasing.

My fingers combed through her hair as her hazels lifted

and met my stare. Voice gravelly and foreign to my own ears, I said, "Fuck me. I need to feel you."

Frozen in place, she gaped as I placed my hand over hers and inched it toward the wetness between my legs. Liz forfeited control a moment and sat slack-jawed as I traced her fingers over my slit. After a few strokes, I shifted forward and thrust gently into her fingers, goading her to take over.

One more stroke and her fingers took control again. My hand shifted to her breast and fondled the plump flesh. As my body crept forward, her fingers tempted and teased my entrance, circling the bundle of nerves above.

She sat up on her knees and aligned herself better with my body, fingers stroking my folds over and over. On the next twirl of her fingers, I drove my hips forward and forced her fingers inside me.

"Yes..." The single word a litany on my lips. My breath faster, harsher.

Liz's mouth crashed down on mine as her tongue dove in and stroked vigorously. Her fingers pumped like pistons in and out of my greedy pussy. But I craved more. I picked up the rhythm and rammed harder as Liz kept pace. Hungry to plunge my fingers inside her, my hands skimmed down her torso and past the skimpy loose-fitting short shorts. Propping myself up, I slid my fingers beneath the inseam and growled when I grazed her hot, bare skin. Moisture coated my fingertips. A new desperation coursed through my veins and I buried my fingers inside her.

Our bodies gyrated to a ferocious beat. Hands and fingers frantic to touch. Orgasms rocketed as friction stroked like a wanton beast. When her orgasm clamped down on me, I no longer resisted my own.

My body ignited like a star being born. Heat incinerated the landscape of my skin, screams ripped from my lips and she swallowed them whole. Liz bit my shoulder and dug her nails into my sides. I loved how impassioned we were when we came undone together.

When she stopped shaking, Liz collapsed against my abdomen. We laid half on the couch, our limbs tangled and the room a haze of rapid breathing and undiluted sex. She scooted up and rested her forehead on my chest, jostling every few seconds to nestle the crook of my neck.

"So much for dinner, huh?" Liz said.

I burst out in laughter, my body shaking uncontrollably. A second later, she joined in. Arms squeezed tight, our bodies trembled in happiness. So much for talking about relationships and emotions. I guess we'd play it by ear and see how the future unfolded.

Bringing her closer to my chest, I added, "That's what they make microwaves for, right?"

SEVEN

DINNER WITH LIZ turned into sex with Liz. Dinner was eaten, but it wouldn't have mattered if it wasn't. After being up far too late, we skipped watching television and talked. We spewed everything we'd bottled up and discovered that we've had more than a simple best friend friendship for quite some time.

By the end of our chat, we decided to keep our previous 'agreement' in place. Both of us had immense feelings for each other, but didn't want a romantic relationship together. Hard to admit, we were both scared to break something perfect. Something completely us.

And though I cared deeply for Liz, I explained my desire to pursue things with Jackson, but needed her reassurance. Her happiness was my happiness. If things didn't pan out with Jackson, perhaps Liz and I would try for more—without ruining years of friendship. But I still had unease about altering the current Liz-Sarah dynamic.

After hours of chatter, the night transitioning into early morning, I decided to stay at Liz's place. In the morning, she'd let me borrow clothes for work. It wouldn't be the first time. After our intense conversation tonight, it didn't seem right to up and leave. Instead, I wanted the press of her warm body against mine, and to have her arms wrap around me and hold me while we slept.

As I stepped out of the ensuite bathroom, my heart raced.

The comforter laid askew on the floor. Liz's almond-hued, nude body sprawled across the bold, red sheets as her fingers rubbed between her thighs. Magnetized, I stared as her fingers circled the spot above her slit with vigor. Her folds glistened from the moisture.

"Oh, god," I moaned as I took in the sight of her.

An ache furled at the junction of my thighs. The intensity almost unbearable. Dampness seeped from my core and slid down my legs. *Fuck me.* Liz stirred things in my body incomparable to anyone prior. I'd been with men and women over the years. But being with a woman was unparalleled. A distinct hunger. One I hadn't known until Liz.

Tugging my shirt over my head and shoving my pants down my thighs, I bared my wanton flesh to her once more. There was no use in denying her, or myself. Although I was eager for what might happen with Jackson, we weren't anything more than two people agreeing to get together at this point. Until that changed, I would enjoy life.

Planting my feet near the edge of the bed, I gawked as her fingers circled her clit then slid between her folds. The ache between my legs morphed into a powerful beast. It clawed and growled and begged me to not hold back.

I slid a hand down my stomach, through the trimmed patch of curls, and ran them along my slick skin. My eyes darted between Liz's lust-spelled gaze and her greedy fingers. Arousal coated my fingers as I propped one leg along the edge of the bed and played with my clit. With each stroke, my fingers disappeared between my folds.

Liz's back arched off the mattress, her fingers moved faster, pumping in and out of her pussy with an insatiable hunger. Her moans louder with each stroke, edging my orgasm further. Our eyes locked, neither of us able to look elsewhere. Both of us chased our orgasms. I pinched a nipple with my free hand, tugging the firm nub and twisting while I drove into my pussy harder.

My eyes scanned Liz's body as she inched into a more upright position. My eyes glued to hers, her fingers worked her clit harshly in my periphery.

"I'm so close," Liz said, her eyes glassy as her face and chest bloomed scarlet. Her legs trembled, a sign she was about to come. An undeniable visual. One I wanted to partici-pate in.

Her jaw fell slack, eyes hooded and focused between my legs. My clit slick as I swiped rapid circles. I moaned, the reverberation raspy in my throat. A second later, Liz whimpered. Our cries of pleasure in sync.

And then she screamed in pleasure—a familiar and alluring cry. The guttural howl sent me over the edge and I rode the high with her.

The air a mixture of her breath and mine, our lungs burning for oxygen. Liz dropped onto the mattress, her legs sprawled with her arms at her sides. Her chest rose and fell in rapid succession.

I want to make her come again.

I planted one knee on the bed, then the other, and crawled up to hover over her. My lips inches from hers as I gasped. "Need to taste you."

She nodded. "Yes."

I kissed her with intimate tenderness, climbed off her body, inverted my position, and mounted her face. Lips to folds. We consumed each other into the early hours of the morning, nowhere near satiating our desires. And without a care in the world.

The hours at work trickled by. Phones at a lull. Reports up-to-date. And my inbox had no new messages. The company frowned upon cell phone usage in the office, unless work related, but I was beyond bored and had another hour before the day ended.

Checking no one managerial hovered nearby, I deduced it safe to sneak a little phone time in without a slap on the wrist. I opened my desk drawer and snagged my cell. After unlocking it, I checked social media and cleared out a handful of notifications. I played my turn on a round of Words with Friends. Then started perusing my surplus of personal emails.

Once bored with my phone, I peeked up at the clock and noticed only ten minutes had passed. This sucked. The monotony endless. Bored out of my skull and tired as hell, I just wanted to go home, slip on some comfy PJs, and crash in my bed. My fluffy pillows and cozy comforter were in for a major cuddle session soon.

A buzz jolted me from the daydream. I glanced down at my phone and saw a text notification. After unlocking my phone, I tapped the notification.

Jackson: Hey, how are you? Ever find out who sent the flowers?

Jackson. Part of me jumped up and down like a fourteen-year-old girl because the boy she liked called her. But another part of me lingered in a strange funk as Liz popped into my thoughts. A twinge of guilt churned in my core at my excitement, especially after what happened between us last night. I didn't want to betray my friend and her feelings, but reminded myself we talked about me wanting to date Jackson. Liz would always be there for me, regardless. It would be idiotic to deny this connection with Jackson.

Sarah: Nope. Probably some lunatic. Who knows? I gave them away. Didn't want to keep them.
Jackson: Didn't think you'd answer right away. Thought you'd be at work.
Sarah: Still at work. Being rebellious. Bored out of my mind. Was messing with my phone when you messaged.
Jackson: Gotcha. Anything new?
Sarah: Same old, same old. How'd your sweat session go?
Jackson: Just another day doing what I do. Sorry I didn't reach out last night. Crashed early. I was beat.
Sarah: No worries. I hung out with Liz last night. Crashed at her place. Stayed up way too late.

After I hit send, I smacked myself in the face. Literally. Did I just tell him I slept at my friend's house? The same friend he saw me making out with. That we were up too late. I closed my eyes, squeezing them tight while I mentally beat myself up. Did I kill my chance before I got one?

Jackson: You two hang out often?

Sarah: Yeah. Best friends and whatnot. We're pretty tight.
Jackson: That's cool. How would I fit into that equation?

I was unsure how he meant the question. Was he asking to be a part of what we had? Or, was he asking what would happen between me and Liz if something happened with him and me? Time to tread lightly.

Sarah: I'm reading that question more than one way. Can you be a little more specific? Sorry.
Jackson: If I asked you out on a date, how does that work? Would you be dating both of us?
Sarah: I told you, we're friends… with a few extra benefits. We have an agreement. Easier to explain in person.
Jackson: Maybe we can grab dinner one night soon and you can explain it to me.

And there it was, right smack in front of my face. The question I'd been eager to hear, or in this case see. And yet the question had my stomach twisted up like a pretzel. Although Liz and I talked last night, I had to share what just happened. That Jackson made his move. The chess pieces in motion. And I planned to accept his invitation.

Sarah: I'd really like that. Between now and this weekend probably isn't the best idea. V day and all.
Jackson: Valentine's Day doesn't scare me. But you're probably right. Every place will be packed. What about next week, Tuesday?
Sarah: Tuesday sounds great. When? Where? Details.
Jackson: All in good time. I'll let you get back to being a rebel. Okay if we talk later?
Sarah: Definitely
Jackson: Cool. Till then…

My cheeks burned as a megawatt smile stretched across my face. If I was ten years younger, I'd be a hormonal lunatic —screaming with my girlfriends, resembling the nerdy girl who got asked out by the quarterback. I wanted to share my excitement with Christy and Liz. Wanted my thrill to be theirs too.

I popped my head up, scanned the sea of cubicles, and spotted no one walking within proximity. Plopping back into my seat, I opened the group chat between me, Christy, and Liz, my fingers jittery as I typed. Christy would be excited, no doubt about it. I only hoped Liz would be, too.

Sarah: Guess who scored a date next week?
Christy: No fucking way, bitch!!! I will need more details.
Liz: That's awesome. The three of us should get together before then and coach you 😜
Sarah: As if I've never dated before 🙄 V day dinner this weekend? Is Rick taking you out C?
Christy: We're going out the day after. Too many people out that day. I'll ask him if it's cool that we hang on V day.
Sarah: Awesome. Keep us posted.
Christy: 👍

The next two days at work snailed along. Liz, Christy, and I had lunch both days, the two of them giving me their best advice on my upcoming date. They behaved as if I'd never gone out with anyone. Ever. It was sad and laughable.

"Give me something to work with here," Christy said over lunch today. She wanted to know all the ins and outs of where Jackson was taking me, hoping she'd be able to rifle through my closet and pick out my attire for my date.

"If I had details to share, you'd be the first to know."

Jackson had yet to disclose where he was taking me. Our texts during the week had been brief. But the second I mentioned we'd been texting back and forth, Christy stuck out her hand and begged for my phone. She was eager to read what our hungry little fingers had typed, word for word, and not my interpretation. As much as I loved Christy, I denied her. If I let anyone read them, besides me, it would be Liz.

I trusted Christy with my life, but her outlook on things was overzealous, and I wasn't mentally prepared for that experience. With things slowly evolving between me and Jackson, I wanted to share things in fractions, not wholes. If she read our text history, I would never hear the end of her over-analyzation. And the last thing I wanted was for things to be picked apart.

The end of the week passed, and the three of us agreed to hang out at Christy's place on Valentine's Day. It was a two-fer. We got to hang out, chat girl stuff, and they could infiltrate me with whatever dating advice they deemed necessary. And Christy would still be home with Rick, in case he wanted more time with her on the cards and flowers holiday.

The whole evening was packed with laughter, good food, and great company. Liz and I sat on the couch, while Christy sat on the floor facing us. Rick joined us shortly after we started eating, cozying up to Christy. They were so damn adorable.

As the conversation flowed, Rick threw out dating tidbits the three of us would never think about. He pitched his version of what would make a great first date from the male perspective. Sex was the one thing I waited to hear but didn't. He told me every first date he'd ever been on, he was super nervous. He worried about every little detail and sex was the last thing on his mind. Call me fascinated.

Sometimes, as women, we forget men are human, too. Behind the bravado and physique, they can be on edge like us, their emotions scattered. A constant wonder if they've said the wrong thing. Uncertain if they should kiss a woman on the first date. It's a challenge to remember we're all capable of the same things in that first moment... Love and fear.

Four-thirty-three. "Could this day be any slower?" I mumbled at my computer. The clock ticked by at a snail's pace as the workday wrapped up. Not checking the time every other minute proved difficult. In less than two hours, Jackson would pick me up from my apartment and whisk me off to a nice restaurant somewhere in the city. Tonight's date had me antsy and over-the-moon. Something about the way Jackson looked at me made my body sing.

We'd messaged back and forth over the last week, talking about dinner and solidifying our plans. There had been light flirting, the occasional innuendo, and consistent interaction. I tried to get a better read on him through his texts, but he didn't give much away. But I was eager for more before he knocked at my door. And he kept me hooked, teasing me with bait on occasion.

Somehow, I made it home in record time, and had more than an hour to look presentable for our date. I reached into the shower, cranked the lever to the far left, and let the water heat. I peeled off my standard Hammond Life polo and khakis before I stepped under the hot stream. Snagging the hair tie I kept in the shower, I secured my hair in a messy top bun.

The water pinked my skin as my muscles loosened and relaxed. I stood there a moment, mind blank, while my body let go of the day's tension. Normally, I wasn't so tightly wound. Was I really that nervous about our date tonight? Maybe. My stomach had been in knots since I woke up.

My last official date/relationship was months ago. And over the last several months, single life had been fabulous. Unlimited time hanging out with friends. Christy and Liz packed my life and heart with happiness, and I wanted for nothing. Dating Jackson wouldn't occupy a vacancy that had magically appeared. More like he was a new branch on our little family tree. At least a small part of me hoped as much.

When I'd told Christy and Liz that Jackson planned to take me to an eclectic bistro, Christy insisted on choosing my attire. As if I were incapable of fulfilling such a task. "I can dress myself," I'd said to them both. Christy rolled her eyes. Liz smiled.

On a wooden hanger, a soft, cream-colored linen dress hung on the back of my door. Thin straps held the halter in place, tied around my neck and exposed most of my bare back. The billowy material skirted over the floor, my khaki flats peeking out as I walked. Sifting through my jewelry, I located the perfect piece to add a little flare and offset the light color.

I slipped the necklace over my head, lifted my hair over the cord, and allowed the chunky, raw lapis lazuli to rest on my sternum. Whenever I wore my lapis, I always felt more connected and energized. I hoped I wouldn't need the extra boost tonight, but a lady could never be too prepared. From the short time we'd seen each other in person, plus the easy flow of conversation through our text messages, a mysterious chemistry ebbed between us. A magnetic aura brought us together and opened our eyes to new possibilities.

For tonight's date, I left my honey blonde locks loose. The strands tickled the skin below my mid-back. As I stared at my reflection in the bathroom vanity, my heart galloped like a pack of wild animals beneath my ribs.

Why was I so nervous?

My ring finger ran across my lower lip as I spread my glossy balm. A buzz from the intercom startled me, and I sprinted for the door. Pressing the answer button on the speaker, Jackson's voice broke the silence in my apartment. "Hey, I'm at the gate."

"Give me a sec." I pressed the button to open the gate, a beep blared from the box. "I'm in the building just before the curve, bottom floor."

"See you in a few." The breeze muffled his voice.

I ran back to my bedroom, going to the full-length mirror beside the bathroom door, my hands brushing down my sides. Twisting left then right, I inspected my appearance from head to toe, and tucked a few strands of hair behind my ears before setting them free again. Before I left the room, I snagged my purse, a loose-fit knitted sweater, and my phone. I plopped down on the couch, my right knee bouncing as I waited for my date to knock at the door.

From the moment we entered the restaurant, I was convinced I'd worn the wrong attire. Saying it aloud would only state the obvious. This place edged closer to fine dining than artsy bistro. I needed more material over my skin. Perhaps something more formal in appearance. Something to cover the mass of bare flesh displayed on my back. Compared to everyone in the room, I was naked. Even if I put on the more-than-comfortable knitted cover-up—which hung limp over my arm—I'd be inadequate. Lacking the coverage I suddenly craved, I wrapped my arms around my center and hugged myself tight. For an outgoing woman, I shied up in an instant.

"You okay?" Jackson's warm fingertips skirted the exposed dip along my spine.

"Uh… I think I'm a bit underdressed," I said and glanced at him. Clad in denim and a dark turquoise button-up, his sleeves were rolled up and hugging the distal end of his biceps. My mouth watered at the observation. The pop of blue accentuated his sparkling eyes as they stared into my soul, my heart ballooning in my chest. I inhaled deep and relief flooded me as I snapped out of my fantasy and realized our ensembles were on equal ground.

"You're not. This place appears more extravagant than it is. One of the reasons I like it." Jackson's fingertips traced up and down my lower back, the soft, subtle motion comforting me. The corners of his mouth curved up, and his smile sparked an unfamiliar heat in my body. A spark which slowly ignited a forest fire.

My arms relaxed as my hands loosened their grip above my elbows. As I scanned the other patrons nearby, I breathed easier and relaxed my shoulders a bit. "Thank you."

"For what?"

"For calming my nerves. And helping me see I blend in. I'm usually not this nervous."

"Sarah, you could never blend in… You're a sunflower in a field of daisies. You light up the room." Heat blossomed on my cheeks. His reference to my favorite flowers, and using them to explain how he sees me, left me speechless. I opened my mouth, wanting to say something other than thank you, but snapped it shut. No perfect words. No witty comeback. My mind frozen. Vocal cords out of service.

The hostess guided us to our table. Various pieces of art adorned the white walls along our path. Paintings, sculptures, drawings. Red curtains connected along parts of the ceiling and created a look like theater curtains. Each wall space had its own art theme—animals, landscapes, fruits, vegetables, wines, abstract, and so on.

If someone explained the interior of this restaurant to me, I would call it gaudy. But it was quite the opposite. Everything on display tasteful. In here, it was all about placement. They used strategy to place each piece. A form of Feng Shui. Once you stepped back, it was easier to see.

Jackson pulled out my chair, his fingertips grazing along my shoulder and down my arm a few inches after I sat. When his touch vanished, my body pled for more.

Crisp, white linen blanketed our table. A large, rectangular candle rested in the center, the wooden wick crackling under the flame. A small vase sat off to one side—dozens of daisies, tall sprigs of rosemary, and stems of a fine leafed fern nestled in the glass.

I scanned the other tables nearby, each of them lit with similar candles but absent of flowers. It'd be silly of me to assume he bought them or had them delivered, but no other tables had flowers. The arrangement was perfect and beautiful, and I itched to lean forward and smell them.

"Did you have the flowers delivered?" I asked, curious.

"Kind of. When I called to reserve a table, I asked if it was possible to add daisies to the table."

Again, for the second time tonight, I had no words. For a woman who spoke openly, it was odd to have nothing to say. Jackson pulled out all the stops and dazzled me. I wasn't a difficult person to impress since I enjoyed the simplest things. But his tactics definitely weighed in his favor.

"They're beautiful. Thank you." My cheeks tightened from my unstoppable smile. Heat bloomed across my face as my eyes diverted down to my menu. What was it about Jackson that brought out this new shyness?

"You're most welcome." The dimple on his right cheek appeared when I peeked up at him.

A server had come and gone, our food and drink orders placed. Under normal circumstances, I wouldn't drink on a first date—wanting to keep my wits about me—but tonight felt anything but normal. I ordered a glass of wine, hoping the burgundy liquid would settle my nerves and fill me with my normal courage. I wasn't a quiet person under normal circumstances, but with this man… everything was different. I was different. In a good way.

Jackson sat across from me, hands steepled at his mouth, elbows on the table, inquisitive eyes boring into mine. His hands lowered from his lips, lips I had trouble looking away from. His tongue peeked out, the tip running over the center of his lower lip, tugging it in and trapping it under his teeth a moment.

As if someone caught me peeping in a window, I gazed anywhere but at his mouth. My line of sight shifted up to his sapphires, their hue brightened by with amusement.

"See something you like?" Jackson asked.

He had no idea. "Mmm…" It was the only response I mustered, reaching for my wine to give my mouth a distraction.

"Perhaps we should distract ourselves with conversation," he teased and poked fun at my lust driven observation. It wasn't my fault he was beautiful, in the most masculine ways. Could any woman *not* stare at him?

An idea hit me. Hopefully it would be enough to distract my wandering eyes. "Perhaps. Seeing as you already know a few of my favorite things, I think it's only fair I'm given the same."

"Fair enough. Ask away." His invitation sat open as he leaned forward and gave me opportunity to ask anything.

"Let's start off with the basics… Favorite color, book, flower, place. The good stuff." I plastered on my best corny smile, knowing he would meet my probing inquisition with humor. I wasn't wrong.

A throaty, deep chuckle bounced in the space between us as his smile crinkled the corners of his eyes. "The good stuff. Let's see. If I had to choose a color, I'd have to say green, like an evergreen or an emerald." He paused for a sliver of time, enthralled, and stared straight into my soul. When his voice reappeared, it seemed as if I'd awoken from hypnosis. "I don't really have a favorite book, but I read mysteries when I pick one up. Flowers… it's really hard for a guy to choose." His index finger tapped his lips as if he were in deep thought. "Purple calla lilies. My mom loved calla lilies, more so of the white variety. They were in the house often when I grew up. I don't really have one specific place I call my favorite, but I love hiking in the mountains. Something

about being away from everyone and everything is invigorating."

"I'll make note later. Good to know a man who isn't afraid
of owning his love for flowers." The words rolled off my
tongue like a whimsical tune as I winked at him.

"A real man isn't afraid to own who he is or what he
likes." My joking extinguished by his semi-serious tone.
"Why be someone I'm not. My turn?"

Interesting. As each layer of Jackson is peeled away, I
became more intrigued. "Ask away," I say, repeating his
earlier words.

"If you could eat anything, contents aside, what would
it be?"

"Italian food. Pastas, breads, all of it. I haven't met an
Italian dish I didn't like. What about you?"

"Without a doubt, good old-fashioned American home-
style cooking. My mom used to make the best shepherd's pie.
She also made a mean biscuits and gravy."

I loved how he loved his mother. Nowadays, people got
caught up figuring out who they were, often separating themselves from their history. In good times or bad, our history
made us who we were today. He'd referenced his love for her
twice in the last few minutes and that warmed my heart.

"She sounds like an amazing woman."

"She was. I've met no one else like her," he murmured,
something in Jackson's tone akin to heartache.

"Was?" I hoped I wasn't rehashing something painful, or
yet something better left buried. We were just getting to know
one another, and I didn't want to stir the kettle of old
emotions.

"She passed away a few years ago. She was outside,
working in her garden, and had a heart attack. My dad didn't
realize what had happened for a short time. By the time she
made it to the hospital… it wasn't good."

I picked up on his desire to stop talking about her. With
each word he spoke, the light in his eyes faded a fraction.
"I'm sorry to hear that happened to her. No doubt she's still
nearby, watching over you."

He watched me as we sat in silence a couple minutes. The
way he studied me was calculated, his eyes working to read

my unspoken thoughts. As with most people, he didn't want pity. And I had no intention of giving him any.

"Thank you. She would've liked you. Before she passed, she told me she wanted me to find a pretty girl. Someone not scared to be herself, no matter who was around."

The sentiment enveloped me in a veil of emotions. Three times. No words. Would anything about him not surprise me? Was there an undesirable bone in his body? I doubted it. Jackson wasn't just a pretty face. His soul seeped out, grabbed hold of mine, and reached parts I didn't know existed.

In an attempt to shift us back to lighter topics, he continued our game of twenty questions. "Favorite type of music?"

"That's an easy one. I love all music. I listen to rock or electronic the most, but I think all music has its place. You?"

"Rock in all forms. Depends on what I'm doing, or my mood. I'll listen to almost anything, though, as long as it doesn't sound like crap."

"I'll agree to that."

It was peculiar. Even though we knew nothing about each other, as I listened to Jackson speak and tell me details about his life, it seemed as if I'd known him years. We were strangers, yet a part of me felt more connected to him than anyone else. It baffled and intrigued me.

Lost in my own headspace, I hadn't realized the server arrived with our dinner until it was placed in front of me. The savory aromas distracted me enough to halt any further questions. For now. I still had so many questions to ask him, but they could wait. Plus, he wasn't going anywhere soon. Not if I had a say in the matter.

Jackson parked his Jeep a few spaces from my front door. He cut the engine and let the darkness encapsulate us. If I considered myself out of place or uncomfortable earlier tonight, I was mistaken. A low hum coursed throughout my body. My thoughts ran a marathon alongside my heart.

I fiddled with my fingers, not sure where to put my hands. Silence stretched the space between us, neither of us sure what to say next. First dates were always tricky. Do you kiss your date? Do you not? There was a mysterious, invisible list of first date dos and don'ts in the world. Depending on whom you asked, different rules would be applied.

Right now… I had zero clue how the evening would end.

I liked Jackson. A lot. He had a great personality. He was charming, funny, down to earth, outgoing, and very nice on the eyes. Just because I thought those things about him didn't mean he reciprocated. I'd have to test the waters, get my feet a little wet, and see where it led us.

"Thank you for a wonderful evening. I had a great time." My voice blended in with the chirping cicadas outside.

He opened his door, exited the Jeep and walked around to my door, opening the door for me. "It was my pleasure. I had a really nice time, too."

Our footsteps clapped against the pavement as we walked to my front door. The pace of our stride nowhere as fast or loud as the beat of my pulse beneath my ears. His fingertips toyed with my bare back, the small strokes flamed the spark in my veins. When we reached the door, I fished through my purse for my keys, then unlocked the bolt before turning back to face him.

Under the soft glow of the porch light, part of his face masked in shadows, the sapphire of his blues burned radiant. My eyes shifted away from his, dropping down and locking on his mouth, watching his lips as he watched me.

His calloused fingers traced my spine, gliding up and stopping when he reached the length of my hair. He flattened his palm against my skin and my body jolted to life. Barely a breath passed between us before he seized my chin with two fingers and lifted my lips to his.

Warmth radiated from every inch of him and poured into me.

His lips on mine was all-consuming. My front porch disappeared. The singing cicadas gone. All traces of the outside world vanished. No sights. No sounds. Just a hint of his scent—a heady blend of spice and fresh cotton.

It was him and me. Kissing as if we were the last two people in existence.

I reached behind me and turned the knob. I backed us into

the confines of my apartment and kicked the door shut. Our lips locked, my hands traced the line of muscles along his biceps as I walked backward and he followed. A moment later, the backs of my knees bumped the couch.

Reality struck Jackson a second later, and he broke our kiss, framing my face in his palms. "You have no idea how bad I want this." His breath heavy on my mouth.

"I'm not stopping you." Truth be told, I may have wanted him more than he wanted me.

"It's not my style to go to bed with a girl on a first date. Or even a second date. But with you… It seems like I've known you my whole life." His words lured me in further, and my desire for him grew tenfold. That he felt the same attraction and familiarity added fuel to the flame.

"I want you. Now." My desperation for his touch spilled out before I stopped myself.

Our eyes locked, the question of what would happen next weighed heavy in the air. I ached for him in a way I'd never ached for anyone else. We barely knew each other, but Jackson filled a void inside me and made it whole. A void I never knew existed. The desire for his connection was powerful and heady.

"I know you do. But not tonight. Not on our first date. I want you to be sure and I want it to be unlike anything you've ever experienced." A smirk lit up his face, then turned serious in an instant. A hint of significance at what was happening between us.

His lips brushed over mine one last time, then he inched back and pivoted to leave. When he reached the door, my words ran after him. "When will I see you again?"

He turned his head, just as he swung the door open. "Soon. I promise. Sweet dreams, my Sarah." And then he walked out the door.

EIGHT

THE MEMORY of my date with Jackson cycled on repeat in my head for days.

I reached up and pressed my fingers to my lips, recalling the heat and intensity of his mouth on mine. He had been such a gentleman the entire evening. As much as I wanted to take our date to the next level, he declined my advances. He wanted to take things farther—desire clear in the way his lips devoured mine—but he needed us to start slow. Get to know one another.

Men like Jackson… they were one in a million. A rare gem. Does this make me lucky? While my head said yes, my body screamed no.

As frustrating as stopping had been, I was thankful for his desire to wait. Instant gratification wasn't all it was cracked up to be. Anticipation… now that made life much more enticing.

Every night this week, I'd gone to bed imagining his lips on my skin. I recalled the way his tongue tangoed with mine. The way his mouth worshiped mine, as if I was his dying breath. If his lips had me that worked up, God only knows how I'd react when his hands caressed my skin and I stripped him bare for the first time. Hell, I couldn't stop daydreaming of what his broad shoulders and strong core looked like under the snug fabric of his shirt. Not to mention the way his jeans hugged his hips and legs, highlighting all the best parts.

"Hey, bitch. We carpooling to the luncheon?" Christy's bubbly voice popped up, and I jumped in my seat, snapping out of my daydream.

"Yeah. Let me grab my purse." My hands fumbled to open the desk drawer while my mind shifted gears back to the present.

"You seem flustered. Everything okay?" Christy asked.

I worked to mask the rising heat in my cheeks and nodded. If I spoke right now, my voice would crack and Christy's questioning would commence.

The annual company luncheon was something they required us to attend, but no one enjoyed. Hours of speeches and slideshow presentations, accompanied by buffet food and boredom. At least it was a change of scenery and I wouldn't be answering any more calls or emails today.

I loved my job, and I performed well. But sitting in a room with close to two hundred people, hearing last year's sales numbers and this year's company goals, was sleep worthy. The only thing we hoped for was a decent selection of food.

I hooked arms with Christy and we all but skipped down the path through cubicle central and headed for the elevator. "Is Liz riding with us?"

"Of course she is. Bitch, you think I'd forget about her?"

Christy and her incessant need to use the word bitch. No matter what kind of day I had, this woman always made me laugh, just like now. "I don't think you could forget about anyone. That's why I love you so much."

Someone's elbow jabbed into my back, a heavy, unwelcome breath heated my neck. The doors to the convention room remained locked for a few more minutes. The mass of Hammond Life employees grouped together like a concert mosh pit, ready to shove when the time presented itself. A gentle weight skimmed the loose locks of hair on my back, followed by a light tug on the strands. As I turned to see who was standing behind me, the large wooden doors opened and everyone propelled forward, eager to breathe cooler air.

"Jesus. You'd think this was a rat race or the running of the bulls," I said to Liz and Christy, who had been driven into my right side.

When we were ten feet into the room, the crowd dispersed and we all breathed a little easier. Everyone split off into four lines. The banquet hall was a spacious room with large, cloth-covered tables and metal-framed, padded chairs. Our names displayed on tent cards in front of each place setting. At the center of the table sat a small bouquet of greenery and simple wildflowers. Banquet employees stood at the head of the four lines, asking our names and directing us to the table number assigned to us.

Christy, Liz, and I were seated at the same table. We appreciated whoever was responsible for the seating arrangement. No doubt I would enjoy the company of anyone at the table, but it was always nice to sit with your favorite people. We had only seen each other a couple times since my date with Jackson, and I missed time with my best friends.

We arrived at table eighteen, our tent cards displayed but not side by side. After moving a couple people around, we ensured we sat next to each other. Taking our seats, we waited while the line diminished. As soon as everyone located their seats, the meeting would begin. The quicker this party started, the quicker the day would end.

"So, I feel like we haven't talked in a lifetime." Christy rolled her eyes, her face highlighted in faux exaggeration. "I neeeeed to know more about your date with the hottie. Details, please." She leaned toward me, her elbows on the table and fingers steepled in front of her mouth. She bounced in her chair—literally. Excitement oozed from her pores.

"There's really not much to tell." My face heated as my legs clenched. Right now, I was thankful the tablecloth hid my lap. "We had dinner. We kissed. He did the gentlemanly thing and went home. The end."

Talking about my date with Jackson made me want to crawl into a hole and hide, which was foreign to me. I was unsure if it was the date's simplicity. Or because I liked him a lot. Maybe I didn't want to prattle off details with Liz by my side. Perhaps it was all three blended together. The urge to share bubbled in my bloodstream, but I didn't want to rub it in Liz's face. Just now, the thought of Jackson's supple lips pressed against mine, my core temperature rose a few degrees. Nowhere in proximity and Jackson affected me.

What exactly does that mean?

"I'm sure there was more to it than that. Why're you being so prudish?" Christy's inquisitive mind was bound to drive me insane. I loved Christy's nature, but couldn't handle the probing right now. Not with Liz here.

"Seriously, there's not much to tell." *Please leave it alone.*

This time, Liz chimed in. "Sarah, are we not best friends? Don't we share everything? Tit for tat. It's an equal exchange. For all of us."

Was Liz sending me a hidden message? Letting me know I could express my feelings for Jackson without hurting her? Our eyes locked as I gauged her mood and the definition behind her words. When she registered my silent pondering, she winked one of her dazzling hazels.

I hadn't realized, until now, how important it was for Liz to accept my potential relationship with Jackson. That she would be okay with hearing me talk about someone else. It was one thing to discuss the possibility of me dating Jackson, but it morphed into something different when I actually went on a date. Knowing she would still be the same Liz either way… it meant the world to me.

I gazed at the white plate in front of me, a cloth napkin folded into a bird rested in the center. My mind drifted, wondering what poor soul had to fold hundreds of napkins a day as their job. Sucking in a deep breath, I spilled the sorted details of my date, my voice growing louder the more I shared.

I told them about dinner. My nervousness when I felt underdressed. How his hands occasionally touched me and it set me ablaze. How much he loved his mother. Our quiet ride back to my apartment. And the kiss. The kiss that had me wanting him like he was my last meal. Part of me thought I had him on the cusp of agreeing to take it farther, but he had been a gentleman. His desire to wait, the most delicious form of torture I experienced. I loved it and hated it.

"For the last week, I've been losing my mind. I've been deprived. We've been talking every night, but his schedule is packed. I hope we can see each other between now and the weekend."

Feedback screeched throughout the room, everyone covering their ears and halting conversation. "Sorry, everyone. Thank you, all, for joining us today to celebrate Hammond Life. In a moment, we'll let you all grab your lunch. Please hang tight while the concierge walks around and signals for your table to go to the buffet. After everyone has gotten their food, we'll begin the conference. Thank you."

We returned to our conversation. They sent tables to the buffet in numeric order, a few minutes elapsing between each. Minutes into our more detailed conversation about my date, a hand tapped my shoulder. Startled, I spun in my chair and spotted Kyle—a middle-aged man whose cubicle butted against the back of mine—behind me.

"Hey, Sarah, how are you? Haven't talked to you in a while."

"I'm good, Kyle, thanks. Been a little busy, but otherwise good."

"Glad to hear it. I saw those flowers you got the other week. They were super pretty. A gift from your boyfriend?" His face shifted for a second. If I hadn't been looking him in the eye, I would not have caught it.

My poker face slid into place. I was somewhat protective about what I shared with my coworkers. An old habit I started years ago. And with the recent delivery, my defensive side appeared more frequently. Staying generic with my response, I said, "They were pretty. But not sure who they came from. Wasn't my boyfriend. So, I ended up giving them away."

I swore, for a fraction of a millisecond, anger glinted on his face. But it vanished before I registered its validity. So, I played it off as my imagination. Maybe all the paranoia about who sent them got to me.

"Such a shame to give away such beautiful flowers," he muttered and turned back to his table as if someone garnered his attention.

My gaze reverted back to Liz and Christy, their eyes glued on me, mouthing *weird*. A slight chill made me shiver from head to toe. Kyle was one of the sweetest guys in the office. He had a handsome face, brown hair, and a full beard. What he didn't have in physical features, he made up for with his kind nature. Sure he was different, but weren't we all? But something about his tone and body language a minute ago didn't sit right with me.

I took out my phone, texting Christy and Liz in our group chat.

Sarah: Not saying anything else. Later, when it's just us.

They both checked their phones and nodded. A man wearing a white dress shirt, black vest and black pants stepped up to our table. "When you're ready, you may proceed to the buffet." I couldn't get up fast enough.

Sarah: How's your day been?
Jackson: Lots of sweat and tears. No tears from me though. First client was having a rough day.
Sarah: Pain is beauty. JK. I hope they're okay.
Jackson: Me too. Life stuff that they're trying to not worry about. How was your day?

Jackson and I had these chats daily now. Although we'd only been on one date, we conversed on a regular basis. Some conversations just idle chitchat. Others more in depth. But with each exchange, my eagerness to see Jackson grew.

Sarah: Boooorrrring. Annual company luncheon. Crap food, long winded speeches.
Jackson: I suppose we must have dinner again. Have some better food to balance it out.

Yes! Now we were getting somewhere.

Sarah: Sounds like a great plan to me. Name the time and the place.
Jackson: You available tomorrow?

Is that even a question? I don't want to come off as desperate, so I paused a moment before responding.

Sarah: Calendar says I am 😃
Jackson: Let me figure out the details. I'll message you in the morning.
Sarah: I'll be patiently waiting.
Jackson: Good night, Daisy.
Sarah: Good night xo

Why did I love it when he called me Daisy?

I stabbed at my salad, spearing the veggies with unnecessary vigor before shoving them into my mouth. My teeth gnashed loudly as I answered Christy's latest inquiry. "I don't know where we're going yet. He asked if I was available tonight and said he'd message me this morning. No other details yet."

"I'm sure it means nothing." Her words tried to soothe me. "Maybe he's just been super busy with work this morning and hasn't had a minute to pick up his phone."

"Christy's probably right. Anyone who ignored my girl would be an idiot." Liz draped her arm over my shoulder and squeezed.

Using my fork to push the remaining contents of my salad around the bowl, I bobbed my head. Their words soaked into my consciousness. "You're both probably right. I've never been this worried about a date before. I feel ridiculous." My juvenile behavior laughable.

"You feel that way because you like him. Just keep sending out the positive vibes and let everything happen how it's meant to." I glanced over at Liz, her words softened my heart more for her. She really was an awesome friend and wanted nothing except the best for me.

We finished the rest of our lunchtime talking about Christy and Rick and how things were in their world. Rick was her happily ever after. Doing small gestures to let Christy know how much he loved her. For their post Valentine's Day date, he arranged an elegant dinner in the park. Heater lamps kept them warm in the chilled air. Followed by a horse-drawn carriage ride. Christy still swooned over the whole evening.

Stepping out of the elevator on our floor, the three of us split up and headed for our designated workspace. After we parted ways, I heard my phone chime in my purse. I snagged it, switched the phone to silent and discovered the long-awaited message from Jackson.

Jackson: You okay with dinner at my place?
Sarah: I'm good with that. Just let me know when and where.
Jackson: Anything you can't or don't eat?
Sarah: Nothing too heavy. Trying to maintain my girlish figure. Not a big red meat eater.
Jackson: Cool. I can work with that.

His address populated the next bubble on the screen, followed by a request for my presence at six thirty. A bevy of doves took flight in my chest as excitement for our date had me a little light-headed. As I reached my desk, I sat down and inhaled a few deep breaths.

I wasn't sure what had me more excited. A second date with Jackson. Or that our second date would be at his place. I pressed my fingers to my lips to hide my exuberant smile from no one. My mind ran laps around the possibilities of the evening ahead. And with each lap, my heart raced a little faster.

I stood outside Jackson's door for at least five minutes. Arriving much earlier than expected, I stared at the grain lines of the large oak door. In a moment of realization, I prayed he wasn't on the other side of the door, watching me through the peephole. Because I surely appeared a fool.

My fingers wrapped around the cool metal door knocker,

tapping it a few times and crossing my fingers he didn't open the door too fast. I ran my hands over my hair and smoothed any out of place locks. By the amount of time it took Jackson to open the door, I determined there was no way he'd witnessed my loitering.

"Hey. Come in, come in." He reached for my hand, enveloping it in his before he pressed a tender kiss on my lips. "Food's almost ready. I'll give you the tour in a sec, just need to watch the stove another minute. Don't want to burn anything." Letting go of my hand, he jogged toward what I assumed to be the kitchen.

I followed behind him, walking through his living room and past a wall opposite the front door, into a spacious kitchen. The walls, cabinets, and floors a mix of black, white, and marble. It was modern and masculine. Beyond the kitchen, a pair of glass doors were open. A screen door kept pests out but allowed the cool evening air to break the heat of the kitchen.

"From what I've seen, you have a really nice place," I said as I leaned against a counter and watched him move around the kitchen. Jackson focused on a task was a delectable visual.

"Thanks. I can only take credit for the decor though. I rent the place. Haven't found quite the right place to purchase yet. I figure something that permanent, I should be ready to stay in one place for years. Know what I mean?"

"Yeah. I love Savannah, but I'm not sure if it's where I want to live for the rest of my life. Who knows? Maybe something will jump out at me one day and I'll know where I'm meant to be."

His eyes studied my face a moment as he assessed my words and held back some of his own. Did I say something off-putting? Did I insinuate? I really hope I didn't just stick my foot in my mouth. How could I break up the awkward silence closing in around me? Around us?

"Is there anything I can help with?"

A dazzling smile highlighted his square jaw, my body temperature rose from the single expression. "The food will be done in a sec. Why don't you go out onto the patio while I plate everything. Pour yourself some wine. I'll be there in a minute."

"Okay."

Sliding the screen door open, I stepped out onto the patio that stretched along the entire back of the house. Off the kitchen, a wooden, planked table had several votive candles illuminating the place settings and an arrangement in the center. Jackson had woven two sunflowers between the candles, along with several daisies scattered around their stems.

At one end of the six-person table, I noticed a metal pail with a bottle of wine nestled in ice. I retrieved the wine from the chilled bucket, liquid courage necessary sooner than expected. Pouring Chardonnay in the glasses on the table, I shot back half the contents of mine before topping it off.

I sat back in the handcrafted, Adirondack-style wooden chair, the grain matching the table, and ran my hands along the lacquered surface on the armrests. The air still crisp as winter lingered, I wrapped myself in the blanket Jackson must've placed in the chair.

I closed my eyes and took a moment to absorb the atmosphere. The mixed scents of Jackson's cooking, his masculine smell on the plaid cotton, and the oak trees beyond the screened porch filled my nose. Miscellaneous forest insects sang to each other as the sun set. My stomach flipped like a hammock as I waited for Jackson to join me.

Tonight was my second date with Jackson and an over-whelming burst of elation soared in my chest.

We'd talked on and off over the last week. Some small talk, work stuff, and a little flirting. From what I could tell so far, Jackson was a pretty laid-back guy. He was also ambitious and gorgeous as sin. I hadn't pegged him as a romantic. Sitting at this table, the glow of the candlelight flickering in my periphery, the decadent smell of our dinner... my heart swelled as butterflies started a hurricane beneath my diaphragm.

The screen door slid open and Jackson stepped out with two plates in his hands. The aroma and artfully displayed food had me licking my lips and my mouth watering instantly. As he set his plate down, he shared tonight's menu. "Shrimp scampi with spinach pasta, maple roasted rainbow carrots, and a small balsamic dressed salad."

I leaned forward, inhaling deeply as the aromas wafted from my plate. "Everything looks and smells amazing. Did your mom teach you to cook?"

His eyes softened at the mention of his mom, his lips curving up into a gentle smile. She must've been an incredible woman to live within him so deep. "She taught me some basic stuff, but mostly she taught me how to cook family recipes. Biscuits, roasts, her version of southern delicacies. I have several recipes. I might have to break them out again sometime." He spoke about her with such reverence. There's no way I could fathom his loss and the pain of missing her.

"I think I would've loved that kind of stuff when I was a kid; making things in the kitchen with my family. My parents lived the hippie life for a while—simplistic. I wouldn't change anything about my childhood, but it would have been fun to do some of those things, too."

The candles flickered with the occasional breeze. Our food disappeared from our plates. The time followed right beside it as we talked more about our lives. Conversation with Jackson was as effortless as breathing. He was open and spoke his mind, emotions included. He seemed passionate about everything in his life. Nothing entered his life without giving him purpose. That concept had me itching to ask him how I gave him purpose.

Why hold back? Curiosity weighed my thoughts as I hesitantly asked, "So, you say that you don't do anything that doesn't give you purpose or have meaning." I sucked in a breath, holding it for five heartbeats before releasing it. "How do I fit into that equation?"

He studied my face, pondered over the words I left unsaid. "When I saw you at the party two weeks ago, you lit up the room. Like a spotlight pointed you out to me."

"Are you sure it wasn't my body rubbing up against two other women that lured you in?" I laughed, the sound bouncing around us.

"Well, I can't discount that. That was hot." A million-dollar smile flashed across his face. "But that wasn't the sole reason. Before you danced with your friends, I saw you. You were wandering around, keeping tabs on everything and everyone. I caught your profile, your smile hiding a bit behind your hair. I wanted to walk up to you, but I didn't. The guy I mentioned that night, he'd been near you for a while. And, although he didn't look like he was your type, I stayed back. It wasn't until I didn't see him anymore that I realized he must not have been with you."

Like was not a potent enough word to describe how Jackson saw me. The way he described that night, he looked at me in an incomprehensible way. He had seen me. Wanted to talk to me. But kept his distance because he thought someone had claimed my heart. *Seriously*, how did I get this lucky?

Date number two. Speechless. Once again.

The rough scrape of his chair legs grated over the concrete floor as he stood. He grabbed his plate and mine. "I'll be back in a second. Grabbing dessert." He pressed his lips to the top of my head and then disappeared into the kitchen, leaving me to swim in the sea of emotions he stirred inside me.

His words from after our first date came to the front of my mind. Ever the gentleman, he didn't want to taint our first date with sex. He wanted to drag out the anticipation, to be sure it was something we both wanted. That it wouldn't hinder us from our future. I peeked over my shoulder and watched him move around the kitchen.

This man was doing everything and anything to impress me. And I fell for every single maneuver. I rose from my chair, the blanket falling behind me as my feet ambled forward, with a single destination in mind. Sliding the screen door open, I stepped into the kitchen, walked up to his back and traced my fingers along his triceps.

He stopped assembling our dessert and his breath hitched. My hands coasted up and down the lines of his muscular arms. Twisting to peer over his shoulder, I glimpsed his profile. Jaw slackened and sapphires sparkling with hunger. He set down our dessert and spun his body to face me. His hands glided up the sides of my face, the gentle touch strong as I leaned into it.

"You are going to make me break my own rules," he stated in a deep, raspy tone. Jackson's eyes smoldered with unspoken desire.

"I want you to break them," I begged as I stood on my

toes and pressed my lips to his. A beat later, his lips parted and his tongue mingled with mine.

His hands danced down my neck and traced my collarbones before gliding down my arms to my waist. He deepened the kiss with a throaty hum as his tongue devoured me. A new synergy formed between us and a fire burned hot in my core. A moment later, Jackson hoisted me up in his arms—my feet dangling a beat before I locked them around his hips—and we were moving.

Our mouths continued to dance in synchronicity as he held me close. His feet padded against the hardwood floor, turning past corners before he stopped. A soft yarn rug warmed my soles when I set my feet down and his hands framed my face as our kiss intensified.

My fingers skirted the firm lines of his back, dipping and tracing before my palms flattened to discover the sculpted tone of his muscles. I fondled my way down his back and hooked onto the loops along his waistline. Slipping my hands under his shirt hem, I hummed my appreciation against his lips. His heated skin seared me like wildfire as I shoved his shirt over his head.

Nothing but our labored breaths floated in the air. With my palms splayed on his bare chest, I leaned forward and kissed the skin below his clavicle. He hissed under my touch, his chest rising and falling faster. Skimming my palms over the pronounced ridges of his abdominals, my tongue peeked out. I licked and sucked over his pec before landing on the taut peak of his nipple. I captured the bud between my teeth and tugged.

His sharp intake broke the silence before his hands gripped my arms and drew me back. A second later, I flew through the air as he launched me onto the bed. Adrenaline pumped through my veins and made me rabid, my fingers eager to remove the clothes shielding the rest of him from me. He opened the bedside table drawer, grabbed a condom and tossed it on the bedding before resuming his position.

His hands glided up the length of my legs, slipping under the loose cotton of my skirt. He hooked his fingers into the tight band of my panties as his remaining digits grabbed hold of my skirt. Quicker than I could say *yes*, he yanked hard and exposed my wanton flesh.

His breath hovered over the apex of my thighs. The rapid exhalation of air from his lungs coated my skin in goose-flesh, driving my appetite to insatiable levels. Jackson's hooded eyes locked on mine, the intensity of the moment causing his sapphires to resemble an onyx.

"Please," I whisper-begged.

The pads of his fingers grazed down the sides of my torso —a trail of sparks in its wake—as he shed the rest of my clothes. His mouth worshipped my flesh, nipping and sucking. My back bowed off the mattress, craving more with each stroke, lick, and fondle.

Fumbling to remove the final barrier between us, I unbuttoned his shorts—my hands and feet working together to push them to the floor. A tidal wave of heat spiked in me when I learned Jackson was naked. *Did he always go commando? Or did he plan for things to progress between us tonight?* Either way, it didn't matter. I wanted him more than anything in this moment and nothing hindered me from having him.

When he pressed his steely erection against my abdomen, a new fever dampened my skin. I reached down and wrapped my hand around his length, watching as he bit back a moan. The action caused him to jut farther into my grip, his length grinding over the tight bundle of nerves between my legs.

"Oh, god," I mumbled as my back bowed and my breasts crushed against his chest.

His mouth smashed mine, tongue thrusting inside; greedy and ready to consume every ounce of me. Jackson's hand slid between us. His fingertips circled my pulsing clit, a slow, lazy rhythm before adding more pressure. Low in my belly, my orgasm grew hungrier with each swipe. Just as I hit my climax, he shifted his fingers and dipped them between my folds, coating them with my arousal before repeating the process.

"Fuck, that's good," I groaned, breathy and loud before I sunk my teeth into the crook of his neck.

"Not yet..." His fingers stopped. Jackson kissed his way

down my body, his tongue leaving a trail from sternum to apex.

I propped myself up on my elbows, my breath shallow bursts, my core begging for release. Jackson's lust-hazed eyes stared back at me, drunk at the sight of me. A second later, his tongue lavished me, flicking the tight bud at my core. His fingers clamped onto my nipples and rolled back and forth, the harsh pinch had me crying out and driving myself more into his eager mouth.

Jackson had a magical tongue. And the way he used it was a superpower. I had no clue what he was doing, how he maneuvered between my thighs, nor did I care. The only thing I cared about was him worshipping my body.

"Holy shit. Don't. Fucking. Stop. Oh. My…" I closed my eyes tightly as I cried out into the darkness.

My core temp was thermal—a volcano ready to erupt. The skill of his magical tongue had me on the brink. When my orgasm hit, it was a sonic boom. Intensity rippled in waves from my convulsing body. The faint tearing of the condom wrapper was barely discernible with my pulse racing in my ears.

A second later, Jackson inched up my body and hovered above me, his eyes locked on mine. After a ragged breath, he dipped down and devoured me. The taste of my orgasm salty and intoxicating as our tongues swirled together in a rhythmic dance. A groan vibrated in his chest and he drove his hips forward, adding the perfect amount of friction between his cock and my clit. My desire to have him inside me escalated by the nanosecond. As if my thoughts displayed on a marquee, he shifted down then thrust inside me. My head tipped back and my torso arched up as I learned what Jackson's strength and prowess entailed.

Our bodies froze—his length fully inside me—as he waited for my eyes to open. He leaned down, his breath hot on my ear. "Being inside you is incredible. Perfect," he said. My groan in response was very unladylike and animalistic.

He reared his hips back slowly, stopping before the tip slid out, and then thrust forward again. Both of us gasped as we took in the moment. My eyes rolled back, and I savored every sensation as Jackson filled me completely.

It had been months since I had been with a man, and my body stretched to accommodate him. Not that any man before Jackson even compared. His magnitude filled me in the most delicious of ways. Each stroke lit me up like the Fourth of July. When he slid out, I dug my nails into his broad shoulders and anchored him to me.

Something shifted between us. His ravenous expression stared down my body before he leaned into the crook of my neck and clamped down, sucking at the tender skin. Hard. One hand, then the other, slipped beneath my butt and squeezed. Tingling started at the ends of my limbs, flowing inward until it converged into a bonfire at my epicenter. My nipples pert. My core ached at the loss of him. Desire ambushed my mind. Delirium on the verge of taking hold.

Before I even said a word, he rammed back into me. Hard. The intensity is incomparable.

My nails dragged down the rippled sinew of his back. With my lungs crying for air he buries his length to the hilt inside me. He reared back—faster this time—and slammed back into my pussy. Slam after slam, he set a fevered tempo that had us both clawing at one another.

His breath hot on my ear, labored and heady. "You… are so… fucking… exquisite." He sucked my earlobe before clamping down and tugging it with his teeth.

Short, high-pitched cries reverberated from my throat and echoed in the room. I clasped Jackson's glutes and relished each of his thrusts. A deep-rooted fire ignited, burning hot and intense, ready to incinerate. It inundated every molecule. My skin pinked and dampened in the darkness. My limbs trembled at the ferocity. And my mouth watered, begging to taste Jackson on my tongue. Every fiber inside me screamed for more.

"Harder. Fuck me harder," I said, my voice indiscernible. My hoarse cries filled the air as I wrapped my legs around his waist and locked my ankles together.

His tempo increased and an electric charge filled the room. One hand encased the back of my neck and locked me in place while he pounded into me viciously. My screams surrounded us, multiplied with each drive forward, and Jackson's growl turned feral.

Pressure and pain and pleasure gnawed my shoulder as Jackson's teeth broke my skin. It was the last straw as I detonated into oblivion. My walls clenched and milked Jackson's cock.

"Holy fuck," he said, breath ragged. A second later, his moan pierced the air as he came inside me.

Holy fuck was right.

NINE

THE BUDDING relationship between Jackson and I had been nothing short of freaking awesome.

To say otherwise would understate the obvious—a once in a lifetime guy. Jackson was more than a pretty face plastered on a magnificent body. So much more. Yes, women got lost for days looking at him, but he had the kindest heart. The way he put others first incomprehensible. Not to mention, his smile warmed my skin and melted my panties.

A few weeks passed since our first date, not a dull moment in our foreseeable future. Jackson mastered the art of wooing. I imagined his mom was the culprit behind how he treated and respected women. He loved her in a way so different from how I loved my parents. My mom and dad loved me to the ends of the earth—and vice versa—but were content being on their own, even in my younger years. The chivalry Jackson displayed was completely natural. A part of him. And everything he did had my heart swooning and my core dampening.

It wasn't just the sex, either. Although, sex with Jackson was a euphoric experience. A high never rejected. Jackson was the whole package. Kind. Gentle. He treated me like a lady in public and a freak in the bedroom. That, all by itself, was a tremendous turn on and made my thighs tremble. I loved how our lives slowly merged. Selfless in nature,

Jackson always thought of us as a whole. Every trait he exhibited made him downright tantalizing.

Since the night we sealed our souls, we went on a few more dates. One at a bar-and-grill during karaoke night. We both learned neither of us could sing worth a damn. Another in the park—our picnic turned into something children's eyes shouldn't be privy to. Needless to say, our picnic ended quick. And, three nights ago, we shared a date night with friends. Me, Jackson, Christy, Rick, Liz, Eric, and Jackson's friend Rob, a personal trainer. All of us had a night full of laughs, beers, and bowling.

Never in my lifetime did I think I'd be so lucky as to find someone like Jackson. My perfect match. You hear stories of your friends, acquaintances or colleagues finding that one person. The one they can't stand to be away from. Someone they call, text, or FaceTime whenever they have a free minute. The one person who is in every molecule they breathe, every beat of their heart, every sensation throughout their body. Someone they can't live without. A person who makes them a better version of themselves.

Our relationship new, our beginning still happening, but I couldn't imagine my world without Jackson. Far too soon for the infamous *l* word, but I was very much *in like* with him. And he was very much *in like* with me. When together… the air in the room pulsated with energy. Raw and passionate and potent.

Hopping out of my Beetle, I walked to the mailboxes for my building and waved at a neighbor. Her chihuahua yipped at me and she scolded him. "Stop barking at the nice lady, Stanley." A second later, she apologized and walked off. Why were the small dogs always the noisy ones?

"Whatever," I said to my mailbox. I popped my key into the aluminum door and discovered a pile of unwanted advertisements along with some envelopes sandwiched in the crease.

As I walked back to my apartment, I flipped through the envelopes.

Crap.

Crap.

Bill.

Crap.

Something. Although, not sure what.

A plain, white envelope sat in the stack, my first name typed in the center. Not typed on a computer and printed from an inkjet. No. Someone typed this on a typewriter, the paper behind the font embossed with faint ink. *Who even owns a typewriter anymore? And how was this in my mailbox?* There was no indication someone mailed it—no return address, no mailing address, no stamp. Only my first name.

My stomach churned at the sight of my name pressed into the paper. Something didn't sit right as I held it in my hands.

I stared at the ominous rectangle as I walked to my apartment. It singed my hands and piqued my curiosity with each step forward. After stepping inside my apartment, I set my keys and purse on the entryway table then opened the envelope, wary to discover what lay inside. A folded piece of paper sat nestled inside the flap. After a moment's hesitation, I retrieved the thin sheet and unfolded it, an entire page also typed on a typewriter.

My beautiful Sarah,

Oh, how I dream about your beauty. The way the sunlight accentuates the golden glow in your hair. How your laughter lights up a room. The way you love others without effort. You are beautiful in every sense of the word. Every time I look at you, you take my breath away. Every time I smell you, you intoxicate me. Every time I hear your voice, I tune out every other sound. You make the world a better place. You make my world worth living in. One day, you will see. One day, you will be mine.

XO my beautiful XO

I dropped the envelope and letter, kicking them away when they landed on my feet, the words blistering my skin. I pressed a hand hard against my sternum as I gasped for breath. A newfound pain seared my lungs and stabbed my heart.

What the hell was this? Better yet, who the hell sent it?

Newsflash... it wasn't mailed. Somehow, some way, a

random person placed this envelope in my mailbox. A locked mailbox. And whoever they were... they knew precisely where I lived. My hands trembled at my sides as a chill prickled my skin, spreading throughout my body. Whoever this phantom was, they made me feel a pervading sense of menace that swallowed me whole.

My life had been invaded, and I shuddered at the idea of someone watching me. I rushed to the door and locked the bolt before sliding the chain in place. Next, I dashed to the four windows in my small apartment, checked the locks, and cranked the handle tight on the blinds. Within seconds, darkness engulfed me. Double checking that the lock on the patio door was secure, I yanked the loose string and jumped as the blinds crashed down.

At a loss, I collapsed to the floor and cried into my palms. *What should I do?*

I should tell somebody. Someone whose cognitive skills function right now. Because mine vanished the moment I read the letter. Someone to give me advice on how I'm supposed to handle a situation of this magnitude. It's not every day you have to deal with someone sending you flowers or creepy notes and letters.

I glanced down at my trembling hands, the tremors strengthened with each passing minute. I stood, wiped the tears away, and inhaled deeply. Step by step, I trudged back to the foyer. When I reached the menacing note, I stopped and stared a moment. *It will be okay.*

Bending down, I picked up the letter and envelope between my thumb and forefinger and held them at arm's length. I walked over to my desk and dropped them, then slowly backed away. Heading back to the entryway, I snatched my purse from the table and riffled through it for my phone. After unlocking it, I opened my contacts and froze.

Who do I call? Jackson? Liz? Christy?

I eliminated Christy first. She would be equally lost. As I squeezed my eyes shut, I imagined her tugging her hair, freaking out, and screaming in my ear. After thirty minutes of screams, she'd tell me to call someone else. Plus, she and Rick were together, and I didn't want to disturb them.

I contemplated calling either Jackson or Liz for a solid five minutes while my eyes seared a hole in the threatening paper on my desk. Liz knew me better than anyone and would rescue me in a heartbeat. But I hesitated over calling her first. Our relationship didn't warrant me going to her when I needed rescuing. We were friends. Best friends. But still friends. We opted to not go down the strings-attached-relationship avenue. And I needed to keep things between us clear. For her and me.

I scrolled to Jackson's name, pressed the phone icon and listened to the slow, torturous ringing. After the third ring, which felt like the twentieth, Jackson answered. "Hey, babe. What's going on?" His voice sweet and charismatic on the other end. I'm happy that I called him.

I remained tight-lipped. What should I tell him? *Hey, I got some creepy letter in my mailbox today. Can you help me figure out how it got there?* I ran through countless stupid lines. Tried to decipher how to speak my unspoken words. But my brain was mush and incapable of decision making.

"Sarah? Are you there? Can you hear me?"

"Hey, sorry. Yeah, I spaced out for a second." My tongue fumbled over my words.

"You okay? You don't sound like yourself," he said as worry etched his tone and concern rang evident.

"Um… I got something strange in my mailbox today. Can you come by? I'm not sure what to do." Normal enough, *right*? A legitimate statement and question. Plain. Simple.

"What kind of strange thing? I'm just finishing up. I can be there in thirty minutes."

"It's easier to show you. You'll understand when you get here." I bit on one of my fingernails, a habit I always found disgusting but I did it without realizing I was doing it.

"Okay. I'll be there soon."

"Thanks."

I checked the clock. Jackson said thirty minutes. Thirty minutes wasn't so long, was it? As I scanned the windows in the living room, I exhaled into the darkness. *I'll be safe until he arrives. He'll be here soon.*

Twenty-three minutes later, a knock at my door startled me. Creeping to the door, I pushed up on my toes and checked the peephole. Jackson. *Thank god.* I unlatched the chain, twisted the deadbolt and turned the knob. As he stepped past me, I scanned the mini front yard and parking lot in front of the building. From what I could tell, no one lingered behind the bushes or stared at my door. In fact, no one was anywhere. Odd? Or was my paranoia hiking up a notch?

"Why is it so dark in here?" Jackson asked as I shut the door. The moment he turned and his eyes met mine, his hands framed my cheeks. He studied my face, seeking answers for my red-rimmed eyes and blotchy skin. "What's wrong? What strange thing was in your mailbox?"

"It's on the desk," I muttered. My eyes shifted to the side as I gestured behind him.

He pivoted and stared at the letter a moment. Two of the folds stood up straight. The envelope beneath. Jackson placed a gentle kiss on my lips then walked over to the piece of paper that shook me to my core.

I bit my nails as his eyes scanned the typewritten lines. His face redder with each word read. By the end, he picked up the envelope and turned it over in his hands. Jackson stared at it and noticed that only my name pressed into the surface with ink. As if I missed something, he lifted the envelope flap and peered inside to look for some missing piece. Another page. Some scrap of evidence I missed, perhaps.

"We need to call the police. Maybe this is the person who sent the flowers." Coming back to me, he cocooned me in warmth. His protective embrace comforted me. And I felt some other nameless, powerful emotion as well.

"I'm afraid," I whispered into his chest. Words I never thought I would say. "What are the cops going to do? File a report? Will a report *catch* whoever this is?" I had no idea. And even fewer answers. Zero. Zilch. Nada. No expertise in this area.

"I have no idea how this whole thing works either, babe." Goosebumps prickled my flesh as he took a step back and held my cheeks in his palms. "But we can't do nothing. We have to try." He leaned back in and placed a sweet, brief kiss on my forehead.

I stared past Jackson to my tattered oak desk, my eyes watering as the disturbing words jumped off the letter and threatened me. My pulse skyrocketed and my limbs shook as panic seeped into my veins. As frightened as I was, Jackson had the right idea. "Okay." I gazed back at him and nodded. "Let's go to the police. But will you drive? Don't think I can."

Jackson's strong arms hauled me forward and pressed me into his chest. His heat encased me like a fleece blanket on a cold evening and slowly eased my fear. "Of course. I'll do anything for you."

We walked out of the police station with a detailed report in hand. Thankful Jackson had his arm around my waist, my body needed his guidance while my brain registered this was actually happening. That this whole situation was real. That I had a… *stalker*. Just thinking the word made me nauseous.

A female officer asked me endless questions, many I fumbled to answer.

"Do you have any former partners where the relationship ended bad?" Not that I can think of.

"Do you know anyone who would want to cause you harm?" No, I was always nice to everyone.

"Have you had any recent arguments or debates with acquaintances, friends or family?" No, like I said, I'm nice to everyone.

The questions went on for two hours. They asked to keep the letter and envelope in the hopes of getting prints other than mine and Jackson's. I happily handed it over to them and told them I had no desire to see it again.

The officer also suggested I behave as if I never received the letter, more so when outside the privacy of my home. She had two theories. The first theory—the letter came from someone with a crush. Perhaps the person wasn't certain how to come forward and speak with me directly. The second theory was more disturbing and had me wanting to lock myself away and throw out the key.

The second theory—this person knew me. Someone in my present or from my past. And this person didn't have a crush, but a deep-rooted infatuation. Disillusioned to the extent they believed I was their girlfriend or lover. Extensive enough that they would do anything within their means to bring us together. Even if that involved hurting someone—including me. With Jackson being a new love interest in my life, it most likely provoked whoever and kick started their initiative.

Neither theory desirable, but I crossed my fingers and sent a silent prayer to whichever deity listened. If I could choose one of the two, I'd pick the first. *Please don't let it be the last.*

The couch cushion dipped next to me as Jackson set a buffet of Chinese takeout boxes in front of us. He grabbed a couple forks and plates from the kitchen, set them on the coffee table, and unfolded all the containers. My stomach groaned and begged me to grab a fork and dive in. My brain, on the other hand, had a million mile per hour marathon on what I should be doing. Eating didn't seem like a priority. Eating was the last thing my body wanted, but I opted to ignore it.

Jackson laid a hand on my knee, his thumb strumming back and forth lazily. As minor as the motion was, the gesture soothed me. "I know you probably don't feel like it right now, but you really should eat something. Your head is probably drowning in thoughts. For a bit, try to resurface."

He was right. As easy as it was to dwell, I had to be strong. This would pass, I just needed patience. I nodded, my eyes glued to the white and red cartons. "I'll try. Nothing too heavy though."

His fingers gave my knee a quick squeeze before they released me to grab a plate. "How about steamed vegetables and a little rice?"

"Yeah. That sounds okay," I mumbled, donning a half smile.

He scooped a spoonful of rice on the plate and added some veggies on the side before handing it to me. "Let's start with that."

Jackson picked up his plate and shoveled food from each box. He covered his dish with more than three times what I had. When he finished building the small mountain, he sat back and scooted as close to me as possible.

Once situated, he grabbed the remote and brought up the guide on the television. After scrolling a minute, he selected a show for us to watch. Jackson chose something that, I'm sure he hoped, would lighten my mood. Tension blanketed the air like a humid summer day. And the television served as background noise while I nudged broccoli and carrots with my fork, the tines occasionally scraping like nails on a chalkboard.

Jackson finished dinner first. I forced myself to eat bite after bite. We curled up on the couch afterward and watched hours of rerun episodes of *Friends*. His face lit up the couple times I laughed. Every once in a while, his strong arms squeezed me tight. After everything that happened today, all I craved was to not worry. Jackson did everything in his power to make this a reality. Mission accomplished.

As my eyes grew heavy, Jackson's weight shifted beside me. Next thing I knew, his arms were scooping me up and I was being carried into the bedroom. Cradled tight against his body, I inhaled his fresh and spicy scent and relaxed.

Our relationship still so new, but he was nothing short of sweet and caring. Jackson helped me undress, then tucked me in under the comforter. He stepped back and toward the door. *Was he leaving?* I didn't want him to go. I didn't want to be alone in the confines of my apartment. Not when someone outside these walls, who had an unhealthy obsession with me, might come after me at any time. Instead, I wanted him to slip under the bedding and lay down beside me. Bundle me up in his protective arms and hold me throughout the night.

I reached out and clutched his hand. I whisper-begged, "Please. Stay with me?"

His gentle eyes studied me, a small pinch glinted the edges. I squeezed his hand tighter as he struggled with staying or leaving. He sighed while bringing his free hand to stroke my cheek. "You have no idea how much I want to stay. I need to know you're safe. But I don't want to take advantage of the situation."

Sincerity laced each word he spoke as his watery eyes stared down at me. Jackson's tender nature astounded me. I had heard stories of women being taken advantage of in times of vulnerability. Far too many. But Jackson wasn't one of those types of guys.

I gripped his hand tighter and pleaded with him. "Please. Just lay with me. Hold me. I just need you next to me." No doubt my gravelly voice screamed desperation, but I no longer cared.

He removed his hand from mine, stepped back and dragged his shirt over his head. A second later, his shorts fell to the floor beside his shirt. I peeled back the comforter and made room for him. The mattress sloped, and I rolled closer to him as he encased me in warmth. I sighed and relaxed into him.

In this micro-blip of time, a stampede of emotions warmed my heart.

I was safe. Someone cared for me. And he would protect me.

"Thank you," I whispered as my eyes grew heavy.

Jackson pressed a kiss to the crown of my head. "Anything for you," he spoke softly against my hair. "Anything."

TEN

Days passed, nothing new came to light. No unannounced gifts. No notes or letters. No updates from the police. It's almost as if nothing had happened.

Aside from work, Jackson and I spent every waking—and sleeping—moment together. For the first time in my life, I craved someone at my side. Hungered for strength and courage from another. And Jackson stood eager to be at the front of the line. Ready to shield me from pain and lift my spirit. To give me the sense of security I so desperately yearned for.

We took the officer's advice and used the weekend as an opportunity to distract ourselves. When it was just the two of us, we were in heaven. But we also didn't want to become one of those couples who shut everyone out. Hanging with friends our livelihood, one of many things we shared in common, and one characteristic neither of us planned to change.

At lunch yesterday, I told Christy and Liz about my and Jackson's plan—a friend's night out. I invited Christy, Rick—if he was free—and Liz. Jackson asked Eric and Rob. Our plan—hit a couple bars or clubs around Bay Street.

Without question, Jackson and I agreed to not mention the letter I received to our friends. The less who knew, the better. We didn't need multiple sets of eyes and ears prying through my life. Plus, if it was someone close to us—which the officer suggested as a possibility—it was better to act as if I never received the letter. Maybe it would lure the culprit out into the open.

"Hell yeah, I'm in, bitch. I'll check with Rick and get back to you." Christy's exuberance lifted my spirits and made my cheeks burn. Too many days had passed since I'd smiled. Days since something other than dread flooded my veins. Christy's energy was the exact medicine I needed filtering through me. If anyone was capable of relieving the stress weighing down my heart, and dulling the craziness in my head, Christy won every time. Never a dark cloud in her blue sky. She always stumbled upon the silver lining or double rainbow in all things. I envied her this.

"Awesome. I really need tonight, ladies," I said.

"Count me in. I've been at home, binge watching reruns for the last two weeks. I could use some time away from my TV," Liz stated, an edge of disappointment in her words. I'm certain she was upset at herself for being such a couch potato.

"Yes!" I wrapped an arm around each of their shoulders, drawing their warmth into my sides and absorbing their positivity. This was the exact piece of reality I needed. A night out with my favorite people. To forget everything that threatened to steal my happiness. A night of the carefree, spirited Sarah.

"Babe, you almost ready? We're supposed to meet everyone in twenty."

I rounded the corner, my fingers fumbling to fasten my necklace as I walked toward Jackson. My limbs had trembled for the last hour, nervous and excited for the evening, and my dexterity had left the building. "Can you help me with this?" I asked.

Spinning around, I faced away from Jackson and swept my honey locks over one shoulder. He eased the eye and clasp from my hands, his nimble fingers hooking the necklace in place. A second later, a warm breath painted my bare shoulder. His feverish, calloused fingers lingering at the base of my neck before he traced a line down my spine. A shiver rippled throughout my body and sparked goose-flesh along my skin.

His lips danced up the curve of my neck, stopping at the sensitive flesh below my ear. "You're lucky I'm seeing you in this top now. If I saw this ten minutes ago, you'd need to get dressed again," he said, a growl ripping from his throat. Jackson nipped at my earlobe before licking and biting his way down my neck and shoulder, a new wave of shivers erupting and converging at my core.

"So you like what I'm wearing?" I squeaked out as I bit my lower lip. My desire alive for the first time in a week.

"Like doesn't even cover what this top is exposing."

He outlined the fabric of my top. The shimmery material edge started at the front of my shoulder, ran down my side, and stopped level with my navel. It only covered my breasts and a fraction of my abdomen. The back was open, with exception to the thin strands which ran across the back and neck and held it in place. A short denim skirt sat low on my hips, the bottom hemline exposing the majority of my long legs.

"I'm glad you more than like it. Maybe later, you can show me how much you more than like it," I teased.

Jackson spun me to face him. His smoldering sapphires locked onto me as he drew me closer, the hunger in his gaze lit my flesh on fire. He ate me alive with his inspection and, for a split-second, I gave serious thought to ditching our friends. If he let me, I'd rip the clothes off his perfect, chiseled body and take him on the floor where we stood.

"If you keep looking at me like that, we won't make it out the door. We should at least show up, seeing as the entire evening was our idea," he taunted with a wink.

"Okay, okay. Fine," I huffed as Jackson chuckled at my pity party. "But mark my words, sir." I tapped a finger on his chest. "This is far from over tonight."

"Yes, ma'am." His face beamed with promise and wonder at what the rest of the night would entail.

People crowded every bar we explored during our adventure. We went from place to place in search of the perfect atmosphere that played good music but with a decent crowd. We wandered in and out of a few places before finally locating one that satisfied us all.

It ended up only being six of us—Rick unable to ditch work. We sent our love to him in the form of goofy, kissy-faced text messages. He responded with pouty-faced texts and a promise to tag along next time.

The six of us stood around a tall table with our drink of choice. Jackson caged me in with his front deliciously close to my back. My body buzzed as the music pulsated around us. Everyone enjoyed a great night out as all dreadful thoughts drifted into the ether.

Christy and I chatted about how fun our next outing would be. "I hope Rick can join us," I said. Just as I asked Christy when Rick finished work, Jackson's fingers traced down my sides. My eyes rolled and slipped shut as his fingers danced over my skin. A moment later, he laced his fingers with mine and towed me onto the dance floor. Jackson walked backwards into the throng of bodies, his eyes locked on mine. A wicked, sexy grin brightened his face in the darkened space.

Before he escorted me to the dance floor, I hadn't paid attention to the song playing. It wasn't until we reached the center of the floor, sweaty bodies gyrating against one another everywhere, that I listened. A sultry bass vibe bounced off the walls and resonated in my bones. Every cell in my body ached to have Jackson's body flush against mine. The tempo flowed like molten lava and seeped into my pores like liquid sex. He spun me and pressed my back against his front, his fingertips igniting a trail of sparks along my skin as he guided us to the seductive beat.

The music pulsated as I stared at other couples giving themselves over to the beat. Voyeurism never interested me, but I gave into the visual stimuli as Jackson lit my body on fire. Calloused fingers roamed and kneaded my stark flesh, from hip to midriff, as he pressed his erection harder into my ass and I melted into him. His breath ghosted the nape of my neck a beat before his lips and tongue bruised my skin. An energy exploded inside me at the contact and flowed through every nerve ending in my body like an electrical grid, pooling at my core. I traced my hands over his forearms and imprisoned his splayed hands near my naval. His mouth continued to assault my flesh as I pressed my ass against his straining erection.

Anyone observing might say we were fucking, right there, in the middle of the nightclub. But I gave no fucks. Freedom surrounded me. An invisible weight lifted away when I was myself, in my element, surrounded by people I cared about. Jackson provided me with the perfect remedy, and I was so thankful.

Turning me to face him, he slid one leg between mine. His jeans rubbed rough on my panties in a delicious rhythm. With each circle and thrust of his hips, my body trembled against his thigh. My breasts smashed to his torso, his hands traced down my bare back and palmed my ass, keeping me upright as we put on a show for hundreds of patrons.

The attention would intimidate some people, but we only saw each other. In this moment, we were completely lost to the world around us. Arms slung around his neck, face buried in his chest, I clutched onto him as he drove the pressure further between my legs. I tipped my head back and Jackson pressed his forehead to mine as our bodies became one, with each other and the music. My hair a veil around us, it shrouded my slacked jaw from onlookers.

"So fucking hot, babe. You're close, aren't you?"

I nodded, and he licked a line over my upper lip, tingles left in his wake. Without shame, I panted against Jackson's lax lips. My fingers dove into his hair and tugged at the strands. The tension in my core wound tighter than a virgin on prom night.

The song edged higher, seconds away from its peak. Jackson drove his hips into me harder and faster as he sucked at the tender spot beneath my ear. In a lucky twist of fate, my orgasm detonated as the song climaxed. As realization dawned and I remembered where we were, I was thankful the music masked my screams.

Bliss and a tinge of embarrassment flooded me as my orgasm dissipated. We just shared one of the most intense and intimate moments while surrounded by hundreds of strangers. No one glanced our way or cared we just dry fucked in the middle of the club. And with that, my embarrassment faded. In its place, a foreign yet desirable thrill took hold.

He sucked on my earlobe, then licked the shell of my ear. "That was the hottest fucking thing I've ever seen," he said, his breath hot and heavy on my ear. "I need to be inside you. Now."

Jackson's hunger a direct line to the saturated flesh between my thighs. Without hesitation, I snatched his hand and led us off the dance floor toward our friends. A brief round of goodbyes to everyone and, in less than five minutes, we were out the door and in the car.

Halfway to my apartment, my body still vibrated from my orgasm. I itched for more. Of him. Of us. My body is bursting with pent up energy as I fidget in the passenger seat. A distraction is necessary. Only one thing popped into my head.

A moment later, I reached across the console and unbuttoned his jeans, the teeth of his fly separated with ease. My mouth watered as I scraped my nails over his erection and slipped my hand beneath his boxer briefs. One stroke, then another, before I removed my hand.

Jackson gasped as he white-knuckled the steering wheel. "I am still driving, you know," he stated. But there was no attempt to stop me.

"I'm aware. But I'm bored. And horny. Don't you think it's time to repay you?" I asked, licking my lips.

His eyes averted from the road a second as my hand kneaded his upper thigh and traced a line up his erection, pausing at the waistband of his briefs. Jackson made no attempt to stop me. Eager to taste him, I tucked my fingers beneath the elastic band and exposed his hard cock. I sheathed him with my hand and stroked his length. The velvety soft skin a juxtaposition to the firm stone of his erection. Arousal slickened my panties again at the thought of him inside me.

I ached for him.

As I stroked him, Jackson's jaw slackened. A harsh pant passed between his lips. A minute later, he drove past the entry gate of my complex, parked next to my car and cut the engine.

Jackson all but ripped my seatbelt off as he yanked me over him and slid his seat back. His pants shifted underneath me and dropped to his knees. I fumbled in the confined space to hike my skirt up and shove the skimpy fabric of my panties aside.

My head slumped forward as the tip of his cock glided between my folds and taunted me. He lifted his chin and our lips met as I seated myself on him. As he slid deep inside me, I dug my nails into his shoulders and clutched him as if my life depended on it. Jackson hissed as I gasped. The air abuzz with static electricity, our bodies statues as we adjusted to our surroundings.

And then Jackson bucked his hips. My body ricocheted up, then plummeted down. I gripped the seat as my eyes rolled back. Jackson inside me was a delicacy. Nothing compared to the way Jackson fit my body. As if we were cut from the same pattern. As if he'd memorized my body before we met, and I'd done the same. In fantasies or a past life.

His hands squeezed my hips, certain to leave bruises by morning. They served as reminders of tonight. Reminders I enjoyed the sight of. He bucked again and sent a ripple of heat throughout my abdomen.

I clawed the seat and rode his cock. My body flickered and ignited as each live wire inside me zapped with current. The world around me disappeared as I orbited earth in the mesosphere. Sex with Jackson an out-of-body experience.

"Oh god. Oh god. Oh my fucking god. Fuck me." The chant rolled off my tongue like a litany. "I'm so close. *Oh god, yes... Fuck me, Jackson."* My plea guttural. A lust-driven command foreign to my own ears.

The car filled with slaps and moans and the undiluted scent of sex. Raw and pure and I never wanted it to end.

"Come for me, baby. Milk me." His direction gruff as his teeth sunk into my shoulder. The bite a sharp sting of lightning that electrified every nerve ending in my body. Another pump of his hips and he knocked me into the abyss, his name vociferated on my lips.

As my climax faded, his cock pulsed inside me. My name

a growl deep in his throat. We stayed in his Jeep a while longer, arms locked in an embrace. After several minutes passed, our breaths and hearts returned to their normal patterns while a light sheen of sweat coated our bodies.

Right here. Right now. The growing affection we shared encased us in our own little bubble. All my worries drifted away. All my fears absent. In this place—our world—everything was absolutely perfect.

Sunlight slithered through the blinds and woke me far too early. I rolled onto my back and stretched my arm across the bed to discover the space beside me empty. In its place, an indentation of Jackson's body.

Propped up on my elbows, I noticed the bedroom door had been closed. A sizzle crackled outside the room, followed by a muffled *shit*. I reached for a tank top and pajama shorts and slipped them on, then shuffled out the door in search of my guy.

From the moment I opened the door, pure deliciousness assaulted me. My mouth watered and my stomach grumbled with a vengeance. I stumbled toward the kitchen, my feet less sluggish with each step. Maple syrup, coffee, potatoes, and the aroma of citrus surrounded me like an invisible force field. My stomach grumbled again, as if I needed a reminder.

I rounded the corner and paused as Jackson stirred something on the stove. With his back to me, I ogled as he alternated between pans and the cutting board. Clad in black boxer briefs that hugged his sculpted ass, an apron string tied at his neck and waist protected his bare torso. What made my mouth water more? The steamy scent of breakfast or the sight of Jackson practically naked in an apron? A tough decision to make this early in the morning. I bit my lip, leaned against the closest wall, and gawked.

A moment later, Jackson went back to the cutting board and busted me. His lips curved up into my favorite smile, the one which made women weak in the knees. "Hey, gorgeous. I didn't hear you. I wanted to surprise you with breakfast in bed," he said as he walked over and placed a soft kiss on my cheek.

"The sun wouldn't let me sleep anymore. Maybe it wanted me to witness this spectacle. I should grab my camera. Because this..." I gestured the length of his body. "This should be a keepsake."

"Picture worthy moment, huh? Better hurry then because it's almost ready. Then the apron disappears."

I bolted from the kitchen and prayed I'd be back in time. Digging through my purse, I snagged my dying phone. A second later, I grabbed a digital camera from the shelf in my closet. Two are better than one. Plus, the camera would capture the visual better than my phone.

I ran back to the kitchen too fast. My feet skid across the tile as I raised my cell and opened the camera. Once my momentum stopped, I tapped the screen twice. Jackson smiled at me in the photo as he waved a wooden spoon my way. Pleased with the image, I set the phone down and brought the camera to my eye. Jackson posed and teased and made goofy faces at the lens.

I snapped a few shots before pulling the camera away from my eye. "Go back to what you were doing. I'm not really into posed photography."

"I didn't know you were such a shutterbug. Just so you know, breakfast will be ready in two minutes."

He went back to focusing on his task. I brought the camera back to my eye and pressed the shutter button over and over. Jackson's body is a rare piece of art. I captured the thick muscles railing his spine, the strength in his broad shoulders, the magnitude of his biceps and triceps, and damn... those glutes. The photos wouldn't need manipulation, only some lighting adjustments.

Just in time, I snapped one last photo before he removed the apron from his chest. "I hope you got what you wanted because breakfast is ready."

Setting the camera on the countertop, I stepped up to his side and rested my chin on his arm. My eyes wandered over the buffet he had assembled. "I did. Let's eat."

He took our plates and headed for the living room. I gathered the coffee pot, mugs, cream and sugar and placed them on a small serving tray. As I sat beside him, I set the tray between us on the coffee table.

"Everything looks and smells amazing. Thank you," I said as I leaned into him and pressed a kiss to his cheek.

"You're welcome, babe. Eat up, before it gets cold."

Buffet a polite term for the mountain of food on my plate. I had difficulty deciding what to eat first. Maple turkey bacon, scrambled egg whites, home fries or the berries and orange wedges drizzled with honey and mint.

Breakfast was orgasmic. And if anyone else would've been present, they'd swear—by the moans and groans—Jackson and I were having sex. No meal is better than sex with Jackson. But his cooking ran neck-and-neck with second place.

And then perversion kicked in. I wondered what it'd be like to eat Jackson's cooking during sex? The food in my mouth all but spewed across the room. My chest heaved as I inhaled food and my body launched into the worst coughing fit. For the best reason.

Jackson dropped his plate on the table and slapped my back with gentle force. "You okay?" I nodded. "Lift your arms up, hands over your head. Did you swallow wrong?" I followed his instruction and nodded again. My face and chest bloomed a brilliant shade of red with each forceful cough of my lungs. "I'm grabbing you some water." He bolted off the couch faster than lightning and returned just as quick with water.

When I gained control of my lungs, I chugged half the water. The cool liquid soothed some of the irritation. "Sorry. Didn't mean to scare you," I said, all harsh and scratchy.

"I know you like my cooking, but please don't inhale it," he teased. His booming laughter bounced off the walls as his hand painted circles over my ribcage.

"It wasn't that. I guess I got lost in thought and wasn't paying much attention to chewing or swallowing. I won't do that again," I murmured as heat pinked my cheeks.

A brow arched as his eyes pinned me. "What exactly were you thinking about?"

Me and my big fat mouth. Oh well, guess it was out in the open. But, hey! Maybe it would be a good thing. Maybe I would actually get the fantasy. "Just day dreaming about eating your orgasmic meals while we had sex. I got a little distracted by the whole idea."

"*Really?* Huh. I may just have to bookmark the idea." A wicked grin highlighted his beautiful face.

God, I hoped so.

ELEVEN

WEEKENDS SPENT with Jackson were comparable to heaven and ended far too soon. Since our second date, we've spent every non-working moment of the weekend together. Our plans determined whose bed we slept in. After the infamous letter, Jackson slept beside me every night. And I had zero complaints.

Once we exhausted ourselves between the sheets, Jackson curled his frame to my back and clutched me tight to his chest. A different warmth spread through my veins. Not arousal. But more akin to snuggles and hot cocoa and unrelenting hugs. Pure comfort. And there was no other place I wanted to be. In such a short span of time, Jackson became my home. A home I never imagined my life without. The sweetest place in existence.

The elevator dinged, disturbing my morning daydream. I walked the short distance to my desk in a haze. Yesterday morning's breakfast feast looped in my memory like an old black and white film. We'd spent hours in my bed entranced with each other. I clamped my thighs tight as I passed my coworkers. An insatiable connection thrived between me and Jackson. A connection I prayed never fizzled.

"Ugh, it's going to be a long day," I muttered to myself.

As I entered my cubicle, I snapped myself back to reality. Before I spoke with any clients today, clarity was needed.

Although we weren't a customer-facing business, Monday was always busy. It was also the time of year when northerners traveled home. And like every year prior, travel plans included questions regarding benefits.

By the time my lunch hour arrived, my stomach was ready to eat me whole. The grumbles certain to alert everyone nearby. I dialed Liz's desk—then Christy's—and whined about my hunger pangs. A minute later, we agreed to meet downstairs at Carol's.

Is it sad that lunch was the best part of the workday? Nothing paralleled to sitting with my besties at a small, metal table with uneven legs. We talked about life and love and whatever the hell floated in our heads.

We discussed our weekends. Each of us enthralled with the other's story. Between the three of us, we exploded with happiness. Our lives full and fun and blissful.

Christy and Rick started to plan their summer vacation. They hadn't decided where, but narrowed it down to two places—the Bahamas or Virgin Islands. Either way, they intended to do a seven-day cruise and forget about everything except themselves.

Liz confessed she'd met someone when we were out the other night. They exchanged numbers and had texted and talked throughout the weekend. "He's super, fucking hot. We're planning to hang out this weekend, maybe grab a bite," she said. Her face lit up like a toddler on Christmas morning. Seeing her like this made my pulse skip. I worried about her once Jackson and I started dating. But her exuberance melted away any residual concern.

Nothing made my heart sing more than these two women and all the wonderful things happening in our lives. A few months ago, this moment would've been a remote fantasy. But now, my heart constricted and my eyes pooled. All of us happy and fulfilled.

"Sometime soon, with your new mister hottie, the six of us should go to dinner. Oooorr…" I said. My hips wriggled in the wooden chair. "Maybe I should ask my personal chef to cook. Who, by the way, looks mighty fine in an apron and his drawers. His mama taught him well." At the mention of

Jackson and his culinary skills, memories of how he looked in my kitchen pinked my skin.

"Sounds like a great idea." Christy tapped her chin as her eyes darted between us. "We could each bring something, so Jackson doesn't have to cook everything."

I aimed a finger at her with my thumb up and clucked my tongue. "Smart thinking. Let's wait till next week, after Liz has a smoking hot weekend, and then sort out the details. Good plan?"

"Yes," they said in unison. Without warning, the three of us burst into a fit of laughter and every pair of eyes locked on us. And we gave no fucks. I loved our terrific trio.

A few minutes later, lunch ended. We shuffled back to the elevator and our floor of cubicles. Our hesitance to exit the car when it arrived was comical. But after a unified huff, we meandered back to our desks.

I leaned into the lumbar support on my chair and inhaled. After two deep breaths, my mind slipped back into work mode. *Only a few more hours to go.* Wrapping the phone's handsfree earpiece around the shell of my ear, I jostled the mouse to wake my computer and entered my password. F1n3@S$mF—if anyone took the time to hack my password, they'd keel over from hysterics.

I clicked on the weekly reports and retrieved my client and prospect lists. After I printed them off for outbound calls, I opened my email inbox and saw a few unread messages.

The first message was from a client sending me thanks for helping them update their policy. I typed out a quick reply and hit send.

The second email was from Marco—carbon copied to Bob in human resources. A congratulations on hitting my sales goal with three weeks left in the quarter. I sent a quick thank you and printed the email, stashing it in my *Go Me!* file in my desk.

The third message had no name or subject line, just a weird blend of letters and numbers.

From: 21LT993YW200054JFQ02399

To: Sarh.Bradley@hammondlife.com
Subject:

My beautiful Sarah,

Under the light of the moon, your skin shimmers like a million flecks of glitter painted across the sky.
In the center of the club, your body moves like no one is watching. No one but me.
I'm always watching. Always listening.
Like when your pussy came all over that guy's leg the other night. I saw the fire in your eyes. Heard the sound of your release, even over the sex inducing music.
And when you fucked him in front of your apartment, your tight little cunt riding his tiny dick like you were at a rodeo, I jacked off in the bushes next to your window.
One day, when you're tired of sir steroids, I'll be the one ramming your juicy cunt with my fat cock. You'll be screaming my name for days. No other name except mine.
I attached a few pictures for your viewing pleasure.

I shoved away from my desk with trembling hands. Tears streamed down my cheeks as my lungs begged me to breathe. I needed to get out of here. Get away from my computer. In the narrow aisle of cubicles, I all but sprinted toward Liz's desk, darting past coworkers on the way. As I stepped into Liz's small space, I clutched my knees and bent at the waist, heaving.

"Sarah?! What the hell's going on? Are you okay?" A bang disrupted the monotony in the office as Liz's chair slammed into her credenza. She bolted to my side and gripped my shoulders.

"Can't. Breathe." I wheezed as my stomach rolled.

Liz guided me to a chair opposite hers. "Sit, sit, sit. Tell me what I can do." Squatting down beside me, she placed a hand on my knee, the other on my shoulder. Her eyes widened with panic as she watched me have a total meltdown.

"I don't know. Maybe call Jackson. I got an email. Tell him

I got an email. Like the letter, only worse." My wheezing morphed into slow, methodical gasps.

"What letter? What email? Talk to me." Her brows pinched together as she silently pleaded for answers.

"Can you just call Jackson for me? He'll explain. Please…" The request faded on my lips.

"Do you know his number? Where's your phone?"

I patted the pockets of my black dress slacks, relieved to find my phone there. I handed the lifeline to Liz with a trembling hand. After she unlocked it, Liz scrolled through my contacts and called Jackson.

Liz's eyes refused to leave mine while my phone was glued to her ear. A flash lit up Liz's face. Shock registered as Jackson greeted her, assuming it was me.

"Hey, Jackson, it's Liz. Sorry to bother you at work. Sarah wanted me to call you," she paused, listening to Jackson's response. "She's okay, I think. She stumbled into my office a minute ago, out of breath. Asked me to call you. Something about an email she got. Said it's worse than the letter."

A moment later, Liz's face transformed from worried to fearful. This did nothing to settle the angst bubbling inside me. The hole in my chest expanded as unease ate away my sanity. My stomach churned again and I begged my lunch to stay down. I assumed Jackson explained the letter I'd received, and let her know that we filed a police report. That he'd been with me during every moment, minus work.

My emotional state registered with Liz. She tried to maintain control and keep me calm. "Sarah, Jackson wants to know what the email says," Liz said in a soothing tone.

I shook my head, unwilling to say the words. Not wanting to see them again, let alone speak them. My fingers quivered as I shoved a loose strand of hair behind my ear. "It's still open on my computer. I can't look at it again. Please, Liz."

She nodded. "Let's walk down there together. Okay?"

Liz stood with my phone still glued to her ear and took my hand in hers. She told Jackson to wait as we headed back to my desk, dropping the phone to her side and hiding it. The closer we got to my tiny square footage of office space, the more nausea churned in my gut. My limbs trembled as bile rose in my throat. A shiver rippled from head to toe as the urge to vomit became inevitable.

Deep breaths, Sarah. DO NOT throw up at work. You'll never hear the end of it.

When we reached my cubicle, I remained rooted at the entryway. Liz glanced to me as understanding washed over her face and she dropped my hand. She stepped around the corner of my desk and sat in my chair. Her eyes darted side-to-side as she scanned the words plastered across the screen.

Her eyes magnified in horror as she peeked up at me, concern etched in the lines on her forehead. I sat down in one of the chairs in front of my desk and dropped my head into my hands. Liz whisper-read the email to Jackson and I forced my fingers in my ears.

Something passed by in my periphery. I chanced a look up as Liz walked to the printer and grabbed a page from the tray before handing me the phone.

I dragged in a breath before I spoke, but still had trouble finding my voice. "Hey." It's all I said. The only word my mouth formed.

"Babe," Jackson said, his voice a soothing metronome. "I'm leaving work in a minute. Liz will stay with you until I get there. Whoever you need to talk to at work, tell them you're sick and need to leave early."

"Okay." My fingers fumbled with the hem of my shirt.

"I'll be there soon. Stay with Liz," he reiterated.

"I will," I whispered.

I disconnected the call and glanced up at Liz. After relaying Jackson's directions, I rose from the chair. I had to leave, but didn't know how. Liz clung to my side and held my hand as we walked to Marco's office. With each step, I considered what to tell Marco. Something that wouldn't prompt endless questions.

Unfortunately, women dealing with premenstrual symptoms had been overused in the office. Some women called off an entire day and tanned their skin by the pool, saying the hot sun was therapy.

Cold symptoms? Maybe. But I'm not sure Marco would buy it considering I was rainbows and sunshine an hour ago. Think, think, think. What else is there?

"Liz. What the hell do I tell Marco? Can't say it's a cold. He won't buy it. I was fine until after lunch. Help me, please," I begged.

Her hand rubbed soothing circles on my back. "Uh… Maybe you can pass it off as food poisoning. Say lunch didn't agree with you and now you're nauseous. That should work."

Food poisoning is a better idea than anything I came up with. My mind started to shut down and run only necessary functions until Jackson arrived. "Thanks, Liz. That'll work perfectly."

We reached Marco's office, his heavy wooden door was cracked open a few inches. I sucked in a breath and straightened my spine as much as possible. Hesitantly, I rapped my knuckles next to the nameplate—*Marco Meyers, Senior Sales Manager*.

"Come in." Authority rang strong in those two words.

"I'll wait out here for you." Liz pivoted to the side, out of Marco's view when I opened the door.

Marco glanced up from a stack of papers in his hands, a pair of reading glasses rested low on his nose. "What can I do for you, Sarah?" He leaned back in his chair, setting the papers on top of his keyboard.

"Hey, Marco. I'm not feeling so hot. Must've eaten something bad at lunch." As if on cue, my stomach grumbled so loud Marco heard it. "Is it okay if I leave early? I'll have someone pick me up."

His sharp eyes assessed me, raking up and down my body to validate my statement. *God, I hope I appeared as sick as I felt.* His fingers tapped the arms of his oak chair, cogs spinning. Second-by-second, I fidgeted in front of him as he accepted my half-truth.

"Yeah, no problem, Sarah," he said, finally. "You don't look so good. Kind of pale actually. Go home, eat some chicken noodle soup, get some rest. If you're not well in the morning, call me. You can afford to miss a day or two."

"Thanks, Marco. I'll let you know." I gave him a tight smile and he told me to get well soon.

I stepped outside his office and gave Liz a thumbs up, relieved I could leave. She yanked me back to her side and hooked her arm in mine as we walked back to my desk. "Let's grab your stuff and I'll walk you down to the lobby. Want me or Christy to bring your car home later?"

I reached into my bottom desk drawer and retrieved my purse, giving Liz my keys. "That would be a huge help. Thanks, Liz. You really are the best." My hand squeezed her forearm a little tighter.

"Anything for you, girl. I'll let Jackson get you out of here, but soon we're all sitting down and having a *family meeting*. You need to fill us in." Concern poured out of her and the worry line from earlier reappeared.

"Soon, I promise. Just give me a day. Maybe come over tomorrow for dinner and we can all talk."

"Keep me in the loop. I'll talk with Christy when I get upstairs, tell her what you told Marco. That way the story jives. We can let her in on everything later. Okay?"

"Okay."

We stepped off the elevator and walked to the lobby and parked ourselves on a bench. I leaned into Liz and rested my head on her shoulder. A deep inhalation later, I shut my eyes, closed out the world, and whispered to the darkness. "Why is this happening to me?"

I meant it more as a rhetorical question, not really expecting Liz to answer. She didn't have answers. No one had them. "Don't know, sweetheart. But between all of us, we'll figure it out. We'll keep you safe. Swear." I hugged myself harder and moved closer to Liz as her words comforted me.

"Babe, I'm here," Jackson said. His hand splayed over my thigh, but I refused to open my eyes. The dark was safer right now.

After a moment, I lifted my head and squinted at the brightness. The receptionist stared at us from her marble-topped desk. "Hey," I croaked. "I gave Liz my keys so they can bring my car home later."

He took my hands in his, stood me upright and pinned me to his chest. "Let's get you out of here." I nodded as he shifted toward Liz. "See you later."

Liz handed a creased piece of paper to Jackson. "In case you need to show it to them." The email. A monster clawed inside my gut.

"Thanks, Liz. I'll let you know what they say."

Jackson steered me to the exit. As we passed through the glass doors, I glanced up. "Let Liz know *who* says what?"

Jackson opened the passenger door to his Jeep and helped me inside. He shut the door and jogged to the driver's side and slid in. "Let Liz know what the police say after we update them."

Jackson maneuvered into traffic and drove past hundreds of people. People not being stalked by some unknown lunatic. Who had normal lives. People not scared to go places or exist outside the walls of their home. Who could be themselves.

People not like me.

I laid on my bed, curled into a fetal position. My work clothes stripped off and replaced with pajama pants and a tank top, courtesy of the best boyfriend in the world. He brushed his fingers over my hair, tucking a fallen group of strands behind my ear.

"What can I get for you, babe? Water? Food?"

He showered me with love like no other. How did I get so damn lucky? "Maybe some water."

"Okay. I'll be back. Then I'll call Liz." He left the bedroom, his stride quick and purposeful. Clinking rang out as ice dropped into the glass, followed by the quieter swish of water dispensing from the fridge door.

He strode back in and settled beside me, offering me the glass. I shook my head and curled tighter into my body as he set the water on the bedside table. "Be back in a minute. I'll just be in the living room." His hand cupped my face and traced the line of my jaw before he stepped out of the room.

A small creak grated from the other room. The same creak I'd heard hundreds of times, but tuned out. As Jackson sat on the couch, I heard every shift of his weight on the weathered springs. I locked onto the glass of water and watched the ice cubes bob. A small pearl of moisture bubbled on the outside of the glass. A moment later, my eyes were stinging and my throat was clogged.

How did I get here? What got me to this point?

This whole situation reflected an unfathomable nightmare. How did a person—who wouldn't harm a bug in her home—happen to have some crazed person following her every move? Sending her 'gifts' and 'love letters' meant to scare her into their 'rescuing arms'. When in actuality, it created the opposite effect. All I wanted was to stay in my apartment with Jackson and never leave until the police captured this nutjob.

Maybe leave occasionally—a trip to the grocery store, perhaps a quick trip to the gym. After all, the gym in my gated community should be safe. With the gate and guard, it wasn't easily accessible. All the stores I shopped at within a mile or two. Which was manageable. I'd be a temporary recluse. At least until an arrest happened.

Jackson's soft rumble carried from the couch to my ear. "I know, Liz. Not leaving her side. I cancelled my appointments tomorrow and I'll have her call off work in the morning." He went quiet a moment—Liz must have been speaking. "We'll be here all night. Just let me know when you're here and I'll let you in."

The room silenced another moment. "We added it all to the police report. The officer said they'll contact the IT department at Hammond. See if the email can be traced." He gave a small *mmhmm* and another *I know*. "Let's shoot for dinner here, tomorrow night at six-thirty. Tell Christy and Rick and I'll get everything else done on this end." Another brief pause. "Thanks, Liz. Talk to you later."

And then nothing but silence. Silence and fear. I needed him here with me. Needed him pressed against me. Needed his embrace to hold me close, to never let go. To soothe my anxiety and promise everything would be okay.

Jackson's bare feet padded across the wood floor, growing louder with each step. I turned my head as he tugged his shirt over his head. A second later, he swathed me in warmth under the protection of my fluffy comforter. His arm slid over my midsection and dragged me into him. His front to my back. Our limbs a snuggled pretzel.

Jackson whispered sweet words in my ear. He vowed to keep me safe. Promised to do everything within his power to end this nightmare. And then his lips pressed a tender kiss below my ear.

My heart fluttered at the unrelenting nature of his tenderness. As I drifted off to sleep in his arms, my hands secured him tighter to me. My mind half awake-half asleep, three infamous words slipped from my lips. *I love you.* And then I drifted off to a place where it was him and me and no one else. A place where monsters didn't exist.

TWELVE

I LAID AWAKE IN BED, wishing for the millionth time to fall asleep. Twisting, I glanced at the clock and groaned. In an hour, the alarm would go off. So much for sleep. Rigid as stone, I tried not to disturb Jackson. I envied his deep, even breaths and occasional snore while he slumbered. As I stared up at the ceiling, a muted amber luminescence from the clock highlighted the room. My eyes lost focus as they gazed at the dusty white paint.

Closing my eyes, I begged the heavens to let me fall asleep. To escape the craziness which currently held my reality captive. To drift off to a happier place. I should be dreaming about Jackson and hiking and mountains. About secluded meadows and picnics and laughter. In this dream, the sun shone high in the sky, its rays bouncing off puffy, white clouds and warming our skin. Flowers and grass and streams perfumed the air. Birds chirped and squirrels scavenged for nuts. No place compared to here. Our happy place. The perfect escape. Too bad it's not reality.

Hot tears pricked my eyes. I held them at bay a moment before the first salty drop leaked out and rolled down to my ear. As best I could, I restrained my sobbing and smothered the whimpers desperate to escape. The droplets continued their unrelenting stream and puddled in my ear. Before much longer, I'd be full-on bawling.

Jackson stirred beside me and he shifted to haul me closer

to his chest. My solo crying session hit full speed as my nasal passages clogged and blocked my ability to breathe. Any moment, I would wake Jackson with my sniffles and tears. But not if I slipped out of the bed gracefully and grabbed tissues. In both scenarios, I'd disturb him and the day would be miserable.

I peeled the comforter and top sheet back and inched my legs to the edge of the bed. With slow precision, I clamped his wrist in my fingers and gently lifted his forearm. Scooting my body inch by inch, I slid out from under his hold.

"You okay?" Jackson mumbled groggy with sleep. Even in my current state of misery, the sex appeal of his morning voice called out to me. I peered over my shoulder; a pair of tired sapphire eyes laser-focused on me.

"Yeah. Just need to use the bathroom." His arm shifted and freed me.

Jackson's fingers skirted over my palm as I stood, a fresh batch of tears activated by his tender touch. The mattress squeaked behind me, followed by a faint thump on the floor. In a heartbeat, Jackson's hands cradled my face as his thumbs swiped the cascading tears away. "Talk to me." Warm lips pressed mine, the lightest of pressure, before he leaned away to study me. "I'm here. Whatever you need. No matter what."

I inhaled deep, barely a molecule of oxygen made it to my lungs, my sinus cavities clogged and complaining. In a very unladylike fashion, I reached up and swiped the length of my hand underneath my nose. It was a disgusting sight, and I was in desperate need of a tissue.

"Come with me. I've got you." Jackson tucked me into his side and walked me to the bathroom.

"I'm sorry." Another snotty inhalation, followed by a river of tears. I'm so pathetic. "I didn't want to wake you. Just couldn't fall back asleep. And then I kept thinking about everything. It's like a rat race in my head. And then, the adrenaline that stopped my crying earlier vanished. Everything crashed down on me all at once. Sorry, I tried hard to be quiet. You looked so peaceful and I didn't want to disturb you."

Word vomit spewed from my lips like bad seafood. It wouldn't stay down, morphing into a vicious cycle of endless words. As much as I didn't want this to burden Jackson, he should know where my head was at. And how I needed his strength since I was utterly weak.

"Don't apologize, babe." He spun me to face him. "I'm here for you. Whatever you need. No matter what time it is. If you need me, even if it's to brush your hair, I'm here."

I nodded as my body relaxed more. "I'll try." He helped me into the bathroom, then stepped away and gave me privacy. I blew my nose; quite an effort on my part. I used the toilet, washed my hands, and snatched the box of tissues on my way out.

Jackson laid under the covers. The down-turned corner exposed him from the waist up. He beckoned me with a curled finger and I crawled back into the bed, and molded my front to his chest as he swathed me in warmth and comfort.

Ear pressed to his sternum, I regulated my breath to the steady rhythm of his heartbeat. His chest rose and fell steadily. His strong arms embraced me as his spicy scent infiltrated and soothed every atom in my soul. This was exactly where I belonged. Beside Jackson. My fortitude. And then I remembered... The three little words that escaped as I drifted off to sleep earlier.

My body became as rigid as stone. My arms curled in closer, tighter to my chest as I closed in on myself. "What's wrong?" he asked, concerned.

Should I tell him? I don't want lies between us. Maybe it was all a dream. Did I really say those three words aloud? "Nothing. Just remembered part of a dream. At least I think it was a dream. It's difficult to know the difference anymore."

Jackson's hand rubbed the length of my back and calmed me, washing away some of the worry. "Tell me. I'll let you know if it was real or not."

I dug deep and mustered up the courage to confess. Perhaps, for the second time. *What if I didn't say it before and I say it now and I scare him away?* I can't lose him. I'd splinter without his strength. But I had to know if I left that sentiment floating in the air.

Dragging in a methodical breath, I spoke on the exhale. "It's all a bit foggy... but I remember telling you something." My pulse throbbed in my ears, a whoosh of blood with each pump of the fast-beating organ. Jackson laid patient and waited for me to continue. "I think I told you I love you."

I cringed. My head and heart ready for the blow of pain and hurt. Prepared for rejection or denial. Seconds mimicked hours as I waited for a response. But Jackson didn't utter a word as his hand continually stroked the length of my spine. Absolute silence. Any second, I'd lose my mind. Time crept. Why wasn't he answering? I blinked to relieve the stinging sensation in the backs of my eyes. A lump lodged in my throat. I had zero expectation of Jackson returning the sentiment. All I wanted was confirmation on reality versus fantasy. Especially now, when much of my life imitated one huge nightmare.

Drawing his arm back, he wedged it between us as he lifted my chin. His sapphires stunned me with their radiance. Jackson guided my lips to his for a blip of time, resting his forehead on mine once our lips parted. "It wasn't a dream," he whispered. One little sentence. Four words strung together. My heart fluttered and my stomach twisted as I waited.

Jackson didn't appear put off, but he wasn't saying anything either. He didn't need to repeat it, not unless he reciprocated. But there was one thing I needed. For him to admit he cared about me. It didn't have to be the infamous *L* word. I accepted that. And respected it.

We laid face to face, Jackson's eyes closed, his forehead rested on mine. His chest pressed mine as he inhaled deep and held it a few heartbeats. Slowly, he exhaled. When his eyes reopened and focused on me, something hypnotic captured me. Sapphire blues scorched my emeralds. The windows to his soul revealed truths without a word spoken. Spellbound and bewitched, I was a slave to him.

We laid there—blue to green—still; soundless. A soft, pink hue outlined his jaw as dawn ascended and the tinge of daybreak emphasized his rugged features. I sighed into the quiet as my emotions skyrocketed toward the peak of my internal roller coaster.

Jackson tilted his chin, and we exchanged a set of small kisses. The kisses morphed, flourished, became impassioned and unstoppable. Hidden meanings bloomed with each pass.

Heat blossomed as his tongue brushed my lower lip. My lips parted and I gasped. Labored breaths and frenzied lips. His tongue stroked mine and I lost it.

We were all hands. Tearing clothes from each other as our frantic kisses drifted to necks and curves and dips. Fuck, I needed him. And this was his way of showing me he adored me. Maybe he wasn't ready to say the words yet, but he could show me. That's the funny thing about love. Some people ached to hear a four-letter word. Begged it be spoken to reassure them. To others, love was an unspoken devotion. Displayed in touch or gestures or the willingness to be present. Right now, Jackson was showing me his unspeakable love.

He rolled me onto my back and hovered inches above me. Our eyes locked as Jackson's erection pressed into me. His cock caressed the slickness between my thighs, but didn't move any farther. He paused. His gaze focused on me as he waited for confirmation. Never wanting to take advantage.

I lifted my hips and the tip of his cock dipped into my wetness before I fell back onto the sheets. That simple reassurance was all he needed from me. A second later, he dipped down and kissed me again. Jackson kissed me slow and sweet as he poured his soul into mine. My fingers weaved through his hair as I held him to me. Slowly, my body stirred back to life and simmered for more. Of him. His taste. His touch.

Jackson bucked his hips, and I gasped as his length filled me. I dug my head into the pillow as he slid out and pushed back in. Jackson's rhythm unhurried as he cradled me to him. We weren't fucking. Or having sex. This… it was making love. We consumed each other from the inside out. And nothing compared.

"Oh, god," I panted.

In a subtle, measured stroke, he glided in and out as he trailed kisses down my neck and licked along my collarbone. A hurricane brewed inside my body. My skin on fire as my heart swelled and punched at my ribcage. Jackson was everywhere—caressing my flesh and branding my soul. And then his forehead pressed against mine and we locked eyes. On the cusp of orgasm, Jackson kissed me like I was his last breath.

I gasped with ferocity as his lips skirted my jawline. A

sweltering heat exploded between my legs and scattered like lightning as my body tightened. He pumped his hips feverishly. Heat prickled every layer of my flesh. Desire and love fused my core. Grunts and pants and moans echoed in the room as our bodies ravaged each other. Both chasing release.

The intensity too much. I buried my nails in his ass as my body free fell off a cliff and into an abyss of euphoria. Jackson leaned into the crook of my neck as his hips surged with force. Deep, labored grunts vibrated in my ear, his moans closer together. And then he was there... diving off the cliff into euphoria beside me.

Jackson's breath beat hot below my ear. A moment later, he trailed kisses up my neck, stopping when he reached my temple, resting his cheek on mine. His scruffy jaw scraped as he whispered. Soft words escaped his lips. They reverberated in my marrow, and it took my brain half a minute to put two and two together. He pulled back and searched my eyes.

"Say it again," I lilted.

"I love you." Three. Little. Words. My chest flooded with helium as the organ beneath my sternum hammered uncontrollably and soared to the heavens.

<hr>

"Do you need help with dinner?" I walked up behind Jackson, wrapped my arms around his midsection, and rested my chin on his shoulder.

He swiveled his head and kissed me quick before returning his attention to the stove. "I'm good, babe. I've got the food if you want to set the table."

"Okay." Reluctantly, I removed my arms from him. After pressing a kiss on his bicep, I opened the cabinet and grabbed plates, then utensils, and set the table.

An unfortunate side effect to my little apartment was the lack of dining room space. I rearranged the living room a smidge and put my two-person breakfast table near the couch and coffee table. It wasn't the ideal setup, but it would work for tonight's dinner. Plus, I'm sure no one cared about the furniture arrangement, as long as we were all together.

Everything in place as the savory scent of garlic, oregano,

and basil wafted through the air. Fifteen minutes and everyone would be here, a cloud of curiosity and questions hovering above them. And no matter how hard I tried, I couldn't keep my eyes off the clock. Nervous energy a virus in my belly. Clammy palms. Bouncing knees. I bit down on my stubby thumbnail.

The living room blurred around me as I listened to Jackson stir and strain. A whoosh of the oven's convection as Jackson opened the door. *Clang-clang.* The sheet pan set on the trivets. *Pfft, pfft.* More oil and garlic spread on the bread. Another whoosh from the oven. Hundreds of thoughts hurtled through my head. Thoughts I didn't want to tackle alone. I needed a distraction. So, I walked back into the kitchen and gawked at Jackson as he added a creamy herb pasta to a large bowl.

"Give me something to do," I blurted, clipped and abrupt.

Jackson glanced up, brows furrowed and eyes pinched, and honed in on my nail biting. With a quick nod, he pointed to the counter next to the sink. "Finish cutting vegetables for the salad?"

I nodded and inhaled deep, relieved to have a task to divert my attention. Sidling next to Jackson, I started to chop. The spring mix already in the wide, wooden bowl. Carrots—sliced thin and on an angle. Done. Tomatoes—cut into wedges. Done. Cucumber—peeled and sliced into rounds and then halves. Done. Avocado—seed and skin removed, cut into chunks. Done.

I placed the veggies on top of the greens and decorated the salad like a floral arrangement. With all the toppings in place, I grabbed two heaping handfuls of blueberries and sprinkled them over the top. Then, I dumped a healthy portion of walnuts onto the cutting board, rough chopping them before scattering them over everything.

A knock at the door startled me from my salad brain. Jackson glanced my way and asked, "Want me to get the door?"

Tracing my fingers over his forearm, I kissed his cheek. "No, I've got it." He nodded, grabbed a pair of hot mitts, and pulled the garlic baguette slices out of the oven. It smelled divine.

Approaching the door, I pushed up on my toes and peeked through the small peephole. My friends stood on the other side of the door, chatting in hushed tones. I stepped back and reached for the knob with trembling fingers.

Taking a deep breath, I plastered a smile on my face. A second later, I twisted the cool metal and opened the door, welcoming my friends in as if nothing was wrong. We exchanged hugs and pecks on the cheek. *Hello's* and *how are you's* passed back and forth. The whole situation reflected a staged show, an air of caution gobbling the energy in the room.

Us ladies went to sit in the living room while Rick headed for the kitchen to shoot the shit with Jackson. Just as we sat on the couch, the guys rounded the corner, both carried serving dishes. The delicious aroma of Jackson's cooking had my stomach growling.

I had eaten little since lunch yesterday. Crazy how an email held so much power over me. Earlier today, Jackson convinced me to drink a nutritional shake. He'd said *At least get something in your system. Maybe if it isn't solid, it won't upset your stomach.* Good call on his part.

Everyone took a seat and loaded up their plates. Fettuccine with a creamy pesto, olive oil and garlic baguettes, sautéed bell peppers and onions, and a salad with balsamic vinaigrette dressing. I picked up my plate, brought it to my nose and inhaled deeply. My eyes closed and Jackson shook with laughter beside me. It was obvious I loved his cooking.

"You better eat." I opened my eyes, caught in his smoldering stare as he zeroed in on me. He leaned into me and whispered in my ear. "Or we'll appear rude to our guests when I haul you to the bedroom."

My breath hitched before I resumed my previous position. I pressed my thighs together and begged for relief, but the polite hostess in me stayed put. I picked up my fork and started to eat my dinner. A twirl of pasta wrapped around the tines, strands of pasta dangled from my fork when I peeked up at my friends, eyes on their plates and shit-eating grins plastered from ear to ear. Slightly embarrassed, I smiled with them.

Jackson squeezed my knee—our signal—and I glanced at

him. His eyes asked if I was ready to talk with my closest friends. Share the story of how some unknown, sick and twisted pervert watched me and sent me creepy messages. My eyes averted, dropping to his Adam's apple as it bobbed, as my head bobbed up and down. One last, stronger squeeze to my knee before splaying it flat.

"Thank you all for coming over tonight. We wish it could be under happier circumstances, but we're still grateful." Jackson held my gaze and steeled himself for what he'd say next. Discussed earlier today, we decided he'd tell them everything. It concerned me I wouldn't be able to say anything because of tears or fear or nervousness, and we had no plan to dance around the subject.

"We need to share some things that've happened to Sarah recently. After it's out in the open, plans will be put in place. With all of us." Three sets of eyes landed on us, hooked on every word. "Liz. Christy. Sarah needs you right now. As much as she needs me. We're not sure for how long, but someone is stalking Sarah. Based on the notes she's received, we—and the police—assume it's a man."

Christy slapped a hand over her mouth and sucked in an audible gasp. "Oh my god, Sarah! I don't know what to say. It doesn't seem right, but I'm so sorry." I nodded and stared down at Jackson's hand on my knee. His thumb drew circles on the inside of my leg.

"I want to let you know what kind of person the police think we're dealing with. That being said, some of what I'm about to share is vulgar." Almost as if a master puppeteer controlled them, the three of them nodded in unison. Jackson's calm tone continued. "A few days after Liz's party, Sarah received a bouquet of sunflowers at work. The card attached had a message telling her how beautiful she was. But whoever sent them indicated they saw her regularly. As in, every day. She had no idea who sent them and asked me because she'd mentioned her favorite flower to me at Liz's party. When I'd told her I wasn't the sender, she gave the flowers away."

Jackson paused a moment, drinking a couple large gulps of water. Everyone ate a bite or two while waiting for Jackson to continue.

"A few more weeks passed and nothing else happened. We started dating and nothing out of the ordinary occurred. Then, about a week and a half ago, Sarah found a letter in her mailbox. Whoever it is typed the letter on an old-fashioned typewriter, and meant for it to read like a love letter. But it followed the same connotation as the card with the flowers. Emphasizing he saw her daily, even smelled her often, and one day she would belong to him. No one mailed her the letter. The envelope only had her first name on it. Somehow, it got into her locked mailbox. After reading the note, Sarah called me for help. We took the letter to the police department and filed a report. Since that day, I've stayed with Sarah after work and on the weekends. The police told us to act normal. Go about our lives. That most of these situations pass without further activity. So that's what we did. We wanted everyone to go out last weekend. We wanted to have fun, forget about everything and just be ourselves with our friends."

Jackson picked up his glass and finished the water before taking a quick bite of garlic bread. Christy and Rick sat hooked on every word. Liz's attention focused on me, since most of this wasn't new to her. After he swallowed the last bit of his bread, he continued.

"Yesterday, Sarah got back to her desk after lunch and checked her email. An email from a strange sender showed up in her unread messages. She opened it and read the beginning, which was somewhat sweet like the previous notes. But as she continued reading, it became lewd and vulgar. The man told her he'd been watching her. Saw us all at the club. Watched us having sex later that night, getting himself off at the same time. And reminded her she'd be his one day. He attached photos, which Sarah hadn't looked at when she'd read the email. When I came to pick her up from work, I had Liz print the email and images off for me, as I planned to file another police report. The pictures contained images of all of us, drinking and dancing at the club over the weekend. The majority of the pictures are of Sarah. Some are close up, catching different expressions on her face. We filed a new report with the police and they're working with security at the office to determine where the email came from."

A low shriek ripped from Christy's lips, her eyes watering

and on the verge of letting go. "Holy shit, Sarah! Oh my god! I can't believe this is happening. I wish I could help."

Rick wrapped his arm around her mid-section and tugged her into his side. "Sarah. Jackson. Whatever I can do to help, tell me. If we need to run shifts, so be it. We need to keep these ladies safe." Rick's brow furrowed as his forehead creased.

"Agreed. No one should be uncomfortable or vulnerable, but let's be vigilant and watch out for each other. This guy seems to have all his focus on Sarah, but the police said that could change if he feels threatened. I'd like us to come up with a game plan. I know we can't always be everywhere together, seeing as we don't all work together or have the same schedule. It'll be easier for the girls, since they work the same hours at the same place. I'd like to set up a group chat, one we use to check in with each other. Thoughts?"

Jackson had so much of this sorted out, and it made my shoulders fifty pounds lighter. My brain fogged more and more as the story went on and everyone pitched in their two cents worth. I sat back in my chair, stared at the pasta as my fork tines twirled the noodles clockwise. I realized, a minute later, the room was suddenly still and silent. I peered up to see everyone's eyes on me, waiting for me to speak.

"I'm sorry, what?" How embarrassing.

Jackson rubbed his hand back and forth over my knee. "We were just asking if you'd be okay with carpooling to work for the rest of the week. Liz offered to pick you both up. Okay?"

Carpooling? Would that really stop this maniac? I doubted it. Giving a non-committal shrug, I said, "Sure, carpooling is fine."

"All right. I'm the only one who doesn't have everyone's numbers. Let's take care of that now, set up the group chat, and dismiss this topic for the evening." I listened as Jackson added everyone's contact information to his phone. A moment later, four cell phones chimed and alerted us to the first group chat message. My brain returned to its foggy state.

Would life be like this going forward? Carpools and group chat check-ins?

The rest of the night flew by. Liz told me she'd be here by

eight-thirty to pick me up. I shuffled to the door with every-one, expressing my gratitude and love, then bid them good night.

When the door closed, I launched myself into Jackson as tears poured out of me. I wanted it all to vanish. He held me there, shushing me and telling me it would be okay. He wasn't sure how it would end, but he kept assuring me he would keep me safe. I stayed there crushed against his chest, my only thought...

I hope you're right.

I stared out the passenger window of Liz's Prius as the city passed by in a blur. No idea how I would get any work accomplished today, but I had to try. When I called into work yesterday and told Marco I wouldn't be in, he asked me to stop by his office the next day. He didn't disclose any details, but I suspected security talked with him and he wanted to talk to me.

The drive from my apartment to the office was short. My eyes scanned the sidewalks and every car. I mentally ques-tioned every man who looked my direction. Wondered if the man in the blue windbreaker was him. Or maybe the guy in the dingy button-down and khaki pants. It could be anyone. We parked in the lot, Liz giddy when she parked in a spot next to a tree. I wish something so simple made me better.

Liz cut the engine, and the three of us stayed put a moment longer. My eyes lost focus. Christy touched my shoulder and snapped me back to the present. "You know we've got your back, bitch, right?"

Laughter bubbled in my chest. Something as simple as using her favorite word lifted some of the tension clouding me. "I love you, Chicky. You and that mouth. I needed a laugh. Thank you." I laid my hand over hers a second, took a deep breath, and opened the door.

As we walked toward the main entrance, Liz said, "If you need us today, for anything, shoot one of us a text. Don't use our group chat. Unless you need Jackson and Rick to know."

Liz wrapped her arm around my shoulders and rubbed my upper bicep.

My eyes bounced between the two. "I will. Hopefully, the day goes by and nothing else happens. It'd be nice to have a normal day."

Walking into the building, the three of us waved good morning to Holly. My face practiced its *I'm perfectly fine* smile as we boarded the elevator. "When the doors open, I'm plastering on the fakest smile. You two go to your desks, I'll go see Marco. He needs to speak with me. We need to pretend everything is normal."

The weight of their stares is like gravity times ten, and my shoulders lock up. Liz nodded and said, "Sure, sweetie. Whatever you want. Just keep us posted."

"Normal. Okay, bitch. If that's what you want, normal it is." Christy shot me a wink, and I shook my head.

A ding signaled our arrival, the doors slid open, and the three of us parted ways. My face screamed happiness and enthusiasm, but my heart shriveled and withered into a dark corner. I walked down the hallway, stopped at Marco's open door, and poked my head inside. "Hey, good morning."

"Morning, Sarah. Come in. Close the door, please." The handle clicked into place, the sound louder than expected and I jumped. "Have a seat. I wanted to speak with you about the other day."

Marco's monotone voice gave nothing away, and I had no clue whether it upset or worried him or neither. "Okay." I sat down in a chair adjacent his and shoved my hands into my lap.

"I had a conversation with Edwin in security." With one line, I knew exactly why he summoned me. "He informed me he received a call from the police department. Regarding an email you received the other day. I won't speak of the content of the email as I'm sure you're aware and don't want to discuss it."

"Thank you." I gave him an impish smile.

"I wanted to share that we plan to investigate this further and to keep an eye on personnel." I scrunched my brow. *Keeping an eye on other personnel? Did they think it was an employee?* He registered my confusion and followed up. "When Edwin did some digging, it would appear someone sent the email from a Hammond IP address. We're still narrowing it down, but are determined to get this sorted out quickly."

Holy shit! It's a *co-worker?* That flew in out of nowhere—complete left field—and slapped me across the face. "What am I supposed to do? Liz, Christy, and I have safeguards in place while here. We've got others when we leave. But I guess I never really considered it being someone here."

A sympathetic smile touched his face. "Good. I'm glad to hear you have friends here. You'll most likely see more management perusing the sales floor. We'll pass it off as goals not being met and the end of the quarter approaching. We'll keep it low key."

"Okay. Do you mind if I keep my cell phone handy? I'll put it on silent. I just want it in case I need to reach Liz or Christy. Can they have theirs close by, too? I would feel better." I rambled, but needed Marco's approval. I wanted him to know that, with everything going on, this was a minor favor I needed him to grant.

"Certainly. You haven't seen it yet, but we sent an email late yesterday. Our floor will have a meeting at nine-thirty today. At the meeting, we plan to mention the whole goals scenario and management stopping by everyone's desk to see what they're doing to stay on track. I would like for you, Ms. Warren, and Ms. Nolan to sit in the front, center table. This will allow myself and Bob to scan the room a little easier, see if anyone on our floor gives any tells. The other floors, two and four, are having similar meetings at ten and ten-thirty. We'll get everything sorted out."

"When I get to my desk, I'll let Liz and Christy know about the table. I really want to get back to work today, but I worry I won't be able to focus. As always, I'll do my best. I just want to let you know where I'm at with this whole situation."

"Thank you, Sarah. If you need to, spend today doing follow-up calls or letters to clients. You're welcome to do emails, also. We've taken the liberty to monitor all incoming and outgoing emails more stringently until they resolve this matter. You will not be receiving another email like that while you're here."

His words brought relief, the knot in my stomach unraveling a little. I closed my eyes and sighed. "Thank you, Marco. You don't know how much this means. Your support is priceless."

"Of course. Now, head out to your desk and try to do your best. If anyone asks why you were in my office, tell them I was checking up on you and your food poisoning, okay?" It seemed as if he had it all mapped out. Perfect explanations for every shift from the office's normal routine of things. My heart swelled and my eyes stung but I held it together. It astounded me I had so many people standing in my corner, willing to do whatever it took to put everything back into its rightful place.

I nodded, stood from the chair, and left Marco's office. As soon as I got to my desk, I typed out a message to Liz and Christy, passing along the meeting table info and that I'd received permission for them to keep their phones nearby. We would have to talk more later, but not in the office.

THIRTEEN

By the end of the week, being at work was a hardship. I had zero focus. Especially after learning one of my coworkers sent the flowers, letter, and email. Although it may not be someone on my floor, the idea had me sick to my stomach.

After lunch on Friday, I spoke with Marco and requested to work from home the following week. In the past, other employees worked from home due to accidents, surgery, or a sick family member and it wasn't a hassle. When I asked Marco, he quickly approved the request.

Before leaving the office, I visited Bob in human resources and received a secure laptop and company cell phone. Marco suggested I stay home until the situation remedied. But he delegated one new task. "Sarah, please keep me up to date on any changes. We will do the same," Marco requested. A small favor to ask in exchange for being allowed to work in a safer environment? No problem.

I shared my new work status in the group chat with every-one. By the reply texts, it was evident everyone agreed with the idea. A huge weight lifted from my shoulders when I walked out the doors of Hammond Life. Hopefully, between the police and Hammond security, the person would be apprehended soon. I couldn't afford to take time off, so this was the next best solution.

The only downfall... long stretches of time alone. Being locked inside my apartment wasn't safe enough in Jackson's mind. He wanted a physical body near me at all times. Honestly, no one in our little family was fond of my eight-hour seclusion. Yes, I'd be working. But no one would be around if something happened. This spooked everyone, including me.

Over the weekend, I planned to speak with the apartment complex management and explain my situation. I'm hoping they'll reassure us the gated community was secure. Because if they said otherwise, I'm lost.

"Yes, ma'am, Ms. Bradley. Thank you for bringing this information to our attention. We'll be sure a guard is at the gate and do regular walk-throughs around the complex. The only reason we're missing a guard is because we let someone go. It's tough finding good help these days."

The owner of the apartment complex, Gerald Chang, smiled while folding in on himself. Apology etched lines in his forehead and bleak expression. I didn't blame Mr. Chang, or the complex, for my stalker problems. Mr. Chang wasn't the reason some lunatic watched my every move. But he assured me and Jackson the situation was a top priority.

"Thank you. I appreciate it, Mr. Chang. The complex's security features were the main reason I became a resident. I'll feel safer knowing extra measures will be taken. Again, thank you."

"It's our pleasure. Everyone should feel safe, regardless of where they are on the property. I apologize for the current lack of a guard, but I assure you I'll have it corrected within twenty-four hours. We have a couple candidates lined up. Perhaps we need both." Mr. Chang smiled then chuckled.

I understood he laughed at hiring two guards, but I wanted to tell him to shut the fuck up. This wasn't a laughing matter. Far from it. Did this creep stalk other women in the complex also? God, I hoped not.

Pushing up from my chair, I shook my landlord's hand, as did Jackson. We left his office and thanked him one last time. My anxiety lessened with each passing minute. My home would still be a safe place. A place I could sit alone all day and not worry if someone watched me through the blinds. A place I could breathe and shut out all the bullshit. My safe place.

"I'm heading out, babe. I'll be back for lunch, if that's cool?" Jackson asked as he slung a duffle bag over his shoulder. Clad in a black t-shirt and loose-fitting, black workout pants, he grabbed his keys and kissed the top of my head.

"Yeah, that'll be perfect. It'll keep my workday somewhat normal," I mused. I leaned against a pillow and powered on the laptop. The new work cell on the comforter beside me, on and ready. My *Miso Awesome* pajama set today's work attire.

"I'll see you around twelve-thirty." A kiss on the lips, and then he left for work.

The laptop's operating system loaded and I entered the password Bob wrote down. Less than a minute later, I logged onto my desktop remotely. The connection rivaled the dial-up internet days. But that was probably because the laptop was older than dirt, hence the archaic load speed. Good thing I started it up early.

I walked to the kitchen, made a cup of hot tea and a bagel with peanut butter, then headed back to my makeshift desk. Plopping down on the bed, I crossed my legs in a variation of a yoga lotus pose. I opened my work email and several messages loaded from the weekend which looked safe to view.

I bit into my bagel, chomped away, and responded to the emails. My work flow ran smooth due to the light workload. Although my current office setting wasn't traditional, I breathed easy and got my work accomplished. Being home is a balm for my soul. For a split-second, I closed my eyes and reveled in the peace.

These working conditions just might grow on me.

I snapped out of my work daydream and dove headfirst into the nitty-gritty. Time flew by quick—emails came and went, calls dialed, reports completed. Before I realized the time, Jackson unlocked the door with the key I'd given him after the first letter.

Some people would say giving Jackson a key after a month was too soon, but who cared what other people thought. I loved and trusted him. With my life. He cared for me and kept me safe. Things I'd never experienced with anyone else. Not to this degree. Sometimes you just know. Sometimes it's better to listen to your heart and ignore the crowd.

I heard a thud as his duffle hit the couch. A second later, Jackson popped his head around the doorjamb. "Sorry. Don't want to interrupt if you're with a client," he stated. After he noticed I wasn't on the phone, he stepped into the room and kissed me. He tugged on my pajamas and smiled. "You're too cute right now. Working in your pj's. Do they help your productivity?"

I leaned into him. "It seems so. I may have to speak with HR about the dress code policy. Who knew wearing comfortable attire and working from bed could make you so productive," I joked, cocking my head and giving him a silly smile.

Loud and throaty laughter spilled out of Jackson. In turn, I smiled bigger than I had in days. "For you, I'm sure they'll take it into consideration. You ready to eat?"

"Yeah. Let me mark myself as away, lock the computer, and I'll be right there."

Jackson walked out of the room and went straight to the kitchen. A couple dishes clanked on the counter before I heard the cutting board come out. I missed lunchtime with Liz and Christy, but a girl could get used to this.

What's better than working from home in your favorite pajamas? When your boyfriend stopped at your place for lunch, made you an amazing salad, and you still had twenty minutes left. So, what do you do with your remaining lunch hour? Sex, of course.

With a few minutes to spare, Jackson gave me one last kiss. "I should be done around four-thirty or five. Be back after."

"Go, go, go. Before I make you stay," I said as I shoved at his chest. His lips brushed against my knuckles. Then he headed for the door. A second later, a low thump echoed through the apartment as he shut the door, followed by the click of the deadbolt.

Best. Lunch. Ever. But alas, back to work.

The only sucky part about working from home was my inability to print reports. At one point, I had six different files open and toggled between them as I worked. It made work a challenge, and tasks took longer to finish, but was doable.

An unfamiliar noise chimed in the room. I unlocked my phone, but I had no notifications. The chime sounded again. I picked up the work cell phone on my bed and noticed two text notifications.

Initially, I thought it might be a client I called earlier. When I unlocked the phone and opened the messages, I learned how wrong I was. The message came from a six-digit number—616263.

I pursed my lips as my lungs singed. How do I breathe? My heart beat a vicious rhythm as I opened the messages.

Unknown: You stupid cunt. You thought you could get away from me. Just because you're not here, doesn't mean a fucking thing.

Unknown: That pretty boy toy you've been playing with, that ends now. If I see him anywhere near you starting tomorrow… Let's just say there will be blood. Yours, his, maybe both.

In a flash, I threw the phone on the bed, jumped to my feet and grabbed my phone, dialing Jackson. I wasn't sure if he was with a client, nor did I care. I had to talk to him now. In less than twenty-four hours, my haven away from the office was no longer sacred.

"Babe, I can't talk. I'm with a client right now," Jackson said when he answered.

He tried to hang up the phone, my shriek stopped him. "Jackson, I need you. Something happened."

"Tell me." His voiced, clipped and urgent.

"Work gave me a cell phone, so I could call clients. Somehow, whoever this is, they got the number. They sent me messages. Threatening me." My chest heaved as I spoke. "Threatening you."

"Fuck! Okay, we got this. Let me make a couple calls real quick. I'll call you back in a few, okay?"

"What do I do till then?" My brain started to shut down, all over again. I needed him to tell me what to do. Because all I wanted was to find a dark alcove and hide until this nightmare ended.

"Call your work. Tell them about the messages. Maybe they can trace them. See if they'll offer a different phone."

"Okay, I will."

"I'll call back soon, babe. Just make sure everything's locked up and the blinds are closed. I love you."

"I love you, too."

And then he was gone. I called Marco, explained the entire situation. He put me on hold a few minutes. When he returned, I heard Bob and Edwin mumbling in the background.

"Sarah, you still there?"

"I'm still here," I said as I paced semi-circles in my darkened bedroom.

"I know this may be difficult for you, but can you read the messages to us? Bob from HR and Edwin from security are with me. We'd like to record it, then come retrieve the device and give you a new one. Also, just as a precaution, can you screenshot the messages and send them to your personal phone and then to my number?"

"Sure," I said, reluctant. I had no desire to read the texts aloud. Having to read them was one time too many. I walked over to the menacing device and picked it up. It burned a hole in my hand as I held it. Unlocking the screen, the message popped up, and I took a quick screenshot and sent it to myself.

When my phone chimed the incoming text, I opened the image and forwarded it to Marco. "I just sent it. If you don't mind, I'd prefer not to have to read it aloud."

Marco's phone pinged on the other end. "Hang on one second, Sarah." The three men talked in jumbled tones, most likely the hands-free microphone covered with one of their hands. "Okay, I've got it. I understand your reasoning and we all accept that. If you don't mind, Bob and I would like to come by, within the hour, and pick up the phone."

"Yes, please. When you get to the gate, the guard will have to call me to let you in."

"We understand. We'll see you soon."

The call disconnected. I walked to my computer, set my work profile to 'away' and logged off the computer. I brought the phone and laptop out to the living room, setting up a new work area. If it were my phone, I'd crush it and throw the tainted device out a window.

Walking through every room, I checked all the window and door locks, as well as the blinds. All secured and closed. I paused in the bedroom and my body shook from head to toe. I tried to calm myself with slow, methodical breaths.

After settling as much as possible, I went to my closet and found something else to wear. It wouldn't be long before I had company. I grabbed the first things I saw—a navy, cotton shirt and a pair of jeans. I stepped into the bathroom, the only room I deemed safe and changed.

My phone rang and Jackson told me he'd be here soon, and that the police were headed to my apartment. The semi-calm state I had obtained from my short meditation... gone. Within the hour, people would swarm my apartment. None of them bad people, but I only wanted one of them here.

As uncomfortable as I was, it would only get worse once everyone sat in the same room. It seemed as if everyone who visited recently, besides Jackson, came here to discuss this crazed lunatic.

Water bottles sat on various surfaces of my living room— some unopened, others empty. From my spot on the center of the couch, my eyes darted from one person to the next. Jackson's hand rested on my knee, his thumb stroking the edge.

My apartment currently occupied six people, excluding Jackson and myself. Marco, Bob, and Edwin from Hammond Life. Mr. Chang from the apartment complex. The two police officers we'd spoken with since the beginning—Sheila Hawks and Shawn Richardson. The six of them discussed the various aspects they were involved in and where things stood on their end.

How was this my life? Sending one last cry to the heavens

to wake up from this nightmare, I closed my eyes and attempted to shut out my surroundings.

All these people in one room. The reason they were here. The walls closed in on me as the air thickened, their voices a collection of white noise. I couldn't take it anymore. A victim in my own life. I rushed to my feet and all eyes instantly zoomed in on me. A second later, I went to the kitchen, needing to be farther away from the chaos that was my current life.

I braced myself by placing my hands on the cool, granite countertop as my head hung low between my shoulders. I inhaled deep and rhythmically, trying to collect myself. When I opened my eyes, I spotted Jackson's shoes. He stood near the kitchen entrance, watching and waiting.

I sucked in another deep breath before I backed away and stood more upright. He closed the short distance between us and bundled me in his embrace. Right here, this was where I wanted to be. But this serenity had been threatened and there's no way I'd let anything happen to Jackson. I wouldn't be able to live with myself if he got hurt because of me. Everything good in my world crumbled at my feet. All because of someone who was too chickenshit to come out of the shadows.

"Jackson," I whispered. "We need to listen to whoever this madman is. So no one gets hurt."

He held me at arm's length as his hands rested on my biceps. Rich blue sapphires zeroed in on me and questioned my logic. "We can't let him win, babe. He wants us apart, so he *can* hurt us. Physically and emotionally."

My eyes stung, tears threatened for the umteenth time in the last couple of weeks. "I wouldn't be able to live with myself if something happened to you." My throat clogged with emotion. But I couldn't let anything happen to him. It would kill me.

His thumb brushed over my cheekbone, wiping away an escaped tear. "Nothing will happen to me. I'm more worried about what he'll do to you if no one else is here." I leaned against his chest and rested my head on his shoulder. Jackson locked his arms tight around me.

Officer Hawks stepped into the kitchen, her demeanor

authoritative yet soothing. "Ms. Bradley, if you and Mr. Ember wouldn't mind returning to the other room. We'd all like to discuss our plan of attack in this situation."

Plan of attack? God, I hoped it was a good one.

"Yeah. Sure." Jackson and I walked back to the room of chaos and I resumed my position on the couch.

Officer Hawks scanned the room, everyone focused on her. "We all decided the best course of action right now is to follow the demands of the perpetrator. Mr. Ember, for the time being, you are to not have physical contact with Ms. Bradley. We believe it is in everyone's best interest you remain in contact, but only through phone calls, text messages, or via computer. We will establish an undercover presence wherever Ms. Bradley goes, making her aware of who the officer will be. Since the perpetrator does not appear to have an issue with Ms. Bradley's female friends, we suggest they spend more time together. Preferably here or one of their homes. No public establishments, with exception to acquiring necessities. Our undercover detective may pose as an old friend who just moved back to the area. Hence why they will be around you more often and perhaps in the same *career field* as you. Ms. Bradley, we'd also like for you, later this evening, to make a *scene* outside with Mr. Ember. If this person works for the same company as you, he most likely wouldn't be nearby for another hour or so. Everyone, including Mr. Ember, will leave here when we're done talking. Mr. Ember, we would like you to go do something, anything, and then return between six and six-thirty. Spend time together, have dinner, whatever you need to do. Around seven-thirty, we'd like the *scene* to go down. We will have an unmarked car close by, watching the building. Although neither of you will mean what is said, you need to convince any onlookers. Make whoever it is believe you're angry with each other and you're breaking up. Remember, we all have a role to play. It is important your role is believable, otherwise things could go from bad to worse in a split-second."

Not ten minutes ago, I told Jackson this very thing. That we needed to do what this maniac wanted. To spend time apart. But hearing the words. Hearing someone else tell me I needed to fake a breakup with the man I'd give my life for.

The only person I'd ever been in love with... I couldn't breathe. My chest constricted, and I wrapped my arms tight around my mid-section.

He tilted my chin toward him. "Breathe, babe. Please breathe." I took a few cleansing breaths, his sapphires the only thing in my tunnel vision as my body shook. "This sucks. Big time. But we have to catch this guy. If this is how we do it, then we have to try. Whatever is said later, we know..." He placed my hand on his heart and his over mine. "We know how we truly feel. I love you and I won't let him hurt you."

I closed the space between us, linked my arms behind his neck, and smothered him in kisses. "I love you, too." I also wanted to say *this person had already hurt me because he stole you from me*. But I kept my lips sealed and enjoyed the short time I had in Jackson's arms.

We sat on the couch, my body draped over Jackson's lap and I clung to his frame. "I don't think I can do this," I whined while I picked at the chipping polish on my nail.

He slid me off of his lap and rose from the couch, extending his hand to help me up. "I know you can. We've gone over everything. We know how everything has to look. Most importantly, we know it's not real and *very* temporary." Jackson took both my hands between his and rubbed his thumbs over my knuckles. "Neither of us have dealt with anything remotely close to this, but we have to believe the professionals know what they're doing. I'm just thankful for FaceTime and texting. We just need to be discreet when we're not home."

His words rang true in my head, but I still wasn't certain this was the best way. I wanted to believe they'd made the best decision under the circumstances, especially considering I had no idea what to do. "I know. It's just that this is the most difficult thing I've ever had to do." I don't know if I can handle this. Any of it. That is what I wanted to tell him, but kept it to myself, knowing it won't change anything.

"Me too, babe. Let's keep the group chats going. I brought

everyone else up to speed before I got back. They all understand everything needs to be as if we broke up."

Ugh, god! Hearing those words, even though it was all show, made me nauseous. "Okay."

We stood at the door, Jackson's duffle bag in his hand, my phone in mine. Our eyes glued to each other, our lips melding one last time in the most passionate kiss, not knowing when we'd actually be face-to-face again. "God, I love you so much, babe." His thumbs stroked my cheeks.

"I love you, too." Giving him one last kiss, I drew in a deep breath, closed my eyes and said silent prayers to all the gods of the universe. *Please let this be over soon.* I twisted the knob on the handle, my eyes laden with tears. Yanking the door wide open, my voice not my own as I yelled at Jackson like I never wanted to see him again.

When the whole scene ended, I shut my front door, turned the bolt, dropped to the floor, and curled into the fetal position. It wasn't real, but it was the worst feeling in the world. I laid there, crying, and waited for Liz and Christy to come console me. But their comfort wouldn't be enough because... half of my soul just got in a car and drove away.

FOURTEEN

JACKSON

"I LOVE YOU, TOO." She took a deep breath and closed her eyes, my way to her soul closing as her lashes painted her cheeks. Her hand on the doorknob as her eyes popped open, red and tear-stained. The door jerked open, her voice boomed —foreign to my ears. "Leave! Get the hell out of here!"

It's not real. It's not real. "You crazy ass bitch! Don't have to tell me twice! Trying to play off your ex as a stalker. I don't need this bullshit! I can replace you in a heartbeat," I belted out as I tugged my duffel behind me, walking away from the love of my life. Tears ran down her face, and I headed for my Wrangler.

God, this fucking hurts.

"I'm sure you have plenty of lady friends to keep your bed warm!" She yelled to my back, and her voice stuttered a fraction. A stutter only I would notice. A stutter which made my heart ache.

"Right back at ya! I seem to remember you love the ladies, too! Good riddance!" I jumped in my Jeep, cranked the engine and peeled out of the parking lot, speeding toward the front gate. In my rearview mirror, I saw her go back inside, the light in her window displayed her shadow as her body collapsed to the floor.

Fuck!

I drove out of the complex and headed to my house, the only place I would rather be was with her. The roads seemed quieter than normal, cars sparse as I turned onto my street. The sky darker as I stepped onto the path leading to my front door. And the moon absent in the night sky.

Void. The same as my heart. And soul. Which I left with her for safe keeping.

I finished putting away the load of laundry I'd washed to pass time. Glancing at my watch, I realized it was close to ten-thirty. Liz and Christy should have left her place by now. By now, she'd be changing into her pajamas and getting ready for bed.

Over dinner, we'd agreed to FaceTime at ten-thirty before going to bed, and again at eight-thirty to say good morning. Between those hours, we'd send texts or random pictures. Although she had the worst part in this whole situation, we both struggled with being separated.

The night she started drifting off, and she mumbled *I love you*, I was scared. Terrified. Fear halted me dead in my tracks. I had been in several relationships, most of them not too serious, none of them ever involving those three words. No use in denying I had strong feelings for Sarah. Stronger than I'd had for any woman. *But love?* In the moment, I had no inkling if it was love.

When she woke the next morning, tears stained her cheeks and she was so adorable with her nose stopped up. Right then and there, all I wanted to do was take care of her. Hold her. Make her feel safe. *Love her.* She'd slid back into my arms, talked about remembering something but not positive if it was real or a dream. I had a sneaking suspicion what she referred to, but wanted to hear her say it.

She recounted her story, telling me how she thought she remembered telling me she loved me. I laid still as a corpse, except for my hand, which was on auto-pilot caressing her back. I didn't want to lie to her or make her believe it wasn't real. She handed me everything. And I had wanted to do the same. But I wasn't sure I could say the words. Not yet.

"*It wasn't a dream.*" I'd told her.

If I wasn't ready to say the words, maybe showing her

was a more viable option. So, I gave her every part of me in other ways. With her, it was never just sex. Sure, some occasions were a lot raunchier than others, but there was always meaning behind every touch. Every taste. Every groan of pleasure.

I poured every drop of myself into that morning with her —making love with her, our connection more powerful than anything science dared try to explain. The bond between us incomparable to any prior—our bodies synchronized, and our passion constructed into a living, breathing entity. No doubt about it, I was absolutely lost in her. Still am. And I couldn't contain it any longer. I refused to restrain the fire she'd lit inside me. Her love fueled my soul. Those three potent words passed from my lips to her ears with ease.

It's a heady emotion. Love. I would obliterate heaven and earth to be with Sarah. And I was willing to suffer and not be by her side if it meant she'd remain safe. Life no longer had a purpose if she ceased to exist. Sarah was worth everything and I would do whatever it took to keep her forever.

My phone vibrated and a picture of me and Sarah kissing flashed on the screen. I pressed the button to answer and a live feed of Sarah lying in bed popped up. "Hey, babe. How are you? I miss you already," I confessed.

She yanked the blanket up to her neck. "I miss you, too. This sucks. I hope they figure this all out soon. I'm not going to be able to live like this." Her hand slid up to her cheek and tucked a cluster of loose hair behind her ear. Strands I wanted to tuck.

"I hope so, too. I've gotten accustomed to falling asleep and waking up with you in my arms."

Her face transformed from elation to sorrow, the shift in expression reminded me of theater masks. "There's no possible way I'm getting decent sleep. Not being alone. Not with that creep still lurking outside somewhere."

God, I wanted to hold her right now. Comfort her. Take away her anguish. It angered me that this asshole was able to go about his shithole existence while we suffered on the sidelines. I tried to not let her see my frustration, it wouldn't do either of us any good. But fuck... this was frustrating as hell.

"All we can do right now is hope the police find this

asshole soon and lock him away. Then we can get back to you and me," I cajoled as I traced a finger over her face on the screen, trying to soothe her fears.

It wasn't the same. Not by a long shot.

I saw her, spoke with her, told her how much I yearned for her. It was nowhere near enough though. Being miles away from her in a crowded city... I forgot which way was up.

If someone told me months ago, I'd be one of those guys—the guy desperate to be with his girl—I would've laughed in their face. I never pictured myself falling madly and deeply in love with someone. Before her, life just did its thing. I woke up, went to work, had drinks with the guys, hooked up here and there. A simple life. Easy. No one ever made me want more. Not until Sarah.

When I wasn't with her, I wanted to be. Every waking thought I had included her. She gave my monotonous existence purpose and meaning. I hadn't told her—and I intended to keep it secret—but I planned to help the police catch this piece of shit. The sooner, the better.

I didn't care what actions needed to be taken. This fucker would pay.

"Jackson? Did you hear me?" she asked, a little edgy.

"I'm sorry, babe. I spaced out a second. What'd you say?"

"Think I'm gonna go take a bath. I wish you were here. Not because I'm about to strip down." A hint of a smile lined her mouth. "I just..."

"Me, too. Go. Take a bath. Try to relax a little. If you want to call or text or video call again, I'm sitting on the other end waiting," I encouraged her.

Her eyes pooled at the corners as her bottom lip trembled the slightest bit. "I love you." A tear rolled down and fell from her chin.

If this didn't kill me, I'd consider myself a lucky man. I desperately wanted to say fuck it, drive back to her apartment, and soothe her. Provide her with the protection she begged for. Hold her close and whisper it'll all work out.

"I love you, too. Let me know when you're headed to bed."

She blew me a kiss and restrained her lingering tears. I returned the sentiment, and then the screen went black.

This shit needed to be over and done with. NOW.

"Have you gotten any updates? I asked Hawks and Richardson, but they didn't say much."

Her forehead and brows scrunched. "I talked to Hawks this morning, she told me there might've been someone ducking in the bushes under my window a couple nights ago. By the time they got there, all they found was an empty potato chip bag. They took it as evidence and are trying to get prints off of it."

Damnit!

Five days blended into one long nightmare. Not that this hadn't been a nightmare from the get-go. Neither of us slept well. Sarah hadn't gotten much done at work. I'd worked, but nowhere near full capacity. I wanted to be easily available if something happened.

"Have they suggested anything? Asked you to do anything different? See if you can lure this prick out. Safely."

Sarah hung her head, hid behind a wall of hair, and spoke with dread. "No, they want me to do things the same as usual. I don't understand how me sitting in my apartment, like a goddamn prisoner, is going to catch this guy," she fumed. Anger saturated every word as her life flipped upside down for someone else's sick pleasure. She had every right to be angry. As did I.

"This is bullshit! Tomorrow, we're doing something. Together. We can figure out a way, coordinate with everyone else if we have to. We can't live like this. We can't let him win."

Her eyes widened and a smile stretched her face tight. Hope glowed on her face for the first time in days. "How? He's watching every move I make."

"Every move *you* make. Not every move *I* make. He can't be in two places at once. I'll put it in the group chat and maybe we can get together at Christy's or Liz's. Have dinner, a game night or movie night. Whatever. And I'll ask Rick to pick me up, so my car isn't there. Rick and I will be there before you. What do you think?"

A glassy haze covered Sarah's eyes as she contemplated the idea over and over. Running through scenarios and how they'd play out. "Yes… we can make this work."

I wanted to throw my hands in the air in victory. Lift her off the ground, press her supple body against mine, and spin round and round. Soon, I would see her again. Hopefully tomorrow night.

"Yes we can, babe. I'll throw it in the chat when we're done. Tomorrow night…"

"Tomorrow, yes…" Her sigh lingered in the electronic energy between us. We sat quiet a moment and absorbed our jubilation. "I won't make it past this weekend without you. Without your touch. It's like part of me is missing."

"I miss you, too. I haven't breathed since we've been apart. My chest is barren without your heart next to mine. Tomorrow…"

"Tomorrow," she repeated. "I love you." Her eyes locked on mine.

"I love you more." And I wasn't afraid to own it.

Mozzarella and garlic perfumed the air as lasagna baked in Christy and Rick's oven. A large, black box containing all the expansion packs of Cards Against Humanity sat in the middle of the dining room table. The only thing missing was my girl. I counted the minutes—seven to go—until Sarah walked through Christy and Rick's door.

Static electricity buzzed my skin at the idea of seeing and touching my girl again. *Fuck.* I more than missed her. Deprivation doesn't even touch the level of loss consuming me. Although our sex life was killer, it was the last thing on my mind.

I sat on a barstool in the kitchen, a foot propped on the lowest peg, and bounced my knee like a hyper child. Checked my watch—two minutes. Why the hell does time move so damn slow when you're waiting for something good to happen?

"Quit looking at the time, man. It's only going to make it worse," Rick said as he passed me a beer.

"I know, but I can't seem to restrain myself. This whole situation is doing a number on us all. I don't know how much longer we'll be able to keep up the charade." Being physically away from each other for almost a week wrecked us. Our relationship is as strong as ever, and our feelings amplified each second we were apart, but as humans… we crumbled to pieces.

It's taking a toll on her that was noticeable in her eyes and when she spoke. Every time we were on the phone, the purple half-moons below her eyes were darker. I wondered if she'd slept at all. When we talked, her voice rasped—and not in the come hither sexy sort of way.

God, I needed her in my arms. Needed that connection with her again. Needed to reassure her we would get past this mountain-sized obstacle. Together.

A low thump sounded as the deadbolt unlocked. I snapped my head toward the door and saw Liz and Sarah walking into the room. All the air sucked from my chest. My stool scraped against the tile as I rose. I stumbled an inch as I set my bottle on the counter. Everything passed in slow motion as I closed the space between us and hauled her into my arms.

I clutched her tight against my chest and relished in her warmth as it vanquished the chill of her absence. A second later, her feet dangled above the floor as I lifted her high and crushed my lips to hers. I didn't give a shit if everyone watched our public display. She was here. In my arms. Where she should be.

Her golden locks shielded us as we made up for lost time. My arms pinned her securely to my chest, but it wasn't enough. She wrapped her legs around my waist and tried to pull me closer.

If our friends weren't here, clothes would've been on the floor already as our bodies rediscovered one another. I hadn't gotten my fill of her, but she stopped the kiss as her soft hands skimmed my stubble. Her face brightened. Eyes glimmered, lips plumped from our kiss, and a smile that fizzled the ache in my chest. God, I fucking missed her smile.

"Hey," she whispered an inch from my lips.

"Hey." I brushed her hair away and exposed us.

Her feet unhooked behind me and slowly lowered to the tile as our eyes magnetized. Sarah leaned in as her arm hooked mine. She laid the side of her face in the crook of my neck and inhaled. A beat later, her body relaxed and the world realigned a little more. We both needed this. And for this momentary blip in time, Sarah and I were whole.

Until tonight, I'd never played Cards Against Humanity. But I decided within minutes, this game would be in our regular rotation. I never laughed so hard or gasped in shock so many times in such a short span. If you played the perfect combination, you either had the hottest, raunchiest, nastiest or most distasteful phrase. I'm officially addicted.

We played our last round of cards and the black card stated ending a romantic dinner with... I glossed over the white cards in my hand—a celebrity name, penis size, incest, superheroes. But my prize-winning choice sat on the right in my hand.

I laid the card upside down for Rick to read, drew another white card, and waited for everyone to choose. Rick picked the handful of cards up, read the black card again and filled the blank with each white card answer. When he read my card, I laughed like an idiot. A romantic date ending with phallic-shaped dessert. To say I was easily amused would one-hundred percent accurate.

We ended the game and Christy won by a landslide, her girly, victory giggle cracked us up. But I didn't want the night to end yet. Not ready to let my girl go back to her apartment. Without me. Alone.

As if reading my mind, Christy announced, "Everyone is more than welcome to stay. Some of us may be more sober than others, but it's also late. There's a bed in the guest room and the couch isn't the most uncomfortable in the world."

I glanced down at Sarah, her arm hooked in mine, as my eyes plead with her to say yes. She squeezed her arm tighter around mine, and I shifted closer to her. Our lips met somewhere in the middle and a bomb triggered inside me. Her lips wordlessly communicated with mine and begged for us to stay.

When the kiss broke, I clasped her chin in my fingers and stroked her soft bottom lip with my thumb. My eyes locked on hers. "We're staying."

Christy slipped into hostess mode and directed us. "Okay, you guys take the spare room. Liz, you staying?"

"Yeah. That way everything seems the same when we leave tomorrow." Liz flashed Sarah a gentle smile.

She made a valid point though. Everything needed to be in sync, and we couldn't leave anything to chance. This creep probably followed Liz here after she picked up Sarah. They should leave together, too.

We helped clean up the game and remaining dishes. When Christy was content, we walked down the hall and headed for the bedroom, fingers intertwined.

Faint moonlight illuminated the room as beams leaked through the thin blind slats. Closing the door, we stood stock still and memorized each other in the darkness. My hands gripped her soft, curvaceous hips as I stepped into her and dipped my mouth to hers, taking what I'd missed over the last week.

Her warm, supple lips molded to mine, sucking and tugging. The rush that faded in her absence flooded my veins. I traced the lines of her body—an arm slid around her waist while the other caressed between her shoulder blades—and pressed her to me. Her mouth bloomed like a flower and opened up for me. Our tongues teased and taunted, only pausing to taste and suck and nip. Heat scalded my solar plexus and fanned out like wildfire.

Sarah stroked the muscles along my spine and up my shoulders before yanking off my shirt. We separated long enough for our shirts to hit the floor. As we stumbled back, her legs hit the mattress, and I lay her down.

She crawled back, and I followed, hovering over her. Slipping my hands under her, I unhooked her bra, yanked it off, and tossed it to the floor. Nimble fingers unbuttoned my shorts as her feet came to my hips and shoved the cotton down.

Every second heated. Every touch memorized. No idea

when we'd be together again and not taking any part of tonight for granted.

Her heels dug into my ass as she thrust up and rocked roughly against my cock. "Fuck," I whisper-moaned, sucking her bottom lip. Her nails clawed down my back and bit my flesh. A thin layer of sweat flared over my body as the painful pleasure swallowed me whole and woke the animal inside. On the next stroke, I slid back further and positioned my cock at her entrance and traced her folds.

"You're so fucking wet, babe," I growled.

Her hunger was a powerful force that beckoned me. A second later, she bowed off the bed in the hopes that I'd pivot forward. As much as I wanted to prolong the moment, my willpower crumbled. As her ass hit the sheets, I jolted forward and hissed when her walls hugged me like a glove.

I froze and absorbed every sensation skyrocketing through me. Hovering as bliss flitted across her face. My cock heavy and to the hilt inside her. A beat later, her head tipped back and pressed into the pillow as an audible gasp escaped her lips. Captivated, I studied the lines of her throat and the pulse below her ear. Leaning down, I sucked the base of her throat and tasted her salty skin, nipping and sucking my way to the sensitive spot beneath her ear. Her breasts pressed firm to my pecs as she muttered, "Oh god…"

When she collapsed against the sheets, her nails bit my skin and carved lines from my ass to my shoulders. As she marked me as hers, the beast inside me clawed up and surfaced. I bucked my hips as a low growl rumbled in my throat. Fervor glowed in her eyes as our bodies synchronized in the dim moonlight.

Her legs clutched my hips as she hooked her ankles. I slid a knee up for more leverage and rammed into her over and over. Before long, her walls clamped me like a vice. As she milked my cock, I fought the urge to come. I wasn't ready for this to be over. Not yet.

I picked up the tempo and pumped in and out of her as I bit her shoulder. She shuddered as her body convulsed around me, screaming loud enough for the neighbors to hear.

But neither of us fucking cared.

I paced my strokes and gave her a minute to come down.

The second she opened her eyes, I kissed her hard and told her to wrap her arms around my neck. When she obeyed, I flipped us over and she straddled my thighs as she lifted herself and then slammed back down on my cock.

Sarah pressed her hands to my chest and clawed my pecs as she circled her hips. She rode me like a bull as I bucked my hips. Fully seated inside her, I hit every tender spot. Her jaw slack as she panted and cried out into the darkness.

I gripped her hips as she clawed me with ferocity unlike any other time. Her hips circled faster and harder. Face tipped skyward. Breath in short bursts. Soft cries on her lips. My hands slid up her sweat-slickened abdomen. When the pads of my fingers clamped onto her nipples, I pinched and twisted and lit a bonfire inside her. Instantly, she pumped her hips wild and feral and met me thrust for thrust. She dropped her head and blonde hairs tickled my abs and lit a new level of intensity.

Almost there, her orgasm on the cusp of explosion. I bucked my hips harder each time she rocked forward and her walls slowly closed in on me. One last thrust forward and she detonated around me, her body shaking uncontrollably. A red flush danced up her chest as she heaved.

Before she caught her breath, I sat up, flipped us over, pulled out of her, and pressed her face into the mattress. She was exhausted, no doubt, but knew she'd let me get one last orgasm out of her. I wanted us in tranquility together.

I gripped her hips, yanked them up and savored her magnificent ass. I bent forward, pressed my cock to her entrance, and whispered into her ear. "One more, babe. Together." She reached between her legs and grabbed my balls and rolled them like a pair of Japanese Baoding balls.

Fuck!

I needed to come, and she edged me. I wanted to go slow and relish every inch of her body, mark what's mine. My hips plunged forward and I sunk inside heaven. My hand flattened between her shoulder blades and pinned her shoulders to the mattress. Her profile slack jawed as she gasped and clawed the sheets. Pure magnificence.

I glanced down at our joined bodies and stared as my dick slid in and out of her wet pussy. Fuck, she ravaged me. I traced her spine to her tailbone then crushed her hips in my grip, pumping in and out her frantically.

God, I fucking loved this woman. Our relationship would never be solely about sex—an added bonus. I loved every part of her. Her beauty. Her charisma. And her desire to see goodness in everyone.

Truthfully, I was the lucky one. The one she chose. Someone she couldn't live without. *Me*. The notion seared my skin with a newly discovered desire.

My skin painted in moisture, electricity fired inside of me, rippled from my limbs to my abdomen and converged in my balls. She mewled as her pussy milked my dick, and I finally let go, fiery and explosive. I grunted loud and guttural, offsetting her whimpers. I collapsed beside her as she dropped her hips and wheezed.

Our eyes locked as we reveled in what just happened. Ten rapid heartbeats later, she whispered, "Holy fuck!"

Goddamn, I loved her.

FIFTEEN

THE OTHER NIGHT at Christy's ran vicious circles in my head. Not just the sex—although it was pretty fucking phenomenal —but how close Jackson and I were for hours. Arms brushing, fingers laced, bodies inches apart, a sweet hum buzzing between us. His arms cocooned me while we slept. It was the first time in almost a week we'd slept through the night.

I don't welcome danger, but how could I not spend time with him. When we woke Sunday morning and the faint light of day replaced the moon, we cuddled and talked for hours.

We devised a plan to see each other, not every day, but three or four times a week. In our plan, we orchestrated other get-togethers with everyone, rotating where we'd hang out so a pattern didn't form. Sleeping in each other's arms a dream, but a tough pill to swallow knowing it wouldn't happen often.

After hours of master-minding, we dressed and joined everyone for a late breakfast, sharing our idea. My heart skipped a beat when everyone agreed. Their smiles of encouragement made this whole situation a little less scary.

In the early hours of the afternoon, we parted ways. The promise of time together in two days put me in a jovial mood. When Liz dropped me at my apartment, I called Marco and said I'd be back in the office the next day. Honestly, I'd probably be just as safe at work as I am at home. Maybe safer.

Either way, this creep still lurked in the shadows.

Harassed me. Tried to rule my life. I refused to hide in the dark like a defenseless, frightened girl. This was my life and I would fight for it. Brave. Strong. Courageous.

———

I slid into Liz's backseat—Christy rode shotgun—and greeted my favorite ladies. Carpooling now the new norm, which grew on me faster than expected. Catching up with Liz and Christy before work one of my new favorite activities. Yesterday, I spent my first day back at my desk, re-acclimating to my workspace and the office noise.

The workday went by without interruption. At lunchtime, the three of us unanimously agreed to eat somewhere besides Carol's since the assumed admirer/stalker worked at Hammond. Later, everyone hung out at Liz's place. Rick brought Jackson over before Christy, Liz, and I arrived. As planned, the guys left after Liz took us home.

The dynamic weird, but if I got to see Jackson, I didn't care. However long, Jackson and I agreed to put up with this crazy routine until an arrest happened. I refused to have my life stolen.

"We aren't at work yet, but where should we go for lunch?" Liz asked, her eyes glued to the road.

"I'm game for whatever," I eluded. Where we went didn't matter as long as it was outside the office.

"Ooh, ooh. What about that new place a couple of blocks from the office? Shelly raved about it. It's Tex-Mex with flair." Christy's hands animated as she painted us a picture.

"I'm good with that. Liz?"

"Good with me."

The day came and went; the colorful Tex-Mex restaurant the highlight of our workday. That night, I told Jackson about the amazing fajitas I ordered and suggested we go there in the future.

Talking about food morphed into a conversation about how much I missed his cooking. How I longed to see him in boxer briefs and an apron again. Our discussion transitioned from my lunch to his cooking to him in an apron to sex in the blink of an eye.

Before long, I stripped bare in front of the live feed. He mimicked my actions, our hands groping our own flesh at the encouragement of the other. I shuddered as he jerked his hand up and down his hard shaft, each rise and fall stirred an ache between my legs. The burn hotter and wetter with each stroke. Jackson tugged faster as he watched my fingers dip and emerge.

Masturbation not foreign to me, but something I'd always done alone. This voyeurism… unexpectedly turned me on. Pure and raw intimacy. Although we'd been completely exposed to each other before, this vulnerability tipped the scales and took us to a new plateau.

My body trembled as I climaxed, not as powerful as when Jackson and I came together, but more potent than any previous time alone. Jackson came seconds later, his sticky seed coating his taut abs and pecs, his muscles taut. And I hungered to lick him clean.

I glanced at the time—eleven-eleven. My superstitious heart begged to make a wish. So, I closed my eyes for a moment and sent a wish out to the universe. *Please let this person get caught. Please let my life go back to normal.*

"You tired, babe? I can let you go."

I was tired. Tired of living in fear. Tired of being a victim. Of being isolated. Of being without Jackson by my side. "Yeah."

"I'll let you go. Try to get some sleep. I'll see you tomorrow." His tone a soft lullaby.

"Love you."

"Love you, too, babe."

Another week and a half had passed and nothing eventful happened.

No calls or texts. No emails or letters. No unexpected gifts. Nothing.

I wondered if the police arrested the creepster and forgot to mention it. One could only hope.

The sun brightened the sky more than usual. Warmer temperatures prickled my skin as a light breeze ruffled my hair. Exultation coursed through me now that it was Friday afternoon and only four hours of work remained.

Liz, Christy, and I perched on barstools at a tall wooden table. Women in tight, short-shorts and barely-covering-their-breasts tops carried trays, weaving between the tables. The smell of fried foods wafted in the air and my stomach growled in delight.

A tray lowered next to us and was set on a stand as the waitress delivered our lunch. The buffalo chicken Caesar wrap I ordered mouth-watering, and I moaned.

"You ladies need anything else?" the server asked. Her auburn hair secured in a ponytail that swayed as she bounced side to side.

"No, I think we're good," Liz answered with a smile and a wink. They eyed one another a moment. Liz's smile slipped to a wicked gleam as her eyes scanned the woman's curves. I'd be an idiot to miss the sexual tension passing between them.

"All right, ladies. Holler if you need me," Tiffany, her name tag read, beamed. As she walked away, Liz scanned the rest of her body.

Playfully, I smacked her arm. "Could you be more obvious?"

"What?" Her pitch an octave higher. "I can't help myself. She's cute. And fuckable." The megawatt smile on her face lit a city.

"Oh my god!" Christy's hand smacked Liz's opposite arm. "Shut the hell up, bitch! People can hear you."

"So what," she retorted. "She's hot. I'm available. Who knows?"

I laughed at my best friend, and former fuck buddy. How I loved her. She lived a carefree life, something I envied her right now.

"Single? What happened to mister hottie?" I asked.

Liz rolled her eyes. "Let's just say, not all men are as great as Jackson or Rick."

"Ouch. His loss. I say, if you think Tiffany's hot, go for it. You never know. Maybe she swings that way. Or both. Either way, you'll never know if you don't ask," I comment.

Liz stared at the grouper tacos on her plate. A smile

brightened her expression as she turned to look at me.

"Thanks. That means more than you know." Her eyes alight with the bond we shared.

I'd said it because the relevance meant the same when she gave me her blessing with Jackson. Oftentimes, I wondered if Liz didn't date because of me. In case things changed between me and Jackson and I needed her again.

The bond Liz and I shared would never change. Our connection always stronger than most friendships. But I didn't want her life limited because of our bond. My future with Jackson wasn't set in stone, but instinct told me—deep in my bones—we would be together years. And Liz should have the same happiness.

Over lunch, we talked about our weekend plans. Christy suggested another game night. Liz mentioned us all ordering an obscene amount of guilty pleasure foods and spending a day doing a movie marathon. I listened to them prattle on, running down a list of options, all indoors and at one of their homes.

Anger flooded me and everything went red. This bullshit had to end. Ugh, I was sick and tired of living according to someone else's desires. I hated feeling like a frightened child, essentially locked away in a closet. I stopped listening. This fucker didn't own me and I should be able to go out with my friends. Be out in the world. Live my life. The threshold of my patience officially maxed out.

"Enough!" I belted out louder than expected. It felt exhilarating.

Both their eyes widened at my exuberance, lips in a tight line. "What?" Liz asked, confused.

"Enough," I said. "I'm tired of this. I'm tired of being a prisoner because of some asshole lunatic. It's been almost two weeks since anything happened. Maybe he got arrested. Or maybe something happened to him. Either way, I don't care anymore. This is my life, damnit. And I want to do something outside the confines of my home, and yours."

"Sarah..." Christy warned. "I don't know if that's really the best idea. We don't know this guy has been caught. Don't you think Marco would've mentioned if someone suddenly stopped showing up?" Although she made a valid point, I didn't care. Why should I be forced to live like this? This creep wasn't stealing my life from me.

"You're probably right, but I don't care. I'm over being held captive. This weekend, we're going out. This weekend, I'm taking my life back," I told them, my mind set.

They stared at me, deer in the headlights, my bold statement rendered them speechless. Surprisingly, Liz spoke first, methodical and orchestrated. "All right, Sarah. Why don't we run this past the guys? See what they think."

Her concern valid. Liz worried about me. But like it or not, this was happening. "Sure, I'll put it in the group text right now. But I'm telling you, regardless, I'm going out this weekend. With or without everyone. I'd prefer it if I had company."

My fingers tapped out the message, and their phones chimed after I hit send. I slipped my phone back in my purse and finished my lunch. They wanted me safe. I got it. But enough was enough.

We finished our lunch in silence. When the waitress came back to clear the table, Liz pulled her to the side.

Tiffany's face transitioned from concerned to someone being seduced by an attractive woman. Her body loosened, her shoulders relaxed, and a crinkle formed at the corners of her eyes as she smiled. Whatever Liz said, it intrigued Tiffany. Liz took out her phone, her fingers raced across the keyboard as she tucked Tiffany's phone number away in her contacts.

When Liz returned to the table, her skin glowed and her cheeks were flushed. It delighted me to see my best friend like this. Happy, excited, giddy over the possibilities. Who knew where things would go with Liz and Tiffany, but at least she took the first step. Sometimes, a single step was all it took to find happiness.

"Babe, I really don't think this is a great idea. It's not that I don't want to go out. I just don't want anything to happen to you. Or anyone else, for that matter." Concern etched Jackson's voice as his brow scrunched inward.

"Nothing will happen. Everything has been quiet for

weeks now. I'm tired of sitting on my couch and twiddling my thumbs, meanwhile the world continues to move forward. Please..." I beg, the word heavy on my tongue. "Come over. Pick me up. Take me out of this place before I lose my fucking mind. Everyone will be there. We can keep an eye out for each other. Please..."

My request didn't sit well with him. He told me so last night. But I begged and pleaded with him. He caved after fifteen minutes and some tears. He understood, as much as I did, how this whole situation wore on me. What it did to my heart. To us. To our sanity.

I stared back at him as we FaceTime talked, and his expression morphed from concern to defeat. All he wanted was to keep me out of harm's way, but accepted he couldn't keep me home tonight. No matter how hard he tried.

"I'll be over soon. Are we meeting everyone at the bar?" he asked, defeat in his voice and posture.

Tempted to jump up and down, I resisted. My enthusiasm on cloud nine. "Yeah. Liz is bringing a date, so there will be six of us."

"Be there in a few, babe," he answered more tender.

"Yay!" My excitement burst at the seams. "I'll see you soon. Love you."

"Love you, too, babe."

***

The bar was packed with patrons sipping beers and fruity drinks as a sea of bodies danced on the floor. A typical Saturday night, but energy surged in my bones. We managed to snag a table, ordered a couple pitchers of beer and some appetizers, and slipped into old times.

Much of our conversation revolved around Tiffany—the newest person in our tight-knit circle. Christy asked the questions most of us wouldn't dare ask, and her lack of intimidation never ceased to amaze me. Tiffany rolled with it, not cowering once during her spotlight inquisition.

Throughout the night, we learned Tiffany attended college to earn her master's in clinical psychology. She worked at the bar-and-grill because tips were great and it kept her head above water. Tiffany wasn't lesbian—yes, Christy straight up asked the question—but she didn't discriminate when it came to dating. Male, female, race, religion. None of those factors influenced her reason behind dating. All she cared about was the person's vibe. Being a psychology major, she vetted most people within seconds.

Jackson and I stayed at the table. His arm slung over my shoulders pinned me to his side, and I loved it. Rick hauled Christy off to dance a couple times. Liz did the same with Tiffany. I curled into Jackson, elated to see my friends smile and laugh and enjoy themselves.

A few glasses of beer later, we were ready to call it a night. Christy and Rick right behind us. Liz and Tiffany hung all over each other and planned to stay until last call.

I hugged Liz and whispered in her ear. "Let me know how everything goes. Talk to you tomorrow."

We parted, and she nodded as we said good night. Tiffany and I exchanged a warm hug. I secretly hoped she and Liz hit it off. Tiffany was so affectionate and honest, and my intuition told me they would be a good match. The group loved her, too. "It was so nice to meet you. Take care of my girl."

"Nice meeting you, too. And don't worry, I will." Her smile genuine. Her heart open. And just like that, I knew she wouldn't hurt my friend. Knew she had an equal interest in her. The thought soothed my soul, and my fondness of Tiffany grew tenfold.

We stepped onto the sidewalk outside the bar, the cool early April air blew strands across my face and the crispness was invigorating. I tilted my chin up and met Jackson's eyes, a soft glow behind his sapphires. "Take me home," I ordered, the sultry demand rolled off my tongue.

I stood stock-still as the soft glow flipped to fiery passion. I may not of said the words, but my tone insinuated what I wanted.

"Yes, ma'am," he replied without hesitation.

We hopped into the Jeep and he drove me home. Stripped me out of my clothes, and he made love to me until dawn. When the sun came up, we fell asleep. His arms embraced me like never before, and we stayed that way until Monday arrived.

SIXTEEN

Two Weeks Later

I WOKE to pans clanging in the kitchen. Something sizzled and the smell of garlic and bell peppers filled the air. I walked into the kitchen and wrapped my arms around Jackson's waist and kissed the back of his shoulder. "Good morning."

He turned and pressed his lips to my forehead. "Morning, babe."

Turning back to the stove, he moved food around the pan to prevent it from burning. "Whatcha making?"

"Western omelets, home fries, and juice."

"Mmm... Can't wait." I scraped my nails over his abdomen before removing my arms and letting him know I would be back after brushing my teeth.

When I walked back into the kitchen, he slid the omelet onto a plate, and carried both plates to the table. I poured us both a glass of orange juice and brought them to the table. We sat in peace-filled silence, his food giving me a foodgasm per usual.

With only a few bites left on my plate, his already cleared, he glanced at me and waited until I finished chewing. "It's supposed to be nice out today. Anything you want to do?"

"Lemme think." I pierced a few squares of potato and shoved them in my mouth. Over the last two weeks, Jackson and I eased back into where we were before the whole stalker situation started.

In the last month, nothing new occurred. No appearances made. No indications the guy hung around. The police backed off a little and told us maybe the guy got his jollies by scaring people and that ship sailed. They asked us to inform them if anything else came up, but until then everything should return to normal.

Normal. I have never loved that word until now. Many people thought normalcy was overrated and boring. They did not understand how great it actually was. To be able to do what you want, whenever you want.

"Let's go hiking. Maybe out at the wildlife refuge. It's been a long time since I've been out there." I scooped up the last bit of my omelet and savored the last bite as it hit my tongue.

"Great idea. You get ready, then we'll head to my place so I can change. Maybe stop and grab something for lunch and make a day of it."

I loved the idea. The refuge along the Atlantic coast had trails and wildlife everywhere in the park. We'd easily spend hours out there and not see the same view twice. Nature was my playground and hiking in the refuge with Jackson was bound to be seventh heaven.

"Awesome," I said and grinned. I stood and bolted for the bedroom. "I'll be ready in ten." His laughter echoed from the kitchen to the bedroom as clothes flew from the closet to the bed.

A long day of hiking equaled no cooking dinner. Both of us spent. I set a bag of food on top of the coffee table, took out to-go boxes, and spread them out. Jackson walked in from the kitchen with spoons in hand. He handed one to me as I gave him a set of chopsticks.

"Bon appétit."

We clinked spoons before slurping miso soup. Bite after bite, my stomach grew into a beach ball, blown to full capacity. Sushi the perfect way to end our day. And as much as I wanted to eat more, I stopped myself.

I slumped against the couch, unbuttoned my shorts, and slid my hand in front of the waistband. Jackson noticed and belted out a hearty laugh, making me smile. Probably thought this was my best impression of an overindulged, old man on Thanksgiving. But whatever. I loved sushi and always stuffed my face.

We flipped on the tv and watched a show about the galaxy on a science channel. Hours later, I woke in Jackson's arms with my body pressed close to his chest. He laid me on the bed, fully clothed, and curled up behind me as we both drifted off.

Seven-forty-seven. Too damn early to be awake on a Sunday. I wrapped Jackson's arm tighter around my midsection, closed my eyes, and tried to force myself back to sleep. Twenty minutes later, I remained wide awake.

I carefully slid from under Jackson's arm—his soft snores adorable—and headed for the kitchen, deciding to make breakfast for him for a change. Nowhere near as creative as Jackson, I whipped up a few of my favorite things.

By the time he walked in the kitchen, I'd cooked a batch of maple, steel-cut oats, sliced up bananas and apples, and topped it with crushed walnuts. Coffee brewed and the tea kettle softly whistled.

He folded me into his arms and inhaled me, planting a kiss on top of my head. "I would've made breakfast."

"Not that I don't love it when you make me breakfast, but now it's my turn. It's nothing fancy, but it tastes great."

He tightened his arms and kissed me once more before letting go. "It smells fantastic. Let me grab coffee."

We ate breakfast, then talked about getting together with everyone else. After breakfast, I sent a quick message to the group chat, which now included Tiffany. Liz and Tiffany converged into a regular duo over the last few weeks and we'd all grown to love her. I texted the group and asked if anyone wanted to hang out.

I peeked up from my phone to Jackson's nude body, his rippled back faced me as he tested the shower's water temperature. I dropped the phone to the bed, peeled away my clothes, and headed for Jackson.

As I stepped into the shower, I marveled at the sight of him as water cascaded down the lines of his neck to his strong pecs and rippled over the ridges of his abdomen. With his eyes closed and his face under the spray, Jackson hadn't realized I had snuck in with him. I reached out, placed my hands on his chest, and stepped into him. Just the heat of his skin on mine stirred the ache between my thighs.

Jackson's chin dropped and a waterfall trickled from his inky hair. A pair of rich sapphires smoldered as they raked over me. Two months together and shower sex, surprisingly, had not happened yet. The idea of him fucking me against the wall lit me on fire. I imagined the slaps echoing off the walls as he rammed into me and I slid up and down the tile. The guttural groan from his lips as I clamped down on his cock. Our moans of pleasure as we climaxed together.

He pinched my chin and tipped it up. For three weighted breaths, Jackson devoured me with his eyes. Then, his lips crushed mine—starved for my taste. A moment later, he nipped from my jawline to my neck, sucked the sensitive spot beneath my ear, and nibbled his way to the base of my throat. I gasped as he bit the line above my collarbone and dropped to my breast, sucking my nipple and biting at the bud between his teeth. An inferno blazed with fury as every nerve ending exploded. When he released my nipple and brought his lips back to mine, I scraped the V leading to heaven and gripped his erection as if my life depended on it.

"Fuck me against the wall," I demanded in a low growl.

My command sent Jackson into overdrive as he clutched my hips and hoisted me against the wall. I wrapped my legs around him and locked my ankles as his cock rammed into me. I gasped as he thrust his cock to the hilt inside me. The fullness and stretch of my body around his girth overwhelmed me in this new position. Delicious and ravishing. He peeled my hands away from his neck and pinned them to the tile above me, holding me in place as he pumped his hips. An insatiable hunger whirled in his eyes and made me whimper.

"You feel so fucking good like this, babe," he said before crushing his lips to mine.

He let my hands go, and I snaked them back around his neck. One of his hands gripped my ass as the other fisted my hair and yanked hard. My body was sparking like a live wire as Jackson dominated every inch of me. Everything new and heated and raw. The passion. The hunger. Undiluted. Insatiable.

"Oh, god. So good, Jackson," I moaned, practically unintelligible.

My breath came out in jagged pants as I begged him to fuck me harder. To make me see stars. In a heartbeat, he yanked my head back, bruised my ass, and thrust in and out of me as if we'd never see each other again. "God, I fucking love you," Jackson grunted between thrusts. The words bled from his lips and I came alive.

I combed my fingers through his hair and balled my hands into fists and tugged. Jackson hissed, and I bit the spot where his shoulder and neck met. Pure carnality unleashed as he fucked me harder, my back burning as the tile rubbed my skin raw.

"Close. So close..." I panted out as my body edged. Jackson growled in my ear as heat shot from every pore of my body and fused in my core. He nipped and kissed his way down and up my neck, sucking when he reached the spot that always sent me over the edge. So. Fucking. Close.

"Let go, babe," he growled, letting go of my hair and clamping my ass with both hands.

One pump, then another, and I erupted around him. My walls closed in and milked every drop of his orgasm as we screamed loud enough to frighten the neighbors. Neither of us cared. It wasn't the first time, and certainly wouldn't be the last.

Jackson pressed his forehead to mine as we worked to catch our breath. "That..." he huffed out. "That was fucking glorious." He pressed a chaste kiss to my nose. "Have I expressed my undying love to you recently?"

I laughed, then nipped along his jawline. "Hmm, I don't know. Maybe you should again, just in case," I teased.

"I love you beyond comprehension, Sarah Bradley." Then

Jackson peppered my mouth and neck and body in kisses, and each stamped my skin for a lifetime.

Something as simple as waking up next to the person you love can make your entire world a better place. I woke before the alarm this morning with the sun barely tinting the sky. I flipped onto my side and faced Jackson and watched his chest rise and fall.

I watched him for close to an hour, completely mesmerized and unable to believe that this strikingly handsome man belonged to me. Jackson Ember could have any woman he desired, yet he chose me. A simple woman with hints of wild and hippie flowing in her veins. Not that I didn't believe we belonged together, it just astounded me how I managed to be the one.

After studying every line and lash and lock, I itched to sweep my fingers through his short, black hair. As he slept, it laid soft against his scalp, free from the product he added to spike it. So soft. So alluring. I tucked my hands under my cheek and resisted the urge.

As I continued my visual perusal, I locked onto the squared angle of his jaw and was spellbound. Stubble dusted his jawline and I yearned to reach out and feel the small hairs scratch my palm, but I resisted and averted my gaze to his lips. Those lips… A girl could get lost for days in his kiss. Full lips highlighted his bone structure, but didn't steal the show from his other features.

But my favorite… I propped myself on an elbow and stared down at this statuesque man. Unfortunately, his eyelids shielded me from his magnificent sapphires. If someone presented me with one option, and I was only able to see one part of him, it would be his staggering eyes. Hands down.

The first time I saw him—walking into the gym and holding the door open—he hadn't noticed me, but he had captivated me. Those magical, alluring blue sapphires. In that moment, a minor blip in time, I caught a glimpse of him. One potent enough to ingrain his soul in mine. The night of the party—the first time he truly captivated me—it was as if two souls found their way back to one another and fused into one.

The story of soul mates has various perceptions. Some said we each have more than one, that soul mates were not limited to just lovers but also friends we held dear in our heart. Other stories showed we have multiple soul mates in the same lifetime, souls who met and shared part of their life, and taught us lessons to lead us to our one true soul mate. Our twin flame.

Jackson was that to me... my twin flame. My joy was his joy. My sorrow was his sorrow. And my pain was his pain. Once we found each other, one couldn't live without the other. A strange concept to explain, but Jackson is the breath oxygenating my blood. Stumbling upon your twin flame compared to locating a person you never realized was missing your entire life. And once you found him or her, being apart was unfathomable.

His body stirred as muscles came to life. Eyes squinting and adjusting to the bright sunlight. He tilted his head toward me—my face casting a shadow over his profile—as he drew me closer to him and painted a sweet kiss across my lips.

"How long have you been watching me?" His shy smile brightened the room more.

"Not long. You looked so peaceful. I didn't want to wake you."

The wailing buzz of the alarm clock jolted us from our sweet moment, the small black box squealed at us to get up and face the world. I drew back the covers, reached over and slapped the disrupting device, rendering it silent.

Reluctantly, we vacated the warm, cozy sheets and dressed for our day. I'd never paid close attention until now, but Jackson and I moved fluidly around each other. The energy surrounding us emulated a human form of synergy as our individual movements complemented the other. There was never any awkward bumping. Never an undesirable touch.

We were one soul, separated by two bodies, moving in harmony. We didn't have to speak a word, we simply knew.

Our morning routine ended with a kiss—I slid into my

car, Jackson in his—and we headed to work. Life beyond perfect. My and Jackson's relationship spectacular. Work had been great, too. Being back in a normal routine relieved all of us, seeing as I no longer required an escort everywhere.

When I reached my desk, two larger than life smiles greeted me. Two pairs of eyes shone brighter than the summer sun. "Hey, ladies. What's up?" Their behavior not completely out of the ordinary, but it was early, and I hadn't caffeinated enough to handle their perkiness.

"Since everything is to be back to old times, Christy and I discussed getting back to the gym. All of us put it on the back burner when all that crazy shit happened. What'daya think?"

I missed my old morning routine with Christy and Liz. My body certainly missed the rigorous workouts. Although, Jackson kept me active and my body in shape. But that stayed between the two of us. "Yeah. That'd be great. Just the three of us? Or anyone tagging along?"

"Ooh, ooh. Great idea." Christy wiggled side-to-side in her chair. "Rick needs to get out more. Maybe if Jackson joins, the two of them can do manly gym things. And we can watch." If her giggle were visible to the human eye, it'd look like pink cotton candy.

"Let's put it out there, in the group chat, and see what everyone says. I love it! I've missed working out with you guys."

"Me, too." Liz nodded. "Just glad we can get back to it."

I tossed the idea into the group chat and everyone jumped on board. We chose a couple days everyone could meet up and a couple days when it'd be 'girls only' or 'guys only'. Another piece of my life given back to me. Halle-fricking-lujah.

I cut the steering wheel to the right and parked my Beetle two spots down from my front door. Florence and the Machine blared from my speakers, and I belted out the chorus before cutting the engine. A gust of wind caught my ponytail and whipped it in my face as I exited the car, essentially blinding me. I shoved the wayward locks aside and turned back to the car.

Reaching down, I grabbed my purse and the brown bag loaded with groceries, and headed for my apartment. Tonight, I would try my hand at cooking eggplant parmesan. Jackson almost always cooked for us. My culinary skills no match for his, but it was time I stepped up and cooked something.

Variety wasn't in my repertoire, but the few things I cooked, I mastered. Luckily, eggplant parmesan made it on the list.

I reached the stepping stones that branched off of the sidewalk and trailed to my door. A teal, wooden chair and a circular table large enough to hold a glass and a book sat on my front porch. Nothing lavish, but I loved the cozy vibe.

A few steps from the porch, a long, narrow box sitting on the chair stole my attention. The outside of the box was decorated in generic images of roses and tulips with a wide blue ribbon wrapped around the center.

My feet sunk into the earth as I kept distance between me and the box. Was it more flowers? By now, if Jackson planned to gift me flowers, he would deliver them in person. Especially after everything that happened.

I set the brown bag down at my feet, peered over my shoulder and scanned the parking lot. With sunglass-shielded eyes, I scanned every nook and cranny. No one loitered in the lot. No clapping footsteps or rustling bushes or birds chirping. I focused on the trees and studied them longer than usual. Nothing.

I faced my front door and the box that flashed bright neon warning signs. I forced my unwilling legs to move—taking two steps, one foot in front of the other—and picked up the box. A label on the front of the box from a delivery service. But if memory served me correct, the first flower delivery arrived from a florist.

With the box in my hand, I stepped away from the chair and purposely exposed myself, in case I needed help. Clutching a corner of the blue ribbon, I slowly tugged the bow free and watched the satin fall to the ground. As one hand gripped the bottom of the box, the other grabbed hold of the top. With precision, I removed the lid and saw a mountain of tissue paper inside. Hesitant, I peeled back the layers and something slimy slithered over my finger. I screamed and threw the box in the grass.

Clutching my chest, I stepped back until I bumped into the wall. In the box, hidden behind folds of tissue, laid a bundle of dead flowers. More specifically, sunflowers and daisies. Roaches, worms, beetles and other insects crawled and squirmed through the flowers. Bile rose in my throat and I pinched my lips tight.

As I stared at the box, a piece of paper flapped with the breeze. I tip-toed through the grass, standing back far enough nothing crawled on me, and quickly tugged on the page.

Hopping back to the porch, I hung my head and flipped the paper over in my hands. As badly as I wanted to read the note, I also wanted to light it on fire and yell at the top of my lungs. My life just returned to normal. Happiness returned to my world. Why was I being forced back into this hellacious fear? Again.

The note felt like a lead weight in my hands. But avoiding it helped no one. I needed to read it and be done with it. The only person who ruled my life, my world, was me. My blood pressure spiked as anger surged in my bloodstream. "How dare you!" I screamed to the heavens, hoping this obsessed, batshit fucker heard me. I was so over the crazed lunatic who threatened my livelihood.

I unfolded the edges of the paper and exposed another typewritten letter. Instantly, my pulse flew off the charts.

Tsk, tsk beautiful little Sarah,
I thought we went over this. I explained myself well enough for you to understand.
I thought you were intelligent. I thought you knew the rules.
But I guess I was wrong. That won't happen again.
Don't think I haven't been watching you. Not a day passes where I don't see you. I have eyes everywhere. You thought you could fool me. Well guess what, my beautiful Sarah. I'm no FUCKING FOOL!
I gave you a chance.
Told you to stop seeing the pretty boy.

Did you listen to me? Not one fucking word was heard, obviously. I know about the little meetings at your friends' houses. I listened, outside that little guest bedroom window, while mister muscles fucked your brains out.
Maybe I didn't make myself clear before.
YOU BELONG TO ME! YOUR CUNT IS MINE!
Tick, tock little Sarah. Before you know it, there will be blood.
Eenie, meenie, miney, mo…
Who will I pick…
You won't fucking know…

I grabbed the brown bag, unlocked my door and threw the keys on the foyer table. With fumbling hands, I yanked out my phone. *This cannot be happening again.* Please, whatever higher power existed in the universe, don't let this happen again.

SEVENTEEN

"Hey, babe. I'm finishing with a client. Should be done with my last one in about an hour, give or take. Then I'll be over."

I wheezed, my lungs unable to draw in enough air as I desperately gasped for oxygen. Jackson was frantic on the other end of the line, shouting my name and pleading with me to answer. After several deep breaths and counting to ten, I located my voice.

"It's happening again! Oh my god, it's fucking happening again!" I shrieked.

"What are you talking about? What happened?!"

Unstable on my feet, the room tilted beneath me. *Why? Why was this happening?* "There was another delivery. A box at my door when I got home."

"You have got to be *fucking* kidding me," he bellowed, his anger evident. Not aimed at me, but to the asshole instigating this. "I'll be there as soon as possible. Call the police. Have them come out and update the case." I nodded as my vision blurred. "Babe, can you hear me? Call the cops."

"Yeah, sorry. I'll call as soon as we get off the phone. I'll let you know what they say," I stammered.

"Please. I'll be there as quick as possible. Lock the doors. I love you."

"I love you, too," I mumbled.

Our call disconnected and my mind drifted into the ether,

wishing Jackson and I somewhere far from here. Why was this happening?

My mind blank. Limbs numb. I heaved and reminded myself to breathe. Everything suddenly surreal. I should call the police, but what good has it done? From where I stood, not a goddamn thing.

With each passing minute, my desire to care lessened more and more. Why not throw in the towel? This madman was determined to ruin my life. I retrieved the officer's business card from my wallet and dialed the number. After three ridiculously long rings, I almost disconnected the call when a woman's voice answered.

"Officer Sheila Hawks, you're on a recorded line."

"Officer Hawks, this is Sarah Bradley. I'm calling to update the police report I've filed. I received another delivery today. With a letter," I sputtered.

"Ms. Bradley, I'm sorry to hear that. We keep hitting dead ends with this guy. I wish I had better news." Silence rang loud and clear. I sat shell-shocked and waited for her to continue. "Would you be able to bring the letter and delivery down to the station now? Best if we dust if for prints as soon as possible. Maybe we'll get something off this new evidence."

"Now?" I asked. I bit my fingernail as sanity slipped from my consciousness. Not sure if driving is such a hot idea right now. But sitting here and doing nothing until the morning was the most absurd idea. She understood the urgency. Officer Hawks didn't have some whack job following her every move and dictating her life. Crushing her soul. But she wanted to do everything in her power to help me and I appreciated that.

"Ma'am, maybe you should wait. It's not a good idea for you to drive right now. You're distraught, and seeing as you called me instead of Mr. Ember, I'll assume you are alone. Perhaps it's best for you not to drive. Take some deep breaths, lock your doors, and try to relax until Mr. Ember can safely drive you. We'll get everything sorted out then."

I understood what she told me and acquiesced. She continued to speak, but I stopped listening. Her voice white noise on the other end. When she finished, we exchanged our goodbyes, and I told her I'd come by later.

Did the police give two shits about my problem? Maybe they had more involved and dangerous cases on their desks. Cases with leads. Cases with a possible resolution. Either way, I refused to be the poor, helpless victim. To sit in my apartment and wait. Desperate to escape and blow off steam, I paced the living room. Ideas whooshed like a hurricane as I contemplated ways to gain my life back.

Heading to my dresser, I grabbed a sports bra and a pair of yoga pants. I changed from my work clothes into the exercise gear and picked up my gym bag. More than likely, I had another forty-five minutes to an hour before Jackson arrived. My nerves firing on hypersonic speed, I needed to center myself. Needed to feel something, anything, besides the numbness. And if I sat in my apartment another minute, I'd lose my shit.

Sarah: Called the police, they said to come down in the morning. Going to the gym for a few. I'll be back before you get here.

Jackson: Babe, that's not a good idea. Stay inside. I'll be there soon. We can go together if you want. I don't want you to go alone.

Sarah: It'll be fine. The gym is usually packed right now. No one will do anything to me. Plus, I'm not leaving the complex. It's a 3 minute walk, tops.

Jackson: Please. Don't go. I have a bad feeling about this. I'm begging you.

This is why I didn't call him. I knew he would disagree with me leaving my apartment. But he didn't understand. This affected me more than him. I refused to just sit idle and wait for the shit to hit the fan. Or stop living because some creepy asshole tried his damnedest to ruin my life.

Sarah: I'll be back before you know it.

I set my phone to silent and tossed it in my bag alongside a bottle of water and walked out the door. Twenty minutes—thirty tops—and then I'd return home. Show him everything was fine. That nothing would happen to me.

That I was safe.

EIGHTEEN

THE DOOR to the gym whooshed open. My ponytail brushed the exposed skin of my back as the air above the doorframe gusted. The gym not as packed as I'd thought it would be, ten plus people spread out amongst the machines. This place resembled my form of sanctuary, and my body relaxed with each passing minute. It was crazy how something so simple brought so much comfort.

I wound my way through the equipment and headed to the treadmills, only one of ten occupied. Setting my bag down, I took out my phone, headphones and water. I left the bag on the bench as I always did and my water parked beside it.

My feet straddled the treadmill belt as I scanned the music playlist on my phone. I searched for something loud and screamy to help me escape reality. After a moment of scrolling, I landed on one and tapped the first song, closing my eyes and breathing deep as the music drowned out everything. "Thank you," I whispered to the music gods.

My fingers jabbed the treadmill buttons as I selected my pace, incline, and time. Seconds later, I was warming up and on my way to a fast-paced walk. Within minutes, my mind would wander away from everything torturous.

Ten minutes into my high-paced walk/light jog, my lungs opened up and drew in more air than I'd breathed in weeks, almost months. The sensation liberated me.

I cranked up the speed a couple notches and eased into a slow-paced run. Working out always provided more clarity and helped me see things in a different perspective. It made me stronger and more capable.

Empowered.

Fearless.

Music blared in my ears as my feet pounded the treadmill. Mileage ticked away as I pushed myself and bumped up the speed again. The treadmill wasn't as enjoyable as running or walking outdoors, but my body kept pace and I forget about the world around me.

Far too soon, the treadmill slowed for the cool down cycle and my pace is now a brisk walk. My pulse hammered in my veins and gave me the adrenaline boost I sought. Confidence inflated my chest and I felt invincible. More optimistic than earlier when I saw the box on my porch. I was ready to tackle anything and everything. Assured I would get through this. *We'd get through this.*

The machine slowed to a stop as my body acclimated to the lack of forward momentum. I stepped off the belt, pulled the towel from my bag, and wiped my brow before taking a huge gulp of my water. I stood next to the bench, drank more water and caught my breath before I picked my bag up and headed back to my apartment.

The gym exit was ten feet away when my head started to spin. The room tilted and spun more with each step. It's like I was on a Tilt-A-Whirl at the county fair. Maybe I overexerted myself. Pushed too hard. *When was the last time I ate?* Hours ago. Shit. As soon as I reached my apartment, I'd eat something.

I slowed my pace, reached for the wall next to me, and put all my effort into staying upright. The room spun a little faster. When I made it back to my apartment, I'd crash on the couch a minute, then eat something. Although, if Jackson saw me passed out on the couch, he might flip out. I don't know.

Don't focus on that now. Focus on getting back to the apartment. One foot in front of the other. You've got this.

I pushed the door open and air rushed around me. The sensation amplified the spinning, and I felt more dizzy with each passing second. I stepped outside and made it a few feet across the sidewalk. What the hell was happening to me? This wasn't overexertion. No matter how much effort I utilized, I wobbled.

Fear coated the blood in my veins. I shielded my eyes as the sunlight blinded me. *What the fuck was this?* Right now, I was scared shitless. Of being out in the open. Of being completely exposed. And *him*.

One minute, I overflowed with confidence. And the next, I drowned in terror.

Forcing all my strength to surface, I attempted to step forward. *Just let me make it home. Please, I'm begging. All I want is to be safe and in my home.*

I took another step forward, my balance shifted beneath me, and my vision blurred. Too late to scream for help, I prayed someone would rescue me.

And then everything faded away as the world turned black. Vanished. No sight. No sound. Total, utter darkness.

NINETEEN

HIM

THE DOOR to the gym opened and there she was. My beautiful Sarah. She stepped inside and paused briefly, scanned the equipment, and noted the small crowd. A wide, purple elastic band trapped her long, soft, golden hair in a ponytail. A few free strands grazed her face and she swiped them behind her ear.

I should be the one tucking those strands away. The one running my fingers through her hair.

Sarah wore my favorite sports bra. The charcoal and peach number. The one that pushed her tits up. Her cleavage more predominant and on display for me. And although they sat snug in place, they still bounced when she walked. Her nipples pebbled beneath the fabric. Nipples I'd soon wrap my lips around. Most of the leggings she wore were similar, but today she'd slipped on a black pair. Mesh slashed across portions of the leg and exposed her skin slightly. And her ass... round and plump and delicious beneath the spandex.

Her fucking curves made me hard. Given the opportunity, I'd stare her down all day. Twenty-four-seven. Three-sixty-five. So fuckable in everything she wore.

On the stationary bikes, opposite the entrance, I tugged the hood on my jacket over my head. Her head was so focused, she never even saw me. But I sure as fuck saw her. I reached between my thighs and adjusted my cock as it lengthened in my shorts. I'd jerk it right here if no one else was around.

Just the sight of her made my dick scream. A drop of pre-cum smeared my lower abdomen. As if she controlled the blood flow to my favorite appendage. Able to get me off without even touching me.

I visually trailed her as she walked to the treadmills. Her go to spot when she came to the gym alone. Always away from other people, if possible. She set down her bag and delivered a fantastic view of her ass. A second later, she placed her water beside the bag and popped earbuds in her ears as she searched for music on her phone.

I pedaled vigorously and psyched myself up for the moment to come. Adrenaline dumped into my veins. The high circulated and jump started my heart into fifth gear.

The treadmill belt started and her shoulders relaxed as she walked. At first, she fast-pace walked until the machine picked up speed. Completely entranced with her curves, my eyes magnetized to every inch of her body.

Her ponytail swung side to side and lightly brushed the exposed skin between her shoulder blades. Her tits bounced in time with her stride. Nipples taut, they begged for my teeth and tongue to clamp and lick. Her ass jiggled as her feet pounded the belt. The curve where her ass met her thigh tightened with each step, and my dick jerked.

Observing her like this—fucking sweet as sin body sweating and bouncing and begging to be fucked—had me on the verge of jumping off this bike, yanking out my dick, and jacking off in front of her. I gave no fucks who witnessed. Hell, I wouldn't be surprised if the other guys here joined in on the action. Every time my hand slid up and down my cock, Sarah flashed in my vision. Goddamn, she was so fucking beautiful.

She'd be more glorious on her knees in front of me, sucking me off as I shoved my cock down her throat. Tears spilling from her eyes as mascara stained her cheeks from the pleasure. Sarah sucked cock like a pro. I witnessed her prowess a time or two.

Maybe bent over in front of me, plump ass in the air,

pussy pleading for my fat cock. With her hands pinned behind her back, and in my grip as I pile-drove her cunt.

Or better yet, cuffed to the four corners of my bed, blindfolded and screaming in pleasure as I fucked every orifice of her body. She'd beg for more. Scream my name. Wish she'd known sooner how much I desired her. Craving me as if it were her last breath.

Soon, she would see. Once I had her in my clutches, she would see. See what she missed all these years. That everything I offered was better than what the muscled pussy she dated gave her. That she should have had me sooner.

Sarah had jogged eight minutes. My guess, she'd be there another ten. Before she finished, the swap needed to happen. Then to the men's room, where my blue balls became a little less blue.

I pedaled slower and eventually stopped before rising from the seat. I grabbed my towel, wiped my brow and neck, then picked up my water bottle. Glancing in her direction, I checked to see if she noticed me get up. Her eyes are forward and zoned out on something not there.

Perfect.

Absolutely perfect.

I walked around the back of the bikes and headed for the row of benches behind the treadmills. My stride swift and eager. I stopped behind her and stood next to her belongings. The sweet scent of her skin blended with sweat and radiated off her in waves as her feet pounded on the machine. The exquisite perfume penetrated my nose and prickled over my flesh.

Fucking delicious. My cock twitched in approval. Implored me to haul her off the treadmill and flaunt what she did to me.

I wiped my towel over my face as a distraction to anyone watching me. I set my water bottle down next to hers, messed with my shoelaces, and picked up her water. After watching her eight hundred and forty-six days, I had plenty of insight on her life. Water was a main staple in her life. This brand the only one she drank.

I glanced over her shoulder and noticed she has nine minutes left. Enough time for me to bust a load and wait for her outside. Rising from the bench, I stepped away and bolted for the men's room.

The locker room is empty and clinical with its white tiled walls. I stepped into a shower stall, yanked down my shorts, spit in my palm, imagined her juicy pussy, and tugged on my cock. Before long, I blew my load. Not a challenge after recalling all the moans I'd heard outside her window. Exploding in my palm, I sprayed my jizz across the stall walls and floor. I reveled in how soon it'd be when I doused her face with my seed.

I wrenched my shorts up, stepped out of the stall, and exited the bathroom. Still on the treadmill, Sarah walked slower as the machine ran the cool down cycle. Another minute or two.

I walked out the gym door, strolled ten feet down the path, and stepped into the tall shrubs and trees decorating the entrance. She would be out here any minute and I had to be ready. My excuse on the tip of my tongue, in case anyone saw me with her. The speech practiced countless times. I reached down and grabbed the duffle I stashed here. A bag too large to carry in the gym.

The door opened and her frame came into view as she stepped out. She stopped moving and tried to get her bearings. I glanced down at the water bottle in her hand. More than half the water missing. She'd collapse any second now.

After a moment, she took a few steps and her knees buckled. A second later, her eyes rolled back as she fell to the ground.

Down for the count.

The time had finally arrived.

I ran toward her, no one nearby to worry over why this woman just collapsed. I opened her bag, threw the bottle inside, and fished out her keys. I scooped her into my arms and walked toward her apartment. Everything would finally come to fruition.

Her front door was in sight when someone strolled past us, clad in basketball shorts, a tank, and running shoes. He paused and asked, "Hey man, she all right?"

I ground my jaw before answering with one of the many lines I'd rehearsed before today. "Yeah, yeah. Too much exertion, not enough food. Not the first time. I'm taking her home," I stated, not halting my stride.

"Need help?"

His concern and eagerness to help is warranted, but he needs to back the fuck up. Did it *look* like I needed any fucking help? *If you left me the fuck alone, she'd already be inside.*

"Nah, man. I got this. Thanks, though." I plastered on a fake smile and hoped it appeased him.

Finally satisfied, the man walked off. *Thank fuck.*

I reached her door and unlocked it, carrying her inside and locking it behind us. Carrying her into her bedroom, I set her on the bed and stared at her body a moment. She should be out for a little longer. The pills I crushed and added to the water were meant to knock her out quick.

I started peeling her clothes away from her body. Slipping my fingers under the waistband of her leggings, I tugged them down to her ankles and deposited them on the floor. The black lace thong hidden underneath stirred at something primal inside me and I couldn't wait to slide them off and run my fingers over the flesh they protected.

I'd save that for last.

I shoved the tight sports bra up and zeroed in on her breasts. Soft pillows of heaven I anxiously waited to sink my teeth in. The bra pinned her limp arms up and I fondled and pinched her nipples. Tweaking them with the edge of my nails.

She laid still as a mannequin.

My balls ached and I reached below my cock and rubbed them.

Lastly, I slipped off the black triangle of lace. Once the scrap landed on the floor, I grazed my fingertips over the sweet mound of flesh below. *Sweet fucking Christ.* Bringing my hand to my nose, I inhaled deep and memorized her sweet, floral fragrance.

Opening my duffle, I drew out four lengths of cord and fastened each of her limbs to a corner of the bed. After they're in place, I tugged them a few times and checked their strength. Once satisfied they restrained her properly, I stood back and ogled every lock of hair, every dip and curve, every line and orifice. My cock saluted in appreciation.

Ravishing.

I lit candles in her room, then retrieved more items from my bag. A thick stack of photos. Images of her at work, in the park, eating lunch with friends, sleeping, fucking. I scattered them beside her on the bed.

Next, I took out two bundles of fresh sunflowers. I removed the wrapping and placed a few beside her before scattering the others all over the bedroom. Glancing down at my watch, I picked up the pace.

She already called lover boy. *Fucking asshole. Always in my fucking way.* It wouldn't be long before he arrived—fifteen to twenty minutes tops.

Taking the small bottle out of my pocket, I cracked open the lid and waved the smelling salts under her nose. She lied still a minute—no reaction. But then a slight change. Her lashes twitched and her eyes pinched tighter. Her body shifted in discomfort as she tried escaping from the restraints. Her breaths pushed and pulled in short bursts of air. Her chest rose and fell rapidly.

Her eyes fluttered open—barely an inch—blinked slowly and repeatedly, and then attempted to focus. A moment later, her head swiveled left to right. More than likely, she figured out where she was.

But how did the drugs affect her vision? Was the room fuzzy?

Did she see me?

Had she figured out it's me in the room with her?

Answers only she knew. But if she hadn't determined it yet… she would soon.

TWENTY

WHAT THE HELL HAPPENED? Was I in some cavernous, sealed off room without walls or windows? Everywhere I looked, it's pitch black. As if I'd fallen off the earth and got sucked into a void.

Surrounded by nothingness. Absent of light or noise. Lost in my own head with no one to help me find my way out. Pressure pierced me from every angle, closed in on me and pulled me under like gravity. Pinned me down and depleted me of life. I've never experienced claustrophobia, but this must be what it felt like. A boulder crushing my bones and stealing my breath.

Wherever this hell was, I had to escape.

Locked in place, my arms refused to respond when I willed them to move. I tugged at my upper limbs again, miffed when nothing happened. As if anchored in place. Exasperated with my arms' inability to function, I willed my legs to walk, to graze the earth below my feet, and learn where I was. But my legs and feet remained rooted in place.

Like a piece of sculpted marble, I was a statue frozen in time. Gravity the strength of Jupiter immobilized me.

Where the hell am I? Eerily quiet. Darkness for miles... Chills surged through my veins and lungs.

Terrified is an inadequate term for the dread consuming me.

Somehow, I got sucked into purgatory. A place packed

with nothing and existence had no expiration. Absent of life, sound, sight, time. Absolutely nothing. Except me.

Alone.

Panic-stricken.

Unsure of what happened to me.

A pungent odor pierced my nasal cavities. Lungs burned from the source. Mouth salivated to rid the new taste. Alveoli worked double time to draw oxygen in and expel the scent. I tried moving my head to one side, then the other, to escape the rancid smell. But it lingered.

As I swiveled side to side, the pervasive stench continuously invaded. No matter how hard I tried, I couldn't escape the odor.

My lids are like weighted balloons, I worked to open them. With each passing attempt, I squeezed them tighter, wetness pooling at the corners. My head thrashed from side to side, propelled backward, tucked into my chest. No matter the effort I exerted, I couldn't break free from the excruciating smell.

The dark veil prohibiting my sight thinned and faded. My eyes fluttered with blurred vision. In a flash, the foul odor instantly disappeared, and my nasal passages and lungs gained immediate relief.

I tested my limbs. Sore, aching, and weak. A sting burned my torso. Exhaustion consumed me. But all I wanted was to shift myself out of this uncomfortable position.

I went to stretch my limbs, roll onto my side, but determined that my body won't budge. My head is a bit groggy, I tugged harder and used every ounce of strength I possessed. But nothing happened. Glancing to my wrists... *shit, shit, shit.* Rope hugged my wrists and bound me to the frame.

Adrenaline spiked my bloodstream. I glanced around the room and my vision sharpened. As awareness set in, I realized I was in *my* bedroom. My hands were bound with a thick, brown rope—the harsh threads chafed my skin with every jerk—connected to the frame of *my* bed.

I thrashed harder and the rope cut my skin deeper. Mind over matter, I ignored the pain from the wounds now forming at my wrists. Panic and fear bubbled to the surface with every breath and consumed me. Dragging in several deep breaths, I closed my eyes and tried to recall my last memory.

The last thing I remembered was walking toward the gym exit. Dizziness hit me in waves, but I thought I'd be able to make it back to my apartment. Then, darkness. As if a machine switched off. Nothing except black.

I lifted my head off the mattress and glanced toward the foot of the bed. Bare, exposed, and one hundred percent vulnerable. I yanked at the restraints again, refusing to be a prisoner in my own home. But my efforts go unrewarded.

When my body settled back against the sheets, I wondered how I would get out of my current predicament. Before any brilliant ideas sparked, I glanced around the room and froze when my line of sight hit the corner. A hooded figure stood absolutely still. His build a little pudgy, stocky, and grotesquely masculine. I closed my eyes tightly, tried to refocus, and implored my eyes to work properly. Like an old digital format buffering, the room sharpened and my sight became crystal clear. The man's face was masked by the hood, his hand feverishly stroking his naked erection.

I attempted to scoot farther away from him, but I was stuck. Bile gurgled in my throat.

Holy fucking shit. I needed to get the fuck out of here. Someone needed to help me. *NOW!*

Speech evaded me as I opened and closed my mouth a couple times to speak. But I swallowed back my fear and rediscovered my voice—my only hope. I parted my lips again and turned my volume to maximum level. *"Help me! Please somebody fucking help—"*

A second later, his hand slapped against my mouth. Hard. He grabbed my sports bra from somewhere next to me and shoved it into my mouth as he removed his hand.

"Shut the fuck up, whore!"

I continued to scream through the material, my voice too muffled to carry. My eyes burned and pooled with tears, the onslaught a river streaming down my face.

The faint sound of a zipper broke the silence, and I watched my attacker as his hands unfastened the front of his hooded sweatshirt. When the pull tab reached the bottom, he shoved the hoodie open, and dropped the hood from his head.

Alan? You have got to be *fucking* kidding me.

The hoodie fell to the floor before he worked the cotton shirt over his head and discarded it. He stood completely nude, less than five feet away from my vulnerable body, spit on his hand, and returned it to his erection.

My stomach churned as acid crept up my throat, inch by inch. Nausea infiltrated every molecule inside me, and the desire to vomit grew tenfold. *I needed to get away from him. From this situation. Whatever I had to do, I needed to get out of here.*

I thrashed harder. Screamed louder. My endeavors rendered pointless. A chill spread throughout my body, down to the bone, as I faced the sick possibility of this piece of shit raping and/or killing me.

"Hush now, my beautiful Sarah." His voice thick with menace, and his sick and twisted version of sweetness. "We don't have much time. Shouldn't we make the best of it?"

He stalked closer to me, stroked himself faster, jaw clenched. The bed dipped, his weight shifting the mattress as he crawled up and rested his knees between my legs.

It was imperative I got the fuck away from him. Who knew what this sick fuck was capable of, and I sure as shit didn't want to find out.

I struggled against the restraints. Jerked my wrists within the binds. Wrenched my ankles, hoping to free myself. Another thrash, another failed attempt. The flesh at my wrists bled. My face was saturated with sweat—the moisture blurring and obstructing my view.

He held up a photo, then another, and then another. Pieces of glossy paper surrounded my body, the edges scraping my skin as he picked them up and tossed them when finished.

"Look at you. You're so fucking beautiful. *Too fucking beautiful.* Don't even know a good man when you see one."

He paused and I assumed he referred to himself. I wanted to scream *"What good fucking man would stalk women and hold them captive!"* His fingers ran along the contours of my face and I tried to jerk my head away from his touch. But he clamped his fingers tight around my chin.

"If only you knew how much I love you, my sweet, beautiful Sarah." His fingers left my face and glided down my neck, down my chest, and then groped my breasts. He hissed his approval of my body and rubbed himself harder with his other hand.

I screamed, *"Don't fucking touch me!"*, but my packed mouth muffled the cries. Intuition yelled at me to quit fighting. It turned him on and egged him further. I refused to give up, but was lost. Inhaling deep, I closed my eyes, shut him out, and prayed to whoever heard me.

Please. Someone. Anyone. Help me. I don't want to die. Please don't let me die. Please help me.

His mouth latched onto my throat, and a growl of excitement ripped from his lips as he tasted my flesh. I was dying, and this was hell. His mouth crept down my body, licked and sucked my breasts, and bit my nipples so hard he probably broke the skin. I cried out, my eyes drained of tears as the ducts ached to produce more. Burning. Singeing.

Someone… please… help me. I didn't want to give up hope, but I wasn't sure how much more of this my body would handle.

He inched down my body, toward my navel. His tongue lapped my skin. His teeth biting with force and piercing my flesh. A moment later, his hands landed on my knees, the skin of his palms rough and scratchy, their weight sliding up my thighs and toward my apex.

Please, god, no. Please don't let him do this to me. I'm begging. Please don't allow this asshole to steal my soul.

He lifted his head to look me in the eyes. A gnarled sneer on his lips, eyes loaded with vicious lust. "This pussy belongs to me. You hear me?!"

My only response was to cry. My body convulsed with each passing second.

My life some twisted version of hell.

He lowered his head and licked me above the small sliver of pubic hair on my mound, his hands roaming closer. He sunk his teeth into my flesh, bit the hair-layered mound with fierce aggression with his fingers millimeters from my most sacred place. I screamed, over and over, and prayed someone heard.

A bang on the door had him upright on his haunches. Jackson bellowed my name from the front door, a snippet of relief exploded inside me. I tried to force the material from my mouth with my tongue, but the fabric only budged a fraction. I screamed at the top of my lungs nonstop, thrashed my body and banged the bed frame against the wall. Jackson's voice boomed louder by the second.

As I continued my efforts, I glanced toward my attacker. His smile stretched his face like the Joker in a Batman movie —as if moments like this were his bread-and-butter. One of his hands furiously pumped up and down on his erection, the other hand reached for the junction of my thighs.

My tongue moved every direction and finally pushed the fabric from my mouth. *"Jackson! Help me!"* The words repeated over and over as Alan's fingers ran up and down the folds between my legs. I thrashed in every direction, exerting every ounce of effort I could to clamp my legs shut and thwart his fingers.

Jackson screamed for me and Alan laughed maniacally as he molested me. *"Jackson! Help me!"* I screamed. Because I won't survive much longer.

TWENTY-ONE
JACKSON

SSTILL NO RESPONSE.

Fuck!

Dizziness consumed me over the number of texts I've sent in the last fifteen minutes. They started out as me letting her know I'd left work and was on my way to her place. When she didn't answer the first after a couple minutes, I sent another.

Then another.

Nothing.

The more I sent, the more frantic my texts became. Still, I got no response from her.

When I called, her phone went straight to voicemail.

She told me she planned to work out at the complex gym for a few—which was not a good idea, especially after another note and delivery—but she wouldn't deliberately ignore me. Not like this. Not after everything that's happened. She definitely would not have turned off her phone.

Fuck! Fuck! Fuck!

I called the police, told them I was headed to her apartment, she wasn't responding to calls or texts, and my concern that something had happened to her. They told me they'd send a unit out to meet me and to wait to enter until they arrived.

Less than a mile from her apartment, and every traffic

light turned red as I approached it. I slammed my fists against the steering wheel, yelled at no one, and screamed to the gods for not letting me get to her faster.

The second the light turned green, my tires squealed against the blacktop as the sign for her complex came into sight. I turned into the entrance; the guard giving me a once over and opening the gate. The metal barrier crept at a snail's pace as my need to yell escalated. As soon as there was enough room for me to pass, I hauled ass to her building, flying over numerous speed bumps, and not giving a damn about my car or surroundings.

I spotted her car, parked a few spaces from her apartment, and parked my Jeep a couple spaces farther down. Jumping out, I jog to her door, looking down to see her watch on the porch, the face cracked.

Shit!

I clenched my fist and brought it up to the door, banging hard. "Sarah! It's me. Open up."

No response.

I bang on the door again, louder this time. I put my ear against the painted metal and hear faint muffled screams on the other side.

Fuuuuuuck!

I yanked out my key to her apartment, slid it in the keyhole, and cranked the deadbolt free from the frame. Turning the handle, the door cracked open, but was halted by the security chain. In the open space of the doorway, I yelled for her. "Sarah! Can you hear me? I'm here." A man's laughter rang loud in my ears.

Son of a bitch!

I stepped back, positioned my footing, then hauled all my weight into my foot as it pummeled into the center of the door. The frame budged slightly. Giving the door another kick, the wood splintered, and the door opened an inch more. One more solid kick and the door crippled under the pressure, allowing me access.

I ran inside, the living room empty. Ran down the small hall and into her bedroom, and everything flickered in slow motion as I entered. Sarah was on the bed, tied to the frame, screaming at the top of her lungs for me to help her. An overweight man sat between her knees and ejaculated onto her body as his fingers moved between her legs.

Everything in my vision went red. *I'm going to kill this piece of shit!*

I bolted to the bed, tackled him away from her, and the two of us hit the floor on the other side. I pinned his body under mine as my fists met his face and pummeled until he no longer moved. Once satisfied he'd stay put a minute or two, I jumped to my feet.

I dashed to Sarah's side and carefully untied the binds from her wrists and ankles, noting the raw skin at each point. She bolted upright, scooted herself off the bed as quickly as possible, grabbed a towel and tightly concealed her body.

Coming to stand in front of her, I slowly reached forward, hesitant to touch her. After a minute, she didn't shrink away from me, and I dragged her to my chest and stroked her hair. I sucked in a deep breath and withdrew from the embrace. My fingers brushed over her cheekbones and cupped her face as I took inventory of her appearance. Eyes red and swollen. Cheeks puffy and stained from her tears. Skin pale and chilled.

I rested my hands on her shoulders, my grip soft yet firm as I controlled my voice, making it as gentle as possible. "I need you to go into another room, I don't care which. Wherever you feel safe. I need to take care of him until the police arrive. Can you do that?"

Her eyes darted back and forth, from me to her assailant. I waited for her to answer, not wanting to rush her. She nodded as her chin quivered. "Yes." That single word loaded with too many emotions. She turned from me and slowly walked into her bathroom and closed the door except for an inch.

Unfastening the ropes from the footboard, I walked over to the psychopath on the floor, flipped him onto his stomach, and wrapped the rope around his ankles and wrists, hog-tying him. He grunted, and I kicked him in the leg. "You don't get to speak!"

"Ms. Bradley. Mr. Ember. Hello?" A man's voice echoed from the front of the apartment. "It's Officer Richardson. I'm not alone and we have our weapons drawn. Can you hear me?"

"We're back here," I yelled.

The police rounded the doorway, guns drawn, and ready to fire if necessary. I held my hands up in surrender and tipped my head toward the bathroom door. "Sarah is in there."

Officer Richardson stepped closer in my direction while Officer Hawks walked toward the bathroom and three other officers entered the bedroom behind them. "I assume this is the guy."

I lowered my hands and peered down to the form at my feet, who was definitely no man. "When I ran in, he had her tied to the bed while he molested her and masturbated over her. I knocked him out and tied him up with some of the ropes."

"We'll need to gather statements from both of you. After we get those, and photographs of the crime scene, you can take Ms. Bradley to the hospital for further examination."

My head bobbed in acknowledgement as I grew speechless. The adrenaline rush I had minutes ago faded away as reality settled in and flooded my heart with dread. After a minute, I coughed and spoke up. "Can I see Sarah?"

Richardson looked over at Hawks, their eyes met and spoke in a silent language only the two of them shared, a minor tilt of her head and I was granted permission. I walked slower than desirable toward Sarah, not wanting to cause her any further panic after everything she'd endured. When I reached her, I brought my hands up to her cheeks and let my palms hover.

Although I had held her just moments ago, I was suddenly scared to touch her now. I didn't know if she'd want any form of touch after what happened. After she'd been separated from the situation and her own adrenaline rush tapered off. I stared into her eyes, her emeralds more translucent than usual, the whites of her eyes webbed with red.

She stepped an inch closer to me, tilted her head to the side, and rested her cheek in my palm. Her eyes closed and a deep sigh left her body as her arms wound around my waist. I wrapped my arms around her mid-section, and pressed her towel-covered body to mine as hundreds of guilty thoughts weighed me down.

"Ms. Bradley?" Officer Hawks's voice soft and kind. "We'd like for you and Mr. Ember to step more into the bathroom." We both glanced at her, confused. "We need to remove the perpetrator from the room. We'd rather you didn't have to watch."

We both grasped the gravity of her words at the same time and inched farther into the tiled safe haven. Once alone, I peered down at her and tipped her chin up. "I'm sorry I didn't get here sooner. I'm so sorry, babe."

A fresh wave of tears rolled down her cheeks as her lower lip trembled. "I should've listened to you. I shouldn't have been so stubborn. None of this would've happened if I'd only stayed here and waited, like you asked."

"No, no, no." I shushed her and ran my thumb over her trembling lip. "You do *not* get to shoulder the blame for this. This was *not* your fault. Do you hear me? This is *not. Your. Fault.*"

Her arms snaked around me and squeezed hard, knocking the breath from my lungs. I kept one arm around her waist while the other stroked the back of her hair. We stood like that, unmoving, until Officer Hawks reentered the room.

"Ms. Bradley. Mr. Ember. We'd like to escort you to the hospital. Can we help you find some clothing? Be sure not to discard the towel. We'll need to confiscate it for evidence."

"Jackson, can you please grab me something to wear? I don't care what."

"Sure, babe."

I headed out of the bathroom with Officer Hawks on my heel. "You may want to grab whatever else she may need for a few more days and any special, belongings she'd like to remain safe. The apartment won't be accessible until the crime scene is cleared. It could be two to four days."

"Of course. I'll grab clothes and see if there's anything else she'd like to bring."

Pulling down the suitcase in her closet, I packed several undergarments, tops, and bottoms. I grabbed a few things off her dresser I'd seen her wear on previous occasions and placed them inside. I brought clothes to her in the bathroom, passed along what Officer Hawks said, and asked her what to grab from the bathroom.

After we gathered everything, I grabbed her purse and we headed out the door. Both of us ready to leave her tainted apartment behind.

TWENTY-TWO

FROM THE DARKNESS of the bathroom, I heard Jackson yell. "You don't get to speak!" His voice followed by a grunt. I wrapped the towel tighter around my body, the terry cloth scraping under my arms. The shield of the fabric nowhere near what I needed.

"Ms. Bradley. Mr. Ember. Hello?" A familiar voice snuck through the crack of the door. "It's Officer Richardson. I'm not alone and we have our weapons drawn. Can you hear me?"

The desire to shout consumed me. I wanted them to know I heard them, but my mouth wouldn't move. My lips unable to form the words. My throat dry and voice hollow.

"We're back here." Jackson's voice bounced off the walls.

Footsteps entered the room as I peeked through the thin line. Jackson held his hands up next to his face as he gestured toward the door. "Sarah is in there."

I spotted Officer Hawks just before her body cast a shadow on the door and blocked my view. Her voice barely a whisper. "Sarah. It's Sheila Hawks. Can I open the door?"

I nod and the door doesn't move. After a breath, it dawned on me she can't see me. I cleared my throat in an effort to speak. With a scratchy voice, I garbled, "Yes. You can open the door."

The door slowly pushed open as her eyes assessed me. I clutched the towel tighter. "I'm not going to hurt you. Is there anything I can do to help?"

I shook my head. *I don't think anyone can help me. What could she possibly do? Comfort me?* Not sure anyone could fill those shoes right now.

"I know this is difficult, but we'll need to get a statement from you. It can wait until after you get examined at the hospital."

I shook my head vigorously. "I don't want to go to the hospital." The words escaped like rapid fire. No way would some random stranger poke and prod my body. I'd already been invaded and violated enough to last a lifetime.

"I know, sweetie, but it's important we make sure your wounds get cleaned up and we get you the proper medications. I know it's scary, but you can have whoever you want in the room while everything happens."

Her final words granted a little relief. At least Jackson could sit with me while the doctors did their evaluation.

"Can I see Sarah?" Jackson asked. After a silent exchange between the two officers, Hawks granted Jackson permission.

Jackson took measured steps in my direction, the way an intimidated child would approach an upset parent. He stopped in front of me as his hands lifted to the sides of my face, but not touching me. His darkened sapphires glassy and on the verge of tears. Not sure I could handle him crying.

I stepped closer to him and leaned into his hand. The warmth of his touch the most welcoming, comforting, and soothing in my world. As I closed my eyes, I let every molecule flee from my lungs. I reached for him, snaked my arms around his torso, and anchored him close. His presence consoled me and I drew myself tighter to his chest as his caress calmed me further with each stroke.

Officers Hawks said something, but I didn't hear her exact words. As I studied her lips, trying to decipher what she just asked, I saw two other officers grab Alan's arms and drag his body.

My stomach plummeted to my feet as nausea roiled in my gut, and my body convulsed. We stepped closer to the shower and lost sight of the bedroom. Once we halted, Jackson traced the line of my jaw with his fingers, so tender, and stopped under my chin. When he tipped my chin up, I registered the guilt written in paragraphs across his face. "I'm sorry I didn't get her sooner. I'm so sorry, babe."

My eyes heated, swelled with unshed tears, and the magnitude of what happened punched me in the gut. My eyes blinked and the tears spilled out, rolled down my cheeks and fell from my chin as my lips quivered uncontrollably.

"I should've listened to you. I shouldn't have been so stubborn. None of this would've happened if I'd only stayed here and waited, like you asked."

Shaking his head, his thumb stroked across my lower lip. "No, no, no. You do *not* get to shoulder the blame for this. This was *not* your fault. Do you hear me? This is *not. Your. Fault.*"

Utilizing every ounce of strength I could muster, I crashed into his embrace, and his lungs exhaled fully. He brought me closer to his chest and ran a hand down the length of my hair, the continuous strokes comforting me. I closed my eyes and allowed myself to get lost in the serenity he provided. His warmth. His kind-hearted nature. His love.

The rise and fall of his chest below me, the steady beat of his heart, soothed me more by the minute.

My eyes refocused on the room and Officer Hawks's voice just outside. "Ms. Bradley. Mr. Ember. We'd like to escort you to the hospital. Can we help you find some clothing? Be sure not to discard the towel. We'll need to confiscate it for evidence."

My entire apartment represented one large piece of evidence. I never wanted to be near or touch my bed again. The bedding contaminated, I hoped the cops threw it in an inferno. Nothing about my apartment—revered as a safe haven once upon a time—resembled the life I desired for the future. Nothing was sacred anymore.

"Jackson, can you please grab me something to wear? I don't care what it is." I wanted out of this place as quickly as possible.

"Sure, babe."

Officer Hawks followed Jackson and told him to gather extra clothing, since I wouldn't be able to access my apartment for days. The notion perfectly acceptable with me. The only time I wanted to return here was to gather everything I owned and either pack it or burn it.

Jackson returned to me, handed me a pair of blue jeans, a loose cotton tee, and the necessary undergarments. "Officer Hawks had me pack some other clothes for you, since you can't stay here for a while. If you grab whatever you need from the bathroom, I'll pack it."

After getting dressed, I grabbed the basic necessities from the bathroom—shampoo, conditioner, face wash, hairbrush, toothbrush and toothpaste. If I missed anything vital, I'd go to the store. My sole focus right now was exiting this hell hole.

I handed everything to Jackson. He slipped it into a bag he'd grabbed and put it in the suitcase lined with days worth of clothing. I reached for my purse, made sure everything I needed was in there, picked my keys up from the floor in the living room, and headed out the door.

On my small patio, I saw my watch on the ground, the glass cracked and glinting in the fading sunlight. I started for it, wanting to take it with me.

"Babe, you need to leave it. For now." My eyes burned as tears threatened for the hundredth time today. "I'm sure they'll return it to you once they've taken care of everything here."

I nodded and ambled forward as Jackson's fingers snaked between mine and kept me glued to his side.

A few steps past the patio, a sound caught my attention, and I turned to locate the source. Two officers stood at one side of the patio, their hands rustling the tall shrub. Seconds later, one of them walked toward the other side of the patio as bright yellow tape screamed CRIME SCENE DO NOT ENTER now spanned the entryway.

I turned back to Jackson and hung my head. "As much as this whole situation sucks, I'm just glad it's over. I can deal with everything else as it comes."

His hand gripped mine tighter. "Me, too."

We traveled the sidewalk, almost to his Jeep, when screaming broke out. My eyes scanned the lot, and my stomach revolted when I stopped at its source. *Alan.* In the backseat of a police cruiser. Kicking and screaming, his face pressed to the glass. A wicked gleam in his eyes.

When I got to the passenger door of the Jeep, Jackson barricaded me from seeing my attacker. And then I heard the words no victim wanted to hear.

"I won't be in there forever. You can't hide from me. I'll find you. I'll scour the earth for you. And when I do... I'll finish what I started. You can bet on it!"

As much as I wanted to escape from all of this, I froze. Rooted in place with fear. Yes, it all happened. And it would haunt me for many years to come, no doubt about it. But right now, it all seemed surreal. Like a living nightmare I couldn't erase.

"Come on, babe. Let's get you to the hospital. Officer Hawks is waiting."

I stepped into the Jeep, fastened my seat belt, and prayed to a higher power. *Please, I'll do anything. Just keep that guy from ever finding me again.*

Being thoroughly examined by someone you don't know— photos taken, swabs run over your skin, ointments and medications given—after a traumatic situation... It's a whole new version of hell.

When the female nurse stepped into the room, she asked my permission for Jackson to stay. I granted it in a heartbeat. She proceeded to explain the entire process of the exam and everything that happened. I signed a document once I agreed, the headline atop the page read *Rape Kit Analysis.*

Although there was no penal penetration by Alan, I wanted to do everything throughout the process. Not certain how all of this worked, but if the analysis was used to keep him in jail, I was one-hundred percent good with it.

Forty-five minutes later, the procedure finished and Officer Hawks entered the room. She sat on a chair, opposite me and Jackson, and said we would need to give formal statements. She retrieved a digital recorder from her pocket, checked the time, and pressed record.

"This is the testimony of Sarah Bradley. Today's date is

April eighteenth. The time is currently nine-twenty-one in the evening. Sarah, when you are ready, you may give us your testimony."

Tears welled in my eyes, and at any moment they would spill. I was so tired of crying over this whole situation. Inhaling a deep breath, I held it a moment and vowed to myself this would be the last time I cried over this. I wouldn't allow this one inhumane person to ruin my life. And I would move on and live my life to the fullest.

When I exhaled, I let it all out. Every single moment. I sobbed while I relived the nightmare as Jackson held me and kept me grounded. When I finished, I wiped away the blubbering tears and listened while Jackson told his side of the story.

As difficult as it must have been for him to hear my side, I never thought it would be just as difficult to listen to him recount his testimony. His voice shook, guilt weighed on him immensely, tears rolled down to his jaw and lodged in the scruff. He was in absolute fear for my life. Devastated by the possibilities of what he might walk in on when he finally got to me.

Never again would I ignore anything this man told or asked of me. He loved me so profusely and I disregarded his requests, wanting to go somewhere and think. My selfishness resulted in me being violated in one of the worst possible ways. If he hadn't arrived when he did, I shuddered at the possibilities of what else could have happened.

My body noticeably shivered and Jackson glanced down at me. "You cold, babe?"

"No." But I curled into him, and his arm snaked around me and drew me closer.

After our statements were given, we left the hospital and went to Jackson's place. He set my suitcase by the dresser in the bedroom and took my hand. "Come with me." His voice soft and kind and full of adoration as he walked me into the bathroom.

We stopped in the middle of the room and his palms framed my face. He wanted to kiss me, but resisted, a war brewing in his eyes. I pushed up on my toes and pressed my lips to his. A gentle exchange between two lovers. Every touch from him healed me a little more. When he pulled away, he glanced down at my body and came back to my eyes. "Can I undress you? We need to shower."

I nodded and granted this wonderful man permission to help me and provide me comfort when I needed it most. He took his time as he removed each piece and eased over the abused areas. He turned away from me and cranked the water on in the shower. A second later, he stripped his clothes, tested the water temperature, and walked us under the hot spray.

I had no recollection of a time when I enjoyed a shower as much as right now. The water mimicked something more potent, not just cleansing my skin, but also washing away everything that lingered from the last several hours. It purified parts of me I didn't realize were tainted. As each droplet hit my skin, a new form of tranquility washed over me. I felt safe. Protected. Loved.

Cupping Jackson's face in my palms, I lowered his lips to mine, kissed him without hurry, and showed him how much gratitude I held in my heart for him. As I broke the kiss, I peeked up and gasped as his sapphires burned into me with compassion and strength and vulnerability, his emotions on full display. Three of the most significant words lingered on the tip of my tongue. Three words I'd never expressed so deeply in my life.

"I love you."

TWENTY-THREE

Sixteen Months Later

"A COUPLE more days till the big day!"

In more ways than one, I missed the high-pitched excitement of Christy's voice when we were face-to-face. The squeaky voice I heard through my phone currently wasn't quite the same.

"Are you excited? What are you guys doing?" Christy spewed out in her usual inquisitive nature.

"I don't know yet. Jackson said it's a surprise. I wish you guys could be here. I miss you terribly," I confessed.

Music played in the background of the call alongside a crowd of chatter. "We miss you too, girl. I can't wait to fly out and see you. Christy and I are trying to coordinate vacation time and see if Marco's cool with it." Liz chimed in, her ear probably glued next to Christy's.

A man in the background started yelling something about someone keeping their hands off his woman.

"Where are you guys?"

"Bar life, bitch. It's cray-cray. There're some hotties up in here, but mostly crazy drunks. Nothing we can't handle."

"Sounds like it. I hope you guys can talk Marco into it. You'd love it here. There's so much to do, so much to see. In the time we've been here, I still feel like I haven't seen anything."

Moving out of Georgia had been both easy and difficult. Painless because it got me away from everything that occurred. Flashbacks infiltrated my mind whether I was awake or asleep, day-in and day-out. No matter how hard I tried, I couldn't escape them.

One night, about a month after Alan's arrest, Jackson made an amazing dinner and crept into the topic of us moving for my consideration. He didn't want to assume that I would want to move with him, but asked if us moving away would make me feel safer. When I didn't hesitate to say yes, we started scouting for places to live.

The most heartbreaking part of moving… I left my two favorite people in the world. Thousands of miles away, at that. When we looked into the various options, we took into consideration jobs for both of us as well as scenery and things to do. I loved working at Hammond Life, but I just couldn't stay there any longer, even after Bob and Marco offered to transfer me to a sister office near where we planned to move.

"Christy and I will see if we can talk any sense into him next week, but it might not be for weeks. A lot of coercion goes into letting two of us take a vacation at the same time." Liz's voice snapped me back to our conversation.

"I know, I know. Just keep me in the loop with what happens. I miss you guys like crazy. I really wish you could be here for my birthday."

Life hadn't been the same not seeing them every day, but Jackson and I knew moving was the best thing for us. We couldn't stay in that city any longer, not with the possibility of Alan being released from jail and scouring the city for me or him or both of us. We couldn't take that risk.

"Us too, bitch. We might just have to do a belated shindig. Besides, more parties are better. Am I right?"

As long as I got to see them, I didn't care what we did. "Sounds fantastic. I'm going to let you two get back to your bar life. Jackson's just finishing dinner. Love you guys."

"We love you, too." They were the Bobbsey twins when they answered in unison. It made me wonder if they practiced doing that, for laughs.

The noise of the bar vanished. My ear met with silence.

The longing to see my friends grew to new heights. Things weren't the same without them.

My hand dropped to my side as I clutched my phone, trying to hold on to my friends a little longer. I stared out the window as the sun dipped in the early evening sky. Sunsets in California stole my breath. The same can be said about sunrises off the coast of Georgia. Something about the sun being close to the water, that monumental glowing ball of fire and energy setting the sky ablaze—rich blues, corals, pinks, oranges, and yellows burning the atmosphere for miles on end. No one could simulate beauty like that. And I couldn't get enough of it.

When we first settled, we spent half of our evenings on the beach at sunset. We packed food and joined the countless others who drove out for the exact same reason. In the process, we met a few other couples, people we saw repeatedly and found the courage to spark a conversation with, and made the start of our new life a little less daunting.

Before reaching Santa Barbara, we elected to never mention the topic of Alan or the stalking unless we'd heard something from the police worth concern. As of now, life was beautiful and fresh and new.

The scent of Asian food wafted my way, and I spun to see what exactly Jackson concocted for dinner. Walking into the kitchen—one more spacious than either of the kitchens we had in Georgia—I stepped up behind him, grazed my hands across his shoulders then down his back, and planted a kiss between his shoulder blades. He glanced over his shoulder, and his glorious sapphires smiled down on me.

"Whatever you're making, it smells unbelievable."

"Found a new recipe for vegan pad Thai online. I thought we'd give it a try, so…"

"If it tastes as good as it smells, it'll be amazing." Standing on my toes, I planted a kiss on his cheek. "Anything I can help with before Judy and Kendra get here?"

His eyes roamed the counter, his thoughts written in the lines of his forehead as he asked himself what else needed to be done. "Maybe open the wine? Let it breathe a little."

"On it." I set off to open the wine, carrying it to the table set for four.

Judy and Kendra were one of the few couples we met at our favorite beach sunset destination. On our fourth visit to watch the sunset, we'd set up our chairs, parked a basket full of cheese, crackers, fresh fruit, and wine between us, and absorbed the show nature displayed.

As we'd settled into our surroundings, the two of them walked onto the beach and laid out a blanket near us. The sun rested a breath above the horizon, and I retrieved my phone to snap a couple photos. One of them spoke up and asked if we'd like to have our photo taken with the sunset behind us. I jumped on the opportunity and returned the favor.

We spent a couple hours that night, talking and getting to know the two of them. Judy was a California native, but lived further north until a few years ago, moving south after she and Kendra met. Kendra had been visiting friends and, while she waited to meet up with them at a coffee shop, Judy walked in the door and the rest is history.

Since that night on the beach, we'd had couples date nights with Judy and Kendra several times. At first, we met up at various restaurants and got to know each other. After becoming better acquainted and comfortable, our home became their home, and vice versa.

Although they could never fill the shoes of our Georgia friends, having them in our lives made us feel more at home than we had in a while. Judy had a brain that would give Liz a run for her money and Kendra had a smile that occasionally reminded me of Christy's laugh. Sometimes I wondered if it was fate that brought them to us, giving us something to remind us of those we missed.

"Wine is officially breathing." I checked my watch, noting we had a few minutes before our guests arrived. "What else can I do, angel?"

I glanced over to see the curve of Jackson's lips push up his cheeks as his tanned skin flushed. I loved watching his reaction to the nickname. Anyone overhearing would think it endearing. It was, but also so much more.

After the fiasco in Georgia quieted. After Alan went to jail. After the world felt like it was no longer spinning out of control. I had time. Time to absorb everything that happened.

How Jackson saved me from who knows what, my body shuddering at the mere possibilities.

We sat in bed, he perused the internet on his tablet and I read. I slid my marker in the page, closed the book and laid it in my lap, staring across the room. He wrapped his hand around mine and asked if I was okay. I'd told him I was fine, but just realized something.

You're my guardian angel, I'd told him. He'd laughed before turning serious. So many times, guilt weighed us down over how that day had unfolded, but I'd told him, *you can't change fate. If it's meant to be, it's going to happen. It all happens for a reason.* I still believed that. The good, bad, and ugly.

We may not love all the circumstances that sent us to the opposite side of the country, but we were meant to come here. To experience this place. To make new friendships. We were meant to do these things together. I don't think any of that would've happened if something so life altering hadn't taken place and shook our world.

My guardian angel. Angel. He would forever be the love of my life. And I his. I would scour the planet to find him, plummet to the earth if I lost him, and lose my way without him. He was me and I was him. We would always be, forever, us.

The doorbell chimed, snapping me back to the present. "They're here."

Jackson tugged his *Kiss the Cook* apron over his head and followed me to the door. His hand rested on the door handle as his eyes met mine, the corners crinkled before his lips upturned.

"I love you, babe." A kiss grazed my temple.

"I love you, too. Angel." My cheeks plumped as I gave him a brilliant smile. "Now, let's not make our friends feel like we're ignoring them." My chin jutted forward and signaled him to open the door.

"Yes, ma'am." His sweet smile slipped into something a bit sexier and my insides puddled.

"So, what's new and exciting at the magazine, Sarah?" Kendra's inquisition, and eagerness for information on the daily activities of my life, felt like I was back in Georgia with Christy. A light, elated sensation warmed the center of my chest.

"Things are good. We're currently designing the October issue, which has been a blast with all the Halloween themed decor and recipes. Everybody is really getting into it. I think it's going to be my favorite since I've been there."

"I can't wait to see it." Bringing her spoon to her lips, the scoop loaded with apple-pear cobbler and coconut whipped cream, pure appreciation hummed in her throat when the treat hit her tongue. "Good, god. I don't know where you found this one, Sarah." She pointed her spoon toward Jackson. "Damn, he is definitely a keeper."

The three of us burst at the seams, and our laughter was sure to be heard outside the four walls of our home. It was the greatest gift—friends you couldn't live without.

Judy set a hand on her wife's shoulder. "Are you trying to tell me something, K?" Working her face into faux seriousness.

"What?" The singular word muffled by the latest shove of dessert between her lips, Kendra turned to meet Judy's eyes. "No, sweets. I was simply noting that Sarah was extremely fortunate to find someone who knows how to cook. That's kinda rare nowadays."

"That's true, I suppose. Lucky for me, I'm partially skilled in the ways of the kitchen, otherwise I might be watching for my replacement." She was joking around, but Judy made a damn good poker face and Kendra wasn't sure if she laid on the sarcasm or honesty.

"Sweets..." Kendra's hands encased her wife's, eyes locked on hers, her face earnest. "You know no one could, or will, ever replace you. Right? No matter what." Her voice dropped lower with each word. "They wouldn't be you. You're all that matters."

Warmth wrapped around my palm as it rested on my thigh, followed by a soft squeeze. I glanced away from the private moment Judy and Kendra shared and peered to the man beside me. His sapphires torched my body instantly.

It always astounded me how Jackson made me feel with just one brush against my skin or a single glance. It started beneath my breastbone, the heat magnifying with each contraction of my heart. Molten lava erupted from the epicenter, trickled its way to my limbs, warmed my fingers and toes, and continually flowed and circulated until it found the finish line. Within seconds, my core temperature was off the charts. I clamped my thighs together and tightened. The yearning for relief skyrocketed as my desire for Jackson clawed at my insides. A relief only he provided.

The walls appeared closer together, the furniture too big for the space, the number of people in the room too many. How did I politely ask my friends to leave? How did I end our evening with them so *our* evening could begin? *Think, think, think.* My mind considered hundreds of possible courtesies, but didn't find one that fit. I would simply have to wait and hope time didn't creep.

Wood scraped on tile, garnering my attention to the other side of the table, as Judy rose from her chair and Kendra mimicked her movements.

"I think we're going to head out. K had a long day, and she starts early again tomorrow. Another big shoot."

Thank heavens, Judy found her way to excuse the two of them for the evening. I'm sure Kendra was filming tomorrow, and that it was for hours on end, but I highly doubted that either of them was tired. Right now, though, I didn't care. The room overflowed with sexual tension and we all needed to end our shared time together.

"Sorry we kept you out so late. Let us walk you out." I scooted my chair back and stepped beside them. Before opening the door, I wrapped my arms around the pair of them. "Thanks for coming tonight. Give us a call and we'll do it again. Soon." Jackson gave each of them a brief hug.

"Soon. Thanks for having us. Everything was wonderful." Judy's voice quieted as she stepped onto the porch and joined the cicadas singing a melody in the darkness.

Jackson and I stood outside the open door, watched our friends back out of the driveway, and waved goodbye. As soon as their car was out of sight, I reached for his hand, walked backward into the house, and tugged him with me.

After passing the threshold, his foot kicked up and shut the door. His fingers locked the bolt, but his eyes never left mine. "We'll clean everything up later." The simple statement set my body ablaze.

He hauled me forward and my chest crashed into him, his hands grabbing my cheeks and his lips crushing mine. Clothes were peeled away at a fevered pace, bits and pieces of fabric littered a trail from the living room to our bedroom.

My feet dangled above the floor as he broke the kiss and tossed me onto the plush cotton comforter on our bed. Instantly, his body blanketed mine. It had been almost two years and the heat and passion and longing for each other hadn't faded one ounce. If I were to describe it, I'd say it amplified with each day that passed.

Jackson worshipped me with his mouth as my hands pawed and scraped his backside. The room an echo chamber of our whimpers, heady breaths, cries for more. I loved the feel of him across every inch of my skin, but I needed more. My body screamed for his. "I need to feel you. Inside. Now."

His sapphires captured me as a growl ripped from his chest and his heat rubbed against me. His lips grazed mine a second before he broke away to observe as he slid deep inside me. My eyes rolled back and my back bowed off the mattress as his hips met mine. We sat unmoving for a beat, his breath hot on my neck as one hand encompassed my hip while the other laced through my hair, his forearm on the bed.

His hips retreated slowly, and then thrust forward once more in a methodical, soft rhythm. A breath later, he whispered in my ear. "I love you, Sarah." Another slow shift of his hips. "More than anything in this world." His hips pumped slowly as the pace grew more impassioned. "I couldn't imagine my life without you." The tempo built with each word he spoke. My orgasm closer to the precipice. His love igniting me. My nails bit his flesh, and his orgasm exploded with mine.

Pure, undiluted heaven. Wrapped in the arms of the person I loved. Our passion an accessory. Our souls united. I couldn't imagine life getting better.

TWENTY-FOUR

JACKSON

My PHONE ALARM WENT OFF, and the metal case buzzed and danced over the wooden bedside table. I snatched it up and prayed it didn't wake Sarah. Silencing the alarm, I slowly peeled back the covers and slipped out of bed. Fingers crossed my absence wouldn't disturb her.

Slipping on a pair of lounge pants, I exited and closed the door behind me. Today's to-do list ran a lap around the block with every minute packed. Thankfully, I recruited help and it would be seamless.

Unlocking my phone, I typed out a new message—one I would delete after it's sent. My fingers tapped across the keyboard on the screen. I peeked up every other second to double check Sarah hadn't wandered out.

Jackson: Morning. Just wanted to check we're on task. She's still asleep. Let me know if you need anything. My phone will be on silent, but I'll answer as soon as I'm able.

I pressed send, waited until the 'delivered' message popped up under the blue bubble, then deleted the message and tucked the phone in my pants pocket. I headed into the kitchen for the first task of the day—make breakfast in bed for my woman. My phone buzzed incessantly against my leg, reply after reply from the friends I entrusted with today's deeds.

After Sarah woke, I'd figure out a way to check them. Until then, I couldn't risk her walking out and wondering who I texted. Raiding the cabinets, drawers, and fridge, I retrieved the necessary ingredients and went about whipping up her first gift.

Moving from Georgia to California was a huge step for us. When we moved here, we'd known each other all of five months. Although, deep in the fiber of my being, it felt as if we had known each other our entire lives. When you had an all-consuming,   I-don't-want-to-spend-a-day-without-you connection, translating or comparing that connection to words was impossible. Sarah was a million fireflies buzzing and sparking in my soul. Friends—hers and mine—questioned us moving to the other side of the country, thousands of miles away, together, not knowing how our relationship would pan out.

We spent countless hours discussing the intricacies of our plan, sifted through every possible scenario or outcome, and had a resolution for each. Never once did the mention of us not being together come into the equation. We loved each other. For us, it was that simple. Neither of us pictured life without the other, so we didn't.

We sat down one weekend and looked at all the potential places to live. Both of us decided we wanted to be in a populous area. Somewhere near water, not specifically the ocean, but that's where we landed. And lastly, we wanted to be in an area that supported all walks of life—young, old, healthy, modern, classic, a little bit of this, a little bit of that.

The internet morphed into a tiresome annoyance, one I wanted to rip out of the computer and incinerate. Who knew it'd be so challenging to find what we were looking for? So we paused a few days, rested our brains and started fresh after time out of the house.

The mini break of city searching triggered opportunity to land in our lap. A client I hadn't seen in months booked an appointment on short notice. During our session, I asked how life was treating him since I'd last seen him. He shared tales of his work travels, how he'd flown all over the country, recruiting new clients and visiting new places.

At the mention of travels, I shared my intent to move out

of state in the near future, but hadn't nailed down the where yet. He understood my need for privacy, but asked what was stopping us.

After a long list of details, he threw a couple of suggestions my way. "Have you looked at Colorado or Santa Barbara, California?" We had looked into Colorado extensively—the area both beautiful and populous. The only turn off. Snow. Lots and lots of snow. Sure, we'd seen snow in Georgia, but it was nothing compared to Colorado.

His other suggestion—Santa Barbara—was where we landed. After some research, we automatically fell in love with the area. The next day, we booked a flight, took a long weekend trip and discovered our new home. Within a month and a half, we secured jobs and a place to live. Everything happened so seamlessly, it was hard to believe it wasn't meant to be.

Sarah in my life was an incomprehensible dream. The sight of her hair fanned across the pillow each morning when I woke. Her warm skin that lit a thousand fires across my skin when we touched. How her eyes sparkled when she looked at me. The way her voice slightly stuttered when she said my name... Sarah was all I wanted. All I ever needed.

The blueberry pancake slid off the spatula and stacked atop the two on the plate. Fresh cut strawberries, melon, and pineapple piled high beside the maple covered cakes. Then I finished it off with strips of tempeh bacon. I positioned the plate on a serving tray alongside a small glass of orange juice, a napkin, cutlery, and fresh daisies to decorate the perimeter. Grabbing the handles of the tray, I set off to accomplish the first task of the day.

Shortly after we moved to California, we made one other big change in our lives. How we lived. We took nothing for granted and experienced everything life offered. Some might say we changed into two completely different people. We say, we simply became a better version of ourselves.

Setting the tray on the table beside the bed, I lit a small candle and kneeled on the floor beside her. Sarah laid curled on her side; her pillow crushed in her embrace, head on the edge of mine as her golden locks splayed across the cotton. Soft, fair lashes rested above her cheekbones and accentuated the light smattering of freckles below them. Her chest rose and fell in a whisper.

With a slight shift, the sheet slipped down to her navel. Her pale breasts on full display, and I studied her golden tan lines in the dim light. I hoped she'd wake up, roll over, notice breakfast, and the day would begin. But now... plans changed. Even with a to-do list longer than Santa's at Christmas, there was no resisting the primal beast clawing inside me.

I lowered my head, wrapped my lips around her areola, and lavished the tender flesh. Her body stirred awake and pressed further into my greedy mouth. I slid a hand beneath the sheet and trailed down her body. From her navel, trekking through the small patch of curls, I traced over her slit and coated myself in her moisture.

One of her hands slid into my hair, curled into a fist, and held on for dear life. Her other slid over mine, and coaxed my fingers to slip inside. I kissed a path across her chest and sucked the other nipple between my lips. She gasped and bowed her back, and pressed her breast farther into my mouth as I dipped a finger inside. I hooked my finger in a *come hither* motion and rubbed against her walls.

"Oh god, Jackson," she moaned, tugging my hair harder.

A light sheen pierced her bare flesh as I explored her with my mouth. I inserted another finger and circled her clit with my thumb as my free hand shoved my pants to the floor. A second later, I joined her on the bed and hovered inches above her. I shifted hands and picked up speed. Within a beat, red blotches bloomed between her breasts, up her throat, and over her cheeks as her body clamped down on my fingers. I leaned down and bit her shoulder as her orgasm ricocheted from her core.

Kissing my way to her mouth, I absorbed her heady breaths and became intoxicated. After coating my erection with her release, I positioned the head of my dick at her folds and stilled as her body trembled under me. Smoldering emeralds magnetized to my sapphires. Her jaw slackened, breath panting. I kissed the corner of her lips, her jawline, the sweet spot beneath her ear. "Happy birthday, babe," I whispered in her ear as I thrust forward. Moments later, we both came unraveled.

"What tricks you got up your sleeve today?" Sitting up on the bed, Sarah's eyes squinted in deep thought, studying me as if trying to read my thoughts. Not happening today.

Today, I was on lockdown. A sealed vault. Poker face securely in place.

"I checked the weather yesterday. It's supposed to be nice all day, so I thought we'd go to the beach for a bit. Pack a picnic, soak up the sun. Maybe see a movie after. Later, though, we've got a dinner reservation."

The cutest and most peculiar expression lit her face. Was she confused or trying to read deeper into the context? *Best of luck*, I thought. I had planned today for weeks. Every detail locked up tight like Fort Knox. No way in, baby.

"Sounds good. Need help with anything before we go?" Desperation laced her words.

"Nope. Just get ready. I've got everything else under control."

Flipping the sheet off her legs, she scooted off the bed and stood a foot away, her sculpted curves on full display. She traipsed a hand over her hip, across her navel and up to her breast, and pinched her nipple. An obvious attempt to distract me. "Are you *sure* you don't need *any* help? You have *everything* under control?"

She toyed with me. Tried to make me cave under pressure. The only thing I'd give into today... fucking her as much as possible. I pushed off the bed, rose to my full height, and molded my body to hers. I gripped her ass with both hands and hoisted her off the floor, warranting a squeal from her.

I carried her into the bathroom, set her down, and turned on the shower. "You know, we don't have to leave the house today, if that's what you want. I'll gladly spend the day fucking you over every surface in the house. It's *your* birthday."

I slid my fingers between her folds and inserted two.

Sarah was insatiable. She gasped, "*Yes...*" A command on her lips.

"Yes, what?"

A moan bubbled deep in her chest. "Take me. In the shower. Now." Each word jagged.

"As you wish." I swept her off the floor, and her ankles hooked above my ass as I carried her into the raining water.

In every direction, the beach was blanketed with bodies. The sun shone bright and warm in the practically cloudless sky. After another hour of side-tracking, we'd finally dressed and left the house. The day mapped out for weeks, I was more than willing to spend Sarah's birthday naked in bed, if she wished it.

The only part that had to stick was dinner. Dinner involved more than us, and it would be selfish of me to leave everyone out. She didn't know it yet, but she'd remember this birthday for years to come.

I laid back against the soft blanket, propped up on my elbows, the sun partially hidden by the dark blue beach umbrella shading my face. Sarah walked out of the surf, feet sloshing along the salty water shallows, hands twisting her wet hair into a bun at the crown of her head. The sun shimmered the water droplets on her body and accentuated her curves. A balloon inflated my chest as a lion growled in my groin.

"The water feels great. You should join me," she pleaded, a gorgeous smile highlighting her cheeks.

The cool Pacific didn't tempt me as much as Sarah, but it was hot as fuck out today.

She stood in front of me as her body shadowed my legs. "Yeah, sure." Extending my hand to her, she helped me up and dragged me toward the surf.

If you'd ever dipped your toes in the Pacific, one thing was certain. It was cold as fuck. Even on a hot summer day, it was frigid. Back in Georgia, every once in a while, we'd drive to the Atlantic beaches. It was incomparable. Sure, it was cold, but not like the Pacific. The occasional trips to the Gulf of Mexico warmer, most likely because it was a smaller body of water.

I waded my way slowly into the water, hissing as I adapted to the temperature.

"You know it's better if you just take the plunge," she giggled.

"What?" I questioned, confused. The frigid water had my thoughts scrambled. *Did she know about later?*

"Just dunk your whole body under the water at once. Get the initial shock of it over and done with." Then she demonstrated.

"It's like ripping a band-aid off. Just be quick about it, huh?" She nodded and waited for me to submerge.

Inhaling deep, I leapt forward and took us both under the water. When we breached the surface, she panted and playfully smacked my arm.

"I wasn't ready for that."

I wrapped her arms around my neck, her legs around my waist, and held her close. "I know. That's why I did it, silly." My lips crushed against hers and pushed all her playfulness aside.

I walked us farther into the water. The depth breaking the water at our shoulders, and the crowd thinning around us. Our lips danced and tongues stroked as the water cooled our heated flesh.

I drew back, the dark lenses of my sunglasses reflecting against hers. "Is this what you want for your birthday? Us, making love and fucking all day?" My question serious and not-so-serious at the same time. "Everywhere we go today, you want us to leave our mark?" The idea stirred deep in my bones. Marking and claiming the city had an unimaginable appeal.

Her arm dipped below the water, her hand sunk between my board shorts and skin, and my dick stiffened further. Her hand stopped when her fingers wrapped around my shaft. She pressed her cheek to mine, her lips a breath away from my ear.

"It seems as if you're good with the whole idea." Her tongue traced the shell of my ear before she sucked the lobe. "I want you to fuck me. Right here. Right now," she whispered. The demand an electrical impulse straight to my cock.

"Put your hands around my neck, babe." As her hand abandoned my dick, I inched my shorts beneath my ass and exposed myself to the elements. I traced her bikini bottoms, ground through the material over her clit before pushing it to the side.

I slid two fingers inside her. *Fuck, she was wet.* I slid my fingers out and positioned her over me. Something about the thought of anyone realizing what we were doing turned me on immensely. Voyeurism had never been a desire or fetish—I never wanted another person getting off watching us—but it was more the adrenaline rush of being caught with our pants down.

I pushed into her, and the water created an unfamiliar friction. Withdrawing a fraction, I thrust forward again and our bodies found an unnoticeable rhythm. She leaned her cheek against mine, the side least visible to the beach goers. Her hot breath panted in my ear as soft whimpers rippled over the waves. I quaked under her as she quietly demanded more.

I widened my stance, trying to gain more leverage, and thrust my hips as I drove her down my shaft. Sex in a body of water was a wholly new experience. Strange and foreign, but also unbelievable and exciting.

Her breathing accelerated as small, high-pitched cries wept from her lips. *Don't stop. Don't stop. Don't stop.* She repeated it as if she knew no other words. A moment later, her body tightened around me and held me in place as my release followed.

"Holy shit!" She pressed her forehead against mine. "That was..."

"Fucking amazing..." I finished her sentence. Exhilaration flooded my veins.

"Yeah." She pulled back and studied me through her sunglasses. "You know I'm never going to look at the beach the same again, right?"

I laughed, thinking how I'll never see the ocean in the same way either. The thought made me love her even more.

"Where are we going?" Sarah asked.

I reached across the center console of the Jeep and encased her hand in mine. I brought her soft, delicate fingers to my lips and kissed each proximal phalanx. My lips had devoured every square inch of her flesh today, but right now, this small intimate touch… beyond perfection.

My eyes veered back to the road as I turned right at a random intersection. I purposely drove us all over the city, burned time, and threw her off to where we were going. Apparently, it worked. In my periphery, Sarah stared out the window and then back at me, her brow furrowed.

She was lost. But me? Not one bit.

"It's a surprise," I replied.

Her reaction exactly what I expected. I felt her eyes roll as she sighed heavily and exhaled with every iota of drama she owned. A gleaming smile split my lips as I worked diligently to suppress my laughter.

"Can I at least get some sort of hint as to where we're going?" Her brilliant emeralds seared my flesh and attempted to seduce me.

Tempted to toy with her, maybe I'd give her a tidbit. A great deal of time and effort went into planning today, no way I'd ruin the surprise. Others would have my head on a platter.

I wanted this birthday to be one she remembered. Always.

We pulled up to a red light, and I glanced over at her and kissed her knuckles. "You'll love it. We should be there in ten minutes or less."

"That's a crappy hint. I don't even know where we are. How can I guess where we're going?"

I shrugged and faced forward as the traffic light turned green. "Sorry, babe. I might get murdered for ruining the surprise."

A quick glimpse at her expression and I laughed loud. Her eyes squinted, brows bunched in, and lips pursed. Her irritation with me absolutely adorable. After she discovered why I kept the surprise on lockdown, she'd overlook any irritation.

I turned the Jeep into the parking lot of Bella and Daisy's Bistro and parked in a space near the entrance. I discovered the restaurant through a client. His endless bragging about how great the food was and how his wife loved the vibe piqued my interest. Days later, I drove by and scoped it out.

I cut the engine and tugged the handle on the door, stepping around the front of the Jeep to open her door. She stared at me, dumbstruck, and then back to the restaurant.

"What is this place?" Her eyes scanned every surface as I took her hand and helped her from the passenger seat.

"Bella and Daisy's Bistro. It came recommended, and I checked it out. I think you'll like it."

She faced me, eyes alight with excitement, her expression softening after a minute. Facing forward again, she squeezed my hand in hers. "It looks wonderful."

I glimpsed the restaurant with her, wanting to see everything how she saw it. From where we stood, the right half of the building was visible, the left masked by a large pergola decorated with vines, small flowers peeking between the leaves. Strewn along the ground, under the pergola, was a mass of colorful river rocks. Different sized wooden tables scattered throughout the gravel. Between all the tables was a fire pit. Adirondack chairs crowded the flickering flames.

To the right of the outdoor seating a small, winding walkway, each slate stepping stone a different shape. To the left of the walkway were tall ornamental grasses with small tufts on the tops. A small pond trickled down a towering stack of rocks on the right. Rows of compact, Edison-style bulbs hung above us as we walked toward the entrance.

Her expression mesmerized me. I loved her awe and excitement as we stepped closer to a set of large glass doors.

I opened the door and gestured her inside ahead of me. Fun, eclectic music crooned from hidden speakers. The scent of fresh herbs and citrus wafted in the air. Walking past a handful of long benches, we approached the hostess.

"Welcome to Bella and Daisy's. Two for dinner?" the brunette asked as her eyes darted between us.

"We have a reservation. Ember."

She ran a finger over the reservations as another fidgeted with her ponytail. She froze a second before her eyes peered up again and her hospitality smile slipped in place. "Right this way, please."

Outside, the restaurant appeared small, as if it could hold

ten or fifteen tables max. When I first checked it out, I got a brief tour and found it perfect for tonight. But now I had the opportunity to really check it out and was more than pleased with my choice.

The restaurant had several tables spread throughout the interior—some for two, others for more. The tables were distressed like the ones outside. Along the ceiling, more of the same Edison bulbs lit the space. With a modern and intimate appearance, I knew my girl loved every part of it.

We wove through a few more tables before turning and walking toward a pair of aged, oak doors, **PRIVATE** decoratively burned into each. The hostess paused in front of the doors, turned to face me, and gave me a knowing look. I smiled in thanks and she retreated.

I faced Sarah, her expression bewildered as she stared back at me. I closed the gap between us and kissed her delicate lips briefly. "Happy birthday, babe."

I opened the door, the room pitch black, and gestured Sarah to step into the room ahead of me. Shutting the door behind us, I flipped a switch on the wall and a group of voices screamed.

"Surprise!"

Her expression went from recognition to shocked to awed to elation… I'd pay every cent I earned for that to happen again.

TWENTY-FIVE

JACKSON OPENED the door and gestured for me to step inside the dark and secretive room. After he shut the door, it was like an endless tunnel without light. His hand patted along the wall in search of the light switch.

A second later, while I stood in the dark and my other senses heightened, a whiff of a familiar scent struck my nose. One ingrained in several memories. One not around often anymore. Before I asked what was happening, lights blinded me, and a sea of friendly faces grinned ear to ear.

"Surprise!"

I rubbed my eyes in disbelief. Everyone I held near and dear to my heart stood in front of me; their excitement and joy to see me flooded me with a rainbow of emotions. My face heated as the corners of my mouth perked up, smiling so hard my cheeks stung. Tears pricked my eyes as a boulder of adoration clogged my throat. I wanted to cry and squeal and jump up and down, but also squeeze the heck out each person here.

I spun to face Jackson, wrapped my arms around his neck, and whispered into his ear. "Thank you for bringing everyone here. This is the best present anyone ever gave me." I kissed the angle of his jaw then retreated and gazed into the eyes of all the beautiful, smiling faces.

Without a word, everyone filed into a zigzag line, ready to hug me and hug or shake hands with Jackson. Christy and

Rick, Liz and Tiffany, Marco, Eric, Rob, Judy and Kendra, Peter and Mark (another couple we met during our sunsets on the beach), my parents—Sally and George—and a man I assumed was Jackson's father because of his striking resemblance.

My mom and dad stepped forward, wrapped me in their embrace, and squeezed me with ferocity. I hadn't seen them since we left Georgia. And although I talked with my mom often—phone calls and FaceTime at least two to three times a week—I missed them terribly. Thousands of miles apart versus twenty minutes was an odd feeling. The three of us separated, and I hooked Jackson's arm with mine. "Mom. Dad. This is Jackson. Jackson, these are my parents. Sally and George Bradley."

Mom stepped to my right; the top of her head barely reached Jackson's chin as she looked up at him with a beaming smile. With her arms outstretched and welcoming, she yanked him into her for a hug. "It's so good to finally meet you in person, Jackson."

"You, too, Mrs. Bradley." His hold on her one of the most tender things I witnessed in our time together.

Mom stepped out of the hug and moved aside as dad took her place with his hand held out, firmly shaking hands with Jackson before he drew him in for a man hug and a strong pat on the back. "Jackson. Great to meet you, son. I've heard nothing but amazing things about you." His dark, amber eyes glanced my way before focusing on the forest greens set in my mother's features. "Thank you for inviting us out tonight. It means the world to the both of us."

"Certainly, sir. I wouldn't want it any other way."

Jackson's formality and expression befuddled me. An abnormal exchange for my father and Jackson. A secret between two men. A quiet sentiment from a father to the man who held his daughter's heart. I had zero time to mull it over as my body was hauled into a tall man's chest and the wind knocked out of me.

I wrapped my arms around his frame. Strong and older, yet familiar. Giving him a tight hug, I took a deep breath and relaxed, his earthy scent comforting. As he broke the hug, his palms rested along my biceps with nearly straight elbows.

"Hey, sweetheart. I'm Bill, Jackson's old man. It's wonderful to meet you. Although it feels like I've known you years, seeing how Jackson talks about you like a schoolgirl."

He smiled, and I instantly knew Jackson's genetics mirrored his father. I studied Bill a moment—the sharp angle of his jaw, the salt-and-pepper sprinkled in his short, black hair, his broad chest. As I examined him, it dawned on me this would be Jackson in the future. The notion plucked at my heartstrings. The only noticeable difference—his eyes. Where Jackson had the most intense sapphires, Bill's resembled more of a steel, metallic swirl. Quite striking.

"It's great to finally meet you, too. I've heard some stories, all good ones, from Jackson. Maybe you can fill me in on stories I haven't heard." I peeked over at Jackson as my brows danced up and down.

"Sure thing, sweetheart. I always love embarrassing my boy. Too bad I didn't bring any old photos. Then we could have some real fun." His laughter shook against me, a deep, throaty bellow. I loved him immediately.

After a mass of hugs are exchanged, everyone took their seat—a table front and center for us faced the group. We headed for our table and Jackson drew out a chair for me while he remained standing.

He picked up a glass of wine from the table, raised it, and cleared his throat; his other hand on my shoulder.

"I wanted to take a moment and thank everyone for being here tonight. I know some of you had to travel farther than others, but it means the world to us you could be here. To our Georgia friends and family, we've missed you deeply. Thank you. We love you." He lifted his glass higher and bellowed out *cheers* before he brought it to his lips.

"Cheers!" Our friends and family echoed.

Jackson sat down beside me, placed his glass on the table, and wrapped his arm around my shoulders. His breath hot on my ear, he whispered, "Happy birthday, babe. Were you surprised?"

"Totally surprised. *You did all this?* This is... *amazing.* Thank you." This birthday would definitely be stored in my memory bank.

"Only for you." He pressed a sweet, tender kiss on my

forehead. "Now let's enjoy some great company and delicious food."

Over the next couple of hours, we mingled with our friends and ate a plethora of appetizers before our dinner arrived. I learned more about Jackson's father—he was a retired carpenter, although he never really stopped working. He loved working with his hands. More or less, he worked as a hobby now and made art for people.

One of the most amazing bits of news, Christy and Liz planned on transferring to the California Hammond Life office. Although it was a two-hour drive from where Jackson and I lived, it was closer—and cheaper—than a long flight across the country. If everything went according to plan, they'd be in California before the year ended. Both of them paused their transfer while Rick and Tiffany sorted out jobs and they all found a place to live.

Life got better with each passing day. My heart was on cloud nine. Ecstatic to have more family closer. Of all the things heavy on my heart when we moved, not being near my parents or friends resonated the worst. At least I would get a chunk back.

Jackson fidgeted next to me—his leg bounced, his attention shifted from Eric to me out of the corner of his eye, then back to Eric. Under the tablecloth, I placed my hand on his thigh and sent calming energy his way. His eyes darted to mine, searching, and a million thoughts flitted across the lines of his face. He rested his palm over mine—his palm sweaty and cool to the touch. His leg stopped bouncing as he gazed into my eyes, a forced, tight smile replaced the nervousness he worked to hide.

I mouthed. "You okay?" Unsure if he had eaten something bad and felt sick. He nodded, but didn't answer.

I watched him another minute. Small beads of sweat glistened the ridged lines of his forehead. His Adam's apple bobbed a beat before he closed his eyes. The wooden legs of his chair screeched against the tile floor, and everyone stopped talking and focused on Jackson.

Peering up at him, I worried over his pallor and damp-ened skin. "Are you sure you're okay?"

He bent down and placed a kiss on my cheek. "I'm fine, babe."

Taking him at his word, I turned back to my mother, ready to resume our conversation about how different the beaches are in California versus Georgia. I assumed Jackson got up to use the restroom, that was until I heard him clear his throat. My attention returned to him, curious what he was up to.

Dwarfed under his height beside me, I strained to peek up and assess him. Sweat painted his face as his eyes danced over everyone in the room as he stood silent. Everyone except mine. Nervous energy cascaded off him in waves. I didn't know what was happening, but I suddenly had a knot in the pit of my stomach.

When he spoke, it was a rattled sound. A stutter on his tongue. "Hey, everyone. Can I have your attention for a moment or two?"

Everyone stopped their chit-chat and directed their atten-tion to Jackson. I gazed at where his fingers rested by his side, the ends tapping his thigh repeatedly.

"Thank you, again, for being here tonight. I know it means the world to Sarah." He locked eyes with me for a second. "It means everything to me, too. It took a lot of man hours, and woman hours," he looked over at Christy and Liz, smiled and tipped his head in their direction, "to get tonight put together. Countless hours and weeks of planning. I couldn't have done it without help. So, thank you. You are the best friends we could ask for."

Christy and Liz lifted their wine glasses and returned the sentiment to Jackson.

"Sarah's birthday isn't the only reason I wanted everyone here tonight." He must have read the confusion on my face, because his smile radiated at my obvious lack of intel. "I brought you all here tonight for another reason as well. I wanted all of you here, the people who hold the highest level of importance to both of us—individually or together—on this memorable evening." Jackson faced me, slid his chair farther back, and dropped to one knee, his hands trembling at his sides. My mouth fell open, hands slapping to cover it as I gasped and my eyes welled with tears.

"Sarah, since the day I met you, a little over a year and a half ago, you have turned my life into this astonishing place. You made me see things a little brighter, your aura like a glowing ray of sunlight. Before you, my skies were gray and life was monotonous. Now, everything is brilliant and bold and screaming with life. You make me feel whole. You make life worth living."

Pausing a moment, his hand dug into his right pocket. A second later, light glimmered off the ring he fished out. Attempting to steady his hold on the band, he held the ring up and presented it.

He glanced over at his father, his eyes wetting before he continued. "This ring belonged to my mother, MaryAnne. I wish you could have met her. She would have loved you immensely." Tears rolled down his cheek, my thumbs swiping them away before they reached his jaw. "But nowhere near as much as I love you. Sarah, today I invited our family and closest friends here for two reasons. The first... to celebrate your birthday. A day that is definitely worth rejoicing over because without it you wouldn't be in my world. The second... I could have held the door open for anyone that day. I was in such a rush to meet up with my client, I didn't have time to pause at the gym doors or say anything to anyone. I thought, in that moment, I'd missed the opportunity of a lifetime. I thought I'd missed my one chance to talk to the most stunning woman I ever laid eyes on. But I didn't know luck was on my side. I didn't know we were meant to see each other again. I wallowed for days, told my friends about the woman I saw at the gym. I tried to make more appointments with the clients that lived in your complex, hoping to cross paths with you again. But nothing happened. Not until days later. I'd been bumming around for days, and Eric was having way too much fun giving me shit for acting like such a girl."

He takes a minute, looking over at Eric and they both laughed a moment before he continued.

"He told me he was going to a party and asked me to come along, that maybe I'd feel better afterwards. Just after we walked in the door to Liz's party, I saw you. Standing in the kitchen. You noticed Eric, but hadn't seen me. Someone had dropped something, and you went into cleanup mode, ignoring everything else. I watched you, waiting for the right moment to approach you and start a conversation. When I did… it was all downhill from there. I was hooked. I've been hooked every moment since. Sarah, I couldn't ever imagine my life without you in it. I never want to. When we're not together, I feel as if a part of me is absent. You fill in all the gaps. You make me whole. You make me a better man. Life without you… it would be cold and dark and empty. You are my light. You are my reason for… *everything*. You make the sun shine and the moon glow. On this day—your day—I ask you the most important question I will ever ask. Sarah Lynn Bradley, will you marry me? Will you be mine forever?"

The spacious room faded away, replaced with a gray fog that clouded everything from sight. Everything except him. It was only me and Jackson. His bold sapphires glassy with unshed tears. Wetness fell down my cheeks as my eyes dropped from his and locked onto the ring clasped between his first finger and thumb.

A silver band, not too thin nor too thick. In the band's center rested a rich, dark sapphire baguette, the precious stone a little longer than wide. Three thin baguette diamonds nestled along both sides of the stone, accentuating the piece and giving it a classic look. The sight of it stole my breath, had my eyes swelling with unshed tears, and froze my voice. Not only did the ring remind me of the specific pair of blues I could never get enough of, but it also held more meaning to him than anything I could ever understand.

My eyes slid up from the ring and locked back onto his. I opened my mouth, tried to form words past the lump in my throat. Never had I been at such a loss for words. My eyes dropped briefly, another batch of tears fell at the quick closing and reopening of my eyes, caught on my lashes and blurred my view.

I waded through the thick layer of emotion that filled the space between us and swallowed. The world around me lightened as if someone lifted a weight off me I didn't know existed. The corners of my mouth perked up, my cheeks rosy from the love and adoration I had for this man. The connection we shared unlike any I had with anyone else. I never imagined my world without him in it. Never wanted to. Ever. He breathed life into me. Was the reason I woke with a smile every morning. The reason I existed. My world was his world and his was mine.

"*Yes*. Yes, Jackson, I will marry you."

TWENTY-SIX

October — The Following Year

I SPIRALED the last fallen length of hair around the curling iron and followed it with a heavy spritz of hairspray. Relaxed spirals loosely framed my face while the remainder of my hair sat secured in an artfully messy bun at my nape. Christy stood behind me and added final touches—a handful of daisies and sprigs of baby's breath. Once finished with my hair, she twisted me in the chair and studied my face.

"Makeup looks fine. Closer to natural is better," I said.

I never wore a lot of makeup. Honestly, the less on my skin, the happier I was.

"Yeah, yeah. Shut up, bitch. This is my time to shine." Christy giggled and it crowded the small dressing room as she playfully shoved my shoulder.

"Be nice now." Liz poked her head out around the tri-fold dressing wall, her eyes pinging between me and Christy like a game of table tennis. "This dress feels all wrong."

"What do you mean? You tried it on and said it was perfect." A tsunami of panic surged from my belly and gnawed its way through my limbs.

Shit! Shit! Shit!

"That's not what I meant." She stepped out from behind the barrier, the soft, teal chiffon complemented her hazelnut skin. A stunning visual I couldn't resist smiling at. "What I meant is… I'm just not a dressy-dress kinda girl." She pivoted side-to-side and the sheer top layer flowed more freely than the thicker fabric below it.

"I think you look stunning. Wait till Tiffany sees you." I glanced up at Christy, her eyes pinched at the corners, and her smile bright. "You're up. Time to change."

"No messing up your hair or makeup while I'm changing," Christy said with a pointed finger and cocked hip.

I stuck my tongue out and saluted her. "Yes, ma'am."

"No need for sarcasm, bitch. The time for you to change is coming soon."

In less than an hour, the ceremony would begin. Instantly, my palms slickened as I stood on the edge of a cliff. I had zero reservations about marrying Jackson. I wanted to be his wife more than I wanted to breathe. The dark cloud of anxiety hovered around my fear of falling on my way down the aisle.

In record time, Christy stepped out from behind the panels and twirled in her dress. In the bust, the material hugged her curves like a glove. From the waist down, it billowed out slightly. Both Christy's and Liz's dresses ghosted the ground when they walked and their shoes peeked out.

"Rescue me. I think I'm going to cry." I fanned my eyes while Christy rushed to my side with a tissue to blot the corners of each eye.

"No tears. Not until pictures are taken and everyone has seen you. Just because the makeup says it's waterproof, doesn't mean shit."

"Okay, I promise. No tears."

Christy and Liz stood back a few feet and studied me. This moment one of the best I shared with them both. Beyond lucky to have them here and sharing another monumental occasion.

Liz squeezed my shoulder. "It's time."

I stared at her and nodded. "Will you guys help me?"

"Wouldn't have it any other way." Christy rested her hand on my other shoulder, the three of us connected. Sisters.

I slid off the creamy, cotton robe, and stood in a nude thong and nude bra adhesives. Liz walked to the garment rack and unzipped the heavy, white dress bag. The three of us had seen my dress a few times, but when the split zipper exposed the material below, we each gasped at my wedding dress.

Some parts of Jackson and I are traditional; other parts, not so much. My dress fell under the less traditional side. It was a soft, creamy rosé hue. The bottom layer of the dress a thick, matte satin fabric, cutting across my bust and sloping down at the sides and plunging to a point at my low back, my bare back exposed. The dress flared out gradually down my legs—not snug; not puffy—and danced across the floor. A thin, delicate layer of matching lace covered the dress as well as the exposed area of my back up to the tops of my shoulder blades, above my breasts to my collarbones, and down my arms. The pattern intricate, the lace hand stitched by an Italian family.

This dress more formal than anything I'd worn prior, yet still wielded my bohemian style. The moment I laid eyes on it on the hanger, I stopped scanning the racks. The moment I tried it on, every particle in my body screamed this was *the* dress.

Gently sliding the dress from the garment bag, Liz carried the dress over to me—Christy noticeably bounced beside me —the length draped over an arm. They both held one side of the dress, Liz's thin fingers trembled slightly as she unlatched the lacy, round buttons down the spine. Once she reached the last button, her hazel eyes gazed at my emeralds as a sweet smile spread across her face and ignited her eyes. The silent exchange between us inflated my heart with joy—she was as happy for me as I was for her.

Most brides got jittery on their wedding day. Although you've seen your wedding dress umpteen times, luxuriated in the fabric against your skin during the several fittings, and smiled like a fool every time you saw it—some women lost all sense of peace the instant the dress left the garment bag.

But I wasn't most women. I definitely wasn't most brides.

My eyes glazed over as I stared at the stunning layers of fabric. All I saw was forever. Forever with Jackson. And forever in love. A bubble of serenity encircled me at wearing this dress and walking toward my forever. If one truth was absolute in my life, it was that marrying Jackson Ember was set in the stars. Love of my life. Guardian angel. The key to my heart.

Stepping into the gown, my arms dipped into the soft, lace sleeves and I wiggled the dress up my body. As I held the lace to my chest, Liz and Christy fastened each button along my spine. As each one connected, a glimpse of my future flashed like an old picture movie. Breathtaking and beautiful and fulfilling. A sharp tug snapped me out of my daydream as Christy and Liz made sure the gown sat in place on my curves. When Liz reached the top button, Christy grabbed my heels—basic nudes with the toe open and a strap around the heel.

I slid my feet into each shoe and held up the dress for Christy to hook them. Once in place, I added one last piece to my ensemble. Grabbing a black box from the vanity, I inhaled deep and lifted the lid. A classic piece nestled in soft satin. My fingers skimmed the precious stone at the heart of a silver chain. A magnificent sapphire rested high atop an intricate silver design. Jackson purchased the necklace. It paired with the ring that once belonged to his mother and now rested on my left ring finger.

With the necklace latched around my neck, the pendant rested at the hollow above my sternum. Liz and Christy slowly spun us to face the three mirrors in the room. No longer concerned about falling over the lace of my dress, I peeked up and digested the three angled reflections staring back at me.

Completely awestruck with my best friends at my side. Tears stung behind my eyes and threatened to spill. I tipped my face to the ceiling and kept them at bay. Again. Overwhelmed by the enormity of my love for Jackson, my best friends held my hands and laughed with me as I refused to shed a tear. Life was complete. Whole.

"Is it time yet? Not sure how much more I can take?" My body trembled with laughter.

Two sets of arms embraced me as *awes* cooed nearby. When we parted, Christy checked the time and announced we should get in position—the ceremony a couple minutes away.

In the blink of an eye, the door opened. Liz and Christy

walked out and my father stepped in. My heart a gooey, toasty marshmallow as he stood in awe before me. After a bated breath, Dad swathed me in love and adoration before kissing my cheek softly. "You are stunning, baby girl. Your mother and I are so happy for you."

I gazed into his weepy, amber eyes and noticed soft lines crinkling the corners. "Thank you, Daddy," I whispered as emotion choked me.

His strong, calloused fingers secured mine and held me tight. "We should make our way toward the aisle. There is a strapping young gentleman waiting for you at the end." A smile that matched my own, one I inherited from the man embracing me, beamed back at me. Pride and love and joy reverberated from his aura and merged with mine. Love only a father possessed for his little girl.

We exited the intimate dressing room and wandered down a pathway to an open set of doors. Outside the building, our shoes clicked along the cobblestone walkway as the muted wedding music played in the foreground. After a hundred rapid heartbeats, we approached an archway blanketed in small red roses, stopped and waited.

Our arms hooked at the elbow, Dad rested his free hand over my exposed elbow and gave me an affirmative squeeze. The music shifted as he locked eyes with me, and his broad smile like a million fireflies brightening the sky. The happiest I'd ever seen him.

"Here we go, baby girl."

I lifted my bouquet—an ornate arrangement of sunflowers, daisies, purple calla lilies, and wildflowers. Had I been in charge of the bouquet, it'd be a hot mess. The florist was our saving grace. I readied myself, took a deep, relaxing breath, and signaled I was ready.

The next thirty-seven steps—yes, I counted each and every one of them—were somewhat of a blur. I remembered people in my periphery, but had no clue who was who and where exactly they were in the ocean of chairs.

The only person I cared to see the entire time was Jackson. His sharp charcoal suit. The teal button-down under his jacket—same as Christy and Liz—unbuttoned at the collar. A boutonniere on the right breast of his jacket matched my bouquet. His black hair spiked, the line of his jaw layered with a thin line of trimmed hair. His hands clamped together in front of him at the groin.

But once I locked eyes with him, everything vanished. No family, no friends, no elaborate decor. It was only me and him. And the glow of his sapphires... their luminescence as I closed the space between us able to vanquish all darkness.

The moment I stood inches from him, the music and chatter faded to white noise. Jackson's hands unlocked, reached forward, and took hold of mine, steadying me. All my buzzing mind thought was—after saying yes in the correct places and speaking our vows—this gorgeous, extraordinary, loving man belonged to me forever. Love exploded in my chest, the shrapnel fiery in my bloodstream as it fueled my soul.

As if psychic, his sapphires glazed over and he mouthed *I love you*. A quiet tear broke the dam and rolled down my cheek just before I mouthed back *I love you forever*.

EPILOGUE
ONE YEAR LATER

I GRABBED another collapsible stadium chair from the back of the Jeep and set it on the beach cart beside me. Towels. Blankets. A bag loaded with several tubes of sunscreen.

"Need a hand?"

I spun around and spotted Tiffany shielding her sunglasses-covered eyes. "Sure. Grab the cooler?"

Sliding the oversized, blue cooler from the Jeep, she set it on the ground and tugged the handle up. Closing the Jeep tailgate, we ambled through the parking lot until the coarse sand warmed our feet.

I paused and scanned the beach for my husband. He—along with Liz, Judy, and Kendra—erected the beach canopy we recently purchased. Seeing as we spent so much time here, especially with friends, it was a great investment.

I trekked toward everyone as Tiffany hauled the cooler beside me. "So, how have things been with you two since the move?" A silly question, but I felt compelled to ask and check on my best friend, as well as her other half. Liz and Tiffany had been living in California for the last year-and-a-half. But I only ever heard Liz's side of life. I wanted to hear Tiffany's, too. It was a big transition for them both.

"It's been really great. At first, I worried I wouldn't find a job. But after a bit of research, I discovered there was tons of opportunity. Probably wouldn't have been as fortunate back home. Us moving here... it was meant to be. And we couldn't be happier."

Her words meant the world to me. Liz assured me everything was fantastic between them—romantically, as well as their careers. Knowing Tiffany echoed the same sentiment put my heart at ease. Beyond happy to see my best friend get her slice of the pie. Liz deserved nothing except the best and it warmed my heart she found her happiness with Tiffany.

As we approached the group, they staked the last corner of the canopy into the sand. Everyone grabbed chairs and blankets and set up our plot of the beach. Jackson stepped forward, wrapped his arms around my waist, dropped his lips to mine and left me wanting when he backed away.

"Is there anything else left in the car, babe?"

"No. Tiffany and I got everything."

Jackson peered over my shoulder. Sand crunched loud, and I turned to Christy and Rick approaching the group.

"Rick, need a hand getting the table?" Jackson spun me so we both faced them.

"Yeah, man. If you don't mind."

The two of them trudged off to Rick's truck, heaved a large banquet table out of the bed, and returned and set it up under the makeshift gazebo canopy.

Moments later, drinks circulated, conversation halted, and Jackson cleared his throat, reining in the group. "Thanks for coming out and sharing our anniversary with us." Jackson leaned in and placed a tender kiss on my temple. "It means everything, to both of us, that we have so many great people in our life. And on that note..."

He paused and left everyone hanging. Tantalizing sapphires sparkled when he pushed his sunglasses into his hair and rested them atop his head. Our next announcement left for me to share.

No pressure. Not really.

After a long pull from my water bottle, I inhaled deep as the cool liquid quenched my nerves a fraction. With my sunglasses in place, the dark lenses a safety net against the knot in my stomach, I peered back at Jackson a second. His smile burned brighter than the sun, and the knot untwisted and my anxiety vanished.

I glanced back to my anxious friends as my lips kicked up at the corner. "We're pregnant!" I announced cheerfully.

For a moment, I swore the earth silenced. But before my mind shifted to overdrive, cheers erupted from everyone. Hugs were exchanged. After everything died down, Liz stated she had news as well.

Beside her, Tiffany glowed brighter by the second. Liz lifted Tiffany's left hand, a diamond rested atop a rose gold band parked on the finger next to her pinky. "We're engaged!"

"Holy shit!" Christy slapped her hand to her mouth before she jumped up and down. "I can't fucking believe it! Soon, we'll all be married." Tears rolled down Christy's cheeks, stress over her and Rick's wedding next month temporarily evaporating.

"Must be something in the water here." I laughed at Christy's exuberance and everyone followed suit, our laughter echoed for miles.

Within minutes, bodies zigzagged here and there, setting up the table with plates and cutlery and mountains of food. I hung out at one corner, shade masking me from the chest up, and ogled the most wonderful people in my life as they shuffled around one another like they knew each other all their lives.

I glanced down at my stomach, a bump protruded an inch, and rested my hand just below my navel. Excited to become a mother, to meet the person who would be a sliver of me and a sliver of Jackson. Eager to teach him or her all the wonderful things I loved about this place.

As overjoyed as I was, a grain of sadness came along with pregnancy and having a baby. My parents lived thousands of miles away and the opportunity for them to see their grandchild would be much less than preferred.

I would more than love to travel back home to Georgia with the baby, but the remote possibility of seeing Alan or him finding out I was there if he got released… it wasn't a risk worth taking.

I hate to say one person still ruled a part of my life, it's not that. Not really. Somewhere, in the depths of my mind, I forgave Alan for what he did. Perhaps it was all he knew. I wasn't the one who needed to worry about such things anymore.

Jackson walked up behind me, his strong arms curved around my mid-section as his hands covered mine on my belly. "You okay, babe?" A whisper of a kiss pressed below my ear.

"Yeah, just thinking about how excited I am to meet our little bundle." I turned my head toward his and our lips met.

"Me, too. Do you want to know the sex ahead of time? So we can plan his or her whole future." His smile beamed, and his dimple peeked out.

"I don't know. I don't think so. Think I'd rather be more focused on what I need to do to be the best for him or her. Unisex stuff isn't so horrible when they're little."

"Whatever you want, babe. Have you thought of any names?"

Both of us stared out at the water, the white-crested waves crashed along the surf. Had I thought of names yet? I hadn't sat down and surfed the web.

"Maybe Alex. For short. That way, if it's a girl, Alexandria. Or if it's a boy, Alexander. What d'ya think?"

His hands rubbed back and forth over my belly, eyes focused as he pondered. "I like it. It's perfect, babe. Baby Alex."

"Baby Alex," I repeated. "Now that we have that sorted out... middle names are your job." I ducked out of his clutches and jogged toward our friends with a wicked grin plastered on my face.

Jackson sat in the chair next to mine and took hold of my hand. In this moment, everyone in my life happy... This was the best love on earth.

Leaning over to his ear, I whispered. "This life, our life, is perfect. And it's all because of you. I love you, angel."

"I love you, too, babe." And then he kissed me as if six of our closest friends were nowhere in sight.

DISTORTED DEVOTION PLAYLIST

Here are some of the songs from the **Distorted Devotion** playlist. You can listen to the entire playlist on Spotify!

In the House In a Heartbeat | Metro Exodus
Need Some1 | The Prodigy
Joanne (Where Do You Think You're Going?) – Piano version | Lady Gaga
Into You | Ariana Grande
Electric | Alina Baraz, Khalid
High For This | The Weeknd
Wicked Game | Emika
Only Love | Ben Howard
Mercy (Acoustic) | Shawn Mendes
Mine | Bazzi
All We Do | Oh Wonder
Every Breath You Take (Re: Imagined) | Denmark + Winter
Release The Psycho | Rowan McLaughlin
Die For You | The Weeknd

ACKNOWLEDGMENTS

First and foremost, thank you to everyone who picks up this book (and my previous)! Your support astounds me and I bow down to you. Readers are invaluable humans and I love you!

Wife! You are the most supportive human I know. You put up with my crazy hours and timelines and read all my words. Really, you're the best! And I can never thank you enough.

To the readers, authors, and bloggers reading my words! Starting an author career isn't a walk in the park. Thank you for being there for me and supporting me. Without any of you, things would be so much different.

Ellie and Rosa at My Brother's Editor! Thank you for editing and proofing this book. Thank you for questioning things I wrote and making me look at it from a different perspective. When I'm in the zone, sometimes I don't see how ridiculous something is. Many thanks.

To everyone in the Inkers Group for answering questions I've had throughout this journey. No author ever has all the answers and I'm so grateful for this group of amazing people who always help one another.

To my family who supports and roots for me! Sometimes it freaks me out when I hand a copy of my book to a family member. Although I'm proud of my accomplishment, it's strange to have someone so close to you reading your work.

PERSEPHONE AUTUMN

BETWEEN WORDS PUBLISHING LLC

PROLOGUE

RICK

Liquid sex bleeds from the speakers in the club. Every inch of Apex packed with slick, bare skin, ready to ring in the new year. This year's turn out is much higher than previous years. Although Apex is invitation or members only, the club has never had a crowd of this magnitude in the five years I have worked here.

As I weave my way through the club, I check in with our regular clients. Since we invited several one-timers tonight, it is imperative our regular clientele enjoys the evening with the same level of comfort as usual. As I approach one of the large, circular couches, I stop and take in the three couples spread across the oxblood leather.

A middle-aged man stands at one end, his entire body exposed to the voyeurs, while a woman half his age rests on all fours atop the couch and sucks his cock like it is her last meal. At her backside, a younger man plows into her pussy while tugging on the chains attached to both her nipples like horse reins.

Off to the side, a third man lays lengthwise with his calves dangling off the curved edge. One woman straddles his hips and rides his cock while another does the same atop his face. The two women kiss, fondle, and occasionally suck the other's breasts, all while being pleasured by him.

Such a magnificent sight. Not quite enough to get me hard, but enough to knock me a notch above flaccid.

After enjoying one last moment of watching them, I walk off and continue my route through the club and touch base with the staff working tonight. Apex has several rules laid in place for staff. One of those rules allows employees to join in on the festivities within the club, but only under strict guidelines. With tonight being one of our busiest nights of the year, the guidelines were reiterated before we opened the doors.

All acts must be consensual for both parties. No ifs, ands, or buts.

You are an employee of the club, on the clock, and expected to work. So, if at any time you are needed, you must step away. Period.

Meeting clients outside our four walls is permitted, but caution must be exercised. They are paying clientele. If things go south with the arrangement outside the club, it is up to the employee to right the wrong. No exceptions.

To date, we have had zero issues with the policy.

"Hey Tink," I holler over the music as I approach the bar. "Doing alright?"

"Yeah. But fuck if it's not busy as shit tonight."

Tink started at Apex in February. Although she has worked several major holiday events since she started, New Year's Eve always draws the largest crowd. She may be bombarded with the never-ending drink orders, but she will be thanking the gods later.

"True. Just wait until you count your tips. You'll beg for every night to be New Year's Eve," I tell her.

Tink throws me a half smile as she pours a line of shots. "You're probably right."

"Anything I can do to help?"

She shakes her head. "Nah, I'm good. Just keep 'em buying, boss."

I nod and settle on the barstool near the wall. At least once per shift, I park here and scan the club. Since the bar takes up a chunk of this corner, I have a great vantage point for most of the club. Everything in Apex is open. With no closed-off rooms. No displays to shadow people in corners. The dim lighting may provide a sense of security to several of the patrons, but I have worked here long enough to see everything around me like a predator in the night.

Just as I finish my visual circuit of the club, I stop when I spot a young brunette at the opposite end of the bar. Her face unfamiliar, but one I would remember without question.

I remain rooted on my stool and observe her a few minutes. Clad in a form-fitted red lace dress, her skin visible beneath the intricate pattern, I notice flesh-colored pasties on her nipples. *Wonder what lies hidden beneath the bar, between her legs.* Her wavy, russet hair frames her round face and black-rimmed glasses and falls inches beneath her shoulders. In a studious way, she is fucking adorable.

After a minute, I wave Tink over. "What's her story?" I ask, jutting my chin toward the woman. The brunette has yet to talk to anyone near her and it fascinates me. *She* fascinates me.

Tink chuckles as if privy to top secret information. Or perhaps at my curiosity. "As far as I can tell, it's her first time here. And she came alone. Tried sparking a conversation with her, but she didn't seem keen on talking."

I nod. "Thanks. She seems a bit out of her element. I'll check on her in a minute."

Tink walks off to pour another drink and mumbles, "I'm sure you will."

Another minute or two passes, and no one approaches her. I abandon my stool and head toward the brunette who holds my interest captive. With each step forward, heat tugs at my cock. Something about this woman stirs at the animal inside me. An animal that begs to come out and play more often than I allow.

When I reach her, I lean in close, rest my hand on her forearm, and drag in the smell of her. A soft floral perfume tickles my nose while a jolt sparks beneath my hand on her skin. A power grid straight to my groin.

"Hey, gorgeous. I'm Rick, manager of Apex. Wanted to introduce myself as I haven't seen you in here before."

She peers down at my hand a second, then lifts her gaze to meet mine. A pair of steel blue tornados shielded by her glasses. Naughty teacher and dirty librarian fantasies zap through my mind, one after another.

Fuck.

"Christy," she says in a whimsical tone. "Tonight's my first time." After a beat, she adds, "Here. My first time here." As if I thought otherwise.

"Welcome. You alone?"

Not that it was out of character, but most women didn't come to Apex unescorted. Christy is safe here, but it wouldn't be difficult to be whisked off by an undesirable. Every once in a while, they slip in unnoticed.

After a sip of her raspberry cosmopolitan, she nods. As I suspected.

"Finish your drink. Then I'll show you around," I tell her. Not necessarily a command, but a strong suggestion. Something tells me she isn't opposed to such demands.

Christy locks eyes with me for one, two, three breaths. Her stormy eyes brimming with questions. The moment her gaze drops to my mouth and she swallows, I have my answer. But like a proper gentleman, I wait for verbal acceptance.

Without preamble, she throws back the remainder of her drink. "Ready when you are."

Quite telling. Color me intrigued.

Stepping away from her stool, I offer her my elbow. She hooks her arm in mine and I weave us through the crowd. Inside Apex, there is no way to gradually introduce someone to the scene. Some couples are more vanilla than others, but there is no escape from the fact Apex is what it is. A sex club. An elite underground sex club. Not just anyone can get in here, so I wonder how she managed.

"Christy, who invited you to Apex?" Management, staff, and VIP clientele are the only individuals capable of inviting non-members.

"This is going to sound ridiculous," she says with a giggle. *Fuck me running.* Her giggle stirs my cock from its slumber. "A woman I work with invited me. We hung out and went shopping," she pauses and makes this adorable goofy face, "and I wanted to go into the lingerie store. She asked if I planned to wear it for someone, and I said no. That sometimes I liked to put on sexy lingerie, take photos of myself, and post them in a chat room. I never show my face, though."

My expression stoic, I ask, "So you enjoy being watched?" If she says yes, I may just come in my pants.

"Yes and no." Close enough. "I've only ever been

'watched' online through posted images. Never a live feed. And never in person. I'm a bit nervous being here."

"Why the nerves? Everyone is here for similar reasons. And there are rules inside these walls. Strict rules." She has no need for fear. Not here. No one does.

"Performance anxiety, I suppose? What if some weirdo pushes himself onto me and things happen I don't want?"

"That will never happen here," I state firmly.

Christy nods. "Glad to hear." Her free hand goes to her hair and she twirls a lock around a finger. "I guess I'm just nervous to do something new."

I stop us in front of a large, round leather ottoman. Four people perform together. A man on his back at the base fucks the woman above him in the pussy. On his knees behind the pair is a man claiming her ass. Standing before her is a third man, who continually pounds his cock down her throat. The four of them have a rhythm all their own. As a voyeur, it is comparable to watching sexual poetry in the flesh.

Out of the corner of my eye, I gaze at Christy to catch her reaction. Part of me is surprised and another not so much.

Christy inches forward, eyes fixated on the act. Her tongue darts out and swipes her bottom lip before she swallows hard. Arm still hooked with mine, her muscles contract as she leans a little closer. Hungry for more. And I want to give her more. So much more.

We stand and watch the group another minute before I speak up. "Come with me."

When she takes a breath, I realize how statuesque her body stood beside me while watching. After she snaps out of her haze, she nods and I walk us away from the foursome. Attached to my side like she belongs there, she inhales sharply halfway across the club floor. If I didn't know any better, I would say she is working to regulate her breathing, undetected. But even through the buzz from her body to mine and the heavy bass of the music vibrating the floor, I pick up on every single detail. Call it a gift.

We reach the roped-off VIP area and step inside. Everything within VIP is visible to the entire club, but only select members have permission to walk past the red velvet ropes. And only a set number of invitations are given. Within VIP, it is less crowded and less invasive. More space to breathe while you enjoy the club. Although all patrons can see you, no one ogles. Call it exposed privacy.

I walk us to a vacant couch and sit us down. Beside me, Christy peers around. Not only is VIP somewhat secluded, it also bodes "accessories." Toys. Implements. Various surfaces, furniture, and swings. Every molecule inside me screams to ask what she thinks of it all. But I hold my composure and wait for her to speak up.

And I don't wait long. Less than a minute passes after we sit and she asks, "Why did you bring me in here?"

She doesn't face me but instead stares at a woman who rides one man's cock and sucks another's. Christy appears more curious than taken aback. This delights me more than imaginable.

I trace her arm, bicep to fingertips, and she shifts her attention to me. "Because it's less chaotic in VIP. From what I can tell, this scene is new to you. I'd rather you not be overwhelmed on your first visit."

After a moment, she squares her shoulders and sits taller. "You speak as if I'll return. What makes you so confident?"

"Everything about you begs for more. The way you lean in to absorb what you see. Your fevered skin and rapid breathing. How you clutch me closer when you're turned on."

"Hmm," she mumbles. "Well, I'd have to be invited or become a member to return. And seeing as I'm not able to become a member—"

"You're a member. Just a matter of semantics. But I'll handle it before you leave."

Her stormy blue eyes spin like a hurricane and I get lost at sea. Taking a risk, I continue tracing my fingers along her body. From her hand onto her knee, I inch my way up her bare thigh. Her lips part as her chest rises and falls in rapid succession. *Has she never been touched like this?*

I stop my trek to heaven and ask, "No offense, but are you a virgin?"

Eyes wide, she verbally slaps me. "What?! No! Why would you ask me that?"

"Wasn't trying to upset you. But your reaction to my touch is indicative."

Christy rolls her eyes. "Well, I'm not a virgin. Sorry to disappoint," she huffs. "Maybe no one has ever let me feel things during sex."

This confuses me for a second. Does she mean no one has touched her except for sticking their dick in her? Or that she has never experienced foreplay? Or, worst of all, has she never orgasmed from sex?

"Care to elaborate?"

With another huff, she says, "Most of the people I've had sex with did what was best for them and didn't reciprocate."

I reach up with my free hand and tip her chin up, locking her gaze with mine. "That will never happen with me."

She sucks in a breath. "How can you be so sure?"

"Because I'm not a prick. Your pleasure is my pleasure." An absolute truth. I lean my face closer to hers as my fingers slowly graze her thigh. With my lips an inch above hers, I whisper, "Can I kiss you?"

My fingers skim the edge of her lacy dress, just at the junction of her thighs. If I moved north another half an inch, I would graze her nude lace panties. Without a doubt, they would be drenched.

"Yes," she whispers, eyes locked on mine.

I crash my lips to hers and she opens up for me—her lips and legs. In a heartbeat, I stroke her tongue with mine and slide my hand the rest of the way up her thigh. Both sets of lips hot and slick and eager for my touch.

Continuing to fuck her mouth with mine, I trace my fingers up and down her lace panties, coating my fingers with her juices. After the third swipe down, she rocks her hips forward in invitation.

I groan against her lips before pushing her panties to the side. Before another second passes, the slick heat between her thighs coats my fingertips. My middle finger circles her clit once, twice, and then dips between her folds. Fuck. So hot and wet and eager for me. I slip my finger out and play with her clit a moment.

Within minutes, her red lacy dress inches higher and higher up her body. Legs spread wide for me, she beckons and I slip off the couch, sit on my haunches on the floor between her thighs, and worship her pussy with my mouth.

After she comes with my mouth on her, I tug the red lace off her body and lay her down. She rubs her hands up and down her body a second before she starts playing with her clit.

As quickly as humanly possible, I strip my clothes and grab a condom from my pants. After I roll the condom on, I kneel down between her legs and slam inside her. She cries out beneath me as I rear back and slam forward again. Her breasts bounce and I glance down to see the pasties still in place. I rip them both away and she cries out again, her cunt wetter.

I lift one of her legs to rest it on my shoulder as I lean forward, plow into her, and suck her nipples. Her hands fist my hair and yank me down to her lips. The way we kiss and fuck is vicious and insane and I never want it to end.

Her breathing shifts into high-pitched cries as her walls clamp down and milk my cock. Un-fucking-believable. I have always been in control during sex, but Christy rips the control away and I come before I can stop myself.

I collapse on top of her and she wraps all four limbs around me. Previous partners are no comparison to the woman below me. There is a purity about her—a virginity to this life—that magnetizes her to me. It is undeniable, and I ache for more. Of her and what we could be together.

"So," I heave. "When can I see you again?"

PART
one

June — Four years later

"I UNDERSTAND why you're moving, but does it have to be across the freaking country, bitch?" I whine to my best friend, Sarah.

Less than two months ago, one of our coworkers—who shall remain nameless—attacked and molested Sarah. For months, he had sent her anonymous gifts and notes. And we will truly never know how long he had been stalking her. Maybe since the day she started at Hammond Life. A shiver rolls down my spine at the notion.

Rick and I have been exposed to a lot of people in our lifestyle. Most of them respectful and respectable. If someone ever did to us what happened to Sarah, I'm not sure I would have it in me to be so vulnerable with others again.

"It sucks to move so far away," Sarah says as she hugs me. "But I need to get as much distance between me and Georgia as possible. I can't breathe here anymore."

I nod. I get where she is coming from. If I were in her shoes, Rick and I would have left as soon as possible too. But over two thousand miles away… not so sure about that.

"Bitch, I feel like I'll never see you again." *God,* why the hell am I such an emotional baby today? Maybe it is my godforsaken hormones.

"Are you kidding me? Of course we'll see each other

again. You're my best friend. That doesn't end because I'm moving."

Point made. But I can't seem to help myself. With Sarah and Jackson—her boyfriend—moving away, it feels as if I'm losing a chunk of my family. My family is small enough as is, I can't lose any more of it.

"Yeah, you're right," I say. "Rick and I will have to plan a trip out to see you guys after you're settled." I peer over at Rick, who is helping Jackson haul larger pieces of furniture from the house to a moving truck outside. He pops a half-smile and winks at me.

Damn, I love him.

"Plus, we'll talk on the phone all the time. No chance in hell you're escaping me." Sarah laughs and I join in. I was so lucky to have a friend like Sarah. Unfortunately, I haven't been able to share all aspects of my life with her. In context, not physically. That ship sailed a while ago.

We finish packing the contents of her kitchen cabinets, then move on to the spare bedroom. It serves as an office and guest room. There isn't much in the room to pack other than the desk contents and two overflowing bookshelves worth of books.

The rest of the packing goes by quick and their house is an empty shell before nightfall. Sarah and Jackson plan on staying with Liz and Tiffany tonight, after their going-away party, and driving out in the morning. As gracious as Liz was to offer hosting the party, I suggested it be at my and Rick's place. That way, if Sarah and Jackson were ready to call it a night, the party wouldn't keep them up. Liz agreed without hesitation.

Liz—my other best friend—recently started dating Tiffany. Tiffany is super sweet and clicks with all of us, like we have known her years instead of months. Before Sarah met Jackson, I suspected Sarah and Liz had a fling going because I caught them making out. More than once. But the topic was never broached by any of us. Oftentimes, I contemplated bringing up Rick and my lifestyle with them, just to have it out in the open, but there was never a time that felt right. So, I kept it bottled up.

The guys join us in the vacant living room and Rick traces

his fingers down my spine before gripping my hip and drawing me into his side. Every time he touches me, a new star burns in the night sky.

"Let's all grab dinner, then head to the party," Rick says.

I press the side button on my cell and check the time. Three hours until the festivities begin. It won't be as lux as Liz's parties, but it will be a good time. "Sounds good." Glancing between Sarah and Jackson, I toss out, "It's your last night here. Where do you want to go?"

They stare at each other a minute, smile, then say, "Barbecue." In sync, like Liz and I did to mess with Sarah months ago. Memories…

"Barbecue it is," I say, laughing.

* * *

"Besides you guys, I am really going to miss the food here," Sarah says from the passenger seat. The guys behind us— Rick driving the moving truck with Jackson's car in tow, and Jackson driving Sarah's car. Which is an interesting sight—a six-foot one, muscular man behind the wheel of a Beetle. Definitely worth a laugh.

"Well at least I get priority over the food," I say, giggling. "You're my best bitch. You know that, right?"

Sarah nods, her eyes welling. "Yeah."

A few minutes later, we park outside our place. We have about an hour before everyone arrives, but I know Liz will be here any minute. Her inner party planner wouldn't have it any other way.

We shuffle inside and start setting up the snacks and drinks. I barely have the cups on the kitchen island before Liz and Tiffany arrive. So freaking predictable. Liz goes to Sarah first, picks her up off the ground, and squeezes the life out of her. Swear to god Liz holds her for an eternity. Did she forget the rest of us were in the room? Her girlfriend included.

I throw my arms wide open and clear my throat. "Am I invisible, bitch?"

Liz and Sarah laugh hysterically before Liz sets Sarah down, they run at me, and tackle me to the ground. "You know we love you," Liz says. "Sarah just gets extra hugs tonight. Don't be jealous."

"Yeah, yeah," I tease.

When I glance over at Rick, a smolder darkens his liquid honey eyes. In an instant, my thighs dampen and lungs heave. An invisible, impulsive chemistry has always existed between us. A bond so powerful, words do it no justice. I reach up and run my fingers over the thin, silver collar around my neck. To an onlooker, the shiny silver is just a unique necklace. Solid with a hinge on one side and a lock on the other. Snug, but not a choker. A small loop on the front most would think is for pendants. But is far from it.

Rick's eyes drop to my throat—my collar—and a wicked gleam shines on his face. The kind that soaks my panties. He clasps his right thumb with his left fingers and toys with the thick, black band. My lips part centimeters and I breathe a little heavier. Simple gestures between us sometimes spark the hottest flames.

Two-and-a-half years ago, just before Rick and I moved in together, he gifted me the collar. In return, I gave him the ring. An effortless exchange, but it meant so much more to us. We were nowhere near ready for marriage—if I'm honest, we still aren't—but the two tokens were representative of our bond to each other. An unbreakable bond.

"Did you hear me?" Liz asks.

I shake my head. "Sorry. What?"

"There's someone at the door. Want me to get it?"

"Sure. We should just put a sign up that says come on in," I joke.

An hour later, our apartment overflows with bodies and the party is in full swing. I haven't seen Rick in a while, but I sense him nearby. His proximity always pops up on my radar. Even the night we met. Rick's soul was a beacon calling out to me.

The music changes—Liz, of course, in charge of music— and my body vibrates to the beat. Before I scan the room, a familiar pair of arms wrap around my waist as his body presses flush against my back. "Hey, gorgeous."

"Mmm, hey." Rick skims his hands up and down my torso, openly fondling me. "Where've you been?" I groan.

"Did you miss me?" he asks before licking the shell of my ear.

"Always," I murmur, grinding my ass against his groin.

"Patience, gorgeous. When the party ends, the real fun begins."

I spin around and stare at him a moment. "Really? Who?" I whisper-ask as if someone will hear our conversation over the music.

Rick hauls my body back to his, slips a leg between mine, and grinds against me to the music. I lace my fingers behind his neck and dance with him. He won't answer me immediately, this much I know. Dragging out the anticipation is part of the pleasure.

When the song ends, he kisses me. He sucks my bottom lip before nipping it and kissing his way to my ear. "Tim and Jill are here," he says.

I moan loud enough for Rick to hear, but no one else over the music. We have only been with Tim and Jill one other time, but it was phenomenal. And suddenly, as eager as I am to spend time with my friends, I want the party to end. Rick senses my mood shift and chuckles.

As if I voiced my desires aloud, several people start leaving. Twenty minutes later, Sarah and Jackson approach me and Rick and say their goodbyes. A lengthy process, but hugs and promises to stay in touch are exchanged. When Sarah, Jackson, Liz, and Tiffany walk out the door, the only people left in the room with us are Tim and Jill.

A scorching fire brushes over my lips as Rick kisses me with unrestrained fervor, his fingers slowly peeling my clothes away. Behind me, Jill and Tim grope one another in similar fashion. Both men still fully dressed. Standing exposed before him, I sigh as Rick strokes his fingertip side to side just above the junction of my thighs with his eyes locked on mine. A dark amber mixes with his honey eyes the more he brushes against my skin. Pausing for a micro blip of time, he draws a line with his finger up my midline, starting at my shaved mound and stopping at my collar. When he reaches the cool metal, he hooks a finger under the silver and tugs me to him.

"Remember who you belong to, gorgeous."

"Always," I tell him.

"Remember who I belong to."

"Yes," I breathe.

He releases me and I spin around to face Jill. Face to face, we are all hands and fingers. Touching and teasing and kissing. A woman's skin is much softer and delicate, and the smooth flesh under my fingertips drives me to explore her terrain. Meanwhile, her fingers drift down, down, down and tease my pussy folds as I pinch her nipples.

Jill has bite-size breasts. Maybe somewhere between an A cup and a B. Not too much, but enough to play with. Unlike my full Cs, which annoy me at times, Jill has the luxury of going braless as often as she pleases.

Her lips break away from the skin above my collarbone and she leans forward to whisper in my ear. "Enjoy fucking my husband again." And then she dips her finger once, twice inside me before walking over to Rick with the taste of me on her tongue.

Tim steps up to me, his t-shirt and khaki shorts securely in place. He traces a line along my jaw with a finger before tipping my chin up and kissing down the curve of my throat. His lips on my sensitive skin amplifying the fire Jill ignited between my legs.

Rick and I have strict rules when with other people. In this life, our rules set boundaries and keep the lines from blurring. The rules are black and white, but there is always space for gray.

First and foremost, no kissing on the mouth. Ever. The act an intimacy only we share. Second, no talking during the act other than guidance, praise, or permission. The reason behind our lifestyle isn't to form intimate connections with other people. It is lust and hunger and a desire to fuck. Plain and simple. Intimacy is saved for when we are alone. Third, if someone does something we don't enjoy, it stops immediately. No ifs, ands, or buts. And last but certainly not least, Rick and I always remain in the same room during every act. Not that we distrust one another, but more so we can enjoy ourselves and protect one another. Baring yourself completely to another person puts you in a vulnerable position. Safety is vital.

After everything that happened with Sarah and her stalker over the last six months, Rick and I tightened our rules and enforced them with everyone who we allowed to step foot into our sex play. If couples were uncomfortable or unable to abide by our rules, we bid them farewell. Nowadays, there is no such thing as being overprotective. Honestly, you never know who is batshit crazy anymore.

Tim kisses along my collarbone as his fingertips dance down my arms, leaving a buzz in their wake, and land on my hips. I reach forward and pop the button open on his shorts, slowly pushing down the zipper. After the slider trails down the teeth to the stopper, his shorts slip down his thick glutes and thump on the hardwood. Beneath, Tim flashes his commando status with pride, and, for a second, part of me wonders if Rick set up tonight with Tim and Jill before the party. Tim seems awfully prepared. And I can't recall if he was bare last time. Not that it matters.

I wrap my hand around his cock and glide up once, twice, before I fondle his balls in my grip and drop to my knees. Behind me, Jill sucks Rick's cock like a gold medalist. Rick fists her hair tight and pumps into her with unmatched vigor.

Tim strips his shirt and tosses it to the side as I suck one of his balls into my mouth and play with it while I stroke him. I pop it out of my mouth and lick the underside of his cock, root to tip, before taking it all in my mouth. The head of his cock hits the back of my throat and I relax my muscles as I bob my head up and down.

Jill's ass brushes against mine, neither of us stops sucking the other man's dick, and I reach between my legs and feel for her pussy. The moment I touch her wet lips, she moans. *So fucking wet.* I slip a finger inside her and she rides me a beat while she face fucks Rick.

In no time, Jill comes on my finger. Her juices coat and run down my finger and onto my hand. Once she drifts back to earth, we stop sucking the guys and climb on the bed. With Jill on her back, head at the edge of the bed, I mount her, press my core against her lips, then lick the length of her slit and suck her taut clit. Breaking my mouth away, I dip two fingers in her cunt as Rick steps up and grabs my hair.

"Suck me, gorgeous," he purrs.

With Rick on my tongue, my fingers inside Jill, and Jill's mouth on my clit, my body goes into stimulus overload. Or so I thought. That is until Tim clutches both my ass cheeks and spreads them wide. *What happens next?* My silent question answered when Tim licks from my clit to the clenched opening between my ass cheeks and circles the tight hole over and over.

My eyes roll back in my head and I forget how to breathe for a split second. White heat lights up every atom in my body. Too much and not enough, all at the same time. Not sure when or how it happened, but somehow I became the center of attention in our foursome. For some reason, everyone wants to contribute to my pleasure. And I won't complain while it happens.

"Such a tight little hole," Tim says behind me as he continues to swirl his tongue over the puckered flesh between my cheeks. "Can I fuck you here?" He lifts his mouth, presses a finger to the center, and pushes in slightly. I gasp around Rick's cock and push back into the pressure.

"Yes," I moan.

Rick tips my chin up before I take his cock again, his eyes intently studying mine to be certain this is what *I* want. The seconds that pass feel timeless. I nod and so does he. Part of our unspoken language. Not just in the bedroom. It came natural to us and formed the night we met, growing stronger with time. Rick knows my boundaries—just as I know his—and when to check in.

Tim coats my rim with my arousal before he dips his cock in my pussy once, twice. *Fuck, he is big.* "Just relax your muscles," Tim says as he grips my hips firmly. A second later, he is there. Cock pressing forward as the hole contracts against the pressure. Jill swipes my clit in small, slow circles, running her finger over my folds every other revolution. In front of me, Rick cups my face in his palm as he strokes my cheek. Rick is what soothes me enough to grant Tim access. No one settles or spikes my heartbeat like Rick.

Once Tim pushes forward, I gasp at the rush of sensation coursing throughout my body. Lust and pain and immense pleasure. A slight burning around the edges until a dollop of moisture coats his skin. He slides out slowly to the crown, then glides back in. Rick's eyes locked with mine, I see an insatiable hunger ignite them. I suck up and down his length for three strokes, peek up at him, and silently tell him to fuck Jill.

A curt nod and Rick retrieves Jill out from under me. He flips her on her stomach and yanks her ass into the air. I refuse to look away as he strokes himself before rolling a condom on and teasing Jill's pussy with the head of his cock. A second later, he thrusts forward and she screams.

Tim bends over me, wraps one arm around my hips and the other at my breasts. He plunges into my ass over and over as he swipes his fingers over my clit. "So fucking wet," he groans. I whimper as he circles my clit again and again, then inserts two fingers inside me.

Jill cries out, her orgasm hitting her quick. But I know Rick isn't done. He can go forever before release. He dips between her thighs and laps at her juices, building her up again with his fingers and tongue. Before I've reached my first orgasm with Tim, Rick has given Jill two and a sense of deprivation washes over me.

Sensing my temperament, Rick abandons Jill for a moment and finagles himself beneath me. Tim stops for a beat, realizing what's happening, and gives Rick a moment. Once situated beneath me, Rick tears off the condom and slips inside my cunt.

A slow rhythm starts. Rick in, Tim out. Tim in, Rick out. Like a seesaw, back and forth. I relax my weight on Rick and he wraps his arms around me before he grabs my ass cheeks and spreads them farther apart.

Rick and Tim work my body like a well-oiled machine as every molecule in my body climbs higher, higher, higher. The hunger and fire raging inside me is intense and addictive and intoxicating. I groan into Rick's neck before I bite his shoulder.

"Feel it all, gorgeous," he whispers in my ear. "Do you know how unbelievably stunning you are right now? Letting someone fuck that tight little ass of yours, and me fucking this pussy. *My pussy.*"

I groan louder. When Rick talks dirty, it dumps gasoline on the bonfire low in my belly.

"You know what would make this hotter, gorgeous? Fucking you while watching this over and over again."

"Yes," I cry out.

Jill, who sits near the pillows finger fucking herself while watching the three of us, gets up and grabs Rick's phone. He unlocks it and opens the camera for her. "If you're okay with it," Rick says to Jill and Tim. "We can set it on the dresser and record. Unless you don't want your face in it."

"Don't care," Tim grunts out. He is so close—the thickening of his cock tells me so—but holds out for my orgasm.

Jill gets the phone set up on the dresser after hitting record and returns to the bed. As Rick and Tim continue to fuck me, she straddles Rick's face and I suck her breasts. Jill rides Rick's face like she's at a rodeo and soon the pitch of her cries changes. She's close again. Rick slips his hand between us and plays with my clit.

Balls slap my skin, cocks piston in and out, Rick circles faster and harder with his fingers. It builds so quick, and I clamp down hard on Jill's nipple. She orgasms on Rick's face as I explode around Rick and he comes inside me. Before a scream escapes my lips, Tim detonates. Both men pulsing inside my body as I visibly vibrate from my orgasm.

"Holy shit," I gasp. "Fucking intense." My voice garbled and skin tingling.

Jill dismounts from Rick's face and I kiss him, tasting her salty tang on his tongue. Slowly, Tim pulls out of me, but Rick and I don't separate. He remains inside me and semi-hard as we kiss the hell out of each other. Right now, I hope Jill and Tim get dressed and leave.

A zipper grates beside us. Feet shuffle on the wood. Rick and I remain connected in every possible way. A moment later, the front door clicks and it is just the two of us.

I sit up, plant my hands on his pecs, and start rocking my hips over him. "Tim not do it for you, gorgeous?"

Back and forth. Back and forth. "Not like you," I tell him as I bring my hands to my breasts and pinch my nipples.

Rick grabs my hips as he hardens inside me. "Tell me what you want, gorgeous."

I bite my lip, grinding down on him. "Fuck my ass."

He reaches around and plays with my hole. "You sure, kitten? You sure it's not tired?" he coos.

I love it when he calls me kitten. That is when I know he holds full control and I am at his beck and call. "I'm sure, Daddy. Fuck my pretty little ass."

He pinches one of my nipples and twists. "Only after you come on daddy's cock pretty kitten." Rick lays back and I press my hands against his chest and ride him until I scream out in pleasure. Then he flips me on my back, grabs a vibrator from the drawer under our bed, turns it on and inserts it in my pussy, and guides himself in my tight hole.

"So tight, kitten." A moment later, my legs are over his shoulders and he's hovering an inch above me, fucking my ass hard.

"Oh, god," I moan. Within seconds, he has me feeling a thousand times more than what Tim did. "I need to come, daddy."

He clutches my shoulders and fucks me harder, faster. With my whines and his grunts, it will be soon. "I'm there, kitten. Let go, gorgeous."

Hot seed floods my ass as I explode around the vibrator. Rick leans back, yanks it out, and runs his fingers up and down my soaked slit. "Who does this belong to, kitten?"

"You, daddy."

"Remember that."

"Always."

TWO

RICK

I WAKE to Christy's bare flesh draped over my body. Leaning my head away, I stare and get lost at the sight of her. *Fuck, she is unbelievable.* How in the hell did I get so lucky? How did I nail down the perfect woman? I am one lucky son of a bitch, that is how. The first night she walked into Apex, it could have been my night off. She could have met someone else. Or left alone after finishing her drink.

But it didn't happen that way. Thank fuck.

The night my eyes landed on Christy, it was as if a light-house lamp lit up and pointed her out to me. Before her, I had been with my share of beautiful creatures, and done countless acts with faceless women and men. But Christy is different for me. Although she is still quite tame in the grand scheme of things, she has an unavoidable radiance I refuse to ignore.

She is a beacon. *My beacon.*

"Quit it," she mumbles and giggles in her sleep. I scan over her face—lips perked up slightly, strands of hair lay haphazardly over her eye, along the side of her nose, and drop off her chin. Even asleep, she is perfection. Wonder what she is dreaming about? Hopefully something involving us.

I wrap my arms a little tighter around her and hold her close. Her all too familiar fragrance pierces my nose and I inhale deep. Peonies and amber and all Christy.

On the first night, I had been skeptical. My radar had failed me in the past and led me down paths I hope to never see again. Sitting at the bar, Christy sipped her drink—so innocent and timid. Her red lace dress screamed for attention while her body language stated the polar opposite. Lucky for me, my radar didn't malfunction with her and I followed Christy's lead. Every day since that moment, she has surprised me time and again. Last night included.

I have tested the water with Christy several times. There were still so many things I wanted to do with her. Claiming her ass being one of them. It sat on a long list with items slowly being tick-marked. My hesitation to try some of them stems from her lack of experience. But after last night, my level of hesitation is slowly going out with the tide.

Tim may have dipped his cock in before me, but he doesn't have what it takes to get my girl off. And that tells me Christy is, and always will be, mine. As I am hers. Sure, we fuck other couples and have a good time. But no one gets my dick harder or makes me come like a god the way Christy does.

After kissing the crown of her head, I strategically slip out from under her and off the bed. Slipping on a pair of boxers, I shut the bedroom door and head to the kitchen. My girl deserves a big breakfast after last night's festivities.

Just as I set the last strip of bacon on a paper towel, the familiar shuffle-thump of Christy's morning strut enters the kitchen. Before I have the chance to spin and face her, her hands hit my hips and skim around my front side, scratching their way to my pecs. I close my eyes as they roll back into my head. Her touch generates a low-lying hum in my veins I would die without. A jolt of life.

"Mmm, smells so good in here," she mumbles against my back before pressing a kiss between my shoulder blades.

"Bacon, eggs, and blueberry pancakes." I grip her hands, lift them, then turn to face her. "Coffee?" I ask the question, although I already know the answer. But why pass up the opportunity to mess with her.

"Is that even a legitimate question?" She rolls her eyes. "Coffee. Please." Christy pads out of the kitchen. "Gotta brush my teeth. Be right back."

If there is one truth in this life, it is that I know my girl. Her routine. The fact that she isn't, and never will be, a morning person until at least eight ounces of coffee is in her system. How she loves her eggs cooked—over medium, so she can poke the yolk and slather it on the egg white. Sometimes she likes to dunk her toast in the yolk, but it varies by day. And how undying her love is for me.

Love… it was never a territorial line I wished to cross. But, within months of meeting Christy, my desensitized heart thumped again. Even in my youth, I had never "loved" anyone other than family. But even the familial love slipped away. Christy knew I only spoke with my parents two or three times a year, during the holidays, but I never told her an in-depth reason why. Not that I don't want to. I do. And one day I will, but I still can't bring myself to say the words. When the time is right, it will pour out of me.

Christy has hinted to me about her family here and there, but just breadcrumbs. And I refuse to pry. Our bond travels boundaries I never imagined possible. When she is ready to let go of her pain, she will. And she will deliver it to me—the guardian of her heart. But I admire her strength and courage. Not everyone rises easily from the ashes. It takes guts and resilience and fire. Qualities my girl harnesses like a goddess.

Just as I pour maple syrup on the pancakes, she swoops in next to me and dives for the coffeepot, filling her mug to the brim. Three, two, one… "Ahhh," she sighs with the mug to her lips after her first gulp. "Thank you." She pushes up on her toes and I lean down and kiss her.

"You're welcome, gorgeous."

I carry our plates to the table and we plop down and eat. When she hits the bottom of her coffee, I automatically get up and grab the pot and bring it to her with the cream and sugar caddy. Her smile beams so full of life, I breathe a little faster. Every day it amazes me how one woman is capable of owning my heart for eternity.

When our plates are empty, I broach a topic I am certain won't sit well with her. "Gorgeous?"

She swallows the gulp of coffee in her mouth. "Yeah?"

"There's no good time to talk about this, but we need to talk about how we're going to handle other couples going forward." Christy tilts her head and furrows her brow. God, she is adorable as fuck. "After what happened with Sarah, I want to be sure we're being as safe as possible."

Understanding settles in her stormy eyes and she nods. "I wondered about that," she says, twirling a lock of hair.

"Going forward, I'd like to look into anyone entering our bedroom. Or us entering theirs. Even people we've been with. We can't be too safe."

"Agreed. What can I do?"

I reach for her hand and take it in mine. For two breaths, I stare at our joined hands and relish in the love I have for this woman. "Let me know if anything off-putting comes up. Tell me who catches your eye. It'd be nice to see new people, but I don't want us unprepared." Stroking small circles on her palm, I bring her hand to my lips and kiss the center. "What happened to Sarah… that *will not* happen to you."

For a beat, a solemn expression flits across her face. But as quickly as it appears, it vanishes. "You'll keep me safe. Never doubted that for a minute."

I kiss her palm again. "Enough with the heavy conversation. What would you like to do today?" And when her face lights up, I have done my job. Fuck, I love her.

After a two-hour walk through the aquarium and some lunch, we head home. With the day half gone, I head straight for the bedroom and get ready for work. Although Apex doesn't open until eight at night, there is prep to be done. Helping restock the bar. Sanitizing the entire venue. Checking all implements and equipment for safety reasons. We also have a small menu of appetizers, so minor kitchen prep has to be finished.

Usually, I arrive around six in the evening and leave between two-thirty and three in the morning. It's a long day, especially now when the northerners aren't here. But I love my job. By no means is it glamorous—to people who care about glamour—but I am in my element and it never feels like work.

Besides, I would have never met Christy if not for Apex.

I slide up the knot on my merlot red tie and fold down the

black collar of my dress shirt. Honestly, the only dress code at work is to be presentable and polished. A button-down and no tie would be completely acceptable, but it comes off too casual for me.

As I put my keys, wallet, and phone in my pockets, Christy walks into the room and whistles.

"Well, hot damn," she rasps. "I love it when you wear black and red." Another thing I know about my girl—the clothes she loves me in. She walks up to me and runs a hand down my tie, tugging it when she reaches the end.

"Careful, gorgeous." She bats her lashes at me. "Coming in tonight?" I ask.

"Yeah. Might see if Liz and Tiffany want to grab dinner first. I'll be in after."

I gaze into her stormy eyes, grab a lock of her hair, and play with it. "Whatever you want. Just let me know." She nods.

Since we helped Jackson and Sarah pack up their place yesterday, my girl hasn't been her usual bubbly self. Hopefully, her sadness will fade with time. Christy and Sarah are much closer than Christy and Liz. Their friendship started more than a year prior. And in that time, Christy and Sarah formed a sisterly bond. Once Sarah and Jackson reach California, and Christy talks with her more often, she will perk right up.

At least I hope she does.

THREE

CHRISTY

Liz and Tiffany agree to meet up for dinner. Thank god.

Today seems like a never-ending trek of loss and gloom. Sarah hasn't been gone twenty-four hours yet and it is as if someone stole a chunk of my family—and my heart—from me. The little bit of family I have left.

Generally, I resonate on the polar opposite of doom and misery. But with Sarah physically absent in our circle, I find it harder and harder to smile already. The misery won't last forever, but last time I lost family, I had friends ready to lift me up. People on the sidelines who jumped in and rescued me. Now, everyone has higher priorities in life besides making mopey little Christy feel better.

This fucking sucks.

I meet Liz and Tiffany at a small Italian restaurant not far from Apex. Another secret. All of my current friends believe Rick works in a restaurant/bar. Honestly, it is the easiest way to explain his weird work hours without sharing he manages a sex club. Anytime Sarah or Liz suggested we "go to Rick's restaurant" for dinner, I always made an excuse.

Just had dinner there last night.

Rick says they're swamped tonight.

Someone called in sick and he's super busy.

Blah, blah, blah.

Don't get me wrong, I love the life Rick and I enjoy together. Couldn't imagine our relationship any other way.

Sometimes, though, it would be nice to share that piece of myself with the people closest to me. To let those people who hold a piece of my heart know the real me. The me that hides who she is outside of specific walls.

But the repercussions of the last time I revealed the real me still scar me today. And I am nowhere near ready to travel down that road again. I refuse to lose anyone else I love because of who I am.

Sitting at a table for four, I twirl my fork and create craters in my napkin with the tines. So intently shredding the napkin, I startle when Liz and Tiffany walk up to the table and sit down across from me. Why the hell am I so spacey? And jumpy? So freaking annoying.

"Hey, girl," Liz says as she studies my face. "You alright?"

I plaster on my big girl smile and answer, "Of course. Just bored waiting for you guys to get here." My cheeks sting from my over-exaggerated smile.

Liz and Tiffany scoot farther into the red vinyl booth, the springs creaking under their weight. Hell, the worn booths would squeak with a thirty-pound toddler sitting on them. But this place is the best Italian restaurant in the area and no one cares how dated the décor is.

Before any of us gets in another word, the server approaches the table, rattles off the specials for the evening, and takes their drink orders. Less than a minute later, she steps off and promises to be back with drinks, fresh bread, and garlic-herb dipping oil.

The table is layered in a blanket of awkward silence as they both stare at the menu. Me? I have been here ten minutes and decided what I wanted nine minutes ago. So, I dig my napkin crater deeper and zone out. Nothing worse than staring at someone without reason. No need for me to make things more uncomfortable.

After the server drops off their drinks and the bread, she takes our orders and disappears again. Maybe she senses the strain on my heart and, by proxy, with Liz. With Sarah gone, Liz is the only close friend I have in my inner circle. But she has Tiffany, and they spend most of their time doing things together... without anyone else. Which is understandable in their newish relationship.

"You sure you're alright?" Liz asks.

I peer up at her from my Swiss cheese napkin and nod. "Sure. Why wouldn't I be?"

"Don't know. But I've never seen you so…"

"Glum," Tiffany chimes in.

Flipping fantastic. Am I really that transparent? Obviously, I wear my heart on my sleeve. Somehow, I need to reign that shit in quick. Last thing I need is to be doted on as the sad one in the group.

"Yes," Tiffany says.

"What?" I ask, unsure of what Tiffany is agreeing with.

Tiffany shakes her head. "You just asked if you were that transparent. And I said yes."

"Shit. Didn't mean to say that out loud."

Tiffany reaches across the table and sets her hand, palm side down, in front of me. "It's okay to be sad because one of your best friends moved away. You, Sarah, and Liz are like sisters. Honestly, it'd be weirder if you weren't sad. But don't bottle it up, okay? Let people know why you're down."

Not that I wanted Tiffany to be my therapist right now, but her insight helped. She had only been a part of our circle for a short time, so she knew the least about us all. An unbiased view. Which turned out to be a bonus in the current situation.

"I will, and thank you. Losing people is challenging for me. Especially those who are close."

"Losing people shouldn't be easy for anyone, sweetie," Tiffany says. For some reason, her term of endearment sits oddly with me. Maybe she is trying to pacify me. Whatever. I really don't have the energy to care right now.

With my brain a monsoon of thoughts, it is a wonder I can function at all. Thankfully, I am saved from potential word vomit when the server brings our meals. Over the next twenty minutes, we eat in silence. Liz slurps her spaghetti, as she always has, and Tiffany cuts her eggplant parmesan with precision. I expect nothing less.

Once we pay our tabs, we walk out together and part ways to head to our respective cars, but not before Liz gives me a huge hug. A hug that swallows me whole and tries to make up for the hugs I won't get from Sarah anytime soon. I wish I had a fraction of her enthusiasm right now. But she remains strong through all this because Tiffany stands to her right. How would Liz be if she came alone tonight? Would she be as miserable as me? After a quick hug with Tiffany, and promises to meet up soon, we go our separate ways.

Secure in my car, I fish out my phone and call Rick. I let him know I'm leaving the restaurant and headed to Apex. Occasionally, the constant checking in irritates the hell out of me. But we do it for a good reason. The same reason Sarah left. Because you never know what could happen between point A and B.

"Drive safe, gorgeous. See you soon."

Ten minutes later, I walk through the door at Apex and smile at the bouncer. "Evening, Ray. Been a good night?"

Ray is a burly, beefy teddy bear. The first time I met him, he scared the bejesus out of me. He towers a foot taller than my five-foot-five and has biceps bigger than my thighs. I was an ant beside him, and his combat boots could squash me in point-five seconds. But he also had the most charming smile and gave the best hugs. Everyone who worked inside these walls was family. It was impossible not to be. With the level of intimacy, safety, and trust required, how could a familial bond not form?

I may not work inside the walls of Apex, but everyone who did considered me family too. So, when Ray bends down, lifts me up, and gives me a hug—my feet dangling a foot off the floor—there is zero awkwardness between us. If anything, Ray is like the older, bigger brother I never had.

"Not too bad, Ms. Christy. You here to see boss man?"

"Yeah. Had dinner with some friends, and it ended sooner than expected."

I step away from Ray as we say our goodbyes. At least his booming nature brought a half-smile to my face. Apex seems quieter than usual tonight, but a decent crowd fills the walls. Weaving my way through a few groups, I sidle up to the bar and try to spot Rick. After a quick scan of the crowd, I land on him twenty feet away. He talks with a couple who look to be in their late forties/early fifties. A moment later, he glances toward the bar and nods for me to go to VIP.

Ordering a drink, I take it and head over to VIP and wait

for Rick. When I first started coming to Apex, it was strange to sit in here and just observe. I thought, *Do these people think I'm a perv or prude because I watch more than participate?* But over time, the worry fell away. I learned several people played voyeur now and again. Especially when bored with their day-to-day lifestyle.

Minutes later, Rick sits down beside me and presses a kiss to my lips. "Sorry you had to wait, gorgeous. New couple." New couples in the club always got the grand tour and were taught the rules and expected behaviors on night one. If they visited other clubs prior to Apex, my guess is the rules would be similar. But I honestly had no idea.

"No biggie. I was enjoying the view while I waited."

He scoops up my hand and brings my knuckles to his lips, kissing each one in turn. "How was dinner with Liz and Tiffany?"

I hunch my spine and huff. Silent a moment, I don't want to say I didn't enjoy spending time with them, but it was lackluster without Sarah. "Alright. Kinda blah, actually. We exchanged maybe five sentences with each other."

More kisses peppered across my knuckles. "I'm sorry, gorgeous. It's probably going to be off for a little while. But it'll get better. Promise."

I nod. God, I hope his words hold truth. Not having people I care about close by splinters my heart. For a few minutes, we sit on the couch. Me sipping my drink, and Rick with his arm draped over my shoulders and rubbing circles on my upper bicep. Such a soothing motion.

Rick runs his nose from the crown of my head to my ear, inhaling deep. "It's slow tonight, and I can take a break while you're here. It's been a while since we've put on a show." He pulls my earlobe between his lips and sucks. Soon, he kisses his way down my neck and I tip my head to the side to give him better access.

White hot heat sears my skin where he kisses me. It travels along my collarbone, from my shoulder to sternum and down between my breasts. Rick slides his hand up my thigh from my knee and my legs automatically open for him.

After many of our first nights together, I learned to love dresses more. With Rick, anytime we were together was an open invitation for intimacy. At home, in the club, out to dinner, or the movie theater. No matter where we went, I prepped for possibility. In my opinion, a girl can never be over prepared.

The tips of his fingers graze my folds and he hums in delight. "Naughty, naughty, kitten." I groan at my pet name. A name used only in this lifestyle. Only between us. "Did you forget to put panties on? Or did you leave them off on purpose?"

He dips the tip of his finger inside and I rock my hips. "On purpose, daddy. Knew it would please you."

Up and down. Circle, circle. Up, down, dip. I rock my hips again and he clucks his tongue at me. "Patience. First things first. Let's get more comfortable, shall we?"

My ribcage expands and contracts faster and faster. "Yes, please."

One by one, Rick unbuttons the front of my red dress. Not quite a sundress, yet not formal—somewhere in between. It hugs my curves and exposes just enough flesh to be flashy, but not trashy. When all the buttons are open, Rick exposes my bare skin to the world.

"Well, well, well. Looks like you forwent the bra as well. I'm not sure if I should punish or praise you, kitten."

Arousal slicks the skin between my thighs and I gyrate my hips as I run my hands up my body and caress my hips and belly and breasts. "Whatever daddy thinks is best."

A few couples in VIP watch us. And let's be honest here, most people stop to watch us. Not that Rick and I do anything as vivid and intense as others, but we have a bond. Our connection is like no other couple's in the room. Anyone can have sex in a room full of strangers. But exposing yourself, being one-hundred percent vulnerable, physically as well as emotionally, is not something you see all the time.

When our eyes connect, a hurricane swirls between us. Everything around us is obliterated. It is him, and me, and nothing in between.

Rick rises between my legs and begins unbuttoning his shirt, draping it over the back of the couch once he finishes. A moment later, his pants follow suit. Beneath his clothes, he is commando. Running my hands up his quads, I follow my line of sight and trace his body with my fingers. Flawless and pristine and not a lick of hair above his knees.

At his nipples, I twist a second before clawing my way down his abdomen. He hisses, "Careful, kitten." It sounds like a warning, but he craves the sting of my nails in his skin.

So, I apologize by leaning forward and kissing the tip of his cock. It jerks under my lips, so I do it again. And again. Until a moment later, I take him between my lips, swirl my tongue around the crown, and suck the head. Rick strokes my hair and whispers words of praise. His encouragement pushes me and I take him further into my mouth and throat. Before I realize it, my fingers slip between my legs and I circle my clit.

Before my body reaches the precipice, Rick breaks us apart. "Lay back, kitten."

I do as he says, spreading out against the wide, cool leather. As he studies me from head to toe, he strokes his cock. Enamored by the act, I miss it when he stops and invites two men to join us. When they step up to us, Rick whispers in their ears and they both nod in agreement. Rick has never had intercourse with another man—as far as I know—but I have watched him kiss and touch other men. So the moment he releases his cock and runs a hand down both their chests and grips their cocks, not an ounce of shock registers in my brain. If anything, my clit throbs harder.

The first man—a thin, clean-cut blond with the whole "boy next door" appeal—steps around to my legs. Number two—a stalky, professional-looking brute with rich brown hair—walks toward my head. Rick stays anchored at my midsection in admiration. As if they have done it a million times, the two men begin. One squats down, licks his way up my legs until his tongue laps at my folds. Two lowers himself slightly and dips his cock between my lips—I give him a slow tease of licks only on the head. I suck the crown of Two's cock like a lollipop, occasionally releasing it and watching it bounce above my lips before taking it again. Before long, One fucks me while Rick and Two stroke themselves and watch.

After One gives me an orgasm, Two takes his place and flips me over, jerks my hips up, and fucks me until I scream. Once they have had their fun with me, Rick sends them away and makes love to me, sweet and slow for all to see. Moments like these are the ones I lock up for safekeeping. When Rick treasures and worships me like a priceless artifact.

Once we are both spent, the length of his bare body lays unmoving atop mine. His chocolate-rimmed honey eyes lock with mine as he plays with my hair. "I love you, gorgeous. You never cease to amaze me."

A symphony plucks my heartstrings. "I love you, too." Out of left field, tears well in my eyes and a lump forms in my throat. I do my best to hide the emotion choking me, but it won't work. Rick is my own personal emotion detector.

His eyes dart between mine as he drops my hair. When his fingers paint a line along my cheekbone, I close my eyes and the traitor tears leak out. Soft and warm, Rick presses a delicate kiss on my lips. "What's wrong, gorgeous?"

My tears feel juvenile. The remnants of a sad, pathetic girl. But if I don't tell Rick what is on my mind, he will be glued to my side until I do. Only, I don't want to be teased. Picked on like a small child who feels betrayed. Better yet, I don't want him upset.

"It's stupid, really," I say, shaking my head slightly.

He kisses me again. "I doubt anything in your beautiful head is stupid."

I roll my eyes and chuckle. "Not so sure about that statement," I joke. After a deep breath and another reassuring glimpse from him, I voice my thoughts. "I was kinda thinking..." *Please don't think I'm stupid. Please don't hate me.* "That maybe we could move."

FOUR

RICK

Of all the things that could possibly come out of Christy's mouth, her telling me she wants us to move was the farthest from the list. What the hell.

I jerk my face away from hers and study every fine detail of her face. Her eyes simmer like a storm on the horizon. Lips tucked between her teeth. A timid tremble at her chin. Not only is she serious, but fear threads through her veins.

Dropping back down, I hover an inch above her face. I stroke her cheek and relish in the way her eyes roll back and close briefly before I kiss her. "You don't need to be afraid, gorgeous. I'll keep you safe. Swear on my life."

Another tear falls from her eye and it is a knife in the gut. She nods and says, "In my heart, I know you'll never let anyone hurt me." Breaking eye contact and staring off into the distance—away from me—she sniffles.

Something niggles my thoughts, and it dawns on me. What if this has nothing to do with Christy feeling unsafe? I automatically assume her safety is what bothers her. But now, I am not so sure. When I stroke her cheek again, her stormy blues come back to me. "Tell me," I whisper.

"God, I feel like such a fucking idiot," she says, inhaling deeply. Her eyes dart between mine as she wages war with herself on whether or not to continue. "I want to move because it feels like my family just left."

If that is not a slap to the face, I don't know what the hell else would be. I bolt off of her and redress without giving her another glance. Un-fucking-believable. What the hell am I? A piece of shit on the side of the road.

Less than a minute later, I'm fully dressed, walking out of VIP and toward the bar. I need a goddamn drink. When I approach the bar, Tink gives me a once over and doesn't say a word. She pours me a whiskey and walks off to talk to other patrons. Funny how well she, and the other staff, know me.

I down the drink and close my eyes as warmth coats my throat and stomach. When I open my eyes, Christy stands inches away from me. Stark. Ass. Naked. Leaning into her, I hiss, "Put your goddamn clothes on."

She rolls her eyes, and for the first time I don't find it adorable. "Why?" she asks, clipped.

"Why? You're joking, right?" She has got to be fucking kidding me. "Because you're walking around the goddamn club like a snack."

Christy flings her arms wide open and crosses her ankles. Now she is intentionally making a scene. And it's pissing me off. "Rick… this is a club where people literally come in to remove their clothes and fuck other people. As if anyone gives a damn whether or not I've got clothes on."

As I scan the crowd, not only has the typical chatter died, but almost every pair of eyes is watching us. *Fuck, fuck, fuck.* I force her arms down to her sides and lean into her, whispering in her ear. "Put your fucking clothes on. Every set of eyes is on you right now. Go home. When I'm off work, we will talk about this."

When I pull away, I study her face a moment. A rosy flush blooms on her cheeks and her eyes are puffy, red, and on the verge of tears. *Goddamnit.* I hate that she is hurting. That she feels like Sarah leaving equals losing someone she loves. But I'm a selfish bastard, and it feels as if she ran over me with a semi.

She may be hurting, but what she said slashed me to shreds.

After a few ragged breaths, she spins around, marches back to VIP, and puts her dress back on. The club remains silent. Well, as silent as a club can be with music oozing from the speakers. Once she zips up her dress, she steps out of VIP with her head high and shoulders back. Every set of eyes locks onto Christy as she storms past me, flips me her middle finger, and walks out.

My heart is a tattered mess on the floor as everyone resumes chatting or whatever they were doing before the whole display. Why can't I breathe? I stumble back and fall onto the stool behind me. We have never fought. Not once. And I have a feeling we are nowhere near finished.

"You alright?" Tink asks.

I hang my head and shake it side to side. "No. Far from okay."

"Tell me to butt out if I'm overstepping. What happened?"

Honestly, I don't want to talk about this with anyone except Christy. But I'm stuck here for at least another five hours. Five hours of nothing except trying to figure out how to fix whatever snapped. "No offense, Tink, but I should talk to her before anyone else."

"No worries. I get it. But we're all here if you need us."

I nod, hand her my glass, and wander off. Only five more hours. It will be over in no time. At least that is what I keep telling myself.

When I walk through the front door, the first thing that grabs my attention is how bright it is inside. Every light in our apartment appears to be flipped on. The second thing I notice is Christy in the middle of the living room, sitting on an over-sized pillow, rocking back and forth with her head tucked between her chest and knees. Although her face is hidden from view, her whimpers tell me all I need to know.

I walk over and squat down in front of her. When I reach out and lay my hand on her shoulder, she jumps. Not just a little. Practically out of her skin.

"Ah! Don't scare me like that," she says, pointing a finger at me.

I sink onto the floor in front of her, ignore the wild look in her eyes, and wipe away the trail of tears on her cheeks. "Sorry, gorgeous. Thought you heard me come in." Wrapping my arms around her, I drag her into my lap and hold her tight against my chest.

We sit like this for a moment. Her tears stain the front of my shirt as her hands clutch the cotton. As much as I don't want to disturb this blip of heaven, we need to talk about what happened earlier. The only way the whole situation will resolve itself is by us opening up and talking about it.

Hesitantly, I break us apart, slip a finger under her chin, and bring her swollen gaze to mine. "I know you're upset, but we need to talk about what happened at the club tonight." Every word a gentle promise that I will do whatever to make this better for her. For us.

Puffy, bloodshot eyes dart between mine in question. How long has she been crying? Hours? After a few seconds, she nods and we move to sit on the couch. It pains me to do or say anything that would hurt her, but it isn't realistic to uproot our lives every time someone else's life changes. That isn't how life operates.

"I need you to talk to me, gorgeous. Tell me what you're thinking and I'll wait until you're done to answer."

She swipes the tears from under her eyes and tucks a few disobedient hairs behind her ears. When she appears to have regained her composure, she starts. "I know she's only been physically gone for a day, but Sarah leaving feels like I lost a loved one. Family has always been a rough subject for me. And when Sarah became family, I never thought something like this would happen. That I'd lose her."

When she doesn't say anything for a minute as she stares down at her fumbling hands, I assume it is fair game for me to speak. "Hey. Sarah has been in your life for a couple years now, so I understand why you're upset. But we can't just pack up our lives and move across the country because our friends moved away. You'll still talk to her all the time. See her on trips. She's not gone forever."

Christy sniffles beside me. "It's not the same," she whispers. The crack in her voice is a splinter in my heart. No matter what I say right now, it will all fall to shit. Is there a right answer?

"I know it isn't, but it's the hand we're dealt."

Beside me, Christy shakes. It starts as this practically

undetectable tremor and evolves to an earthquake. And then she bolts upright. "No," she screams. Not just a simple increase in volume. More on the level so the heavens can hear the authority and disparity in her voice.

"No?" I ask. Honestly, I'm not sure what else to say or ask.

"No. I'm sick and tired of being the one left behind. *It's okay, Christy. Everything will be fine.*" Her tone mocking, but of who I'm uncertain. "Well it's not *fine*. Why does everyone else get to be happy, except poor little Christy?"

I have no idea what the fuck is happening with her right now. This side of her is completely foreign. Where the hell do I begin? "What the hell does that mean?" It is the only sane question to ask. Because I have no goddamn idea right now.

"What does that mean?" she asks. "It means that I always draw the short end of the stick when it comes to love."

What in the actual fuck? Since the day I met Christy, all I have ever done is love her. I may not have classified it as love in the beginning, but that is exactly what it was. And now she is suggesting she has no one to love or to love her in return. If I don't calm the fuck down, my fist might rip through the drywall any minute.

"Care to elaborate? Because if I'm understanding you correctly, you just insinuated no one loves you. And that's fucking bullshit." It is almost four in the morning and the volume of our conversation is reaching levels loud enough to wake our neighbors. I wouldn't be shocked if someone pounds on the walls or front door soon.

"Well, right now, it feels like I'm standing in the middle of a dark forest without a light. In the cold. All alone."

"Wow. So your best friend moves away. She's gone less than twenty-four hours. And no one else is good enough for you. Thanks," I yell. "Thanks for throwing me in the trash."

Her eyes bulge as recognition hits her. But it is too fucking late. She may be upset or distraught over her friend moving away, but she handled the whole situation wrong. Beyond wrong. I should be her strength. The one person she leans on. Who she tells all her secrets to and believes will never leave her side. But she has contaminated that. Laced it with poison. And force fed it down my throat.

She steps toward me and I step back. For the first time

ever, I don't want her touch. Nor do I want to be swayed by the potency of our bond. A bond which I thought could never be tampered with. "No." I put my hand up, then point to the bedroom. "Go to bed. I can't do this right now."

Another step toward me, and I back up farther. Her eyes beg me to forgive her. With every ounce of me, I wish it could be so simple. But she didn't just hurt me. She cut out my heart with a spoon, dropped it in the earth, and stomped on it for good measure. It will take time before I heal from her wounds.

Tears rip from her eyes like an avalanche. She walks backward from me, eyes glued to mine, chin trembling as she mouths, *I'm sorry. I love you.*

When our bedroom door shuts, I breathe for the first time in minutes. Dragging a deep breath in through my nose, I exhale the anguish and heartache she just inflicted upon me. For a split-second, I almost lost my shit in front of her. Now that she is tucked away in our bed, I close my eyes and relish in the quiet. If one thing holds true, I never want to see Christy as I did moments ago. Once she realized what she had said, once I threw it back at her, her stormy eyes said it all. That she made a mistake. A huge fucking mistake.

I head to the spare bedroom, shut the door, and drop onto the bed. Half a minute later, I bring my hands to my face and cry into my palms. My heart shrivels and beats cold in my chest. Fuck this hurts. No matter what, I plan to do whatever it takes to make things between us better.

But how the hell do I fix this?

Four days have passed since our fight. Four days and we haven't spoken a single word to each other. No morning interaction. No texts during the day. Nothing. When I come home from work, she is locked away in our bedroom with the lights out. When I wake in the morning, early on the off chance I will catch her, she is already gone for the day.

Not a single sound in the apartment. No kisses or hugs goodbye. No notes on the fridge.

Nothing.

I miss her so fucking much. A light has been extinguished between us and I haven't the first clue how to reignite it. Tonight, I plan to make this right. If not right, definitely better than what it is now. There is no way we can continue living like this. No matter how hard she tries to hide it, I hear her muffled tears when I come home. Neither one of us is sleeping well, if at all, and it ends tonight.

While she finishes her workday, I head out to run errands. After a quick workout at the gym, I stop at the grocery store and pick up ingredients for dinner. On the drive home, I pass Christy's favorite florist shop and turn around.

Generally, flowers and chocolates have never been something I showered on Christy. I am more a man of passion and actions and words. Not to say I have never purchased flowers or gifts for her, but it isn't on the normal rotation in the affection department. Maybe if I had seen my father do such things for my mother, I would be more apt to pass it on. Maybe if I'd had the opportunity to see Harriett as a young woman, my outlook might also be different. But neither of those things happened, so the point is moot.

After I spend my life savings in the florist shop, I drive home. On my to-do list today... whatever it takes to get my girl back. Dinner and flowers seems like the perfect way to start.

FIVE

CHRISTY

"Ms. Nolan? Did you hear me?"

I shake my head and snap out of my foggy state to see Marco standing on the opposite side of my desk. Arms crossed in front of his chest. Head cocked to the side. A blend of scowl and sympathy stretch across his face.

At the sight, I slump farther into my chair. "Sorry. What?"

This week has sucked at work. Between Sarah being gone and the absence of Rick, I haven't been able to think straight, let alone function. My eyes are tired, sore, and swollen from several nights of crying. God, I am so sick and tired of the endless tears. Why can't I be one of those people who suffers from dry eyes? Now would be the perfect time to have such a problem. Unfortunately, my tear ducts seem to have a never-ending supply of sadness.

"I asked if you were doing okay. But you answered without saying a word. Why don't you go home, take tomorrow off, and have a long weekend to recover from whatever has you down."

Sincerity laces Marco's voice as his arms unlatch and he shoves his hands deep in his pockets. The offer to take time off warms my heart and has my eyes stinging. I blink rapidly to keep yet another round of tears at bay. *I will not cry at work. Especially in front of my boss.* As much as I would love to leave, half the work day remains and I have a mile-long list of shit to get done. Shit that I have ignored for far too long during my emotional stupor.

"Let me finish some stuff today. I'll take you up on tomorrow, though."

A gentle smile lifts the corners of Marco's lips. "You miss her. We all do. If you're as close as I think you are, you'll see her again. Don't doubt that, Christy."

And just like that, the dam bursts wide open. I nod and click the mouse, pretending to do something productive on my computer. "Yeah, I know," I mumble over the emotion lodged in my throat. After a beat of silence, Marco nods, steps out of my cubicle and walks back to his office.

The moment he is out of sight, I close my eyes and take a deep breath. *Just get through the rest of the day.* Surrounding me, fingers tap keyboards like wildfire. A cacophony of chatter swirls around as if I am in the center of a tornado. I open up the instant messaging application on my computer and shoot a quick message to Liz.

Christy: You eat yet?
Liz: No. Want to grab a bite downstairs?
Christy: I'll be ready in a minute.

Liz meets me at the elevator two minutes later and we ride down to Carol's Deli in silence. For a deli who caters mainly to the workers of Hammond Life, the place is always packed. We order our food and locate a table near the window. For a moment, we sit and stare out the window. People shuffle along the sidewalk—some enter the building, others just pass by. Although I don't look in her direction, I *feel* Liz's eyes on me. How she senses my unusual disposition. My less than perky self. And I don't think she is quite sure how to handle me.

"I miss her," I say, diving straight into the deep end as I face her.

Liz reaches across the table and sets her hand over mine. "Me, too. But I get why she had to move. If I were in her shoes, I would've left sooner."

I tilt my head to the side and study Liz for a moment. Her screaming red hair recently dyed black. "Really?" Not sure why I ask her this, but Liz doesn't peg me as someone to run away from danger. If anything, Liz seems the type to get in danger's face and shove them in the chest.

"Why do you sound so shocked? I may be badass, but I wouldn't want to stay in the same town and be reminded of some guy who did horrible things to me."

When she puts it in that context, I see where she's coming from. "I hadn't thought about it like that, but I guess you're right."

She squeezes my hand and I glance up at her. "There's no right or wrong here, Christy. But we should respect that Sarah struggled to smile every day after all that bullshit happened. It's not fair to her for us to be selfish. I miss her like crazy, like you, but I'm not going to tell her that. It would just add an unfair layer of guilt. Right now, she needs to figure out how to start all over again. And that's hard enough, especially in a new city."

Staring down at where Liz's hand still rests on mine, I mull over her words. On so many levels, Liz is spot on. My urgent desire to move away all stems from a selfish urge to keep Sarah physically close. But, in the process, I forgot about what everyone else needs. Rick, especially. I skipped over his feelings and only considered my own. On my solo path to what should have been happiness, I created a major rift between us. A rift that has splintered my heart more with each passing day. A rift I need to settle and heal.

I hang my head, refusing to cry at my idiocy. No more tears. My body can't handle it. "Thanks, bitch," I mutter. "Only you tell me like it is and I actually listen. Now I have to make things better with Rick."

"Hey." Liz jostles my hand. "What happened with you and Rick?"

Shaking my head because I am the biggest idiot to walk the earth, I tell her, "Four nights ago, I told Rick I wanted to move. Less than a day after Sarah left, and I told him that. Needless to say, it didn't go over well. We had a huge fight." I pause a moment and gaze into Liz's hazel eyes, once again on the verge of crying. "We've never fought before, Liz. And it's all my fault. All because I couldn't handle losing Sarah."

"But we haven't lost her," she says.

And for the first time since Sarah left, I understand this now. But after all the bullshit with my own flesh and blood family, it hurts to have someone I care about slip away.

"I know. It just felt like it. In some ways, it still does. Probably will for a while."

"Once she settles in, you know she's going to invite us all out there. It may not be anytime soon, but we'll get to hug her again." Liz smiles and a small weight lifts from my heart. This is the most we have talked since she and Tiffany became serious. "On another note... It's great to hear you call me bitch again. I started to wonder if you only reserved that for when Sarah was here."

I laugh loud enough to turn several heads in our direction. And for the first time in a week, I smile. A true, genuine smile. Oftentimes, I get teased for tossing my favorite word around like a whore at a free-for-all. *Bitch*. Don't remember the first time I used it so casually, but Sarah and Liz called it my signature. I just laughed and called them bitches. Little do they know, I *only* use it with them.

"Sorry I haven't been myself, bitch. Promise to bring her back to life. On one condition, though."

Liz tilts her head and narrows her eyes, intrigued. "And what's that?"

"That I don't lose you to Tiffany." Liz's eyes soften and she squeezes my hand harder. "Seriously. My family did some fucked up shit to me and I can't lose the only family I have now."

A tender expression crosses her face. "You won't lose me, girl. And if it feels like I'm slipping away, set me straight. Okay?"

"Yeah, okay."

I walk through the front door just after six and stop in my tracks. Walking up, everything looked dark behind the blinds on the windows. So, when I step inside to candle light, hundreds of peonies, and the aroma of herbs floating in the air, I'm taken aback.

Doesn't Rick work tonight?

Slowly, I walk from the foyer to the kitchen. At the stove, his back to me, Rick stirs a large pot of something on the burner. He doesn't turn to face me. Just keeps stirring whatever he is cooking. Best guess, he didn't hear me come in because I didn't announce myself. Usually, there is no need to because he is at work when I get home.

For a moment, I lean against the doorjamb and watch him. Clad in a snug black shirt and a pair of khaki cargo shorts, his feet are bare. Rick has many qualities that are beyond attractive. Not only is he physically good looking—long, almost black hair slung to one side, buzzed from the ears down; so tall he towers over me like a tree when I stand barefoot; lines and bulges of sinew in all the right places—he also lures me in with his mind. So incredibly smart with a wicked and talented tongue.

He checks his watch, then wipes his hand on the towel slung over his shoulder. Probably wondering when I will get home. Like a spy, I stand silently off to the side and wait for him to spot me. Before I finish the thought, he spins around and startles when he sees me ogling him.

Slow and steady, he saunters toward me. A lion hunting his prey. When he stands less than a foot away, he reaches out and strokes a finger along my cheek and jawline. Without hesitation, I close my eyes and breathe him in. Leather and bergamot and sandalwood flutter up my nose and settle my soul. I sigh as my shoulders cave forward. God, I have missed him. Us. This.

"Didn't hear you come in, gorgeous," he whispers as his lips ghost mine. I shudder beneath him and his lips curve into a smile against my skin.

"Usually pretty quiet when I get home. Plus, I wanted to see what you were up to."

When I open my eyes, the hunger swirling in his knocks the breath from my lungs. He plucks a lock of my hair and plays with it between his fingers. So intimate and tender.

"I've been so lost without you this week."

I study the lines of his face a moment, making note of the shadows beneath his eyes and how much his usual buzzed beard has grown out. He looks as exhausted as I feel.

Inching forward, I kiss him. Soft and sweet. "Missed you,

too," I breathe. He presses his lips to mine again and my world seems more even keeled. He breaks the kiss far too soon and walks back to the stove. The instant he steps away, I crave his warmth and the rough touch of his skin on mine. So, I push off the wall, walk up to his backside, and wrap my hands around his waist. "Need help?"

He peers over his shoulder at me and winks. "I got this. Go get comfortable. Dinner should be ready in a few."

I kiss him between the shoulder blades, happy to finally be close to him again, then head for the bedroom. When I flip the light on, a massive sea of pink hits me.

Scattered on the dresser, bed, and every available surface in our bedroom is countless peony flowers. My favorite flower. To say he spent a pretty penny on flowers would be delicate. The number of flowers in here and throughout the apartment, he spent hundreds. For someone who isn't big on flowers and candies and clichés—neither of us are, to be honest—he sure went out of his way to do something special for me.

Stepping farther into the room, I pluck one of the flowers off the bed and bring it to my nose. Such a subtle fragrance. As I gaze at all the pillowy, blush-colored bulbs, warmth blossoms in my heart. There is nothing this man wouldn't do for me. No bounds he wouldn't push to keep me happy and by his side. The splinters in my heart slowly suture back together, and a wholeness only Rick provides settles deep in my bones.

After I slip on one of Rick's t-shirts and a pair of boxer shorts, I walk out and see him waiting at the dining table. Methodically, he glances up and down my body. A wicked gleam lights his face, and it is all the praise I need.

While we enjoy the pesto fusilli, salad, and garlic bread he prepared, we talk about our days. How work has sucked for me. His trip to the florist—who thought him insane for buying a hundred plus of the same flower. He still won't disclose how much he spent. Not that it matters.

When we finish, he takes our dishes to the sink before we settle on the couch. The elephant in the room standing tall and proud and eager for us to speak.

"I'm sorry," I say, staring at my clasped, sweaty hands in my lap.

Rick slips his fingers beneath my chin and tips my head back as he holds me prisoner with his gaze. "Don't be sorry for telling me how you feel, gorgeous. If anything, I should be apologizing to you. It was out of place for me to talk to you like I did. I will never raise my voice like that again." He slowly leans forward and presses a kiss to my lips.

I nod. "You weren't the only one fired up, but I don't ever want us like that again. This week has been the worst. Not sure if I ever fell asleep without you in our bed."

He plays with the ends of my hair. "Me either. I never want another night without you in my arms. And I never want us to fight. Ever." I agree with him before he continues. "And I've done some thinking. I'm making no promises, but I will look into other opportunities that might allow us to move. If that's what you really want."

My eyes bug out behind my glasses. "Are you serious?"

"I wouldn't bring it up if I weren't. But I need to ask you something first."

The room swirls around me with excitement. "Okay."

"Please tell me about your parents." His honey eyes dart between my steely blues. "It's a touchy subject for you, but I need to understand it better. As open as we are about us, we've never shared that side of ourselves. And I respect your desire to keep it tucked away, because there are reasons we never see my family either."

Rick and I have been together four-and-a-half years and neither one of us has brought up our families. And neither of us questioned the other regarding our silence. In some relationships, your significant other may find this quite odd. But because we obviously both had issues with some or all of our family members, it isn't in our nature to ask or pester.

And I want to share this part of my life with Rick. Be completely transparent with him. But fear has crippled me over the years. Fear of losing more people I love. If something happened to Rick or us, and we couldn't be together... the world would become a dark hole.

But in my heart, deep down in the depths of my marrow, I know I can tell Rick about this. And when I finish, he will still be here. With me. Keeping me safe and guarding my heart as he has since the first day we met. I inhale deeply and settle every nerve in my body.

"When I was sixteen," I start. "I lost my virginity to a guy named James. We weren't dating. In fact, I met him at work. He was older than me. Too old to have sex with a sixteen-year-old."

Rick holds up his hand and I stop for a moment. "Do you know how old he was?"

I nod. "James was twenty-eight at the time." Rick growls beside me, but I ignore it and continue my story. "Anyway, we worked together, but he was in a different department of the store. Every once in a while, our paths crossed. And from time to time, we'd sit together and eat on break. He was a nice guy, easy to talk with. Over time, my attraction toward him grew. After all, I was sixteen and my hormones were all over the place." I roll my eyes for dramatic effect and Rick laughs. "One day, during our break, he broached the subject of sex. Part of me shrunk away from the topic, while another part of me screamed to learn more. Most of the girls from school had already lost their virginity and bragged about how amazing sex was. But, for some reason, no one seemed interested in sweet, little Christy."

Rick smiles at me briefly. "That's because they didn't know how amazing you truly are."

I wave him off and continue. "So, when James took an interest and wanted to talk about sex, I talked. Within a few short minutes, I spilled the beans about still being a virgin. But that didn't perturb him. If anything, his fascination with me grew stronger. He asked, *'How is a beautiful girl like you still a virgin?'* All I could do was shrug. You can't help how things pan out. We continued these talks for weeks. Most of the time, it was me asking him questions."

"So how did it go from an innocent conversation to you having sex with him?" Rick asks. He means no disrespect; I sense it in his tone. More or less, he is fascinated by how I volunteered to sleep with a man almost twice my age.

"One day, while we sat in the break room, he asked if any of the guys at school caught my eye. Completely honest with him, I said no, but someone outside school had. No lie, at the time, I was enamored by him. He was the first guy to take an interest in me. A man. His attention boosted my self-esteem like no one else had ever done. So, when he asked who I was interested in, I told him. But he wasn't fazed by my attraction to him. Not excited or put down. James simply smiled and told me he was attracted to me also. From that day forward, our conversations were quieter. Our legs or hands brushed against each other time and again. For two weeks, we had the most intense version of foreplay."

A half-smile kicks up the left side of Rick's mouth. "Indeed. But how did no one else see you together? Surely other people took breaks at the same time."

"The store had a break room and a small cafe. Most of the employees ate in the cafe, so we only had company on occasion."

Rick waves his hand. "Continue."

He leans on his palm as his elbow presses into the back of the couch. Gazing at me with such admiration and awe. The more I share with him, the lighter my heart feels over the past. But we haven't gotten to the root of the matter yet, and my pulse hammers in my chest as I continue.

"After weeks of flirting and secret touching and conversations about sex, I was tired of talking. I wanted to know what all my girlfriends had been raving about. Plus, I figured saving your virginity was just my religious parents' way of keeping me *pure* for whoever they wanted me to marry. I was ready to give it up, though. Ready to see what all the whispering was about. So, I told James I wanted to have sex with him. At first, he hesitated. Not sure if it was the age thing, but I quickly reminded him the age of consent in the state of Georgia was sixteen. Once I stated that little fact, the relief on his face was visible for miles. Soon after, we started making plans. Arranged sex. Super intimate, right? But I didn't care."

I pause a moment and take a sip of wine. Rick is fully invested in listening to my story, waiting to see how my relationship with James leads back to my parents. It surprises me he hasn't put the pieces together yet. Maybe he has, but he's reserving his assumption so I will share my story.

"We figured out a day when my shift ended early and James was off work. I lied to my parents and said I was going to a friend's house after work and that I would stay the night there. They were none the wiser. When my shift ended, James picked me up and we went back to his place."

My stomach twists in a knot and a light sheen pricks my lightly fevered skin. Although it was a lifetime ago, my heart beats viciously against my ribcage. But I keep reminding myself this was years ago. Years before Rick and I knew one another. And he would never think less of me because of a choice I made when I was sixteen. It isn't his nature.

"At first, it was like two friends hanging out. We sat on the couch, ate snacks and watched television. He flipped through the channels until he landed on a pay-per-view movie. Essentially, soft core porn, but I didn't know that's what it was at the time. After he paid for the movie, we sat back and watched. Half an hour later, his hand skimmed up and down the inside of my thigh. Another ten minutes in and we started kissing. When the first sex scene popped up on the screen, he hiked my shirt up and yanked my pants down. In less than an hour of the movie starting, I learned what it felt like to have a man inside me. Learned how incredible sex was and what I'd been missing. We had sex for hours that night. The next day, I struggled to get out of his bed and could barely walk. When I returned home, my parents asked why I was limping and I blamed it on too much exercise. Sixteen-year-old girls are obsessed with their figure and it seemed like a good enough excuse."

Beside me, Rick bends at the waist, clutches his stomach, and laughs hysterically. Without a moment's hesitation, I join in. Reliving that last part is worth every painful chuckle stemming from my diaphragm. God, I was such an idiot back then. But as I mull over the whole scenario, my parents were pretty naïve. How in the hell did they believe my fib about too much exercise? They must have never thought their daughter would ever lie to them. Or… maybe they really believed it at the time. It doesn't matter now.

"It was a half truth," I say. "But after that day, James and I hooked up several times. Through him, I learned sex wasn't just about sticking a dick in a hole. It was, and is, an art. A talent that develops and improves with time and routine practice. Something you wet your lips with, but didn't devour immediately. Because of him, I craved sex more than love. He taught me that sex and love could co-exist or be separate entities. I never loved James, but my infatuation for him was strong. And that's when the slip up happened. One Saturday morning before work, I packed a duffel bag like I had for the last several weeks. My mom walked in my room and asked who I was staying with after work. Instead of telling her I was sleeping over at Jenika's house like I had every other time, I said James. I prayed she didn't hear me right, but within seconds I had my answer. She stormed out of the room, hollering for my father. Nothing like a Marine to shape up a disobedient child, right?"

Rick brushes his knuckles up and down my bicep, soothing me. As if he knows what is coming. Although the situation has long since passed, just thinking of the way my parents handled the whole thing, and how they treated me, boils my blood.

"Needless to say, I lost my job because I'd been grounded to my room and my parents called my work and said I would not be returning. They confiscated my cell phone and drove me to and from school each day. My life became a prison sentence. *'No little girl of mine will be a whore on the streets.'* That's what my father told me. After a week, I asked a girl at school who'd worked with me if she could deliver a note to James. He and I were far from serious, but I wanted him to know I was okay. She agreed. What I didn't expect after the note delivery was for James to show up unannounced at my house. He and my father got into a pissing match on the porch. I witnessed the whole event from the living room window. My father's sole mission was to triumph over James because *he was my dad*. While James actually spoke up *for* me and never said a selfless thing. James was the first person outside of my family to care about me. But he was also the reason my parents kicked me out of the house."

Rick jerks his head back, eyes wide as a haze of red slowly creeps up his neck and onto his ticking jaw. "Are you fucking kidding?" If looks could kill, Rick would have killed my parents in a heartbeat.

He may not have known me all those years ago, but he still jumps to my defense regarding the scenario. His devotion to my happiness makes my heart stutter and my breath catch. I shake my head. "No."

"If I ever meet your parents, I'll personally let them know what kind of trash they are." I don't doubt Rick or his promise for a second. Given the chance, he would defend me to the death.

"Honestly, I never want to see them again. After they kicked me out, I stayed with James for a while. But over time, it wasn't hard to figure out we would never be more than just sex. And I wanted more. He was generous, wouldn't let me pay rent, so I saved every penny for as long as I could. After the first year, we became more roommates than lovers. When the second year passed and I graduated high school, we were simply friends who lived together. He saw other women; I dated a couple guys. No big shake. Matter of fact, we were still living together that first night I was in Apex."

"Really?" Rick asks, jealousy dilating his eyes and dancing on his tongue. "Do you still talk with him?"

"He checks in every six months or so, making sure I'm okay. Other than that, we don't talk."

What happened between James and I was a lifetime ago. When I met Rick, I was twenty-four and James was in his mid-thirties. A lot had changed since I first met him at sixteen. For a time, James was my only trustworthy friend, more like family. Keeping in touch with him over the years only seems fair, after everything he did for me.

Rick nods with a loose fist pressed to the corner of his mouth. Intrigue swirls in his eyes and I fall victim to the hypnotizing sight. "Dare I say I'd like to meet him?"

His interest snaps me back to reality and I laugh. "You sure about that?"

What would it be like to have James and Rick in the same room? The man I willingly surrendered my virginity to next to the man I love and share sexual partners with. Hmm, I sense a struggle for power in the future. What a chest pounding, snarl inducing match that would be. Although James and I haven't been anything other than friends for more than a decade, I easily picture him sizing up Rick and running down an invisible checklist to see if he is worthy. It makes me smile.

"Yeah, gorgeous." His tone softens. "I'd love to meet the man who rescued you from hell. And thank him."

That's a one-eighty from where I thought this was going. "Thank him?"

He nods and drops his hand from his cheek. "For not wanting to keep you. Because then you wouldn't be mine."

A bevy of doves takes flight in my belly, soars up, up, up, and steals my breath. When did Rick become so swoon-worthy? "If you're serious, I'll ask." Face straight, eyes locked on mine, Rick nods as he reaches forward, grabs a lock of my hair, and plays with it. "Okay then," I say. This whole conversation has been equally exhausting and relieving. "So, now do you get why losing people hits me a little hard?"

Rick closes the space between us and presses his lips to mine briefly. "I do. And now I'm willing to compromise."

"Compromise?" What is he talking about?

"Yeah, gorgeous. I'm willing to see what job options are available in California."

I jump off the couch and throw myself onto his lap, peppering him with kisses. Although we don't say the words often, in my heart, Rick will always be mine and I will always be his. Our bond is electric and instantaneous and persistent. There will never be another person who jolts me to life the way Rick does. And there isn't a single thing he wouldn't do for me, or I him.

SIX

RICK

I CAN COUNT on one hand how many times in my life I let my nerves get the best of me. Tonight is one of them.

Nothing about Chad intimidates me—physical or demeanor. But before heading into work, I shot him a text and asked if he could meet me at the club. Every time a boss hears those words, it is the same as your girlfriend saying *we need to talk.*

So, when I walk through the front door at quarter to six, it doesn't surprise me when I spot Chad behind the bar helping Tink restock. Something I normally do. As my shoes clack against the hard floor and announce my arrival, Chad peers up from the cutting board and calls me over to the bar, telling Tink to take a break. Hesitant to leave, she studies the pair of us for a minute. When neither Chad nor I say a word, she tosses her towel down, walks out from behind the bar, and heads to the back.

Once Tink leaves and the back room door closes, the nervous energy encapsulating me doubles. "What'd you want to discuss?" Chad asks, not beating around the bush.

Hands stuffed in my pants pockets, I hold his gaze. "Some stuff happened to a friend of mine recently and it has my girl a little spooked."

Chad stops slicing limes, sets the knife down, and comes around the bar. Pulling out a stool beside me, he pats my shoulder. "Sorry to hear, man."

"Thanks." I nod and prepare myself for what I haven't said yet. *This is just Chad, get ahold of yourself.* "Since then, she's got her heart set on us moving. Out of state." Chad's brows shoot up to his hairline. Glad I am not the only one surprised by such a notion. "Yeah. But I told her it all depended on both of us securing jobs. Can't move unless that happens."

Chad twists on his stool and faces me head on. "So, where do I fit into the equation?"

"Right, so I was wondering if you had any connections in Cali? Nowhere specific out there." It is a longshot, but Chad is the only person I know to ask. It's not like businesses such as this put help wanted ads in newspapers and online job search engines.

He swipes his index finger over his lips a moment. "I'll make some calls. See what I can find out and let you know."

"Thanks, man. Appreciate it."

"Sure thing. Least I could do." He rises from the stool and slides it back in line with the other untouched stools. "Be back after opening. Let me know if we need anything while I'm out."

I nod and thank him again. Once Chad leaves, Tink walks back over and asks what just happened. Now is not the time to divulge the fact I may leave, so I tell her I needed a word with Chad, but everything is fine. Management stuff. Tink pinches her eyes in a tight line and stares at me, trying to suck the unknown out of my head. When I don't budge, she gives up and we go about our usual pre-opening setup, and the time passes without notice.

Just after ten o'clock, Chad returns and loiters with the clientele. Not too often, but on occasion, Chad indulges with the patrons. Tonight happens to be one of those times. After an hour of play, he unties a woman from a table, kisses a man as if he'll never kiss anyone again, and heads my direction. In all his glory.

For his age, Chad is attractive as hell. Mid-forties. Silky chocolate skin. Frame of a bodybuilder. Hung like a beast. But his frosty blue eyes steal every woman and man's breath. Even I am not immune to his presence. Christy only met him once, and we all kept our clothes on. If she saw the rest of him, I have no doubt my girl would want to sample the merchandise. Hell, the temptation to call her down here now weighs heavy in my groin.

Sitting on the stool next to me, his erection slowly taming, Chad orders a drink. After Tink delivers the shot of whiskey, he tosses it back and glances at me. "Got a name and number for you."

"Quicker than I expected," I say.

"In our industry, most of us know each other or can connect us. It was a matter of making the right calls. When I find my clothes, I'll get it to you." He laughs, staring across the room at the couple he walked away from. The woman up on all fours while the man takes her from behind.

After a few circuits of the club and several conversations, I take my break. I go into the back storage area where the music from the club is quietest. More than likely, night life is just ramping up in California. Taking the slip of paper with Chad's scribble out of my pocket, I dial the number and fidget as the phone rings in my ear.

"This is Rocco," a man with a throaty voice says.

"Rocco, hello. My name is Rick. Chad Wexler gave me your number in reference to a job opportunity."

The line is silent for a beat and I pull the phone away from my ear to be sure the call didn't drop. "Ah, yes. Chad near Savannah."

"Yes, sir."

"Good guy. Well Rick, I will have an opening in the near future. A current bar and night club I own is prospering, so I thought it was time to expand." Rocco proceeds to tell me about his current business. An upscale bar on the main floor called The Sophisticate. Beneath the bar, though, is P.I., an exotic night club. He opened the businesses seven years ago and they are thriving much quicker than he'd expected, hence he's decided to open a new establishment.

"Will the new place mimic your current?" I ask for more than one reason. One—I don't care to manage a strip club. Not really my thing. Too much drama. Two—I was under the impression the California offer would be for a job exactly like the one I hold.

"Yes and no," Rocco states. "Yes, because it will structurally appear the same. The main floor, where patrons enter, will be a fine dining restaurant with hints of sensuality. Nothing obvious to those not in the life. No, because instead of an exotic dancer's club, there will be a club similar to what you work in now. I'm not going to call it a sex club, but, in essence, that's what it will be. The restaurant, Opulence, will cater to a set crowd just as my bar does. It's imperative we filter out the undesirables. There is a strict dress code and a contract to be a member of the club. The same will apply at Boundless, the new lifestyle club. From time to time, myself or people I deem suitable will "interview" patrons in the restaurant. If we find them compatible to possibly joining the club, we offer them a one-time invitation. Several of the members from P.I. plan to join Boundless, so there will be a base when we open."

Wow. Opulence/Boundless is a dream job. In a haze from everything he shared with me, I remain speechless when Rocco pauses. When I manage to form words, I ask, "When will the new business open?"

"Doors open in December." Elation kicks in. December is less than six months from now. "Next year," he adds. Now I'm flat on my back. A year-and-a-half. For this job, I would be more than willing to wait. But will Christy be open to waiting so long? Fuck, I hope so.

"Say you hired me. When would I start working? I imagine you'll need me prior to the doors opening." *Speak as if you already have the job*—the best advice I received from my first boss. It tells owners and interviewers how serious you are about the position.

"Right you are. If all goes to plan, I would need you to start—if hired—three months prior. If you're open to it, I'd love you to fly out, show you around The Sophisticate and P.I., and we can do a formal interview."

Holy fuck. One phone call and I have an interview. Not just any interview, but an interview for one of the best possible jobs. Am I in the *Twilight Zone*? How the hell does this even happen?

"Definitely. Tell me when works best for you and I'll coordinate with Chad."

"The number you called from, is it your cell?"

"It is," I answer, maybe a little too quickly.

"I'll text you dates that work for me once I'm back in my office and we'll go from there. Good with you?"

Hell yeah it is. "Perfect."

"It was a pleasure speaking with you, Rick. Look forward to meeting you soon."

"Likewise, Rocco. Thank you for your time."

The call disconnects and I stare at the phone in my hand for a moment. Holy shit. I landed the opportunity of a lifetime. Managing a club from the startup. With a man who sounds more like a mentor than a boss. Christy will flip her shit when I share the good news.

SEVEN

CHRISTY

Rinsing the last of the soap off me, I shut off the water and step out of the shower. The moment my phone pings with an incoming text, I perk up. After drying off somewhat and wrapping the towel snug around my torso, I amble over to the bed, snag my phone, and unlock it.

Rick: Exciting news. Will you be up when I get home?
Christy: No, but wake me.
Rick: Get some sleep, gorgeous. See you soon.

I start typing out what a tease he is for leaving me hanging, but know it's not intentional. Obviously, whatever he wants to share is better in person than via text messages. So, I delete the unsent message and toss my phone back on the bed.

Back in the bathroom, I brush the tangles from my hair, finish drying my body, and toss the towel in the hamper. Rick and I own nightwear for when we have guests stay over or when it gets really cold—which is almost never, if I'm honest. Otherwise, we sleep how nature made us. Bare.

After brushing my teeth, I shut off the lights, snuggle under the plush comforter, and read my current paperback. A rom-com by one of my favorite authors. Suddenly, I startle awake with the book flat on my chest. *At least I didn't lose my page.*

Sliding the bookmark into place, I set the paperback on

the bedside table and shut off the light. Before long, Rick slips into bed beside me. Face to face. Inching closer to him, I weave my legs between his as he wraps his arms around me and inhales deeply.

"You can sleep," he whispers into the darkness.

I skim my fingertips along the front of his throat, down his sternum, over the ridges of his abs, and clutch his cock. He thrusts forward and moans in my ear. In a heartbeat, I straddle him and rub my clit over his fast growing erection. Teasing him with strokes up and down his length, I finally cave when he bruises my hips and tattoos my flesh with his grip. Slowly, I push him inside me, dig my nails into his biceps, and ride him until we both come undone.

Once our breathing settles, he bundles me in his arms and holds me close to his chest, chuckling. I sit up enough to see his face in the illumination of the alarm clock. "What's so funny?"

"You were passed out cold when I got in bed. Now, we're both wide awake."

"Worth it," I mumble as I fall back against his chest. "What did you want to tell me?"

He rolls us over, so he hovers above me. Tugging on a strand of my hair, he smiles. "I have a job interview next week. In California."

It takes a moment for all my synapses to fire, but once they do, I squeal. A little too loud for the late hour. "Really? When? Where? I need details."

Rick laughs above me, fingers still toying with my hair. He goes over all the details from the call he had earlier and what job he is interviewing for. The only kicker, if hired, the job wouldn't begin for a little more than a year. As far away as that is, it's a timeline. Rick stares down at me with trepidation, uncertain if the prospect makes me happy. Which it does. Another year will pass between now and then—because he *will* get the job—but I can handle it.

But he needs my reassurance. "This is great news. So excited for you. For us. How awesome to be at the startup of a lifestyle club. You get to help create something new."

"Most of the night, I was so worried the time between

now and then would bother you," he admits. "A year is a long time. Especially if you're unhappy."

"Only part of me is unhappy." I brush my fingers over his jawline and relish in the prickliness of his stubble. "A small part. But having a possible timeline, it gives that small ounce of hope." Closing the space between us, I press a soft kiss to his lips and say, "You own the biggest part of me. Not just my heart. Many people can own slivers of that. No, you have my soul. The piece of me no one else will ever own."

Rick slams his mouth to mine and steals my breath. Renders me speechless with his kiss. Takes control of my body with his capable hands. And with every kiss and touch and inkling of intimacy, he possesses every ounce of my soul. As I possess his.

***

Over the next week, life is back to normal again. Our version of normal, anyway. We go to work, spend as much time together as possible, and get lost in each other at Apex. Rick mentally preps for his trip. He will only be in California two days, but he says his schedule should be packed the entire time.

The night before his flight, I walk into Apex wearing his favorite dress. All black with a corset top and a leather skirt that hugs my hips. Attached to my collar is a thin chain. Rick has never outright told me, but I know he wants to dominate me more than he actually does. Honestly, I think he holds back because he isn't sure if I would enjoy it.

But I want to give him what he truly desires.

Weaving through the crowd, I perch on a barstool and order a drink. After Tink delivers my martini, I sip on it and scan the sea of bodies. Tonight appears busier than usual, and there are several unfamiliar faces.

After a few minutes of people watching, I spot Rick across the club. He sits slouched in a chair by himself and watches two men as they whip and fuck a petite blonde. Typically, seeing Rick like this wouldn't bother me. Considering our lifestyle, it takes a lot for jealousy to surge in my veins. But something sharp jabs my chest, stabbing me as I sit on the opposite side of the club and watch him stroke himself through his pants. The stiffness of his erection is quite evident. His expression screams how desperately he wishes to join them.

The sole reason my heart thrashes like a wild beast is because he has no idea I stepped foot in the club tonight. I never want to question his loyalty to me, but seeing him like this... sweat highlights my skin as jitters shake my limbs.

A few minutes pass as the scene becomes more intense. More assaulting. More heated. And I can no longer sit on the sidelines and be a silent observer. I slip off my stool and step up to a pair of men a booth away. "Care to escort a lady?" I ask, popping my elbows out.

Each of them rises and takes an arm. Slowly, I guide them through the club. When we are twenty feet away, Rick's eyes leave the ménage and land on me. His hand flies to his side and he sits taller. If expressions were written in words across someone's face, Rick's would say *how long has she been here? What did she see?*

When we reach Rick, I thank each of the men with a peck on the cheek and a groping of their balls. Rick doesn't utter a word. Not until the two men walk away.

"When did you get here?" he asks before kissing me.

For a moment, I stare at him, make him sweat a little, and remain utterly silent. It takes a lot for Rick to crack, but if there is one thing he hates, it's silence. When I have dragged out the torture long enough, I give in. "Maybe fifteen minutes ago. Looks like you've been enjoying yourself." I glance down at his groin, where his erection stands proud and tall behind his zipper.

"It's nothing, gorgeous. These guys asked me to watch. Nothing else."

I believe him. Really, I do. But there's a small piece of the whole scenario that eats away at me. His hunger to join. To get off with others. Without me. Dilated pupils and insatiable strokes up and down his fly told me as much.

Rick and I don't have your typical, "normal" relationship. We fuck and make love like every other couple. We also fuck other people. And get off while watching other people fuck. But we always do it together. *Always.* There has never been an occasion when we spent time alone with another person or couple for sex. Ever. Hence why my blood simmers as I stand in front of him a bit peeved.

"I don't doubt they asked. But for me to sit at the bar and watch you stroke your cock in your pants for more than five minutes…"

Pivoting, I walk away from him. I have no intention of leaving the club, but I need to breathe something other than him for a minute. Walking into VIP, I pass a couple sprawled out on a large ottoman. The woman is nude, clamps on her nipples and clit, chained together, and gripped by the man fucking her ruthlessly.

I sit in a chair beside them and get lost in the visual. The longer I sit here and absorb their energy, the more my clit throbs. The heavier my breasts grow in my corset. Spotting Rick out of the corner of my eye, I rub my hands over my thighs. His stare burns through me, but I ignore it.

When the man tugs the chain and the woman cries out, I slide my skirt up and expose my bare wanton flesh. When she begs him for more, I circle my clit then coat my fingers with my juices. And when she cries out in release, I dip my fingers inside myself.

"Enjoying yourself, kitten?" Rick hisses from behind me.

"As much as you were, *daddy.*"

In a flash, Rick yanks me upright and steers me toward the large X on the wall. Anger vibrates off him with the pulse of the music. *Why does he get to be angry?* I only did what he was doing when I walked in. Tit for tat.

He rips my clothes away and straps me to the Saint Andrew's cross. Before I get to ask how this is remotely my fault, he walks off and toward a wall of implements. After selecting two, he returns and steps up to me.

Grabbing the chain connected to my collar, he yanks my neck forward. "For that" —he points to the chair I sat in a moment ago with a leather whip in his clutches— "you will be punished."

He takes three steps back and rears his arm, then brings it forward and whips me. Sharp stings prick over my lower abdomen and mound where he struck me. Only comparable to a thousand shards of glass piercing my skin. Not enough to bleed, but enough to feel their presence. When he does it again, the bite to my skin is more brutal and I scream.

"So, it's okay for you to get off watching others alone? But not me?" I bite out after I catch my breath.

The whip cracks my skin again and I hiss. He doesn't hold back and it hurts worse than expected. "I never got off, kitten."

His words infuriate more than the physical punishment he doles out. "Neither did I, asshole."

He freezes and just stares at me. His expression shifts. Eyes dilated. Posture taller, prouder. Gaze icy. I shiver under his scrutiny. Stepping toe to toe with me—if my feet actually touched the floor—he barks out, "What did you just call me?" His tone is as frigid as the arctic.

Un-fucking-believable. "Ass. Hole." When he just stands there, I continue. "How dare you. How dare you get pissed at me for doing exactly what you did. At least I had the decency to keep you in my line of sight the entire time. You... you were so enthralled with the blonde and her two brutes, you had no idea what was happening around you." I huff and slam my head back. "Is that what you want? Someone completely unlike me? A pretty little toy?"

I drop my head and let my hair shield my face as tears spill down my cheeks. Seconds pass and neither of us says a word. I'm still restrained to the cross as every emotion drains out of me. My body is exhausted and quivering from the onslaught of sobs that I couldn't hold back. Dozens of eyes are fixated on us and this whole showdown. Although we aren't yelling, we are most definitely fighting. And we both swore to never fight again. How did we get here again so quickly? Oh right, his earlier groping session.

A tug at one ankle gets my attention, then the other, followed by my wrists. I let gravity take me as I fall into Rick. He cradles me in his arms and walks away from the crowd. After he passes the chatty crowd, we step through a door and the music is muffled. When I peek up, I spy a cluster of black metal lockers, a small dining table with four chairs, a fridge and some cabinets, and an oversized couch. The employee's lounge. Rick places me on the soft cushions and drapes a blanket over me before he paces the length of the couch.

After a beat of silence, Rick walks over to the small table and leans his backside against it. "Is that what you think?"

I wrap the blanket tighter around me and peek up at him. "You'll need to be a little more specific."

He pushes off of the small table, walks across the small space, and squats down in front of me. "That the blonde woman is what I want?"

"Yes. No. I don't know." I shake my head, confused by it all.

Rick reaches up and plays with a strand of my hair, tugging the end when he reaches it. "Hey," he says when I break eye contact. "Her." He points toward the door. "She is *not* who I want. You are the only one I want. But I'm not going to lie and say I wasn't enjoying watching the two men with her."

I nod and sit silent, pondering over his admission. He doesn't want *her*. But he wants someone *like* her. Someone willing to do things we have not. Things I wish he would ask to do with me, but has yet to. And I refuse to always be the one to reveal all the cards in my hand. He needs to be equally willing to do the same.

"Am I enough for you?" I whisper-ask.

The room remains silent for far too long. And with each passing second, a new pain mars my heart. A knife stabbing me again and again. Each thrust adding a new scar to the slow-beating organ. *Will I ever be enough?*

His knuckles stroke my jawline and I close my eyes. I count to myself—*one… two… three…*—before he tips my chin up and waits for me to open my eyes. When I do, his golden gaze sears my soul.

"I love you," he says. *Not a confirmation I am enough.* "And I love who I am because of you." *Still avoiding the answer.* "But do I wish we could be more? Sometimes, yes."

Hot branding iron to the chest. God, this fucking hurt. Not that I expected him to answer differently. But hearing it aloud is a vicious slap to my confidence.

The door swings open and Tink steps in with my clothes. "Someone brought these to the bar," she says, holding them up.

"Just set them there, please," Ricks says, pointing to the table. She sets them down, stares at us a beat, then steps out.

I rise from the couch and drop the blanket on the floor. Ambling over to the table, I redress then head back to the couch, fidgeting and avoiding eye contact with Rick. It's silent for several minutes beyond comfortable and I am more than done with the night's events. Done being in this place. Just done.

Walking toward the door, I stop and glance over my shoulder. "Have a safe flight," I mumble, all energy drained from my body. "See you whenever you're back." And before he responds, I turn the handle and exit.

EIGHT

RICK

WHEN I GET HOME from work, I head for the bedroom and twist the handle to open the door. But it doesn't budge. I try it again. And again. It takes me a minute, but it eventually dawns on me Christy has locked me out of our bedroom. She shut me out after what happened tonight.

What the actual fuck is happening with us?

I love this woman fiercely. Like no other. Would give up everything for her. Hell, I'm flying to California for a job interview for her. Yet she infuriates me at times. Her fire is one of the traits I love most about her. But as of late, it seems we are constantly fighting. And I hate it. Hate the expanding hollowness beneath my sternum.

Her question tonight... *"Am I enough for you?"* threw me for a loop. How the hell could she doubt her worth to me? Christy is a vital, essential piece of me. My life would be absolute shit without her. Questioning my devotion to her was a slap to the face. And a knife to the heart.

After she left the club, I was tempted to run after her. Tempted to drag her back into the lounge and hash things out, right then and there. But I stopped myself. She needed time to sort out her emotions, and I needed time to reevaluate what happened.

When I sat down and really mulled it over, it dawned on me how badly I fucked up. I violated one of our rules. A rule I was adamant over when we started seeing each other. *Never be a part of an act without the other present.* Although I wasn't physically participating in the act in the club tonight, I was on the cusp of coming as I stroked myself. And honestly, that is equally as bad as participating.

Once I realized how at fault I was, I typed out a text to her, but didn't have the balls to send it. I fucked up and didn't want us in this questionable place before I left for California for days.

I walk into the guest bedroom and flip on the light. My suitcase and clothes for the morning, which were originally on our bed before I left for work, now lay sprawled out on the guest bed.

"Fuck," I whisper-hiss.

Taking my keys, phone, and wallet out of my pockets, I set them on the dresser and see a folded piece of paper with my name on it in Christy's swirly penmanship.

R,
Travel safe. Have a good interview.
C

The note cold and lifeless, but exactly what I deserve. Flipping off the light, I set the alarm on my phone then lay back on the bed. The wall isn't the only thing dividing me and Christy, but I attempt to sleep over the next five hours as my thoughts whirl in a never-ending cyclone of sadness and confusion.

The wheels hit the tarmac at LAX and I jolt in my seat. Flying never bothered me, but today felt different. Edgier. Unsettling. Not just because I have an interview for a dream job. But also because I didn't get to kiss Christy goodbye before I left. Our disconnect a constant dull pain in my solar plexus. Once I disengage airplane mode, I type out a quick text to her.

Rick: Just landed. Love you.

Notification after notification populates my phone screen,

but not a single one of them is a response to my earlier text letting Christy know the plane was in cue for takeoff. The hollowness in my chest swells. She has every right to still be mad, and I understand her reasoning, but I just wish she would acknowledge she received my texts. From what I see, she either hasn't read them, or she turned the read receipt function off.

I wind my way through the maze that is LAX and locate the pickup area. Rocco told me he would send an employee out to pick me up. He also offered a room at his home while I stayed here—which I gratefully accepted.

I step through the sliding doors and the first thing that hits me is the smell of the city. Savannah is no small city. But it is far from being a metropolis. The Los Angeles air is drier. I inhale and capture a blend of salty ocean air, a soft floral perfume, marijuana, and a hint of burning wood. It's a strange mix, but not unappealing.

A man in black dress slacks and a black button-down stands beside a car at the curb and holds a small sign with "Matheson" in black marker. I head in his direction and offer my hand when I reach him. "Hi. Rick Matheson."

The man shakes my hand. "Ben." After he wheels my carryon to the back and stuffs it in the trunk, we get in the car and drive away from the airport. One of the first things I notice as we drive through Los Angeles is how busy and alive this city is. Savannah compared to Los Angeles is minuscule. The sea of people and commuters isn't as intimidating as I thought it might be. In fact, the bustle invigorates me.

Wrapped up in all the sights, time flies by and soon we park in front of an opulent building. Stone and pillars and perfectly manicured foliage. Ben gets out and retrieves my luggage. We walk up to the entrance of the building and another man greets us. A man twice the size and a hell of a lot more intimidating than Ben. He nods at us and we step past him.

Ben leads me through a bar/lounge, up a set of stairs, and down a small corridor before he points to a large, wooden door. "Rocco is in there." Other than offering his name, that is the most Ben has said to me since picking me up. Either he is not much of a conversationalist or his job requires him to be a man of few words. I nod and head for the door as Ben leaves.

Staring at the door, I close my eyes and take a deep breath. *You got this*, I repeat in my head. After a few inhalations, I knock and wait a millisecond before I'm invited in. I turn the handle, step inside, and Rocco rises from behind his large mahogany desk and smiles wide. "You must be Rick," he says, walking around the desk and shaking my hand. "Pleasure to meet you."

"No, the pleasure is all mine. Thank you for having me."

We exchange pleasantries for a moment, then get down to the formal part of the interview. Questions for a job of this nature are not quite like those in a typical job interview. Sure, he asks some of the familiar questions. Job history. Why the big move. What my boss and employees would say about me. But when we surpass those, we broach the ones some people may cringe hearing.

What sex acts have you witnessed? Are you straight, gay, bisexual, pansexual, non-defined, other? Elaborate. Have you witnessed a sexual act that made you cower? If so, what was it? Tell me the most hedonistic scene you've been witness to. How did it make you feel?

The questions go on for more than an hour. Once he has asked me a mile-long list of questions, Rocco walks me around the bar and introduces me to several of the staff. We sit at a table in the lounge, eat lunch, and have a drink while discussing his and my lifestyle.

Hours pass and the crowd inside The Sophisticate multiplies. We chat and mingle with patrons. Rocco points to a couple—woman and man. "I'm going to talk with them in a minute, and I want you to listen. See how I filter out people I'm willing to allow into P.I. The only people who know about P.I. are those who have been invited in. They are told not to discuss the club outside these walls. If members want to bring friends, we allow them a one-time opportunity to bring a guest into the club. Names are taken and we track every person who sets foot in P.I."

I nod. "Got it."

We reach the couple and Rocco asks them how they are enjoying themselves. He introduces me as one of his managers, then continues speaking with them. Basically,

Rocco asks them questions to check their integrity and determines if they would act civilized in the exclusive area of P.I. Some of his questions also ascertain if P.I. would be something they would be interested in. It is somewhat similar to what we do at Apex, only this is more personal.

Rocco invites them to join us in an elite area of the bar. He doesn't divulge specific details, but tells them it is a club. When the couple agrees, we head toward a guarded staircase. Rocco tells the bouncers the couple will be guests for the evening. After the bouncers check their IDs, they are let in and we follow.

After descending a lengthy stairwell, we land in a dark corridor. Music vibrates the walls and light slowly seeps in. When we reach the open space, another bouncer lets us pass. The moment I scan the room, I remain rooted in place, awestruck.

If a strip club could receive star ratings, P.I. would get them all.

We walk over to the bar and take a seat. A nude woman pours Rocco a drink and offers me one as well. Once we both have drinks in hand, Rocco asks my opinion on the place.

"First of all, this place is stellar. I've never seen a business of this nature appear so *classy*. Now I'm eager to see your plans for Boundless. Is there only dancing here?"

Rocco points to a space to the right of the stage. Sheer curtains cascade and form a sense of privacy, but every person can see everything in the open area. "Most lap dances happen there, but the girls will stay at the tables if the patron accepts." Next, he points to a long wall with several doors. "Those rooms are for private dances. Only the dancers can take someone in them. And they are in control of what happens. No one except them and the patron are privy to what happens inside."

He tells me more regarding the club and the girls who dance here. Just as Rocco is very selective with the clientele, he is even more so with the staff and dancers. Everyone receives a full background check and is given a probationary period. If anything undesirable happens in the first ninety days, the person is let go without notice.

After a couple hours in P.I., Rocco and I leave and drive to his home. Less than thirty minutes later, I strip my clothes away and take a quick shower. Once I hit the sheets, I send Christy another text. It's just after midnight in California, which translates to after three in the morning at home.

Rick: I miss you, gorgeous. Had a great interview. I love you. Sleep tight.

I plug my phone in and lay it on the bedside table. Just after I turn the light off, my phone vibrates and lights up the room.

Christy: Miss and love you, too.

Thank fuck. If we didn't exchange any form of communication during my entire trip, I was ready to throw in the towel on this offer. Why put in all the effort to move out of state if we're not in an amiable place?

The next day, Rocco takes me to where Opulence/Boundless is being constructed. Similar in nature to The Sophisticate, it has a few differences. Where The Sophisticate has touches of creams and browns in the bar/lounge area. Opulence is bold with black and silver on the exterior. On the interior, the base a slate gray with pops of purples, blues, reds, and occasional touches of silver. Describing it sounds like a disco ball, but visually it screams fine dining with a hint of sex.

We walk the floor plan and I see the restaurant slowly coming to life. Rocco points to a long wall on the left. "We'll have a bar along most of that wall." Then he points toward the back right corner. "An open kitchen there, with a doorway that leads to a closed off prep area and refrigeration." As we reach a stairwell similar to the entrance to P.I., Rocco stops. "And this will be the patron entrance to Boundless. The only traffic to enter and exit through other means is strictly staff or emergency personnel."

I nod, and we head down the stairwell. The entry mimics

P.I., which I prefer. This way, there are no surprises or questions regarding the safety of everyone inside.

When we step into the massive open space, Rocco asks, "How do you envision Boundless?"

Whoa. Completely unexpected and humbling. I gaze around the vast interior and try to picture a club the way I would love it. Currently, there is absolutely nothing here. Just concrete, dust, and the beginning stages of drywall being hung. Spinning around, I point toward the farthest wall. "A bar spanning the majority of the wall. Slate or concrete to match the color scheme in the restaurant." Rocco nods and waves me to continue. "Along majority of this wall" —I point to the longest wall that butts against what could be the bar— "couches, chaises, and chairs with low tables. Same material as the bar top. With tables, couches, and chairs sporadically placed throughout as well. At Apex, we have a VIP section. Perhaps we could create a similar set up here. A secluded area where higher paying clientele or more frequent members can lounge more comfortably and be doted on more."

"I like the idea of having a VIP. We also intend on adding closed off rooms here, like in P.I., where people can explore new things without watching eyes. Not everyone is as adventurous their first time. At least two of the rooms, though, will be specifically for spectators."

This has my interest piqued. "Wouldn't everyone here be privy to the happenings of everyone else?"

"Yes," Rocco confirms. "But the voyeur rooms will be equipped with specialty items from different lifestyles. Bondage, D/s, fetish items, stimulation devices, and so on. Depending on what it is, we will also allow clientele to bring in their own items for play. But they must be approved by myself or club management. The voyeur rooms are intended to be more intense in nature than what happens on the club floor."

Boundless truly is a dream job. This place is everything I've ever wanted out of working in this industry. Freedom to express who I am without criticism. To be in a like-minded environment and not be shamed or made to feel guilty for being who I am. Other than Christy, nothing has ever felt so right.

"Rocco, I don't know what to say, except I hope you'll consider me for the job. I understand if you need time to—"

Rocco cuts me off. "Rick, after talking with you on the phone last week, I made a few calls. Several conversations later, and it was just a matter of meeting you. If your vibe fit what I was seeking, you were my man. And, I'd like to extend you an offer. Would love to have you join the family."

Floored. Absolutely floored. I met this man a day ago, shared nervous conversations with him, and just like that he is ready to bring me on. Speechless and stunned, I shake off my incredulity. "Yes. Let's discuss going forward."

That evening, I sit at the bar inside P.I. A young woman with long dark hair dances across the stage. If I had to guess, I'd say she is Native American. Her beauty rare and subtle. I sip on a glass of whiskey and bask in the day's events. The whole offer still blows me away.

Pulling my phone out of my pocket, I type out a text to Christy.

Rick: Best news, gorgeous. He offered me the job.

The little bubble pops up and the three little dots dance in the gray box, and it thrills me she is awake and responding.

Christy: I'm so excited. You'll have to tell me all about it when you get home. What time is your flight tomorrow?
Rick: 2:30 p.m. CA time. Think I land close to midnight.
Christy: I'll be waiting.
Rick: Fuck, I miss you. Love you, gorgeous.
Christy: Love and miss you more.

I glance at the time on my phone. Just after eleven. Which means it is after two back home. Honestly, I'm somewhat surprised Christy is still awake. But happy I got to chat with her a moment. It was one thing to have her in the room next to me after we had our fight. If I wanted to bad enough, I could have jimmied the lock, walked in, and laid with her. Being thousands of miles apart in a foreign city, though... there is no such possibility.

Honestly, I just want to wake up next to her, study the

lines of her face, get lost in her expressions as she dreams, smell that distinct floral scent of hers, trace my fingers over her curves, and bask in her stormy blue eyes and supple body when she wakes.

Sometimes, it takes distance and not having someone completely accessible to grasp how much they truly mean to you. I have loved Christy for years. But I think time has made us comfortable and complacent with each other. Not having her curled up next to me at night—not even in the same living space—is lonely and cold and unsettling.

After I finish my drink, I exit the club and head back to Rocco's home. Never have I been so eager to jump on a plane and fly back home. Home is wherever Christy is. And if my girl wants to move to the opposite side of the world, I will go with her in a heartbeat. Because wherever Christy is is where I need to be.

NINE

CHRISTY

THE BED DIPS beside me and a draft sends shivers across my skin. I groan into the darkness and yank the comforter higher on the bed.

Just as I drift off again, warm lips graze my temple, my neck, my collarbone. I moan and roll onto my back. Best dream ever. Wet lips kiss down my sternum, across my breast, and wrap around my nipple. When his teeth grind together, I bow my back off the bed.

"I missed you, gorgeous," Rick mumbles around my nipple, his fingers dancing down to my navel and dipping lower.

I open my eyes and see a head of dark hair sweeping over my ribcage. Still believing it's just a dream, I comb my fingers through his hair, make a fist, and tug. Hard. His teeth and lips part, freeing my nipple as he hisses.

A second later, he inches up my body as his lips crash onto mine and it is a battle to the death. When our lips break apart, he slips under the comforter and licks his way down between my legs. His tongue circles and laps my clit, over and over, like a savage beast. But the moment he inserts two fingers and pumps inside me, I let go.

"So sweet," he says, muffled by the blanket. "Fuck, how I have missed the sweet taste of your pussy, kitten."

He crawls his way up my body and hovers above me for a second before kissing me senseless again. The sweet and salty tang of my release hot on his tongue. As he breaks the kiss, he slowly pushes inside me.

It isn't often Rick makes love to me. Yes, our sex is intimate and passionate, but I wouldn't classify most of it as making love. We fuck. A lot. It's intense and hot and euphoric. And the majority of the time, it is straight up fucking.

But what's happening between us right now. How he rocks his hips with slow precision. The way his lips brush softly over my skin and ignite an inferno in my soul. This is so far from fucking, and tips the scale much closer to lovemaking. The pace at which he slides in and out of me. The passion whirling in his eyes. Yes, lust is present. But his longing to touch and see me is a million times stronger. Taking precedence. As does the tender kisses he presses to my lips, my forehead, and my chin.

More intimate than any other time we have been together. Our bodies in sync, this dance we're doing nothing short of hypnotic. I can't get enough of him.

We make love for hours. Kissing. Touching. Reacquainting ourselves with each other after days apart.

Not quite sure what happened while Rick was in California, but he seems different. More appreciative and affectionate. Saying I missed this intimacy would be just the tip of the iceberg. Over the last few months, things between us have been off. Maybe us moving across the country isn't such a bad idea after all. Maybe it is exactly what we need.

In the morning, we stumble out of bed after making love again. After a late breakfast, we dress, hop in the car, and then Rick says he has a surprise for me. We chat throughout the entire drive—Rick telling me every last detail of his time in California. Before I realize it, he drives up to and parks at a small airport, and we board a helicopter.

"Where are we going?" I ask as I buckle myself in and tug the belt as tight as it will go.

Rick winks at me. "You'll see. Figured it'd be fun to have a change of scenery."

After the pilot finishes the preflight checks, the helicopter lifts off the ground and we are high above the streets of Savannah. Beside me, Rick chuckles as I attach myself to the window and watch the city and trees change. In the sky, the world is an entirely different place. Quiet. Peaceful. Sure, all the chaos still happens below us, but it looks like ants marching in the forest. In the clouds, perspectives change. People change.

After we leave Savannah airspace, I sit back in my seat and wrap Rick's hand with mine. With no idea of what he has planned, a fresh wave of excitement ripples in my chest. Rick kisses my knuckles before drawing me closer and pressing his lips to mine. When he strokes my tongue with his, the world vanishes.

No helicopter. No pilot. Just him, and me, and the connection that magnetizes us and always will.

Less than an hour passes and we descend toward Atlanta. The city bustles with life, its energy a massive bubble luring me in. Before the helicopter hits the ground, I assault Rick with kisses. A couple years shy of thirty and I have never traveled very far outside of the city limits of Savannah. Most of my life I was sheltered, and in the years since meeting Rick, we've stayed close to home. Not because neither of us wanted to travel, but we just never had anywhere we dreamed of going.

A car sits idle near the airstrip, and I glance over my shoulder at Rick. His larger than life smile plucks the strings of my heart. "When did you do all this?" I ask.

He shrugs as we slip into the backseat. "I had some free time on my trip. Thought it'd be nice to take you somewhere new. Have a change of scenery. Things have been difficult the last month, and I missed seeing your smile."

I hop on his lap and kiss the hell out of him. After we are both breathless, I inch back into my seat and buckle my seatbelt. "Thank you," I whisper. "You don't know how much I love this."

Dropping a chaste kiss on my nose, he says, "Anything for my girl."

After we grab lunch at a chic cafe, we wander hand in hand through the streets of Atlanta. Rick steers us into a couple stores. The first stop, a jewelry store named Compulsion. Not your typical diamonds and gold bands jewelry store. But I love it the moment we step inside.

Rick drops my hand and lets me walk ahead of him. My eyes light up at all the pieces on display. Silver, platinum, titanium. Collars, cuffs, clamps. The small store is packed with a plethora of jewelry that would be appealing to people from all walks of life. Bands and gemstones and chains glint under the lights in each case.

When I stop in front of a case, a set of silver cuffs sparkle in the display. Simple and beautiful, yet so much more. The bracelets a half inch wide and a quarter inch thick. A small chain links them together, but is removable for normal daytime, public wear. Almost a perfect match to my collar.

Rick leans forward and presses his chest to my back. "Something catch your eye, gorgeous?" I nod and he laughs. "Haven't quite mastered reading your mind yet, so you'll have to tell me."

I swallow and clear my throat. "The cuffs," I mutter.

He leans in closer, his groin thick on my lower back. "Mmm… those would match this" —he brushes a finger along the edge of my collar— "quite nicely. Would you like them?"

I twist to get a better look at him. His honey eyes simmer, lips kicked up in a slight smile. "Really?" I ask. After a beat, his smile widens and reaches his eyes. "Yes, I would love them."

Rick signals for the clerk and, ten minutes later, we walk out of the store. Me with matching bracelets on my wrists. Rick holding a small bag with a chain and a few clamps tucked inside.

While I stare awestruck at my new accessories, Rick guides us into a second store. As soon as we step inside, the distinct scent of leather and latex grabs my attention and I snap my head up. Rick and I have experienced so much together, sexually. We also play a lot in the fetish department. At least I think we do.

For the most part, we enjoy sex together and with other couples. Yes, we have done things deemed not "normal" by the average person or couple. But we haven't introduced an arsenal of accessories. Honestly, that is why I lost it when he strapped me to the Saint Andrew's cross at Apex.

Was I turned on? No doubt about it. But the humiliation rang much louder and stole all the pleasure from my body.

We have never been shy, but our lifestyle wasn't centered around exhibitionism. So, when he caused a scene and everyone stopped to watch him—us—a piece of me shattered. A piece I pray is mendable.

I peek up at Rick, his eyes alight as he scans the store. "Why are we here?" I ask.

Kissing my forehead, he answers, "We have plans tonight. Thought you might enjoy a new club, for a change."

Staring at bodysuits, corsets, and crotchless panties, I zone out a second. When I come back to, I ask, "What kind of club?" Because we don't make a point to wear leather or latex in Savannah.

"Rocco told me about it." When I stare at him confused, he clarifies. "He wanted me to check out other clubs. More ideas for Boundless."

Ah… so this isn't just time away with your girlfriend for fun. This trip to Atlanta is also a work assignment. Don't I feel fucking special.

"Do we need to wear some of this?" I ask, waving my arm at the miles of fetish attire. A few pieces catch my eye and I wouldn't be opposed to wearing them. But there are several things I don't know if I'm quite ready to experience yet.

"No. But I thought it might add some flair." He bends down and kisses me on the lips. Slow and sweet. "And I didn't think you'd be opposed to trying something new."

Am I against it? Yes and no. Should I have to put on skintight, unbreathable material to turn Rick on? I hope not. But slipping into the second skin also adds a new layer of desirability. The chance to be someone new. Someone different. In a sense, wearing leather and latex is a form of role play. For us anyway, being new territory and whatnot.

"Okay," I acquiesce.

After what feels like hours of searching the aisles and racks, I chose a black leather cage bodysuit. Thick black straps span over my neck, breasts, abdomen, and between my thighs. And they are all that will mask my nipples, clit, and ass crack. When I pick it up and survey the design, Rick practically drools beside me.

I drape it over my arm and smile up at him. "What are you wearing?"

We walk to the men's attire and he lifts a pair of leather pants from the rack, hanging them over his forearm. We head to the dressing rooms and try on our selections. Needless to say, the cage bodysuit is a winner in my book. Can't wait for Rick to see me in it later. Before we head for the checkout, Rick walks us down a few more aisles and snags more toys for our collection.

Once we pay and leave, a gleam I have never witnessed lights up Rick's face. And it makes me wonder, once again, if I am enough for him.

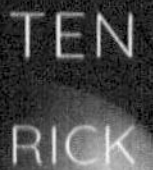

TEN

RICK

We step inside Entrapment and a rush explodes in my bloodstream.

Entrapment isn't a sex club like Apex. It is notches above.

The floor plan is twice the size of Apex, but smaller than the space for Boundless. A small bar sits off to the left of the entrance, dim red lights glowing along the liquor shelves. Black, studded leather couches, chaises, and ottomans spread throughout the open floor. The back third of the space lined with cages, suspension equipment, and varied restraints.

A buzz hums across my skin as I soak in every square foot.

I inhale deep as my eyes close and wrap my arms around Christy's waist. This is what I need. The energy. The lechery. Countless people with insatiable desires, dying to fulfill their utmost fantasies. This is what I want for Boundless.

Walking slowly toward the bar with Christy on my arm, I absorb every heady inch of Entrapment. A seductive beat echoes throughout the large floor plan. It vibrates beneath my feet as heat and lust ripple through my limbs and up my spine. The dim lighting adds another layer of allure to the club. The air is thick with leather and sex and sweat. Pure fucking bliss.

When we reach the bar, Christy orders us both drinks and sits on a stool. Sexy as fuck in the caged leather piece, I can't wait to peel it off her body. But as I wait for my drink and study her body language, I register her discomfort. Legs tightly crossed. Arms banded over her breasts as she fiercely grips her biceps. Head tipped down, eyes on the bar top.

This isn't my girl. Not one bit.

I tip her chin up and force her stormy eyes to meet mine. "You okay, gorgeous?"

The bartender sets our drinks down and her eyes dart toward them. Sliding her glass closer, she locks eyes with me again. "Yeah. I guess. It just feels..." She trails off and scans the men and women in the club. For a split-second, her eyes widen. "Everything is so different here."

Bending down, I kiss her gently. "Yes, it is different here. Things will be different at the new club in California, too." I paint a finger over her cheekbone and down the side of her neck. "Sometimes, different can be good, gorgeous."

Christy stares at me with questions in her eyes. Questions she refuses to ask. A huge part of me wants to introduce her to more than the tamer shit we have done. More than sex with other couples. Because the animal that has always lived inside me, the one I cage up and bury deep, yearns for more.

Not corporal punishment or open wounds. I understand the desire others have for that, but it doesn't resonate with me.

What I thirst for is more kink. More delayed gratification and foreplay. The ability to let go and release the beast clawing inside me. I want to be savage and rough and watch Christy's skin redden under a whip or paddle. I want to clamp her nipples and her folds, chain them together and yank them while I pound into her.

And I want Christy to want this with me.

"I suppose. But I feel so out of my element here. People here are more—"

"Intense," I finish for her.

"Good choice." She nods then sips her drink.

Was bringing her here not such a great idea? *Fuck.* I hope she is open to this. To being in a place similar to this. To experimenting with new things. Boundless will mimic the vibe here and I want her to accept the concept before I work there day in, day out. Christy means the world to me, and I want her to be comfortable with more beyond sex with other couples.

"Are you okay with the intensity here?" I pose the question and pray she says yes.

Taking another sip of her drink, she scans the crowd. Her eyes zero in on a group, and then another, before coming back to me. "I'm not narrow-minded. This is just a lot to take in without warning, I guess."

I mentally slap myself for being so vague with her today. But I wanted to surprise her. Show her the world wasn't just black, white, and gray. Splashes of color existed and it is okay to let droplets dye your skin.

After taking a sip of my drink, I kiss the crown of her head and leave my lips there a moment. Her amber-floral scent pricks my nose, and I close my eyes. "Sorry I didn't tell you, gorgeous," I mumble into her hair. "Just wanted you to be open to new possibilities. Boundless will be more like Entrapment than Apex. I'd rather you be shocked now."

Christy's arms snake around my bare torso and she tugs me closer. Cheek pressed against my pec, she says, "Okay, I'll try to enjoy the evening." She sighs, and a layer of goosebumps pop up on my skin. "Just please don't be upset if I don't want to try certain things."

I inch back from her, take her chin between my thumb and forefinger, and lock eyes with her. "I will never make you do anything you're uncomfortable with. Ever. And it won't upset me. All I want is for you to enjoy yourself. Okay?"

She nods. "Yes."

We finish our drinks and I wrap my hand around hers, guiding us around the club. Tucked close to my side, Christy gazes at couples and groups as they explore one another. When we get closer to the back of the club, where the cages, harnesses, and other contraptions reside, Christy pauses.

For a few minutes, we stand rooted in place and just watch. If I'm not mistaken, Christy seems a little more than curious. Her gaze is locked on the couple in front of us. A good sign.

A tall, lanky man stalks circles around a young woman. If I ventured to guess, I would say he is in his mid- to late-forties, and she appears barely legal. Age is easier to define when you aren't wearing clothing. Both their ages evident in the lines and curvature of their flesh. But in a place like this, as long as consent is provided, no one judges your tastes.

The young woman's ankles and wrists are cuffed and latched to a square, metal frame mounted to the floor. Her body is stretched completely and fully upright. A ball gag is buckled at the back of her head. Her breasts are small and the nipples pert, her thighs are glistening with arousal. As the man circles, he cracks a leather paddle over her body. With each thwack, the young woman jolts in the cuffs and my dick throbs behind my zipper.

I peek down at Christy. Her widened eyes haven't strayed away. From my current angle, it is difficult to tell how all this registers with her. As badly as I want to know, I don't wish to come off as pushy. More than anything, I ache to explore new things with Christy. Incomparable to any other woman I've ever had, it's imperative I know she is happy with our life and open to new possibilities.

When I can no longer bear standing here unaware, I ask, "How does this make you feel, gorgeous?"

She fidgets beside me a minute, her eyes still fixed on the man and young woman. Twirling a lock of hair around her finger, she answers, "Not sure. Guess it depends on what he does next. Right now, though, I don't want to look away."

This is a good sign. In the realm of possibility. Hopeful.

"Do you want to keep watching?" I ask.

"Yes," she whispers. "Please."

I release her elbow and step behind her, wrapping my arms around her waist. With my lips at her neck, just below her ear, I start kissing a trail down and across her shoulder. Her body trembles beneath my lips, and I trace my fingers along the cage straps on her belly. Soon, she audibly pants and starts grinding her ass over my groin.

Fuck yes.

The man switches out the paddle for a riding crop. As he circles, he stings her nipples, clit, and each butt cheek. After a few passes, the young woman's skin blossoms a glorious shade of red. A red I wish to paint Christy's skin.

"Does this turn you on, kitten?" I murmur.

Christy gyrates her hips and rubs her ass over my erection. "Yes, daddy."

Thank fuck. "Do you want to play, kitten?" I trail my fingers down her belly and between her legs.

"Please. But be gentle."

We step away from the suspension exhibition and wander. After a few minutes, we spot a couple on a couch. They're still mostly dressed, with the woman bound to the couch while the man flogs her. For a moment, we observe before introducing ourselves.

When the man glances over at us, I nod and he stops. Extending a hand, I introduce us. "Name's Rick. This is my girl, Christy."

The man shakes my hand. "Jason. And this fine specimen" —he points the flogger at the woman on the couch— "is my wife, Rachel."

Christy speaks up. "Nice to meet you both." Her smile illuminates the darkest night and the shadowed parts of my heart. Fuck, I love her.

"We wondered if you'd care for company," I state.

Jason walks over to his wife, leans down, and whispers in her ear. She glances our way, nods then kisses her husband. When Jason returns, we discuss our conditions for play. Once everything is laid out, I saunter toward Rachel on the couch.

Near her knees, that are bent over the seat edge of the couch, is a bamboo cane. Christy and I have never played with whips, canes, or similar items. The harshest implement we have introduced was a paddle or crop. I have wanted to try something *stronger*, something with a little more *bite*, but am worried Christy won't enjoy it. Hopefully tonight will change that.

I pick up the bamboo cane and scrape the end over Rachel's body—up her thigh, along her torso, tracing her collar bones. When I stand on the opposite side of her, I lift it up six inches and whip it back down over her breasts. Rachel bows off the couch and moans in pleasure.

Immediately, my cock stiffens and groans for relief behind my zipper. It isn't so much that Rachel turns me on, it's the pleasure she receives from the pain.

Stepping between her widespread knees, I lift the cane again and whack it against her clit.

"Fuck yes," she mewls. Between her thighs, moisture

pools at her folds. Not yet, but I need to fuck the hell out of this woman.

I glance over at Christy and Jason. For a beat, my pulse roars in my veins. Jason has her spread wide on an ottoman, hands and ankles bound at the furniture legs. Clamps attached to her nipples, a chain linking them together as he holds the center in his clenched fist. He sweeps the leather tassels of a black flogger over her still caged body. Christy wiggles when the leather grazes between her thighs, and he tugs the chain.

When she gasps, eyes rolling back in her head as her mouth hangs open in pleasure, I freeze. *Have I been too scared to push harder with her? Maybe she wants more, and I have been resistant for the wrong reasons.*

An unfamiliar anger builds inside me. Not anger at Christy. Anger at myself for what has been lacking in our relationship due to my concern. A concern I plan to voice when we are alone.

I refocus on Rachel and take out my aggression on her with the cane. The fact she enjoys it only makes me angrier and my cock harder. Once I have licked her skin with the cane several times, I grab the paddle at her feet, undo my pants, and roll on a condom.

Jacking Rachel's hips up, I slip my knees beneath her ass and line myself up with her folds. She watches me with unadulterated lust in her eyes, and it makes me wild. Sneaking a side glance at Christy and Jason, I stare a beat as he rubs his thumb over her clit and slides in and out of her ass.

Motherfucker.

I whack Rachel's breasts with the paddle and she bucks beneath me, forcing me inside her. So fucking tight. After a moment, I find a rhythm of fucking and beating. The harder I hit Rachel, the louder she cries. Beside us, Christy appears to be enjoying herself more than past exchanges.

In a heartbeat, I see red.

In a heartbeat, I fuck Rachel like a rag doll. Except her limbs are frozen in place. I bang the fuck out of her. Punish a woman I only just met for circumstances beyond her involvement. Beat her with the paddle and mentally scream at the top of my lungs in rage.

Why is this eating me up?

The answer is simple. Christy is mine. She is mine and I have limited our relationship due to fear. Fear of rejection. Fear she will detest me. But most of all, fear she will leave me. Because a life without her isn't a life worth living.

And with all this building up inside me, I explode inside a woman who means nothing to me. A woman who I hope got off, because I lost focus and am not sure she did.

But the worst part of this whole debacle… Not five feet away, my girl is screaming out the most intense sound I have heard leave her lungs. And I suddenly hate myself.

PART
two

ELEVEN

CHRISTY

August—One year later

RICK AND I, along with a dozen other people, sit in a dark private room at Bella and Daisy's Bistro. In a matter of minutes, Jackson and Sarah will walk into the pitch black room as Jackson pretends that just the two of them are having a private birthday dinner for her. Sarah has no idea we traveled here for her birthday. The other night when Liz and I talked on the phone with her, we played off our loud night out in the city and told her we were partying. A half truth. We were out at a bar drinking and dancing, but unbeknownst to her we were only a few miles from her house.

The moment she walks through those doors, her reaction will be picture worthy when she sees us all here. God, I have missed her face. Missed her carefree demeanor and smile. Talking with your best friend on the phone regularly is one thing. Being able to hug the hell out of them is so much more.

The door cracks open, and Jackson and Sarah step inside before the room goes dark again. Sarah is ten feet away and it takes all my willpower to not jump forward and plow into her. A few seconds tick by before the light flicks on. After a quick adjustment to the brightness, we all holler "Surprise!"

Sarah remains stock still with wide eyes. After realization dawns, she smiles so big the room glows brighter. I snap a few quick photos. The moment is one-hundred percent priceless.

After we all line up and give hugs to the birthday girl, we settle at our tables and spark conversations. Everyone made a special trip here just to see Sarah on her birthday. Sarah's parents, Jackson's dad, Liz, Tiffany, me, Rick, Eric, and some new friends they have made since their move to California.

Smiles light up every face in the room. Laughter ricochets off the walls. Family, friends, and the best of times. In my heart, nothing gets better than this. Well… I glance toward Jackson. Just as I suspected, pale as a ghost. I wriggle in my seat and lean toward Rick. "It's almost time," I whisper in his ear.

Rick pauses his chat with Jackson's father and glances at me with confusion etched in the crease of his brow. "Time for what?"

Sworn to secrecy, I haven't shared with Rick that Liz and I have been helping Jackson coordinate tonight. The pièce de résistance coming in five… four… three… two… one.

Jackson rises from his chair and Sarah peeks up at him. Concern mars her forehead as she studies his sweat slickened pallor. She asks if he feels okay and he brushes it off, kissing her cheek. When she returns her attention to her mom, Jackson clears his throat. "Hey, everyone. Can I have your attention for a moment or two?"

The room quiets and every pair of eyes hones in on Jackson. Poor guy. Sweat glistens along his forehead. His breathing is jagged and heavy. His fingers tap the outside of his leg as if he's playing a drum solo.

"Thank you, again, for being here tonight. I know it means the world to Sarah." Jackson gazes down at Sarah as if she is the sun, stars, and moon wrapped into one. "It means everything to me, too. It took a lot of man hours, and woman hours —" Jackson pauses and tips his head to me and Liz "—to get tonight put together. Countless hours, that turned into weeks, of planning. I couldn't have done it without help. So, thank you. You are the best friends either of us could ever have."

When I raise my wine glass, Rick leans into me. "You've been helping Jackson plan this?" Rick almost hisses, and I just ignore his pissy demeanor and nod. Rick and I have been *off* as of late. Not sure if our upcoming move to Los Angeles is to blame. Or if work has been a stressor for him. Either way, our relationship teeters on a slippery slope. A slope I wish would flatten out and right itself.

"Sarah's birthday isn't the only reason I wanted everyone here tonight." Jackson's lips curve up and display his bright smile. Gah! I have been waiting months for this exact moment. "I brought you all here tonight for another reason as well. I wanted all of you here, the people who hold the highest level of importance to both of us—individually or together—on this memorable evening."

Jackson pivots, shoves his chair back, and drops to one knee. I slap my hand over my mouth and gasp. Although privy to the planning for this very moment, I still shake my head in disbelief that it is actually happening. Tears threaten to rain down my cheeks any second. I'm so happy to be here to witness one of the happiest moments of my best friend's life.

"Sarah, since the day I met you, a little over a year and a half ago, you have turned my life into this astonishing place. You made me see things a little brighter, your aura like a glowing ray of sunlight. Before you, my skies were gray and life was monotonous. Now, everything is brilliant and bold and screaming with life. You make me feel whole. You make life worth living."

Jackson fishes a ring from his pocket and presents it to Sarah. After a shared, teary glance with his father, Jackson continues. "This ring belonged to my mother, MaryAnne. I wish you could have met her. She would have loved you immensely." Sarah wipes a tear from Jackson's cheek. I swipe at my own, not able to fight the urge to let them run free.

Jackson explains why he flew so many of us out here for tonight. Not just for her birthday, which he holds in high regard. "I could have held the door open for anyone that day. I was in such a rush to meet up with a client, I didn't have time to pause at the gym doors or say anything to anyone. I thought in that moment, I'd missed the opportunity of a lifetime. I thought I'd missed my one chance to talk to the most stunning woman I had ever laid eyes on. But I didn't know luck was on my side. I didn't know we were meant to see each other again."

Jackson explains how he whined to his friends for days about the beautiful woman he spotted at the gym. How he practically begged clients in her complex for another appointment, all in the hopes he would see her again. The story plucks at my heart as he shares his point of view.

"Eric was having way too much fun giving me shit for acting like a girl." Jackson glances over at Eric and they laugh a moment before everyone joins in.

As Jackson carries on, he shares how he ended up going to Liz's birthday party. Where the two of them met and spoke for the first time. "I watched you, waiting for the right moment to approach you and start a conversation. When I did… it was all downhill from there. I was hooked. I've been hooked every moment since. Sarah, I couldn't even imagine my life without you in it. I never want to."

I zone out for a moment and ponder over Jackson's confession to Sarah. How his life is incomplete without her. And part of me saddens at the reality of where Rick and I are right now. In some strange limbo. Do I love him? Without a shadow of doubt. Am I completely happy? In this very moment? I want to answer yes, but my hesitancy is answer enough. Whatever has shifted us off kilter, I want to force it back into place. Realign us. Piece us back together and make us whole again.

When I snap out of my introspection, Jackson says the one line most women swoon over. "…will you marry me? Will you be mine forever?"

The room goes silent. Utterly engrossed with Sarah and Jackson, I startle when Rick rests his hand on my thigh. Sometime after Jackson started his speech, maybe while I sat here deep in thought, Rick inched closer to me. For the first time in weeks, Rick displays a level of affection that's been missing from our relationship. Affection I crave on an unhealthy level. And in public, no less. Taken slightly aback, I peer at him out of the corner of my eye. I stare for a moment, wondering what circulates through his head as he watches our best friends get engaged.

Has Rick ever given thought to us getting married?

It crosses my mind for the millionth time. Sarah and Jackson have been together less than two years and he is proposing to her. Rick and I have been together five and a half years, and I wonder if he has ever thought of me beyond the term *girlfriend* or *kitten*.

At times, it feels like we're strangers. Passing each other in the thin timeline between our work schedules. Honestly, I can't remember the last time we had sex. A wild guess, at least three weeks to a month ago. Ever since that night at Entrapment last year, Rick has slowly distanced himself from me. I don't have it in my heart to assume he would cheat on me, but oftentimes my thoughts wander down that path. With his distance, how could they not?

When your partner prefers the company of everyone except you, it isn't difficult to believe you are the issue. Truth or falsehood.

The room booms with congratulations. I wilt in my seat, pissed, because I was so wrapped up in my own head, I missed the key part. Where my best friend accepted the marriage proposal. Not a second passes before a lone tear rolls down my cheek. Not from joy for my friends, but from the notion I may never have this. A happily ever after like Sarah and Jackson.

Rick reaches up and wipes the tear from my cheek. "Happy tear?" he asks as his eyes search mine.

A huge part of me wants to lie and tell him yes. But we swore to always be honest. Always. Although our relationship may not be in the best place, I never go against my word.

"No," I whisper. *Please don't let me ugly cry. Not here.*

He tugs on my chair and spins it so I face him. "What's wrong, gorgeous?" Gone is his pissy attitude from ten minutes ago. Now, a layer of charming and sweet sits out in the open. The sudden shift is like whiplash to my heart.

Damnit. I don't want to lie to him, but I don't want him to do a one-eighty when I spill my honesty. Whatever. "Being here... are we okay?" I ask.

My question broken and vague, but he knows exactly what question I'm asking. There is no way he doesn't see or feel the distance growing between us. A gradual barrier erecting and widening with each passing day. If he doesn't recognize it, then we need to have a more serious talk.

His thumb draws small circles on my bare thigh beneath my dress. The motion soothing and equally disheartening. "We should talk later, but yes, gorgeous, we're okay."

I survey the lines of his face. Study his eyes with intensity. Drop down and stare at his lips. He gives nothing away. If there is one thing I have learned over the years, it is that if Rick doesn't want you to know something in a particular moment in time, you won't. He keeps secrets better than Area 51.

The rest of the party goes by uneventfully. Sarah flashes her engagement ring to me and Liz, and a boulder sinks deep in my gut. Flashes of being nothing more than Rick's *girlfriend* pop in and out of my head the rest of the evening. Nothing sets the tone better than a *"we should talk"* moment.

Bile rises in my throat and I excuse myself. Sarah and Liz offer to go with me, but I tell them I will be back in a minute, then walk away alone. Once in the locked bathroom stall, I sit on the seat, hang my head in my hands, and cry.

Cry for my relationship, which is going south faster than a snowbird leaving Canada for Florida. Cry for my best friend, and the jealousy that runs in my veins like a drug every time I bear witness to her happiness. And I cry for myself, and the life I thought I would have but can't seem to grab hold of no matter what I do.

After I dry my eyes, I walk back to the party with my eyes downcast. If I keep them down long enough, maybe no one will notice their red and puffy state. The last thing I want is to ruin my best friend's birthday/engagement party.

An hour later, our Uber parks at the entrance of our hotel. We step out, walk to our room in silence, and head inside. The quiet irks me more than anything. Lack of communication is the devil taunting me. If I know Rick at all, he will bring everything up as soon as I hit the sheets.

I turn on the shower and start stripping out of my clothes. The continuous silence kills me as I watch Rick remove his clothes. Once undressed, I step under the hot spray, close my eyes, and sigh. A river of tears sits restrained by my internal dam. I refuse to cry. Not now. Not when it won't solve a damn thing.

As I run my hands through my hair, cool air licks my skin for a beat before Rick grabs both my hips. It has been too damn long since the last time he touched me intimately. I hate to admit it, but I have almost forgotten what it feels like to be caressed by Rick. After another pass through my hair, I swipe it to the side and Rick peppers soft kisses from the base of my skull to the edge of my shoulder. So sweet. So gentle.

At any given moment, that internal dam I built is going to shatter.

His strong arms wrap around my belly, tug me out of the spray, and spin me around. Then his lips graze mine. "I'm scared," he whispers.

My eyes pop open and lock on a swirl of golden fire. I reach up and frame his face. "Why?"

For the first time in weeks, the bond that brought us together flickers. "I'm scared to leave Georgia. It's where my life came together. What if us moving out here tarnishes that?"

I shake my head and press a chaste kiss on his lips. "It won't. We won't let that happen."

"How can you be so sure?" The way his voice cracks... it breaks my heart.

"Because you are the strongest man I know. And if you want something, you go after it."

His brow furrows as he stares into my eyes with uncertainty. "Not that I've purposely withheld from you, but there are skeletons in my past I don't wish to unearth. And moving might do that. My lifestyle—" I cock a brow at him. "Our lifestyle, sorry, is an outlet for me. And if we're being truthful, sometimes what we have isn't enough for me."

"Like what?" I challenge.

Rick starts playing with my hair. "After Jackson and Sarah's engagement today, and seeing the way your face lit up when he asked her, it was a knife to the heart." His eyes wander to where his fingers toy with the strands. "I love you, Christy. More than I love anyone else. But sometimes I wonder if we give each other what we need."

I inch back from him and his eyes refocus on mine. "What is that supposed to mean?" I bite out.

"Please don't be upset." He pauses, eyes bouncing back and forth between mine, and he takes a deep breath. "What I mean is, I'm not sure we're both satisfying the other physically."

My blood boils. *Is he serious right now?* "We have to have sex for that to count."

He flinches, then nods—my words a slap in the face—and returns to playing with my hair. "After that night in Atlanta, a light came on. I'd never seen you so euphoric during sex—with me or anyone else. At first, I disregarded it and blamed it on my imagination. But the next time we had sex, it replayed in my head. How much you got off with that other guy. Your cries. The way your body begged for more of *him*. For the first time ever, I felt inadequate."

I lean back, my hands still on either side of his face, and study his eyes. Rick's eyes hold the keys to all his secrets. "You feel inadequate? I don't understand how that's possible. Especially seeing as I never give you what you need."

He slowly shakes his head, eyes watching my lips a beat before they come back to mine. "Christy... you *are* everything I need."

Pressing my lips to his, I kiss him as if I never will again. "Are you sure?" I hold his gaze. "Because that club in Atlanta... The new club in LA... They're so different than what I'm used to. And you're not the Rick I've known in those places. White hot fire blazes in your eyes in that setting." Inhaling deep for three breaths, I continue. "Baby, I want you to be happy. If doing things I'm not quite comfortable with makes you happy, I'll do them."

He strokes his knuckles over one cheek while his other hand tinkers with my hair. "That's not what I want, gorgeous. I don't want you doing things, especially uncomfortable things, to make me happy. This isn't just about me. It's about us. What we enjoy individually, and together. You're in control, more than me."

His words seep into my consciousness and filter through every molecule. As much as I would love to believe I hold more control in our relationship, it isn't true. Yes, I love the thrill of having new sexual experiences and partners. But it isn't the end all, be all. If Rick told me today he no longer wanted to have another person in our bedroom—so to speak—I would stop for him. And I hope he would react the same. It isn't strictly the thrill of a different partner, but also what they do and how they behave.

Hard to explain, but it is a yearning deep inside that begs to be fulfilled. A hunger. An insatiable drive for more. Could Rick give me what I need? No doubt about it. And that is why I am willing to experience new things. Besides another shape or set of hands on my body. If I expose myself to more, maybe I can be enough for Rick. Be enough for him to not need another in our bed.

I shake my head. "No baby, we're both in control. And all I want is to love you."

For the first time in weeks, Rick makes love to me for hours. As if it were our first time. And I fall asleep with his arms wrapped tight around my waist. Sated and peaceful.

TWELVE

RICK

Walking through Boundless, I scan the floor as workers lay planks of graphite gray tiles. The walls coated with fresh paint two days ago. Once the floor is finished today, another set of hands will come in and construct the bar. Everything is coming together quickly, and it is hard to believe the doors will open in a month and a half.

After looking over the concept drawings for Boundless, Rocco and I added our opinions and notations. Within days, we had contractors and workers lined up. Everything kicked off faster than expected. Watching it all come to life is unreal. The pull I have in decision-making even more surreal. Rocco instills an unfathomable level of trust in me, and every day I work with him I am beyond thankful.

Christy doesn't start at the California Hammond Life office until Monday. So, over the next few days, she spends her time going through box after box and unpacking our home. Liz and Tiffany are scheduled to arrive week after next. At first, I considered it odd Liz also wanted to move. But then again, I never shared a bond with friends like the three of them do. The only person I have ever been somewhat close to —on that level—was Harriett.

"Mr. Matheson?" One of Opulence's bartenders calls across the room.

"What's up, Jake?"

He points a thumb over his shoulder toward the stairwell. "There's someone upstairs. Says they have an interview."

I nod. "Thanks, Jake. I'll be up in a minute. Get them a drink, please."

Jake spins on his heel and heads for the stairs. Taking my phone out of my pocket, I type out a quick text to Rocco.

Rick: Next interview is here.
Rocco: Be there in a minute.

I head for the stairs and up to the restaurant level. Opulence/Boundless has a third, upper level dedicated to office space for Rocco, myself, the restaurant manager, and shared space for our backup managers. I consider myself the club manager, but Rocco corrects me each time. "You're not strictly the club manager, Rick. You're also my number two. My right hand." When Rocco isn't here, employees come to me in his stead.

Today, we are interviewing for the open managerial roles. Tomorrow, we will see a long line of people applying for positions within Boundless. Bartenders, bouncers, drink servers, dancers, security, janitorial. The list goes on and on. We have seven managerial interviews today—an hour blocked for each. But the interviewees tomorrow will get fifteen to thirty minutes max, especially with the mile-long list.

When Rocco rounds the corner, I wait for him to join me. Together, we walk over to where a man sits. Before we sit, I quickly observe him. Bouncing knee. Palms wiping his thighs beneath the table. His eyes dart to me, then Rocco, then back to me. The glass of water on the table in front of him half full.

Why the fuck is he so nervous?

After talking to Mr. Scared Shitless for twenty minutes, I give a pointed look to Rocco. Something tells me this guy has never worked in a place like this before. Part of me questions whether he has ever seen a naked woman in person. Or if he's even been with someone else. Honestly, I pray we don't attract an obscene amount of pervs. I don't have it in me to deal with them.

We dismiss him and let him know we'll call him sometime next week. As soon as he walks out, I turn to Rocco. "We need some sort of signal. Something to tell the other we don't like the candidate."

Rocco laughs. A harsh, genuine roar. "Thought it was just me. How about this?" He brushes the side of his index finger knuckle against his nose. The gesture could pass as an itch. Vague enough only he and I would understand it means more.

"Perfect," I say. "If either of us feels we need to cut the interview short, we signal the other."

"Agreed."

The next three interviews come and go. Two of them potentials. One a dirty old man looking to get off. Wasn't hard to detect. If I have seen one, I have seen them all. Wrinkled button-down and slacks. Greasy hair slicked back. Cologne strong enough to smell a mile away. But that wasn't the worst of it. That belonged to the devious smile—sans a few teeth—and the glint in his eyes every time we mentioned anything sexually related. Within five minutes, Rocco and I both rubbed our nose.

Fucker.

Three more to go. Hopefully, they will be more professional. Rocco and I discuss the two potentials as we wait for our next candidate. We both agree we prefer Grayson over Charles, but both have potential. Once we finish discussing them, Rocco starts asking me personal questions.

"So, tell me about you and your girl. Christy, right?"

"Yeah. She's my light. Things have been a bit rocky since her friend moved to Santa Barbara a little over a year ago. But I hope we're on the upswing."

Rocco nods. "Me, too. I wouldn't imagine either of you moving thousands of miles with the other if things were bad. You love her?"

"With everything I am. But we both have our demons, and every once in a while they make us doubt the other's happiness. Couldn't imagine life without her, though."

"So why isn't she more?"

I cock my head. Not wanting to assume, I ask, "How so?"

"If I remember correctly, you said you've been together almost six years. No ring?" Rocco gestures to my left hand.

Twisting the ring on my right thumb, I shake my head.

"Not yet. Funny thing, I know she'd say yes if I asked. And it's not that I don't want her forever. But before I ask her to be my wife, I need to eradicate my demons first. Demons I haven't shared with her."

"Take it from me," Rocco says as he taps the table, "don't wait too long. You love her. She loves you. The longer you wait to share, the harder it will be. Plus, her trust in you may change."

"You speak from experience?"

"Yes and no," he tells me. "My wife and I have been married almost twenty years. She spends a lot of time with her family in New York—her mother isn't well. At times, it's hard on us, but we're completely open. Do I miss her? Every goddamn day. She misses me too. But for the longest time, I kept my tendencies to myself, and she didn't tell me about her mother's illness. It wasn't until we'd been married a few years—we dated four years—that I introduced my kinky side. Needless to say, she was shocked. Initially, I hid it from her because I didn't want her to leave me. Not that I thought she would, but you never know. She is sweet and gentle, and I feared losing her."

I sit beside him, running a finger over my upper lip. "Christy only knows half the kink I enjoy. I introduced her to more last year and she seemed open to some of it. My worry is she'll see me in a different light and leave me. Plus, we haven't talked much about my past. It's a touchy subject for me, and every time I think about telling her about it, I chicken out."

"Dive in head first. Get it over with. Thinking about the what if's will only have you questioning everything. If you're constantly in your head, she'll think the worst. And you'll never know her reaction unless you bring it up."

I nod. "True. Thanks for the advice, Rocco."

The last of the interviews pass and thank fuck there aren't any other assholes. Once we have spoken to everyone, Rocco and I go into his office and narrow down the candidates. Between the seven candidates—well, six because the perv was automatically eliminated—we narrow it down to four people. Through a second interview, those four will dwindle to three. A manager for the restaurant and each of our assistant managers.

Rocco hands me a few small slips of paper and I write their names and numbers down. Tomorrow, I plan to do call backs and schedule second interviews. All in all, the day went much smoother than expected and we are on par with our opening timeline.

After a long day, I park in the driveway at home. Christy and I found a small, two-bedroom home just outside the city. The cost of living in California is dramatically different than Georgia, but Rocco offered me a substantial salary and Hammond gave Christy a cost-of-living pay increase. It worked out perfect and we're financially more stable than before.

As opposed as I originally was to us moving across the country, everything has fallen in line. I have never been a firm believer in destiny. Not after what happened to Harriett. And with Sarah. But the concept grows on me more with each passing day.

When I walk in the house, Christy bangs pots and pans in the kitchen. From the sound of it, you might think she is cooking for a party. Tiptoeing from the front door to the kitchen, I stay out of her line of sight and watch her a moment. She must not have heard me walk in. Obviously slaving over the stove to make us dinner. Christy enjoys cooking, always has, but cooking doesn't like her.

I lean against the pillar that breaks up the open floor plan. The kitchen sits opposite the front door, foyer, and small breakfast nook. Off to the other side of the front door is the living room. Our black leather couch with a chaise on one end dominates one corner of the room. The television is mounted so it swings out from the wall and points toward the couch, but otherwise it is flush. Across from the living area, but next to the kitchen, is the formal dining room. Not a huge space, but our table expands to seat ten comfortably.

We have yet to set up the bookshelves or hang photos and art. But that will come with time. And we have plenty of that ahead of us.

A frustrated huff puffs up a tuft of hair over Christy's glasses. On both of her denim-covered butt cheeks is a flour handprint. Only a small island separates the kitchen from the open space. On the island lies the evidence of where her flour prints came from. She stirs a large pot on the stove before lifting the spoon out and tasting the contents.

"Shit," she yells, tossing the spoon in the pot and slapping her fingers to her lips.

I push off the post and walk toward her. "Did you burn yourself?"

Christy jumps with a shriek before spinning to face me. "Holy shit! You scared the bejesus out of me." She play slaps my chest and leaves a flour handprint over my left pec. But I give two shits about the handprint. Whether or not she burned herself is far more important.

"Are you okay?" I drag her closer to me and inspect her lips. Before she answers, I kiss her. She tastes like herbs and chicken with a hint of her sweet honey flavor.

When the kiss breaks, she inhales deeply. "Yeah," she says, breathily. "Just hotter than I expected."

"Mmm. Whatever it is, it tastes good." I kiss her again, dragging her body closer and erasing all space between us.

After I devour the taste of dinner off her tongue, I break the kiss and head to the bedroom to change out of my work clothes. Christy walks in a minute later and slips on a cute, skimpy pajama set. Whether dressed to the nines or in her frumpiest outfit, Christy is drop dead gorgeous. A glowing burst of love and energy. She owns every room she steps in. Most of all, she owns my heart.

I twist the band on my right thumb and admire her. Christy is the reason my heart beats. Why I have purpose. The years before we met, I filled the void in my life with countless sexual partners. To be honest, I don't remember a single one of their faces, let alone their names. That probably makes me a cold prick, but the truth is what it is.

Without Christy, days trickled by and felt lackluster. Hell, I probably fucked half or more of the patrons from Apex before meeting Christy. From the second I laid eyes on her, life transitioned from a cold, cloudy existence to a sun-laden paradise. For years, my heart was this hunk of frigid stone in my chest. Unmoving. Never warming. Until the night she walked into Apex. Even at the lowest points in our relationship, she jumpstarted my heart with just her presence.

There is no way to explain the way she lifts me up. All I know is, my life would be shit without her.

We sit on the couch with large bowls of chicken and dumplings and watch *Meet Joe Black*. Christy loves this movie on an unhealthy level. A few years ago, I bought her the digital copy after the DVD got scratched and she ugly cried for an hour straight. Just couldn't bear to see my girl in such agony. She enjoys the love story most of all, but I find the rest of the storyline intriguing. So, we both get sucked in every time.

Curled into my side with a blanket over her legs, her body sinks deeper into mine and her breathing evens out. The movie has another hour to go, but I shut it off. I scoop her up from the couch, cradle her to my chest, and walk down the hall to our bedroom.

Once in the bed, she lies on her side and gravitates toward me. I sweep fallen hairs off her cheek after I set her glasses on the bedside table. She sighs in her sleep and leans closer to me. It is moments like this that I treasure. The ones only I get to keep locked tight in my heart. The ones where I am most tender with her.

I kiss her softly on the lips and whisper, "Love you, gorgeous. Sweet dreams." She stirs beside me and drapes her body over mine. This is all I need in life. Christy in my arms.

THIRTEEN

CHRISTY

"I have never wanted to go to work so much in my life," I say.

On the other end of the phone, Sarah laughs. "Just wait till you're at your desk tomorrow and you have five thousand emails to answer. Plus, meeting new coworkers. Being home might not be so bad then."

"Bitch, you think I can't handle new people?" I tease.

Her laugh intensifies to hyena level. "If anyone can handle a crowd, it's you." She has no idea. Me and new faces—we go together like chocolate, marshmallows, and graham crackers. But not everyone knows such things.

Rick and I arrived in California a little more than a week ago. Hammond was more than generous and gave me ten days off to transition from Georgia to California. The drive stole a couple of those days and exhausted the hell out of us, but we made it.

Marco, my manager in Georgia, gave me a company laptop before I left. Although I wasn't required to work during the transition, I had the option to do so. So, when I needed the occasional break from unpacking, I cleared out emails and responded to clients. That little bit of work would make my first day at the new office less stressful.

"What's that supposed to mean, bitch?" I ask.

Since moving closer to Sarah, my favorite word has resurfaced. Honestly, I only threw *bitch* out with Sarah and Liz.

After Sarah moved, and Liz stayed home with Tiffany more often, I stopped saying it. Throwing my favorite word out felt wrong. They were my *bitches*. No one earned it like them. Saying it with one of them gone was a betrayal.

"Nothing bad. Just that you have the ability to make a crowd fall in love with you," she confesses.

"Thanks," I mumble. God, why can't I find the nerve to tell her more about who I am. About my and Rick's lifestyle. Sarah rejecting me for who I am isn't something I picture. At least a big part of me believes this. But until I know for certain she will accept the other side of me, the side I shelter from half of my life, I plan to keep it to myself.

With the phone pinned between my ear and shoulder, I toss towels into the laundry basket and walk it to the washing machine. Sarah continues talking to me about her new job at a magazine as I add clothes to the washing machine.

I pick up a pair of Rick's work pants and something crinkles in the pocket. Fishing out a piece of paper, I unfold it and freeze. Is this real? I pinch my eyes tight, take a couple deep breaths, then open them again. Sarah still talks in my ear, but the last thirty seconds are a blur.

"What the fuck," I blurt out.

"Christy? You okay?" Sarah asks.

I stare at the small slip of paper, dumbfounded. "Yeah, I'm... I'm good. Uh, I got to go. Talk to you later?"

"Sure," Sarah says, a hint of confusion lacing her voice. "Call whenever. Love you."

"Love you, too." I disconnect the call and throw the phone down on the dryer.

What the actual fuck? Why the hell does Rick have this?

Scorching my hands is a small slip of paper with the name *Elizabeth* and a phone number written on it. In Rick's handwriting. Beneath the number, he has written *Monday 1:30*. Is he meeting up with this woman tomorrow? And who the hell is she?

My eyes refuse to look away while my thoughts scream *Rick wouldn't cheat on you*. I pinch my eyes shut as a vise tightens around my ribcage. I work to control my breathing, but it refuses to calm down. This cannot be happening. We are better. Things between us are better. Not as great as they once were, but on the upswing.

I snatch my phone off the dryer and vigorously type out a text to Rick.

Christy: Hey, for my first day back tomorrow, want to have lunch together?

Generic and innocent enough. Every once in a while, Rick would have lunch with me on his off days when he worked at Apex. So my asking wouldn't be out of the ordinary. Especially after our move.

Rick: Sorry, gorgeous. I have a meeting tomorrow. Tuesday?
Christy: Okay. Tuesday.

I shove my phone in my pocket and finish loading the laundry. Once done, I walk to the kitchen, grab a bottle of wine and a glass, and plop down on the couch. My head drowns in thousands of crazy thoughts and I have no idea which one I should believe. My heart tells me Rick would never mess around. But the paper scalds me like a branding iron.

Two bottles of wine and hours later, Rick walks in the front door. His body silhouetted by the outside lights. Since opting to drink my feelings, I haven't flipped on any inside lights. So, the second Rick flips on the light switch in the foyer, I squint and shield my eyes as if the sudden contrast burns my retinas.

"What are you doing?" Rick asks as he walks in my direction.

I bring the bottle of wine to my lips, tip my head back, and drink straight from the bottle. When I finished the first bottle, I left the glass in the kitchen sink. Honestly, using a glass just made extra work.

Rick sits on the couch beside me and studies my face. Etched in the lines around his eyes as he half-squints is worry and confusion. As far as he knows, everything is on the up-and-up. I stare at him a beat before glancing at the paper on the coffee table. When I don't look back at him, he follows my line of sight. His body deflates next to me.

"Who is she?" I ask.

He picks up the weathered paper. I crumpled and straightened the small slip several times over the last few hours. At one point, I was half tempted to call the number, but stopped myself. What would I say? *Who the hell are you and why does my boyfriend have your phone number?* I'm not some lovestruck teenager. No, I'm a grown ass woman, and we don't make petty phone calls. We get even.

"Really?" Rick stares back at me, a fire roaring in his eyes. "Are you sitting in the dark because of this?"

"Not an answer." I take another swig from the bottle. "Who is she?" I ask again.

"Is this why you asked me to have lunch with you tomorrow? Because you found this." His face reddens and he is on the verge of yelling, but I give no fucks. Because he still hasn't answered my question. His evasion like poison in my veins, slowly eating me alive.

"Lunch would've been nice on my first day back, but yes," I hiss.

Rick rises from the couch, stares down at me, and shakes his head. "No words." He turns his back on me and walks to the bedroom as if his non-answer is acceptable.

Are you fucking kidding me? Not answering me adds fuel to the fire blazing beneath my sternum. I bolt up from the couch, slam the bottle on the table, and hold my hands out in front of me to stabilize myself. Whoa, I definitely drank too much. But it was the only thing to do that made time not drag by.

Once the room stops spinning, I storm toward the bedroom. I step past the threshold and see Rick stripping, then heading for the shower. Following in his wake, I stare at him through the fogged stall glass. He still looks pissed. But I don't fucking care.

"Why won't you answer me?" I ask, loud enough to be heard over the shower.

He stands under the spray, unmoving. The water pounds his face and torso. His eyes pinched shut as he grinds his jaw.

Fists clenched at his side. After a minute, he turns his head in my direction. Eyes sad and red. Deflated and small.

"Do you think so little of me?" He mumbles so soft I almost don't hear his question.

Is he crying? Fuck. What have I done? Did I take something and spin it completely out of context?

He hangs his head, chin an inch above the hollow of his throat, and lets the water rain over him. I strip out of my clothes and hop into the shower behind him. Running my palms down his back, I wrap my arms around his waist. He doesn't move. Not an inch. And I simply hold him.

"I'm sorry for assuming. But why won't you answer me?" I whisper against his skin.

After a minute, his arms band over mine and he tugs me closer to his backside. "The fact that you thought I'd cheat on you shatters me. The name on the paper" —he slowly spins around and looks me in the eye— "she was someone Rocco and I interviewed. I had her number so I could call her back in for a second interview."

Stupid, stupid, stupid. How could I be such an idiot? And why the hell did I automatically jump on the cheating train? Yes, our relationship has been a bit wishy-washy recently, but I never doubted Rick's loyalty to me. Ever. So, why now? Maybe because we are in a new place. A new life. And our whole world is a hot mess.

I close my eyes and mentally berate myself. "I'm a jerk. A goddamn idiot. Sometimes I wonder why you're still with me," I admit. "Recently, all I seem to do is cause problems between us."

"Hey." He tugs my chin up and waits until I open my eyes. The usual fire in his golden irises is a dull amber. I hold his bloodshot, somber honey eyes. For a moment, the world fades away as we get lost in each other. "You still don't get it, do you?"

No, I don't. I don't get why this beautiful, intelligent, and highly desirable man chooses to stay with me. Not after so many others rejected me. Rejection is a strange creature. Has the ability to twist your mind and make you believe you're not worthy. Worthy of trust or love or happiness. How could you be worthy when every person who mattered left?

The only person who repeatedly sticks by my side is Rick. And when I found that paper in his pocket, I automatically assumed the worst. Assumed he was sick of me. Of all the shit I have dished out in the last year. Of my lack of willingness to do more physically. And he was ready to move on with someone less drama-laden.

"No," I mutter. "What's so great about me? When you can have so many others who will give you more than me, how do I believe I'm it for you?" Especially after spending so many years together, and our relationship not evolving. Then again, we have never sat down and discussed our relationship being anything more than it is.

"Christy, I don't want anyone but you."

I shake my head. "That's not true. If it were, we wouldn't live the life we do." We wouldn't have sex with other people is what I really want to say. As exciting as it is, sometimes I just want it to be him and me.

"Fucking other people... I'd quit if it meant that much to you." He leans down and kisses me. "When we're with other couples, the only reason I get off is because you're with me. Before you, fucking was fucking. With you, it's so much more. I won't deny the pleasure I get from us fucking other people. But if you weren't in the same room, if I couldn't watch your face, imagine my cock inside you, it wouldn't matter."

His confession has me awestruck. "Why?" It's all my mind can conjure.

He shakes his head in disbelief. As if I should be aware of the answer. "Christy, you make my blood sing. Before you, sex was an outlet. With you... you breathe life into me."

"Will you tell me?" Rick hasn't told me much about his past. And I haven't pried. But this is the second time he has alluded to it. Almost as if he wants to tell me, but hasn't found the nerve.

"Let's finish showering."

He drags me under the spray and kisses me fiercely. When he releases me, we take our time washing each other. Hands and fingers touching and caressing as we lather and rinse. After we finish, he dries off before wrapping the soft cotton around me and toweling me dry. Rick walks into the bedroom, goes to our dresser, and fishes out nightwear for both of us. Once we dress, he curls me to his chest on the bed and holds me impossibly close.

After a sweet press of his lips to my forehead, he speaks up. "During my senior year of high school, I started using sex as an escape. Not that it was the first time I had the desire to be more *brutal* in the bedroom. Honestly, I think the urge has always been there. But most high school girls weren't into being strapped to the bed and hit before getting fucked. So, I found older women who were interested."

"What changed that year?" I ask as he dances around telling me.

"My sister," he whispers.

I lean away and peer up at him. "You have a sister?"

He nods. "I *had* a sister." Tears pool in his eyes. "Just before senior year started, sophomore year for her, she was hanging out with a new group of friends she'd made during freshman year. My parents and I never questioned anyone she was friends with. Harriett was a good kid. Made good grades. Was ambitious. Dreamed of traveling the globe and photographing all different walks of life. She wanted her photos in *National Geographic*. So, when my mom got a call from the police department telling us to come to the hospital, we were shocked."

I wipe away the tears rolling down his cheeks. He trembles beneath me, and I realize I have never seen him like this. So vulnerable and scared and disarmed. So different from the strong, always-in-control man I always see.

"Twenty minutes later, when we got to the hospital, it was too late. How can someone die so quickly?" he mumbles to himself, and I don't answer. I'm not meant to. "The *friends* she'd been hanging with were into drugs. If Harriett smoked weed, I wouldn't care. There was no harm in it. But obviously it wasn't weed. After we could walk again, the doctor brought us to her in the ER bay. They'd draped the sheet over her entire body, but my parents wanted to see her. They refused to believe she was dead until they saw it with their own eyes. I'll never forget how blue her skin was. Ash blue. After the toxicology report came back, we learned she took a mix of pills with alcohol. The cops spoke with the other kids' parents and learned they regularly had pharm parties. And a boy Harriett had a crush on dared her to take the pills. Told her how amazing it felt. We'll never know what actually happened, but I assume she wanted him to really like her and caved. Five pills. That, and a few ounces of vodka, is all it took to take Harriett's life."

Rick tips his head back and smacks the headboard. Eyes glued to the ceiling, he silently cries for Harriett. For the sister he lost and will never hug again. Will never tease or give advice to again. For the life she would never have because of a boy she crushed on. I squeeze him tighter, whispering how sorry I am over his heart. Words will never replace the loss he has suffered. Nothing can make up for the pain he has endured. And I understand why he needed an outlet. How else can someone get through such a tragedy?

"Sex was the only healthy way to release my anger. After the way Harriett died, there was no way I'd resort to pills or alcohol for reprieve. A few weeks after Harriett's funeral, I met a woman at my job. I worked part time at an auto body shop. Basically, I was a bitch boy while I learned about auto mechanics. A woman brought her car in for routine maintenance, and something inside me sparked. She was several years my senior, and looked at me like she wanted to eat me alive. After her car was finished, she slipped me a note with her number. When I met up with her, I fucked her in the backseat of that car. It turned her on when I wrapped my hand around her throat and clamped down. We fucked several times over a three month period. That's when I wondered if other women like her existed. Women I could take my aggression out on and get off on it. Turns out, there're tons."

He chuckles beneath me and I wring my arms tighter. "Do I give you the outlet you need?"

Tipping my chin up, he presses a sweet kiss to my lips and nose. "I don't really need the outlet now like I did then. Do I enjoy rough kink? Yes. No lie, the rougher it is, the harder I get. But, do I need it? No. As long as I have you, I don't need it." He slides down the bed and lays eye-to-eye with me. "Christy, you fill in all the gaps. You make my life remarkable. Worth every beat and breath and minute. As long as you're by my side, life is complete."

I comb my fingers through his hair and he melts into my

touch. "Well, just so you know, I like the kink. And I'm willing to try new things. Okay? I see how turned on you get with some of it."

He kisses me as one hand comes around the back of my neck and the other traces down the curves of my body. Slipping a leg between mine, he grinds his hips against my pubic bone. The second he breaks the kiss, he stares into my eyes and strokes a thumb over my lower lip. "How did I get so lucky?"

"Is it you who's lucky? Or is it me?" I propose.

"Gorgeous, I don't know how, but you're making me believe in fate," he says, twirling a lock of my hair around his finger.

For the next several hours, we exhaust each other between the sheets. Just him, me, and the bond we have shared from the start.

FOURTEEN

RICK

EVERYONE SCURRIES around the restaurant and club frantically.

Upstairs, bottles are dusted and lined up on the glass bar shelves. Candles, salt and pepper shakers, and a single red rose in a small glass vase sits at the center of each table. Black cloth napkins are intricately folded and sitting on silver-rimmed white plates. Warm, ambient lighting brightens the restaurant with an array of wall sconces, while fairy lights drip from the ceiling. Opulence screams its namesake.

Downstairs, the bartenders and barmaids stock glassware and check that all the liquor is accounted for at the club. Janitorial staff does a last once over, wiping down all the furniture and cleaning the floors. In the club, there is less to straighten out and manage. The bar and the basic janitorial cleaning will be the biggest things to prep each shift.

Tonight, we will have a soft opening. Family, friends, and members of P.I. invited to enjoy Opulence and Boundless before heavier crowds occupy both. P.I. members will be offered special pricing if they opt to have a membership at both clubs. Rocco and I sat down, crunched numbers, and came up with what we thought was a hell of a deal. Hopefully, they will think the same.

Hours pass faster than seconds, and it's not long before Christy strides in. Glancing at her from head to toe, I openly check her out, swallow and adjust my cock. With the soft opening for both the restaurant and club, I asked her to dress accordingly. As always, my girl never disappoints.

Clad in a sultry yet classy dress, she smirks knowingly when I bite the inside of my cheek. The base layer of her dress is a nude fabric that hugs her body in all the right places. Over the top is a layer of black lace. From a distance, the nude material is unnoticeable. Sleeveless, the neckline plunges and displays just enough cleavage to keep it semi-appropriate. The material stops mid-thigh and accentuates every curve, dip, and groove like a second skin. Her toned legs are bare and glistening under the amber lighting. But it's her black heels that pull it all together—long leather straps wind up her calves to her knees.

When she reaches me, I exhale and pull her to me. "Fuck, gorgeous. How am I supposed to work?"

Christy laughs and I bask in the sound. Over the last year, she hasn't laughed as much. Part of which was my fault. But she was also sad with Sarah gone. Now, it feels like my girl has returned. Her smile, her laughter. You never realize how amazing those small tidbits are until you don't get them on a regular basis.

She brings her lips to my ear and whispers, "Wait until you see what's underneath." Kissing the angle of my jaw, she inches back and flaunts a wicked smile. "I want to play tonight."

One line is all it takes. One line and my dick strains against my zipper. I grip her tighter and hold her hostage. Lips at her ear, I whisper-hiss, "You can't walk in here dressed like a goddess and say things like that. Now you have to stay put until my cock calms down."

She clucks her fucking tongue and it does nothing to settle my erection. "Patience. I brought a couple things with me." Lifting her oversized purse, she raises her brows. "Where can I set this down?"

I walk her downstairs and introduce her to the club staff. Since it's our soft opening, everyone works tonight. After introductions are made, I show her the staff only lounge/breakroom. It's a complete kitchen, bathroom, a small wall of lockers, and two couches. In the center, a table where employees can sit and eat. A work version of a tiny home.

Rocco wanted to be sure the staff had a place to relax and get away.

Unlocking my personal locker for her, I give her the combo, and Christy tucks her bag inside. We walk out together, and I direct her to my office on the upper level. Inside, I get her an access bracelet. For tonight and the first few visits, members will have these bracelets. Once officially signed up, we will issue member ID cards. Rocco has already ordered cards for employees and their significant others, but they didn't arrive in time for tonight's event.

When we reach the restaurant floor, I hook Christy's arm on mine and walk her to a table. I pull her chair out and she glides onto the leather. "Stay here, gorgeous. I need to make rounds and shake hands. Order dinner for both of us. I'll be over soon." I bend down and kiss her. As much as I don't want to, I break the kiss and hold her gaze a beat. "Be back shortly."

The next thirty minutes involve a lot of schmoozing. Several members of P.I. arrive and they chat with myself and Rocco. I wouldn't go so far as to say we are brown nosing, but it is pretty damn close. A key foundation for Boundless is dependent on current P.I. members and their word of mouth. Although our lifestyles aren't exposed for everyone to see, we know people in the life. And people in our circles talk.

After speaking with a couple who has been with Rocco since the start, I head over to where I left Christy and join her for dinner. Before taking a seat across from her, I kiss the crown of her head. "Thank you for waiting, gorgeous. What'd you order?"

As she relays our dinner order, I bend over the plate and inhale. "Garlic and caper grilled salmon served with dill creme fraiche and a side of roasted herb root vegetables."

I peek up at her. "You could've started eating without me."

She waves me off. "It's been here maybe five minutes. Besides, I had salad and bread to tide me over until you got here."

We eat our meal and I pass on who some of the guests are. Christy asks me questions about P.I. and I explain how it is basically an upper-class strip club... with benefits. When it comes to the benefits, the dancers run the show and dictate what they are willing to allow.

Soon, dinner ends and Rocco says a few words of thanks to everyone who came out tonight. He announces anyone present is allowed to stay and join us downstairs in Boundless. Tonight is a one-time glimpse for everyone here. Their one chance to see Boundless without membership. He continues to explain membership, how it works, cost and the rules while downstairs in Boundless. At any point in time, anyone can be removed from the club, if their behavior is deemed inappropriate.

Rocco reiterates, several times, that Boundless is a safe space and environment. If anyone does not feel this way while inside, they are to seek out management or an employee immediately. Rocco and I pride ourselves in keeping Boundless a place where people don't cringe when they express their sexuality. Instead, they feast on it and share it with others.

After his speech ends, everyone rises and ambles down the stairwell at the back of the restaurant. As we hit the final steps, I clutch Christy closer to my side. Adrenaline hits my bloodstream like an avalanche. Beside me, Christy bounces on her toes. Music thumps and vibrates the walls. Low lights illuminate the corridor. A mysterious and alluring vibe oozes from the walls.

When we reach the end of the corridor, I breathe in the visual masterpiece laid out before us. Seeing Boundless with all the overhead lights on is one thing. Seeing it how we want everyone else to see it is a wholly new perspective.

Industrial Edison sconces glow around the room while large Edison bulbs hang from the open ceiling, dimly lighting the charcoal walls with an amber radiance. The entrance sits off to one side with the club management office in the small crook beside it. Fifteen feet into the club, a concrete bar top starts and spans for thirty feet, connecting with the wall to form a large rectangle. Just past the bar is a sectioned off area for VIP members. All in all, VIP is about three hundred square feet and is for selected clientele. The small nook has minimal furniture but has a suspension grid and wall restraints. Along the back wall, and slightly onto the wall opposite the bar, is a variety of furnishings—poles, long, padded tables, cages, more suspension options, as well as an array of tools and implements. The second half of that wall and part of the entryway wall has a handful of private rooms, which can be utilized for up to thirty minutes. The rooms are generally utilized by people who haven't gotten up the courage to be so open and/or explicit. Two of the rooms are completely private. The others have a small adjoining room with a two-way mirror for voyeurs. In the center of it all, leather couches, chairs, chaises, ottomans, and concrete topped tables. Small clusters of candles illuminate each table, which can be decorative or for play.

Boundless is beyond what I expected and I hope Christy loves it.

Once inside, we head to the bar and order drinks. Slowly, everyone wanders in and breathes in the piney leather polish and amber scented candles lining the bar and tables. A few minutes pass and Christy tells me she is going to change and will be back in a moment.

While I wait for her, I prop a foot on the stool behind me and sit. People watching in the clubs always fascinates me. Always a fifty-fifty with the crowd. Half are eager and ready to rip their clothes off. The other half wander in circles and watch the people ready to rip their clothes off. Eventually, though, most people open up and free their mind. In no time, there will be more bare skin than clothed skin.

Out of the corner of my eye, I see a pair of toned, delicious legs. Legs I have memorized and would know in the darkest of nights. They don't just belong to any woman. They belong to my woman. But when I scan my eyes up her body, my mouth goes dry and I swallow hard.

Fuck.

Christy struts toward me. No longer in the dress I saw her in less than ten minutes ago. The closer she gets, the more my cock swells. Fuck, she is gorgeous.

Thin leather straps cage her thighs and calves, hooked to a garter belt at her waist. Black, strappy panties shield a small patch of her flesh. Nipples marked with an "X" in black tape, she wears a sheer black top. Another set of leather straps cages her breasts and torso and hooks onto the belt around her waist. Her long, russet curls hang loose and drape the front of her body.

But the thing that shocks me the most. The single thing I can't rip my eyes away from is her eyes. Stormy blues stare back at me, but not through her glasses as usual. *Is she wearing contacts?* What incinerates my blood in this very moment is the mask covering half her face. Black. Leather. *Kitten.*

Christy is sex fucking personified. Every set of eyes in the room is on her, watching as she slowly saunters across the club and in my direction. My heart swells as much as my cock and only one thought runs through my head. *This woman belongs to me.*

An inch away, she stops and I can't avert my eyes from her cherry red lips. I don't move. Not a breath. My limbs forgetting how to operate. As she leans into me, I gasp and beg for her to touch me. Kiss me. *Fuck me.*

"Hey, daddy," she purrs. "Kitten wants to play."

When she inches back, I lock eyes with her. A hurricane spins around her pupils and makes landfall on a path headed straight to my groin. I adjust myself and tug her back into me, whispering in her ear. "Good girl, kitten. Come," I extend the crook of my elbow to her, "let's go play."

As if we're the power couple in the room, patrons step aside and allow us to pass. We walk in leisure, reaching the wall of toys. After I slip a few items from their holsters, I walk us to one of several couches nearby.

"Do you know what seeing you like this does to me, kitten?"

"Tell me, daddy," she cajoles.

Lifting a hand, I pinch her chin between my thumb and forefinger and tip it up. When her stormy blues land on my lust-laden honeys, I keep her stock still a moment. There is something to be said about a non-verbal exchange between lovers. Bonded couples, such as ourselves, exchange a million sentiments without uttering a single word.

We don't have to.

Eyes connected, I take her hand in mine and drag it over my erection. Fingers contracting around my length cause me to swell even more, I watch her lips part and her eyes that dare to close. But they won't. She yearns for our connection as much as I do.

"This is what you do to daddy, kitten." I rub her hand up and down my length. "Are you ready to play? Do you want to play new games tonight?"

Her breathing spikes. "Yes, daddy. Teach me some new games."

With her invitation and permission, my chest heaves and cock pulses. I'm not quite sure what shifted with Christy, but this is new. It hardens my cock to steel. Has me ready to come in my pants. Maybe it's the mask. Maybe it's her unprovoked exhibitionism. If I am honest, perhaps it's a combination of the two and the fact that she has never been so eager to please me.

Before I sit on the couch, she reaches around her backside and retrieves something. Once in her hand, she extends it to me and I take her offering. The cool metal is a light weight in my hand, and I glance down to see the leash. *Her leash.*

I can count on one hand the number of times we have used this. The tally wouldn't tick off all digits either. For Christy to dress like this, to hand this to me… A rush of blood whooshes behind my ears like white noise. The gush all I hear. But beneath my sternum, a war wages between my heart and lungs on which organ can pump fastest. Currently, my heart takes the lead.

Stepping into her, I brush my lips against hers, then clip the leash onto her collar. She sighs as her eyes close for a blink. Her satisfaction shoots adrenaline throughout my body. How long has my girl needed this? Craved this? And I neglected to give it to her. All because I didn't know if it was something she desired. In essence, I disregarded us both under the assumption she didn't want this in our relationship.

Obviously, I was wrong.

Over the next several hours, I tease and torture and do questionable things to Christy. With each lick of the paddle, she begs for more. While suspended by her wrists, I whip her flesh and revel in the pinking and sting marring her alabaster skin. Her whimpers and cries all in the name of pleasure. A pleasure only I fulfill.

Several people crowd around and ogle us. Voyeurs fucking and petting as they watch our interaction. It sets me off, and I am certain it urges Christy on too. The evidence is in her dilated pupils. As she bows her body and silently pleas for more. In her slack jaw and parted lips. And the dampness soaking the flesh at the apex of her thighs.

Never have I seen my girl aroused to this degree. As I stare at her now exposed skin, sans the black tape over her nipples, I relish in all we have done together. All we have done here, tonight. She never ceases to amaze me.

I unclip her and slide her body down the front of mine. Walking her over to the nearest couch, I bend her over the back of it, and whisper in her ear. "Fuck, gorgeous. You have no idea what it does to me knowing you're mine."

Christy peers over her shoulder, mask still in place, and grins wickedly. Her hand dips between my thighs, clutches my balls and massages. "And you're mine. Always." She faces away from me and grinds her ass against my erection. "Now fuck me."

In seconds, my pants hit the floor and I wrap my hand around her throat as I ram into her from behind. The world disappears as euphoria clouds around us. Just me and my girl. Savagely fucking like beasts. Her cries of pleasure the only sound in my ears.

It will always be her. Only her.

FIFTEEN

CHRISTY

"Where do you want the sweet potatoes?" I yell from the dining room.

I spin around in search for an open space. Any open space. So far, there is zero to be found. "On the side table, next to where Tiffany's sitting," Liz hollers back from the kitchen.

Scanning the side table, I shake my head. The side table is already stacked with a mountain of mashed potatoes and cranberry-orange relish. If I scoot things around, the sweet potatoes still wouldn't fit. How on earth did Liz think we would have enough space for all this food? So, I glance back at the four-person, square dining table and ponder what I can shift to create more space. We still need space for the rolls, butter, and green beans.

"We need another table," I say, walking back into the kitchen after countless attempts to shift plates and glasses and serving bowls. Liz bustles around like a maniac, washing dishes and wiping down countertops. She pauses and stares at me with tightly pinched eyes and deep creases in her brow like I requested her left lung.

She shakes her head and breezes past me. If Liz has a better solution to the table setup, I would love to see it. You can only fit so many platters and casserole dishes on the space provided. If the table had space for another two people, we would have more than enough room today. But it doesn't. So we don't.

I follow her back to the dining room and watch as she shifts cups, plates, and dish after dish. Exactly what I did before coming in and telling her it wasn't possible. Minutes later, she steps back and points to the tiny open spot she created. "There. Put it there."

"Okay, bitch. But where the hell are we putting the rest?" A fair question. One that any normal person would ask. But a second after I ask, I wish I could retract my question.

Liz huffs, rolls her eyes, and throws her hands in the air. She looks like a bomb ready to detonate any second. "Why am I the only one figuring all this out? Where the hell is Rick and Tiffany?"

I shrug and bite the inside of my cheek. No chance in hell I would tell Liz she frightened them with her *perfect Thanksgiving* demands. Last I saw, Rick and Tiffany were on the back patio. They stepped out an hour ago, just after Liz's first "this is how you baste the turkey" moment. It came with a full tutorial of how much of the drippings to suck into the baster and where the best place was to disperse it.

Liz isn't a perfectionist. Just... particular. And when it comes to holidays, events, and parties, it kicks up a notch. Sarah and I always ignored her neurotic tendencies. It is the only way party planning ever gets accomplished. I love Liz, but her demands can be over the top at times. Rick never joined in during the planning phase, and Tiffany is still somewhat new to it all. She and Liz have only been together a little more than a year.

"Um." I squint as my lips tighten into a straight line, exposing my teeth. "On the patio," I say hesitantly.

She rolls her eyes again, groans, and storms back off to the kitchen. "Maybe *they* should help you figure out the table situation."

Not mad, but definitely peeved. As soon as we all sit down to eat, she will relax and enjoy the day. Until that moment strikes, though, Liz will be a twisted ball of yarn, wound tight and ready to fall apart any second.

I head for the sliding glass doors and step out onto the patio. A shiver rolls up my spine as the cool air whips my hair across my glasses. The smell of wood-burning fireplaces trickles through the air. Nothing like cozying up near a fire on a cool fall day.

Rick and Tiffany stop their conversation and glance up at me. Apologies written in their eyes and the lines crinkling their faces. For a moment, I sit beside Rick and take a deep breath.

"Would you guys mind helping me in a minute?" I ask.

Tiffany's shoulders cave forward. "Sorry," she says. "Didn't know Liz got like this. Last year, we went to friends and family during the holidays. She gets so flustered, and I just feel like I'm in the way."

I nod. "Yeah. She just wants everyone to have a good time. Which equals everything being perfect." Peering over my shoulder, through the glass doors, Liz is a madwoman cleaning the kitchen. "Help me?"

Rising from the loungers on the patio, we walk on eggshells once inside. I tell Rick and Tiffany a few more dishes need to be brought out and we need to shift things around to make room. After a minute of our best Tetris skills, Tiffany pauses and her eyes light up.

Without a word, she turns on her heel and walks away. A minute later, her feet pad across the floor and she walks in with a small side table. Thank God. If we had to spend another second squeezing and semi-stacking dishes, I would pull my hair out.

Tiffany sets the table off to the side. The second the legs hit the ground, I set the mashed potatoes, balsamic roasted Brussels sprouts, and brown sugar candied carrots on top. With all the food made, we had enough to feed a dozen people. Leftovers inevitable. But leftovers were one of my favorite parts of holiday meals. Some foods just tasted better the next day.

"Thank you, Tiffany. You saved the day." I pull her into a full body hug. "If Liz is ready, I say we eat."

When I release Tiffany, she ambles to the kitchen, hesitant. So cute how gentle she is with Liz. Not wanting to agitate the lioness. "Baby, whenever you're ready," Tiffany coos.

Once we all sit around the table, laughter and smiles and chatter consume us. Plates piled high with tons of delicious food. Wine glasses full to the brim. Banter all around. This is the perfect gathering.

Tiffany updates Rick and me with her job. After finishing her master's degree in Georgia, she scoured for open positions. For months, she had zero luck. When the topic of moving west came up, she and Liz were open to the idea. Low and behold, Tiffany was equally lucky as Rick in acquiring a job before the move.

Her job at Lewis House is more rewarding than imaginable. The facility, armed with several psychologists and psychiatrists, is an organization which helps teens and young adults up to age twenty-five who deal with or have dealt with depression and/or suicide. An admirable practice. The organization was founded a few years after a fifteen-year-old boy, Taylor Lewis, ended his own life. Tiffany astounds me. The fact she works with individuals who feel no one cares, and then guides them down a path of hope. Not just anyone can do what she does. I applaud her and the others working at Lewis House.

After our bellies are full and we clear the table, we all slump on the couches with heavy eyes. Eventually, Rick flips on the television and engrosses himself with the football game while Liz, Tiffany, and I chat.

Liz and Tiffany banter constantly. The way they are with each other is adorable. "If you don't behave, I'll tie you to the bed later," Tiffany teases. My eyes widen and I stare between the two of them. They smile like idiots.

Kinky? Let's find out.

"I love being tied to the bed." The bait set.

Liz stares at me like she doesn't know who I am and I squirm. Beside me, Rick sets a hand on my thigh and strokes his thumb against my skin in a slow, measured motion. Although his eyes haven't left the game, he listens to everything. Always. The weight of his hand meant to comfort me. Since Rick and I don't discuss our lifestyle with friends not in that circle, this is a big step. One I second guess.

Other than the game commentator screaming from the television, the air around us remains eerily silent. My lungs burn as I patiently wait for someone to say something. Anything. My stomach shrivels and sinks like a lead weight. The silence and not knowing how she feels about what I just said is a dull knife to the torso, again and again.

All I ever wanted was acceptance. Especially by people close to my heart. For them to know me. The real me. And not just a fragment. But every aspect of who I am. And love me just the same. Ever since my family disowned me for being myself, the desire for acceptance and love has been the biggest reason I shelter my life. Rejection, especially from someone close to me, would shatter me.

Time ticks by as if days have passed and not seconds. The room spins and I remind myself to breathe. Just as I inhale, Liz tips her head back and laughs at the ceiling. A rich, hearty, everyone-within-a-mile-will-hear-her laugh. Is this good? God, I am so fucking confused.

"Don't tell me how, but somehow I knew you were a kinky bitch," Liz states. She belts out another torrent of laughter. "Call it intuition. Maybe it's your extroversion. Who the hell knows. Maybe it's because you never talk about sex. *Ever*." Liz glances at Tiffany. "What is it they say… it's the quiet ones who are the kinkiest."

I throw a pillow at Liz's head and hit her smack dab in the forehead. "Have I ever been quiet?" A stupid question. But I threw it out more teasing than anything. Her laughter was exactly what I needed. The perfect antidote to settle my anxious heart.

"Not in general, no. But you never talked about sex with me and Sarah. Most girlfriends do. Sarah and I did. A lot. But you… you just sat there and listened and never said a single word about your sex life."

"That's different and you know it." I give her a pointed stare. Before Sarah and Jackson got together, Liz and Sarah hooked up all the time. They never brought it up around me, but after I caught them making out one day, it was rather obvious.

"Guess you're right. But it still holds true."

Not that I need his permission, but I peer over my shoulder at Rick. A smile spans his cheeks while his eyes follow the football game on the screen. Before I turn back to Liz and Tiffany, he squeezes my thigh. His way of telling me it is okay to talk about who we are as long as *I* am comfortable.

And I am. This is Liz. One of my best friends. Someone I trust my life with.

"Whatever, bitch. You want to hear me talk sex? Better grab some more wine. You have no idea what you asked for," I tease.

For the next few hours, I divulge just how kinky my and Rick's life is. Liz and Tiffany sit completely silent and captivated. They ask questions, truly interested in the answers. Rick inches closer to me and adds more pressure to my side. His way of supporting without hovering.

By the time we leave, I feel twenty pounds lighter. An unknown burden lifts off my shoulders and floats away. But that is by far the best part. Which happens to be the fact my friends still accept me. Us. And this year, I am thankful for this life. A life of love and acceptance and happiness.

SIXTEEN

RICK

Servers bustle around the dining floor, fold napkins, set them on the plates on tables, and add silverware. Bartenders with pen and paper scan inventory, fill ice, and wipe water spots off glassware. In the kitchen, chefs in tall white hats chop, dice, and julienne vegetables. Roasts and whole birds cook in the oven for hours, the back of the restaurant smells of lemon and garlic and rosemary. Another group of chefs off to the side are putting the final touches on dessert plates.

I slap a hand to my stomach as it growls, begging for a morsel. *Later.*

After surveying the dining area one last time, I head downstairs.

Inside the walls of Boundless, loud music pours from the hidden speakers in the walls. A low, sultry beat throbs at the pace of my heartbeat. For the next nine hours, Boundless will stir to life. After the soft opening two-and-a-half weeks ago, we added over two dozen members. Some of them members of P.I., others referred by those members.

If all went as projected, Boundless would have close to a hundred members by end of year. We set a maximum membership number to one thousand. For now. As it stands, Boundless can comfortably hold a thousand people at one time. With room to breathe. After we determine the pattern of our regulars, we plan to gauge whether or not to increase membership capacity.

But being exclusive has its perks. Not just anyone can walk inside Boundless. The membership a pretty penny, but worth every cent. Worth having a safe space to express yourself amongst similar individuals. What we offer is not comparable to any other establishment within a three-hundred-mile radius. Rocco and I did our fair share of research.

A few hours after Opulence and Boundless open, Christy waltzes in. She goes to the end of the bar nearest the entrance and club office. After a glass of merlot is set in front of her, she sips it and scans the club. Catty-corner to where she sits, she spots me after a minute. She blows me a kiss and I wink at her.

Once I make another circuit around the club, talking with several patrons and thanking them, I head over to where Christy sits at the bar.

"Hey, gorgeous." I kiss the crown of her head. "Did you eat yet?"

She shakes her head. "Figured I'd eat with you when you have a break."

The club is somewhat quiet, so I tell the bartender, Cheyenne, I am heading to the kitchen to grab dinner, but will bring it back down here to eat. After I hook Christy's arm with mine, we head upstairs and make a bee-line straight for the kitchen. Christy and I wander past the swinging double doors and I order us chicken, risotto, and whatever vegetable is on the menu tonight.

In no time, we walk back downstairs to the club's office and eat our meal. The office set up with a two-way mirror of sorts. Inside the confines of the office, I see everything happening in the club. But from outside the office, no one sees in. Instead of a mirror on the club side, the glass is made to look like the wall. Don't ask me about the fancy tech behind it all, but I love it. Able to monitor all activity in the club while doing other managerial tasks.

Once we finish eating, I lock the office door, bend Christy over the large mahogany desk, twist her hair around my wrist, and fuck her senseless. Sure, I could have fucked her on the club floor. Had every pair of eyes in the club on us. But tonight, I wanted Christy all to myself. What can I say... I am a greedy bastard sometimes.

"How long you staying?" I ask as I zip up my pants.

Christy straightens her dress and combs her fingers through her hair. "Thought I'd stay until midnight or so. Want to people watch in a new place."

At times, Christy enjoys being the voyeur more than the exhibitionist. She teeters back and forth, giving equal love to each. Another astonishing quality I love about her. An equal opportunist.

"Staying at the bar? Or you want to sit in VIP?"

"The bar for a little longer. Then I'll hang out in VIP."

She continues to mess with her hair, doing her best to settle the wayward strands. I grab her hands, lower them, and kiss her forehead. "You're perfect, gorgeous." Her body melts into my touch and, for a beat, I don't want to leave this room. For a minute longer, I want to hold her in my arms and kiss the hell out of her.

I love her warm skin against me. The way she leans into me as if I am the only solace she needs. And I love the way my heart jackhammers when she is in proximity. No one has kickstarted my heart the way Christy does.

We leave the office. I mingle on the club floor while Christy sits at the bar with another glass of wine. By the time I make it to the VIP lounge, Christy has already made her way over. In a tall-backed, leather throne chair, she sits like a queen. *My queen.*

I join her and another couple she has been chatting with for a bit. Ella and Thomas. Like us, they enjoy the company of other couples. The four of us talk about Boundless. All the walks of life inside these walls. I mention Apex, and how different that club is compared to Boundless. Christy jokes about her boring day job and how tiring it is to sell life insurance to people. Although, she does admit to hearing some of the oddest stories. Ella tells us she owns an indie bookstore just outside the city. The traffic was slow going at first, but sales have picked up drastically in the last quarter. Thomas works at a law firm in the city. Jokingly, he says he won't bore us with the details.

Thomas and Ella are easy to talk with. Comfortable. No strange vibes. Almost as if we have known them years. I ask my standard list of questions in casual conversation. And I take note Thomas does the same. Obviously, we are both interested in each other, and our exchange easily goes from minutes to hours in no time.

On occasion, I excuse myself and meander the club. Each time I glance at Christy with Ella and Thomas, all I see is smiles or laughter or in-depth conversation. Since moving to California, things hadn't been what they once were. But seeing Christy so at ease in her own skin, hope surges in my veins. Before Ella and Thomas leave tonight, if Christy hasn't already asked, I plan to extend an offer to meet up outside of the club.

As I make one last circuit on the way back to VIP, a woman steps in front of me and halts my path. "Hey, sugar." The bleach-blonde places her hand on my chest and pets me. Immediately, anger simmers in my blood and I step back.

"First things first," I say, giving her a pointed stare. "Without permission, you do not touch people here. Understood?" It is a fundamental rule in Boundless. Although everyone in these walls enjoys sex, not everyone wants other people touching them. And everyone needs to respect that. We aren't all into the same lifestyle.

A gleam lights her smile. "Okay, sugar."

I cringe and bite my cheek a second before I say something unprofessional. "Second of all, I'm not your *sugar*. Do not address me as such."

She steps closer to me and pops her breasts closer in the tacky, tight one-piece she wears. "Bossy one, aren't you?" Not a question. Her tone is intended to be sexy and appealing. Honestly, it makes bile rise in my throat. "I like them bossy."

I clench my jaw and take two steps back. "If you'll excuse me."

But before I turn to walk off, she reaches out and touches my bicep. I glance down at her hand, curl my top lip, and look back up at her. The acid in my stare tells her I'm not fucking around and she yanks her hand away. Thank fuck. "Sorry. Just looking for a good time."

Obviously, this woman can't take a hint. Stepping farther away, I point at the crowd around us. "There are plenty of options here. But I'm not one of them. And just a reminder, if you cannot abide by the rules of the club, you will be asked to leave and not allowed to return."

Her wicked gleam makes its return. Tongue jetting out to lick her lips. A single lick of the lips usually sparks interest for me, but with this woman, there is not an ounce of attraction. If anything, the more she tries, the more turned off I become.

"I'll do my best." She winks then walks off. Finally.

When I rejoin Christy, Ella, and Thomas, my girl is talking about previous partners we have had in our bed. I sit on her left, hand wrapped around hers, and we chat. Another hour passes, the conversation flowing smoothly, and all I want is my shift to be over.

By the time Ella and Thomas stand to leave, Ella and Christy have exchanged phone numbers. An unspoken agreement that we'll meet up in the not too distant future. With certain people, we find it more comfortable if the women meet up alone in a public setting, and the men too. This way, we get our own vibes without disruption.

Not long after Thomas and Ella leave, Christy decides to head home. It's well after midnight when I kiss her goodbye, and I promise to be home in a couple hours.

Minutes after Christy leaves, my hackles rise. A pang twitches in my gut. Sharp and nauseating. I scan the club and spot the bleach-blonde staring at me. Strapped to a wooden table. A man yanks a chain attached to her nipples while he fucks the hell out of her. But she stares at me, licking her lips. Disgust swims in my gut. *What the hell is with this woman?*

I shake my head and go to the bar. "Cheyenne, keep an eye on the blonde on the restraint table. I'm getting a bad vibe from that one. I'm going to the office for a bit."

She pours a beer from the tap, nods and doesn't look up. "You got it, boss."

With that, I head into the office and shut the door, bolting the lock. I stare out at the club floor, my eyes landing on the blonde. Although she can't see me in here, she stares where I stand. It sends a chill down my spine—and not the ball-clenching, explosive type I enjoy either. *Who the hell is this woman? And why is she so fixated on me?*

Hopefully she's not a member. More than anything, I also hope to not see her inside these walls again.

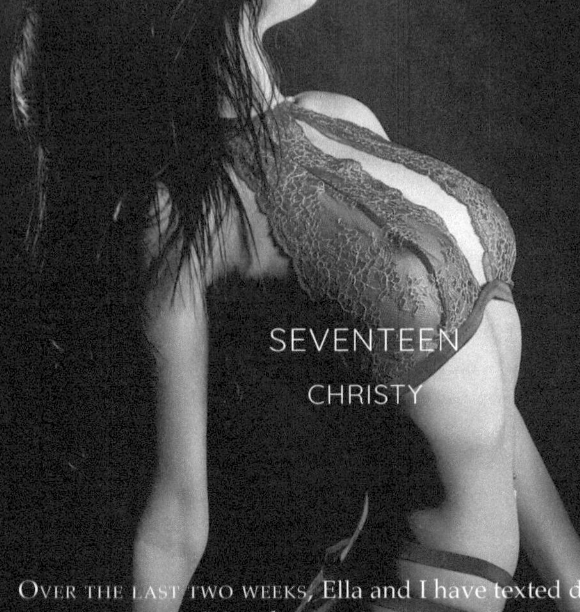

SEVENTEEN

CHRISTY

Over the last two weeks, Ella and I have texted daily.

It is wonderful to have a friend to talk about everything with. Although Rick and I haven't met up with her and Thomas outside the club yet, we have chatted in VIP a few times now. Mostly, when Ella and I text, we discuss normal life stuff. Work, best places to eat, annoying habits our significant others have. Plain Jane normal. Getting to know one another. And it makes me so happy.

Two nights ago, at Boundless, I finally learned where Ella's bookstore is. Actually, not too far from our house. Now that we have developed a level of trust, I want to see Ella outside the club walls. See her in her element. Her love for books and how she interacts with others. Which brings me to here and now.

I park under a shady tree and stare at the hand-painted oak sign over the bookstore. Cozy Corner Books. The storefront has large glass windows and white painted brick with a pillar supported overhang. At either end of the store, an iron post sticks out from the wall with a matching store sign hanging from two rings. On the front door is the store name in a font that matches the signs. An appealing blend of modern and antique/vintage. Quaint. Unique. I love the vibe.

Cutting the engine, I loop my purse over my shoulder and step out. The bookstore is freestanding but has a coffee shop next door as well as a bakery and delicatessen. The area is busy yet quiet. A perfect place to grab a coffee, pastry, and read a good book. Ella has it made here.

I tug the wood and glass door open and am hit with a smell I haven't inhaled since grade school. Fresh paper and ink. Binding glue and worn leather. I inhale deeply and close my eyes. Bookstores and libraries are high on my list of favorite places. The paper grain against my fingertips. The weight of the words in my palms. Nothing replaces a good paperback novel.

Aisles and aisles of six-foot oak shelves fill the space. Along the walls, the shelves go to the ceiling. I spy a rolling ladder on each packed wall. At the front of the store, several distressed tables sit stacked with new releases or sale priced books. Off to the far right is a small reading nook with a few couches, chairs, and a large window that looks out on a small patch of greenery, trees, flowers, and a fountain.

Is it possible to fall in love with a store? Yes. Because I just did. I don't know how Ella leaves here every day. But I can definitely see why she loves it.

As I wander past some of the tables in the front, Ella walks up from farther back in the store. "Welcome to Cozy—" she pauses a second "—hey, Christy!" Ella steps up to me, wraps her arms around my shoulders, and hugs me like we have known one another years instead of weeks. "What are you doing here?" Her excitement to see me warms me like a mug of hot cocoa on a winter day.

"I had some free time and wanted to check out your store. Think I'm in love." I swoon at the shelves and she laughs.

"It's pretty great. Have you seen much of it yet?"

"Nope. Walked in a minute ago."

Ella grabs my hand and yanks me. "Let me show you around." Her jubilance is palpable. I practically stumble behind her as she drags me through the store and points to this and that. Her two favorite parts are the reading area— inside and out—and the indie author section. The way her eyes light up as she gives me a tour, you would think this was the first time I'd been in a bookstore.

She tells me to wander and check things out but invites me to have lunch with her in thirty minutes. After I scan hundreds of book spines, not even a quarter of the way through the store, she finds me down the indie romance aisle. After I store the books in my hands behind the clerk counter, we head to the delicatessen for lunch.

Once we pay for sandwiches and drinks, we take them to the outdoor garden by the bookstore and sit at a picnic table. The air whips my hair and sends a chill throughout my body. Although it's winter, it has been unseasonably warm. Noticing my shiver, Ella cranks on a small outdoor heater next to us. Within minutes, the air warms as we start eating.

"So," I start, "I stopped by to ask if you and Thomas would like to join Rick and me for dinner."

Ella finishes her bite of roast beef and wipes her mouth with a paper napkin. "I'll check with Thomas, but I'd love to. When were you thinking?"

"Rick has tomorrow off. If that's not too soon for you."

She nods and takes a sip of her water. "Should work for us. After I check with Thomas, I'll text you."

"Cool," I answer.

We eat the rest of our lunch, and I reiterate how much I love Ella's store. When we finish, Ella gets back to work. I purchase the books I stashed behind the checkout then head home. Energy zaps and funnels through my veins on my drive home. The same sensation I get every time when we plan to meet up with a couple. The natural chemical high is addictive and intoxicating. And with Ella and Thomas, it feels ten times more powerful.

***

Chopping a plethora of veggies, I add them to a large wooden bowl filled with lettuce. Lemon and garlic wafts throughout the kitchen before Rick adds shrimp to the scampi sauce. After he tosses the shrimp a moment, he drains the cavatappi pasta and adds it to the shrimp and sauce. Just as he pulls garlic bread and roasted carrots from the oven, the doorbell jingles.

Tossing the final slices of red onion in the salad bowl, I rinse and dry my hands, then go to greet our guests. Before opening the door, I face the mirror in the foyer and fix my hair. After a quick swipe down the sides of my dress, I open the door with a warm smile.

"Ella. Thomas. Please, come in." As each of them steps in, we exchange hugs. Of all the couples Rick and I have been with, none have resonated with us like Ella and Thomas. With them, life clicks into place a little more.

Giving Rick a moment to finish in the kitchen, I play tour guide and show Ella and Thomas around. The tour doesn't last long and when we reach the dining room, Rick is placing dinner on the table.

"Hey, man," Thomas says as he and Rick shake hands and do a one-arm bro hug. Slap on the back included. "How've things been?"

"Good. You?"

"Good. Feels like you and I have been missing out. Our girls chatting all the time." Thomas laughs and Rick joins him. Ella and I shrug, not caring that we have been talking day in-day out, and join the laughter.

We all sit, eat dinner, and chat. In such a short period of time, Ella and I have developed a wonderful friendship. Our daily texts just typical girl chatter. I love how easily we have come together. Other than Sarah, I have never had a friendship form so quick and simplistically.

After we finish our meal, we make our way into the living room with wine. The guys talk sports for a bit, while Ella and I discuss a book we have both read. The conversations flow and the time breezes by.

When the wine is gone and the conversations simmer down, Rick sets his palm on my knee and gives it a light squeeze before sliding it up my thigh, slow and steady. Midway up my thigh, he turns in his seat to face me head-on.

While his hand continues toward my center, the other cups my jaw and he kisses me. Twisting to face him better, I spread my legs and give him better access. Rick savors me with his tongue as his fingertips dance over my wet folds. Completely absorbed in his touch, I startle when soft lips graze the top of my shoulder. Ella.

Opening my eyes, I peer to my shoulder as Rick kisses me. Ella slides the thin dress straps off my shoulder and kisses from where the material vanished and further up my neck.

Thomas stands behind Ella, sweeping her curly red locks off her neck. Kissing her neck, his hand cups her breast, squeezes, then glides down her abdomen.

I can't see, but I know Thomas's hand dove between Ella's legs. Behind me, her hips circle. Begging for more. Her eagerness shoots a bolt of lightning to my core. I want my fingers between her thighs. To taste her on my tongue.

"Oh, god," I moan.

Rick circles my clit. Once, twice, thrice. I gasp, breaking our kiss, and rock my hips forward. In an instant, two digits slip inside me. Reaching down, I hike the skirt of my dress up my hips and gaze between my thighs. Watching as my hips rock back and forth, Rick's fingers sliding in and out of my folds.

Shifting my weight, I press my back against the couch and gain a better view of everyone. Beside me, Ella moves onto her haunches as she kisses along my collarbone and Thomas plays with her clit, occasionally dipping his fingers inside. I run one hand up Rick's thigh, gripping his cotton-covered erection, then run my other hand up Ella's thigh. Her knees slowly part the closer I get to the junction of her thighs.

When I reach her slick core, Thomas removes his hand and lets me take over playing with her. A zipper unlatches in the room, and I assume it's Thomas undoing Ella's dress. My assumption answered a second later when the top and bottom of her dress bunches at her waist. Thomas kisses his way along Ella's collarbone before he dips down and wraps his mouth around her nipple, sucking and teasing the pert bud.

Under my touch, Ella thrusts forward and I pump my fingers in and out of her. Rick continues to finger fuck my pussy as he slowly peels my dress away. Once my dress drops and exposes my breasts, Rick slips off the couch and sucks each in turn. My breasts grow heavy with need. My nipples taut and begging for more after Rick releases his grip on each. Rick kisses his way down my abdomen, biting the sensitive skin below my navel. I pause my fingers inside Ella long enough for Rick to rip my dress away.

Beneath the soft cotton, I'm bare. No panties. No bra. Not a lick of hair on my body.

As I resume pumping my fingers inside Ella, Rick spreads my knees wide and bites his way up the inside of my thighs. With each nip, I jerk forward and hiss. By the time Rick reaches the apex of my thighs, I have scooted to the edge of the couch.

His mouth clamps down. Tongue swirls. Heat pulses through my limbs and soars where he continues to taste me. "So fucking sweet," he growls.

Thomas stops teasing Ella's tits and replaces my fingers at her folds. I paint her juices over her lips before sucking them off my fingers. Damn, she is divine. Like honey and cinnamon.

Rick laps at my pussy while Thomas does the same to Ella. Beside me, Ella mewls. Whimpering as Thomas licks and sucks her clit. Watching the two of them spikes my high. I grip Rick's hair and grind against his face. Hard.

Leaning toward Ella, I pinch her nipple and roll it between my fingers. Soon, she tips over the edge. Not long after, I follow suit.

The rest of the night progresses much the same, except we transfer to the bedroom. Hours later, when we are all spent and it seems impossible to stay awake another minute, Rick and I offer the spare bedroom to Ella and Thomas. They thank us for the offer but decline. Their departure is far from awkward. If anything, there is more of a level of comfort with them than any previous partners we have been with.

After Rick closes the door behind Ella and Thomas, he faces me and walks us back to the bedroom. "We got lucky and found great new friends," Rick says, kissing the top of my head.

"Agreed." Hope soars as my heart flutters. California went from originally being a questionable idea to being one of the best decisions we have made. Fate. Because I feel like Rick and I are finally home. In the place we belong. Together.

EIGHTEEN

RICK

The clientele at Boundless has been gradually growing. Just as Rocco and I predicted. As business booms downstairs in the club, it also booms on the floor above. Rocco is a smart businessman and has mastered the art of prospering.

Oftentimes, Boundless patrons dine upstairs and flaunt their wealth in well-tailored attire and flashy jewels. Once they have enjoyed dinner, they descend the "members only" stairwell and step into the club for dessert.

Since having Ella and Thomas at our place three weeks ago, things have flourished between the four of us. Christy smiles more often. As do I. Our relationship, and happiness, has never felt more alive and electric.

Thomas and Ella stop by Boundless once or twice a week. Most nights they're here, so is Christy. When I'm able to join them, we sip on drinks and chat inside VIP. On my last night off, the four of us went out on a normal date—dinner and a movie. After we stepped out of the theater, Thomas invited us back to their house for a nightcap.

Best damn nightcap I ever had.

We also spent time together over the holidays. It was so… normal. The most normal our lives have been in a really long time.

I love how easily our ladies mesh together. Christy and Ella are two peas in a pod. They text or talk on the phone all day, every day. Thomas and I exchanged numbers after the first night we had them over at our place. We occasionally catch up, talk about football and the girls. Occasionally, we bring up our past, but nothing too heavy. After our times together and the conversations Thomas and I have had, one thing holds true. I trust Thomas. As a man. As a person. And with my girl. There is no doubt in my mind that he would admit the same.

Trust is challenging in our lifestyle. We have to test the water with so many people. Some just don't click, while others only pretend to be into the life just to get in your bed. But it soothes my insecurities that Christy and I have found the level of trust we crave with Thomas and Ella.

"How you two doing back here?" I ask Cheyenne. Currently, Cheyenne is training our newest bartender, Xander. Between the two of them, they have served thousands of drinks over the last week. They keep up and never complain. We are lucky to have them at the club, and I try my damnedest to let them know how much I appreciate their hard work every chance I get.

"Good, boss man." Cheyenne pours a shot of Patrón and slides it in front of a middle-aged man with salt-and-pepper hair. "But looking forward to my day off."

"Both of you" —Xander glances over at me— "keep up the great work. Never seen a bar tended this perfect."

A heap of flattery, but I meant every bit of it. Over the years at Apex, Tink poured drinks faster than my eyes could keep up with. But Cheyenne and Xander... I never see their hands. Drinks just magically appear in front of people. I have mad respect for them both and their abilities.

I sit at the end of the bar, near the office, and survey the crowd. As per usual, hundreds of bodies tempt and tease and dance. Bass shakes the walls. The scent of salt and sex whirl in the air. Skin slaps skin as lungs gasp for breath. Whiskey lingers on the tip of my tongue after I down a shot Cheyenne places in front of me.

Turning the glass over and setting it on the bar top, I signal to Cheyenne and let her know I'm going in the office for a bit. Unfortunately, a stack of invoices with my name on them call out for my attention.

As I close and lock the office door behind me, the music

fades away. Not completely, but enough for me to focus on the pile of paperwork on my desk. This room, as well as the break room, had special insulation added to semi-soundproof them from the club. A bit more professional to have phone calls that don't involve loud music, screaming, or moaning pleas for more.

The invoices slowly shuffle from *to-do* to *done*. Just as I finish inputting figures from the invoice in my hand, I glance up from the computer and out onto the club floor. A man in tight-fitting leather stands at the bar, waiting for a drink. On his elbow… the bleach-blonde.

Fuck.

I don't have time to deal with pests tonight. Especially those who don't respect others or rules. And I refuse to be holed up in my office because some woman is incapable of controlling herself. I take a deep breath, promise not to let this annoying woman rain on my parade, and continue working on the task at hand.

An hour later and I finish the last of the invoices. Surveying the club through the two-way window before I exit, I see no sign of the blonde woman. Perhaps I got lucky and she left. One can only hope.

I straighten my shirt and slacks, step out of the office, and start my rounds of the club. Halfway through my first circuit, and a handful of conversations, I spot the blonde near the wall. I shift my trek and walk closer to the center of the room. Twenty feet later, a small hand grips my elbow and I spin around to see who it is.

Goddamnit.

Why won't this woman leave me the hell alone? What the fuck is her deal?

"Last warning," I tell her, glancing at her hand on my elbow. "You touch me again without permission, and you'll be banned from the premises."

She removes her lanky fingers from my elbow and coos, "No need to spit out threats."

I grind my jaw and hold back what I really wish to tell her. That threats are undelivered promises. I deliver on my promises. "What is it that you need?" I have lost my patience with this woman. She is a thorn in my side.

Leaning far too close to me, yet not touching me, she says, "Someone to fuck me hard."

I step back from her, annoyed at her presence. Five seconds away from booting her out, the man from the bar latches on to her side. Completely oblivious to what is happening. Another step back, I create a wider gap between us. "If you'll excuse me."

Before I take another step, she steps into my personal space. Again. Her hand running down my side and pissing me the hell off. "Think about it," she purrs.

"Actually," I pause and lock eyes with one of the bouncers. I signal him over. When he reaches us, I stare coldly into her eyes and speak to her as if she were a child—slow and exaggerated. "There is nothing to think about. You are banned from Boundless and Opulence. If you are caught on the premises again, we will call law enforcement and have you arrested. Jake will escort you out."

I turn and walk back to the bar. First person to be kicked out and banned from the club. Joy and happy day. Open for two months and the aggravations are already popping up. Hopefully we don't see any more for a while. I never enjoy dealing with these situations.

The rest of the night goes smoothly. I shoot Rocco a text and let him know I had to ban someone. His response—*won't be the last*. Too true.

The club shuts down for the evening and we all go about our closing routines. After the tills are locked in the safe, and everything is ready for the janitorial crew, I walk Cheyenne and Xander to their cars. Xander told me he was more than capable of walking to his car alone, but it's a habit from over the years. Just because he's a man, doesn't mean I can't extend him the same courtesy as the female staff. Once their cars start up, I head out of the lot and home to Christy.

Since starting at Boundless, my schedule has been a bit wonky. But since things are starting to level out, the management team decided it was time to set regular shifts/days off. Day after tomorrow, I officially have weekends off. Which means more time with my girl. Which also means a sense of normalcy in our lives.

Finally, everything is falling into place for us.

The next morning, I wake to Christy sucking my cock under the sheet.

Her hot, wet tongue glides up and down my shaft as she fondles my balls with her fingers. I growl when she takes me to the hilt, and she fists my balls tighter.

"Fuck, gorgeous." I comb my fingers through her hair and fist a cluster of locks, holding her head in place as I plunge down her throat.

"Mmm," she muffle-moans.

The faster I pump my hips, the more she moans. As my cock swells in her mouth, she rakes her teeth over my shaft and I explode down her throat.

"Goddamn. Son of a bitch. Motherfucker." I prattle off the curses as she takes everything I give then licks me clean.

When she pops out from under the sheet—hair a disheveled cute mess and eyes bright and wide—she licks her lips like the goddess she is and singsongs, "Breakfast. Best meal of the day."

I yank her down to my chest and wrestle with her a minute. Her giggle floats around the room and my heart bursts with joy. Best goddamn sound in the world. One of them, anyway. The second being her whimpers as she comes on my cock.

"Shouldn't you be getting ready for work?" I ask, tickling her sides.

"Yeah. Just couldn't resist going in the tent on our bed. Only time I really enjoy camping." She laughs and I join her.

Can't help I'm hard half the night. Happens when you sleep next to a woman like Christy.

Pushing up onto my elbows, I suck her bare nipple a second, slap her ass, and shoo her away. "Go shower, gorgeous."

The most adorable pout jets out her lip and creases her forehead. "Fine," she huffs. "I'll get ready for work." She takes her sweet time slipping off the bed, purposely strad- dling my cock and grinding for a beat.

Before the shower starts, I fall back asleep. When I wake, there is a note on the bedside table.

Looking forward to the weekend. Should we see Ella and Thomas?

I am one lucky son of a bitch. To find someone as amazing as Christy and live a life we both enjoy. Grabbing my phone from the charger, I shoot Christy a quick text.

Rick: Yes. Want me to set it up?
Christy: Nope. I'll take care of it.
Rick: Love you, gorgeous.
Christy: Love you, too.

NINETEEN

CHRISTY

Tossing dirty laundry into the washer, something crinkles in Rick's pocket. Déjà vu strikes as I reach inside and pull out a slip of paper. This paper is different than the previous, though.

Folded on a Boundless receipt is a phone number, smeared lipstick, and a message.

You want a real woman? Call me.

I stand frozen, staring at the wrinkled slip of paper. Who the fuck is *this* bitch? And why the hell is this in Rick's pocket? When we were in Georgia, this shit never happened. Ever. As great as California is, it seems the place comes with new challenges.

I drop the note and pants and go locate my phone. *Breathe, Christy. Assume nothing.* If Rick was actually trying to hide something from me, he wouldn't leave notes from other women in his pockets for me to find. Plus, the context of this note is somewhat juvenile. Similar to a note a girl would slip a guy in high school.

After I snag my phone from the charger in the bedroom, I shove it in my back pocket and sit a moment. Once my thoughts have simmered down, I walk back to the laundry room. With trembling hands, I slide my phone from my back pocket and lean against the washer. I pick up the paper and flatten it out on top of the machine and snap a photo. Opening up my and Rick's text history, I attach the photo and type out a brief message.

Christy: What is this?

While at work, Rick doesn't always feel his phone vibrate when I text. Sucking in a deep breath, I slip the phone back into my pocket and go back to my chore, doing my best to ignore the menacing slip of paper. He will text back as soon as he sees the message. No doubt.

An hour and a half later, almost every surface inside the house sparkles and glows. Clean cotton wafts in the air from a lit candle in the living room, mixing with the artificial lemon scent from the floor cleaner I used not long ago.

Sometimes, when I get a touch frantic, I clean. And not just a little cleaning here, a little cleaning there. More like shit-can't-possibly-get-any-cleaner OCD cleaning. The clothes are twenty minutes away from finishing in the dryer. Then I'll swap the bedding from the washer into the dryer while I fold and put away the items from the dryer. I swept, vacuumed, and mopped every room. Dusted every surface above ground level, especially those pesky floorboards. Cleared out any old leftovers in the fridge. Washed the dishes. Wiped down the shower, toilet, and bathroom sink. Swiped wood polish over the dresser, bookshelves, entertainment center, and tables. Changed the sheets on our bed as well as the spare bed. Reorganized the linen closet, then decided to reorganize our bedroom closet. Shredded all the mail I couldn't throw in the trashcan.

Now standing in the middle of the living room with my hands on my hips, I spin around and look for something else to do. Maybe reorganize the books on the shelves? Should I alphabetize them? Sort them by color or author or genre?

I still haven't gotten a response from Rick and I'm losing my freaking mind. Ugh! It never takes him this long to answer me. Of course, every second that ticks by right now feels like a week passing.

Part of me is half tempted to jump in the car and drive to

the club. Business has picked up, from what Rick told me, but he still gets breaks and does office work.

Just as I slip on my shoes and throw my purse strap over my head, my phone pings with an incoming text.

Rick: Not sure. Could be from this crazy bitch I booted out the other night.
Christy: Crazy bitch?
Rick: Yeah. She got in my face one too many times. Propositioned me. I kicked her out.
Christy: So how did this get in your pocket?
Rick: Beats me. But she kept touching me. Maybe she slipped it in my pocket.

Deep, steady breaths, Christy. You know what they say about assuming. So, don't be an ass.

Rick: I swear, gorgeous. Didn't know she did that. She's actually made work a pain in the ass. Until I banned her.
Christy: Good. Glad you banned her. Otherwise, I might have to kick her ass.
Rick: There's my girl. Gotta go. See you in the morning.
Christy: Love you.
Rick: Love you, too.

Just breathe. Everything is fine. God, I need to quit jumping to conclusions. Especially when I don't have enough information. Nothing is going on. Nothing except crazy bitches in the club trying to steal my man. Another day in the life. But I definitely need to chill the hell out.

I crumple the paper and toss it in the trash bin. Once my heart settles, I fold and put away the laundry, make myself dinner, and head to bed. Soon, Rick will be home. Soon, we will share our first weekend off together since moving here. And it will be absolute perfection.

We meet Ella and Thomas at a bistro near the beach.

The chic decor grabs my attention as soon as we walk in

the door. Oil and watercolor paintings hang sporadically on the walls. Most of the art naturalistic. Botany. Flowers. Pops of yellow and blue amongst the creams and greens. Chunky tables resemble smooth driftwood. Matching chairs draped in cream crocheted blankets and fluffy pillows. A cluster of tea lights glow in the center of each table beside a small fern filled vase.

Rick pulls out my chair for me. After he scoots me forward, he presses a kiss atop my head and sits in the chair beside me.

"This place is super cute," I comment. "Thanks for inviting us."

Ella waves off my gratitude. "Someone in the bookstore mentioned it after sitting in the reading nook. And you never need to thank us for an invite."

My heart swells. Rick and me being here with Ella and Thomas is so normal. A couple's date night out. Although the four of us have been intimate, tonight isn't about that. For the first time, we thought it would be a nice change to have dinner and enjoy the company of one another. As great as the sex is, it doesn't rule our lives.

Thomas discusses the crazy case he just landed. Says he will be bombarded for months unless a miracle happens. His client suing a large corporation due to one of their employees driving under the influence and running them off the road. The client's spouse passed away less than twenty-four hours after the accident. Now they're suing for negligence, pain and suffering, and how the loss will affect the living spouse's future financially.

The more he shares—as vague as possible—the more I tremble. If anything ever happened to Rick, I would be absolutely devastated. He has been my rock. The only solid foundation I have known. Once upon a time, my parents were my foundation. But the moment they shamed me, the earth tilted on its axis and shattered beneath my feet. Lucky for me, Rick righted my world, slowly sealed those cracks, and gave me a solid place to set my feet.

As if he senses my wayward thoughts, he clutches my hand and strokes his thumb softly over my palm. His assurance through touch that nothing like this will ever happen to us. And I want to believe it, so I let all my anxieties fall away.

We order dinner. Chat about life before we met. Enjoy each other's company and share laughter.

Before Ella owned the bookstore, she worked several retail jobs. In her words— "nothing of significance."

"So, how did the bookstore come to life?" I ask out of curiosity. Rick and Thomas carry on a separate conversation beside us.

"Sheer luck. An older woman lived next door to us. Grace. Such a sweet and kind-hearted woman. Unfortunately, her children only visited during the holiday season. She wouldn't confess it, but I think they only showed for the check she put in their card." Ella shakes her head and purses her lips, obviously upset over the matter. "Every day, Thomas or I would go check on her. Visit with her for an hour. Sometimes, we'd make enough dinner for the three of us. It saddened me that her family basically sat on the sidelines and waited for her to die."

I slap my hand over my mouth and shake my head. Working at a life insurance company, I know just how often this happens. It always shocks me when people call in and ask to cash in the policy. Their loved one barely gone, and their only concern is the check they will receive. Unfathomable.

"What happened?" I ask.

"Grace passed in her sleep a few years ago. I went to check on her in the morning. When she didn't answer the door after a couple minutes, I let myself in with the key she gave us. She laid so peaceful in her bed. Afghan tugged up to her chin. Not an ounce of suffering on her face. I kissed her forehead, said my goodbyes, and called the non-emergency number for the police."

Ella swipes a tear off her cheek. And it isn't until she does this that I realize I started crying at some point. She sucks in a jagged breath, then continues. "Anyway, a month later, Grace's attorney called. Asked us to come down to their office. A few days later, we learned Grace altered her will months prior and left Thomas and me her savings. She'd left the house to her children and instructed them to sell it and divide the proceeds. In the end, her four children sold her house for a quarter of what she left us. They were bitter, but we ignored them."

"Wow," I say. "Sorry you had to deal with the drama, but after all you did for her... what a wonderful gift she left you."

"Yeah. Grace loved books. Always had one nearby. The man who previously owned the bookstore had been in the red for some time and put the store up for sale. After weeks of negotiating, Thomas and I became the proud owners of Cozy Corner Books. With some of the remaining money, we gave the store a facelift and made it more inviting. Soon, the coffee shop and delicatessen moved in and business has boomed since."

I love this story. Although the part about Grace was sad, it tells me what kind of people Ella and Thomas truly are. Considerate. Loving. Generous. Rick and I are more than lucky to call them friends.

After we finish dinner, the four of us bundle up and walk down the street to Confectionate. One of my coworkers bragged for ten minutes straight about the sweet shop's pie selection. The second I mentioned it to Ella, she told me it wasn't far from the restaurant and we should go.

Once we have our fill of sugar, chocolate, and fruit, we call it a night. For the first time, we don't take the evening any further. A flutter erupts in my solar plexus. Ella and Thomas are so perfect for me and Rick. Not only do we pair well as sexual partners, we also bond perfectly as friends.

There isn't a single couple Rick and I have ever had a relationship with that was similar to this. Fate is a strange creature, but I believe everything happens for a reason. Ella and Thomas fit into our world so simply. Like the missing pieces to our puzzle.

With each passing day, life here gets better and better.

TWENTY

ALEX

A BLOCK AWAY, he opens the passenger door for her. Kisses her. A little too long for my liking. Then shuts the door and gets in on the driver's side.

The black Audi starts and pulls onto the street. Behind them, another black vehicle. A BMW SUV with the other couple. They both drive away but turn opposite directions at the traffic light down the street.

As soon as they are out of sight, I crank the engine of my dying sedan and veer into traffic. Five minutes later, I drive three cars behind the Audi. My eyes lock onto it and watch its every movement. It turns left, and I follow suit. Then takes a right a few blocks later, and I continue behind them but keep my distance.

On the quiet neighborhood street, porch lights glow and highlight well-manicured lawns. Houses decorated with wreaths on the doors or accent lighting showing off their prized plants. It is all a little too prissy for my taste.

The Audi parks in a driveway, and the couple steps out and walks hand in hand to the door. Once they go inside, I drive slowly up to the house and stop in the street, staring at the large windows.

That should be my house.

A light flips on inside and their silhouettes come together and blend into one.

That should be me in there. Lips crashing and hips slapping. Me.

Soon… soon it will be.

Might not see me coming, but they will soon learn.

TWENTY-ONE

RICK

TONIGHT, we closed Boundless for a private event. A fucking bachelorette party to be more precise.

The squealing women and shit ton of glitter everywhere has me ready to puke. *If I ask Christy to marry me, would she behave like this at her bachelorette party?* An errant thought I shake off.

The bride paid a pretty penny—five thousand, to be exact—to make Boundless hers for the evening. Currently, she and twenty of her closest friends dance naked in the vacant space. Body glitter on every lick of their skin, shimmering like a disco ball under the lights. And spreading onto every surface they touch.

Honestly, I hate that the janitorial crew will be cleaning twice as long tonight to get all this shit off the furniture and floor. They will no doubt hate us by the time they clock out.

But Rocco told me the bride is a close friend to one of his dancers, and that is the *only* reason he allowed it.

Two men walk out of the entry corridor, half-dressed as law enforcement, and I roll my eyes. I really have no desire to stick around and watch what is about to unfold. Amateur hour with a couple of scrawny dweebs and women who obviously don't get pleasured often enough.

Walking up to the bar, I look at Cheyenne and she rolls her eyes. She loves tonight just as much as I do. "Cheyenne, I'll be in the office. Let me know if you need anything."

She harrumphs and nods. The last thing she wants to do is spend the next several hours watching these women as some ridiculous male dancers twirl their cocks in banana hammocks. At least Rocco agreed to pay her a normal night's salary. Which is the only reason she hasn't stormed out yet.

"Yeah, sure," she says, then goes back to slicing lemons and stocking the bar. At least tonight will give her a chance to prep more for tomorrow.

After I weed through a stack of invoices on my desk, I call Christy. Before leaving for work, I forgot to tell her we were closed for the party. If she walked in and saw the flock of sparkly women mobbing the male dancers, she would probably turn around, walk out, and call me with a million questions.

"Hey," she purrs, answering the call.

"Hey, gorgeous. Forgot to tell you tonight the club is closed for a private party. We'll be out early."

"Yay." Something shatters in the background and she curses.

"What was that? You okay?"

"Dropped a glass. I'm fine. Just need to clean it up," she huffs.

"Just a glass. It's replaceable. Don't cut yourself." A gust muffles her phone speaker and I imagine her blowing her hair off her face. So fucking adorable. "I should be home in a couple hours."

"'Kay. Love you."

"Love you, too."

I walk Cheyenne to her car before I slip into mine.

After five hours of squeals and hollers and enough glitter to wipe out the unicorn population, the bachelorette party ended. Thank fuck. Seriously, if Christy ever has a bachelorette party, I know it would never be packed with all that fake bullshit. Not even sure she would ever have a bachelorette party, to be honest.

I shake my head. There I go again. Imagining Christy as my wife. Not that I don't love her with every beat of my heart, or enough to want her as my wife, but her in such a traditionalist role seems odd to me. Matrimony doesn't quite fit our mold. But what really does?

Marriage has always set me off-kilter. Not in a bad way. Never comprehended the point, I guess. Why do two people need a piece of paper and words uttered before other people to be committed? In my eyes, they don't. Christy and I have been committed to each other for the last seven years. We don't need a government certificate to validate our love. At least I don't.

But does she?

For the first time, I consider she might dream of such things. At Sarah's birthday party, she bawled as Jackson proposed to Sarah. Starry-eyed, she smiled at me in a way I had never seen before. She cried that night and I assumed it was happiness for her friend.

Maybe it was more than that? Maybe she wished for the same. To have a ring on her left hand. To flaunt it to the world and lay claim to me. Little does she know, she claimed my heart seven years ago.

"Am I blind?" I ask the steering wheel.

I twist the black band on my right thumb. Have I failed this part of our relationship?

Sure, we have had our ups and downs—like every couple. But I don't imagine a single day of our lives apart. Ever. From the second I laid eyes on her in Apex, Christy was mine. She would always belong to me. We may share ourselves with other people, but only our bodies. Never our hearts. Hence why we don't allow kissing. Far too much intimacy comes with kissing.

Christy has never given me any indication she isn't happy. With me. Or our relationship. But I can't help but wonder if I deprive her of what she truly wants.

Years ago, we discussed other important life topics. Mainly children. Thankfully, we were both on the same page. Neither of us wants children. When she eventually told me about her parents, it made more sense. She never wants to expose another life to the pain that comes with rejection. Especially from family. The people who claim to love you the most.

Me? The minute I lost Harriett, my perspective on life changed. Mom shut down. Dad finished a bottle of whiskey every other day. Neither of them gave two shits about me anymore. Their baby died and nothing else mattered. Not even their living, breathing son.

I never want to suffer a loss like Harriett's again. She may not have been my daughter, but she was my world then. We never bickered like most siblings. If anything, we spent more time with each other than our friends. Harriett wasn't just my sister, she was my best friend.

Losing her flipped a switch in my brain. A switch that turned off my emotions and erected a wall. A barrier to shield my heart. I never wanted to get close to anyone again. Never wanted to love someone again. Because love equals loss.

But Christy scaled that wall, wrapped her warm arms around my heart, and jump started the slow beating organ.

"Holy shit," I whisper into the darkness as I park in our driveway.

I sit in the car a minute and wrap my mind around this revelation. True, I may never have imagined myself married. But with Christy, my imagination runs wild.

After clearing my thoughts, I go inside to greet my girl. Barely after eleven, and she is sexy as fuck on the couch. Curled up with a knitted, heather gray throw blanket, head propped on the arm of the couch, she snores softly as movie credits scroll up the television screen.

For a moment, I squat beside the couch and watch her chest rise and fall. Steady, even breaths. A lock of her russet hair drapes her left eye. Glasses cock-eyed on the bridge of her nose. Her eyes dart behind her lids and I wonder what she dreams about. Wishing it would project onto the screen and show me her inner desires.

She inhales and sighs in her sleep. "Always," she mumbles.

The corner of my mouth perks up. She's dreaming about us. Often, I dream of her. Of us. My heart inflates and jack-hammers behind my ribcage as I stare at my girl. My gorgeous, amazing girl.

I click off the television and scoop her up in my arms. Automatically, she wraps her arms around my neck and curls into my chest. Even asleep, her body clings to me. As does mine to her. Like second nature.

After laying her in the bed, I undress and slip under the comforter. A second later, her arm and leg are draped over me. I tug her impossibly closer and kiss her forehead. "Night, gorgeous. Love you," I whisper into the dark.

Her body hugs me tighter. "Love you, too," she mumbles.

Am I really here?

Thomas stands next to me and pats my back. "Overwhelmed?" Overwhelmed is putting it lightly.

I stare around the small, independently-owned store. There isn't much to look at, but there is plenty. And everything fucking sparkles. Every. Goddamn. Thing.

"Uh, yeah."

After my revelation a few nights ago, I shot Thomas a text and asked for his help. Not that I am incapable of doing this type of thing on my own. Just thought it would be nice to have support since I'm swimming in uncharted territory.

"Any idea what she likes?" Thomas asks as he scans the blinding jewels in one of the cases.

Did I know? Christy never wore anything flashy. Most jewelry she owned was simple—not plain, but not a piece someone would shriek over either. "Classic. Silver. Nothing gaudy."

We survey a few of the cases before he points out a selection to me. "How about these?"

Walking over to him, I scan the rows and rows of sparkling stones. If there aren't spots in my vision when we leave, I will be shocked. All the twinkling and prisms is starting to make every one of them look the same. And it is a little much. Ready to give up after scanning a few more rows, I freeze.

Locked in my gaze is a platinum, antique filigree band. At the center, the two-carat, round cut black diamond sits high. On either side, woven into the band, is five vibrant, red rubies. Absolutely stunning.

You have heard of women seeing a wedding dress and

instantly knowing it is "the one". Right now, staring at this small, delicate piece of jewelry, one truth is absolute. It was crafted for Christy.

After shelling out a small fortune, I leave the store with the black velvet box tucked in my pocket. My palms sweat and my throat dries. Nervousness has never struck me this hard. Like a closed fist to the sternum.

Am I *ready* for this? To propose to Christy? What if proposing fucks everything up between us? Will she say yes? God, I hope she does. More than that, I hope I don't make a fool of myself. But what if she says no? I love her more than anything, and it would shred me if I ask and she says she doesn't want to be my wife. Not sure how we would move forward after that.

Thomas and I grab a quick bite to eat before he heads back to the office. The entire time, he shares how nerve-wracked he was before proposing to Ella. He had the same fears that currently wrench my heart in a death grip. Before we go our separate ways, Thomas does his best to soothe my distress and tells me to call him if I need help.

After lunch, I head to Boundless and lock Christy's ring in the safe upstairs. Only Rocco and I have the vault combination, so I know it will be secure. Once I'm in my office, I sit at my desk, surf the web, and distract myself from the torrent of *what-if* questions.

An hour later, the perfect date is planned for proposing and I breathe a little easier. My nerves seem to have settled a fraction, thank fuck. Taking a deep breath, I mutter, "She'll say yes. Quit worrying."

I speak nothing but truth. No doubt Christy will say yes when I ask her to marry me. Our love is endless. Timeless. And we have proved it time and again with every obstacle that has hit us.

So then why is there still a boulder lodged in my gut?

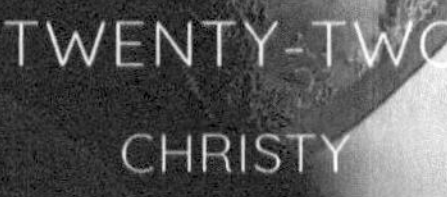

TWENTY-TWO

CHRISTY

RICK HAS BEEN ACTING WEIRD.

I let him sleep a little longer while I cook us breakfast. After tearing open the pack of maple bacon, I lay several strips on a drip pan and put them in the oven on low. While they start, I dice up potatoes, onion, garlic, bell pepper, and avocado.

Once the onions caramelize, I remove half and add the potatoes and garlic. As I start whipping the eggs for omelets, Rick wraps his arms around my waist. I freeze mid-whisk and close my eyes, basking in his warmth. He kisses the back of my head and I shudder as tingles run down my spine.

"Morning, gorgeous. Smells good."

I set the bowl down on the counter, twist in his arms, and kiss him. "Ten more minutes."

He nods, presses his lips to my shoulder, then walks off. "Gonna brush my teeth."

Over the last few days, Rick has lavished me with more kisses than normal. Soft, sweet kisses. Not that I don't love them, but they aren't the typical sort of kisses we share. Yes, he has been tender with me. And it is not as if I don't enjoy the softer side of his affections. But the ratio between gentle and harsh kisses is a ten-ninety split. Not the opposite. It's as if everything has suddenly flipped.

What the hell changed?

Before I delve too deep into my wayward thoughts, he

walks back into the kitchen. "Need help?" Another shoulder kiss.

"Coffee?"

He nods and heads for the single brewer, popping a mug under the drip, loading a pod, and starting it up.

Once everything is plated and the coffee is ready, we sit at the small table in the breakfast nook. Silence stretches out the minutes like an overused elastic band. I want to scream. Ask him what the hell is going on. But, instead, I sit in silence and keep my thoughts to myself.

I shovel another forkful of omelet into my mouth, ready to lose my shit and fling the pronged metal at him. Just as I work up the nerve to blurt out and ask him what the hell is going on, he figures out how to speak again.

"Made us plans for Valentine's weekend."

I shake my head. *W-w-what?* "We never do anything on Valentine's. Always agreed it wasn't a real holiday."

"True. But indulge me. Please?"

I tilt my head to the side and study him for a beat. Is this why he has been acting weird? Because, for the first time in seven years, he planned a Valentine's Day surprise. Was he reluctant to tell me? Possibly.

"Sure," I say before eating another bite of omelet. "What did you have in mind?"

He taps his temple and smiles, the corner of his eyes crinkling. "It's a surprise. Can you get the day off? Would be nice to have a long weekend together."

Valentine's falls on a Friday. If Rick wants a long weekend together, I assume he already asked for the day off. Which means he has put in more effort than imaginable to make our first celebrated Valentine's Day one to remember. I study him as he eats another bite of potatoes and wonder what he is up to.

"I'll email Ingrid after breakfast," I tell Rick. "She should be good with it."

Ingrid is the new Marco. My direct supervisor. Her dedication to Hammond Life is admirable. She isn't just a boss, but also a leader. Honestly, I didn't understand the difference until I met her. When it comes to work-life balance, she advocates as if it was the most important part of the job. Lucky doesn't describe how fortunate I am to work for her. Someone who urges employees to take time off at least once per quarter —whether one day or five.

"Good." Rick winks then gobbles down his forkful of potatoes.

After we clean up the kitchen, we dress and head out for the day. Once Rick mentioned he made plans for us on Valentine's, a weight lifted. Obviously, he was worried about how I would react. But I'm happy he finally spit it out and things feel like our version of normal again.

Rick steers us through traffic, his hand wrapped around mine as he draws circles with his thumb over my skin. A small smile perks up the corners of my mouth as warmth radiates from our joined hands. Before we left the house, Rick asked if there was anywhere I wanted to go today. I told him to choose. So, our first destination… the zoo.

Although nature is less than a couple miles from our home, the outdoors in California is vastly different than the outdoors in Georgia. The air thinner and lighter on my skin. The trees a more pungent pine and the earth damp and musky. When the sun beats down on me, I enjoy its warmth rather than melt into a puddle. Also, elevation is a legit thing here—not that it wasn't in Georgia, but the difference is noticeable. And the wildlife—no comparison to what we normally saw in our neck of the woods in Georgia. Life out here is just… different. And I love it.

After Rick parks the car, we follow the other zoo-goers and head for the entrance. Once we have our wristbands and step through the turnstile, I feel like a little kid for a moment. Twenty feet in and the scent of cinnamon and sugar and buttered popcorn wafts under my nose and has me searching for its source. A vendor sits off to the side with churros, popcorn, cotton candy, and a variety of drinks.

It doesn't take much to convince Rick we need junk sustenance. "Thank you," I say as I bite down on my churro.

He pays the young man behind the cart then laughs at my gluttony. "You're welcome, gorgeous." Before I can yank my churro back, Rick chomps a bite twice the size of mine.

"Hey. That's my churro. Get your own, mister," I tease as I tuck the confection behind me.

After I finish eating my morning snack, we stroll hand in hand along the paved paths and check out the lemurs, tigers, and hippos. At each animal enclosure, we stop and read the posted signs. All the animals here were rescued from horrendous circumstances. Injured or loss of habitat. Rejected by their herd. The zoo takes them in, rehabilitates them, and provides them with a better place to live.

Before we leave, I coerce Rick into a small photo booth to take pictures with me. We make goofy faces in the first two pictures. The other two are much more passionate as he kisses me deeply. Thank goodness for the booth curtain. Normally, kisses like the one we just shared don't bother me. But the zoo is packed with kids and our kiss was nowhere near a PG rating.

As we step out, I run my hands over my dress then do my best to fix my hair. I stand near the drop chute where the pictures print out. Don't need any curious children and pissed parents peeking at them. When the small sheet of images drops, I snatch it and smile at the photos.

I brush my finger over my lips. That kiss. The intensity. The way he cradled my face and held me prisoner while he expressed how deep his feelings for me run. Why have those been so far and few between recently? Does he think I want gentle and cute? On occasion, soft and tender fits a special moment. But for us, it isn't often. Maybe he needs a reminder how much I love it when he is rough and assertive. How I love it when he kisses me like he will never have another opportunity.

Shortly after leaving the zoo, Rick drives us to a café and we eat lunch. As we sit across from each other and eat paninis, I grant him a little more time. I plead with the universe for any sign his saccharine behavior has changed. No such luck. If anything, it has gotten softer. Wispy touches. Hushed tones. Delicate kisses on my shoulders, knuckles, forehead.

So tender.

So wholesome.

So not Rick.

When we get back in the car and drive toward home, he strokes the backside of his fingers up and down my bicep. Gah! I love it and hate it, all at the same time.

That is it! I can't deal with this anymore. "Are you okay?" I ask bluntly. Better to get right to the point. Really no sense in pussyfooting.

Rick takes his eyes off the road for a split-second and glances at me. When he looks forward again, he says, "Yeah. Fine. Why?"

I shift in the passenger seat to face him and tuck my feet under my butt. "You've just been acting strange the last few days. Everything okay at work?"

His grip tightens around the steering wheel for a blink. So quick I almost miss it. But Rick and I learned to watch each other's body movements years ago. With our lifestyle, knowing when your significant other is unhappy is vital. His eyes pinch tightly as if he is upset with himself. Why would he be mad? What is he hiding? Rick and I have always been open and honest with each other. Not sure what has changed, but it is eating me alive not knowing.

In an instant, I'm a hawk and he is my prey. Eyes locked on target and tracking every move. If he shifts an inch to the left, I will know. His every move an instant blip on my radar.

"Work is fine. The bachelorette party was a waste of time and money, in my opinion. But Rocco is the ultimate decision maker in those instances. Nothing else has happened."

I narrow my eyes and study him as we drive through Los Angeles. After a beat, I retract my claws and let him drive without me being a distraction. The last thing we need is Rick to glance over at me and cause an accident because I stir the pot.

"Has something else happened with that person you kicked out?"

We exit off the highway and wind our way through the city. Rick waits to answer until after he navigates us to a street with less traffic. When we stop at a red light, he faces me. "Haven't seen her again. Hopefully we won't. We take copies of IDs and have marked hers as "no entry permitted". She shouldn't be an issue."

I stare into his honey-swirled eyes, searching for clues. Any clue. Something to shed light on his recent change in behavior. Rick isn't someone who changes without just cause.

But he also has one of the best poker faces. When necessary, he is a master at masking the truth. He isn't lying to me. Just skirting around the truth.

"That's good," I mumble. "Still doesn't explain…" I let my words trail off as I spin to face forward. If this conversation isn't going anywhere, I am done talking. No sense in making us both upset.

His knuckles brush my forearm before he laces his fingers with mine. "Does it bother you? Me more tender."

I whip my eyes back to his just as the light turns green and he has to look away. "Yes and no," I confess.

"Tell me why, gorgeous."

Gazing down at our joined hands, I fumble over what to tell him. Will I come across as an idiot? Embarrass myself? Both equally possible. "It's just… not us. Yes, I adore the sweetness. But usually it comes in small bouts. When it's days, I wonder if something happened. If I did something wrong. Or if you did. So, I question it because we aren't a softhearted, mushy couple. Not ninety-five percent of the time, anyway."

He turns the car right, then left, and a few minutes later, he pulls into the driveway. Throwing the car in park, he faces me full on. "It's true we aren't gentle lovers," he says, chuckling. "But every once in a while, it's nice to be like this. Don't you think?"

My brows furrow as my eyes narrow. "Yes. But what brought it on?" Because I truly want to know. As if a coin flipped and Rick went from heads to tails without warning.

"I had lunch with Thomas a few times recently. He said some things that resonated with me. Guess part of me is opening up. Trying things a little different. Should've brought it up with you, but thought *that* would be weird."

Trying new things? I suppose that is possible. But would we enjoy life the same if we did things different?

What if our relationship suffers? What if trying to be something we are not, knocks us down? God, I cannot imagine a life without Rick. Nor do I want to. I shake the horrible thought away and swear to not think it again. *See the bright side, Christy. Stay optimistic.*

Optimistic.

What if this change is exactly what we need? Will it make

our love stronger? More powerful? Unbreakable? These are the questions and ideas I need floating in my head. Notions that scream positivity and love and strength.

"You're right. It would've been weird," I say, giggling. "Let's give this sweeter side a try. But we need to talk about it. Weird or not. So we're both on the same page."

Rick spins in his seat, opens the door, and exits the car. Before I grab the door handle, he opens my door for me and offers his hand. "Perfect plan, gorgeous," he coos. "Now let's go inside. I need to make love to you."

And with that, we bolt to the front door like two horny teenagers who can't keep their hands off each other.

TWENTY-THREE

ALEX

This is fucking bullshit!

Sitting in cold ass temperatures and watching them. As if I don't have better things to do. Complete. And utter. Bullshit. How the hell did I manage to get myself coerced into this?

If it was only me involved in this whole operation, things would already be next level. Strides would be made. Not this amateur stalking shit. Honestly, wouldn't shock me if they knew they were being followed.

People sense that shit. Intuition and whatnot. Not much of a believer in it myself, but sometimes you can't explain how you just know that shit. So saying you had a "gut feeling" fits the bill.

With these two, I can't be sure. Maybe they are oblivious. Maybe they are that fucking stupid. Answers will come with time.

Not much longer, though. Soon, shit will hit the fan. Soon, I will get to twist rope around their wrists and ankles and throats. Tie them down on chairs and play my little games. That is when all the real fun begins.

My cell pings in my lap and startles the shit out of me. "Fuck!" Ever since this whole stalking game started, I have been a live wire. Been far too long since my last fix. And it can't come quick enough.

L: Anything to report?

"If there was anything to report, you'd know. Dumb ass," I say to the screen sarcastically.

Alex: Same shit. Different day.
L: Keep me posted.
Alex: Yep.

"Nah. Thought I'd sit here day after day for shiggles." I roll my eyes at the screen then toss the phone on the passenger seat.

The last thing I need is to be patronized. I volunteered for this gig because it would fulfill the urges living deep in my bones. Not to mention, I would do anything for L. The bond we share has proven it time and again. This isn't our first rodeo. Definitely won't be our last.

I suck down the last of my energy drink and toss the can onto the passenger floorboard. Leaning the driver's seat back, I undo my pants and stare at the house's far right window. The one I know is their bedroom.

Daydreaming of all the things soon to come, I fist my cock and tug hard. When I was a teenager, I got off on inflicting pain. After the first few people in my bed, word spread quickly and most steered clear of me. *The sicko with a torture fetish.*

Can't help what you love.

And soon, I will satiate the beast inside me.

TWENTY-FOUR

RICK

Nervous fucking wreck.

The only logical way to explain the thunderstorm of nerves brewing inside me right now. And I don't understand it at all.

Christy and I have been together seven years. Seven. Years.

The only other time I remember being remotely this nervous was in the beginning. When our relationship status was questionable and I had no clue as to what kind of person she was. A guessing game as to the level of her desires. Didn't take long to learn what my girl liked, though.

Hopefully, I guessed this right too. If not, I am royally fucked.

Beside me, Christy stares out the passenger window and bops to the music playing. Is she nervous too? Maybe keeping this so under wraps wasn't the smartest idea. Both of us on are on edge, and neither of us are speaking.

I reach across the console and twine our fingers together. Her eyes glance away from the passing scenery and stare at my jawline. She draws faint lines with her eyes along the angle of my jaw to my chin. Subtle and heated.

"Where are we going?" she asks.

Over the last forty-eight hours, she has asked me about this weekend again and again. I simply smiled at her and tapped my temple. From the glint in her eye, I know a part of her is excited. But another part of her wants to bite her nails off and spit them at me. Surprising Christy is not something I do often. Not like this.

"Not much longer and you'll see."

She sighs and it is the cutest thing. I tuck the sound away, hoping it's not the last time I hear it. "Don't know why you still need to be so secretive. We *are* on the way there."

I laugh, and she smacks my forearm. "Why ruin it now? After all the effort I put in, I'm not caving when we're minutes away from it all starting."

Her eyes snap up in attention. Like a child, she peers out the window and searches for invisible clues. As if a neon sign will flash in the distance and point out our destination. Once I pull onto the Pacific Coast Highway, I know the restaurant is roughly five minutes away. Watching her—giddy and excited —makes tonight, and this weekend, worth every second of anxiety I suffered.

When I drive up to the valet attendant, Christy ogles the restaurant. The valet opens her door and helps her out. Another attendant does the same for me before handing me a ticket. I walk around the car to Christy, offer her my elbow, and we stroll down a small path toward the restaurant.

I lean into her, my lips a breath from her skin, and whisper, "What do you think, gorgeous?"

She stares at the creamy stacked rock exterior. Along the roofline, planks of mahogany add a pop of warmth. We walk along a boardwalk path, winding through tall grass plants and perfectly manicured bonsai. Near the entrance to the restaurant is a small deck with muted gray outdoor couches, matching ottoman-style tables, and wide cream canvas umbrellas overhead.

From where we stand, you can see nothing but the Pacific Ocean for miles. The cirrus cloudy sky tinted cornflower blue with hints of peach, watermelon pink, and ruby as the sun starts to sink closer to the horizon. Absolutely perfect.

After a minute of getting lost in the scenery, I take out my phone. "Let me take a picture with the sky behind you," I tell Christy.

Just as I snap the photo, a man steps up beside me and offers to take a photo of the two of us. A few clicks later, I thank him and we head inside. At the podium near the entrance, I inform the hostess of our reservation. Probably not the first person to say this, but securing a reservation at a popular restaurant on Valentine's Day is a pain in the ass. But when the night ends, it will be worth every hassle.

The hostess seats us at a table near a large window with an ocean view. On the opposite side of the glass, outdoor heaters warm the patio seating. I considered us sitting outside when I made the reservation but wasn't sure how the weather would be. Our current table is perfect for the two of us. Neither Christy nor I have ever been the type to need fancy or over-the-top.

Once alone, Christy peeks over her menu at me. "Rick, this place is expensive." Her brows pinch together with concern. It only makes me love her more.

"If the cost was an issue, I wouldn't have brought us here. So, please, don't let it bother you, gorgeous. Find something you want to eat and ignore the price."

She chews on her bottom lip a moment and studies me. Once she sees my resolve, her shoulders drop and she sinks further into her seat. "Okay."

We order our meals and a bottle of wine. Christy slowly unwinds and enjoys the view and ambiance. Below the table, my hand swipes back and forth over the lump in my pocket. Each time my hand passes over the chunky band, my palm sweats a little more.

When dinner arrives, we dig in. After we both have a moment to savor our meals, we agree a walk by the surf after dinner would be the perfect way to end our night here. Originally, I hadn't planned for us to go down by the water. Now, it seems like an excellent opportunity. Before long, we finish our dinner, order dessert, and drink a little more. I drink only enough wine to settle my nerves, but not enough to inhibit my driving.

"Ready?" I ask as Christy drinks the last of her wine.

She nods. "Yeah."

Fifteen minutes later, I park at a beach access lot. The

closer we get to the water, the more Christy's hair whips across her face and her dress threatens to fly up. The sun set over an hour ago, but the sky hasn't turned ink black yet.

Hand in hand, we stroll near the surf. A hundred yards away, a group of people sit in a circle around a bonfire. The flames lick the sky and light the beach where we stand.

I bring us to an abrupt halt, jerking Christy in the process. "Sorry," I mutter.

"Everything okay?"

This is it. Right here. Right now. In this exact spot with the waves crashing behind her and the bonfire brightening her skin. Her russet locks pelt her cheeks and mask her glasses as she faces me.

I nod. "Yeah, gorgeous." Pulling her to my chest, I brush her wild strands away and kiss her. Soft at first. My tongue painting delicate lines on her lips and tongue. Once the taste of her hits me, I frame her face in my hands and kiss her harder. Christy moans and fists my shirt, dragging me impossibly closer.

Fire and lust and my need for her drive me forward. But before things get out of hand, I break the kiss and press my forehead to hers. Her breasts rise and fall as she gasps for air.

"Why'd you stop?" she whispers against my lips.

Breathe Rick. You got this.

"Because there's something I need to say. And if we keep doing that, I'll never get it out." I laugh nervously, holding her face in my palms as I stare into her stormy blue eyes. "Valentine's has never been a day we've celebrated. But this year, I wanted to do something special."

"You didn't—" I press a finger to her lips and cut her off.

"Let me finish." She nods and I remove my finger. "We've been together seven years. Not a day goes by where you're not on my mind. Since you walked into my life, your happiness is what makes me whole. More recently, things have been challenging. But there is no other person I'd want beside me during those challenges. And just when I thought I had you figured out, you surprise me in all the best ways. You make me a better man. No one loves me the way you do. And that's why I wanted to do something special tonight. Because you deserve to be celebrated and adored and cherished."

A tear escapes her eye and I swipe it away. I close the space between us, kiss her sweet and tender, and reach inside my pocket. Then I drop to one knee and take her hand in mine. "Christy, no one has healed my heart the way you have. No one, but you makes me whole. And I would be honored for you to be my wife."

I pinch the ring between my thumb and first finger and present it to her. She slaps her free hand over her mouth as tears flood her cheeks. "Oh my god!" She squeals.

Seconds tick by. Waves continue to crash along the surf. Chatter from the bonfire floats in the air. My heart expands and contracts at such a rapid pace, I wonder if a heart attack is imminent. Just when I am about to stand up—cause fuck if I didn't plant my knee on a rock or shell—she nods.

"Is that a yes?" *Please let her answer yes.*

She continues to nod. "Yes! A thousand times, yes!"

I rise from the sand and squeeze my arms tight around her waist, lifting her off the ground and swinging her in circles. She cups my cheeks, hooks her ankles at my back, and kisses me fiercely. The idea of fucking her on this beach—here and now—crosses my mind. But, after a moment, I plant her back on the sand and take her left hand. Sliding the ring on her ring finger, I smile so big my cheeks sting.

Fuck. Nothing compares to the symphony playing in my chest cavity right now. The zips and flutters and whirls as my pulse thumps, thumps, thumps. Never would I have thought I could feel so many emotions in a split-second.

Elation. Joy. Beholden.

Only one person gives me everything. And she just agreed to be mine for eternity.

The weekend ends far too soon.

After I asked Christy to marry me, I swept her off her feet —literally—and brought her back to the Airbnb I rented us for the weekend. The place is cozy and cute, but Christy didn't see a square-foot of it until Saturday morning after I woke her up with my head between her legs.

We stayed inside all weekend, minus one trip to a grocery

store for food. After fucking on every surface of the small cottage, we watched movies, fed each other chocolate-covered strawberries, soaked in the tub, and laid around naked. Pure heaven.

The best part… Christy stared at her ring every chance she got. Better yet, her smile never faded. Nothing has ever made me this happy. Nothing.

With an hour left at the Airbnb, we relax on the couch and watch television. Christy manages to find a channel dedicated to weddings. And it has been on for the last three hours as we packed and ate breakfast. Her excitement palpable. Hopefully she picks up on mine too.

"Do you have ideas for our wedding?" Part of me is scared to hear her answer. But another part of me jumps internally at what her answer will be. The wedding getup doesn't matter to me, so long as I get to marry her. We could be as fancy or plain as she wants. As long as she says yes at the appropriate moment.

"I'd like to get one of those planning books to organize everything. But I was thinking we'd have a small ceremony. You, me, and a few close friends. Nothing fancy. Never been one of those girls who dreamed of the poufy white dress. A red dress to match my ring feels more appropriate."

Her response is exactly what I expected—and hoped— from her. "So why are you watching all these bride shows?"

She laughs. "Just for fun. Big weddings may not be our thing. Watching these reminds me why. Too much drama. No, thank you."

Less than an hour later, we are on the road and driving back home. Out of the corner of my eye, I spot Christy staring at and twirling her ring. The way her eyes light up when she stares at it… I picked the perfect one. If one thing holds true; I know my girl. Inside and out.

As we turn onto our street, I glance up and spot a tattered, champagne-colored sedan in the rearview mirror. The same sedan I have seen a dozen times over the last week and a half. Never close enough for me to see the person behind the wheel or clearly read the license plate. And I'd chalk it up to being a neighbor, except I see the car in various places around town in my commute. No way a neighbor drives *all* the same places I do.

The car turns left on the side street before our house, and I breathe easier. Maybe it's nothing. Or maybe that person travels a lot and it's a coincidence I see them as often as I do. Maybe.

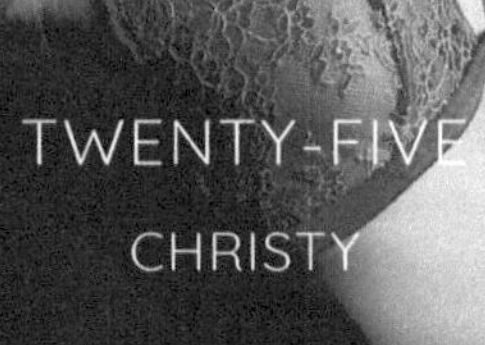

TWENTY-FIVE

CHRISTY

After I finish up at work, I decide to stop by the mall. Although neither Rick nor I desire a large, elaborate wedding, I also don't want our magical day to be a hot mess. Hence why I currently stand staring at a wall of wedding organizer books in the bridal boutique. The whole decision-making process of which planner to go with is a bit overwhelming, but I'm determined to find the one for me.

Three times, a sales associate has approached me and asked if I need help. And each time, I declined. Maybe I should have taken one of them up on their offer. As much as I would like to pick out the planner for me, I really have no idea what I'm searching for.

"Excuse me," I say, walking up to the first woman who offered to help me. "Can you help me find a planner book thingy?"

She smiles, and the way her lips curve up is endearing. "Sure thing." We walk back toward the wall of a million magazines, books, and organizers. "Anything in particular you're looking for?"

"Just something simple. We plan to have a small wedding. So I need an organizer for the basics. A place to keep track of dates, phone numbers, appointments, and so on."

The woman taps a finger over her lips and scans over the plethora of options. Her eyes scan the wall a minute longer before she bends down and scoops up a small planner. "Take a look at this one and tell me what you think."

She hands me the planner and I open the cover. Soft paper grazes against the pads of my fingers as I flip each page. Inside, the planner is divided into several sections. Each is packed with pages and pages of things I might easily forget. Since we want a small ceremony and reception, these checklists are exactly what I need. After skimming through each section, I nod to the clerk. "This is perfect. Thank you. I would've been here another five hours without your help."

"That's what we're here for. Glad to help."

Back at the register, I pay for the planner and leave the shop with a little pep in my step. Something as simple as an organizer has made my day all that much better. After window shopping a few other stores, I exit the mall and head for my car.

As I weave through the rows of cars, I glance over my shoulder a few times. A shiver rolls down my spine and I can't help but feel like I'm not alone. Each time I look behind me, there is not a soul in sight. I tremble again. Somewhere in this lot, someone is watching me. No denying their eyes are on me, burning my skin.

Picking up the pace, I dash to my car and slip inside, quickly locking the doors. As soon as I start the engine and back out, I inhale deeply and shake off the layer of unease.

There was no one there. No one was following me. I'm fine. Just imagining things.

Driving away from the mall, I swing by the grocery store. Usually, we grab groceries on the weekend, but since Rick swept me off my feet, asked me to marry him, and held me captive all weekend, it never happened. But you will hear zero complaints from me.

In the store, I grab a cart, pull out my shopping list and a pen, and start my rounds. While waiting at the bakery counter for my loaf of sliced bread, I spot a woman out of the corner of my eye. Staring at me intently. I play cool and pretend to not notice her. But her eyes bore into me like a drill mining for oil and I keep an eye on her in my periphery. The level of intensity she exudes in my direction is unnerving.

The baker hands me the bread and I set it in my cart,

happy to step away from this woman. I drift over to the deli area for lunch meats and cheese. After tugging a number from the deli ticket dispenser, I spy the same woman in my periphery again. Her eyes are locked on me like a hawk swooping in on her prey. Just as I suck up the courage to face her and ask why the hell she keeps staring at me, the deli clerk calls my ticket number.

"What can I get for you this evening?" the man asks.

I deposit my ticket in a small basket on top of the case. "One pound of applewood turkey and half a pound of Havarti, please."

He nods and walks off to slice my order. In the reflection of the case, the woman stares at me. Top lip curled in disgust. Eyes pinched tight. Hip cocked out with her hand resting on it. Studying her reflection in the glass, I try to place her, but come up with nothing. Nothing about her is familiar.

Perhaps she had a bad day and is one of those people who project their anger onto others. Who knows.

After I collect my order, I wander off and pick up the rest of the items on my list. During the rest of my time in the store, I never see the angry woman again. Thank god. I can't quite put my finger on it, but something about her just didn't sit right with me.

When I mark off the last item on my list, I make my way to the checkout lines. The grocery store on a Monday night is such a pleasant experience. Honestly, the lack of foot traffic and people bumping carts in the aisles is a delight. Perhaps I will change our grocery shopping day to Monday. Rick wouldn't care. He just tags along to be with me.

The bagger sets my bags in the cart and offers to help me to the car, but I decline his gesture. Parking the buggy in the corral, I heave the canvas totes on my shoulders and walk to the car.

Staring out at the vacant and dark parking lot, I change my mind about shopping on Mondays. It may be a quick and stress-free trip inside the store. Alone in the dark parking lot... I'm not really keen on that. If Rick were with me, I wouldn't care. But he isn't, and the feeling I had earlier—like someone is watching me—returns with a vengeance.

Fifty feet away, my brilliant red SUV gleams at me. I

scurry across the lot and press the unlock button on my key fob. Almost there.

I open the hatch, unload the bags from my arms, and set them in the back. Just as I close the hatch, boots thud loudly behind me. Before I spin to see who walked up, the world around me goes black.

TWENTY-SIX

ALEX

"LOAD her in the backseat and drive her car to the meet," she demands.

What the fuck? "Since when do you make all the decisions? And since when do you tell me what the fuck to do?"

She rolls her eyes and cocks her head to the side. "Just shut the hell up, get in the car, and go. We need to get out of here. I'll meet you there after I make a quick stop."

I growl under my breath before shaking my head. "Whatever. Don't be long."

Sliding into the driver's seat, I start the car and back out. I tip the mirror down low enough to see Christy draped across the backseat. Her long hair hangs over her face, matted in clumps with blood. The gash on her temple is only a couple inches long but is enough to spill blood everywhere. Nothing bleeds worse than the face. From what I have noticed, anyway.

Twenty-three minutes later, I park near the warehouse entrance. I slip out of the front seat and open the back door. For a moment, I stare at her unconscious body. So pretty in her red and black swoop neck dress. The material hugs her curves and stops at her knees. Right now, with her completely out of it, I'm half tempted to push the dress up and see what is hidden underneath. If I ventured to guess, I would say nothing. Just her bare, pink flesh. Hot and wet and begging to be touched.

I rub my palm against my zipper and try to settle my eager cock. But the only way my hard-on will fade is after I finish this.

Grabbing her hand, I sit her upright before cradling her in my arms. Dead weight in my clutches, I carry her inside and set her in one of two wooden chairs. The chair with ropes secured at the legs and armrests. Quickly, I secure her limbs to the chair. Then I take a longer rope and wind it around her torso. Lastly, I tie a piece of rope to the top of the chairback and secure the end in a loop around her throat, creating a noose effect. That way, if she jerks forward in an attempt to free herself, she will instantly stop before choking.

Once she is fully bound, I step back, take out my cell, and snap a picture. I attach it in a text message and send it to L.

Alex: Let me know when you get the pic.

Less than a minute later, my phone dings.

L: Got it. Be there soon.

Lowering myself in the chair opposite her, I scan up and down her body. When I sat her down, I purposely hiked the skirt of her dress up to her waist. For my benefit and to up the ante with the photo. Beneath the tight fabric, her panty status is just as I suspected. Absent.

So while I wait for L to arrive and for the real party to start, I jack off to the delicious view of her pussy staring back at me.

TWENTY-SEVEN

RICK

THE LAST PERSON leaves the club and I itch to get the hell out of here. If I had it my way, the club would have closed hours ago.

After the most amazing weekend of my life, I'm dying to leave and get home to Christy. Our life has never been so stellar. Head over heels in love. Unbelievable sex—just the two of us or with Thomas and Ella. And as much as I never considered marriage, I am more than ready to run down the aisle and call Christy my wife.

Mrs. Christy Matheson.

Once everything is wrapped up, I hop in the car and push the gas pedal a little harder than normal. The traffic is minimal at this hour and I arrive home in no time. Just before I pull into the driveway, I notice Christy's car isn't parked in its usual spot. *Maybe she parked in the garage.* I hop out, open the garage, and bug out when the space is empty. I shake my head, confused as to why her car isn't home.

Where is she?

After closing the garage, I step inside and stop abruptly while my eyes adjust. Not a single light inside is on, which is normal when I get home this late. Although, after this weekend, I expected Christy to be up. I tiptoe through the house and go straight for the bedroom. When I open the door, my heart drops to the floor.

The bed is perfectly made and there is no sign of Christy.

My pulse thrums loud behind my ears as I leave our bedroom and check the guest room. Nothing. Sweat pricks every inch of my skin and my hands start to shake. Next, I reach the living room and scan the couch. Not there.

As I go room to room through the house, I flip on every light and check every possible nook and cranny. "Christy," I shout. I wait but get no response. Nothing except the echo of my own voice. "Where are you, gorgeous?"

Yanking my phone out of my pocket, I call her cell. It goes straight to voicemail. What the *hell* is happening? She didn't leave me, did she? After everything this weekend, did she freak out and bolt? Not possible. She was just as giddy about my asking to marry her as I was.

Rick: Gorgeous, where are you? I'm worried.

I wait a few minutes, but she doesn't text or call back. Where is she?

After a few minutes pass without response, I call Liz. Maybe she went over there after work and they drank too much. Wouldn't be the first time. But when Liz answers, her voice thick with sleep, I immediately apologize. "Hey Liz, sorry to call so late. Early. Or whatever. Is Christy there?"

"No," she groans. "Why would she be here?"

"Don't know. But she isn't home and I'm worried. Tried to call her, but it went straight to voicemail. Then I texted, but she hasn't answered."

In the background, I hear Tiffany ask who called. Liz puts her hand over the speaker, but not completely, and tells her it's me.

"Haven't seen her since lunch today. Where she flashed her ring at me. Congrats, man."

If Christy flaunted her ring to Liz, that means she is over the moon about us getting married. There is no way she would show her best friend her engagement ring if she wasn't serious about us getting married. Which worries me more now. *Where is she?*

"Thanks. Hey, if you see her first, tell her to call or text. Please?"

"Of course. Sorry I'm of no help."

"'Night, Liz."

"'Night, Rick."

I disconnect the call and ponder over calling Sarah or Jackson. She could have gone there, but that would have been a heck of a commute after work. So, I hold off on waking them.

Instead, I wander around the house and look for something. Anything. A note. Her phone. Any clue. Once I scour each room for the third time and come up with nothing, I hang my head in frustration.

I'm sick of asking myself the same question over and over, but *where the hell is she?*

My head pops up with an idea. Not sure why, but my gut tells me to check the front porch, seeing as I came in through the garage. Maybe I missed something out front. I walk through the foyer, unlock the door, and flip on the porch light. After I swing the door open, I step out and am greeted with a bunch of nothing. Not really sure what I expected, but I hoped to find something.

Hanging my head again, I stand at the threshold and stare at the ground. A solicitation near the bush catches my eye and I bend down to retrieve it. It's a request for canned goods for a local, quarterly food drive. When I flip it over and see our address on the back a light kicks on in my head.

How did this fall out of the mailbox?

I spin and face the mailbox beside the door and lift the lid. Inside, a pile of mail sits waiting. I pull out the stack and walk back inside the house. For a moment, I fumble through the envelopes and advertisements, and weed out the crap. Almost to the bottom of the pile, I freeze.

An eight-by-eleven-inch piece of copy paper is folded in thirds, catching my eye as my jaw drops. I drop the other mail and unfold it, reading a note scribbled in black Sharpie.

We got your girl.
When you get this, text 555-876-3590.
Maybe we'll tell you where she is.
If you call the cops, she's as good as dead.

What. The. Fuck.

Why in the hell would someone abduct Christy? She is the

sweetest person on the planet. Wouldn't hurt a goddamn fly. Behind my sternum, my heart thrashes like a wild beast for a new reason. Rage. Pure, undiluted rage. Whoever did this… Whoever took her… They are dead. Fucking dead.

I whip my phone back out of my pocket and start a fresh text message.

Rick: Who is this? And where the fuck is my girl?

Not up for any games, I get right to the point. Less than a minute later, my phone dings. When I glance down, I see an image of Christy strapped to a chair with a rope around her neck, head lulled to the side. From the picture, I have no way of telling if she is unconscious or worse.

Instantly, everything goes red.

Unknown: Come to the warehouse on 4th & Main. Look for her car. Come alone.
Rick: If you hurt her, I will fucking kill you.
Unknown: That's rich. You don't even know who I am. Good luck. Better hurry.

Before I bolt out the door, I run to the bedroom and grab the gun out of the safe tucked in our closet. Until now, the gun has never left the safe except for the occasional cleaning. When I purchased the gun years ago, I hoped to never use it. The same holds true now.

I check that the clip is loaded and lock it in the grip, pull back the slide, then tuck it in the back of my pants. Yanking my leather jacket off the hanger, I shoulder it on to conceal the gun in my waistband.

Bolting out the door, adrenaline surges through my veins as I speed down the highway. As I drive toward my girl, I pray this asshole hasn't hurt her in any way. If one goddamn hair is out of place… If there is even a scratch on her… There will be hell to pay.

In no time, I veer onto Main. Slowing down, I gaze up and down every side street. Still a few blocks from 4th street, I park my car and step out, opting to walk the rest of the way. I creep in the shadows along the street, most of the sidewalks dark or dimly lit. None of the businesses along here are currently open, so the whole street has this creepy movie vibe going on.

When I hit 4th street, I slowly peer around the corner. Fifty feet away, I spot Christy's car. In front of it, an old warehouse is lit up inside. Inhaling deeply, I close my eyes and pray to the universe that my girl is all in one piece and has no injuries.

A moment passes and I step out of the shadows then head for the door. As I twist the knob and crack the door open, a familiar head of brown hair comes into view. But that isn't what shocks me most. No, it's the person sitting across from her which has my jaw hitting the floor. The one with a big smile stretched across his face.

What. The. Fuck?

Darkness blankets everything around me like eternal night. The air thick with mildew and stale cigarettes. I open my mouth and try to speak, but my tongue rests heavy and no words come out. No matter how much I beg my voice box to project—something, anything—it doesn't budge.

I need to get out of here. Wherever here is.

When I go to step forward, nothing happens. I glance down at my legs, and it is then I realize there is nothing there. No legs. No arms. And no body. As if I am a pair of eyes floating in the void. But would eyes have conscious thought? Honestly, I have no idea, but my first thought is no.

Maybe this is a dream. What a weird fucking dream.

What is the last thing I remember? I shuffle through my thoughts slower than dial-up internet and come up with nada. Why can't I remember anything?

"It's okay, Christy," I subconsciously whisper. "What *do* you remember?"

I stare into the darkness and dig deep into the corners of my mind, searching for clues. Who knows how much time passes—this place null of seconds or minutes or hours— before a speck of light appears. From where I stand—or am I floating?—it seems miles away. But I see it.

When I work to move closer to the speck, another appears. Then another. Soon, the specks form small clusters similar to constellations. I lose myself in the display, mesmerized by the illumination. Until it hits me. A memory.

At the end of my workday, I gathered up my things and headed to the wedding store for a planner.

One of the stars burns brighter in the darkness.

Inside the wedding store, I eventually asked one of the workers for help because I was so overwhelmed by all the options. She found exactly what I needed, rang me up, and then I left the shop.

Another star brightens.

Maybe these aren't stars. Maybe they are my memories. Memories of all the thoughts fogged over in my head right now. If a star burns brighter each time I remember, I need to try harder to conjure up what happened before I got here.

I pinch my eyes tightly and think, think, think. "Come on, come on."

When I open my eyes again, the star memories glow a brilliant white in the void surrounding me. Filling the dark space like pieces of an incomplete puzzle.

After the wedding shop, I went to the grocery store. There was a strange woman watching and following me. She freaked me out, but she disappeared after the deli. When I finished checking out, I bolted for the door and hauled ass to my car. I made it to my car and then... Nothing. As in I have no clue what happened after I reached my car.

The room around me slowly comes into view. My ankles and wrists are bound to the arms and legs of the chair I sit in. But it's as if I'm not in the chair. More like I'm hovering above it. When I glance down the length of my body, it feels as if I am staring into a mirror. Except the version of me in the chair isn't awake.

Am I dead?

Shit. Oh my god! Am I fucking dead?!

No way. No fucking way! There is no chance in hell I am fucking dead. Who the hell would strap a dead girl to a chair? Not anyone I know of. What would the point be?

I glance around the room and try to figure out where the hell I am. The space is huge. Maybe the size of two football fields. The exterior walls are concrete, as is the floor. Tall metal beams break up the space every hundred feet or so.

Along the ceiling, water pipes with small sprinkler heads form a grid, occasionally dripping to mold-stained spots on the floor below. A single light fixture hangs from the ceiling where I sit, making it a central focal point, and it is sparse throughout the rest of the space.

Voices murmur around me, but I can't see anyone. I drift closer to myself.

How do I do this? How do I get back in my body and wake up?

This is the weirdest shit ever. Hovering inches from myself, I clamp my eyes shut and wish, over and over, to wake up. Whatever is happening, it cannot be good if I'm strapped to a chair.

"Please, please, please. Let me wake up," I mutter.

After a moment of pleading, a damp coolness pricks my lungs. Pain throbs at the back of my skull. Shrouded in darkness again, I crack my eyes open and the bright light stings my pupils. The mildew and stale cigarette smell is more pungent in my nose. Eager to get away from the unpleasant odor and this place, I go to stand. But a voice stops me.

A familiar voice. "He should be here any minute. You ready?" Who is that? And how do I know his voice?

Keeping my eyes shut, I jog through my memories and try to place the low timber of the man who just spoke. It isn't one I've heard much, but I swear it's familiar.

"More than ready." A woman's voice. And I have no idea who it belongs to.

Heavy boots clamber on the floor, quieting the more steps they take, and I assume the man walks away from me. "Go over there." He pauses. "Don't want him seeing you when he walks in. It'll ruin all the fun."

The boots trek back in my direction and panic inflates my lungs like helium. Is he going to hurt me? When I hear him settle not far from me, I breathe easier. *Just sit here and pretend you are still unconscious. Maybe they will leave you alone.*

Time ticks by in torturous silence. The man scrambles across from me, there is a faint crinkle before a scratching. Then, the faint odor of tobacco floats in my nose. I hold my breath and fight to not move as I inhale the unwanted smoke.

Another unfamiliar noise grabs my attention. *Splat. Flick. Splat. Flick.* Every part of me screams to open my eyes and bear witness to what the hell is happening. But a small voice in the back of my mind reminds me to remain quiet and stay put. I trust that small voice and don't move an inch.

I count another thirteen splats and flicks before a loud creak echoes behind me. Metal scraping metal. The clacking of shoes, growing louder and louder with each step in my direction. As badly as I want to spin around and learn where the sound came from, and who made it, I pretend to still be unconscious.

Then the room goes quiet again. Too quiet. The rapid beating of my pulse whooshes behind my ears and renders me deaf. Until I hear his voice.

"What. The. Fuck?" Heaven or hell. In life and death. I would recognize that voice anywhere. *Rick.* "Xander, what in the actual fuck?"

Shoes clack against the concrete floor again, louder with each step, and I picture Rick in the dress shoes he wears to work. Then he stops. Too far back. I wish I wasn't so scared to just open my eyes. But it may make this whole situation worse if I do.

"Don't move another step." That must be Xander. "And it's Alex, actually."

I wrack my brain and try to place Xander or Alex—whichever the hell he is. *Think, think, think.* As I search my memory bank, a light kicks on. Xander—who is actually Alex—is the new bartender at Boundless.

What the hell?

"Why the fuck is my wife strapped to a fucking chair, *Alex*?" Rick seethes, his voice thick with venom.

For a split-second, I forget about everything happening around me. Rick just called me his wife. Behind my breastbone, the small, fist-shaped organ surges with new life and a tear slips from my closed eye.

"Since when is she your wife?" Alex roars. Wood scrapes against the floor a second before Alex's boots thump past me. Before Rick answers, Alex continues. "The price on her life just went up tenfold."

The price on my life? What the hell is going on?

On a whim, I crack my eyes open and hope Alex doesn't notice. The muscles in my neck are stiff as a board from hanging between my shoulders for so long. I angle my chin a little in the direction where I heard Rick, and peek at him and Alex.

"Who the fuck do you think you are? If you think you can put a price on her" —Rick points at me and his eyes widen when he sees mine open— "you're stupider than I thought."

"Oh, there's a price. But you won't be paying it in cash."

Rick shakes his head ever so slightly and narrows his eyes at Alex. "Don't be cryptic, fucker."

Alex chuckles just as a new tip-tap enters the space. *Tip-tap, tip-tap, tip-tap.* Curious, I glance toward the sound and she catches me looking. The creepy bitch from the grocery store. I should have fucking guessed it.

"Look who's awake," she singsongs. Walking toward Alex and Rick, the woman exaggerates the sway of her hips. No clue who this woman is, but the way she carries herself indicates she thinks her shit doesn't stink. When I get out of this chair, I plan to show her how much it does.

At this point, I sit up straight and roll my neck until a rope tugs my windpipe. Not only am I tied to the damn chair, I'm completely bound.

The woman walks up to Rick and brushes her hands over his shoulders. Instantly, he steps out of her touch. "What's the matter, sugar? Gun shy now that the misses is here?"

"You're a sick bitch," Rick tells her. "What? I don't cave to your desires in the club, then I throw your ass on the street, and this is what you do? You bribe one of my employees and kidnap my wife? Really, you are a stupid cunt."

She waggles her finger in Rick's face. "Tsk, tsk. Might want to bite your tongue. Don't want me angry. Not when I control her fate." The stupid bitch points back in my direction.

"As I said earlier, you hurt her" —Rick glances over at me — "I will kill you."

The woman steps closer to Rick, and I want to scream for her to back the fuck up. But, right now, I sit helpless and at the mercy of Alex and this psychotic bitch, waiting to see what Rick will do next.

"I warned you," she hisses. A second later, she stands beside me and glances down. "Nice to meet you, *Christy.* I'm

Lexi. Your replacement." Then she runs the end of a scalpel over my forearm and slices a four-inch wound in my flesh.

"Argh!" I scream. Bound to the chair, I have no way of adding pressure to the wound or covering it. "Bitch!"

Lexi laughs and the sound reminds me of the cackle of a witch in a movie. Maniacal and lifeless. A shiver slithers down my spine as bile threatens to come up. "You ain't seen nothing yet," she says, looking at me then Rick. And a huge part of me believes her. If this woman is as crazy as I think she is, she will kill me to get to Rick.

So, I play into her game. "Go ahead," I say, glancing over at Rick. "Take him." Rick's eyes on me, mine on his. The instant the psycho bitch shifts her gaze from me to him in my periphery, I widen my eyes at him. *Play along.*

It takes a beat, but when it clicks, Rick gives the slightest nod. He spins the ring on his thumb—our first bond exchange —with his index finger. When I spot the movement, I nod.

"Was ready for a change anyway," Rick says. He steps closer to me and Lexi, fixing his gaze on her. "But I'm not sure if you can handle me."

"Me?" Lexi points at her chest for emphasis. "I've done it all, baby. You want a real woman? Here I am." She lifts her hands over her head and spreads them wide. "But you need to prove you want me."

"Yeah? And how would I do that?" Rick steps up to her. If he moved two inches to his left, he would graze me.

"Fuck me," she says and Rick rolls his eyes. "In front of her. Now."

You have got to be fucking shitting me.

Rick lowers his eyes and studies me. The corner of his mouth twitches. His way of telling me he has a plan. Telling me not to worry. I swallow, drag in a deep breath, and close my eyes.

"Yeah, sure."

My eyes shut out the world as Rick's shoes tap a step closer to her. The contents of my stomach rise in my throat and the sudden urge to vomit creeps dangerously close. I refuse to open my eyes though. Refuse to watch what is about to happen. Might as well tear my heart out and stomp it into dust.

The room is quiet. More than quiet. And a sick part of my brain begs me to peek through the cracks of my lids and discover what the hell is actually going on. As peaceful as the darkness is, the unknown terrifies the hell out of me.

Just as I crack open my eyes, a hiss echoes through the air. A whoosh of air blows against the cut on my skin. Bodies shift beside me. Fast. Way too fast. And all I see is red.

TWENTY-NINE

RICK

My gorgeous girl. Her head bowed in fear of seeing what I may do with this woman. But my plan isn't what she thinks. Not by a long shot.

I step up to psycho bitch and plaster on an exaggerated smile. One she has no clue is as artificial as her tits. She smirks and tucks a strand of her bottle-dyed blonde hair behind her ear. When I'm as close to her as possible without gagging, I tip my head slowly her way and watch her eyes close.

Bingo, dumb bitch.

In a flash, I grip the hand with the scalpel and twist her wrist and arm, then pin it behind her back as I step behind her. The scalpel falls to the floor and I bend down, her wrist contorted in my grip, and pick it up from the floor.

"Ow! Ow! Ow!" she howls.

Xander or Alex—whatever the hell his name is—steps closer and I bring the scalpel to Lexi's throat. "Don't come any closer. I'll slit her throat," I warn.

His eyes dart from me to Lexi, again and again. Obviously, she means a lot to him. Otherwise, he would have already told me to kill her. His hands ball into fists at his sides as he scorches me with his stare. He has no idea what to do.

"Get her," Lexi hisses.

Alex shakes his head. "No, Lex. I can't. He'll kill you."

"I'm dead either way. Might as well not be for nothing," she demands.

I push the scalpel closer to her skin and a drop of blood trickles down her neck, below her jawline, and stops at her collarbone. "Alex, it's not worth it. Is your life worth what *she* wants?" I coax. "Is *she* risking her life for *you*? Or is she risking it for me?"

Alex pops his eyes up to mine. "She's my sister. I'd do anything for her." Although what he says may hold truth, there is a chink in his armor. Something underlying that has him doubting himself.

"Alex, I understand doing everything and anything for a sister. It's how things were with mine. But sometimes, we can't save everyone."

For so many years, I beat myself up over Harriett's death. Blamed myself for not being a better big brother. If I would have spent more time with her, talked to her more about what types of people to avoid, maybe she would still be alive today. For almost two decades, I blamed myself for her death and for my family falling apart. It wasn't until recently that it dawned on me how wrong I had been.

"But she's my sister," he whispers.

Just as I open my mouth to tell him he isn't responsible for her anymore, the door is kicked in and more than a dozen police officers run in with guns aimed our way. Immediately, I drop my arm from Lexi's neck and push her forward to Alex.

"That's them," I say to the officers as I point at Lexi and Alex.

"You'll pay for this," Lexi hisses at me and Christy.

"Shut the fuck up," Alex barks at her.

Officers cuff Lexi and Alex, pat them down and read them their rights. As Alex and Lexi are shoved out of the room, I cut the ropes binding Christy with the scalpel. As soon as all the binds are severed, she launches herself into my arms and suffocates me in hugs and kisses.

"God, I love you," she says, tightening her arms around my neck. "I love you, I love you, I love you."

I chuckle beneath her. "I love you too, gorgeous. And I hope you know I'd never let anything happen to you. Ever." She nods furiously in the crook of my neck.

"Excuse me, ma'am. Sir. We need to get a statement from you both."

An hour and a half later, Christy and I walk out of the warehouse. After giving the officers both of our sides of the story, letting them know how Alex and Lexi came to know who we were, then getting Christy's arm cleaned and bandaged, we are given permission to leave.

As we approach Christy's car, I tell her we will come back for it tomorrow. An officer overhears and offers to have it towed to the house at no cost to us. We accept the offer and tell them our address. Just as we walk off, Christy clutches my arm and stops me.

"The groceries are in the back."

Laughing for a beat, I say, "Just leave them. We'll grab them later."

Christy yanks on my arm harder. "No, there's perishables in there."

"Fine. I'll grab the bags."

Of all the things to worry about after being kidnapped, tied to a chair, and cut open. Leave it to my girl to worry more about the damn groceries.

After grabbing a quick bite to eat, followed by a hot shower, Christy and I climb into bed. Who the hell knows what time it is. And I refuse to check the clock. It's either really fucking late or super fucking early. Either way, I just want to lay in our bed and hold Christy in my arms for days.

She scoots back and molds her back to my front, clutching my arms as tight as they will go around her belly. In my arms, she trembles and I squeeze her impossibly tighter. "Thank you," she whispers into the dark comfort of our bedroom.

I kiss the back of her head and let my lips linger on the surface of her hair. The scent of her floral shampoo seeps into my senses and has me closing my eyes while my chest flutters. "You never have to thank me for saving you, gorgeous. It's my responsibility to keep you safe. And I will. Forever. Just wish I would've gotten to you sooner."

Christy slowly spins in my arms until she faces me. Her

stormy blue eyes glisten with the threat of tears. Our room is blanketed in darkness, but enough light spills in from the streetlight outside to highlight the curves of her face. And without words so much is spoken between us in this quiet moment.

Fear and pain and so many unanswered "what if" questions. But most of all, it is her love that shines brightest. Love and trust and promise. My girl has been through so much in her life. So many highs and lows. And I consider myself a lucky son of a bitch to have her by my side.

No other woman seals the cracks in my heart like Christy. No other woman fulfills my desires and needs and life like Christy. Since the very beginning, she has been a bright burning star in my night sky. Navigating me to places I never knew existed. My compass.

"Sleep, gorgeous." I kiss her forehead and nose and lips. "I've got you."

Then she curls into my chest, kisses to the left of my sternum—just over my heart—and falls asleep in my arms. The only place she will ever be.

THIRTY

CHRISTY

My EYES SNAP open and I take a deep breath, trying to calm my racing heart.

A week has passed since Alex and Lexi abducted me from the grocery store parking lot. And for the last seven nights, I've bolted awake with the smell of mildew and stale cigarettes lingering from my nightmare. Breaking out in a cold sweat when the flashes of Lexi cutting my skin appear behind my lids.

Lexi and Alex are sitting, uncomfortably I hope, in a jail cell while awaiting trial. Although I know this, it terrifies the hell out of me they could get out. The cops and our attorney have assured me, time and again, they won't be free anytime soon. Since both Alex and Lexi were involved with my kidnapping, they will each receive eight years. Add in Lexi cutting me and threatening to kill me, she may never leave the state penitentiary. Alex, on the other hand, will probably get parole, but not for more than a decade. Hopefully by then, he will have other things on his mind.

All in all, I truly believe Alex was a pawn in Lexi's grand scheme to get Rick. But just because someone you love asks you to do something heinous, doesn't mean you say yes. Life is a balance. Yin-yang. Black-white. Yes-no. Right-wrong. During childhood, most parents work to ingrain their morals on their children. Unfortunately, not all parents know good from evil. Even worse, not all parents care.

Yet another reason why I chose not to bring life into the world. Do I know right from wrong? Yes, I would like to say I do. But that doesn't mean shit nowadays. Too many outside forces clamber in and strip all the good away from young, impressionable minds, then fill them with lies and hate and greed. Not to say this happens with every child—because there are some really great humans in the world.

But it is a war I have no desire to fight.

Next to me, Rick stirs and tugs me closer to him. I rest a hand in the center of his chest and trail it down until I reach a few inches below his navel. Since the incident last week, sex has been absent from our life. Not because I don't want it. In actuality, I ache for it. But Rick is worried I want to use sex as an outlet instead of talking about my feelings.

My response… there isn't much to say. I may not be one-hundred percent comfortable walking or driving alone since everything happened, but fear *will not* hold me prisoner. I refuse to allow it.

"Morning, gorgeous." His voice is raspy and thick with sleep before he peppers kisses on my forehead. "You sleep okay?"

I drag my fingertip side to side an inch above his well-groomed pubic hair. "Yes and no," I answer, peering up into his lust drunk honey eyes. "Nothing to worry about. Promise." I zigzag my finger lower and graze the base of his dick. He shudders at the touch as his eyes roll back in his head.

"You should talk to me about it," he says, huskily. "Get it out in the open."

Leaning forward, I kiss along the dip above his collarbone as I skim my hand lower. "After," I say.

He growls beneath me. "You can't keep avoiding this, gorgeous." I bite my way down to his nipple. "We should talk about it."

I clamp onto his nipple. Hard. And he hisses loudly as I wrap my hand around his cock and yank. "I said, after. Please," I beg. "I need you."

Inching my hips closer to his, I rub the tip of his cock over my pussy. "Fuck, you're wet."

And within seconds, Rick brings me one step closer to paradise.

After we shower, Rick makes us breakfast and we talk. Mostly, I talk.

I tell him about my dreams since everything happened. Sometimes he wakes when I do, but most of the time he doesn't. I spill out every heart pounding, sweat inducing moment I have had since that night. And the great guy that Rick is, he sits there and listens to every word without interruption.

When I finish, he reassures me there is no more reason to worry. That Lexi and Alex will never bother us again. His certainty soothes any remaining panic and settles me in a way only Rick can.

After we finish washing the dishes, Rick spins to face me. "Why don't we go down to the courthouse today?"

I stare at him with narrowed eyes, thoroughly confused. Did I write down a wrong date for Alex and Lexi's hearing? Damnit. I swear I wrote them all down correctly.

When I don't say anything for several minutes, Rick brings both his hands to my face and cups my cheeks. "It's okay, gorgeous. Nothing to do with them. Alright?" I breathe deeply and nod. "I was thinking maybe we could go there and get married. Today. I have the band for your engagement ring set tucked away. And I may have already bought my band."

All the air gets sucked from my lungs. *Did he say what I think he said?* For us to get married today? "I… uh…" At a loss for words, I stand dumbfounded, blinking rapidly as the world around me turns fuzzy. He doesn't push me to answer. Just simply holds me and waits until I gather the courage to answer. A moment passes, then I snap out of my foggy state. "Yeah, okay," I whisper.

He squats down so we are eye to eye. "You sure? Don't say yes for me. Say it for you." I nod.

Although I wanted to spend some time planning out a wedding and deciding on small things like flowers and colors with Rick, going to the courthouse just feels *right*. On a later date, we can have the fancy party with our friends. And until then, the only people who need to know is Rick and me.

"I'm sure. Let's go."

We amble back to the bedroom, hand in hand. In the room, we break apart. Rick goes about dressing in black dress slacks and a black button-down shirt, leaving the top two buttons undone. I slip into a merlot red dress with three-quarter sleeves and the skirt ending just beneath my knees. The dress isn't as snug as others I own, but my curves are visible.

After I brush out my hair, I add a hint of product and leave it down. Once I add a light touch of makeup, I put my glasses back on and join Rick in the living room. When he glances up at me from the book in his hands, his eyes glaze over in a new light. Not lust or hunger or the urge to rip my dress off. No, a much stronger and deeper emotion blazes in his eyes. An emotion solely reserved for me. Call it love, if you will. But the way he looks at me, it is something so much greater than love.

He rises from the couch and saunters toward me. When he reaches me, he kisses each of my cheeks. "You look stunning. Ready?"

I nod. "Yes, more than ready."

The drive to the courthouse seems much quicker than any other drive in the city. Less than thirty minutes after we leave the house, Rick parks the car in the lot beside the courthouse. Rick gets out and comes around to open my door. When he offers me his elbow, I hook mine with his and we walk to the statuesque structure.

Ten minutes later, and we are sitting with a clerk, filling out the marriage license after providing our identification, and listening to her ramble on about marriage and divorce in the state of California. After we finish the license paperwork, she tells us to take a seat and we will be called in shortly for the ceremony.

We sit on a glossy oak bench in a long corridor. Other couples nearby chatter with one another while we sit in silence, cuddled close. Over the years, Rick and I developed our own language. One that requires no words. One based on trust and body language and expressions. With one slight change, Rick reads my every need, ache, desire, or pain. And it is moments like these—where we don't utter a single word —that the most thoughtful moments occur.

So while we sit in this chatter-filled space completely silent, Rick expresses how much he loves me, and I do the same. With light touches and occasional kisses and close proximity.

"Christy Nolan and Richard Matheson," a clerk yells from a room off to the right.

Inside the small room, a desk swallows up most of the space. The clerk tells us to stand on the side of the desk with no chairs. She verifies our identification once more and tells us the judge will be in momentarily.

When the door opens again, a rotund man wearing a black robe enters. "Ms. Nolan. Mr. Matheson. I'm Judge Jenkins. This is Clerks Roberta Johnson and James Townsend. They will be witnesses for the ceremony." He sits in the chair. "Let's begin."

The judge goes through a spiel that feels longer than it took us to drive here. When he finishes, he offers us a chance to say vows.

Taking a deep breath, I start. "Rick, for the rest of my life, I will honor and cherish you. I promise to take care of you, however necessary." I pause and waggle my eyebrows. Rick shakes his head and grins ear to ear. "But most of all, I promise to love you for eternity."

The judge nods, then waves his hand to Rick. "Mr. Matheson."

After a quick, rattled breath, Rick starts. "You are the most brilliant star in the night sky, Christy. A life without you isn't a life at all. I vow to protect and respect you. Promise to keep you safe and hold you close. To love and worship you until my dying day, and every day after."

A moment later, we exchange our "I do's", slip on our wedding bands, and Rick kisses me as if no one else is in the room. After everyone has signed and notarized our marriage license, we leave the courthouse. Once my feet bounce off the bottom step, Rick hoists me up in his arms and spins me around like a teenager.

"Time to celebrate, wife."

This is the first time Rick has called me his wife... when we were actually married. I don't wish to rehash the first night I heard him say it. That night is tainted. But hearing it now, every molecule inside me bursts into flames.

"Yes, husband. Let's celebrate."

THIRTY-ONE

RICK

Christy and I step out of the shower and towel off. Five minutes ago, she screamed my name so loud, it wouldn't shock me if the neighbors three houses down heard. Once dry, I hang my towel and smack her ass as I step out of the bathroom. She doesn't yelp. Not my girl. She moans.

After I dress in jeans and a shirt, I leave her in the bedroom to get ready while I start dinner. In the kitchen, I take out all the ingredients for chicken cordon bleu, roasted root vegetables, and a side salad and get to work.

I chop all the vegetables first. Then toss the root vegetables in olive oil and herbs and put them in a roasting pan in the oven. Next, I assemble the chicken cordon bleu. Just as I pin the last one with a toothpick, Christy comes in and works beside me on the salad.

For a moment, I stare at my wife. *My wife*. Stunning in her sleek black maxi dress. Hair in a messy, wet bun on top of her head. If there weren't other things in life to do, I would get lost in her nonstop.

"Everything won't be ready on time if you keep staring at me like that," she teases.

I step up behind her, my hands pinned at my back, and whisper in her ear. "They would understand." Because it is true. Thomas and Ella wouldn't be upset if I told them I stopped cooking to fuck Christy against the countertop. If anything, they would tell me to turn the stove and oven off and continue.

Christy pauses her assembling of the salad and groans. The vibration as needy as her ass that grinds against my groin. I kiss the curve of her neck and back away. Dinner first. Then, no holds barred.

Shortly after I put the chicken in the oven with the vegetables, I clean the kitchen and wash up. As I'm pulling the food out of the oven, Christy walks in with Ella and Thomas on her heels. Smiles and hugs are exchanged before we head to the dining table and sit.

After the incident two months ago, I wasn't sure how Christy would handle being near other people for a while. For more than a week, she clung to my side. Her job had been generous and gave her time off to recuperate. During that time, she was never more than a few feet away. Also during that time, I worried the most. Worried that what happened to her at the hands of Alex and Lexi—which we later learned, during their hearings, were Alexander and Alexis, twins— tweaked something inside her. Similar to what happened to Sarah in Georgia. And every night I prayed my wife would heal from all of it.

Christy is so much stronger than I have ever given her credit for.

Within two weeks, she smiled and laughed and teased me like nothing ever happened. Just after she told me about every nightmare she'd had since the incident. Once she got it off her chest, it was as if she had permission to heal and be herself again.

And although she and I have had sex several times since everything happened, tonight is the first time Thomas and Ella have joined us since that night.

She hasn't told me, but my gut says Christy confided in Ella with some of what happened to her. And the idea of them discussing it makes me smile. Christy needs someone, besides me, that she can talk with and free her burdens. Thomas and I have somewhat done the same. The friendship and bond Christy and I have developed with Thomas and Ella is invaluable.

"Everyone up for dessert and a movie in the living room?" Christy asks as we clear the table.

While I finish loading the dishwasher, Christy takes the pan of cherry cobbler she made earlier, plates, and forks to the living room. As I'm putting the last of the dishes in, I hear the movie cue up in the living room.

Two portions of cherry cobbler and an hour of the movie later, Christy starts traipsing her fingertips up and down my thigh. Not something we set up, but it is sort of her cue she wants to play now.

I shift on the couch and face her, cupping her cheek and kissing the hell out of her. Her moan vibrates against my tongue and my eyes roll back in my head. Is it possible that making her my wife makes her that much more delectable? For me, it does.

When I open my eyes and peer over at Thomas and Ella, I see them kissing while Thomas strokes his fingers back and forth between Ella's thighs. My lips grow more urgent on Christy's as I slide her dress up, graze my fingers up her thigh, and dip them inside her hot, slick folds.

Tonight, Christy holds the reins. Until she signals she's ready to have another person touching her, only I touch her. Over the last few days, we discussed our comfort levels with Thomas and Ella. It is imperative Christy feels safe no matter what. So, when she told me she felt as at ease with them as she did me, I offered up something we had never done.

Going forward, Christy and Ella have free rein to kiss. If either of us had the urge, Thomas and I could as well. But I would still not kiss Ella, and the same held true for Christy and Thomas. The four of us are on the same page with that.

Christy whimpers in my ear. Her breath jagged, and her body begging for release. I slip the top of her dress down and expose her glorious breasts. Perfect lift. Plump. Firm. Nipples the color of summer licked skin. I take a taut bud into my mouth and suck and nip as my fingers slide in and out of her.

"Yes..." she moans as I grind my teeth over her nipple.

The moment she comes on my fingers, I slip them out and suck them off. So fucking delicious. Swear to God, she tastes better as my wife.

Once Ella comes beside her, Christy kisses her then lays her flat on the couch. In a blink, Christy and Ella are stripped bare and lapping the cum off of each other.

Unzipping my jeans, I drop them to the floor, followed by my shirt, and stroke my cock. Thomas follows suit as we watch our wives suck on each other.

Not that it has never happened, but it has been years—years before Christy—since I did anything with a man. But watching our wives. Seeing his arousal while I'm stroking mine in my clenched fist. I want more from this relationship we share with them.

In two short strides, I stand inches from Thomas. Both of us stroking ourselves. I glance down and watch his hand as he strokes up and down his cock. A hunger simmers low in my balls and trickles up my spine. With each pump of his shaft, greed licks a fire in my veins. But it isn't until Thomas reaches forward and lifts my chin that I see the ache inside him. An ache solely directed at me.

His jaw slackens and, in my periphery, his fist jerks harder. With hooded eyes, he steps into me, releases his cock, and slams his mouth onto mine. I open up and his tongue dives in, licking and sucking and mouth fucking mine.

There is something so completely different about kissing or touching a man than a woman. Kisses with either can be tender and sweet, or desperate and needy. A woman's lips are soft and supple, her jaw less rigid and angular, her skin smooth and scent sweet. Whereas a man's lips are firm and plump, his jawline sharp and strong, the skin of his neck and jaw gritty and rugged, his scent woodsy and rich.

Both divine. Both send a surge of white hot energy straight to my cock.

I break our kiss, slip my fingers into his hair and make a fist, and yank his head to the side. Running my tongue from the base of his ear to the curve where his neck meets his shoulder, I clamp down and suck the toned musculature beneath my lips.

"Fuck," he hisses. Against my hip, his cock jerks and I palm it.

My hand glides along his rock hard shaft—once, twice—

before he inches back. For a moment, it crosses my mind that maybe Thomas doesn't want this side of the relationship and I overstepped my boundaries. I hadn't considered that maybe he had never been with another man before and only enjoyed the female aspect of our lifestyle.

But all thoughts go out the window the second he drops to his knees in front of me.

He reaches up, palms my balls, and rolls them in his hand like a pair of Chinese Baoding balls. I lean into his touch and hang my head, eyes fixated on his every move. After one, two, three rolls of my balls, he glances up at me with fire in his mossy green eyes. With his eyes locked on mine, hand massaging my sac, his tongue darts out and licks the crown of my cock. A shudder ripples out from his touch and spreads over every square inch of my body like an electrical grid.

Before I tell him how spectacular his hot tongue feels circling the head of my cock, he grips my hip and takes me in his mouth.

"Goddamn," I grunt out. Thomas massages the underside of my cock with his tongue as he goes from the root to the head. I grip his hair and hold him in place. "So. Fucking. Good."

Sucking cock has previously been added to his resume. No one sucks a man's dick like this without previous experience. While I hold his head in place, my hips piston and drive my cock in and out of his greedy mouth. As I thrust my cock to the back of his throat, I stare at his right hand as it pumps his own.

Fire licks hotter in my veins. Scorching me from head to toe. Sweat seeps from every pore. Building. Climbing. Winding around my spine and tightening. Before I explode in his mouth, I pull out and bring him to his feet. As much as I'd like to shoot cum down his throat, I'd much rather pump it into my wife's cunt.

Just as Thomas is about to question why I stopped, I grab hold of him and shove my tongue down his throat. After he strokes mine a few times, I lick and bite my way along his jaw, to the front of his throat, and down to his sternum. I pause my descent to give some appreciation to his lean, fit body. Drawing circles around each of his nipples with my tongue and then nipping the pert nubs.

As I run my lips and tongue over the ridged surface around his navel, I dig my hands into his ass cheeks. Below my chin, his dick jerks and grazes me. A wicked idea surfaces as lick over the shaved skin around the base of his cock.

I glance up at Thomas, my cheeks stinging from the wide grin plastered on my face. "Everything fair game?" I ask.

He cocks his head to the side and studies my face a beat. A moment passes before he nods, cups my jaw, and says, "Suck me."

Fisting his cock, I lift it and run my tongue from his balls to the tip before taking him deep in my throat. Thomas has the perfect dick. When aroused, his length easily hits the back of my throat with a couple inches to spare. And girth… just enough to stretch my lips tight, but not painfully so. For a woman, it may be a different experience. Not too veiny. Deep ridge lines around the crown—perfect for rubbing the elusive spot most men can't find in a woman's body.

Would it be odd to say I have cock envy?

As I bob up and down Thomas's cock, taking him all the way to the root, our wives cry out beside us. And for a split-second, we both forget about us and stare at how glorious they are on the couch. Currently, Ella lays on her back with one leg draped over the back of the couch while Christy rides her face and plays with Ella's clit. By now, I'm certain they have both orgasmed several times. But Thomas and I have ignored their cries in an effort to chase our own.

Just as Christy bends back down and puts her mouth between Ella's thighs, Thomas continues to fuck my face. His hips jerk back and forth, and his groans grow louder with each lap of my tongue. And that's when I stop.

The moment he is no longer in my mouth, he glances down at me in question. I point to the ground beneath us. "Lay down," I tell him. Without hesitation, he drops and lies on the floor, resting his head on his hands.

I position myself between his thighs, spit onto my fingers, and watch him as I spread it between his ass cheeks. If possible, his mossy green eyes immediately shift to an almost black-green as his lids grow heavy.

"New territory?" I ask.

He nods. "Never been comfortable with anyone else there," he answers.

I jut my chin toward our wives. "Not even Ella?"

He shakes his head. "Never been brought up." His eyes roll back as I swirl my index finger over the tight hole and press slightly. Part of me relishes in the fact I will be the one to break this cherry. That I will claim his ass before anyone else.

I lower myself, hovering less than an inch above the tip of his cock, and take him back in my mouth as my finger slowly presses against the tight pucker of his ass. When I breach his body's initial resistance, his cock jerks in my mouth. "Holy fuck…" he hisses.

He fists my hair as I suck his cock in measured strokes and finger fuck his ass. As my pace picks up with my mouth, seconds later, it picks up with my fingers. Saliva coats his cock and rolls down his balls to his ass and lubricates my finger as it plunges in. His grip on my hair tightens with each tongue stroke up his shaft.

In my mouth, his cock grows impossibly thicker as his climax nears. Thomas's grunts and breathy cries come faster. And I know he is close. As if on cue, a hint of saltiness hits my tongue and I growl around him, picking up speed.

"Oh fuck. *Fuck, fuck, fuck…*" he hisses.

Then his hips press into the floor as he yanks my hair and holds me in place. Hot cum shoots to the back of my throat and I continue to suck him off as I withdraw my finger from his ass. When his orgasm calms, I climb up his body and kiss him roughly. Once our lips break apart, I rub the tip of my cock against his ass. "One day, it won't be my finger in your ass," I promise.

A wicked gleam lights his face. "Better be a man of your word." Something about the challenge in his words ignites me. "Let me finish you," he offers.

I glance over at our wives—our beautiful as fuck wives—and watch them a beat as they finger fuck each other, lips locked in a vicious battle of lust. As much as I would rather cum between Christy's legs, nights like this aren't just about the two of us. It's about all four of us. The bond we share.

The connection we have developed that continues to flourish.

Scooting back to lean against the couch, I spread my legs, stroke my cock, and invite Thomas to finish what he started. And it doesn't take long before I spurt down his throat and taste my cum on his lips.

After hours of sucking and fucking, the four of us crash—Thomas and Ella staying at the house. Our sleep the best it had been in years. And an idea sparks when I wake in the next morning.

As everyone congregates in the kitchen for breakfast, I lure Thomas away from the girls. "You mind if I run an idea past you before mentioning it to the wives?"

He nods. "Shoot."

"What are your thoughts on the four of us living together?"

Ella and Thomas celebrated their ninth wedding anniversary November seventh—a little more than a month before the four of us met. They had been in a relationship for two years prior to marrying. When they first met, Ella was barely eighteen and Thomas seven years her senior. Of course Ella's family stirred up trouble, but as soon as she was able to leave home, she moved in with Thomas. The rest is history.

We may not know everything about one another, but both Christy and I are absolutely comfortable with the two of them. And my instincts tell me Thomas reciprocates.

The four of us living together probably seems odd to the outside world. The world of man-woman, single-partner relationship enthusiasts. But to us, living together is ultimate trust. Just as with a relationship with any two people, everything boils down to compatibility, trust, companionship, and desire.

Not every night would involve sexual acts with the four of us. Just as I want nights solely with my wife, Thomas and Ella will want the same. With cohabitation comes other factors. Safety and security. Stronger bonds—friendship and sexual. Companionship when others work odd hours.

Thomas rubs the tip of his finger over his lower lip. Eyes zoned out as they focus on something in the distance. "It would have its perks," he says. "Of course we'd need to sit down and hash out some things. With the four of us, rules, and where we'd live."

A smile kicks up my lips. "If you're good, we can talk logistics later. But first, let's see how our wives feel about the whole idea."

EPILOGUE

CHRISTY

Three years later

ELLA WALKS into the open shower and steps under the second stream of hot spray. As her head tips back and the water trails down her body, I inch closer to her and trace my fingers from the top of her sternum to her pubic bone.

Although I have zero intention of fucking her in the shower right now, it is only natural to touch her every chance I get. Since we met Ella and Thomas, life has only gotten better.

Ella and I developed a fast friendship. Our bond rivals my other friendships, but each has their place in my life. Two and a half years ago, Ella, Thomas, Rick, and I moved in together. We found a house more suitable for all of our needs. One that gave us space, if we wanted to be with our respective spouses, but also brought us together when we so desired.

Shortly after we all moved in, I invited Liz and Tiffany over, as well as Sarah and Jackson. Having so many people who love me nearby grips my heart in unspeakable ways. But on that night, I fidgeted more than any other time in my life. It stirred up past memories of rejection and heartbreak.

In the end, everything worked out perfect.

"Thanks for coming over tonight," I say, my eyes bouncing between Sarah, Jackson, Liz, and Tiffany. "It means so much to me

and Rick." At his name, Rick squeezes my thigh and presses a kiss to my shoulder. The perfect balm for my shaky nerves.

"I wouldn't miss a chance to spend time with you," Sarah tells me. "We're not as close, distance wise, as we were in Georgia, but it's not a hike to get here."

Nodding, I take a deep breath and remember one of the main reasons why I wanted everyone here tonight. Before everyone arrived, Rick and I asked Ella and Thomas if it was okay if we shared who we all were with my friends. Not that I needed the world to know I occasionally enjoyed the company of another woman or man, besides my husband. More like I didn't want to hide who I was from the people closest to my heart. And sharing who I am is important to me.

Acceptance is important. A peace of mind I have needed for years.

I swallow down the building lump in my throat, take a drink of water, then tell my two best friends about the side of my life I have never shared with them. "Sarah. Liz. Jackson. Tiffany. I introduced you to Ella and Thomas when you first got here." Their heads bob in acknowledgment. "What I didn't tell you is that the four of us live here. Together."

For a moment, Sarah and Liz stare at me in slight confusion. Certainly they are curious as to why we have "roommates" when we can afford to live on our own. And by Thomas and Ella's outward appearance, so can they.

"Okay…" Sarah says, judgment free but still unsure of where this will lead.

But when Liz's eyes light up, it is obvious she knows where this conversation is going. After all, I did mention Rick and I were kinkier than people realized. Perhaps she just couldn't grasp the gravity of it all.

"Ella and Thomas are married," I say. "And, occasionally, the four of us sleep together."

The room is so silent you can hear every breath I take. A voice screams in my head for someone to say something. Anything. For my friends to tell me they hate me. Or, hopefully, the opposite. When the silence stretches out and no one moves an inch, I pinch my eyes closed and mentally berate myself for this whole admission.

Stupid, stupid, stupid.

You should have just kept your mouth shut and left things as they were. Now you have probably lost more people you love. A boulder slowly crushes my soul.

"Well damn," Liz says. "You told me you were kinky, but hell." She glances between Rick, me, Ella, and Thomas and shakes her head. "This here." Liz waves her finger in front of us. "This is fucking hot."

I exhale the longest held breath on earth and laugh. Leave it to Liz to turn a tense moment into the polar opposite. Bless Liz and her craziness. "Thanks, Lizzy. Can always count on you." I wink at her.

"Christy," Sarah speaks up. Her emerald green eyes study my stormy blues for a moment. Curiosity and sadness prick her expression. "Were you afraid to tell me—us—this?"

Sarah's genuine kindheartedness has always plucked my heartstrings. I shouldn't have been worried about her reaction—or Liz's—but I was. They are my sisters. The only two non-romantic family I have. Counting their significant others is off the shelf until they fully commit. And because of what happened with my flesh and blood family so many years ago, I lived in fear of receiving that rejection from Sarah and Liz.

I nod. "Yes."

Sarah reaches across the table and sets her hand down, palm up. After I place my hand in hers and she clutches mine with a strength I didn't know she possessed, she says, "Nothing you say or do will ever make me not love you. We are family. Jackson and I may not be as wild in the bedroom as you all" —a smile lights up her face— "but we are far from tame. If this is who you are, I'm happy you found Rick. And I'm also glad you both found Ella and Thomas."

My heart is a hot air balloon, inflating bigger and bigger, and soaring in the clouds. A tear rolls down my cheek as I stare at my best friend. The woman whose opinion means more to me than I fathomed. "Thank you."

After we finish washing up, I turn off the shower and we step out. As we towel off, I stare at us in the floor to ceiling mirror in the bathroom. Tonight, the four of us are going to a party hosted by another couple we met through Boundless. It is their third party, and each has been successful as far as attendees.

"What are you wearing?" Ella asks, snapping me out of my foggy trance.

I glance at her in the mirror. "Red lace. You?"

"Was thinking maybe I'd wear that black piece I got the other day when we were shopping."

That little black piece had my panties wet in the fitting room we shared. Ella stood five inches taller than me. Her tits more than a mouthful, and her hips curvy as hell. Not that I didn't have curves of my own, but hers were sinful. In the little black number she tried on… she was sin personified.

"Yes," I say all breathy. "Definitely the black."

She drops her towel to the floor and saunters over to me. Stopping in front of me, she swipes a finger between my legs and closes her eyes. "So fucking wet. Shall I clean you up before we finish getting ready?"

We shouldn't, but I want her tongue on my skin. Cleaning the juices between my legs. "Yes," I breathe.

Ella dips two fingers inside me and starts walking me backward toward the attached bedroom. When my knees hit the mattress, she slides her fingers out and pushes me onto the bed. Fifteen minutes and several orgasms later—for us both—we crawl off the bed and finish getting ready.

Ella and I get ready for the party in the joint bedroom and bathroom. When the four of us moved in together, it was key to find a house with adequate space for everyone. We ended up with this magnificent three-story, five-bedroom house with a four-car garage, an oversized kitchen, and an open floor plan. The third level is intended to be attic space, but we converted it to office space for us all. Both couples have a bedroom. The third bedroom hosts a California king bed for nights when we all want to sleep in the same space. Most of our time together is spent in the third bedroom. Bedroom number four is the home gym. And bedroom five is a library —because that's what happens when one woman owns a bookstore and the other loves books.

All in all, this home is everything I dreamed of. Beautiful. Elegant. Comfortable.

Once we are dressed, Ella and I meet the guys in the living room. Rick and Thomas eye us up and down, and hunger floods my veins. Rick rises off the couch and walks toward us. Dressed in all black, I eat every inch of him up with my eyes.

When he reaches us, he wraps his hands around me, bends down, and kisses the spot beneath my ear. "You look delectable, gorgeous," he purrs. Glancing at Ella, he points at what she's wearing and says, "Love the new piece."

Thomas steps up to Ella and runs his hands down her sides. "Fuck, baby. Not sure this will stay intact on the way there."

I glance over at Ella and mouth, "Told you."

After Ella and I slip on our coats, we pile into the car. Rick drives and I sit up front with him. During the forty-five minute drive, Thomas and Ella explore each other in the back-seat and I turn sideways in the seat to watch them. Legs spread as wide as possible, I play with my clit while Thomas devours Ella's pussy. On occasion, Rick reaches across the console and dips his finger in me.

When we pull up to the party, we park along the street and head inside.

These parties are strictly invitation only. For the most part, the number of people here is limited as well. Less crowded and more enjoyable.

Once the front door closes, Rick removes my coat. Beneath the red trench coat, equally vibrant red lace hugs my body like a second skin. The strapless piece has a straight bustline at the start of my cleavage, while the bottom hem sits an inch below the apex of my thighs. There is no underlay. The simple piece is just lace and a zipper at the back. Every inch of my skin is on display beneath the soft material.

"Stunning," Rick says as he traces up the inside of my thigh.

Beside me, Thomas removes Ella's coat. The second it's off, my mouth waters and I want to lick every dip and curve of her body.

That little black piece has me chomping at the bit. Honestly, there is almost no fabric in the first place. Just a web of one-inch strips of leather joined with rivets and rings. It starts and ends in almost the same places as the dress I'm wearing, with the exception of the crotch. Which is exposed.

We meander through the party, grab some wine and hors d'oeuvres, chat with other couples while music plays low in the background. The hosts—husband and wife—walk around and chat with everyone before everything begins. They're such a fascinating couple—and how they met even more intriguing—and the six of us have recently bonded. But they have a strict rule. They don't join other couples. Just watch.

A few minutes later, the music pours louder from the speakers. The signal that everyone has arrived and the party can begin.

Rick, me, Ella, and Thomas wander over to a puffy cloud of large pillows on the floor. After Ella and I step onto the makeshift lounge area, I spin and face her. "Time for me to repay the favor from earlier." I drop to my knees, spread her legs and lick the length of her slit.

Rick steps behind Ella and fondles her tits while kissing the curve of her neck. Thomas squats down behind me, scoots my feet further apart, and drags his finger over my slit before dipping it inside me.

It doesn't take long before Ella and I lay completely exposed. Rick and Thomas slowly peel off their clothes and join us on the fluffy pillows. We watch other couples in the house lick and suck and fuck. Something each of us gets off on seeing.

Over the last three years, some rules each of us established has fallen away. Some still hold true. The husbands don't fuck the other's wife unless all are present. That is a hard rule we all agreed will never change. But kissing is the one that has relaxed the most.

Since the four of us started living together, and, for all intents and purposes, are bound to each other, it is only natural for us to exchange that simple intimacy. Thomas's kiss will never light my soul on fire like Rick's does, but it fulfills the bond we share. The same for Ella and Rick when they kiss. And the four of us stated in the beginning how important it is to have an open line of communication. We have no room for insecurity or jealousy in our relationship.

Thomas lines his cock up between my legs and strokes himself along my slit. "You ready, kitten?" he whispers in my ear.

Something else we all share… pet names. Ella and Thomas never exchanged pet names before us. Both men now answer to daddy, and Ella and I respond to kitten. At first, it turned my stomach, but then it dawned on me that it's just a name. Roleplay. It doesn't define who I am, just the role I play.

"Yes, daddy."

Thomas rubs the head of his cock up and down my slit again, slow and steady, then thrusts inside me. "So fucking tight, kitten."

He pumps his hips as I clutch his ass. Thomas has a magnificent cock. Nothing gets me off better than Rick, but Thomas is a close contender. As if the universe knew Ella and I needed more to be thoroughly satisfied in life.

"Fuck me harder, daddy," I moan.

Thomas hikes my legs over his shoulders and drives into me harder. Beside us, Ella rides Rick's cock like a rodeo champion. As I watch her grind on top of my husband, a molten heat boils in my core. Her eyes glance my way and we stare at one another. And for a beat, it is me and Ella.

Seconds later, I come on Thomas's cock and Ella shudders over Rick.

When we float down from the clouds, Thomas goes to his wife and Rick joins me. As I mount Rick, I moan at the pressure of his girth stretching my walls. Thomas may have a magnificent cock, he may be able to make me come undone, but nothing will supersede the way Rick feels inside me. As if he was made specifically for me. Thomas and Ella lay on their side facing us as he props her leg up and enters her from behind. Such a sight to behold.

As I claw Rick's pecs and grind my hips over his pelvis, he sits up and kisses up my neck. When he reaches my ear, he whispers, "Remember who you belong to, gorgeous." His hand trails up my spine, grips the hair at the base of my skull, wraps it around his wrist and tugs.

"Always," I answer.

"Remember who I belong to."

"Yes."

No matter who enters our lives, one factor holds true. Rick Matheson belongs to me. And I belong to him. Until my dying day, regardless of whatever challenges life throws at us, he will always have my undying devotion.

NEVER DID I think Thomas and I would ever find another couple like us. Two people who enjoy exploring their sexual fantasies the way we do. A couple so open and compassionate and generous. No one Thomas and I have been with compares to Christy and Rick. Chloe and Dominic were close, but our connection with them was strictly primal.

Before Thomas and I met, I had been with my fair share of people. Men and women both. I started exploring my sexuality at the ripe age of eleven. I remember my first experience was with my best friend at the time. Brianna and I were both curious about what we had heard some of our older friends talking about. Sex and masturbating. Although we were young and inexperienced, we wanted to see what the big deal was.

One day after school, Brianna and I walked home to my house. My parents wouldn't be home from work for hours. At first, we had no clue what to do. So, we listened to music and sat on my bed like we normally did.

"Are you nervous?" I asked her.

"A little," she told me.

Slowly, we inched closer and closer to each other. A few songs played before her arm brushed against mine. Another song ends and my fingers traced over her denim-covered thigh. As each song started and ended, we made another move.

Excitement flashed in my veins as her fingertips explored my small breasts through the cotton fabric of my t-shirt. No one had ever touched me like this. And no one made me tingle the way Brianna did.

Thirty minutes in, I experienced my first kiss. It was wet and sloppy and exhilarating. I didn't want to stop kissing her. So we kept kissing.

Ten minutes later, I ran my fingers through another person's pubic hair for the first time. Although it was soft and curly like mine, I enjoyed the texture of it so much more than my own. Course and velvety at the same time.

Another ten minutes later and I dipped my fingers inside a girl for the first time. Slipped my fingers in and out. Memorized the ridges inside her walls. Gloried in the warm wetness dripping from her core. And relished the taste of her on my tongue.

After that day, Brianna and I remained friends. But we were never anything else. Exploring my sexuality with my friend first is something I will never forget. When we started high school and Naomi stepped into the picture, I saw less of Brianna. From time to time, we still catch up, calls or texts, but not much else. A few years back, she married a guy she met in college. A month ago, they welcomed their first child into the world.

Brianna was my first sexual experience. Before I met Thomas, there were easily dozens more. I never kept track. But after learning what sex tasted like and how my body reacted to it, I hungered for it. It didn't bother me that guys in the school told other guys I was a freak in the bedroom. Nor did it bother me that girls either hated or envied me.

But the day I met Thomas is one I will never forget.

Naomi and I just graduated high school. To celebrate, she wanted to go out and party.

Going to clubs or bars was nothing new for us. A guy she dated a couple years back made us fake IDs and we'd been getting past bouncers for two years. We never drank, just had a good time.

That's what I thought we were doing tonight. Going to a night club.

This was a club alright. Just not the typical places we went. Nope, this one is packed wall to wall with varying degrees of nudity and lots of sex. I am far from a prude, but this… I wasn't prepared.

After giving Naomi the third degree, she swore to stick by my side. That lasted all of five minutes. Naomi, my best friend, ditched me in an underground sex party. She texted her apology and I replied with how much she sucked.

I bought a drink, found an empty couch and watch a woman give oral to a man. It wasn't long before some old pervert sat next to me and tried to cop a feel. Across the couch circle, Thomas saw my discomfort and swooped in for the rescue.

He asked my name and I'd given him my fake name. He pinned the lie immediately. Minutes passed as we chatted. Our attraction was immediate and irresistible. In no time, he'd peeled my clothes from my skin and took me in that grungy warehouse.

I'd had sex in front of others before, but not people I didn't know. It was awkward and liberating. When we left the party, Thomas invited me to his place. Reluctant as I was, I caved. Best decision I ever made. Because after that night, and some tense moments with my parents, Thomas and I were inseparable.

We fucked like fiends every chance we got. And two years later, Thomas asked me to be his wife. Saying yes was as easy as breathing. Saying I do on our wedding day had been even easier.

The rest, as they say, is history.

I walk into the third bedroom in our house—the joint bedroom. Christy lays naked, sprawled across the sheets on the bed built for all four of us. Her legs spread wide, her fingers circling the bud between her thighs. Majority of the time spent in our house is without clothes on, and we all love the freedom.

Crawling onto the bed, I go straight to her and kiss my way up the inside of her leg. When I reach her apex, she lifts her hand away and I eat her pussy like it's my last meal. Christy tastes divine. Like no other woman I've had my mouth on. Sweet as berries with a hint of salt.

As I lick her clit and finger her cunt, the light padding of two sets of feet enter the room. I peek up over Christy's shaved mound and watch her tweak her nipples. Her lusty eyes look over my shoulders at the two men who entered the room. Our husbands.

I spread my legs farther apart and push my ass into the air as I finger fuck my girl. 'Cause that's what Christy is—my girl. Just as I am her girl. Her walls clamp around my fingers and I lick her faster. As she comes, I withdraw my fingers and suck her folds.

Behind me, the mattress dips. I lift my ass as high as it will go and wait. When I finish sucking Christy off, she shifts position and slides down beside me.

With my face pressed into the mattress, Christy traces a line from my neck to the end of my spine, down my ass crack —where she stops and teases my hole for a moment—and along my slit. I haven't determined if it's Rick or Thomas behind me yet. They're just out of my line of sight.

Christy continues to run her finger over my folds for one, two, three strokes before she dips inside. She finger fucks me slow and steady for a minute before running her fingers back up to my tight ass. Painting circles around the hole, she slowly pushes inside and I gasp.

Once she finds a rhythm, she kicks her legs back and is on her knees and one hand. With her finger pumping in and out of my ass, a cock slides inside my pussy.

"Fuck, you're wet," Rick groans.

I push up onto all fours and repeat the same Christy just did with me. Soon, we are ass fucking each other while we both have cocks filling us.

No possible way life could get any better.

***

THOMAS

Ella's finger pumps in and out of Christy's ass as I fuck the shit out of her pussy. Honestly, I want my dick in her ass. I tap Ella's hand and she peeks up at me. I jerk my chin to the side, silently asking my wife to remove her finger. When she does, Christy's hole stays open a beat as I spread her cheeks wide.

I grab the bottle of lube we keep near the bed and squirt some down her crack. It slides down and I smear it around her hole.

Christy sucks in a breath and peeks over her shoulder. "Fuck my ass, daddy," she purrs.

She always called Rick daddy when they played, but Ella never called me anything and I only called her pet. The first time we allowed the pet name exchange between us all, I wasn't sure how I would feel about it. The first time it fell from her lips, my cock got a new surge of life. Has happened every time since. Occasionally, Ella calls me daddy, but it has a different effect than when Christy does it. For Ella, the term daddy has a dark history. Her saying it shocks me. But Christy truly is a kitten when she begs for daddy.

"You want daddy's fat cock in your tight ass, kitten?"

"Please, daddy. I need your fat cock deep in my ass."

Fuck my life.

Since Ella and I met Rick and Christy, I have never fucked so many times in my life. Ella and I went at it like rabbits before, or so I thought. But with Ella's and Christy's appetites under one roof, we fuck several times a day.

Rick pounds into Ella while I fuck Christy's tight, plump ass. Our women scream and cry out in pleasure. The salty scent of sex fills the spacious room. After Christy's third orgasm, I spurt into her ass. Ella begs for it harder, coming on Rick a moment later for the second time and he releases inside her.

After cleaning up, we all collapse on the bed and pass out for a time.

When I wake, the room is dark. Everyone still in the bed, but I hear Ella and Christy kissing and playing with each other. Rick lies behind me, but from what I can tell, he is still asleep. I slowly stroke myself in the dark under the comforter. The more I stroke my cock, the more my hips rock and my ass bumps Rick.

Quickly, I learn he is far from asleep. And his cock is hard as steel.

I inch my ass closer to him, rocking back and forth as I stroke myself. When the head of his cock grazes my ass crack, I clench my cheeks and pinch the head slightly. With each rock of my hips, I bring myself closer to him. He doesn't move, but his hand runs up and down his shaft. Every few trips up, his fingers run up the length of my crack.

A few more rocks back and the head of Rick's cock presses firmly against my ass. My back to his chest. He wraps his arm around my waist and grabs my cock in his hand. "You want this?" He whispers in my ear.

I push my ass into him farther as my answer.

Ten minutes and a shit ton of lube later, and I have never come so hard in my life. Beside us, the girls lay quiet, eyes locked on us.

If it wasn't official before, it is now. We are one. And fuck if I have ever been happier.

Ella wakes me the next morning. "Hey, sleepyhead. Time to get up. Big day ahead of us." I groan and roll out of bed. We have been planning this day for months, best not to ruin it by oversleeping.

After a quick bite to eat, I shower and get dressed. When I come down the stairs, Ella, Christy, and Rick wait near the door. Our wives both radiant as ever. Ella wears a sage green backless dress that ties at her neck. Christy in her classic red, the dress the same style. Rick clad in his typical all black, same as me.

We all hop into the car and Rick drives us to Boundless. Today, the club is closed for our gathering. A small intimate get together to celebrate us. We invited our closest friends to join us. On the way there, the girls discuss how excited they are about sharing tonight with whom we consider to be family.

Once Rick parks the car, we head inside and go downstairs. In the bright lights, the club is a whole new place. The walls still ooze sex, but it is less in your face. Either way, I love this place. It is where the next chapter of our lives began. For me, Ella, Rick, and Christy.

One after another, slowly our friends make their way inside. Light chatter fills the open space as soft music plays in the background. After everyone arrives, Rick signals for Elizabeth to start.

"Can I have everyone's attention, please," Elizabeth shouts. After everyone quiets, she continues. "Thank you for being here today. And for honoring Rick, Christy, Thomas, and Ella."

Elizabeth waves us to the front of the room. Everyone else sits on couches or chairs positioned to face the front of the room. Ella and I stand on one side of Elizabeth while Christy and Rick stand on the other. Once we all stand in the right place, Elizabeth faces our friends and family then begins.

"Today, Rick, Christy, Thomas, and Ella have asked you all here to witness their special day. Although under the eyes of the law, this ceremony is not recognized, it holds significance for them and their future together. Today, we join these two couples—Rick and Christy Matheson and Thomas and Ella Reynolds. Call it a marriage of sorts. Between them, they vow to uphold all the promises they exchanged before arriving here today. The same that holds true in any bond formed. Safety. Love. Honor. Commitment. Devotion."

Elizabeth pauses and I glance down at Ella. Her smile brighter than the summer sun. Since the heated start of our relationship, I never imagined we would be standing here today. Utterly devoted to each other. Both of us in love with the couple across from us.

When I gaze at Rick and Christy, two of the most beautiful souls stare back at me. Two souls who mimic mine and Ella's. Two souls who love fiercely and give completely. Luck is the only word I can use to describe the chances of our finding each other.

"Today, Rick, Christy, Thomas, and Ella make an unbreakable promise before the people who matter most in their lives. The promise of loyalty to each other." Elizabeth hands us each a box. We open them and each slip out a ring. Christy and I have our rings, and Rick and Ella have their rings. As we exchange rings, placing them on our right ring fingers, I kiss Christy, and Rick kisses Ella. After I kiss Ella while Rick kisses Christy, then me and Rick and Christy and Ella. "Before your loved ones, I now pronounce you husbands and wives."

After Elizabeth announces the final declaration, my heart jackhammers between my lungs. For the first time ever, a sense of absoluteness fills me. Similar to what I felt when I found Ella. She filled in all my missing parts. But once we found Rick and Christy, it was as if they sealed our hearts and gave us new life.

A new life we will all enjoy together. Always.

UNDYING DEVOTION PLAYLIST

Here are some of the songs from the **Undying Devotion** playlist. You can find and listen to the entire playlist on Spotify!

Wallflower | Kimberly August
What You Need | The Weeknd
The Wall | PatrickReza
Lover. Fighter. | SVRCINA
Holocene | Bon Iver
Voyeur Girl | Stephen
Do It For Me | Rosenfeld
All I Ever Need | Austin Mahone
Forever Ain't Enough | J. Holiday
BBY | Two Feet

ACKNOWLEDGMENTS

Readers are the best humans! Thank you to each and every one of you for reading my words. It still blows my mind that I'm publishing. Thank you times a million. If I could hug you all, my tentacle arms would squeeze you tight.

Bloggers!! I would be nowhere without you! Thank you for reading my words and promoting my books all over the internet. YOU ROCK!!

To my ARC review team! Thank you for taking a chance on me. Thank you for wanting to read my books and supporting me. And thank you for every review—they are GOLD! Without any of you, things would be so much different.

Ellie and Rosa at My Brother's Editor! Thank you for editing and proofing this book. Thank you for making my manuscript better than it was before I sent it to you. Your input is priceless!

To every author I have bugged with questions. It amazes me how wonderful the writing community is. To belong to a community where every person wants everyone to thrive and succeed… I love it and you!

WIFE!! Thanks for being my alpha reader. Thank you for sharing your brutal honesty and cheering me on. And thanks for never getting aggravated over my non-stop schedule.

To my family who supports and roots me on! It freaks me out when I hand a copy of my book to my dad or daughter. Although I'm proud of my accomplishment, it's strange to have someone so close to you reading your work. Especially this book… eek!

DEVOTION SERIES

PERSEPHONE AUTUMN

BETWEEN WORDS PUBLISHING LLC

For the women who have been through hell and come out on the other side. For the couples who battle against the norms and don't let it get them down. For love… because love knows no boundaries and will always conquer in the end.

TRIGGER WARNING & AUTHOR'S NOTE

Beloved Devotion is romantic suspense story. Graphic content, domestic violence, physical assault, miscarriage, sexual violence, and/or partner manipulation in certain scenes may trigger emotional distress in some readers. If you are sensitive to the above listed triggers, this story may not be for you.

Please use your personal judgment before proceeding.

When I initially set to write more books in the Devotion series, I didn't know the ins and outs of book 2 or 3. When I sat down to start plotting and writing Beloved Devotion, I didn't have the full picture right away. But slowly, Tiffany's story came into focus and although her history isn't pretty, I had to tell her story.

On average, 24 people per minute are victims of rape, physical violence or stalking by an intimate partner in the United States—more than 12 million women and men over the course of a year. Nearly half of all women and men in the United States have experienced psychological aggression by an intimate partner in their lifetime (48.4% and 48.8%, respectively). Females ages 18 to 24 and 25 to 34 generally experienced the highest rates of intimate partner violence. ****Statistics from National Domestic Violence Hotline****

If you or anyone you know are in an abusive relationship, please seek help. If you are not able to seek help online or through the phone, but know someone who can, please push them to do so. And never give up the fight.

I have never been in a physically abusive relationship, but have witnessed one for years as a child. They are scary and chip away at you. But please know there is a way out. There are people who want to help. Who will be a voice for you.

- https://www.thehotline.org
- 1-800-799-7233
- 1-800-787-3224 (TTY)

PROLOGUE
TIFFANY

L ɪ z and I stroll hand in hand along the sidewalk near the Santa Monica pier. The salty Pacific air sticks to my skin as the waves crash and create a soothing melody in the background. Battered and deep-fried sugary treats pierce my nose and make my mouth water. Bright lights glow from the rides on the pier as the sun starts to dip under the horizon. Children and families laugh and squeal with delight.

We step onto the boardwalk and weave through the dense crowd as we take in all the sights. It's our first trip here and I immediately understand why the small amusement park is so popular.

"Want to share a funnel cake?" Liz asks with the widest smile before she clamps down on her lower lip.

I pat my stomach. "Maybe in a little bit. Still full from dinner."

She nods and rubs her palms on the sides of her legs, just below her hips. For the past few hours, Liz has been on edge and I have no idea why. As badly as I want to pry the truth from her, I don't say a word. I would rather not appear to be "on duty" in normal conversation. This is date night, not a therapy session.

Winding our way through the small amusement park, Liz stops in front of the Ferris wheel and tips her head back, staring at the oversized ride. The spokes glow blue and pink in the setting sun as the wheel spins at a leisurely pace. Liz whips her hazel eyes back to me and flaunts the sweetest smile my direction.

"Let's go on the Ferris wheel," she says, her tone whimsical and giddy.

It isn't often I see this piece of Liz. The piece that reminds me of bubbly young girls experiencing something new with friends. Not that Liz is a Debbie Downer. But she also isn't unicorns and glitter, either. Beneath all the black attire, beneath the party and rock music, Liz is a quiet romantic. How on earth can I deny her right now? Especially when her jubilance is on display for the world to see.

"Okay" —I clap my hands together and rub them— "let's go." At least on the Ferris wheel, I have zero worries about my dinner making a reappearance.

After two more loops around, the ginormous wheel stops. One car at a time, each bucket empties and refills. A couple glued at the hips gets in two cars ahead of us, while a father and daughter get in just before us. After the attendant secures the lock on the car before us, the wheel turns slightly. A woman and two teenage boys climb out before we slide into the bucket and latch the door shut. Once a few more cars switch riders, we float up into the lilac-coral-peach blossom twilight.

I tug my hoodie sleeves down my elbows to my wrists as goosebumps decorate my skin. A light shiver trembles in my chest as the unobstructed breeze whips my hair across my cheeks. Brushing the strands from my sight, I peer over at Liz, about to ask her if she feels chilled too, when I notice her almond-colored skin looks more like coffee with way too much creamer. Her blanched pallor throws up warning flags. Is she really afraid of heights and ignored it to ride something calmer? Is *her* dinner not sitting well? Oh, god.

"Hey," I speak up, tapping her forearm. "You okay? Look a little pale."

She shakes her head and bites the inside of her cheek. "I'm fine. Just that…" Her words trail off and I wait for her to finish telling me what exactly is bothering her.

When the Ferris wheel does a third loop and she has yet to say anything, I slip my index finger under her chin and lift it, bring her line of sight back to me. Once eye to eye, I ask again. "Sure you're okay? You're starting to scare me."

Her eyes dart back and forth between mine. Hundreds of questions itch to be asked as I hold her gaze. Sucking in a deep breath, Liz leans forward and presses her lips to mine. Warm lips with a hint of lime from her margarita earlier. The kiss is soft and sweet as I melt into her body. As quickly as the kiss began, it ends. Liz's sudden shift back to her seat, the way she scoots as far away as possible, gives me whiplash. I lick the hint of lime from my lips as a sting builds in my chest.

But before I comprehend the why behind her actions, Liz awkwardly drops to one knee in the bucket. A buzz whooshes behind my ears as my pulse races for the finish line. I may faint one hundred and thirty feet in the air above the Santa Monica Pier. *Breathe, Tiffany. Breathe.*

"Tiff, I have been battling with my own words for days. Trying to come up with the perfect way to do this. But saying romantic things isn't my strong suit. So, here comes my version." She laughs, the resonance slightly off-kilter. "From the moment I laid eyes on you, in those barely-there, skin-tight shorts and snug little top that displayed one of your best features—" She stops, winks, and I laugh. "—I knew you were the one for me. Quickly, I learned how witty and sexy you are, and I fell in love. Hard."

I bite my upper lip and work to hide the smile stretching my face taut, but it's no use.

"You make every day worth getting up for. Your smile and kind words. Your astonishing ability to help others. I never thought I would be so lucky as to have someone like you in my life." The blue flecks in her hazel eyes shimmer as she searches mine for one, two, three breaths. "And I'd like it to stay that way. Forever."

My cheeks sting from smiling. Tears prick the backs of my eyes and threaten to spill. And in less than a minute, my heart has relocated to my throat, clogging it with raw, heavy emotion.

I don't dare say a word. Liz implying she wants to marry me is one thing. But she has yet to actually ask me. If I just blurt my answer when she hasn't proposed the question, I may make the biggest fool of myself. And I don't want to steal her spotlight.

Liz reaches into the front pocket of her jeans. I hold my breath and keep my eyes on her hand. When I see her trembling fingers again, a thin rose gold band with a sparkling diamond rests between her pinched thumb and forefinger. Nothing fancy. Just simple. Perfect. Exactly the type of ring I would choose for myself.

"Tiffany Page, will you marry me?" Liz holds the ring up higher and watches my every move.

I glance between her and the ring. Liz is, by far, the best thing that has happened to me. No way I would move across the country with her if I didn't see us being together for the long haul. She has this uncanny ability to make me love life more and want to be a better person.

So, why does it feel like there is a time bomb sitting on my chest right now? Slowly pressing all the air from my lungs and rendering me speechless.

Why can I not give her an immediate answer and scream *yes* for everyone to hear? Without a doubt, I want to tell her yes.

But I can't.

Because it's complicated.

The nervous and jumpy expression on Liz's face slowly starts morphing into concern and fear. The corners of her eyes crinkling as the corners of her mouth point down. I need to answer her. Need to not let her think I don't want this. I do. Just need to clear up some history first.

I unclench my sweaty palm and stretch my fingers in her direction. "Yes!" I blurt, my voice scratchy and cracking.

Liz audibly inhales before her shoulders drop, and I just realize she had been holding her breath this whole time. "Thank god," she professes, relief coating her words. "For a minute, I thought you were going to say no. Was about to lose my shit."

I laugh, and it sounds forced. Vacant. "Please don't lose your shit."

Liz pushes up off her knee and presses a chaste kiss to my lips. Then she slips the dainty band onto my finger and kisses the knuckle distal to the band. "I love you, Tiff. Can't wait for the day I can call you my wife."

I smile at her sweetness, then stare down at the band as I twirl the underside with my thumb. The stone slides side to side, occasionally grazing the inside of my pinky and middle finger.

"Can't wait either," I mumble as emotion chokes me.

The Ferris wheel loops again and we pause at the top as people switch out the buckets. Liz looks out at the water, her smile bright enough to light the night sky. And I love how perfect this moment has been. Like a modern fairy tale.

I stare down at the classic cut diamond on the rose gold band and a fierce pain stabs me beneath my breastbone. Nothing excites me more than marrying Liz. Being her wife and dubbing her as mine forever.

I may have said yes to her proposal, but there is one thing I forgot to mention. I can't marry her. Not yet, anyway.

But there is no chance in hell I am speaking that aloud.

The day will come soon. Swear it will. But I have a lot of work ahead of me. And if I'm completely honest, all of it scares the hell out of me.

ONE

LIZ

"What do you mean she's acting weird?"

I finish chewing the bite of food in my mouth and swallow. How do I tell one of my best friends that I think my fiancée *doesn't* want to marry me? A knife twists in my heart at the thought of Tiffany *not* wanting to be with me. Of her only agreeing to marry me out of guilt or pity.

"Ugh, I don't know, Christy. Call it intuition. Or maybe it's the fact that I asked her to marry me almost four months ago, she said yes, and now she acts as if I never asked at all." Fuck. This is beyond frustrating. Honestly, I'm not even sure my thoughts are properly translating into words. I ball the hand in my lap so tight my nails practically break the skin.

Christy spears her salad as if it were her archnemesis, then shoves the forkful in her mouth. A couple days ago, I shot her a text message and asked if we could meet up. I needed some best friend time and maybe someone who could decipher what was happening in my life. Because I sure as hell had no idea. And I had to get this two-ton weight off my chest, even if only for a moment.

Without hesitation, Christy agreed to meet up. Granted, we see each other almost every day at work, but it isn't the same. Talking with Christy is effortless, always has been. But it doesn't feel right. The two of us sitting down for lunch and hashing out problems like this. Problems such as your fiancée not wanting to participate in the preparation of your eventual marriage. Problems such as your fiancée always skirting around the topic of wedding or marriage or being together for the rest of our lives.

Talks such as these require more than our one-hour lunch break time slot. Plus, I don't need the prying ears of my coworkers nearby.

"Maybe the idea of being married scares her." Christy shrugs as if it's the simplest conclusion. To me, it is much more complex. "Some people believe marriage isn't for them. Hell, Rick and I had been together seven years before he proposed to me. Honestly, I never thought he'd ask."

"And look at you now." I wave my hand in front of her as my eyes trail down to the black and red rings on her left, fourth digit. The knife in my heart twists a little more. "Actually got married without inviting your friends." Christy's cheeks and neck bloom a brilliant shade of pick as I clasp my hand over my chest and faux-gasp. "But at least you're still doing a ceremony for everyone to be a part of."

The green beast deep in my belly roars louder with envy.

I love Christy and Rick, no matter what. God, jealousy flows through my veins at the fact that not only are they married to each other, *but* they also married—in their hearts because it isn't legal—another couple, Ella and Thomas, that they felt they couldn't live without. *Double marriage.*

All I ask for is one. *One.* Am I asking too much?

"Yeah… when Rick first proposed, I wanted to wait and do the big shebang with everyone around. But life happens. Shitty people happen. So, we didn't want to wait any longer. We did what was right for us. At the end of the day, that's what matters."

Months ago, when Christy and I took our lunch break together, I noticed an additional ring on her left fourth digit. The one you usually get once the marriage ceremony occurs. When I questioned the flashy new jewelry, she regaled the story as to why she and Rick opted to get married so quickly. Can't say I blame either of them. If I were in her shoes, I would do the same.

"True. I just wish I understood why Tiff acts as if I never asked. As if the whole proposal is a figment of my imagination. Sometimes I glance down at her hand and double-check she's wearing her engagement ring." And every time, the diamond catches the light and beams back at me. Teasing and taunting. "Did I do something wrong, Christy? What if she has second thoughts about us getting married? I don't fucking know a damn thing and it's slowly killing me."

Christy reaches across the wooden picnic table in the garden area of Cozy Corner Books and brushes her thumb back and forth over the top of my hand. The motion soothes me, but not enough to wipe away the pain. The thought of Tiffany not wanting to marry me hurts on an unfathomable level. What possible explanation is left other than she doesn't want our relationship to go down that path? If she said yes to appease me, to not hurt my feelings in the moment… well, that is so much worse.

As if reading my mind, Christy says, "I'm sure Tiffany has a perfectly good explanation as to why she's acting the way she is. Maybe work is stressing her out. Maybe all the legwork leading up to the actual wedding is freaking her out. I don't know, Liz. And neither will you until you sit down with her and talk it out."

Sit down with Tiffany and talk it out.

Yes, that seems like a good game plan. Plans start rolling through my head about how to approach this. Could make us dinner tonight. Delicious food and some wine might be the perfect way to loosen her up and get her talking.

"Thanks, C. You always know what to say."

"What can I say, bitch." Christy flashes me her profile as she raises her hands to either side of her face. "I'm a guru. Why do you think everyone loves me?"

I shake my head and chuckle. "All right, somebody's let their ego inflate a little too much recently. Jump down from your high horse and join the rest of the population."

"Pff. You're just jealous of my amazing ability to find solutions like that." Christy snaps her fingers and blows me a cocky kiss. "But you still love me, bitch."

Isn't that the truth. I do love her. Couldn't have asked for a better friend. She and Sarah both. No matter what life throws my way, both of these women—my two best friends—will be right by my side. My cheerleaders. Always rooting for Team Liz.

"I do. Now let's finish eating so you can show me every-thing you love about this bookstore." I rub my hands over my biceps and send a silent *thank you* to Ella for having heaters in the bookstore's garden.

As if I demanded her to eat, Christy starts shoveling salad down her throat like a starved animal. All I do is watch, shake my head at how crazy her antics are, and slowly finish my sandwich. Utterly bananas, but she owns her version of crazy while wearing a crown. How can anyone not love her?

No one would ever peg me as a romantic. Not with my love for all things black and the screamy rock music I blare when we aren't partying. Down to the core, though, isn't that what every person wants? To be loved. Whether from another person. Or even a pet. To form a connection and flourish from the bond created. Whether it is friendship or intimacy, we all push for some form of attachment.

I may not be your typical roses and candies and touchy-feely romantic. But, admittedly, I love the jitteriness and flut-ters and all-consuming-I-can't-live-without-them feeling. The emotion which swallows me whole and consumes every molecule in my body. The way my heart sprints for the finish line and my breathing vanishes when she walks in the room.

Call me a closet romantic, I suppose. Grand gestures aren't so much my modus operandi. But I have my ways.

One way I have always expressed myself when someone matters… food. For as long as I can remember, I love being in the kitchen. Getting my hands messy and creating something everyone will enjoy. Both Grandma Winston and Grandma Warren had a hand in my love for cooking. My mom, too, but she doesn't share the same passion as my grandmothers and I do.

And my love for cooking is precisely why I am shuffling between the cutting board, the pressure cooker, and the oven at this exact moment. Apron over my head and secured at the waist. Hair in an elastic at the nape of my neck. Perspiration slowly beading on my temples. Next up—the stove.

In the oven, a crumb-topped pie is baking for dessert. And

for the last fifteen minutes, I have been tortured by the delicious smell of apples and cinnamon and sugar as I cut chicken and vegetables for stir-fry.

A loud squeal bounces off the kitchen walls. I glance at the pressure cooker, a light on the display flashes indicating it finished. "Yeah, yeah."

After I release the pressure valve, I turn on the range and set the wok on the burner. Once I chop the last of the vegetables, I test the temperature of the pan with a drop of water. Hot enough, I toss sliced carrots into the wok. One by one, as things cook, I add more vegetables to the pan. Scooping them all out once they are cooked, I add the chicken in the pan with a hint of toasted sesame oil. As the small slices sizzle and start to brown on all sides, I toss the veggies back in and bring it all together with a homemade savory sauce I whipped up.

Just as I coat everything in the sauce, the front door opens and Tiffany walks through. "Lizzie, I'm home. What smells so good?"

"In the kitch—" Tiff walks into the kitchen and cuts off my hollering. She wears a button-up white dress shirt—not tucked—and a pair of black dress slacks that cover the majority of her four-inch heels. The role of doctor, albeit a clinical psychologist, suits her. As if she was born to fill these shoes. Shoes she looks amazing in… without the dress pants.

"Hey." She presses a kiss to my cheek before scanning the contents of the pan. "Looks and smells amazing." Tiffany waves her hand over the steam and wafts it in her direction as she inhales.

"Just finished everything. Go change and I'll dish it up."

"'Kay, be back in a sec." She kisses my cheek again then heads to the bedroom. I stare at her ass as she walks off and appreciate her curves for a beat.

Turning off everything, I grab a couple of the large bowls we use for stir-fry nights and portion out the rice, chicken, and veggies, then sprinkle it with gomasio. After I set the bowls on the dining table, I fetch a bottle of wine from the fridge and two glasses from the cabinet.

As I set the glasses down and uncork the wine, my eyes dart across the center of the table. *Should I have lit some candles?* They would set a pleasant tone during our dinner, but might be overkill and Tiffany would be more suspicious I was up to something. After all, we don't light candles during dinner any other night of the week. Only special occasions.

Good call on no candles.

Tiffany walks back into the room and moans. "God, it smells so damn good in here. Did you make something besides stir-fry?" She moans as she slips into her chair at the table.

I smile and shrug. "Made us pie for dessert. It has another ten or fifteen minutes in the oven."

"Well, it smells heavenly."

Glancing at her across the table, I melt a little in my chair from the smile on her face. "Thanks."

After a few bites, she asks, "Is there a special occasion I forgot about? Been jogging my memory and came up with nothing. Please tell me I didn't forget an important date." Her cheeks tighten as her lips form a straight line, eyes squinting as if preparing for a slap across the face.

If I had to guess, she almost seems… afraid. But why? I would never freak-out over missing an anniversary or holiday. Honestly, not even my birthday. She knows all the important dates in our relationship. I have seen them written in her planner. So this shift in her demeanor is odd.

"No special occasion. Just wanted a nice dinner. Over pie, I thought maybe we could talk about wedding stuff. Nothing major. But it would be nice to pick a date and discuss how many people we'd like there."

Tiffany shovels way too much food into her mouth and gives a noncommittal "Mmmhmm." Again, it seems as if she is purposely avoiding anything and everything to do with the wedding. And it pinches tight and twists in my gut. But until proven to be true, I refuse to believe she doesn't want to marry me.

Dinner ends and we clean up the kitchen as the pie cools. The way Tiffany and I move around each other in the kitchen —and everywhere else—feels fluid. Natural. Symbiotic. We don't have to utter a word. We simply ebb and flow. As I slice the pie, Tiffany grabs plates from the cabinet.

"Want a scoop of ice cream with yours?" I ask, setting the slices on plates.

"Is that a real question?" Tiffany scoffs. "Do bears shit in the woods?"

I stare at her a moment, poker-faced, as elation soothes my heart. This girl right here. This is *my girl*. *My* Tiffany. Full of spunk and not giving a shit what anyone else thinks. Being unapologetically herself and voicing her mind.

"Not sure," I answer. "Don't generally stick around and wait to watch bears shit."

A loud clang echoes off the tile backsplash as the forks in Tiffany's hand drop and smack against the granite countertop. She throws her head back and laughs. Louder and harder than I have seen or heard her do in months. I love and hate it in equal measure.

Love it because seeing her like this—being the open and free woman I met years ago—has a colony of bees buzzing to life beneath my sternum. Hate it because since the day I asked Tiffany to marry me, this side of her has been snuffed out and faded to the background.

An endless list of questions float in my head and I continually add more to that list. Today, I will add *why haven't you laughed?* to the list.

Tiffany kisses my temple once her laughter subsides. "I love you, Lizzie. And I'm sure bears shit wherever the hell they want. But, mostly, it's in the woods."

Once pie and ice cream are plated, we take our dessert out to the living room and plop down on the couch. Tiffany tucks her feet under her butt and wiggles her way back into the pillows. The maneuver a quirk she does every single time we sit on the couch with dessert or, on occasion, dinner. Little mannerisms like the way she scoots back on the couch hold a special place in my heart.

Generally, I had never been someone who bookmarked habits or mannerisms. Not until I met Tiffany. That first day, when Sarah, Christy, and I stopped for lunch at the bar-and-grill restaurant, there was no denying the way she lured me in. Before Tiffany, I never foresaw myself being one of those people in a serious relationship. Someone who yearns to spend the rest of their life with the same human.

But the way her auburn hair swayed in her ponytail as she went from table to table. How her ice-blue eyes heated and melted everything south of my diaphragm. I wouldn't call it love at first sight, but there was definitely an intense level of lust at first sight.

Half our pie and ice cream gone, I chance a look at her and notice her eyes glued to the plate in her hands. *Now or never, Liz. Just spit it out.*

"Tiff?"

"Yeah?" she question-answers, not lifting her eyes to meet mine or even look in my general direction.

I pinch my eyes shut and swallow the boulder of emotion lodged dead center in my throat. "Do you want to marry me?" The words leave my lips so softly, I wonder if she heard me. My raging pulse drowns out all sound and I open my eyes.

Out of the corner of my eye, her fork hovers above her plate for three heavy breaths before she sets it down. Then, she leans forward and sets her plate on the coffee table, grabbing mine next and setting it beside hers before sliding back into her spot on the couch.

Her gaze burns every inch of my profile. I have yet to shift and look at her head-on. Scared of what I will see on her face. Sadness. Regret. Who knows? And the not knowing is the scariest part of it all.

"Liz, please look at me."

We sit in silence a minute as I stare down at my fumbling fingers. I want one more minute without the truth. Because whatever her truth is, whatever the reason she is so hesitant for us to move forward, it will hurt. But I need to know. No matter how much it hurts, I need the truth.

You can do this, Liz. Just look up at her.

Rotating to face her, I lift my eyes to hers and what I see swallows me alive. Her icy blue irises bore into my hazels as if she's trying to tell me something telepathically. Not an ounce of regret or sadness rests in her brilliant blue orbs. Perhaps, a hint of guilt, though.

"Lizzie, I have no regrets about agreeing to marry you." Relief swells in my chest as a weight lifts from my shoulders. "But I won't lie to you. Getting married scares the shit out of me." The solace from seconds ago deflates as my heart shrivels.

"Why? Is it us? Me?" If she discloses the reason behind her fear, perhaps I could help her counteract it.

Tiffany shakes her head before reaching forward and taking my hands in hers. "No. It's—" She stops and doesn't say another word. Leaving the open-ended answer hanging out there like a dangling carrot. Taunting and teasing me.

What is it? What secret could she be keeping from me? For someone who wants nothing but honesty in a relationship, what skeletons is she hiding from me? Whatever the root cause is, it has to be huge. Crawling into a corner and hiding from the world isn't Tiffany's style. At least not the Tiffany I know.

"What is it, Tiff?" I rest my hand on her leg and she glances up at me. "You can tell me."

Her icy blue eyes melt into puddles as she stares back at me. A sharp pain lances me as her eyes dart back and forth between mine. Whatever she isn't telling me, it scares the hell out of her. Literally. The last four years Tiffany and I have been together, not once have I seen her like this. Curled in on herself and withdrawn.

Tiffany is one of the strongest women in my life. Sarah and Christy tied in for runner-up. Seeing her timid and frightened has me questioning why I haven't gotten her to open up about her life before us. Small snippets are all she offers whenever the past gets brought up. Enough to appease me.

Now, I need to ask invasive questions. Questions that will make us both uncomfortable, I'm certain.

"It's... I... can't. Not yet."

"Can't what? Tell me?"

She glances down at our hands and shakes her head. "I will soon, but I'm not ready to tell you yet. Soon." Her voice breaks on the last word and my heart cracks a fraction.

The more her spirit plummets, the more I ache for answers. But I can't pry them out of her. Tiffany needs to do this at her own pace. Tell me piece by piece of her own volition.

"Okay." I clasp her hands between both of mine and clamp down. "Whatever it is, when you're ready to tell me, I'm here. And I'm not going anywhere."

Tiffany nods. Leaning into the empty space between us,

she presses her lips to mine. "Thank you." I kiss her again, framing her face in my hands. Her lips salty from the few tears that escaped and sweet from dessert. "We can set a date. But I have one request."

My heart ping-pongs between my lungs. "Name it."

Inches from kissing her again, I stop myself when she answers. "The wedding needs to be a year or more away."

Hurt creeps up from my belly, clenching my heart like an angry fist and evaporating the air in my lungs. Obviously, I wear my pain on my face because Tiffany flinches. I haven't the slightest idea how to respond to her. So, I give her a generic answer.

"Sure, Tiff. Whatever you want."

The fist around my heart tightens, another crack forming. But I will do this for her. Anything for her.

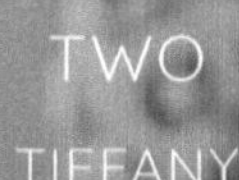

TWO

TIFFANY

Last night was more than uncomfortable.

Every molecule in my body screamed for me to tell Liz. To confess the burden which has plagued me for the last decade. But when it came down to it, I couldn't do it. Couldn't get the words past my lips. As desperately as I wanted to relay my past, I sat frozen and weak.

I help people with similar situations on a regular basis, yet can't do the same for myself. Probably should set an appointment with my own therapist. Soon. Dishing out the advice and expertise always seems easier than utilizing it. When it is you with the issue, the countless hours and years of training and knowledge fly out the window.

Poof.

"Hey, girl," Chloe says, stepping into my office. "Doing all right? You look exhausted."

Chloe Lewis. My boss. The owner of Lewis House. A kind and generous soul with a past she refuses to let run her future. I wish I had her strength.

She opened Lewis House thirteen years ago, three years after her fifteen-year-old son, Taylor, committed suicide. Chloe doesn't work on the psych side of things, but wanted to provide a safe place for people, of any age, to discuss alternatives to suicide. Slightly conventional, but more relaxed and welcoming than a typical psychiatry office or hospital psych ward. Lewis House has on-sight patients as well as former patients who come for follow-up sessions. On occasion, we also see new patients who are "on the fence" and need someone to guide them down a healthy path.

"A little on the tired side. Had a rough night. Think I need to sit down with Trina."

Chloe nods. "Need time off? You know you can have it anytime, right?"

"I know, but no. I'll shoot her an email and chat with her later. Working helps."

"Okay. Well, let me know if anything changes."

"I will. Thanks, Chloe. What did you need?"

Chloe hands me a small stack of file folders. "Just wanted to give these to you. Recent discharges. You always like to be the first to touch base with them."

One of my tasks at Lewis House is to check in with discharged patients. Although it isn't officially in my job description, it gives me peace of mind to follow up with each of them. And the other doctors on staff don't seem to mind I take on the task.

"Thank you. I'll keep you up to date with each of them."

Chloe heads for the door but stops just on the other side of the doorjamb. Her shoulder-length medium-blonde hair sweeps over her sunny-yellow blazer. "Want to grab lunch today?" A slight smile perks up the corners of her lips.

Her sincerity is warm honey coating all the sore parts inside me. "I'd love that, Chloe. One good with you?"

"Yes. I'll meet you in the café at one."

Chloe shuffles out my door and goes left, probably finishing her rounds for the first half of the day. Working at Lewis House has been a blessing in more ways than one. Not only do I have the opportunity to help others—mostly teens —but I get help in return. Not just the free, in-house psychia-try. There is something magical about helping other people that alleviates the ache harboring in my soul.

It is no secret we all have personal issues. Really, who doesn't? My past was this dark cloud hovering overhead and following me no matter where I went. But after hours and hours of chatting with my old psychiatrist, and some major life-changing decisions, here I am. Life isn't always laughter and hugs and sunshine, but it is a hell of a lot better than it once was.

Honestly, if I hadn't made those choices when I did, there is no telling how my life would be today.

I sift through the files Chloe handed me and make a list of who I will call and when. Calling the previous patients is one of my favorite parts. To hear their voice on the other end, full of light and life and exuberance. One of the best and fulfilling parts of this job is seeing the impact we make on someone's life. That they choose to live and go forward. That they rediscover all the joys around them and find new ones.

After I call Trina and make an appointment for later this afternoon, I check my patient roster for the day. Only one patient meeting before lunch today, Jensen Pastor. Jensen has been with Lewis House for a week now. We have sat down together twice, in which I did ninety-five percent of the talking and he sat there stone-faced.

Jensen arrived at Lewis House the day after he was admitted to the emergency room with a bottle's worth of sleeping pills in his stomach, body limp, and incoherent. As of now, Jensen will be an inpatient with Lewis House for at least the next couple of months. If not longer. Followed by extensive outpatient treatment.

Most facilities don't keep patients as long as Lewis House does. The reason we opted for longer periods of time was because evidence has proven our patients show better signs of improvement with the extensive treatment and easy accessibility to a health care provider.

I open his file on my tablet and review my notes from our previous visit. Today, my goal is to get him talking. Even if only a few more sentences than our previous visits, it would be an improvement.

Once I have everything ready, and my head is clear and in the right frame of mind, I rise from my desk and walk down the hall to the patient wing.

Lewis House is huge. No lie, the building is easily fifteen thousand square feet. Maybe more. The bottom floor is where the majority of the doctors, nurses, and executive staff have offices. Also, on the bottom floor is where the red-flagged patients are housed. Red-flagged patients are those with the highest risk of self-harm. After extensive therapy, they graduate to green-flagged and relocate to the second floor.

The second floor houses fewer doctors, but has nurses on staff twenty-four seven. Patients on the second floor are in the process of going home and having outpatient appointments. The ultimate goal of Lewis House is to give every person who walks through our doors a reason to want to leave. A reason to move forward and love the life they were given.

I swipe my keycard through a slot next to the double doors of the first-floor ward, then place my palm on the scanner below it and enter a code onto a keypad. Once my credentials are verified the door buzzes and I walk onto the ward.

The space is vast when you first step through the doors. Walls painted a soft, pale yellow. Art strategically placed on the ward—behind the nurse's station, along the halls, and in the communal area. The pieces placed high on the walls so they cannot easily be reached. Some of the pieces painted or drawn by previous patients, others simply inspirational pieces Chloe purchased from local artists.

In the communal area, the furniture is simple. Soft, cream couches with no harsh edges. Matching and equally comfy chairs. A handful of card tables with collapsible chairs. On a far wall, shelves are built into the space and have a plethora of games and books.

At Lewis House, Chloe didn't want it to feel like a penitentiary. Although the patients are here because of extreme circumstances, they shouldn't be punished for how they feel. Being unhappy with your life shouldn't be a punishment, and our goal is to help them all see the optimism in the world. Even when it is most challenging.

Walking up to the nurse's station, I greet and wave at each of them. "Hey, Patrick. Gina. Juan. How are things today?"

"Morning Dr. Page, the ward has been quiet. Nothing noteworthy to report," Juan answers. Juan is one of the senior nurses on staff.

"Glad to hear it. I'm speaking with Jensen this morning. Anything I need to know since my last visit?"

Juan glances to Patrick and Gina, both of whom shake their head. "No, Dr. Page. He still keeps to himself. During communal time, he sits alone on the couch and doesn't speak or interact."

I nod. "Thank you, Juan." Making a couple notes in Jensen's chart on the tablet, I wander away from the nurse's station and down the hall where each patient on the floor has a bedroom. Most rooms are individual, but a few rooms can house two patients.

When I reach room one-thirteen, I knock on the door frame. None of the rooms on the first floor have doors. Privacy is a luxury not awarded until patients move to the second floor. There are nooks that hide them from the hall, where most of them change clothing. Restrooms are also semi-exposed to the hall, but the actual toilet and shower not visible unless someone makes an effort to look into the bathroom.

"Jensen? You awake?" I ask as I step into the room.

The rooms are basic. A bed with no headboard or sharp edges or corners. A bedside table with two deep drawers—also no noticeable corners—where they store four sets of undergarments, socks, and scrubs provided by Lewis House. All the patients also provided with shoes which require no laces. Laundry washed every Tuesday, Thursday, and Saturday. Towels provided at time of need. There are no mirrors, glass, bars, or metal. All of which is pretty standard on most psychiatric wards.

One thing Lewis House does not have, but you would find at most psychiatric facilities, is the clinical smell. Bleach and chemicals and sanitizer galore. Nope. Chloe searched long and hard for cleaners which held the standard for health facilities, but were calming and pleasant. Lavender and jasmine and rosemary and peppermint. We rotate through each of the scents weekly.

Besides the scents, Chloe also added subtle relaxing music. It plays quietly through speakers in the ceiling twenty-four seven. Waves crashing on the beach shoreline. Birds chirping. A trickling ravine. Wind blowing through the trees and rustling the leaves.

Thanks to my parents—insert sarcasm—I knew what a psych ward looked like at an early age. What parent thinks it is okay to bring their child to work, on a psych ward, at the brimming age of four? When your mind is so impressionable and things are engrained so easily. My father, that is who.

Not that my mom was much better. Always poking and prodding me as Dr. Elaine Page, pediatrician, rather than hugging and cuddling with me as my mom. Dad thought it wise to teach me early on that not everyone was "normal". His word choice, not mine. As a psychologist, you would think my father would know how much that experience scared the shit out of me. But nope. Between the ages of four and eleven, I visited psych wards so often I wanted to be checked in.

My father believes the reason I became a clinical psychologist is strictly because of his efforts in my youth. I let him believe his truth. But I know differently.

"Jensen?"

I walk farther into the room and spot Jensen on the bed, curled into the fetal position and facing away from the door. The universal sign for "leave me the hell alone." But I ignore it.

Stepping past the bed, I stand in front of him and scan his face. Eyes open and staring at the wall in front of him. The wall has a small window which starts around the seven-foot mark. Only two feet tall and five feet wide. Just enough to allow light to come in the room during the day. No curtains or blinds. The mid-morning sun lightens his already sun-bleached blond hair and glints in his smoky topaz eyes, but his solemn demeanor dulls both.

"Jensen, will you come sit with me in the communal room? I'd like for us to chat for a bit."

A minute passes, I don't move an inch and neither does he. I refuse to cave and allow him to lay in here and wallow. After a few minutes, Jensen realizes I have no plans to leave and rolls his eyes shut.

Sucking in a deep breath, he huffs out, "Fine." No enthusiasm or sarcasm or emotion whatsoever.

After he rises from the bed and leads the way out of the room, we walk to one of the couches in the communal room and sit on opposite ends. Jensen draws his knees to his chest and hugs them tight, setting his chin atop them.

"Jensen, today I would like us to both talk. Okay? I know

being here isn't what you want, but there are worse places. Today, I'd like you to start. Talk to me about what started the path to you ending up here."

We sit in silence on the couch for countless minutes. Jensen stares past me, more than likely hoping to return to his room without exchange. Not happening today. Today, I will get more than five words out of him.

While he remains quiet, I type notes into his chart on the tablet. Out of the corner of my eye, I notice his arms shift and his legs slide down into a cross-legged position. *Finally.* I finish the note then glance up at him.

Jensen studies me a moment, slowly tilting his head side to side. For someone who plays coy during every interaction, Jensen is smart. Highly intelligent, actually. When I initially scanned his file, I glimpsed his education history and his IQ. A score of one-twenty-two doesn't just pop up every day and shouldn't be taken for granted. Jensen, more than likely, could outwit most people. He has attempted to outwit me more than once. But I know his tactics.

After a solid five minutes, our visual stare-down ends, and Jensen finally speaks.

"Why?"

Not that I expected anything different to come from his mouth. "It matters to me, Jensen. Although we didn't know each other then, I would like to know what brought you to this point. What hurt you so much, you opted to harm yourself."

Jensen rolls his eyes before looking away from me and stares out the window facing the outdoor gardens. Gardens only visited by staff and second-floor patients. His eyes zero in on a young girl on a bench under a tree. The image of her slightly hazy through the polycarbonate window.

"Have you ever felt like everyone depends on you to make their life better?" His thoughts spill out in a whisper laced with pain. He doesn't look back at me, but continues to stare at the girl in the garden.

"Yes, Jensen, I have. Does someone make you feel this way?"

The corner of his mouth twitches for a split-second. "You could say that." He stares at the girl a moment before bringing his gaze back to me. "The day my parents had me tested for the gifted program was supposed to be a happy day. Instead, it became one of the worst days of my life. The day I went from being Jensen, John and Margot's cute son, to being Jensen, John and Margot's ticket to millions." He rests his chin atop his knees again, a tear slipping down his cheek. "God, I was nine, for fuck's sake. A damn kid. I'm still a damn kid. But they didn't care. Still don't care. They shoved me in every possible free program that would benefit *me*. At least what they told everyone. It wasn't until I hit high school that I really noticed their motives."

Jensen swipes at his cheeks and sniffles. Already today, he has amazed me. With his bravery and strength. It takes a hell of a lot of courage to open up and share what shreds your heart.

"Did they do something in particular at this specific point in high school?"

He pinches his eyes together tightly. Hugs his legs even tighter. Obviously, this is not easy for him. Not that it should be. How does a child recover from deceit? Especially deceit from someone significant in their life.

"After school one day during my sophomore year, I came home to my parents and a guest. A man who could help me fulfill *my potential*. That's what my parents called it. It was weird, but I sat down and listened to what he had to say. Basically, he was recruiting *kids like me* and had *opportunities to better my future*. Like the good son I am, I listened to every word, took the pamphlet, and researched him after he left. After hours of surfing the web, I learned my parents wanted to ship me off to the middle of nowhere, where the children helped with scientific research, and the parents were handed a fat check. When I confronted my parents, they denied knowing about the financial end of the deal. But I'm no fool and saw past the dollar signs glowing like a neon sign in my parents' eyes. One day when I was home alone, I dug through every drawer and hiding spot in the house. Eventually, I found what I was looking for. The letter."

Jensen stops, sits up straighter, and buries his face in his palms. Tears streaming down his cheeks. More than ever, I wish it wasn't unethical to hug him right now. To give him the comfort he so obviously needs. Has needed for a long time. But I sit stock still and wait for him to regain his composure. Wait for him to be ready to let go of the pain wrenching his soul.

A river of tears later, Jensen wipes his nose against the sleeve of his shirt and continues. "Most parents would say their child is priceless." He shakes his head as an empty laugh spills from his throat. "Not my parents, though. They put a price tag on my life and were ready to ship me away with a complete stranger. With no idea if we would see one another again. Who the hell does that? Who the hell sells their kid for two-hundred-thousand dollars?"

In some respects, I relate to Jensen. Relate to having parents who are willing to sell a piece of you for money or image. But I lock up my personal issues and listen to Jensen. This is not the time or place to allow my mind to wander to such thoughts.

"How long ago was it that you found the letter?" I ask.

After a few deep breaths, Jensen closes his eyes. "A few months ago. The letter said my parents would receive the check from the institute upon my delivery. On the letter, there was a date. They were scheduled to take me two days ago. So, I stopped them—the institute and my parents—from winning."

God, all I want to do is tell Jensen it will all be okay. That he will survive this and be stronger than ever. And somehow it will all work out for the better. But I can't because everyone processes things differently. He will get past it, but who knows how his life will be on the other side.

"Jensen, do you have any other relatives or friends you can stay with after you leave Lewis House?"

I have to know whether or not he will have a safe place to go when his time here is over. There is no way in hell I will allow him to go back to his parents. Not two people willing to sell their child for no reason other than greed. Utterly disgusting.

He shakes his head. "No. I don't think so, anyway. When my parents got together, my mother and her parents became estranged. They didn't approve of my father. And I've never met or heard mention of his parents." He pauses and sniffles again. "As far as friends, I'm kind of a loner at school. Most kids my age are more concerned with social media and sex, not libraries and learning as much as possible."

Glancing at the time on the tablet, I note that Jensen and I have been sitting here for just over an hour. And today, he did the majority of the talking. Not only am I proud of his strength and bravery, but also this major step he took. Trusting me with the pains piercing his heart.

"I make no promises, Jensen, but I will do what I can to make sure you do not go back to your parents. Sending people back into a toxic environment is the opposite of what we are trying to achieve here. Just hang in there. Listen to the nurses and don't miss appointments or opportunities to talk. Okay?"

Jensen nods. "Yes, Dr. Page." He sighs heavily. "Thank you for making me talk today. I feel better."

I smile as I close the cover on the tablet. "You are most welcome, Jensen. I'm glad you were able to talk with me."

We rise from the couch and walk separate directions. Jensen back to his room. Me down the hall and out of the patient wing. My time with Jensen today was groundbreaking. He released so much pent-up anger and hurt. Little does he know, he also inspired me to want to do the same.

Lunch with Chloe was uneventful. We discuss patients. Touch on some new ideas for Lewis House. Chloe asks my opinion on having therapy animals come to Lewis House twice a week. Allowing lower-risk patients to spend time with them. Honestly, the idea is fantastic. So many patients recover quicker and easier when therapy animals are introduced into the mix.

When we part ways, Chloe has an extra hop in her step. I love her devotion to helping others. It doesn't make up for her loss, but helps counteract it to some degree. Unfortunately, Chloe and her husband, Stanton, missed so many of the signs their son, Taylor, displayed. In no way are they over losing their only child, but they will do whatever they can to make sure they save as many others as possible.

Shortly after returning from lunch, I head down to Trina's office. Dr. Trina Long, senior psychiatrist on staff, has been helping teens for over twenty years. Her loyalty astounds and inspires me. One day, I hope to be where she is today.

I knock on her office door and wait. The door swings open seconds later. "Dr. Page. Tiffany. Please, come in." She steps aside and waves her hand toward a set of chairs in her office.

Trina's office is warm and inviting. Creams and tans and rich browns. Hints on lemon and leather and lacquered wood. Most of the doctor's offices look identical—desks, chair, book-shelves, and electronics. But each of us adds our own touches. Trina's office has brass-studded, brown leather chairs with a matching couch. An espresso-lacquered oak table is parked in front of the couch with a small potted fern in the center. A few watercolor paintings hang on the walls which depict ponds and trees.

Every time I step into Trina's office, a warm embrace wraps around me and holds on for a beat. Walking in, I take a seat and cross my legs at the ankle. "Thank you for seeing me today, Trina. I appreciate it."

Trina sits down across from me. No notepad or pen or tablet. Although this is a professional session, between the staff here, we don't officially record our sessions. We do these sessions as a courtesy to one another. Each of us knowing we need to get things off our chest just as much as the next person.

"Of course. What did you want to talk about?"

Dragging in a deep breath, I exhale slowly. "Liz is upset because we haven't set a date for the wedding yet." I close my eyes for a moment before reopening them. "And I'm the reason we haven't set a date."

Trina nods, hands crossed in her lap, and studies my expression. "Are you scared to get married?"

A vicious rhythm vibrates in my chest as sweat pricks my skin. *Just tell her. She can't tell anyone.* No, I can't say anything. Not yet. "Yes and no."

Trina sits stoically across from me. "Care to elaborate?"

Internally, I berate myself for holding back. Trina won't pass along a word I say to Liz. With absolute certainty, I know this. So why am I terrified to tell Trina the truth? I wish I could scream it at the top of my lungs. But my lips remain glued shut.

"There're some past issues I need to resolve first. Once I fix those, I will be able to move forward. Until then, it's not fair to give Liz a date when I may not be able to follow through."

She nods again. Trina spends a lot of time during every session nodding. Her version of acknowledgment without stealing the spotlight from the person who should be speaking. If anything, I have learned to mimic this trait during my sessions more and more. It drives results.

"Why wouldn't you be able to follow through?" Trina prompts. "What holds you back?"

"Ugh." I clamp my eyes tightly together. "God, I want to tell you. Tell someone. But..." I trail off.

"What?"

"I... I can't..."

Why can't I fucking say the words? Why can't I complete this one specific sentence? It unnerves the hell out of me. Pisses me off that this one predicament still rules my life. After all these years, I am still a prisoner. Even thousands of miles away.

"Tiffany, I have no idea what it is you are harboring. Whatever it is, until you find a way to let it go, you will never get past it. Ever. Some situations stick with us for years. Decades. But it doesn't have to be that way. When you're ready, we're all here for you. Liz, too."

She is right. Deep down in my bones, I know she is. But when I abandoned that part of my life, I never thought it would resurface. And I never thought I would have to revisit its headstone. Yet, here I am. Standing in the cemetery of my past with a shovel, slowly digging holes.

I just hope I don't end up in a plot when all is said and done.

SINCE OUR WEDDING conversation last week, where hope soared for one second before it was squashed like a pesky insect, Tiffany has spent more time than usual at work. Out the door a half-hour or more early. Home an hour plus late.

The irrational side of me believes she is purposely avoiding me. Finding reasons to stay away so I don't force any future conversations regarding the wedding, *our wedding,* down her throat. Not that I would do such a thing. Would it be nice to *actually* plan the day we vow to be with each other for all eternity? Yeah, it would be more than nice. But I refuse to force Tiffany to do anything.

On the other hand, my sensible side says Tiffany is working hard. For her to be putting in extra hours, a new patient must need her attention. She does everything within her power to help countless kids who need someone when they potentially have no one. I get why she does it. Why she helps them. Her drive to save others. It's one of the reasons I love her.

Then the little green monster in my head pops up and says… *What about me? What about us?*

Doesn't our relationship require nurturing and work and help and love just as much as her patients? The last thing I want is our relationship to be classified as a job, but, as of recent, it seems to be more work than any job I collected a paycheck from. And I refuse to be left to the wayside.

Forgotten like a sticky note buried under a stack of folders on a desk.

I matter, damnit.

I count.

Picking up my phone, I click the side button and check the time. Ten after six. She should have left work over an hour ago. Each day, she leaves later and later. By the time she gets home, we scarf down our dinner with minimal conversation before she complains how tired she is and heads for the bedroom. We literally have zero time together. Quality time, anyway. Sometimes, we are more roommates versus lovers. Being engaged seems more a formality than a reality.

Frustrated as hell, I type out a text to her, smacking the screen harder than necessary with each word I write.

Liz: Planning on being home for dinner? My stomach will eat me soon.

I stare at the screen and zone out as I wait for her to respond. The screen dims and goes black before the little bubble pops up. Five minutes later, my phone pings as the screen lights up.

Tiff: Leaving in a sec. Sorry. Was talking with Trina.

Trina. One of the shrinks at Lewis House, I know for a fact, she talks to when she needs to get shit off her chest. Shit she doesn't want to talk to me about. Shit she *should* be talking to me about. Her goddamn fiancée. Probably told her the reason why she hasn't helped me pick a date for the wedding yet.

Suddenly, every inch of my skin ignites as my blood heats like a lava river under the surface. Every thought in my head flips and tells me Tiffany is just prolonging the inevitable. That she doesn't want to marry me. That she only said yes out of pity.

Fucking bullshit.

Liz: Still doesn't answer my question.

Not that I expect you to is what I want to add after the fact, but I keep my fingers at bay. As badly as I want to yell and scream and shake the hell out of Tiffany—maybe the answers will fall out of her—I suck it up and pretend as if her noncommittal to a date isn't killing me.

But it's a lie. I'm dying inside.

Tiff: Want me to grab takeout? Might be easier.
Liz: Guess so. Don't care what you get. You know what I like.
Tiff: Walking out now. Be home soon with dinner.

And just like that, one crisis—my Venus flytrap of a stomach—averted. With Tiffany bringing dinner home, it gives us a little more time together and less time cleaning up. Maybe I can wiggle some information out of her and learn what she has been talking to Trina about.

If I get lucky, maybe she will tell me why she is so hell-bent on not picking a date.

After we stuff our faces with Thai food, Tiffany plops down beside me on the couch with an ice cream bar. We both devoured more than one serving of our meals, plus spring rolls. How the hell does she still have room for dessert?

Peeling back the brown and green wrapper, she brings the chocolate-covered confection to her lips, bites down, and moans. I love her moans. The throaty way she begs for more. Too bad that ice cream bar is getting more action than me.

"Wish I was an ice cream bar," I tease.

Tiffany looks over at me and smiles, guilt creasing her brow. "Sorry," she mumbles around the chilly treat.

"Can I ask you something?"

Her shoulders sag as she huffs. "Sure." Tiffany did her best to give me a confident answer, but the edge of her voice is laced with irritation. Irritation that is really starting to piss me off. If anyone should be irritated, it's me. I'm the one who sits around with unanswered questions. I'm the one giving and giving and not getting anything in return.

"What are you talking with Trina about?" Mentally, I stare

up to the heavens and pray to whatever deity will listen. *Please give me something. Please tell me you're trying to fix whatever is stopping you from wanting to marry me.*

"Can't say much, but recently we've been discussing a new patient of mine. She's helping me work through some countertransference."

"Counter-what?"

"Countertransference. It's when a therapist feels a connection with a client. Happens way more often than most people realize. Trina is guiding me through the proper channels to try and turn it off. So to speak."

"Can I ask what type of connection you've been feeling?"

Rules of doctor-patient confidentiality… you cannot say anything that would divulge privileged information in reference to a patient. The only time that rule doesn't apply is if the patient's life is in danger—from themselves or someone else.

"Uh." Tiffany looks up to the ceiling and taps a finger on her chin. "Specific instances with his family have stirred up past emotions for me. They've also brought irrational thoughts to the surface."

"Irrational thoughts?"

Tiffany winces. "I gave serious consideration to adopting the kid once he's out of the program."

"Is that even allowed?" I shriek. Why the hell would Tiffany think about adopting some kid? How random is that shit? Better yet, why the hell hasn't she mentioned this to me *at all*?

Beside me, Tiffany bites her ice cream bar and shrugs. She seems so nonchalant about this whole scenario. Does she not think this is odd whatsoever? Wanting to adopt a child without speaking to your significant other. If our roles were reversed, no doubt she would be freaking the hell out next to me.

"You don't know? Or you don't care?"

She swallows the bite of ice cream in her mouth. "Don't know."

"I don't want to get into a fight, but can you please explain to me, as much as possible, why you haven't brought this up to me once. Isn't this something we should've talked about?

Sometimes, I wonder if you ever take into account how I'd feel at all." The last part comes out in a mumble, but I couldn't resist putting it out there.

Taking her sweet ass time, Tiffany sets the wrapper and stick to her dessert on the table. "I didn't bring it up to you because it seemed irrational. Oftentimes, therapists develop feelings for patients. It's not uncommon. But it's inappropriate. Honestly, I thought it would be easier to have Trina help me counteract what I was feeling. Although, it doesn't appear to be working much." She frowns and sags into the couch more.

Tiffany stares at her lap as her fingers fumble with the hem of her shirt. Seeing her like this, so unsure of herself, is so off-putting. Especially when she exudes confidence when it comes to her work.

"Irrational or not, I really wish you'd talk to me. Ever since I proposed, it feels like you have jumped ship and left me to drift alone at sea."

For the first time in weeks, I let Tiffany know how much her reluctance to be an active part in our relationship has weighed me down. She has a past. I get it. Not like I don't have history either. But to let her past eat her alive and hold her hostage from being happy ever again... is preposterous.

Living in your own head will never fix problems. The only way to counteract your past is to share the burden with others. To let them listen. To let them help you through the trenches so you come out on the other side with minimal scars.

Tiffany reaches across the space between us and takes my hand from my lap. Bringing it closer to her, she cradles my hand between both of hers. "I'm sorry if it feels like I've abandoned you. Believe me when I say that is the farthest from my intentions." She continues staring at my hand encased in hers as a tear rolls down her cheek. "So sorry I've been so wrapped up in stuff," Tiffany whispers.

With my free hand, I tip her chin up. "Hey. Please don't cry. I hate it when you cry." Tiffany nods. "But I need you to talk to me. I'm going crazy over here. Thinking up every worst-case scenario as to why you don't want to pick a date.

Why you don't want to marry me. Why we talk less and less with each passing day."

Eyes as blue as a glacier stare back at me, melting. Spilling all the hurt and pain of her past down her cheeks. Whatever happened in her past, it is bad. Not just bad. Crazy bad. For Tiffany to withhold the details from me, that is the only viable reason. Whoever did this to her, she is terrified it will happen again if she says anything. Maybe I should try another tactic with her. Maybe I can *guess* the answer and she won't have to speak a word of it.

"Tiff, maybe there's another way for us to get past this."

Her eyes perk up. "Another way?"

"Yeah. What if I guess whatever is bothering you, and you tell me if I'm hot or cold? Is that doable?"

Her eyes glaze over for a moment as she ponders over the possibility of me guessing what has her so petrified. After a few jagged breaths, she slowly nods.

"That sounds like something to try." She tells me it's okay to go forward, but her expression screams a million other things. The most prominent tells me she hopes I don't figure it out. Part of me hopes I don't. But at least she is trying.

The fact she is willing to give this a shot, willing to find a way to resolve this gap dividing us, gives me conviction. Now, here comes the shitty part. Me trying to think of all the possible things that could've happened to her. Horrible things.

"You ready?" I ask.

Tiffany inhales deeply. "Think so."

I squeeze her hand in mine. "Were you mugged?" It's a long shot, but I have to start somewhere.

"Cold," she answers.

"Bullied?"

Tiffany teeters her head side to side. "Lukewarm."

Lukewarm on being bullied. Perhaps it wobbles on the edge of bullying.

"Abused?" The second the word leaves my lips, I hate I asked her this. Pray her answer is no.

"Hot."

Fuck. I work to control my expression. To not let it slip and show how much this pains me and also pisses me off. Who would hurt Tiffany like that? And why?

No wonder why she is skittish about being fully committed to someone. *Hot.* This explains a whole hell of a lot. Inhaling deeply, I prepare to trudge forward, hoping she will continue to answer.

"Parents?"

She closes her eyes for a heartbeat. "Lukewarm."

Damnit. If the abuse wasn't mainly her parents, it doesn't leave many other options. Neither one of us has ever mentioned having siblings. As an only child, I don't often consider the fact that other people have siblings.

"Sibling?"

Tiffany shakes her head. "Cold. Although I do have a brother and a sister." Her face lights up for a second before a gloominess takes back over.

"Someone you dated?"

"Hot."

In the blink of an eye, everything in my vision goes red. No idea who did this to Tiffany, but if I ever meet the mother-fucker, I will kill them. No one has the right to hurt another person. Not like this.

As I attempt to restrain the anger boiling in my veins, Tiffany cries harder beside me. Her body visibly shakes as the pain of her past wracks every inch of her body. Pain I wish I could erase and replace with love and passion and a life without tears. Except for happy tears—those are completely acceptable.

Guessing game time is over. Seeing her like this is unbearable.

"Come here." I open my arms wide and beckon her forward.

Tiffany scoots closer and flops into my embrace, sobbing endlessly. I hold her impossibly close and hug her pain away as much as humanly possible. It irks me to no end that someone did this to her. Someone who she chose to be with. Who she trusted on such an intimate level. They stole a piece of her and refuse to return it. Refuse to set her free. What kind of hideous person does such a thing?

Seconds turn into minutes. Minutes feel more like hours.

Eventually, Tiffany stops crying and falls asleep clinging to me. Never in my life have I wanted to tear someone apart, limb by limb. I have never hated another human so much in my life. And I have never met the person.

But whoever did this. Whoever hurt my girl. This isn't the end of it. Not by a long shot.

FOUR

TIFFANY

I STARTLE AWAKE DRENCHED in a cold puddle of sweat. Lungs heaving. An icepick piercing my heart. Body shaking uncontrollably. Nightmare fresh in my memory.

Fuck.

Years have come and gone since the last time I had one of *those* nightmares. The ones where I am back in Florida and *he* is there. Hovering over me with a snarl of his lip and eyes as black as death. And no matter how many times I blink or breathe methodically or shake my head, *he* is still there. Lurking. Waiting.

I don't blame Liz. She means well and just wants to help. But the only plausible explanation for my nightmare to rear its ugly head is her guessing game after dinner last night. The game where Liz probed into my past and learned a little more about where I came from. And to be completely honest, it's a past I never want unearthed. Not fully, anyway.

"You okay?" Liz asks, raspy with sleep, as she touches my arm.

I jump at her touch and scream. "Argh! Shit! Sorry!" I spin my body on the bed and dangle my feet off the side of the mattress. Hanging my head, I cover my face with my hands. "Didn't mean to scream. Or yell. Sorry," I mumble.

Liz brushes her knuckles up and down my spine, in an effort to soothe my obvious fear and anxiety. After my breathing settles, she asks, "Did you have a bad dream?"

I chuckle without humor. "That's putting it lightly."

She continues her soothing strokes on my back and I close my eyes as I get lost in her touch. "Is this because of last night? Because I asked all those questions."

Lifting my head, I turn back to face her. A grimace mars her face before her chin dips to her chest and her shoulders sag forward. Clearly, Liz harbors guilt over my nightmare. Since we have been together, I haven't experienced a single nightmare. The night I open myself up, even for just a taste of what happened years ago, and reveal one of the skeletons in my closet, I wake up dripping wet and freaking out. So I get why she feels guilty.

I won't lie to her. Won't sugarcoat the past or the truth. Sugarcoating it doesn't resolve a thing. "Yes."

If possible, her back bows further as she slumps closer to the mattress. "Damn, Tiff. I'm so, so sorry. Had I known this would've been the result, I wouldn't have tried to guess."

The last thing I want Liz to feel is guilt over something she has zero control over. She can't control what *he* did as much as I could've in the beginning. She also can't control the fact it is part of who I am. "You didn't know. How could you? It's a good and bad thing. At least now you know."

Liz drags me into her arms and holds me tighter than ever before. "At least now I know."

The alarm clock flashes beside me and I become mesmerized by the two dots between the hour and minutes. No matter how many times it flashes, I don't look away. But eventually we slip out of bed, knowing neither of us will get any more sleep. Not tonight—well technically, this morning.

Liz hauls me to the kitchen and has me sit at the breakfast bar as she flips pancakes on the griddle pan. Maple and simmering apples and cinnamon float in the air. Watching Liz move around in the kitchen is a sight to behold. I'm a voyeur as she creates magic and plates love. Although, at times, she can be a little neurotic in the kitchen—I learned this quickly when we hosted Thanksgiving the first time—she is an extraordinary cook. Occasionally, she uses recipes from online or a cookbook or something passed down from one of her grandmothers. But most of the time, she just wings it.

Liz's best friend, and my friend since Liz and I have been

together, Sarah, always insinuates Liz should attend culinary school. No matter how many times the idea is mentioned, Liz always waves it off, telling us she wouldn't love being in the kitchen quite the same if she let it become a technical skill or her job.

Liz plates buttered pancakes, douses them in maple syrup, cinnamon cooked apples, and plant-based breakfast sausage. After she sets our dishes on the placemats, she brews us each a coffee. She adds cream and sugar to mine and leaves hers black.

Minutes pass as we dive in and guzzle down all the deliciousness. Once our plates are empty, I clean the dishes. Since it's Saturday, and we both have the day off, we plan to go hiking.

Shortly after we arrived in California, Liz and I grabbed every tourist brochure and guide we got our hands on in a ten-mile radius. Over the last couple of years, we have slowly ticked off various different adventures. Too many expeditions lie in our backyard, so to speak. And we are eager to explore them all.

After we shower and dress, we hop in the car and drive toward Runyon Canyon Park. Several people we have met and chatted with during previous hiking excursions recommended the trails in the park. Needless to say, both of us are over the moon to hike the trails and get lost in the park. According to the weather forecast, today is predicted to be perfect. Sunny. Warm, but not hot. A slight breeze. Barely a cloud in the sky. Through the tint of my sunglasses, the forecast is proving accurate.

Liz weaves through a lot and parks the car. As soon as we are out of the car, we grab our CamelBaks and the small backpack with snacks from the trunk. Suited up, we trek through the lot toward the entrance for the park's foot traffic.

At the trailhead is a wooden sign with the entire trail carved and painted into the grain. The massive sign makes me feel small, but not as small as standing next to a redwood. All in all, we learn there is actually three routes for the trail. Beginner, experienced, and extremist. Those are the names someone wrote on a paper and attached below where it says 'easy, medium, and challenging'. We opt to walk the medium trail, ready to up our hiking game, and grab a map from the holder on the post.

I study the map a moment as we stroll along the trail, hand in hand. The first half mile of the trail is open. Blue, cloudless sky stretches for miles above us. Once we pass this segment of the trail, most of the path will be littered with shrubbery, various-sized trees, and abundant animal life. The higher elevation without tree canopy grants us a bird's-eye view of the city. Up here, things are different. Life is different.

The air is lighter and cleaner. Sun pinks your skin easier. The scent of dusty earth and evergreens and elderberry wafts up my nose as the breeze whips my ponytail against my cheek. A sense of peace wraps its metaphorical wings around me and takes hold—helping me breathe easier and relieving me of my burdens.

This is exactly what I needed. Time away from the incessant noise and to be surrounded by nothing but nature. No cell phone access. No people buzzing nearby. Nothing except me and Liz and the earth beneath our feet. Absolute perfection.

"Thanks for suggesting we come here today, Lizzie. For the first time in days, I can breathe again."

Liz squeezes my hand and glances over at me. Eyes hidden behind her sunglasses, her stare bores into me as her smile beams and cheeks glow. With minimal effort, Liz makes my heart bang, bang, bang beneath my sternum. Never takes much to send my heart skyrocketing into the stratosphere when it comes to Liz. When we met, I instantly knew she was different than anyone else I'd dated.

Liz exudes confidence as easily as breathing. Her confidence isn't overwhelming or domineering. It doesn't assault or belittle you. If anything, it lifts you up and boosts your own confidence.

"I thought you might want to get away from everything for a little while. Step away from all the people and commotion."

Between us, I swing our hands back and forth. "It's perfect." I spin us so we face each other, tug her into me, and plant my lips on hers.

We stop moving, the kiss starts off gentle and sweet. My

heart sprints down the trail as the intensity of our kiss builds and burns hotter with each swipe of our tangled tongues. The warmth and taste of apples and cinnamon on Liz's lips has me melting into her embrace. Until someone brushes past us and giggles, reminding us where we are. Our lips break apart before Liz rests her forehead to mine with a bright, toothy smile on her face. Public displays don't bother or stop us from expressing our affection for each other. And the extent of our displays has gone much farther in the past.

Once we compose ourselves, we continue walking the trail with our fingers laced together. Every now and again, we point out various birds, wildlife, and intriguing plant-life along the trail. Parts of the trail edge near the famous Hollywood sign. Up close, the sign is colossal. But I'd much rather see the hawks and snakes—from a distance—and deer. Watch the wind blow the treetops and kick up bits of earth.

Thirty minutes into our excursion, Liz directs us off the main trail and down a valley. "Where are we going?" I ask as I halt my next step forward and lean to the side and peer down the valley. The park posts signs on the trail for reason informing hikers to not veer off.

"There's something I want to show you. Saw it online and thought you would love it."

We walk a hundred feet down the small valley, trees and bushes shrouding us from every direction but where our feet step, before it opens up to a vast open stretch of land. I stop and suck in a breath. The view is incredible.

Blue skies and bluer water for miles. Trees and earth and silence stretch out all around us. In the center of the large rock platform we're standing on is a tremendous mandala created with rocks and branches. Beautiful is the only word my brain can form to describe the sight in front of me.

The sight steals my breath as a mass of energy vibrates throughout my body. As if I'm standing in the epicenter of an energy vortex and nothing but love and light and strength surround and consume me. It lifts me up and provides me with a sense of wholeness instantly. I close my eyes and absorb every magical vibration around me.

We stay at the rock mandala formation for close to an hour. Up here, in the middle of the trees and soft sounds of nature, life is less stressful. Less crazy. Less scary. Slowly, all my anxieties drift away and are replaced with nothing but exhilaration and love. Occasionally, it baffles me how something as simple as sitting near a rock formation can bring me such solace. But I know it is more than that. Something unexplainable and much bigger than me. I don't question. More like I respect it.

As we walk away from the rock mandala, I tug Liz closer. "Promise me we'll come back here. Often."

Liz's chestnut lips perk up at the edges as she wraps an arm around my shoulders. "I promise." She presses her lips to my temple. "We can come up here as often as you'd like. Just say the word."

With the promise of returning, we head back for the trail. As we stroll along the remainder of the trail, a renewed sense of peace fills me. Powerful and potent, it provides me with the boost I need since confessing part of my past to Liz.

Only Liz would know exactly what I need to move forward. What it takes to get me into better spirits. And one day, I hope to share the rest of my sordid tale. But now isn't the time.

FIVE

LIZ

After I lead Tiffany to the rock mandala on Saturday, she appeared in better spirits. Her body relaxed more. Her smile more radiant and on display. The bounce in her step more noticeable and frequent.

Thank god.

The conversation we had on Friday—the guessing game—was draining for both of us. Tiffany shed countless tears in my arms while I did my best to console her. But how on earth do I show compassion when what happened to her is beyond my level of comprehension?

I may not have the exact answer now, but I will stop at nothing until I do. Even if I have to go to counseling for significant others who have been abused. Tiffany is my entire world and I will do whatever it takes.

Obviously, whoever did this to Tiffany, whoever hurt her to this extent, scarred her for the rest of her life. A scar no one sees on her flesh except her and runs deep to her soul. When I resurrected a piece of her history, I also released the abuser front and center. I'm no shrink, but I recognize terror and pain when I see it. The person who did this to her, traumatized Tiffany.

Going forward, all I hope is to unearth a way to help her jump the hurdles of her past. To leap high over them and beat them to the finish line. And I will constantly remind her that I'm here for the long haul.

The phone on my desk rings, startling me. I glance down and see Christy's extension illuminating the small screen. "You rang," I greet.

"What? Why are you so weird sometimes? Can't you just pick up the phone and say hello?"

I laugh. "And why would I do that when I can be weird? It's funner."

"Funner? Is that even a word? Liz, you're weirder than usual today," Christy says.

"Thanks. Best compliment I've gotten all day. Did you dial me for a reason other than picking on me?"

"I'm not… never mind. Yes, do you want to grab lunch at one?"

"Hmm. I don't know. Are you going to keep picking on me?"

"God," Christy huffs. I imagine her rolling her eyes on the other end. "Do you want to have lunch with me or not, bitch?"

"Ah, there's my girl. Yes, I will have lunch with you. Meet at the elevator?"

"See you at the elevator at one."

Before I can mess with her any further, Christy hangs up on me. "Rude, bitch."

For the next two hours, I call close to a dozen clients and sell a couple new insurance packages. A sense of accomplishment surges throughout my body and has me on cloud nine. Since Saturday, life has steered toward a more positive direction. Tiffany's lighthearted behavior sparks more assurance than anything else. Hopefully, everything will keep going up, up, up.

Five minutes to one, I lock my computer and set my earpiece on the charger next to my desk phone. Grabbing my wallet, phone, and keys from my desk drawer, I exit my cubicle. As I approach the elevator, Christy taps the toe of her pointy flats on the tile as she studies her watch, then me.

"It's about time," she teases as she perches a hand on her hip.

Checking the time on my cell—twelve-fifty-eight—I roll my eyes at her. "Bitch, I got here with two minutes to spare.

Shut the hell up." Then I stick my tongue out at her for good measure.

She shoves me, almost knocking me on my ass, then pushes the down button for the elevator. Christy, Sarah, and I always live to mess with each other. If Sarah still worked with us, she would be crammed into this tiny-ass elevator with us and five other people. Although we miss working with her, Christy and I completely understand why she had to leave the company. If either of us were in her shoes, we probably would have done the same.

When the elevator doors swoosh open, we let everyone exit before us. Once we can breathe again, I probe, "So, where we headed for lunch?"

We step out of the building and make a beeline for Christy's SUV. She presses the button on her fob and we slip inside. "Thought we'd hit up the new market a couple blocks up. Cindy said it was hella good."

I spin in my seat and stare at her wide-eyed. "Did you just say hella?"

Christy shrugs and quirks up a corner of her lips. "Cindy's word, not mine." Cindy is one of our coworkers. Her cubicle is directly across from Christy, so the two of them chat frequently.

"It may be Cindy's word, but you could have said *really* or *awesome*. But you snuck hella in there so naturally. Sounds like you're losing a little of that Georgia accent too. Dare I say it, but I think you're becoming a west coast girl."

Christy play-smacks my arm. "Shut the hell up, bitch. Not like you haven't changed since we moved out here."

"True. But my lingo is still as it was before."

"Booooring. You need some diversity in your life," Christy teases.

I widen my eyes and pop my lips. Time to mess with her more. "You're joking, right? How could I possibly be any more diverse than I am? One… I'm a black woman with inter-racial parents. Not to mention, I am in an interracial, lesbian relationship. How much more diverse can someone get?"

Christy stares at me like a deer caught in headlights. I'm just fucking with her, but she hasn't figured that out yet. I bite the inside of my cheek and stop myself from laughing a little longer. When I can't stand to see her suffer any longer, I burst out laughing.

"I'm yanking your chain, bitch. Lighten the hell up. For someone who is all about free love and shit, sometimes you take me way too seriously."

Christy shakes out of her stupor. "That's because sometimes I can't tell if you're being legit or messing with me. I'd rather take you seriously first."

"I'll have to remember that."

A few minutes later, we park near the market and wander to the entrance. There's barely room to breathe with all the bodies inside. Plus, it smells incredible. Hints of soy sauce and Italian herbs and something roasting with rosemary. A mishmash of heaven all in one place.

We trail through a line and grab different small plates of food. By the time we reach the register, my tray is overflowing with mini plates. After paying a small fortune, we search for a table. Winding our way to the back, we finally spot a free table, sit down, and start demolishing our lunch.

"So, anything new with you, Rick, Ella, and Thomas?"

Shortly after I, Tiffany, Christy, and Rick, Christy's now-husband, moved to California, Christy had a confessional moment with all of us. Sarah and Jackson included. She invited us all to her house and spilled the beans that she and Rick were, for all intents and purposes, swingers. For years, she kept this little tidbit to herself, worried none of us would accept her, or Rick, for who they really are.

After she confessed one of her most hidden secrets to us, and we accepted her all the same, she became much more open with us about things occurring in her life. No lie, when Christy and Rick sat us down and hesitantly explained they were forming a new relationship with another couple, my jaw fell to the floor a split-second. It's one thing to love kink and sleep with other people, but the concept of those two couples becoming one unit seemed odd to me. But they loved Ella and Thomas. Everyone did. And after being in a relationship with them for months, they all decided moving in together was the next step. So they bought a new house.

The dynamic of their relationship is definitely different than most I'm used to. Uncommon. But it doesn't mean I harbor any negative feelings toward the bond they share. Their individual happiness is all that matters. And here in California, their relationship is easily accepted. Georgia would have been a whole different ball game.

"Nothing new. Rick says the club raised the number of members allowed and they've already sold out. Ella's bookstore is booming, as you saw when we were there. She has several local authors hosting talks and signings. Thomas has been busy at the firm, but things have been going well. You know..." Christy taps her index finger to her lips, eyes looking past me as she sits deep in thought.

When she continues to stare off into space and doesn't finish her thought, I imagine myself grabbing her shoulders and shaking her while I beg her to end the sentence she started. Instead, I sit on the edge of my seat, breathe in and out slowly before prompting her to continue. "What? You know, it'd be nice if you actually finished what you were saying."

Christy shakes her head and holds her hand up. "Patience, bitch. What I was going to say before you so rudely interrupted me" —my jaw drops as my eyes go wide— "you and Tiffany should come out to Boundless sometime. Once a month, they invite a limited number of nonmembers to check out the place."

I stare at Christy for a moment, completely shell-shocked as I try to form words. By no means am I a prude, but Tiffany being in a place like Boundless has my stomach in knots. Maybe because of the guessing game. "You're joking, right? Not like I'm opposed to the idea, but I don't think a sex club is Tiff's scene."

"Never know until you experience it. Keep it in mind. If you guys want to come in, let us know. Rick can get you in without issue."

"I'll remember that."

"Now, on to more important matters. Any wedding updates? I expected you to be in full bridezilla mode by now."

I reach across the table and knock her fork out of her hand. Christy stares at me as if she can't believe I just did that to her. But I did. Because how dare my friend call me a goddamn bridezilla. Just because I'm organized and want special occasions to be perfect... some nerve.

"First of all, why the hell would you call me a bridezilla? Have you seen those crazy bitches?"

Christy throws her head back and laughs obnoxiously loud. When her eyes level with mine again, she shakes her head slightly. "Um, yeah. And I could so see you being exactly like that. All *super* controlling and yelling at florists and venue staff."

Leaning back into my chair, I squint as my lips twist and release. I bite the inside of my cheek and resist the urge to laugh. "You were going to say hella, weren't you? Instead of super, you were going to say hella. Admit it."

"Never. Now shut up and answer my damn question." She waves her hand in front of me.

I was really hoping to avoid any wedding talk with Christy, but that's not an easy feat. Especially when she knows you're engaged. And have been for months. Normally, most couples would be discussing wedding details shortly after the proposal. They'd sit down and hash out some of the details. What to wear. Where they imagine the big day happening. Who will be in their wedding party. Most of all, by now, the couple would have set a date when the nuptials would occur.

But the path Tiffany and I are taking is lumpy and winding and unknown.

"No updates. We haven't chosen a date. Tiff has had some stuff come up with work and we're working around it. But as soon as I have a date, you and Sarah will be the first to know."

"You swear, bitch?"

I draw an X over my heart. "Swear."

We finish lunch and thank god the topic of weddings does not come up for air again. By the time I reach my desk, the high I felt from hiking yesterday has completely evaporated. Over the next few hours, I finish a long list of tasks on my computer while trying to let go of all the sadness that crept up during lunch. When I leave work for the day, I text Tiffany and let her know I'm on my way home. She responds with a heart-eyed emoji.

And for the next twenty-five minutes, I think about our hike on Saturday and the permanent smile Tiffany had plastered on her face when we left the rock mandala. When I put the car in park and make my way inside the apartment, some of my dread from earlier vanishes.

Although it isn't fair for me to want to, part of me wants to play the guessing game again. Part of me wants to dive into more of Tiffany's past since she's in a better headspace. But it's too soon. I shouldn't be selfish and use games to get information out of my fiancée.

It wouldn't do any good. For Tiffany or me. Or better yet, our relationship.

FOR THE FIRST time in who knows how long, I arrive home before Liz.

Her text message fifteen minutes ago said she was on her way home. I sent her my usual response, but didn't tell her I left work early today. After all the extra I've put in recently, I thought it would be nice to surprise her with a little extra time together. Hopefully, her face will brighten when she walks through the front door and sees me.

Since the engagement—and my avoidance of picking a wedding date—our relationship has felt strained. Harder. More work than it should be.

Which is all on me.

And I need to set our relationship straight. Right our wrongs. Get us back to where we were before I flipped out mentally over marriage. *Liz is not him. She will never be him.*

The one way Liz fixes a situation is with food. So, I will attempt to do the same.

By no means am I as great in the kitchen as Liz. She moves so gracefully around the kitchen. Like an artist with a paint-brush swishing oiled hues on a canvas. I slip on my Liz "hat" and put my best foot forward, which has to count for some-thing, right?

After I scour the internet for recipes, I rummage through the cabinets and fridge, plucking out all the ingredients and cookware I will need to make dinner. Since my talents in the kitchen rely on recipes and visual aids, I set my iPad up next to the stove and watch step-by-step instructions so I don't burn anything.

Once everything is chopped, sliced, and measured, I tidy up the counters. A sweet fragrance from the honey-glazed carrots blends with the floral perfume of the jasmine brown rice. It floats in the air and mixes with the earthy aromas seeping from the oven where two herb-crusted chicken breasts sit in a roasting pan.

Better believe I pinned all these damn recipes. If they suck, I'll delete them later.

The timer on the oven screams like a whiny child and I smash the off button with a little too much enthusiasm before I take the chicken out of the oven. As I'm setting the pan on a trivet, I spot Liz out of the corner of my eye standing opposite the breakfast bar.

"Hey, I didn't hear you come in."

"Didn't want to interrupt you. Was nice watching you in the kitchen for a change." A mischievous grin lights up her face as she cocks a brow. "You look cute in your knee-length skirt handling hot pans and stirring pots."

I stare at her slack-jawed for a beat before tipping my head back and laughing at her kitchen fantasy of me. "Keep dreaming, baby. Not sure how often you'll catch me doing this. You're lucky the internet exists, otherwise we'd be just starting dinner."

Liz pushes off the wall and saunters around the counter, eyes locked on mine. The closer she gets, the faster my chest rises and falls. A mere inch from grazing my body with hers, she reaches forward and grabs my hips. Her lips a breath from mine. "I am lucky," she whispers. "But it has nothing to do with the internet."

She doesn't give me an opportunity to respond before hauling me against her and kissing me. Hard. Harder than she has in a while. I melt against the potent ferocity of her lips pressed to mine. Our tongues tangle and twist and battle to devour the other. A hint of her saltiness on the tip of my tongue.

I groan into her mouth and clutch her polo shirt, fisting it like I may never have the opportunity to kiss her this way again. Liz paints a line up my spine with the tips of her fingers before spreading them wide at the nape of my neck. Her fingers dive into my auburn locks as my heart jackhammers in my chest. She grips my hair like a savage and yanks my head to the side. Before the gasp leaves my lips, her lips skirt along my jaw, down the column of my throat, and over my clavicle.

My eyes roll back as I work to breathe. "Oh, god. Feels so fucking good," I moan.

This moment... the way Liz touches me, the way she lights me on fire... I love how my confession to Liz during the guessing game hasn't changed her feelings toward me. Toward us. Me asking her to delay our wedding was shitty. The guilt continually rattles me. But I couldn't be more thankful she is okay with waiting—to set a date and have the ceremony. Just have a couple demons to vanquish before we take us to the next level. Top level. Once they're gone, everything will be perfect.

Tugging my head to the opposite side, Liz kisses her way up my neck until she reaches my lips. One peck. Two. A third. And I feel her urge to keep kissing me before she breaks away. Her forehead against mine, she works to calm her breathing as she curls strands of my hair around her finger.

After our breaths quiet and heartbeats resume their normal rhythm, she says, "I just had to kiss you. Seeing you in here, making dinner for me. For us. With the biggest smile on your face. All I thought about was kissing you."

"I love you, too," I whisper against her lips. "Dinner is ready. Do you want to change first?"

Liz shakes her head, shaking mine along with it since our foreheads are still connected. "Nah. Let's eat and watch a movie. I need some cuddle time with my girl."

Once we physically separate, we move in symbiosis beside each other. I collect plates from the cabinet while Liz slices the chicken. I pour each of us a glass of wine while Liz portions food onto our plates. Minutes later, we plop down on fluffy pillows in the front of the coffee table with full plates and warm hearts. Liz grabs the remote and surfs through Hulu until we decide to watch The Handmaid's Tale rather than a movie.

"Tons of people at work won't shut up about this show," I say as I spear a slice of carrot and chicken onto my fork. "Hope it's as good as they say."

An hour later, our plates sit empty on the table. We lean against the couch completely discombobulated over what flashed on our television the last hour. I glance over at Liz and notice her glassy expression. *What the hell did we just watch?* And why do I immediately want to watch another episode?

"Thoughts? Feelings? Opinions?" I ask.

A moment of silence passes before Liz spins to face me. Mouth slightly agape. Pupils dilated. Brows lifted. "Um… already addicted." She laughs and shakes her head. "Christy said she read the book and just started the second book. Can't put it down. I kind of understand why."

I nod. "Agreed. And as much as I would love to sit here and watch more, I vote we get ready for bed."

Liz studies me for a moment before we rise from the cushions on the floor. She grabs both our plates as I toss the pillows back onto the couch before taking our wine glasses to the kitchen.

"You tired?" Liz asks as she rinses our plates and sets them in the dishwasher.

Coming up behind her, I set the glasses on the counter. I sweep her long, black hair aside, wrap my arms around her at the bra-line, and kiss the nape of her neck. "Not tired," I murmur as I kiss the back of her neck, nipping and tasting her salty skin.

Liz moans and grinds her ass against my front, circling her hips. In a flash, Liz whirls around in my arms, frames my face in her palms, and devours my mouth with hers. I fist her shirt and draw her closer. Heat radiates off every inch of her body and incinerates me from the inside out. Her hands slide down my neck, grazing my shoulders before one cups my breast and the other latches onto my hip. When she rolls my nipple between her thumb and forefinger through my shirt and bra, I break our kiss with a moan.

And then we become a frantic mess of hands. Gripping and yanking at our clothes as we fumble in the kitchen. Smacking against counter edges and fridge doors and walls.

Nothing but lips and tongues and the adrenaline coursing through our veins as mouths and hands explore each other.

One small step in front of the other, I guide us to the bedroom. Our lips locked the entire trek past the living room, down the small hallway, and into our bedroom.

Liz's knees smack against the edge of the bed a split-second before she grips my hips and tosses me onto the comforter. The mattress dips as Liz crawls over me, lips brushing against my skin and leaving a trail of fire in their wake. On my knees. Up the length of my thigh as she shoves my skirt to my hips. Her teeth nip the edges of my panties as her nimble fingers unbutton my blouse and peel it wide open.

I sit up and all but rip my clothes off. After I toss my shirt to the floor, Liz stands and yanks hers over her head. As I wiggle out of my skirt, Liz drops her pants to the floor. Clothes in a heaping pile on the rug, Liz hisses as her eyes appraise my body. "Damn, baby." She bites the corner of her lip. "You look damn pretty in white lace. Sometimes I forget how much you love lingerie. And I love how much you love it."

I've never explained to Liz why I love lingerie to the extent I do. She probably thinks it's for vanity or sexuality. But the truth is far from either. I wear certain styles of lingerie as a form of power. To take back power once stolen from me. Power I will never lose again.

Liz starts her trek up my body again, lifting my leg and kissing the arch of my foot. Torturous and slow, Liz sucks and nips up my calf, skirting along the inside of my thigh, skipping over the small triangle of white lace at the apex of my thighs. Before I pout and whine, her lips graze the upper hemline of my panties and head north to my navel. Nip. Lick. Up to my lace-covered breasts, where she clamps down on each nipple in turn. Then she's at the hollow of my throat, nibbling up the column of my throat as she drags her nails up the sides of my torso.

My back bows off the bed as I gasp, unable to absorb so many sensations all at once. I reach out, grip her bicep and tug her down until her breasts brush against mine. "Make love to me," I whisper just before I rock my hips against hers.

Her lips crash down on mine as her knuckles trace left and

right over the skin just below my navel. Sometimes, I wonder if Liz gets off on teasing the hell out of me. Every inch of my skin is licked with sweat. Trails of fire blaze where her lips and tongue and fingers have touched me. The pulse between my thighs throbs, sending a ripple of vibration throughout my body. My mind loses all sense of focus. A scream ready to rip from my lungs. A desperate plea for Liz to put her mouth between my legs and take me to heaven.

At this point, I am not above groveling.

Just as I thread my fingers through Liz's hair to shove her down between my thighs, she kisses a path back down my body. The descent is slow, but it sets every nerve in my body into overdrive. By the time she peels away my panties and licks up the center of my folds, I practically come on the spot.

"Shit, baby." She hums against my flesh. "You are so damn wet."

I groan and grind my pelvis against her face. "Shut up and make love to me."

Her lips spread into a wide smile against my skin. "Yes, ma'am."

And for the next several hours, Liz and I drift in and out of heaven.

Chloe knocks on my door, standing in the archway of my office. "Knock, knock."

"Come in. What can I do for you?"

She steps inside and sits down in the chair across from my desk, crossing her legs and resting her hands on her lap. "Just wanted to check in and see how Jensen is progressing."

I love Chloe's dedication to each person who walks into Lewis House. The level of care she demonstrates for each one makes her loss that much more tragic. No doubt she provided more love and attention to Taylor, her son, before he passed. And it breaks my heart she didn't recognize the signs of his depression.

"Better. We had a breakthrough last week. Since then, he's been a little more forthcoming with his past. Slowly, but surely, we're getting there."

Chloe brings her hands together in prayer position at her heart as her face alights with joy. "Oh, thank goodness. For a while, I was concerned we wouldn't see improvement with him. It makes my heart happy to hear he's talking."

"Agreed. I never want to give up on anyone, but he was being stubborn for all the wrong reasons. After he got a lot off his chest, opening up seems easier now. He's even been interacting with some of the other patients. Playing games. Reading books. Juan told me he glimpsed a smile on his face last night. He really is a great kid. Just in a shitty situation and didn't know the right way to handle it."

"How are you dealing with it all? I read your notes. Did his parents really want to sell him to some ranch place for two-hundred-thousand?"

I nod as my lips form a tight line. "Yep. It astounded the hell out of me too. Who the hell would do such a thing? Who would sell their own child?"

Chloe shakes her head as she gets lost in the scenery outside my office window. "Tiffany, we can't let him go back to his parents. Whatever it takes, we have to find another solution." Her voice seems far away as her mind processes the type of people Jensen's parents are.

"Glad we're on the same page," I say. Because no matter what Jensen's future holds, I don't want him returning to the toxicity he came from. "Honestly, I told Trina how I've given thought to adopting him after he finishes the program."

Across the desk, Chloe's solemn demeanor shifts as she straightens her spine and eyes me with interest. "Really? Would you do that? Can you?"

The idea has constantly niggled the edges of my mind. But it's something I need to sit down and have a serious conversation with Liz about before remotely moving forward. I also don't want to have such a serious discussion with Liz until I can commit to a wedding date. It wouldn't be fair of me to not commit to marrying the woman I love, yet ask her to adopt a seventeen-year-old boy with me.

"I need to have an in-depth chat with Liz. More than anything, I'd love to say yes. He's a great kid and has so much potential. He was just handed a shitty homelife. Thank goodness he came to Lewis House. Hopefully we can turn his life around."

"I have no doubt you will."

Chloe is one of the most generous people. It's a shame places like Lewis House didn't exist when her son needed someone to turn to. From everything she has told me, she was the most attentive mother. Always asking about his day. Checking in on any potential loves in his life. She asked questions. Showed she was there. She just didn't know what signs to look for when it came to depression or suicidal tendencies. And, unfortunately, some people hide the signs better than others. Not wanting to be a burden. As it is, most feel like a hindrance. And when it gets to that point, giving up seems easier than asking for help.

"It's not just me who leads him down the right path. We all have a hand in his recovery. Every single person in Lewis House. Including you."

Rising from the chair, Chloe walks toward the door with the soft pitter-patter of her dress flats tapping the tile. "If you say so," she says as she spins to face me. "But honestly, Tiffany. You do so much for him. More than anyone else here. Don't disregard that, okay?"

I nod and try to swallow the sudden lump in my throat. "Okay."

Chloe exits my office and my mind whirls at her words. My commitment to Lewis House and these kids is parallel to breathing. It isn't a job. More like a calling. My duty.

My cell phone rings, snapping me out of my introspection. Sliding open my desk drawer, I glance down at the illuminated screen. A number I haven't seen in years flashes on the screen. A number I hoped to never see another day in my life.

No, no, no.

And as badly as I want to ignore the call, as much as my insides scream to disregard the person on the other end, I go against my own better judgment and pick up my phone. The speaker continues to blare my ringtone, the volume seemingly louder, as my finger hovers over the answer button.

My stomach churns and my mouth goes dry as I tap the green button and press the phone to my ear.

"H-hello?" And I instantly hate how feeble I sound. How frail I become.

"Just because you moved away, doesn't mean I don't know where you are. I've always known where you are, *Princess*. And you will never hide from me."

The phone slips from my hand and clatters as it hits the floor. My hands visibly shake as my body climbs higher up the Richter scale. "No!" I whisper-scream.

Beneath the desk, I hear the vile echo of his laughter through the phone as I shrivel and collapse in on myself.

What the hell is wrong with me? Why the hell did I answer the phone?

SEVEN

LIZ

I THROW the car into park and step out with a smile on my face when I see Tiffany's already home. What I'm not prepared for is the sight before me when I walk inside.

Not five feet in the apartment, I notice her purse and work bag on the floor by the front door, her keys tossed in the middle. The apartment is dim with light only spilling in from the blinds-covered windows. I scan the semi-open floorplan until my eyes land on the couch.

In the middle of the couch, Tiffany is curled into a tight ball, arms wrapped around her drawn-up knees, as she rocks in place and mumbles incoherently.

I bolt over to where she's lying and drop down in front of her, swiping loose tendrils away from her face. "Baby? Tiff? Can you hear me? What's the matter?"

A void I have never witnessed consumes Tiffany's eyes. Her usual glacier-blue irises are practically white. Devoid of emotion. She rambles on and on. Muttering under her breath as her body trembles. The only words I comprehend are *not happening again.*

Resting a hand on her forearm, I speak in soft tones. "Tiff, what's not happening again? Did something happen to you today? Baby?" I brush my fingers over her forehead as my pulse whooshes behind my ears.

She continues to rock back and forth, and seeing her like

this—frightened, terrified, having a meltdown—scares the shit out of me. Makes me feel helpless. In our four years together, Tiffany has never acted this way. Lifeless. Fearful. Repressed. How do I even begin to mitigate what's happening to her? I don't even know what triggered her emotional state in the first place. So, how does one handle something they have no information on? How does one handle a panic attack when they don't know what started it in the first place?

Tiffany always exuded confidence. Stood strong with her head held high, back straight, and shoulders squared. Until the day I proposed. And now.

"Tiff? Baby? Talk to me, please. You're scaring me. What can I do? Tell me how to help." I stroke her disheveled auburn locks. Trace a finger along her shoulder, down her bicep, along her forearm. But she just keeps rocking.

And then she stops.

Her eyes shift and lock onto mine. Slowly, the dilation of her pupils shrinks and her whitened irises transition back to the bewitching blue I love so much. Her breathing settles. The mumbling stops.

Without warning, she sits up and smiles at me as if nothing I experienced in the last ten minutes occurred. "Hey, Lizzie. Didn't hear you come in. How long have you been home?"

What. The. Fuck.

Am I missing something here? What in the actual fuck just happened? Less than a minute ago, Tiffany was lying on the couch in the fetal position, a babbling, frightened mess as she rocked back and forth. Now, she acts as if she'd been sitting here patiently waiting for me to come home and nothing for the last ten plus minutes happened.

"You okay, Tiff? You were..." I point to where she was freaking out on the couch a moment ago. "Did something happen at work today? You looked—" I pause and choose my next word carefully "—*upset* when I walked in."

Tiffany's brows pinch together as she squints and studies me. "What are you talking about? Just been waiting for you to get home. I'm fine. Work was fine. Everything is fine."

I may not be the most feminine female on the planet, but I

know anytime a woman says she is *fine* it is far from the truth. As badly as I don't want to push the issue with her, I want to grip her shoulders, shake her, and snatch the truth from her brain. Because *something* happened to her today. And whatever it was, it scared the hell out of her.

"Okay, baby," I soothe. "How about we make dinner?"

Her smile grows exponentially bigger as she stands from the couch. "Let's make dinner. Want me to help?"

I weave my fingers with hers and kiss her temple. "I'd love nothing more."

Once in the kitchen, Tiffany asks how she can help. After grabbing the butcher-wrapped salmon and carrots from the fridge, I hand the carrots to Tiffany.

"Clean these, and four potatoes from the basket, and chop them up into big chunks so we can roast them in the oven."

Tiffany bobs her head like an overeager adolescent. She bounces on her toes as she walks to the sink with the root vegetables in her hands. Smiling too big as she turns on the faucet and runs a carrot under the running water. Bopping back and forth as she wipes it dry with a towel.

Seeing her like this—so completely night and day from the Tiffany I have grown to love—throws me off-kilter.

This morning, she was her usual chipper self. Singing in the shower. Swaying her hips to the music spilling out of her phone as she dressed for work. Slipping her fingers into the loops of my khakis and tugging me closer as we kissed each other goodbye for the day. All of it so blissfully normal.

But this—I glance toward the sink where she barely scrubs the carrots and potatoes clean—this isn't my girl. This is someone else. Maybe another side of Tiffany. A side she keeps hidden or a side she thought was vanquished years ago.

As Tiffany gingerly chops the carrots and potatoes into bite-size chunks, I take out the tall mason jar of quinoa from the cabinet. While she cubes, I measure. Just as I turn the burner on, Tiffany whispers something unintelligible.

"What'd you say, Tiff?"

I snag the dill from the herb and spice drawer, then the Dijon mustard from the fridge. Squirting a squiggly line of mustard on the salmon. As I'm about to smear it into a thin layer, I realize Tiffany still has yet to answer me.

When I peek over at her, she stands frozen. Eyes locked on the knife in her right hand as the blade rests inches above her left. *What the hell is she doing?*

I have never wanted to move so quick in my life, but a voice in my head tells me to proceed with caution. So, I take measured steps until my hip almost connects with hers.

"Tiff? What're you doing?"

She stands motionless and continues staring at the blade. That voice in my head from a moment ago, the one that told me to proceed with caution. Right now, that voice screams at an unprecedented volume and says *fuck caution. Get the damn knife out of her hand.*

Tiffany has never presented herself in any manner that would make me believe she would harm herself. But tonight, I witnessed more than one different version of Tiffany. Versions that make me question how well we really know one another. Versions that stack question on top of question in my mind.

I'm about to ask her for the knife. Make up some bullshit excuse that I need it to cut the salmon. But before I do, she speaks up with a strange hollowness in her voice. "This is a great knife, Lizzie. No wonder you love cooking."

How do I even respond to her? What the hell is going on inside that beautiful head of hers? And why won't she *talk* to me?

"Thanks, Tiff. Can I use it a sec? Need to cut the salmon." I extend my hand out between us.

She glances at my hand, then up to my eyes, before going back to my hand. For a beat, she nibbles on the inside corner of her lower lip. Why does she need to think about this? Before I ask again, she hands it to me.

"Of course. What should I do with the carrots and pota-toes now?"

It's as if I'm in the kitchen with a grade school child who is learning to cook for the first time. Tiffany and I have cooked dinner together on countless occasions. Although she prefers it when I do all the cooking, she knows her way around the kitchen and can make several dishes without guidance. Including the side dish, I asked her to prepare.

Going with it, I collect the olive oil and herbs for the root vegetables and set them on the counter beside her. I instruct her on how much of each to add to the veggies after she puts them in the roasting pan. Then tell her to toss everything together and make sure everything gets evenly coated.

While Tiffany finishes with the veggies, I smear the mustard on the salmon and sprinkle a thin layer of dill. I set the pan of fish by the toaster oven and preheat it. As I wash my hands and put things away, Tiffany starts whisper-singing as she tosses the vegetables.

I turn off the water and take my time drying my hands as I listen to her sing. At first, I don't make out the lyrics to the song. So I step up to the stove and check on the quinoa. The water ready to boil any moment, I catch a line from the song. It's the chorus verse to "You are my sunshine."

Listening to her sing the chorus perks up the corners of my mouth. Until she hits the next verse, and it's not a verse I've heard before. I furrow my brow as I lean closer to her.

She sings the lyrics in a hauntingly sweet tone. Lyrics about leaving someone. About regretting the decision.

A shiver ripples down my spine and spreads to my limbs. Those are not the lyrics to the song. Are they? I make a mental note to look up the song when I'm alone.

And the way she sang the words... her voice unfamiliar and foreign—eerie—to my ears. Worrisome and beguiling.

I lean into her, press my hip and bicep into hers. She stops singing. Stops mixing the potatoes and carrots between her widespread fingers. Stares at the pan. Waiting.

"Did I do good?" she asks.

I glance over the pan and pretend to study her work. In actuality, a sliver of my heart wilts at her behavior. "Yeah, baby. You did great," I choke out.

Tiffany claps her oily hands together and bounces in place for a second. I want to rest my hands on her shoulders and calm her down, but I have no clue if that will make whatever is happening with her worse or better or not change a damn thing. So, I opt to ignore the idea.

"The last part of the song you were singing, where did you hear it from? I've never heard those lyrics in the song before."

She finagles the faucet on and pumps soap into her palm.

Running her hands under the water, she rubs them together into a lather, over and over. For a moment, I wonder if she heard me. But then she answers. "It's the original version. Most people sing the happier lines nowadays. But I learned the original lyrics a long time ago."

I nod, unsure of what to say next. Who would teach someone such morbid lines to an otherwise happy song? So I ask, "From your parents?"

Tiffany hasn't talked about her family much. The only thing she has mentioned is they live in Florida somewhere. She told me she left Florida to attend college in Georgia and loved it so much she decided not to move back. I assume she keeps in contact with them, but she only mentions them if I bring up the subject. Maybe they had a falling out, and she feels better not discussing them. Maybe they aren't as nice as I portray them to be in my thoughts. But, honestly, I have no idea. How can I?

She shakes her head. "No. My parents never believed in 'conventional' upbringings. The kind where kids are told fables and falsehoods. They said it was inappropriate to lie to children until they reached a certain age and learned the truth. My father said it set a standard and told the world it was okay to lie."

I jerk my head back and purse my lips. *Seriously? What the hell?* "So, no Santa Claus then?"

Tiffany laughs and it sounds hollow. Empty. Nothing like the laugh I have generated from her throat and lips over the years. "Are you kidding me? While my classmates went on and on about Santa and the Tooth Fairy and every other folklore, I was the girl in time-out because I told all of them it was a lie. My parents told me Santa was just an excuse for stores to sell more toys for children. It was also a ploy for parents to keep their kids in line. So, I told everyone else the same. Needless to say, I was never allowed to participate in holiday activities at school. Name a holiday, I was alienated."

Holy shit. How can I have known Tiffany for this long and not known this part of her life? Maybe she is ashamed of it. Does it riddle her with guilt? Perhaps the years of suppressed memories somehow unlocked at work today. Something triggered her old memories to life. Memories she tucked away in the corners of her mind and hoped to never unearth again.

But she said her parents didn't teach her the song. So it begs the question, who did?

"If your parents didn't sing the song to you, who did?"

As she wipes her hands on the towel hanging on the stove, she looks up at me and tilts her head. "Huh?"

"Who sang that version of the song to you?"

Tiffany narrows her eyes and furrows her brow. She stares at me a minute. Almost through me. "What song?"

Woah. Hello whiplash. What the hell is happening? Did we not just spark our conversation minutes ago because of this particular song? Or am I losing my goddamn mind?

"The song you were singing a few minutes ago. I asked if your parents sung it to you and you said no. So I asked you who did."

She shakes her head as if she doesn't believe a word I'm saying. "I wasn't singing."

Okay. This is all getting to be a little too strange for my blood. All of a sudden, it's as if another switch has been flipped. Maybe I should try another line of conversation. A different tactic altogether. Maybe she isn't lost in her headspace anymore.

"How was work today?" I ask.

Picking up the roasting pan, she opens the oven door and slides it on the top rack before closing the door. Nodding, she says, "Good. Nothing eventful happened. How was your day?"

What am I missing here? Over the last thirty minutes, Tiffany has gone from practically comatose to a robotic, more innocent version of herself to, dare I say it, normal. At least I'm guessing she is back to her normal self. *Fuck*, I am so goddamn confused right now.

The toaster oven dings to let me know it's done preheating. I ignore putting the salmon in, knowing it only needs to cook for a short time. Instead, I lean against the counter and stare at Tiffany as she tucks her hair behind her ears.

"I'm going to ask you something, but you have to promise me you won't freak-out. Okay?"

She tilts her head to the side and shrugs. "Sure."

All I want is answers. If Tiffany has health issues—mental health issues—I need to know. How else can I care for her when she has an episode? Is it even called an episode? Fuck. Does me asking her make me an asshole? We have never discussed anything like this before. Never had a need to. But now it seems necessary and urgent.

"Tiff, do you remember me coming home?"

Generic enough. Doesn't tell her I walked in on her in total freak-out mode. Doesn't remind her she was curled into a ball, rocking back and forth, and muttering in fear.

She brings her thumb and forefinger to her chin, puckers her lips, and looks to the heavens. She taps her chin a moment before bringing her eyes level with mine and she shakes her head. "No." Confusion wrinkles her forehead and crimps the corners of her eyes. "Was I asleep?"

I take a few measured steps forward and lessen the space between us. "No, baby." God, how do I say this? Ugh. How do I tell her she was wasn't *herself*? "You were…" I pause and suck in a breath, holding it until I'm able to speak the words I desperately don't want to say. "You were curled into a ball on the couch, shaking from head to toe, staring at the wall."

Tiffany is close enough for me to reach forward and take her hand in mine. But I don't. I allow my words to seep in. As they do, she stumbles back. Her hips smack against the granite countertop, but she doesn't flinch. Her magical blue eyes hone in on my hazels while she shakes her head in disbelief. "No," she whispers. "No, that's not true. It can't be. I was asleep. I fell asleep on the couch."

I step into her and eliminate the last ounce of the space between us, curling my arms around her waist and tugging her close. "Tiff, I wouldn't make something like this up. You scared the shit out of me. And if I'm being honest, you haven't been yourself until a few minutes ago."

She watches me vigilantly. Blue eyes a pool of questions. And before I get a chance to say anything further, she yanks her body out of my hold and bolts to the opposite side of the room. "You're lying. Why would you say such things to me?" She starts crying and balls her hands into tight fists at her sides. "I wasn't doing what you said. No…" She trails off and starts shaking. "No. Not again," she whispers.

Without warning, Tiffany collapses to the floor and fists her hair. Tugging it hard.

I bolt to her side and drop down to my knees. "Please talk to me, baby. Please help me understand what's happening. I want to help you." I stroke one of the hands in her hair.

Face smashed to the tile, she yanks her hair harder and screams. Loud and shrill. It vibrates through every pore in my body. Bleeds into the marrow in my bones. Has my body trembling as my heart shudders. Fire burns hot in my lungs. A breached dam spills from my eyes. Desperation consumes me. I want to reach out and take her in my arms. Soothe her and steal whatever pain ravages her soul.

She releases her hair and starts shaking her head side to side against the tile. The longest ticks of time pass before an empty, eerie laugh fills the room. It's haunting and dead. "I wish you could help me," she mumbles to the floor.

Taking a chance, I reach out and place my hand in the middle of her back. "If you will let me, I want to try. But you need to tell me what's happening. I'm lost here."

Tiffany presses her palms flat to the floor and hoists herself up slowly. Eyes red and veiny. Her captivating blue irises dull. Cheeks blotchy. A foreign desolation steals every ounce of her joy.

"Lizzie, I love you."

"I love you, too, Tiff." I gather one of her hands in both of mine and hold on tightly.

"There's something I haven't told you. Something I was hoping to resolve on my own. So we could get married."

Her hesitance with us getting married isn't solely because she doesn't want to. *Thank god.* A hint of relief settles in my chest and I am instantly lighter.

"Okay. Well, if you want me to, I will help."

She shakes her head. Over and over. "Wish you could. But this is something only I can do."

A million ideas run through my head as to why she has to do this on her own. If it's her mental health, I will do whatever is necessary to help her get well. No matter how challenging. Take her to appointments. Joint counseling. Learn how to notice her triggers and work through them. Because that's what you do when you love someone.

Tiffany swallows and brings her gaze to mine. "The reason why only I can handle this is because…" I sit frozen and wait for her to finish. The anticipation is eating me alive. "I'm… I'm already…" She drops her eyes to our hands. Her shoulders fall as she exhales audibly. "I'm already married."

What. The. Fuck.

EIGHT

TIFFANY

DID I actually say that aloud? Did I just confess one of my darkest, wish-it-wasn't-real secrets? A secret I hoped to correct on my own before Liz found out.

Stumbling back, Liz stares at me as if I am a complete stranger. Maybe I am. After all, me being married is a major bomb to drop on your fiancée. But being married isn't the worst of it. Not by a long shot. For now, though, the marriage bomb is enough. Hopefully, the other fragments can remain buried.

Almost black, Liz's hazels widen further in disbelief. A vacancy taking over her soul as she repeatedly opens and closes her mouth. I struck her with a branding iron. Stole every possible thought or word from her mind. If our roles were reversed, I imagine my reaction would be similar. Maybe worse.

"Wh-what do you mean?" Her eyes drop to my lips—watching, waiting—then lift back to meet my eyes. "You're... you're." Not finishing her thought, Liz shakes her head furiously as her fists tighten and loosen at her sides. Grinding side to side, the muscles of her jaw flex beneath her cheeks. Her skin flush and damp. Within seconds, her expression morphs from questioning to upset to anger.

Instantly, my heart lurches into my throat and I take a few steps back. Liz has never been violent. Not to my knowledge. Never screamed at me with menace. Never raised a hand in violence. But currently, her body language screams every warning sign. A predator ready to pounce on its prey. And I just so happen to be the prey.

Pounding with a rhythm so vicious, I slap my hand to my chest, just over my heart, clutch the cotton beneath my palm and gasp. Pain. Piercing. All-consuming. Hole puncturing pain. I can't breathe. My vision blurs as I choke on fear.

No, no, no. This can't be happening. Not again. Not with Liz.

In a heartbeat, I crumble and hit the floor. The coolness of the tile a welcome sensation against my fevered skin. I don't move. Not an inch. My sensory response to protect myself to curl inward has abandoned ship.

Liz darts toward me, dropping to her knees. She strokes my hair and cheeks and jostles my shoulder. Over and over, she says my name. Waits for me to respond. But my lips won't move—the muscles not functioning. Voice won't escape —a wad of fear blocking all form of sound. I simply stare at the ceiling and crawl back into the corner of my mind. The only safe place I know.

The place I go when my world turns upside down.

"Tiff. Tiff. Please talk to me. Come on, baby."

Liz continues to shake me, but I lie here. Lifeless. Counting the specks on the ceiling. Noticing the imperfections in the paint. The dust in the corners.

Beside me, Liz talks, but I zone out and don't comprehend a word she says. An arm slides under my neck and lifts me up. Liz wraps my arms around her neck and tells me to hold on. Then she slips an arm under my knees and draws me close to her chest. A shaky moment passes before I'm hoisted into the air. Slowly, Liz carries me to the couch, holds me close and whispers in my ear.

Lowering us to the couch, Liz draws me impossibly closer and runs her hand up and down my back. "Shh, baby. Everything will be okay. Don't worry, baby. You're safe. I got you."

She whispers to me, over and over. I latch onto her as if my life depends on it. In some respects, it does. Liz whispers about safety and hope and love. And I drift off, praying her words hold truth.

I startle awake to find Trina sitting on the couch next to me and Liz. Still nestled in Liz's lap, I snuggle closer to the crook of her neck and inhale. The soft and distinct blend of coconut and ginger—a fragrance only Liz possesses—calms my startled state. Before Liz, no one provided me with comfort. Not even my family. Mom and Dad were too clinical to give emotional comfort.

"Trina? What are you doing here?"

My dry, tired eyes dart between Liz and Trina, wondering what the hell is happening.

"Tiffany," Trina starts as she reaches forward and rests a hand on my thigh. "Liz called me a little bit ago and asked me to stop by."

Liz squeezes her arms tighter around me, smashing me against her frame. I curl tighter into her warmth and take a deep breath.

"For what?" I ask.

Thinking back, the day starts to play back in my head. Images flash in my mind's eye like a movie reel. Except this movie jumps from one point to another then another. There's no fluidity. Chunks of time missing here and there. As if someone took the film off the reel, cut out the important pieces, and Scotch-taped it back together.

Missing time frustrates the hell out of me. Downright pisses me off. There is nothing worse than living your life and not being included in what *you* are doing. Unfortunately, this isn't the first time it has happened. The last time this happened.... The last time I missed fragments of time— anywhere from minutes to days—was when…

No. That was a long time ago.

"Tiffany, what's the last thing you remember?"

Fidgeting in Liz's lap, I think over her question. What is the last thing I remember? Being at Lewis House. My conversation with Chloe. Shortly after she left my office, I must have left work for the day. But I don't actually *remember* leaving. The drive home is also a blur. Dinner flickers in and out like images captured under a strobe light. An image here. Blackness. An image there. Blackness. Over and over.

Fuck. So much after my visit with Chloe has vanished into thin air. A phantom in the night.

I don't want to lie to Liz or Trina, but if I tell them most of the evening is hit or miss, who knows what will happen next.

They will ask more questions. Questions which will stir up my past. Questions I am far from comfortable answering right now. Not that I don't want Liz or Trina knowing the truth. But I don't need them seeing me as a helpless victim. Not now. Not ever.

"Um, I remember talking with Chloe before leaving work. Liz and I having dinner." I shrug and don't say anything else. Short, sweet, simple. In this instance, maybe less is more. Maybe less will help my cause.

Beneath me, Liz stops breathing. *Shit.* Something bad happened. Something I don't remember. Something I haven't said, but Liz is fully aware of.

Shit, shit, shit.

"Tiffany, do you remember when Liz got home from work?" Trina studies my every flinch, breath, and eye movement. Psychology training in full effect. She may be here as a friend, but she is staring at me as if I'm a patient.

I'm screwed.

Peeking up at Liz, I hope the sight of her will spark a memory. Stir up the moment she walked in the door. The moment we exchanged our *welcome home* kiss. No such luck.

I shake my head and bring my line of sight back to Trina. "No." A tear rolls down my cheek. "I just remember having dinner together."

Trina nods and pats her hand on my knee. Most people would enjoy the sentiment. A small pat. A gentle swipe of the hand. A connection between people. But my educational background parallels Trina's—minus her years practicing. The hand pat is meant to reassure the recipient. To appease them. In this instance, it only skyrockets my anxiety to the troposphere.

"First things first. You know whatever we talk about is strictly between us. Right, Tiffany?"

I nod as another tear rolls down my cheek and falls from my chin. "Of course, Trina."

"Are you okay with Liz being here while we talk?" As Trina asks the question we're trained to whenever someone is in the room with a patient, every inch of Liz goes rigid. But Trina has to ask. And it's not done to be hurtful.

"Yeah. It's fine."

Limb by limb, inch by inch, Liz's frame relaxes beneath me and I clutch her tighter. It has never been my intent to have secrets between us, but some parts of my past are better left exactly where they are. In the past. Buried. No sense in rehashing painful memories.

Trina pulls her hand away and nods. "Liz tells me when she got home, you were on the couch."

"I must've fallen asleep waiting for her."

Liz tucks me closer to her chest and rests her cheek on the crown of my head. The move is protective. Her hand on my backside strokes up and down my spine. If the situation were different right now, I would find the gesture endearing. Instead, a layer a discord coats my skin.

"You weren't asleep, baby," Liz murmurs against my hair.

What does she mean I wasn't asleep? Of course I was. I would remember waiting for her to come home if I was awake. I would have been in the kitchen, doing a shit job at prepping dinner. But I have no recollection of being home before her. She must've woken me after she started cooking. Right?

"I don't understand."

Honestly, I have no idea what is happening. And it scares the shit out of me.

Trina places her hand on my leg again. "Tiffany, when Liz came home from work, you were on the couch. Awake. Curled in a ball and shaking. Liz said you kept repeating something over and over. *Not happening again.*" Trina pauses and studies my face. Waits for a brow lift or furrow. For a pinch of eyes or twitch of my lips. A change in my pallor or sweat on my skin. I work to contain all these signs and pray she doesn't spot the dread taking hold. If she does, I don't think she will acknowledge it. Not right now. "What does that mean, Tiffany?"

A chill sweeps over my body and I shiver. Absent is the comfort I usually have in Liz's arms. Bringing my legs closer to my chest in her lap, I lean more into her body, inhale her comforting scent, and wish for her warmth and love to provide me with the strength I need.

"I... I don't know."

The lie rolls off my tongue with ease. Years and years of

practice will do that—make fibbing second nature. But the lie isn't to hurt anyone. If anything, the lie protects. Not only me, but everyone I love too.

"You don't have to be scared, Tiff. You're safe here. With me, and Trina. Nothing will happen to you." As if to seal her vow and protect me from my demons, Liz kisses the crown of my head.

I wish it were that simple. A kiss to secure my safety.

But it's not. And I won't risk anyone I love getting hurt. Never again.

"Lizzie, you know I love you. Right?"

Her arms banded around my chest tighten as she nods against my hair. "I do, baby."

"Then, please," I beg. "Please, just let this go. It's nothing. Old news."

Trina stares at me with sad eyes. She knows exactly what I am trying to do. That I'm skirting around the subject to avoid admitting the truth behind my obvious freak-out. The split-second cock of Trina's eyebrow also tells me the two of us will be discussing this more in the future. But that is easily avoidable.

"Tiff, I can't get the images of tonight out of my head. How am I supposed to forget? How am I supposed to move past this?"

Liz shifts her position so we are more eye to eye. The soft patch of skin between her brows scrunches as she narrows her eyes. Her head shakes side to side infinitesimally.

Somehow, someway, I need Liz to forget whatever happened tonight. Or at least let it go until I can get things figured out.

The very last thing I remember before seeing Trina on our couch was telling Liz I was married. And the anger on her face. Anger *he* used to flaunt as if it were a luxury, not just a weapon.

"Do it for me. Please? I have everything under control. Promise."

Liz clenches her teeth before glancing over at Trina. An unspoken exchange happens between them and my heart beats faster. *What did they discuss when I was out?*

Hanging her head, Liz shakes it in defeat before sliding

out from under me. As soon as she is free, Liz leans down, kisses the top of my head, bids Trina goodnight, and walks off to our bedroom.

What just happened? What did I miss?

"Trina, what was that?"

A sad smile pushes up the corners of Trina's lips a fraction. "Tiffany, when Liz came home, you displayed all the signs of an abuse victim. Now, I didn't tell her that. But the way she described everything to me—the rocking fetal position, the constant mumbles, the way you shut down when she became angry at your confession tonight. I don't need to go into detail, you know the signs just as I do."

No. No, no, no.

This will not rule my life. Not again. I refuse to let it.

"It was a long time ago. And something I buried deep."

"Not deep enough if it's making a comeback. What happened today? Something obviously triggered you. Did you have a bad session with a patient?"

Thinking back on the day, I replay each session and nothing comes to mind right off the bat. "No," I say. Then I pause as a memory trickles back in. Like a car collision in slow motion. The phone call. "Wait," I say and hold up a hand. "After Chloe left my office, I got a phone call. From my ex."

"Your ex?" Trina studies my reaction, and I give in to my emotions.

I hang my head, shake it a moment, then meet her gaze. "Yeah. Usually, I ignore the calls. I've blocked his number, and changed mine, several times, but he always finds me. He probably called because I filed for divorce. Again. And he's probably pissed. I shouldn't have answered the phone. A little part of me hoped he would be different. But he threatened me, as per usual. Probably what set me off."

In all honesty, I don't remember a word of what he said to me on the phone. He doesn't have to say anything of importance to set me off. Which is why I have ignored his calls over the years.

Trina does the knee pat again. "Please come and talk to me. I don't care how often, just do it. You can't hold all this in.

Maybe I can help. You, of all people, should know the resources we have to help in these situations."

Nodding, I answer. "Just didn't want to push my problems on to someone else. Thought I could handle them on my own. Obviously, I was wrong."

"Hey, you know it's okay to ask for help. Just because you know how to deal with these types of situations, doesn't mean you have to do it alone. Plus, coaching ourselves is never the same as coaching others."

Trina rises from the couch and I follow suit. A sudden wave of exhaustion consumes every muscle in my body. We exchange hugs and she reiterates how I don't have to go through this alone. I promise to come and see her in a day or two and talk more.

When Trina is confident I will speak with her again, she bids me goodnight and leaves.

I flip off the light in the living room and walk down the hall. I tiptoe into the pitch blackness of our bedroom, and I hear Liz's soft cries against her pillow. Stripping out of my clothes, I crawl under the covers and spoon against her—my back to her front—and she embraces me wholly.

"You really scared me tonight," she whispers after minutes of silence pass. "Don't know what happened to make you so frightened, but I hope you believe me when I say I'm here for you. That I'll always be here for you."

I band my arms tight over hers. "Yes, I believe you. Sorry I scared you, Lizzie." Loosening my grip, I turn in her arms and face her. After adjusting to the darkness, I spot the glossiness coating her eyes. The tears I created. Tears I am responsible to wipe away. "It's just... I've been trying to fix this—divorce him—for years. I didn't want to drag you into my mess."

"Baby, your mess is my mess. If there's anything I can do to help, I'm here. You know I am. Just say the word."

Liz pushes back a few stray locks of my hair, tucking them behind my ear. She is so much better than I deserve. More than I ever expected to have. More than I imagined. Sometimes, I pinch myself to make sure what we have is real. Not just an illusion my mind is feeding me to get through another punishment from *him*.

Closing the space between us, I press a gentle, chaste kiss to her lips. Absorb her heat. Taste her salty tears on my tongue. Inhale her distinct scent. "I know. But please let me try to do this myself. It's my mess, and I need to clean it up."

My heart expands and contracts so quickly, it feels as if it will explode from my chest cavity. I hold my breath, waiting and pleading to the heavens for Liz to let me do this. Not just for the sake of doing it, but also for closure. More than anything, I *need* closure.

Liz strokes her knuckles slowly along my cheek. Back and forth. The rhythm soothing. As my eyes grow heavy, Liz whispers into the darkness. "Okay, baby. As long as you promise to ask for help if you need it."

My eyes flutter shut. "I promise."

"Love you, Tiff." Liz presses her lips to mine.

"Love you, too, Lizzie," I tell her as sleep takes me under.

"She's what?" Christy shouts a little too loud as she spews salad from her lips and across the table at me. In a split-second, dozens of eyes land on our table. Heat floods my face at the level of attention Christy has attracted.

I widen my eyes and clench my jaw, staring at her with a *shut the fuck up* expression. As if it's not embarrassing enough to tell one of your best friends that your fiancée is currently married. Honestly, I am positive my life could not get any worse. Actually, I rescind that thought. It can get worse. Because whoever the asshole is that still lays claim to Tiffany, he traumatized her in ways I have yet to learn. Ways I am petrified to learn.

"Lower your damn voice," I whisper-hiss. "Jesus. There is no reason to yell."

Christy drops her fork and it clangs almost as loud as her voice a moment ago. For fuck's sake. Moments like this, I wish Sarah still worked for Hammond. Sarah was always a good buffer with Christy. Tapered her boisterous energy a little. Funny thing though, around Rick, Christy never seemed as bubbly. As if he tamed her over-exuberance. Either that or she dumped it all on me.

Holding both hands up in surrender, Christy winces. "Sorry. It's just…" She trails off and stares at me. Pushing her glasses up the bridge of her nose, she takes a deep breath.

"You guys have been together for *years*. How could she not mention this ginormous fact until now?"

This is what I have been asking myself for the last eighteen hours. There have been way too many opportunities for Tiffany to mention it. On several occasions, we have stayed up late at night, especially in the beginning, and bled our pasts to each other. Or so I thought.

Thinking back to those late-night conversations, curled up in her bed or mine and getting lost in each other's eyes, there are gaps. Vague mentions of her parents—how her mom, a pediatrician, and dad, a psychologist—treated her more like a patient than an actual child. Their relationship was, and probably still is, quite clinical. The way she talks about them, I have an inkling I will never meet them. Or at least not until our wedding or thereafter.

Aside from the small frequency in which she mentioned her parents, Tiffany doesn't discuss much about her past relationships. I get that it's awkward to talk about exes with your current partner, but unless it's your first relationship, we all have history.

"My thoughts exactly. But I'm sure there's a good reason. Just need to learn what it is," I say, mumbling the last line.

"Look, Liz. I don't want to sound like a know-it-all, but secrets ruin relationships. Not like I am the queen of relationship advice, but this is something Rick and I instilled from the get-go. Secrets are like poison. They slowly kill you from the inside. And by the time you figure out the culprit, sometimes, it can be too late."

I hang my head and nod as I poke at the salmon filet on my uneaten salad. Christy is right. But how do I bring up the topic with Tiffany without her losing her shit again? Seeing her on the couch when I came home... then later in the kitchen...

I shiver, pinch my eyes tight, and cock my head. Whatever happened in Tiffany's past, whoever did this to her, fucked with her head in ways I cannot comprehend. Ways I am scared to hear.

But isn't part of healing exposing all your wounds? Ripping the bandage off and peeling back the scab. Cleaning the wound and letting fresh air heal it.

I want to help Tiffany. Need to help her. But how can I be there for her if I have no idea what I'm dealing with?

"It can't be too late," I whisper, not looking up from my lunch. "We've barely just begun."

Christy reaches across the table and lays her hand on mine. Lifting my head, I bring my gaze back to hers. Behind her black-rimmed glasses, I see her sadness for me. See how badly she wants to dive in and save me from this new version of hell I'm living in. And Christy doesn't know the half of it because I will not tell her about the two instances where Tiffany was far from herself. It's not my place. And I would never betray her confidence. Never expose all her skeletons.

"Everything will work out," Christy says as her thumb rubs small circles over the top of my hand. "It has to. You both love each other. Fiercely. I've seen it. If your love is powerful enough, it will slay all the demons of the past. You just have to be willing to fight."

Am I willing to step up and fight for Tiffany? To defend her on the battlefield? Damn straight. Tiffany is the best thing to happen to me. And I will take anyone out who tries to steal her from me.

Just wish I knew what I was up against.

The several days that follow fly by uneventfully. Tiffany has been her normal, chipper self. As if nothing happened in the first place. And it has me a little on edge, constantly watching her to see if she gives any other signals. But I have yet to catch a single one.

Hopefully, she has taken time to talk more with Trina and get whatever bothers her out in the open. I hate to think she has locked up everything in her mind and tucked it away in the hopes it won't resurface. No matter who you are, no matter what has happened in your past, packing up your problems and shoving them into a dark corner never works. Never.

But, as a loving partner and someone Tiffany leans on, I do my best to be a positive force in her life. Someone she wants to share her life with.

So, rather than bring up the topic, I drop it and we discuss life as we used to. Our days at work. Adventures we hope to go on soon. Crazy conversations with friends and coworkers. Plans to hang out with our friends. Maybe normalcy is the medicine she needs.

On Saturday, we join Christy, Rick, Ella, and Thomas for dinner. The restaurant is small, but not too small. Quaint. A wall of windows faces the street, lined with several tables for two or four. After the hostess connects two of the tables, she leads us to our table and promises a server will be with us soon.

Inside the restaurant, across from the long line of tables, is a bar with at least a few dozen stools. Between the tables and bar are three long tall-top tables, wedged in the middle of large square pillars, with stools on either side. Hundreds of people bustle in the space, chatting loudly over one another and cheering on the sports games on large televisions on the bar's wall.

Tonight isn't about finding a snappy place to eat or having quiet conversations. Christy said none of them had been out anywhere except for Boundless in far too long and she needed a change of scenery. She had no idea how much Tiffany and I needed an excuse to go out too.

Before Tiffany and I were serious, I went out three or four times a week. Either that or I was hosting parties at my place. I don't miss—or not miss—the parties and booze and variety of people between my sheets. But I do miss the change of pace and excitement and high I felt during those days.

I figured if we at least got out of the house and had a night of fun, like we did so often in the beginning of our relationship, it would add another layer of happiness in Tiffany's life, and mine.

Tiffany has acted as if everything is ducky. And who knows, maybe she has hashed a lot of her past out with Trina. But she hasn't brought it up to me whatsoever, and neither has Trina. I don't expect Trina to call me and report this, that, or the other. But I would hope, especially after Tiffany's meltdown, Trina would keep me in the loop if she and Tiffany had sessions at all.

After we order, everyone branches off and starts talking

with each other. Since I see Christy five days a week at work, I spark up a conversation with Ella and Thomas while Tiffany chats with Rick and Christy.

"So, how are things at the firm?" I ask Thomas.

Thomas recently made partner with the firm. A major promotion for him. Christy rambled on for ten minutes without taking a breath, telling me how awesome it was to see his name on the outside of the building. They should all be proud. Countless hours of blood, sweat, and tears were poured into such an accomplishment. Making partner is a hell of a victory in his career.

"Beyond amazing. Things have been hella busy, but I love it. Business is at an all-time high and I am exactly where I want to be. Couldn't ask for anything more."

I laugh internally at his use of hella. Reminds me of Christy and how quickly she has picked up the term. She blamed it on a coworker, but I have a sneaking suspicion Thomas and Ella influence the word usage more.

"Congrats again on the promotion." I glance over at Ella, who is beaming beside him. "And the bookstore is doing well, yeah?"

Ella's face glows bright as the sun. "So good. I swear we have more and more people in the store every day."

I love her excitement. One day, I hope to have a job I love and feel equally as passionate about. Honestly, my dream job would be owning a restaurant. Several times, Sarah and Christy have suggested I go to culinary school and follow my passion. Each and every time the subject came up, I waved them off. More than anything, I would love to leave the insurance industry and follow my heart. But what if I don't love being in the kitchen after it becomes my job? What if my passion fades and I am stuck? What if I fall out of love with cooking? It's not a regret I am convinced I could handle.

"The store was swamped last time I was there. So happy business is going well. Mind if I ask a question?"

Ella shrugs and tilts her head. "Shoot."

This is me, putting it out in the universe. *Please universe, don't jinx me.* "How do you keep the bookstore something you love instead of it becoming just a job?"

Sipping her water, Ella's eyes smile, followed by her lips

as she sets her glass down. A sneaking suspicion tells me Christy has told her about my love of cooking. Not that it bothers me. Actually, it is cute how bonded the four of them are. It's one thing to catch minor glimpses here and there. It's another when you notice small tells.

"It didn't happen right away, if I'm honest." She leans forward and laces her fingers together on the table. "When we first bought the store, there was a ton of work that needed to be done. The previous owner hadn't done much to keep up with the store as a whole. The outside was shabby, and the inside was worse. Unkempt, dusty, and there was a mysterious odor which took months to get rid of. But one thing held true throughout all the craziness."

I leaned in closer to her. "What?"

"My love for the written word and how this was the opportunity of a lifetime. My dream. For as long as I can remember, I've loved reading. When I was a little girl, I used to take all the books in our house, stack them around the room, and pretend I was selling them." Ella laughs and shakes her head at the memory. "As if my younger self knew what was meant to be."

Across from Ella, I nod as I absorb her words. As a little girl, I remember being in the kitchen. Cooking and baking with either my mom, Grandma Warren, or Grandma Winston. Each of them showing me something new or different. From mom's chicken cordon bleu to Grandma Warren's homemade bread and Grandma Winston's love for pies. They only shared the whole recipes with me. Whenever family friends asked for them, they always left out a key ingredient or two. As a child, I didn't understand why. As an adult, I laugh about it. But they instructed me to always do the same. *Recipes stay in the family*—a repeated phrase from each of them.

"Yeah," I mumble. "Sometimes you just know early on."

The rest of dinner is filled with good conversation, great laughs, and an all-around sense of happiness. Tiffany sits beside me, hand in mine on her thigh, with a smile that rivals the brightest of stars. Tonight is exactly what we needed. A dose of normal. An effortless evening out with our friends. A night chock full of love and laughter and good memories.

After we say goodnight to our friends, Tiffany and I head

home. Her smile from our night out a permanent, glowing fixture on her face. Seeing her happy, watching her face light up, it is all I need to keep moving forward. All I need to know everything will be okay.

TEN

TIFFANY

Exiting Lewis House, I head for my car in the lot, press the button on my fob, and get in. I crank the engine and slip my sunglasses on before backing out of the space. In a flash, I drive off and head for an appointment.

A month has passed since my meltdown. The same meltdown where I spilled to Liz about my current marital status. A marital status I wish never existed.

Not as if I really wanted to marry *him*. That status came at the behest of my parents. Somehow, *he* swept my parents off their feet and had them swooning with his smooth words and suave appearance. When my parents learned *he* was a doctor, it was the tip of the iceberg. My parents fell in love with *him* and the idea of me being the wife of a prominent and up-and-coming doctor.

They loved *him*. At one point, I thought I loved him too.

Until I saw the other side of *him*. The real side.

Less than a month after meeting *him*, we were engaged. He showered me with sweet talk and pretty trinkets and promises of the best life. A beautiful home, children, the career of my dreams with him on my arm. To some, our age difference was questionable. But my parents' circle of friends were equally enamored by him.

Ten years wasn't that big of a deal, right? That's what we all thought.

Fresh out of high school with a handful of college credits

under my belt, I was eager to follow in my father's footsteps. Although my childhood wasn't like most, over the years I developed a love of psychology. Working to decipher how the mind works, how one person interprets a scenario different than another person, and how I would have the ability to help others resolve problems in their lives.

With *him* by my side, I believed my dreams of becoming a well-respected psychologist were written in stone.

Five months after our engagement, a month before my nineteenth birthday, we were married. Looking back, it truly was a beautiful wedding. The ceremony held at a high-end resort on Long Boat Key. Twinkling lights, miles of sheer white fabric draped from the ceiling, a ballroom packed with a few hundred of our family's closest friends and loved ones. My wedding was nothing shy of magical. And *he* looked at me as if I handed him the world with the two simple words.

Everything was perfect. Until it wasn't.

A week into my college winter break, the ink on our wedding certificate barely dry, that's when *he* showed his true colors.

I shiver at the mere thought of seeing him again. Thankfully, my attorney said I should be able to handle everything without needing to. The attorney started drafting divorce paperwork two weeks ago. After an endless stream of questions, my attorney told me he would have everything ready for me to sign today.

Part of the challenge, since I abandoned the marriage, is how he may be able to contest it and drag it out longer than necessary. It wouldn't shock me one bit if *he* made this whole situation more unbearable than it already is.

Ever since Liz asked me to marry her almost six months ago, I have wanted nothing more than to sit down with her and plan the perfect wedding. One so very different than my first. Where we ogle dress fabrics and collaborate on our guest list, opting to keep it small with only the people who are most important in our lives. The way we'd both want a simple yet elaborate ceremony.

And after we exchange our vows, things with Liz will be better than they were with *him*. Because this time I was cautious. This time, I did my homework and took my time and spent years with Liz before we got to where we are today. I asked questions and innocently probed for answers. Answers to tell me what type of person Liz is. Answers to tell me Liz is exactly the person I want to spend my life with.

I pull into the parking lot, park close to the entrance under a shady tree, and cut the engine. Inhaling a deep breath, I grab the file folder on the passenger seat and step out of my car. My stride steady and purposeful as I head for the entrance.

The exterior of the office is nothing special. Wooden paneling painted a neutral slate gray. A white sign beside a set of double wooden doors lists names of the office personnel. I tug on the heavy door and step inside.

"Can I help you?" A busty brunette woman sitting tall behind a glass top desk glances my way as I enter.

I approach the desk, hiking my purse higher on my shoulder, and lean forward. "Yes, ma'am. I have an appointment with Mr. Kelly. Tiffany Page."

The brunette clicks the mouse on her computer a few times, then looks up at me again. "Have a seat Ms. Page. Mr. Kelly will be with you in a moment. We have coffee and water available, if you'd like."

"Thank you."

I walk over to a small vanity-style cabinet and scan the options for the Keurig. After brewing a hot chocolate, I sit and wait to be called.

Just as I sit down with my hot chocolate, a young man calls my name and has me follow him down a long hall. He directs me into a conference room with an oblong oval table and we sit. Neither of us says a word while we wait for whoever else is joining us.

The room has a clinical vibe—white walls, minimal generic art, a handful of pens and a landline phone in the center of the conference table. The distinct smell of pine cleaner and Lysol floats in the room. Lewis House is ten times more homey than this place. Maybe our next meeting should be in my office, where they can pick up some décor ideas.

The door opens, a silver-haired man and a younger blonde woman with similar facial features stride in. After they reach their seats, the man extends his hand across the table.

"Anthony Kelly. Pleasure to meet you, Ms. Page." I shake his hand. "And this is my daughter" —he gestures to the blonde woman— "Andrea Kelly. She will be assisting with your case."

After we exchange handshakes, the real work begins. Discussions regarding what I should expect with the case. How long they believe it will take to have the divorce finalized. As of now, they foresee everything wrapping up in less than six months.

As soon as the timeline is announced, my breathing settles a notch and my heart beats easier. Slower. *This is exactly the news I need to hear.*

An hour passes faster than a twenty-minute commute to work, and before long I'm signing paperwork to initiate the whole process. With the final flick of the pen, a light brightens at the end of a very long, dark tunnel. Relief is in sight. I want to stand up, scream to the heavens, and celebrate a moment I never thought would come.

Mr. Kelly slides the paperwork into a folder in front of him, offers his hand, and we shake. "We'll be in touch, Ms. Page. This should be wrapped up soon."

Rolling the chair back, I stand and grab my belongings. "Thank you for everything, Mr. Kelly. Ms. Kelly. I appreciate all you are doing for me." More than they will ever comprehend.

With the meeting over, I walk out of my attorney's office with a pain-inducing smile plastered across my face. The sun beats down on my skin as I tilt my head back and close my eyes. Time drifts by and I simply stand there and absorb the warmth of the sun. Allow it to seep into my skin and heat my bones. Allow relief and joy to flood my veins as fear and pain filter out.

For the first time in years, a deep-rooted chill evaporates and exits my body. A chill which has loomed in the background for far too long. A chill I will never know another day of my life.

Now, it's replaced with something stunning and earth-shattering.

Freedom.

"Are you sure?"

I have never been more sure in my life. "Absolutely."

Liz stares at me, her hazel eyes darting back and forth between my blues. Then, she bolts upright and squeals at the top of her lungs with her arms overhead and hips wiggling side to side. I tip my head back and laugh at her exuberance.

In a heartbeat, she launches herself at me and tackles me. Back flat on the couch, Liz peppers me with kisses as she frames my face in her hands.

"Ohmygod, ohmygod, ohmygod! Now? Can we pick now?"

I stare up at her plumped cheeks, smile for days, and dazzling eyes. Who knows what I did to deserve Liz, but I am thankful for every touch and smile and heartbeat we share together. She is the only person I have met who says what she means and means what she says. Open and honest and so sweet behind her tough-girl façade.

Smiling back at her, I feign a cough. "Can't breathe," I rasp, only to mess with her.

"Sorry, sorry, sorry." Liz pops off me instantly and I dramatically drag in the air. For way too long. And she catches on quicker than I expect. "Tiff! Why are you messing with me?" She jostles my shoulder.

I laugh. "Because I can." Sticking out my tongue, I scrunch my eyes and nose. "And to answer your question, yes. Yes, we can pick a date now."

Liz wraps her arms around me again, lifts me off the couch so I hover inches from the floor, spinning me in circles. Between the physical motion and the rapid pounding in my chest, I feel like a little kid at the playground going round and round on the metal merry-go-round from my childhood. Whirling until dizzy. Both elated and nauseous at the same time.

But I wouldn't exchange the exhilaration for anything.

After Liz wobbles a little, she sets me down, plants her hands on her knees, and laughs. Such a beautiful sound. A sweet pitch with a hint of baritone.

As I stare down at her bent form, a new sensation bubbles

beneath my breastbone. If euphoria could morph into tangible existence, it would radiate from every pore of my flesh. Not a single person in my existence has given me this gift. The gift of hope and wonder and unconditional love.

Liz bolts upright, stares at me with wide eyes for a beat, then runs across the apartment and into our room. In seconds, she reaches my side again, grabs my hand, and hauls me back to the couch. We plop down and snuggle into the cushions. Liz fumbles with a binder in her hands. A very large, pearl-finish binder with dozens of tabs and colored fabrics hanging out the edges.

Sucking in a deep breath, I swallow and glance up at Liz's swirly hazels. They swirl a little like the merry-go-round in my chest. This is it. We are finally going to pick a date. We are finally picking when forever begins.

"You're absolutely sure?" Liz studies my expression, waiting for me to show signs of doubt. And after months of making her sit patiently on the sideline, I have absolutely no doubts. I want to call Liz my wife more than I want to breathe.

"Never been more sure about anything in my life," I tell her without an ounce of uncertainty.

Swirls of blue and green and a hint of gold stare back at me with a sparkle I have never noticed before now. A spark fizzes above my diaphragm, building and growing more powerful with each rhythmic pump of the fist-sized organ in my chest. Rising and swelling in my throat until it's difficult to swallow. Tears sting the back of my eyes and threaten to spill any moment.

Damnit. If I'm this much of an emotional wreck already, no telling how much I will cry when the actual wedding happens.

One corner of Liz's mouth pops up long enough for me to catch it. A pop that translates everything she isn't saying aloud. How she believes me. Knows what I am feeling in this exact moment. Because she feels it too. Before she asked to be mine forever, and now sitting next to me. She feels the nonstop ache to hold me in her arms and never let go. To kiss my lips as if they were the most precious piece of me. To whisper sweet—and naughty—sentiments in my ear as we lay in bed.

She knows.

Liz flips open the binder of intimidation and flips the first tab to the left. Behind it is a page with a large loopy font. *Our forever starts…* Beneath the words is a blank line begging for one of us to scrawl our date. The day when we plan to start forever.

"Any requests?" Liz asks, her fingers brushing over the page as she stares down at it with pen in hand.

I wait for her to look up at me. Wait for her to see understanding when I tell her. When I don't answer immediately, she glances up and nods. As if she knows this is a serious moment.

"Just not November."

She drops the left side of the binder on my lap and takes my hands in hers. "Not much of a November girl anyway." After a slight nod and a squeeze of my hands, she releases me and starts tapping her lips. "It's March now. And we should give a fair amount of time for planning and finalizing everything."

The way Liz says "finalizing everything" has me thinking she's talking more about the divorce paperwork, and not the organization of dresses and color and flowers and venues. Either way, I love how she doesn't mention any of it. As if she believes it will trigger another episode. Will it? I have no clue.

"Maybe we should do a spring wedding. The first day of spring. A perfect time for new beginnings."

I don't remember the lead up to it, but suddenly Liz's lips are attached to mine. They tell me how much she loves me. How she will do anything and everything for me. Love me. Honor me. Protect me. From anything or anyone who wishes me harm—mentally, emotionally, or physically.

Without hesitation, my love for Liz skyrockets to worlds unknown. There isn't a doubt in my mind, Eliza Warren is my savior. The one person meant to heal me and make me whole again.

"March twenty-first it is," Liz states.

"March twenty-first," I repeat before I kiss her senseless.

ELEVEN

LIZ

Since setting the wedding date, Tiffany and I have been full steam ahead with planning. We have talked colors and food and who will attend. Hours spent together hovering over the massive wedding binder. The whole experience has been nothing short of dreamy.

The toughest decision so far—will we both wear dresses, or just one of us. Maybe neither of us. With so many beautiful options between dresses and dress suits, I am constantly changing my mind. The way Tiffany has been ogling all the dresses in the magazines, I have no doubt I'll see her in tulle or satin or organza. With every page flip, she becomes more and more starry-eyed. And I love every glimpse of it.

Which brings us to now. Me sitting on a plush loveseat staring at a trifold of mirrors with a platform in front of them. Tiffany behind a curtain-closed room to my right, slinking on the first dress out of a small stack the attendant pulled from the racks.

The curtain slides to the side, and I get sucker-punched in the solar plexus. All air evaporates as I take my girl in. *Dear, god. Tiffany is the most beautiful creature I've had the pleasure of knowing. Of seeing.*

Stepping out, she clutches both sides of the skirt and lifts it as she walks forward with her eyes on the floor. Seven steps closer, she releases the skirt and I watch it billow to the floor before she peeks up at me. "What do you think?" she mutters, then bites her bottom lip.

What do I think? I think I want to take her face between my palms and kiss the hell out of her right now. Sweep her off her feet, twirl her in circles, and squeeze the hell out of her.

I blink and blink, working to stop the tears biting the backs of my eyes from falling. I open my mouth to speak, but nothing comes out. A thick ball of cotton lodged in my throat. Opening my mouth again, I relocate my voice—although it scrapes like sandpaper. "Perfect." There is no other way to describe Tiffany in that wedding dress in front of me. Absolute perfection.

Tiffany steps up onto the platform surrounded by mirrors and runs her hands down the skirt as she stares at the lace and tulle in the mirror. No matter the cost, this is Tiffany's dress. The bodice and skirt a soft champagne. A silver belt at her waist shimmers under the light. Light white tulle embroidered with lace overlays the skirt. The lace covering the bodice is more intricate and tight-knit before spreading down her back and down her arms to stop at her wrists. The back brought together by a long row of satin-covered buttons.

Her beauty ravishes me, and I have to remember how to breathe. How to speak and function like a human.

A consultant from the shop runs to her side and starts pinching in fabric at her backside before adding large clamps. Tiffany stares at herself for a few minutes, twisting and turning to see the dress at different angles. All while I ogle this gorgeous woman who will soon be my wife. Maybe not as soon as I would prefer, but soon enough.

"Is this the dress?" the attendant asks Tiffany.

Tiffany meets my gaze in the mirror, silently asking me the same question. "You look stunning, baby. But you have to love it. The choice is yours."

A twinkle I haven't seen before sparks in Tiffany's eyes and brightens her expression. I'm not sure what provoked the change, but I love seeing the glow on her skin.

Swiveling to face the attendant, Tiffany nods. "Yes, this is the one." When she turns back to the mirrors, her lips perk up and slowly spread into the most incredible, blinding smile.

The attendant takes Tiffany's hand, guides her off the platform, and tells her to change out of the dress and into under-garments only, but not to remove the clamps. Once she has changed, the woman takes several measurements to have the dress properly fitted. After she finishes, Tiffany gets fully dressed and both women look at me.

"Your turn," Tiffany says, bouncing on her toes while clapping.

Uh, what?

"Not sure I want a dress, baby. I didn't come prepared to try anything on."

Tiffany reaches forward and clasps my hand, yanking me off the loveseat. "So what. You should still try something on. I want to see what you look like in a dress."

I swallow and slowly retract into myself. Not that I have never worn a dress before, but I wasn't expecting to try on anything today. And I have no idea what to look at. Sure, I have stared at bridal magazines for months, but that's just breezing through pages and sparking ideas.

"Um, okay," I say, reluctantly.

Tiffany and the attendant both clap in glee. Their smiles bright while I force my lips up. Although the idea excites me, it also binds my stomach into a trucker's hitch knot. The woman asks what ideas I had in mind for the big day. When I share my ideas, she stares at me wide-eyed for a beat before scurrying off to find something to meet my specifications. Tiffany tugs me back down to the loveseat and I whisper how gorgeous she is—in her wedding dress and in general.

Ten minutes later, she returns with three options. I gawk at each of them, stunned into silence. Not often will I slip on a dress or wear more feminine clothing—mostly, I just love being comfortable. But these dresses spark something warm and profound and life-altering in my core. A legit awareness that this is happening. Tiffany and I are getting married.

Rising from the loveseat, I stroll over to where the atten-dant hung the three gowns. Each of them different fabrics and cuts. All of them contenders for the big day. All of them awe-inspiring.

Stepping up to the first dress, I trace my fingers over the material. The satin smooth and soft under my touch. With a sash just beneath the strapless bust, the top and skirt the same satin material, it flows smoothly to the floor and fills out like the most elegant ball gown I have ever seen.

With reluctance, I inch down the line to the second dress. This one slimmer fitting until it hits the knees. The organza delicate and elegant. It reminds me of a mermaid. At least the darker tales of mermaids with the color of the fabric. The dress equally as alluring as a siren of the sea.

But the final dress stands out above the other two. Screams at me to wear it on the big day.

When the attendant asked me what ideas I had in mind for the ceremony, I told her I'd either wear a feminine and revealing tux or a bold dress that makes a statement. Whether a tux or dress, my wedding attire would be black. Far from traditional on every level, I long to express my individuality on the most monumental day of my life. To be myself. The closet romantic who isn't so feminine has a strange addiction to all things black, and listens to off-the-wall music from time to time.

So, as my hands graze and caress the multiple layers of black tulle, something whimsical ignites inside me. A whirl of foreign emotions inflates beneath my ribcage and my heart floats in a cloud of bliss. Before this moment, I thought I had experienced every spectrum of love. Thought I'd been exposed to euphoria. Tiffany has given me that gift. The gift of love.

But brushing my fingertips over the soft layers of this dress changes everything. A quiver sweeps up my limbs, tingling its way up my neck and spreading across my torso, before the sensation converges just above my diaphragm and jolts my heart.

"This one," I whisper. "Want to try on this one."

A wide, toothy smile brightens the attendant's face before she takes the third dress to a changing room and hangs it on a hook.

"If it doesn't fit you, don't worry. Put it on as best you can and we can take it in or let it out wherever necessary."

Walking past her, I nod and slink into the seven-by-seven changing room and close the curtain. Quickly, I strip out of my clothes and finagle the poufy dress off the hanger. I undo the buttons at the neck and down the back then step into the skirt. Hands on the sides of the skirt, I wiggle my hips as I hoist it up. Once in place, I loop my arms in and start to button the back as much as possible.

After I fumble with the buttons a moment and have most of them connected, I spin to face the mirror which takes up an entire wall of the changing room. I stare at the woman in the reflective glass and gasp. Not that I have ever considered myself an ugly duckling, but I have also never thought myself a beautiful swan either. In this dress, knowing what it symbolizes and how it will change my life, my breath comes and goes in sharp bursts as my heart thrashes viciously in the cage holding it captive.

Sucking in a deep breath, I spin around, clutch the dressing room curtain, and shove it aside. Tiffany and the attendant chat as they look over her dress. I step out and try to calm the buzzing cicadas whirling in my belly.

Tiffany spins to face me after catching me out of the corner of her eye and slaps a hand to her mouth. "Oh my god!" she mumbles into her hand as her eyes well with unshed tears. "Exquisite. Dazzling." Her words soft on her lips as the first tear rolls down her cheek.

I hoist up the dress, walk over to the platform, and step up to see myself in the mirrors. The attendant scurries over to me and begins latching the buttons I was unable to reach on my own. Once the dress is fastened, the attendant stands off to the side behind me and peers over my shoulder into the mirrors.

"What do you think?" she asks while fluffing out the skirt more.

Taking in the entire dress from multiple angles, a sting pricks my eyes as my throat constricts with emotion, and I sigh. This dress is what princesses wear—if black was in their wardrobe. A fairy-tale dress. It doesn't need jewels or accessories or anything glitzy to accentuate it. All on its own, the dress is perfect.

And the fact that Tiffany and I both found *the* dress is all the proof I need to know our marriage is meant to be. Call it fate or destiny or kismet—whatever terms float your boat—but this seals the deal more than any other circumstance.

"It's the one," I whisper. The woman nods then clasps her

hands in prayer position at her lips. Her joy reminds me of how my mother might react if she were here. Which reminds me to call my mom when I get the chance.

Half an hour later, Tiffany and I leave the store. Both of our measurements taken, paperwork completed, and deposits made. We drive a few miles before stopping for a bite to eat. Our conversation flows easy and we talk all things wedding related. For the first time in months, life feels normal again. Normal and happy and balanced. And I want the moment to last forever.

But something sits in the corner of my mind, sporadically reminding me that we haven't discussed her meltdown again. We haven't peeled back the layers and gotten to the root of the problem. What triggered it all in the first place. Her being married—separated—can't be the sole reason for how she behaved. During the guessing game, she admitted someone from her past hurt her. Was it her ex? Is there something more to it? Something she doesn't want to share.

However possible, I need to show her, that no matter what demons she has in her past, I love her and will always be here. Regardless of her scars.

After spending the last two weeks swamped in wedding plans, Tiffany and I agree we need a night off. So we invited everyone over to our place for dinner, drinks, and maybe a movie as background noise. It's no party or game night like we had years ago, but all my favorite people will be in attendance. Which is all that matters.

Just as I pull the baked parmesan-crusted chicken out of the oven, the doorbell rings. After setting the pan on trivets, I pop dessert in the oven—a new recipe for a rustic strawberry peach tart I dug up online.

"I got it," Tiffany calls out as I close the oven door.

"Thanks, baby," I tell her as I grab the tongs and flip over vegetables roasting on the grill-top burner.

Within minutes, the open floor plan is packed with bodies and noise. Hugs and greetings are exchanged. Sarah and Christy both deposit different bottles of wine on the kitchen island. In unison, they jog up beside me and encase me in a fierce hug.

When I can breathe again, we all laugh. Since Sarah doesn't live as close as Christy and I do, we don't spend as much time together as we did back in Georgia. Although I have gotten used to it over the years, having everyone together makes my heart happier than imaginable.

"Need any help?" Sarah asks as she peeks at the pots and pan on the stove, waving the steam toward her nose.

"Not in the kitchen. But if you guys want to figure out how we're all going to eat at that small ass table," I point to the small dining table we own that seats four, "that would be excellent."

Christy slaps a hand to my back. "Don't worry, bitch. If we figured out that first Thanksgiving, we got this."

I roll my eyes at her. The Thanksgiving she refers to was a hot mess. After spending hours in the kitchen, slaving over the oven and stove, doing everything I could to make the day perfect, Christy came into the kitchen and told me there wasn't enough space on the table for everything and she needed help. Tiffany and Rick had since abandoned her because of my desire to have everything just right. By no means am I a perfectionist. But I can't help the fact I want nice things and for everything to turn out as close to perfect as possible. It's who I am.

"Just so you both know, we don't have to sit at the table. As long as we're all together, that's all I care about."

Sarah and Christy nod then wander off to game plan how and where we will eat.

With a minute left before the risotto finishes, I open the oven and pop a pan of small dinner rolls in to warm up. Once everything is ready, I dish the food onto large serving plates and bowls, and set them on the island. Dessert still has another ten minutes in the oven before it's done. By the time we get to it, it will still be warm.

"Hey, kids. Dinner is ready."

Everyone files into the kitchen and portions out a plateful of food. We congregate in the living room where Christy, Sarah, and probably Ella set up places to eat. Once we all settle, I glance around the room and smile. There are several things in life to be grateful for, but oftentimes those minor details get overshadowed by something bigger in the moment. Having my friends—if I'm being honest, I would dub them family first and friends second—here today, it pumps my heart with incredible joy. A lot of shit has happened over the years, but no matter what, we remain rooted. Strong.

"If I could have everyone's attention for a minute," I announce. Seven sets of eyes flick my way. "Before we forget, Tiffany and I have an important announcement." I set my plate on the end table beside the couch and reach for Tiffany's hand. "We have a date!"

The room is dead silent. Considering no one was talking when I made the announcement, the vacant silence feels like an eerie mist closing in on me. Six pairs of eyes gawk at me as if I just declared war. Why are they looking at me like this? Like they have no clue what I'm referring to.

I jog my memory bank and double-check that everyone here knows Tiffany and I are engaged. Sarah and Jackson—check. Christy and Rick—double-check. Ella and Thomas—yep. Everyone knows. So why are they all looking at me like I have two heads? When no one says anything for far too long, a few pieces click into place.

Christy knew about Tiffany's current marital status. Only Christy. I never told her to keep it to herself. So as the chain goes—Christy told Rick, and probably Ella, which equals Thomas as well. No doubt Christy also mentioned it to Sarah in one of their five million text messages, who then told Jackson. Regardless, everyone in the room is fully aware Tiffany and I cannot get married yet. But Tiffany probably has no clue they all know this snippet.

Just great. Way to go Liz.

As if the awkward silence isn't bad enough, Christy adds a dash of kerosene to the fire. "What date?"

Seriously, what the hell? Beside me, Tiffany shrinks into me and the couch. It isn't difficult for her to pick up on everyone's strange behavior. Hell, she has a master's degree in psychology.

But I try to push us out of the weird funk.

I glance at Tiffany a beat, smiling big as she holds my

gaze. "Our wedding date. Duh. I wanted to tell you all at the same time before we sent out 'save the date' cards."

The weirdness turns up a few notches when no one says anything right away. Just as I am about to jump in and rescue the situation, Tiffany lets go of my hand and rises from the couch. She stares down at me with disbelief etched in her expression.

"You told them, didn't you?" Her tone far from accusatory, but laced with melancholy.

This moment should be a happy one. When you tell everyone important in your life the day you plan to start your forever. But me confiding in my friend—which I should have known would circulate in no time—about something so private was not a smart move on my part.

Damnit.

"I was frustrated and didn't know if I could talk to you about it. I'm sorry, baby." I reach for her forearm, but she tugs it back.

I fucked up. Big time.

"It is what it is. No sense in worrying about it now." Tiffany winds her way through everyone in the living room, pausing once she passes them. Looking over her shoulder, she adds, "March twenty-first, in case any of you were wondering." Then she walks back to the kitchen, sets her plate down, and heads straight for the bedroom.

Once Tiffany closes the bedroom door, Christy locks eyes with me and winces. "Sorry. Didn't know it was top secret. I hope you guys don't hate me."

I shake my head. "No, Christy. You don't get to shoulder the blame here. I should've kept my mouth shut, or at least asked her if it was okay for me to talk with someone about first. Didn't think it would be a big deal."

"So, March twenty-first," Sarah says. "Any significance?"

Nodding, I answer, "Yeah. New beginnings." Hopefully, I didn't fuck it all up.

TWELVE

TIFFANY

"Tell me how that made you feel," Trina prompts from the chair across from me.

Today marks the fifth session I have had with Trina since *he* called. Although we haven't gotten down to the nitty-gritty, we have discussed a lot over the last two-and-a-half weeks.

"Like I have no control. And I need control."

"Why?"

"Why?" I repeat her question back. She is trying to dig deeper. Trying to get me to open up more. But opening up scares the ever-loving shit out of me.

"Yes, why?"

I huff and adjust my position in the chair. Although I have been more forthcoming in the last few weeks than I have been in the last decade, I'm still not ready to expose myself to that level of vulnerability. Soon, but not quite yet.

"Because there was a time when I had no control whatsoever. It had been stolen from me. And I refuse to live like that again."

Trina watches me closely. Checking for tells as she scans my eyes, the lines of my forehead, level of perspiration on my skin, tightness of my jaw, pulse at my throat, and the rise and fall of my chest. And although this whole situation makes me want to puke, I do my best to maintain my composure.

"I get it, Tiffany. But if there is one thing you take away

from our talk today, let it be this. Don't think you are in this alone. It may have started off as only your burden, but now you have a whole team of loved ones who want to help you move past this. It's okay to let them in. To let them help. Whether for a hug, a shoulder to cry on, or just someone who will listen. Don't push them away. Not when you need them most."

Everything she mentions, I take it in, absorb it, and try to comprehend it *not* from a therapist's perspective. Unfortunately, I have been dealing with this whole fiasco alone for so long, I'm not quite sure I know how to let others help.

"Any suggestions on how I do that?"

"Start with Liz. Sit down and put as much as you're comfortable with out in the open. Let her know why you keep so much of it to yourself. She'll probably understand things better if you explain why it's been this way for so long."

I nod. Trina's right. For years, I have had to shoulder everything that happened with *him*. Took every ounce of pain he delivered and carried the burden on my own. Even though people would say I am strong for walking away after everything that happened, I don't necessarily feel strong. I have always thought running away from my problems made me weak. And although I earned a degree in psychology, and spent hundreds of hours learning about people like *him*, I still find it difficult to let it all go. To be strong when it comes to my own life.

Maybe it all stems from the fact we are still married. I never took his last name, but that doesn't mean anything. You would think, after all these years, he would be just as eager to divorce me and move on. No doubt he has bedded countless women since I ran off. Hell, I wasn't stupid when we were together. More days of the week than not, he came home with a different perfume on his skin. A different shade of lipstick on his collar... or elsewhere. And he didn't give a fuck if I smelled it on him or noticed the rouge.

Actually, he seemed *proud* to flaunt it in my face.

His control knows no bounds. Hence why he never signs the divorce papers sent to him. This will be the third attempt over the last nine years. And I always use an attorney so he doesn't have my actual address.

I never doubted he had some rough idea of where I was. But now that I found happiness, now that I am ready to move on with someone who brings me more joy than I knew existed, I fear he *will* find me. And if he does...

"Yeah, I'll figure out a way to talk to her. I just... I don't want her to look at me differently. And I don't want her fighting my battles for me. It took a long time to gain a sense of independence and learn who I am as a woman. If that fades, it will put me right back to where I was."

Trina stares at me, sympathy pinching her brow. "Maybe you need to tell Liz that, too. It's okay to tell her why you've kept this to yourself throughout your relationship. If you don't say anything, how will she know your boundaries? How will she know if she's overstepping?"

"Once again, you're right." I laugh and shake my head. "Thanks for this, Trina. You've helped me so much these past weeks. Maybe I can repay you with dinner at our house one night. Liz is a guru in the kitchen."

She waves me off. "You're my friend, Tiffany. And we're all here for each other. We have to be. I'll keep dinner in mind, but I don't expect anything in return except the reward of helping out a friend."

I rise from the couch and run my hands down my thighs. Talking to Trina these past weeks really has lifted some of the burden off my shoulders. Whether she likes it or not, I will repay her.

As I head for the door, Trina calls out to me and I turn back to face her. "Hey, have you talked about Jensen with Liz yet?"

"Not yet."

"You may want to do that soon."

I tilt my head. "Any particular reason?"

"Chloe talked with his parents earlier today. They're trying to sign him out of Lewis House. Something about him moving soon."

"Damnit," I curse under my breath. "I don't care what it takes, I won't let them."

Trina eyes me with interest before pointing a finger at me. "That right there," she states. "That fire inside you to help him. Use it, not just to help him, but to help you."

"What?"

"Something about Jensen shoots your passion up tenfold. Hone the intensity and use it to help him, but also to fight your own battles. Fight for you, but also fight for him. What he could possibly mean to you and Liz."

I get it. Use the lit fuse to ignite what needs change in my life. "Thanks again, Trina. For everything." I bolt out of her office, grab my things, and leave Lewis House.

No matter what, I will not let Jensen return to his parent's custody. He deserves better, and hopefully Liz and I can give him that. Now all I have to do is convince her.

"You want to what?"

I sigh and fall back against the kitchen counter. Rosemary and thyme and garlic waft my way in a pillow of steam while Liz stirs a large pot of chicken and vegetables, glaring at me. She slowly pours in chicken stock and another small dose of herbs. It smells like heaven.

"Please, just think about it. Jensen is a great kid. And I think adopting him would be wonderful. For him and us."

Liz adds a little flour and cornstarch to milk and stirs it a minute before adding it to the pot. It's hard to concentrate on the topic at hand with her concocting a huge pot of deliciousness.

She stops stirring and glances over at me. "I'm sure he's great—your judgment isn't something I question. But we don't have everything sorted out with us yet. How are we supposed to adopt a child? A grown child, no less." Liz turns the burner down then starts combining biscuit mix and water in a bowl.

"Lizzie, we may not be married, we may have a lot of shit going on, but we can still adopt him. I know plenty of people who can help us. All I need to do is make some phone calls."

Pulling the dough mix out of the bowl, Liz cuts it into bite-size chunks. "Please don't take this the wrong way, baby." Liz inhales deeply, closes her eyes for a split-second, and exhales slowly as they reopen. "I don't think now is the right time."

"Why?" I whisper-ask.

This is not the answer I expected to hear from Liz. I thought she would be in my corner, cheering me on and bouncing with excitement. When in actuality, it is the polar opposite. We have never discussed children—maybe the reason is obvious, we're both women—but I didn't think she would dismiss the idea so quickly. I hoped she would at least think about it for a minute or two.

Liz drops the bite-size pieces of dough into the lightly bubbling soup mixture, gives it a stir, then faces me. Her brows pinch closer while her eyes take on a sadness. "It's not that I wouldn't want to have a child with you, Tiff," she says so softly I almost don't hear it. "But what if we went through the process of adopting him and something went south? What if your ex tried to pull something seeing as you're still married? If that happened, that poor kid would suffer even more."

I widen my eyes at her questions. My thoughts have been swimming with every possible way to help Jensen, I never considered the fact that my marital status could create an issue. A major issue. The last thing Jensen needs is to be put through an even worse scenario. Not that there are many scenarios worse than your parents basically selling you for a payout.

"I... I don't... How did I not think about that?"

Wrapping her arms around my waist, Liz tugs me close and presses a kiss to my lips. Slow and warm and perfect in every way. Her kisses are my lifeblood. When she breaks the kiss, she rests her forehead on mine.

"One of the things I love about you, Tiff, is your passion. The way you fight for what you want. It's the part of you I fell in love with first. I may have made the first move with us, but you sealed the deal. Until you, I never thought I'd find the one."

Most people have no clue what a romantic Liz is. Lucky for me, I caught her eye. "Must've been the short shorts and tight midriff top that helped." I laugh and, seconds later, Liz joins in.

"Wish you still had that outfit. We could role-play."

"Role-play, huh?"

"Um, yeah. You were sexy as fuck in that outfit. Role-play

would be easy. I cook, then sit, and you serve me in that barely-there outfit. I grope you and it evolves from there."

I shake my head. "How long have you been thinking about this role-play scenario?"

Liz shrugs. "For a little while. Maybe."

"Sounds like more than a little while."

She shrugs again. "What can I say? I'm a sucker for your curves." Liz laughs—silly at first, but then it falls away. "In all seriousness, though. I would love to adopt Jensen with you. And that's saying a lot, considering I haven't met the kid. But you need to make sure it's possible with everything going on. Maybe ask your attorney."

"Probably a good idea. I'll call in the morning." Liz walks back to the pot and stirs the chicken and dumplings, flipping each piece of dough and checking to see if they're done cooking. I press against her backside and rest my chin on her shoulder. "Thanks for loving me enough to want to have a child with me. Even if most of the parenting is done with him."

Liz turns her face and kisses me. "I love you, Tiff. Truly, madly, deeply. And if having a child makes you happy, I'm all in."

Relief washes over me at hearing her words. Until this very moment, I hadn't realized how much I needed to hear her affirmation. To hear that she wanted everything life had to offer as long as that life included me. Over the years, through my work, I have heard countless tales of couples not lasting because they didn't realize their desires in life. They loved each other but didn't want the same things out of life. In the back of my mind, I worried constantly if that would happen with me and Liz.

Did we have a solid foundation built on love and trust? Without a doubt. But that didn't mean I would never question how she felt, whether it was being married or having children or exploring whatever our heart's desire.

My past had taught me to never believe in fairy-tale endings. And I have spent every day after abandoning that life to believe otherwise. Liz helps bring me closer and closer to believing dreams and a happily ever after are possible. I praise the heavens every day that she walked into the bar-

and-grill and was seated in my section. The instant attraction between us was electric.

"I love you, too, Lizzie. More than I could ever put into words." I press a kiss to her lips. "Thank you."

"For what?"

"For being everything I ever wanted but never thought I would have."

Her eyes soften for a second before her arms snake around my waist and draw me close. "If I was capable of giving you the world, Tiff, I would. In a heartbeat. But until that day comes, I'll give you as much of me as possible. Your happiness is my happiness."

Liz kisses me—soft at first, but intensifying with each thump of my heart. Her hands squeeze my hips a beat before dancing up the sides of my torso, across my shoulders, up the column of my throat, and winding into my hair. A trail of fire tingles every inch of my skin as Liz drags me closer. Kiss deepening. A silent demand for more.

I clutch her cotton shirt in my fists, needing her closer. Not an inch of space exists between us. Then Liz breaks away and disappointment washes over me. But it doesn't last.

Liz turns the burner off on the stove, places a lid on the pot, and turns back to me. Slipping her hand in mine, she doesn't say a word as she guides us out of the kitchen and straight into our bedroom.

THIRTEEN

LIZ

TIME CHANGES the dynamic of a relationship. People get comfortable. The adrenaline rush in your veins from the excitement of something new starts to fade. Complacency wiggles its way in and alters the way you think, feel, and act. All of it part of the natural cycle in every relationship.

Before Tiffany, relationships never stuck. Mostly, I coasted through life and had a good time. My longest relationship before Tiffany lasted five months. And even that was a stretch. I never counted the friends-with-benefits relationship Sarah and I had. It was nothing serious, and we both knew it would stay that way.

At some point, I resolved maybe a long-term relationship wasn't in the stars for me. No matter who I met, no matter how many dates I went on, it never *felt* right with anyone. Until I laid eyes on Tiffany. Her auburn locks and glacial eyes kick-started the wilting organ beneath my sternum. Her hour-glass curves an added bonus. And from the moment we connected, when every synapse in my brain galvanized, I instantly knew I would do whatever necessary to make her mine.

Lucky for me, she had the same idea.

As I guide us into the bedroom, her hands grip mine a little tighter. With her tense behavior since I proposed, intimacy has been at an all-time low. I don't blame either of us specifically. More of a combination of circumstances that have had our heads elsewhere.

But the second I glimpsed the heat in her gaze, the perspiration on her skin, how her breath came in short bursts, and the intensity of our joined lips—it was time to break the cycle. Time to show Tiffany, for the first time in far too long, how much she means to me.

Closing the space between us, I frame her face in my hands and press my lips to hers again. Warm and soft and sweet. I trace her lower lip with my tongue and she gasps, opening up for me. Her arms snake around my backside, palms sliding down and gripping my ass. She kneads each cheek, driving my hips closer and closer to hers. With each swipe of her tongue, my restraint falls to the wayside faster and faster.

I need to taste her. Now.

"Tiff," I groan before spinning us around and pushing her down on the bed. "I need you on my tongue."

"Oh, god."

She scoots up the bed while kicking her shoes to the floor. Planting a knee on either side of her legs, I crawl up the bed and straddle her as I unfasten her pants and start wiggling them, along with her thong, down her legs. As they thud against the floor, I press my palms on the inside of her knees and spread her wide. Light spills into the room from the living room and highlights the dampness between her thighs. I bite my lower lip and swallow. Damn, she is mouth-watering.

I crawl up the mattress, a lioness hunting prey. Tracing my fingers up her toned thighs, Tiffany vibrates against me and I pin her hips to the bed as I kiss my way up, up, up. An inch away from her glistening folds, I pause and inhale deeply. Her scent a heady combination of pheromones and tang and an unnamed sweetness which has me licking my lips.

Hovering an inch above her mound, I pant heavily and breathe in the taste of her. Beneath me, Tiffany trembles as my hot breath paints her skin. Her hips rocking gently and begging for my touch.

Reaching down, Tiffany laces her fingers through my hair, makes a fist, and tugs. "Taste me," she demands. "Put your mouth on me. Now." She tilts her hips and forces my face between her thighs.

"Yes, ma'am."

My lips brush against the heat at the junction of her thighs. I kiss her dampness chastely, again and again. Teasing and driving her wild. On the seventh kiss, I part my lips and run my tongue the length of her slit. Her tanginess on my taste buds so fucking sweet.

Wiggling at my tongue, Tiffany fists my hair taut and moans. I peer over her mound, her body silhouetted by the faint light outside the room, and take in every ripple of her body. Still clothed from the waist up, I itch to rip her top off. Ache to watch her pert breasts tighten and nipples harden as I lap at her clit.

I kiss my way up her body—she groans and I laugh—and shimmy her top up the sides of her torso. When she realizes what I'm doing, Tiffany sits up and tears the top away as I reach around and unhook her bra. Once removed, I nip her lower lip before trailing my way lower, sucking and biting. Paying attention to each of her breasts, clutching the soft skin as it spills over my palms.

Trekking down her midline, past her navel, I lick a path to the lush patch of curls reminding me of heaven. Hands still clutching her breasts, I bite along the perimeter of her mound. She jerks beneath my touch before pushing into me further as I roll her nipples between my thumb and forefinger.

"Liz," she moans my name like a litany.

Releasing one of her nipples, I drag my nails down her abdominals, past her hip, and along her thigh. Her back arches off the mattress and she claws at my hair with a vengeance. Grazing the inside of her thigh with my fingertips, I insert two digits into her hot pussy. The moment I'm inside her, her hips grind into me harder, and my own arousal slides down the inside of my thigh.

"Yes," she hisses.

I gaze up her body, her tits at attention, a light sheen glowing on her skin, back lifting from the sheets as she grinds harder on my face. Her cries of pleasure music to my ears and I pump my fingers in and out of her folds.

Pitch higher. Screams louder and closer together. She

trembles as her walls grip me like a vise. Hands fisting my hair tighter. I suck her clit faster, harder, and within seconds she detonates on my tongue. Continuing to pump in and out of her, I lift my mouth and watch as the orgasm ricochets throughout her body.

When her body comes down, I withdraw my fingers and suck them off.

"Fuck, you taste amazing," I grunt out as I roll my eyes closed.

Before my eyes crack open, Tiffany's hands are on me. Yanking my shirt over my head. Tugging me forward and shoving me down on the mattress. Ripping my pants away. Devouring every exposed inch of my skin. Her animalistic need to have me jolts my arousal to an all-new crescendo. When I reach out for her, she takes my wrists in her hands and slaps them down to the mattress above my head.

"My turn. Be a good girl," she demands.

"Promise, baby." I wink at her.

Hours pass as Tiffany and I make up for all the missed nights of intimacy. All the nights we just went to bed, turned off the light, and fell asleep untouching. All the kisses we missed out on. Our tapered fire.

Over the last two weeks, the bond between me and Tiffany rediscovered its flame. Every opportunity we have to touch or kiss or cuddle, we do. Our relationship resembles more of what we had in the beginning. The insatiability. The hunger to be near each other at all possible times.

After a lengthy discussion with her attorney, and Tiffany having an even lengthier conversation with Jensen, Tiffany and I have started the process of adopting Jensen. Tiffany's attorney explained that the divorce is an undesirable obstacle during the process, but won't deter it. Because the adoption application will have only her name and mine on it, we are the only people involved. Her ex can try to stir up shit, but it won't stop things from happening. And he also won't have any rights to Jensen—something Tiffany was extremely concerned about.

Tiffany has been on edge the last two days. On the first night, I asked what had her so riled up.

"The divorce papers get served tomorrow." The words barely a whisper on her tongue.

I wish I knew why this guy scared the shit out of her. Have I had fucked up relationships in the past? Of course. Who hasn't? Hell, high school and college are full of nothing but bad choices—not that I got the true college experience.

But the way she shrivels at the idea of him, I know he fucked her up more than comprehensible. The woman I met, the woman I fell in love with, is strong and brave and has the sexiest confidence I have ever seen. Somehow, this man drained all of that from her, once upon a time. Hopefully, he doesn't do it again.

I stare up at the ceiling, the morning sun a couple hours from rising, and do my best to not worry. Tiffany sleeps beside me, occasionally mumbling words that make no sense when strung together. Words like "storm" and "picture" and "closet." No matter how I spin them, I can't piece them together in a way that makes any sense. And I refuse to ask her what she dreams about.

Something tells me she won't be forthcoming.

So, I slip out of bed, grab my phone from the charger, head to the bathroom, and text Christy.

Liz: You up?

A minute passes before the text bubble pops up.

Christy: BITCH, IT IS 5:21. IN THE MORNING. ON A SATURDAY.
Liz: Sorry. Need some gym time. Join me?

Sitting on the toilet lid, I stare at the three dots dancing in the bubble on the screen. It disappears then reappears. *Is she typing out a damn novel?*

Christy: Meet you in 30.
Liz: Thanks, girl.

I dress in leggings, a sports bra, and a loose-fitting tank before slipping on my hoodie and sneakers. Although winter ended weeks ago, the morning chill seeps in your bones this early in the day. Quietly, I grab my gym bag out of the closet and make sure my towel and water bottle are inside.

Once I have everything, I walk out to the kitchen and grab the pad of paper magnetized to the fridge. I write a note to Tiffany, peel the paper off the pad, and walk it back into the bedroom and place it on my pillow. One last glance her way, her auburn locks splayed behind her as she faces where I would be if in bed, I blow her a kiss and head out.

Twenty minutes later, Christy and I straddle treadmills at the twenty-four-hour gym between her house and mine. We tap a few buttons and soon the belt starts spinning. Christy knows most of what has been on my mind recently—which has gotten better. So, right now, I'm sure she wonders why I'm running like I need a punishment. But she doesn't ask. Doesn't question why I woke her so early on a Saturday.

The best part about best friends, they know when to ask questions and when to wait patiently for you to speak up.

After forty-five minutes and a gallon of sweat, we jump off the treadmills and wipe our faces dry.

"Mind if we do bikes for a few?" I ask. She has already run at least a 10K beside me, and I know me asking more out of her is a stretch.

"We doing a triathlon, bitch?" Her teasing is exactly what I need, she knows it too, and I laugh.

I wave my hand in front of us. "Do you see a damn pool? Not me. Maybe just a duathlon," I tease.

She rolls her eyes and shakes her head. "I guess. But don't expect much out of me. My legs are already jelly."

"We've run more than that before. You getting weak in your old age?"

Christy play-slaps my arm. "I'm not old, bitch. If you really want to know, it's from the sex marathon we had last night."

Every set of eyes within twenty feet snaps our way. "Will you shut up," I whisper-hiss.

She laughs. Head tipping back, hand slapping to her chest, nonstop laughing. When it dies down a smidge, she stares at me with amusement glinting her eyes. "When did you become such a prude, Liz? I'm not ashamed of who I am. Not anymore. And if I have *lots* of sex, it's my prerogative. If these people are embarrassed" —she points at everyone staring at us— "that's their issue. Not mine."

And then she walks off to the stationary bikes, leaving me to stand here with countless people staring in disbelief. I simply shrug and follow in her wake.

We start pedaling—me twice the speed of Christy—and I push myself hard. Five minutes pass and I finally locate the courage to speak what is on my mind.

"I'm scared."

Christy stops pedaling for a moment, then starts back up. "Why?"

Neither of us looks at each other. We don't need to. Being friends for almost six years has built our foundation. We don't need eye contact or to see body language to understand one another. She hears the quiver in my voice. Knows my eyes would be glassy if she peered over.

"Things have been going really well between me and Tiffany these last weeks."

"That sounds like a good thing. That shouldn't make you scared."

I bite the inside of my cheek, hesitant to spill too much, but also knowing I need a friend's advice. Maybe if I just hint around it. I don't need to divulge specifics to get my point across.

"Have I ever told you Tiffany talks in her sleep?"

Now is when Christy chooses to glance over at me. Her eyes wide behind her black-framed glasses. Head shaking slowly. "No. What did she say?"

I reach for my water bottle and take a swig. "Most of what she says is broken up. Random words that don't make sense. Not to me anyway." After another drink, I set the bottle back down. "Some of the things I've heard more recently..." I trail off. There's no simple way to say what I'm thinking. Also, I don't want to betray Tiffany's trust, or secrets, if what I am thinking is true. "Her ex, I think he *hurt* her."

The words taste sour on my tongue and I instantly regret saying them.

"Physically?" Christy asks barely above a whisper.

"I don't know. Maybe. She won't talk to me about it. I get that talking about it stirs up bad memories for her. But my mind is racing at all the possibilities of what it could be."

Christy stops pedaling altogether and stares at me. "If that happened to her, Liz, you need to let her do things at her pace. You can't force her to do anything. She'll pull back if you do."

My legs halt as I get lost in Christy's words. She is right. If I start demanding answers from Tiffany, she will shut down. Or worse, leave me. Even if my only desire is to help her.

"Yeah, you're right." I sigh. "What do you think I should do?"

"Wait it out." Christy winces. "I know that's not the answer you were hoping for, but when she's ready, she'll say something."

"What if she never does?"

"Then you leave it alone. It's her past, Liz. She's the only person who decides to tell it. And if she doesn't tell it, maybe it's because she has made peace with it."

"Or it's avoidance," I mumble.

"Maybe," Christy says. "But, again, it's her choice."

I nod and stare past her. Just let it all go. When Tiffany is ready, she will tell me. Regardless of what happens, I have to remember this. It would be unfair of me to expect her to spill demons that unsettle her.

"Thanks, bitch," I say. "Thanks for always telling me what I need to hear. Life wouldn't be the same without you. And please don't pass this on. Tiffany would be embarrassed."

Christy smiles sweetly. "Promise."

We get off the bikes and head for the exit. The walk to our cars is quiet, but exactly what I need. After we say our good-byes, we get in our respective cars and drive off. Traffic has picked up, and the extra time gives me a chance to mull over Christy's advice.

By the time I walk in the front door, my mind is set. I will do this. Be Tiffany's strength and not ask her to uproot her past. I will give her what she needs. Time. And hopefully, one day, she will gift me with more of her in return.

FOURTEEN

TIFFANY

Two weeks have passed since Liz and I started the adoption process for Jensen. Initially, when I mentioned the idea to Jensen, he looked taken aback. Questioned why I would want to adopt him when he would turn eighteen in less than three months. I explained my reasons to him—because he deserved better. Simple as that.

Since then, we have talked almost daily. About his progress. How he is feeling. How he thinks his parents will react to the whole situation.

The entire situation has been quite therapeutic—for both of us, if I'm honest. As a therapist, I shouldn't be on the receiving end of therapy when with a patient. The concept is highly frowned upon within our scope of practice. But because life has progressed beyond the typical therapist-patient relationship with us, I have allowed myself to become more invested in all things Jensen.

I round the corner and head for the first-floor wing. After entering all my credentials, I come to an abrupt halt when I spot a couple at the nurse's station. Although I haven't met them in person, I have seen pictures of them. In Jensen's file. Jensen's parents are here. In the patient wing. Talking with Juan.

Parents shouldn't be permitted onto the wing without the patient's doctor being notified. In this instance, that would be me. Chloe insists parents or guardians be allowed in—as a measure to help the patient heal. But Jensen's parents won't help in the healing process. If anything, he will spiral after having contact with them.

Unsure what has provoked their visit, I take a deep breath and compose myself. Once I slip my doctor face on, I step toward the nurse's station.

"Good morning, Juan. May I speak with you a moment?" I focus on Juan, divert my eyes from the couple, and he gives a slight nod. We step to the other end of the nurse's station, Jensen's parents still in view. "Why are they here?" I whisper.

He peeks at the couple out of the corner of his eye before locking eyes with me. "Said they're here to check Jensen out. That he has a plane to catch," Juan whispers back.

Son of a bitch. Bile rises in my throat as I ball my fingers into tight fists. These people know no bounds, will stop at nothing to get a payday off their own flesh and blood. They make me physically sick. How the hell do they sleep at night?

Stretching my fingers out, I inhale deeply and try to calm my irate pulse. "How long have they been here?"

Juan checks his watch. "Five minutes. Told them you would be here shortly, and that they would need to wait." I nod. "Also overheard them say today was the last day. What-ever that means."

Today is the last day. Juan and the other nurses aren't privy to everything going on in Jensen's life, only pertinent things that help them do their job. Unless they searched Jensen's file, they would have no clue what his parents were up to. For Jensen's sake, I wish they were up-to-date.

"Thank you, Juan. If you wouldn't mind, will you please go to Jensen's room and let him know I will be with him soon. Do *not* let him leave his room."

Juan raises his eyebrows, studying my expression for a moment. From his tone and posture when I walked in, he knows something isn't right. And without a word, Juan puzzles out that I will tell him more after they leave.

"Yes, Dr. Page. Let me tell Kayla and Tom I need to step away."

I nod. Kayla and Tom are additional nurses we have on staff. The nurses currently manning the station. After Juan tells them he has to step away, I step forward with my most composed doctor face and mentally prepare for a war of wills.

"Mr. and Mrs. Pastor," I greet, extending my hand to them. Mr. Pastor reaches forward and shakes my hand, followed by Mrs. Pastor. "Why don't we have a seat." I gesture to one of the couches away from the nurse's station.

We all walk over and take a seat. Me in a single chair, the two of them on one of the couches. The first thing I notice is their discomfort. Not with being here. But with each other. The couch seats three adults comfortably. Most loving couples would gravitate close and sit side by side. In places like Lewis House, parents would embrace each other with an arm around the backside of their significant other. Lay a hand on the other. Hold hands. Display worry or fear or devotion for their child. They do none of the above. If anything, they sit as far apart as possible. Literally on opposite ends of the couch. Their expressions blank.

Another oddity I plan to solve.

"We're here to pick up Jensen," Mr. Pastor states firmly. "He's been in this nuthouse long enough. Time for him to come home and move on."

Move on? Wow. This guy really is a piece of shit.

Who comes to a wellness clinic for people who have inflicted harm on themselves and demands them to leave and "move on"? Someone who doesn't give a shit, that is who.

I swallow, straighten my spine, and square my shoulders. "Mr. Pastor, Jensen isn't ready to leave yet. He hasn't completed the program yet." I glance down at my tablet as if to check Jensen's file—which I'm not. "Jensen still has at least another month before we can release him from our care. Lewis House has specific protocol we follow when someone is admitted."

"Well, that doesn't work for us," Mrs. Pastor snaps. "He's signed up for a special *c-camp* and he's scheduled to fly out tomorrow morning." I don't miss the way she stutters and emphasizes the word camp. As if Jensen is eight-years-old and this is summer space camp. It boils my blood at how easily these people plan to sell their child.

Giving them a hard smile, I shrug. "Sorry. Jensen won't be leaving until we feel he is no longer a danger to himself. If you call the camp he is attending, I'm sure they'll give you a refund considering the circumstances." I add the last part, knowing they haven't paid a cent for Jensen to go where they intend to send him. Quite the opposite.

Mr. Pastor bolts up from the couch, fists balled at his sides as his face reddens. "He's *our* son, and I say we're not leaving here without him." His elevated tone grabs the attention of Kayla and Tom, who look to me, silently questioning if I need assistance. I nod slightly.

I rise from the chair, set down the tablet, and lift my chin a half-inch higher. "Mr. Pastor, you need to calm down before I have you escorted off the property."

He looks me up and down, curling his lip and muttering under his breath. "You can't keep me from taking my kid out of this shithole. I said he's leaving with us, and I meant it. We aren't leaving without our boy."

My arms and legs shake as my pulse sprints for the finish line. But I refuse to let this man break me. Refuse to let him walk all over me and hurt Jensen. For Jensen, I will stand my ground and fight. Assholes like John and Margot Pastor will not ruin another life.

I tip my chin and hold up my index finger to Kayla and Tom. A non-threatening gesture to anyone on the ward, a gesture that appears as if I'm telling them to give me a minute, but it's one of many signals we have in place. This one basically states *Security needs to escort these people out.* Kayla nods and presses a button on the phone.

"Once again, Mr. and Mrs. Pastor, Jensen will not be leaving today. If you care about Jensen's well-being, I ask you to let us do our jobs. Please, you need to leave the premises. Do not return without calling prior and setting an appointment."

At this, Mrs. Pastor shoots up from the couch and stands toe-to-toe with me. Finger jabbed in my face. "You can't keep us from our boy, you stupid bitch."

My breakfast threatens to make another appearance as I swallow. But I don't move an inch. I don't back down or cave to her intimidation tactics. I will not be bullied into a corner. Never again.

"If you don't wish to leave in the back of a police cruiser, I suggest you take several steps back and lower your hand." I hold my breath as I wait for her to retreat.

Security enters the ward and steps up to the three of us. "Dr. Page?" Zach sidles up next to Mr. Pastor as Paul comes to stand near me and Mrs. Pastor.

"Zach, Paul, please escort Mr. and Mrs. Pastor off the property."

I don't flinch or breathe or shift my eye contact from Margot Pastor, who still stands an inch from me. The woman growls at me—literally growls—then spins around and walks off with her husband and security on their heels.

As soon as they disappear from the ward, I bend at the waist and brace my palms on my knees. I can't breathe. Can't speak. After a moment, I collapse into the chair, yanking the tablet out from underneath me, and work to settle my nerves.

That was my first interaction with Jensen's parents. First impressions say so much about a person, and theirs told me they only cared about one thing. Money. If I hadn't been privy to what Jensen told me, things might have been slightly different. But not much. As I told them, Jensen isn't ready to leave yet. That much is true. Although he harmed himself because of the way his parents were treating him, he still made the attempt. And that is never taken lightly.

Once my blood pressure levels out, I walk over to the nurse's station. "Will you please make a note in the system. John and Margot Pastor are not permitted in Lewis House without a security escort and either myself, another doctor, or Chloe being notified as soon as they step through the front door."

"Yes, Dr. Page." Kayla types away on the keyboard and Tom does the same. Each of them making notes in different locations in the system.

"I'm going to check on Jensen. Juan should return in a moment."

Heading down the corridor, I stop in front of the open doorframe of room one-thirteen. Jensen's room. God, I hope he didn't hear his parents. With how they raised their voices, it wouldn't shock me if it echoed off the walls and down the corridor to his room.

I knock on the frame, although Juan stands five feet away,

and step into Jensen's room. Jensen sits on his bed, facing away from me, while Juan stands with his legs wide and arms crossed at his chest. A barrier. A shield. A protector.

"Hey, how is he?" I ask Juan.

Juan drops his arms and slumps slightly before shaking his head. "We heard most of the conversation."

I nod and pat his shoulder. "Thank you, Juan. I'll take it from here."

Glancing over his shoulder at Jensen, Juan nods then leaves the room. "Let me know if I can help, Dr. Page."

"Will do."

Once Juan leaves, I slowly step farther into the room. Inching my way closer to Jensen. His back is taut, arms rigid at his sides as he grips the blanket on his bed, head hung low between his shoulders. With every molecule in my body, I want to reach out and drag him close. Hug him like he has never been hugged prior. Show him that good people do exist. That not every adult is like the two who gave him life.

But I don't. I can't. Not yet. Not until things settle and become finalized.

If one thing holds true, even if I am not his mother, I will protect him as if I am.

"Jensen," I say, my voice hoarse. "Talk to me." I sit down beside him, keeping a professional distance between us.

His grip on the blanket tightens and I wonder what is going through his head. Poor kid has dealt with some heavy shit. Things no child should ever have to worry over. Especially from their parents. My parents were not ideal, but at least they didn't try to sell me to the highest bidder.

At least I don't believe they did. But now that I'm away from them, and *him*, life has a wholly different vantage point. What I once saw as normal, I see in a whole new light. My parents wanting me to be with a man because of his title and status in the doctoral community—not to mention his paycheck—isn't so very different from Jensen's parents. Just different circumstances.

"Thank you," Jensen croaks out, his head still low between his shoulders.

"For what, Jensen?"

He peers up at me, his eyes damp and swollen and veiny-red. Releasing the blanket, Jensen lays his hand over mine. A softness filters his smoky topaz eyes as tears spill down his cheeks. "Standing up for me."

A splinter pierces my chest and I can't seem to find a noteworthy thing to say. It stuns me that any parent wouldn't do what I did for Jensen. But after meeting his father and mother, it doesn't shock me. Saddens me more than anything. How long has Jensen had to deal with them like this?

"Jensen, you don't need to thank me. Part of my job is standing up for you. Being strong for you whenever necessary. I'm sorry you had to hear all that." I point in the direction of the communal area. "I promise you, they will get nowhere near you without my permission while you're here."

Sniffing, Jensen wipes his nose on the sleeve of his shirt. "What about when I leave?" His eyes on mine, but looking right through me.

"I'm working on that. If everything goes according to plan, all should be taken care of by the time you're ready to be discharged."

He squeezes my hand briefly before resting his in his lap, his head drooping between his shoulders again. "I hope you're right. Because I will *not* go back with them. No matter what."

The way Jensen states this has me up off the bed and pacing in the confined space. I don't like the edge in his voice. Like he would take drastic measures again, if it was the last option he had, rather than be with his parents. It pisses me off. Shoots my adrenaline sky high. Makes me want to scream and shake the living daylights out of whoever so I can keep him safe.

I stop pacing and squat down in front of Jensen, waiting for him to make eye contact. His eyes remain pinched tight until I rest my palms on his knees. When his smoky topaz irises meet my icy blues, I give him a sad smile. "I will do whatever it takes to keep you safe, Jensen. Please don't say such things. Okay?"

A tear slips down his cheek as he nods. "Okay, Dr. Page."

I give his knees a light squeeze before I stand back up and head for the door. Peering over my shoulder, I ask, "Would you like to talk in the garden today?"

His head whips around, eyes wide and mouth slack. "Really?" It's the first time I have heard excitement in Jensen's voice. A new warmth builds between my lungs and I smile.

"Yes, really. Since you've been making great progress, you deserve time outside."

Jensen bolts up from the bed, swipes the back of his hands across his cheeks, and sidles up beside me. We walk down the hall and I inform the nurses Jensen and I will be in the garden for an hour.

After we pass through two locked doors, we step out into the garden. The fenced-in area is roughly ten-thousand square feet. Tall oaks, evergreens, and cypress shade various sections of the garden. A variety of flowers, ferns, bushes, and grassy plants decorate the ground—under trees and out in the sunlight. Bird feeders hang from a handful of trees with flocks swooping in for a taste. Water ripples in a small pond as a fountain continually spills over stacked rocks. I close my eyes for a moment and inhale deeply. Rich earthiness from the trees and a gentle sweetness from the flowers fill me. Brings me a sense of peace. Being in the garden is one of the best places on this property, and I am grateful Chloe opted to add it.

We amble over to a bench under a lush, forty-foot oak and sit. For a few minutes, we remain silent in the shade and scan the natural habitat surrounding us. Being out here, taking a break from the world, is just as therapeutic as screaming at the top of your lungs. The silence gives you a moment to breathe. A moment to think without disruption. An opportunity to just exist.

I glance over at Jensen out of the corner of my eye. His feet up off the ground and crisscrossed on the bench. Palms facing up and resting on his knees. Eyes closed. Chest rising and falling at a steady pace. He needed to be out here just as much as me. To step away from all the chaos in his life and breathe.

Giving him an uninterrupted minute to just be, I stare up at the sun through the limbs and focus on the way the beams dance amongst the leaves. After a beat, I close my eyes and listen to the birds chirp and the rustle of the leaves in the breeze. Peace flows in and flushes out the negatives from earlier. Nature has always been my solace and moments like this remind me how infrequently I experience it.

"Jensen." I peel my eyes open and turn toward him. "Would you like to talk about earlier? What you heard your parents saying?"

Drawing his legs up and close to his chest, wrapping his arms around them, he shakes his head before resting his chin on his knees.

I reach over and lay my hand on his shoulder. "It can't be easy to talk about, but keeping it all inside isn't any better. Please, will you try?"

He grinds his chin on his knees a moment before replacing his chin with his cheek and casting his eyes my way. "It hurts, Dr. Page. Knowing the two people who should care for me most want to sell me." His sorrow is a hot blade melting my heart. The backs of my eyes sting, and I remind myself I can't cry. Not now.

"Jensen, I cannot fathom your pain. Although I have experienced some painful things in my life, this is not one of them. But I will do everything within my power to help you."

"Are you sure you want me?" He swallows as tears pool in the corners of his eyes. "I mean, in less than three months I am free to do whatever I want. Live wherever I want. Be who I want."

What he says is true, but the last thing I want for Jensen is to feel like he still has no one he can turn to when life becomes challenging. He may not need a parental figure at all times, but we all need someone we can lean on. To guide us through the rough patches. To celebrate with us when we achieve something. Life has ups and downs, and it's comforting when you have someone trusting to share them with.

"Yes, and true. Your eighteenth birthday may be right around the corner, but life doesn't magically shift on that day. Yes, you will feel different. More yourself. But at the same time, you'll feel exactly the same. Age doesn't make the past vanish. Only time can help do that. And I would be honored to be someone at your side to help you with that. If you'll let me."

He faces the garden and lifts his head higher. The corners

of his lips slowly perk up—not to a full smile, but a noticeable glint of happiness. Second by second, his body relaxes more into the bench and his legs slide back into a crisscross again. His chest rises and remains full for three beats before he exhales and hums softly.

A bird chirps above us and Jensen tips his head back to watch the rock dove flutter and coo. "I would like that. A lot." He breaks contact with the dove and brings his line of sight back to me. "Does your wife want me too?"

The simple question sparks a pang in my chest. No child should ever have to ask if they are wanted. Ever. But with everything Jensen has dealt with, I don't blame him for asking such questions.

"She does, Jensen. And she would love to meet you. When you're ready, I will bring her here and maybe we can come out in the garden again and get to know each other better. Sound good to you?"

He nods. "Yeah. I'm ready to meet her whenever you bring her."

I pat his shoulder and he glances my way. "I'll make the arrangements. She just has to coordinate it with her boss."

For the next fifteen minutes, we walk around the garden. The silence between us is peaceful as we soak up the sun and listen to the trees and animals. After we head inside, Jensen joins the other patients in the communal area and starts a game of chess with a young girl, Samantha. For a moment, I observe the way they interact with each other. Both Jensen and Samantha smile. Something neither of them do much when apart. A weight lifts from my chest and I internally pump my fist.

I don't know the dynamic or relationship Jensen and Samantha share, but a bond has formed between them. A bond I plan to bring up the next time we chat. A bond I hope he retains once they both discharge from Lewis House.

Who knows... maybe one day Jensen and Samantha will be more. The idea warms my heart.

Everything is on track. With the wedding. With Jensen. And damn does it feel good.

Mr. Kelly, Tiffany's attorney, has assured us things with the divorce documents is moving forward without issue. The attorney on Tiffany's ex's end has stated he will sign the papers tomorrow. As soon as Tiffany learned this, I instantly noticed a change in her demeanor.

She slept easier—her somniloquy disappeared. Smiles flash up on her expression more often than not. Her posture more relaxed.

Honestly, I have never seen Tiffany so light and buoyant.

Today, after lunchtime, I meet Jensen for the first time. Tiffany has told me so much about him—without breaking doctor-patient confidentiality—and I cannot wait to meet him in person. If all goes according to plan, Jensen could be our son a week before his birthday. Under normal circumstances, the process would take a few months longer. But because of Jensen's age and the circumstances with his family, not to mention the connections Lewis House has, the process is being expedited quicker.

I check the time on my computer and notice I have only been at work a little more than an hour. The morning is going to drag until it is time to leave. Ugh.

Shooting an instant message to Christy, we agree to lunch before I head to Lewis House. I take a deep breath, open my email and a few reports, and get to work. Hopefully drowning myself in work for the next two hours will make time fly.

As I wrap up a call with a client, Christy appears at my cubicle doorway. The second I click the button on my earpiece, she steps in and sits in one of the empty chairs across from me.

"Ready for lunch, bitch?"

It's then that I notice she has her purse hanging across her body. Checking the time on my computer, I jerk back an inch, wide-eyed. Two hours passed much quicker the moment I stopped looking at the clock.

"Yeah, just let me sign off." I log off my computer. Grab my keys, wallet, and phone before locking my desk. "Let's go."

We meet up at a small mom and pop diner a few blocks from the office. The food is good, and the service is faster than any other place nearby. After ordering, Christy and I chat until the food arrives.

"You psyched to meet him?" Christy asks.

"I never imagined myself with a kid, you know. But adopting Jensen is incomparable to anything else I've felt. Even though I haven't met him, it already feels like he's mine. Tiff says he is the nicest kid. Just comes from a fucked up situation."

The server delivers our lunch and we dig in. After Christy demolishes half of her BLT, and I polish off a healthy portion of my salad, we continue our chat.

"Poor kid. But at least he has two people who care about him enough to adopt him."

I nod as I chew and swallow my bite. "At first, I wasn't sure how I felt about it all. Like I said, I never pictured myself having kids. But this is different. He already means so much to Tiff. And if he means that much to her, I know he'll mean a lot to me too."

As we finish our lunch, Christy updates me on Rick, Ella, and Thomas. Although the dynamic of their relationship seemed odd to me at first, it quickly grew on me. After the four of them moved in together, Christy invited everyone over and explained their relationship. The way the four of them regard each other, it is obvious, even as an outsider, how much they care about each other. Seeing them together taught me love comes in many forms. Love is far from black and white. And love overcomes any obstacle.

After we pay, Christy tugs me into her arms and hugs me hard. More than five years have passed since I met Christy at Hammond Life in Georgia. She, and Sarah, accepted me easily. Most people weren't so quick to befriend the black girl with stop-sign-red hair and an unhealthy obsession with black clothing. But they welcomed me with open arms and we have been inseparable, to some degree, ever since.

"Good luck," Christy whispers in my ear. As if saying it too loud will tarnish our meeting.

I hug her tighter to my chest for a beat. "Thanks, Christy. I'll let you know how it goes."

And with that, we part ways. Christy back to the office, and me toward Lewis House.

I park in the only remaining shady spot in the lot of Lewis House. A few rows over, I spot Tiffany's car and take a deep breath.

Flipping the visor down, I pop open the mirror and stare at myself a moment. "This is it," I mutter at my reflection. "You're about to meet your future son." I take another deep breath and close the mirror, flicking the visor back in place.

I type out a quick text to Tiffany and let her know I'm here. She replies almost instantly and says she will meet me at the reception desk.

Inhaling one last deep breath, I exhale, tug on the door handle, and exit the car. Thirty-seven steps later, I lug open the heavy glass door and step inside Lewis House. The door closes behind me, but I don't move an inch. Tiffany has worked here for a while now, but this is the first time I have set foot inside.

Scanning the vast reception area, I survey a cluster of chairs off to the left—maybe a dozen altogether. To the right is a set of double doors with opaque, wired glass on the top half. Beside the doors is a keycard scanner, a blank panel, and numerical pad. I swallow and shift my eyes forward, seeing the reception desk for the first time. The large granite desk roughly four-feet tall. Behind the ten-foot-wide desk is a woman and man who watch me with curious smiles. Off to the side of the woman is Tiffany, a wide smile shining bright on her face.

Taking a deep breath in through my nose, I exhale and step up to the reception desk.

"Hey, Tiff," I greet.

"Hey." She steps around the desk and sidles up beside me. "This is Ron and Greta." She gestures to the man and woman behind the desk. "Ron, Greta, this is my Lizzie."

The way she says *my Lizzie* accelerates my pulse. Obviously, she has mentioned me to her coworkers. Although it is such a normal behavior to mention your partner to coworkers, it isn't always normal for same-sex couples to bring it up. Same-sex relationships may be more accepted than they once were, but that doesn't mean everyone accepts it. Knowing she is comfortable enough to share our relationship here shoots adrenaline through my bloodstream and sends tingles throughout my limbs.

I lift my hand and wave. "Nice to meet you."

Tiffany hands me a badge. "Clip this on." *Visitor—Eliza Warren* reads across the badge face in bold red font.

After I attach the badge to the belt loop of my pants, we leave reception and head for the double doors. At the doors, I watch Tiffany as she swipes her work badge, places her hand on the blank screen, then enters a long string of numbers on the keypad. The level of security consoles and disturbs me at the same time. It's great such severe measures are in place, but it saddens me it has to be this way.

We pass through another set of similar doors after walking down a long corridor of offices. The new space we enter is different and I instantly know we are on one of the wards. Tiffany walks us up to another desk and speaks with the people behind it.

A man, maybe a few years younger than me, rises from his chair and walks off down a hallway. Less than a minute later, he returns with a young man. With his golden locks and constant eye contact with Tiffany, I take in Jensen for the first time.

Aside from his sunny asymmetrical and naturally messy hair, his eyes captivate me immediately. A soft lavender surrounds his pupils, blending into a light gray until it reaches the edges of his irises, which are a bold, deep gray. His beautiful eyes hold a sadness no child should bear, but one that will strengthen his soul one day. Something else I observe about Jensen is how thin he is. Too thin. Other people might say he is so thin because of his height, but height has nothing to do with Jensen's gaunt appearance.

His hands continually fidget, trying to figure out where to rest as he pinches the ends of his shirt. Tiffany hooks her arm in mine and walks us closer to Jensen. In three strides, we close the distance between us and stand two feet in front of him.

"Jensen, this is Liz." Tiffany smiles at Jensen, then faces me with the same wide, toothy smile.

Releasing the hem of his shirt, he lifts his hand and purses his lips. "H-hi. Nice to meet you," he mumbles.

I swallow down my nervousness and do my best to moisten my dry throat. "It's great to finally meet you, Jensen," I say with confidence. "Tiffany—" An elbow jabs my ribs and I wince. "Sorry, Dr. Page. Anyway, I've heard a lot about you."

Jensen's eyes dart back and forth between us. "You have?"

"Yep. In fact, Dr. Page won't shut up about you." I laugh, and after a second, he joins me.

The air around us lightens. Relief and ease taking hold. My initial nervousness at being here, at meeting Jensen, slips away.

"Let's go out to the garden and talk," Tiffany suggests.

Releasing my arm, Tiffany leads the way and we fall in step behind her. Out of the corner of my eye, I catch Jensen peeking over at me. Surveying me. Assessing me. What does he think about me? Am I what he expected? Not sure what and how much Tiffany told him about me. Obviously, she probably only told each of us minor tidbits. That way we could get to know each other on our own.

When we reach a stone table with benches surrounding it,

the three of us sit down. For a moment, we don't speak. Tiffany and Jensen have seen each other regularly for weeks. They have a familiarity that we have yet to share. To say I am nervous would be an understatement. Jensen isn't an infant or toddler or of an age where he doesn't quite have a grasp on the world. Far from it. Soon, he will be eighteen. An adult. Of an age where he can make choices about life-altering things.

At this stage of his life, even I questioned Tiffany's reasoning for adoption. She could just find ways to keep him at Lewis House until his eighteenth birthday. Then his birth parents wouldn't be able to do what they're trying to. His voice would count. And if he wanted to leave here, he would have that right.

But Tiffany explained it to me from a different perspective. How it isn't necessarily about us raising Jensen. After all, he is weeks away from adulthood. The adoption is more about giving him a true family. People who he can lean on or ask for guidance or just spend time with as he transitions into manhood.

He was dealt a shitty hand, but Tiffany wants to provide the opportunity for him to still come out ahead.

Jensen tears apart a leaf he picked up from the table. His eyes trained on the little bits beneath his palms. I bite the inside of my cheek and inspect the mossy branches above us. Seeing as this is an opportunity for me to get to know Jensen, and vice versa, I should initiate some form of conversation. Out of the two of us, this *should* be easier for me.

"So, Jensen, I have a super important question to ask you."

He stops ripping the leaf to shreds and slowly brings his timid eyes to mine. "Y-you do?" It's odd to have a kid as tall as Jensen—his height easily towering four inches over my five-foot-ten—appear apprehensive. Voice faint and shoulders slumping forward, it is easy to detect his unease. And it breaks my heart.

"Yep." I aim for easy-going as I continue. "What kind of music do you like?"

Eyes wide, Jensen openly stares at me. His lips tight and twitching side to side as he considers his answer. The question wasn't meant to challenge him, just break the ice between us. Something light. To find a common ground. He isn't aware, but I pretty much love all music. I just happen to love a couple genres more than others.

Drawing his hands off the table, he tucks them under his thighs. "Alternative rock," he answers, squinting almost as if he is unsure it's the correct answer.

"Awesome," I say, holding my hand up for a high five. After a beat, he slaps his palm to mine. "I love rock music, and some other types. But mostly rock."

For the first time, I glimpse a smile from Jensen and some unfamiliar emotion erupts in my chest. An almost indecipherable sensation. A strange combination of physical commotion. Like the high that floods your system when you plummet down your first roller coaster drop. Mixed with the dizziness of realizing you are in love with someone. Add in the jumpstart of my pulse and it's the perfect blend.

Over the next hour, I learn more than imaginable about Jensen. Aside from his love for rock music, he also learned to play the guitar in school. Tiffany told me he is smart, but until we really started talking, I hadn't realized the extent of his intelligence. Once the initial discomfort faded away, Jensen used words I'd never heard a day in my life. After I leave, I'll probably sit in the parking lot for a solid twenty minutes googling each of them online.

I also learned he didn't have anyone special in his life but had dated two girls early on in high school. He mentioned there was a girl he liked, but didn't know if anything would come of it. No names were given, but at the mention of said girl, Tiffany glanced my way with a twinkle in her eye. She had an idea of who he talked about, but didn't call him out.

Before long, it was time for Jensen to go inside and for me to leave. Leaning in close to Tiffany, I ask, "Am I allowed to hug him?" She bites her lower lip as her eyes glaze over and she nods.

Stepping closer to Jensen, he watches my every move as the space between us slowly disappears. Inches away from him, I start to extend my arms forward and he picks up on what I'm doing. Slowly, I wrap my arms around his waist as he folds his around my shoulders, and we stand stock still for ten rapid heartbeats.

Holding Jensen in my arms... aside from having Tiffany in my life, nothing else has felt this natural. Before releasing him, I take a deep breath and memorize his clean, soapy-lemon scent.

He may not be my son via biology. We may not share the same color skin or eyes. But hugging him right now, joking with him moments ago... everything clicks into place. I have experienced love in different forms—love for a friend, love for a parent or grandparent, and romantic love. But none of those types of love compare to the swell beneath my sternum right now. The never-ending expansion of my pericardium as the chambered organ encased inside pumps faster and faster.

Within an hour, I love this young man as if he were my own. And the instant we break apart, I swear to do whatever it takes to keep him safe. To give him happiness. To love him every day going forward.

He may not be my son through biology, but he is mine. He is ours.

SIXTEEN

TIFFANY

Life is on the upswing.

Today, *he* will sign the divorce papers. In a few hours, he will whip out his overpriced, fancy pen and flick it across the documents that will set me free. Today… freedom rains down from the heavens.

I have never wanted to jump and spin and vomit all at the same time as I do now. This day has been almost a decade in the making. When said and done, I plan to drag Liz out for a night of celebration. Who cares if it's a weeknight. Victories like this don't happen every day and they are worth celebrating.

Scanning over my list of patients, I organize my time with each of them for the day. After arranging my day, I review all my previous notes for each patient. Aside from Jensen, I currently tend to six others—Janet, Sean, Kenny, Leanna, Cole, and Samantha. They range from twelve to seventeen in age. Each of them here for different versions of the same reason.

Just as I collect my tablet and stand from my desk, Chloe knocks on my open door. "Got a sec?"

I check the time on my watch. Five minutes until I meet with my first patient of the day. "Yeah, but not much. What's up?"

Chloe steps inside and closes the door behind her. That can't be a good sign. "Just wanted to check on how things are going with Jensen. His parents continue to call and toss out threats."

For the love of all that is good in this world. Why will these people not give up? Why won't they just let him be a goddamn kid? Their greed obviously knows no end.

"My attorney is expediting the adoption as quickly as possible. Sorry about the parents. Do you know why they're so eager to get him out of here?"

Occasionally, Chloe reads the doctor's notes, but sometimes she just skims. I have no idea if she has read Jensen's file. And if she has, I don't know to what extent.

When she starts shaking her head, it is all the answer I need. "All I know is they came in and were hostile on the ward."

"Chloe, they aren't good people. After my talks with Jensen and the way they behaved last time they were here, I know Jensen is telling the truth. His parents are on a time crunch. From what he told me, they were planning to ship him off to someplace out of state in exchange for a lot of money. Basically, they're selling their son. And since he turns eighteen soon, they're running out of time."

Chloe slaps a hand over her mouth as she gasps. "Oh my god, Tiffany. Who the hell does that?"

I nod. "My thoughts exactly. That's why I kept them away from him when they were here. And that's why I'm doing my damnedest to stretch things out. I'm keeping him safe."

In a flash, Chloe straightens her spine and squares her shoulders. A fire sparks in her eyes as her jaw tics. If I had to name this new look on Chloe, I would dub it her fierce mom persona. Momma bear. After her son Taylor passed away, she made an oath to protect every child she possibly could. To help them in ways she wasn't able to help her own son. Occasionally, I catch that glint of sadness in her eyes. The sadness that will lessen, but never leave her completely. But she is one of the strongest women I have the pleasure of knowing.

"We will all protect him," she states with certainty. "Tell me what I can do to help."

"Help me keep him here as long as possible. At least until the adoption goes through. And we need to do whatever we can to keep the parents out of here. They're the reason he did what he did."

Chloe nods sharply. "On it."

I check the time again. "Sorry to cut this short, but I need to meet with Samantha. We should talk more later. Lunch?"

"Lunch is perfect. Text me what time works for you. See you then."

As quickly as she breezed in my office, Chloe disappears. I collect myself the best I can as I walk down the corridor to the first-floor ward. Passing through the door, I take a deep breath and slip my game face on. Samantha deserves my full attention. Plus, she can't pick up on anything going on right now. She is one of the only people Jensen interacts with—most likely because they are only months apart in age.

I check in with Willis, Sheila, and Gina at the nurse's station and get an update on how everyone has been overnight. A moment later, I sit in the communal area with Samantha. She updates me and smiles more than ever. I'm certain Jensen is the reason for her influx of smiles.

As she continues to talk, I smile and nod and hum in agreement at all the right times. Unfortunately, my mind drifts in and out of focus with our conversation. I hone in on all the pertinent points Samantha tells me. But in the corner of my mind, all I keep thinking about is Jensen's parents and their determination to ruin their son's life.

Thankfully for Jensen, I am equally determined to improve his life. And I plan to go down fighting.

Chloe and I drive to a café ten minutes from Lewis House. After we're seated and place our lunch orders, Chloe starts prattling off all the added safeguards she is putting in place to help protect Jensen. Her Momma Bear status has my heart leaping out of my chest. I'm glad more people are team Jensen in this whole messed up situation.

Since our talk this morning, she has personally gone and spoken with every staff member in regards to the situation. Those not at work spent a solid fifteen minutes on the phone with her, by the sounds of it. Now that everyone is abreast of the whole Jensen situation, Lewis House is a fortress. It will take an act of god for Mr. and Mrs. Pastor to even pass the front entrance.

When Chloe wants something enacted, consider it done.

We finish up lunch shortly thereafter and head back to Lewis House. Walking in the doors, a new level of respect and awe wash over me. When I was a young girl, I dreamed of becoming a psychologist like my dad. Although our relationship wasn't conventional, it was all I knew. Dad talked about his profession like the world couldn't live without it. That's when I first fell in love with the idea of becoming a psychologist.

If I'm capable of helping just one person, if I'm able to help them create a better life for themselves, I have done what means most to me. The reward of helping someone improve their life is the biggest perk of this profession. To have a patient walk in on day one and tell you their life doesn't matter, then turn around months later and tell you the polar opposite—it sparks so much hope in my heart.

Although Chloe doesn't run Lewis House from the doctoral perspective, she brought it into existence out of love. And that love bleeds from the walls. Is in every ounce of effort expended to help each patient that sets foot on the property. Losing her only son put life in a different perspective. It changed her relationship with her husband—unfortunately for the worse. Their marriage remains intact, but is held by a thin thread.

Before we part ways, Chloe gets my attention. "I emailed the entire staff and got them up to speed on the Pastor's. Even though I talked with everyone, I wanted it all in writing. Just in case. When you get a minute, will you read it over and let me know if it's missing anything?"

"Definitely. After I have a session with Janet, I'll give it a read."

Chloe surprises me when she leaps forward and hugs me hard. Her petite frame swathes me tighter than a football quarterback. "In case no one has told you recently, you're the best."

As quick as she jumped at me, Chloe releases me and heads toward her office.

The remainder of my day at Lewis House breezes by and before I know it, it is time to go home. Just as I reach my car and set my purse on the passenger seat, my phone rings. I dig through the oversized purse that I now wish I never purchased in the first place. *I really need to downgrade this thing.*

Before my phone goes to voicemail, I yank it out and answer. "Hello?" The process of locating my phone has me flustered and slightly out of breath.

"Dr. Page, it's Anthony Kelly. Do you have a moment to talk?"

"Of course, Mr. Kelly."

As my breathing settles back to its normal rhythm, my heart rate spikes at Mr. Kelly's non-responsiveness. I pull the phone away from my ear to make sure the call didn't drop. Still connected. Just as I'm about to speak up again, Mr. Kelly jumps in.

"Tiffany, he wants to see you."

Instantly, my body turns ice cold. My limbs begin to numb. I can't breathe. Can't speak. And my vision starts blurring as my pulse whooshes loudly behind my ears.

"No," I whisper-croak. "Mr. Kelly, I… I can-can't see him." *No, no, no, no, no.*

On the other end, Mr. Kelly sighs as if he knew this would be my response. It isn't a sigh of anger or disbelief, but leaning more toward pity or sympathy. "Tiffany, he says he won't sign the papers until he sees you. It won't be just the two of you. I will be present, as well as his attorney, and you can bring anyone else you'd like."

Great, I can bring whoever. Who the hell cares?

I honestly thought I would never have to lay eyes on him ever again. Being on complete opposite sides of the country is still too close to him. Although having thousands of miles between us has made life much more bearable.

As badly as I want to fight this and figure out some alternative way to force him to sign the papers, I have confidence that Mr. Kelly has already done everything he possibly can up to this point. If he wants to see me again before signing the papers, I will cave to his request. But only on my terms.

"Um, okay. I guess. But I have conditions."

Mr. Kelly audibly exhales into the phone. "I'd be shocked if you didn't."

With my free hand, I grip the steering wheel until my knuckles whiten. Deep breath in through my nose. Exhale slowly through my mouth. I can do this. Once I'm as calm as possible in the current situation, I dole out my terms.

"We meet in a public place. Somewhere busy. Also, somewhere far from where I live or work." Thankfully my name doesn't appear on anything within public access. Partially due to my profession, but also because I try to stay under the radar as much as possible. "You and his attorney are present at all times. I can bring *whoever* I want. And no matter what, he is not allowed to be alone with me. Ever. Not even to talk privately. No excuses."

For a moment, Mr. Kelly doesn't respond. In the background, papers shuffle and I know he remains on the call. "I'll get it set up. Is there a day that works better for you?"

"The sooner this is done, the better. I can tweak my schedule, if necessary."

"As soon as we hang up, I will call his attorney's office and get things rolling. When I have a date and time, I will email you. And Tiffany?"

"Yes, Mr. Kelly?"

"It'll all work out. Just hang in there. We're in the home stretch."

God, I want to have faith in his statement. But I know my past, and I won't believe anything is final until I see it with my own two eyes. When you know someone's history the way I know *his*, it is difficult to believe anything will work out.

So, I send a prayer to anyone listening. *Please. Please let this end quickly. Let it be painless. And let it be final.*

"Okay, Mr. Kelly. I'll be waiting to hear from you."

At some point, I crank the engine to life and drive home. The entire drive is a blur, but I make it home safely and in one piece. As soon as I walk in the door, Liz runs to my side and wraps me up in her embrace. I recap the call with my attorney. Liz clutches me impossibly closer and whispers in my ear, telling me everything will be okay. That it will be over before I know it. That, soon, I will never have a reason to think about him again.

And I want to believe her.

But she doesn't know him.

Or what he is capable of.

SEVENTEEN

LIZ

Tiffany didn't sleep much last night. Neither did I.

Throughout the night, she tossed and turned, mumbling random words. Words that gutted and angered me. Words like *fist* and *stop*, followed by body jerks or shivers.

I desperately want to wake her. Soothe her. Settle the crazy thoughts spinning cyclones in her dreams.

But I don't. I leave her to sleep in bed. Alone.

After slipping on a pair of pajama bottoms and a tank top, I exit our bedroom, shut the door, and go into the kitchen. The display on the stove lights up half of the room and I squint to read the time. *Fuck.* Three-twenty-one. At this point, is it considered really late? Or really early? Either way, it sucks.

Walking farther into the kitchen, I flip on the lights under the upper cabinets. The small strips of LED lights instantly blind me and I wince as I slam my eyes shut. Slowly, I crack my lids open until my eyes adjust to the brightness.

I plant my palms on the cool granite, hang my head for a beat, and breathe slow and steady. Thank goodness tomorrow —well actually, today—is Saturday and I don't have to be at work. I would be dead on my feet. Probably still will be, but at least it'll be in the comfort of my own home.

Once I garner my thoughts, I step over to the fridge and snatch the magnetic notepad off the door, along with the pen we keep in the drawer near the fridge. Staring at the lined page for a minute, pen hovering an inch in my hand, I ponder a mile-long list of things to do to preoccupy my mind.

Eureka strikes, an imaginary light bulb popping up over my head, and I jot down dish after dish. Ideas supersede my weary body and I scribble as if sleep is the last thing I need. When the lined sheet is full, I step back and nod.

"Time to get to work," I whisper to the paper as I tear it off the pad.

For the next four hours, I stress cook and bake, cleaning up after each mess and remaining as quiet as humanly possible. When seven-thirty rolls around, I yawn and survey the additional meals and treats on the kitchen island. Quiches loaded with maple sausage, caramelized onions, mild cheddar, and rosemary. A batch of both oatmeal chocolate chunk and peanut butter cookies. Quinoa, balsamic roasted carrots and Brussels sprouts, and grilled herb-crusted chicken—all divided into containers for three lunches. The remaining chicken, vegetables, and quinoa in broth and ready to be heated for soup. And piping fresh from the oven is a pan of peanut butter swirl brownies.

I had yet to scratch biscuits, potstickers, cinnamon rolls, scones, cucumber salad, and stuffed shells off the list. Some of the items just prepped to bake later in the week. Others made and frozen after the fact. But I will make them later.

Stumbling over to the couch, I plop down and yank the throw blanket off the back, tugging it up my body. With heavy lids, I close my eyes and drift off.

"Lizzie," Tiffany says softly near my ear. "Go lay in bed."

I grumble and shift on the couch, facing the back and yanking the blanket over my head. "So tired."

Tiffany lightly strokes my hair. "Did I keep you up?"

Rolling back to face her, I squint at the faint light sneaking in through the blinds. "No, baby. Just had difficulty sleeping and didn't want to wake you." Pushing the blanket down to my waist, I reach up and take her hand. "What time is it?"

"Just after eleven."

I groan and force myself to sit up. Extending my arms and legs, I stretch my limbs out before twisting my torso left to right. A little over three hours of sleep. It sucks, but sleeping all day will only throw off my whole body clock.

Begrudgingly, I rise from the couch. "Have you eaten yet?" I ask.

Tiffany shakes her head. "Woke up a little bit ago and saw the buffet on the counter. Wanted to wait for you."

I loop my arm in hers and we wander into the kitchen. In the daylight, my overnight kitchen extravaganza is more jaw-dropping. How the hell will we eat all of this before it spoils? Both of us need to take some of this to work.

"Where to begin?" I mutter.

Tiffany twists to face me, a colossal smile lifts her lips which plumps her cheeks. "Not sure about you, but I'm eating half a quiche with a brownie appetizer and cookie dessert." Her smile is infectious and soon I'm smiling too.

"Good choice. Think I'll have the same."

While the quiche reheats in the oven, we dig into the brownies. After a healthy portion of chocolate, peanut butter, and sugar, I dish out the quiche while Tiffany makes us coffee. We demolish the quiche in no time. With food and coffee in my system, not to mention some sugar, my body wakes up more. I won't be working out anytime soon today, but at least I no longer resemble a zombie.

"Anything you want to do today?" I ask as I start covering and stashing food away.

Tiffany hands me the other, now lidded, quiche. "Honestly, it would be nice to hang at home in PJs. Maybe have a movie marathon and eat more cookies and brownies. If we get bored, we can make the other stuff on the list on the counter."

I close the fridge and step up to Tiffany, snaking my arms around her waist and dragging her flush to me. I kiss her nose then rest my forehead on hers. "Sounds like the perfect Saturday."

We settle on the couch and decide to have a *Matrix* marathon. For the first two hours, we snuggle under the blanket and stretch out on the couch. When the credits roll up the screen, we get up, stretch, use the bathroom, and grab sweet provisions from the kitchen.

Halfway through *Matrix Reloaded*, Tiffany's phone rings and I pause the movie. She bolts off the couch, answers her phone in the bedroom, and slowly ambles back to the couch.

Plopping down next to me, she drops her head in her free hand as she listens to whoever talks to her. "Okay, I understand," she mumbles, sighing heavily. "When?"

Instantly, Tiffany straightens beside me. Back ramrod, jaw clenched, eyes glassy. Must be the attorney discussing her ex. In the time Tiffany and I have been together, nothing has freaked her out. Nothing except *him*. She still hasn't told me what he did to her, but I want to run a blade through his chest. Whatever he did to Tiffany… he is a real piece of shit.

"Set it up. I'll clear my calendar with work. This needs to be over now." Tiffany is silent a moment as the attorney responds. "Thanks, Mr. Kelly. I owe you so much."

Tiffany disconnects the call and tosses her phone on the coffee table. Resting her elbows on her knees, she drops her face in her palms, hair curtaining her profile. I gently press my palm to her back and rub up and down. Beneath my touch, Tiffany trembles.

"What did he say?" I mutter.

We sit in silence for a few minutes. I absently watch the screen saver on the television while I continue rubbing her back. Slowly, her trembling wavers and she takes a deep breath, speaking on the exhale. "The meeting has been arranged."

"As much as it'll suck, at least we can get it out of the way." It's my best attempt at finding the positive in the situation.

She nods. "Yeah, I suppose."

"When is the meet?"

Lifting her head, Tiffany peers over at me. "Friday. Five o'clock. At some Italian restaurant in downtown. Mr. Kelly is emailing me the details."

"Friday," I whisper as a tingle ripples up my spine. "So soon."

Tiffany nods. "Yeah, I told Mr. Kelly the sooner, the better. That way we can move on from all this." She drops her hands in her lap and I reach for them.

Our fingers fumble a moment before I firmly hold hers in mine. Lifting our joined hands, I kiss her skin that barely peeks out. "Smart thinking." After a thought, I perk up and smile at her. "Just think, by this time next week, it will all be over."

That gets her smiling. "Thanks, Lizzie."

"For what, baby?"

"Always knowing what I need. Always being here for me and loving me. No matter what."

"You say all this as if I have a choice."

Her smile brightens. "We all have a choice."

I lean forward and press a chaste kiss to her lips. "When it comes to you, I never had a choice. Because you're the other half of me. Only wish I found you sooner."

"Love you bunches, Lizzie."

"Love you more, Tiff."

EIGHTEEN

TIFFANY

Liz and I spent the weekend at home in our pajamas.

For the first time, we grocery shopped using one of those home delivery apps. By Sunday afternoon, we demolished all of the brownies and half of the cookies. With some guidance from Liz, I helped make the biscuits while she made the potstickers and stuffed shells for another night this week. We also whipped up cinnamon rolls, strawberry shortcake scones, and cucumber salad.

Mostly, I sat on a stool on the opposite side of the kitchen island while Liz stirred and blended and sliced. Every once in a while, she would lug me around to her side and make me get my hands dirty. I never knew how therapeutic cooking and baking could be. Now, I understand one of the many reasons why Liz loves being in the kitchen.

When I sit back and observe, I pick up on the love and passion Liz holds for the culinary world. For the umpteenth time, I mention her going to school. She simply waves me off. Little does she know, I did an internet search for culinary schools and have requested information from the three closest schools to us. And any day, the brochures will hit our mailbox. Can't wait to see her expression when they do.

Too soon, Monday arrives.

This morning, I wake to a sharp stabbing pain beneath the right side of my ribcage. I bolt upright on the mattress, shove the bedding down my thighs, lift my tank top and inspect my torso. In the faint morning light, the skin appears normal. I shoot off the bed and head for the bathroom, shutting the door and flipping on the light. After my eyes adjust, I examine my body again.

Running my hands over the piercing pain, I shake when I see nothing there. *It was just a dream. Just a dream.* I pinch my eyes shut and shake my head over and over. Looking at myself in the mirror, I whisper, "Just a dream."

A knock raps on the door and I scream before slapping a hand over my mouth.

"Tiff, are you okay?"

Emotion clogs my throat as I try to answer Liz. I sniffle and swallow. "Yeah," I choke out.

Liz pushes the door open and steps in the bathroom. She doesn't say another word. Just walks past me, cranks on the shower, and starts peeling away my tank top and boy shorts. Once we're both bare, she guides us under the hot spray. The water loosens my tense muscles slightly as she combs her fingers through my hair under the showerhead.

Once my hair is wet enough, she squirts shampoo into her palms and works it into a lather in my strands. Her fingers massage my scalp as the soap suds grow. After she rinses out the shampoo, she follows the same process with the conditioner. Next, she adds bodywash to a loofah and washes every inch of my skin. Every touch tender and gentler than I have ever felt from her hands.

When I'm all washed and rinsed, Liz cleans herself quickly. Then she turns off the water and grabs us towels. She towels me off and swathes me in the soft terry cloth before doing the same to herself.

We walk back into the bedroom hand-in-hand and she sits me on the bed. Tucking her forefinger under my chin, she tips my head back so we connect—her hazels to my blues. "I know you're scared, baby," she says. "But I'm here. For whatever you need. A hug. Someone to cry or scream or laugh with. Whatever it is you need, I will always be here. Even if you just need to get something off your chest."

Tears sting the back of my eyes, the lump in my throat from earlier makes a comeback. I nod and nod and nod. Even if I had something semi-intelligent to say right now, my mouth can't seem to form the words.

Liz kisses the crown of my head, her lips lingering on the spot for a moment. When she stands straight again, she spins around and goes to the closet. I follow her with my eyes and remain silent in my spot on the edge of the mattress. She tugs one of her work polos from the hanger and a pair of khakis. Next, she slides my silky, cream top from its hanger, then a pair of gray slacks and the matching jacket.

By the time she returns to my side, she hands me a bra and panties, setting my attire beside me on the bed. I dig deep, locate an inkling of energy, and rise off the bed. Slinking into the lacy undergarments, I slowly dress myself.

Although my head isn't in the game today, not going to work isn't an option. It's better than sitting home and constantly being in my own head. At least work will provide somewhat of a distraction. People at Lewis House need me, and I refuse to let them down for selfish reasons.

After Liz dresses and finishes up in the bathroom, she wanders out of the bedroom. A pan clanks on the stovetop and I hear her whisking something in a glass bowl. I love how Liz is here for me, but also gives me space to breathe. Not too clingy, but here to help me when I ask.

I amble into the bathroom and stare at myself in the mirror for a beat. Time ticks on as I fixate on the exhausted woman in the reflective glass. At thirty-one, I should be bursting with energy and life, not mopey and frail. When I tire of staring into my own eyes, I sigh, snag a seamless head-band off the counter, and slide it into my hair. Picking up my makeup sponge, I get to work on applying my daily mask. The mask sheltering my true reality.

Less than fifteen minutes later, the bags under my eyes are now invisible and my complexion is smooth and natural. A hint of freckles accentuates the contours of my cheeks and bridge of my nose. The smoky eye shadow adds a pop to my features and distracts anyone from seeing my constant melancholy expression.

I brush out my thick tendrils before twisting them all into a low bun. Once secured with a handful of bobby pins, I survey my overall appearance in the mirror. To an onlooker, I was dressed for the job. Professional. Perfect makeup. Not a hair out of place. Nor a wrinkle in my attire. Respectable.

But appearances can be misleading.

On the inside, I rest on my haunches with my head in my hands and beg for this nightmare to end. Inside, I scream into the vast darkness; a void plaguing my mind. In the darkness, I yank at my hair as mascara smears down my cheeks. Beg for silence and peace. Plea for the insanity to end.

But no one will see this particular side of me. Not even Liz. It's a side I reserve only for myself. A side where I question my sanity and if I can actually handle life. Liz doesn't need to bear such heaviness. Liz needs to remain in the light, so she can bring me there with her.

I meander from the bedroom and go to the kitchen, where Liz whips together breakfast. Coming up behind her, I wrap my hands around her waist and rest my chin on her shoulder. "Anything I can help with?"

Liz rotates her head my way and kisses me briefly. "Nah. Everything will be done in a sec." I sag against her then pull away. "Will you grab plates and forks?" Obviously, she detected my need to do something. Anything. Just sitting idle is like nails on a chalkboard.

"On it."

By the time the plates hit the counter beside the stove, Liz starts divvying out the spinach, onion, and cheddar omelet, sliced berries, and avocado toast. She sprinkles the omelet with herbs and the toast with Himalayan salt and pepper.

Breakfast ends faster than expected and soon we head out the front door. Liz tugs me close, hugs me fiercely, and kisses me sweetly. She wants to lift my spirits and help make this all end as quickly and painlessly as possible.

"Try not to think about Friday. Focus on those kids at work and do them proud."

I nod. "Promise." Leaning forward, I press my lips to hers again. Just being like this—in a gentle embrace, followed by a chaste kiss—Liz soothes my weary soul.

"Love you, baby."

"Love you too, Lizzie."

Work comes and goes. I see my usual Monday patients. Spend some time talking with Trina, and later with Chloe. By the end of the day, my anxiety has tapered from level ten to five. At this point, I don't think I'll be free of the constant twist in my gut until Saturday—when all of this is finally in my past.

When I get home, Liz is cooking dinner. Although Liz concocted tons of food over the weekend, we ate quite a bit of it. And what we didn't eat was reserved for lunches during the week.

Liz doesn't hear me come in since she has music playing and I use this to my advantage for a moment. As quietly as possible, I slide out a barstool at the kitchen island and take a seat. For the next seven minutes, I ogle my fiancée while her back is to me. How her frame shifts and tightens when she stirs, chops, or samples whatever is in the pot on the burner.

It's not until she spins around and sets two bowls of salad on the island that she spots me. At the sight of me, she jumps slightly. Slapping her hand to her chest after putting the bowls down. "Scared the shit out of me. I didn't hear you come in." She huffs a moment before lowering her hand. "How long have you been home?"

I smile at her surprise. "Not long. Less than ten minutes."

"Why didn't you say anything?"

Now it's my turn to smile. "Was enjoying the view. I like watching you in the kitchen. The way you move in here… your passion shines."

Liz pops an eyebrow up and cocks her head. "You don't say."

"Can't deny that you love being in the kitchen. I mean, you did cook enough food for the week a couple nights ago."

A smile creeps up her lips. "Is that why two packets came in the mail today from culinary schools?"

Heat blooms up my neck and spreads to my cheeks. "Um. I may have reached out to three or four schools."

"Three or four?" Liz asks wide-eyed.

I wince and shrug. "It's just information, not pressure to enroll. Thought maybe you might like to read over more information. See what you need to do to get in, if that's something you're considering."

Liz walks around the island and stops in front of me as I spin to face her. She steps between my legs and takes my hands in hers. A soft glint hazes her eyes. Her lips curving up slightly at the corners.

"You did this for me?" she whispers a breath away from my lips.

"Being in the kitchen, creating all these amazing dishes… it's your dream. I want you to live your dreams. And if this is it, I will do whatever I can to help you achieve them."

Leaning impossibly closer, Liz rests her forehead on mine and locks her hazels on my blues. Awe flows from her and into me. She drops my hands and frames my cheeks in her palms.

"Tiffany Page, you are the most astonishing woman I know. How did I get so lucky?"

"Ditto."

A moment later, Liz jolts back and dashes to the stove. "Shit." She vigorously stirs the contents in the pot on the stove. "Oh, thank fuck."

I step around the island and sidle up beside her at the stove. "Everything okay?" Glancing in the pot, I spy one of my favorite dishes. Leaning over, I wave the steam toward my face and inhale. The salty, sharp scent of Gouda, Gruyère, and Brie cheeses float up my nose and I melt. "You made my special mac and cheese?"

"We haven't had it in a while." Liz shrugs as if it's no big deal.

Mac and cheese is my ultimate comfort food. When life is shit, I eat my weight in mac and cheese. Before Liz and I started dating, there was this fancy restaurant in Savannah that I bought double orders of mac and cheese from each week. It was my one splurge each week. When Liz learned how much I loved their recipe, she played around in the kitchen until she created something similar. Honestly, Liz's version is ten times better. Especially when she crumbles crispy bacon over the top. I'm somewhat surprised she didn't make it during her cooking marathon this past weekend. Either way, I'm giddy she made it now. And a shitload of it.

I throw myself at Liz, fling my arms around her shoulders, and squeeze her tight. "You really do love me," I singsong.

Liz laughs. "Is Tiff's Special Mac and Cheese the only way you know I love you?"

I drop my arms, scoot back an inch and play slap her bicep. "No, silly. But it's something special you make only for me. So if that's not love, I don't know what is."

While Liz pokes and prods at the garlic and herb chicken in the oven, I steal the spoon for the mac and cheese and shove a mouthful between my lips. The cheese scalds the roof of my mouth, but I don't care. I melt on the spot and moan aloud.

So damn good.

Soon, we dish out dinner—Liz's plate with equal portions of chicken, mac and cheese, and steamed green beans and carrots. My plate, on the other hand, is seventy-five percent mac and cheese, ten percent chicken, and fifteen percent veggies.

When my plate empties, I scoop two more spoonsful of mac and cheese onto my plate and call it dessert. Once I can no longer pack any more in my belly, I tap out and Liz laughs at me. We cuddle up on the couch and watch an episode of *Virgin River* on Netflix. By the time bedtime rolls around, my heart is lighter and my mind is quieter.

Liz is my personal miracle worker. She always knows how to make me feel whole. Better. More myself.

And tonight, when we hit the sheets and Liz holds me close, life feels less stressful and more intact. Soon, everything will align. Soon, my past will be nothing more than that. My past. By next Saturday, it will all be over. Finally.

NINETEEN

LIZ

My phone vibrates in my desk drawer at work and I sneak a peek at the screen. Generally, Tiffany knows not to call my cell while I'm at work, since we aren't supposed to have them out. Back in Savannah, Hammond was much stricter on the policy. Here in Los Angeles, work flows a bit smoother. Not necessarily fly-by-the-seat-of-your-pants smooth, but definitely more laid back. As long as you get work completed and are on target to meet your goals, no one here cares about cell phone usage.

An unfamiliar number flashes on the screen. With everything going on—wedding planning, the adoption, Tiffany's divorce, and my recent culinary school inquiries—it could be one of several people calling. Although we are given permission to answer our cell phone at our desk, my heartbeat turns erratic at the possibility of getting caught.

Before it goes to voicemail, I tap the green accept button on the screen and lift the phone to my ear. "Hello?"

"Good morning. I'm looking for Ms. Eliza Warren, please." A man with a raspy edge to his voice speaks up on the other end.

Definitely not someone who knows me personally. The only time someone speaks my full name is when it's either my grandparents or a person meeting me for the first time. Since preschool, I have gone by Liz. Unless, of course, I was in trouble or met someone professionally.

"This is. Who's asking?"

"Wonderful. Tyler Reed, and I'm reaching out from the Chef Apprentice School of the Arts here in Los Angeles. My call today is in response to an inquiry about our program. Do you have a moment to speak with me?"

"Yes, Mr. Reed. Th-thank you for responding to my email."

Over the next ten minutes, Mr. Reed asks me a slew of questions. Questions regarding my interest in culinary arts, my level of experience in the kitchen, what I hope to gain by attending culinary school, and, of course, my financial situation. He prattles off the curriculum, what hours and length of time I would attend the program, if I moved forward.

The more he talks and hypes up the program, the more eager I am to start this next step in my life. He points out the slow progression of the program, but the pace is perfect for learning every facet of the profession. A twenty-three-week course. Less than half a year. Completely doable. Plus, they offer financing if I don't wish to deplete my savings in one fell swoop.

"Mr. Reed, I… I don't know what to say."

He chuckles into the phone. A gruff reverberation, and I easily picture Tyler Reed as a man in his late-forties or early-fifties. A man who has experienced life. Who lives it to the fullest with a smile playing on his lips. "Say you're ready to sign up and get started."

Now it's my turn to laugh. "I'll speak with my fiancée tonight, solidify a plan, and call you back tomorrow. But I'm certain we'll be discussing paperwork when I call tomorrow."

In the background, a clap echoes and I picture his hands rubbing together with glee. "Perfect. I look forward to hearing back from you. Have a wonderful day, Ms. Warren."

"And you."

The call disconnects and I have the sudden urge to bolt up from my desk and scream at the top of my lungs. *Ohmygod! Ohmygod! Ohmygod!* This is really happening. I am really taking steps to make my dream job a reality.

I bolt up from my chair and knock it back with my knees. It clambers against the credenza behind me and I slap a hand over my face-splitting smile. After glancing to my nearby cubemates and noting their obliviousness to my excitement, I awkwardly speed walk to Christy's cubicle.

As I enter her space, I bite my cheek and glance at the minimalist décor on her desk—a complete one-eighty from her desk in Savannah. While she finishes up with a client on the phone, I plop down in one of the chairs across from her and start bouncing my knees and picking at my fingernails.

Christy wraps up her call, piercing me with a vicious, penetrating glare. "Why are you so bouncy? It's... weird." Her eyes narrow as she studies me.

"I have news. Can we grab lunch in a bit?" Checking my watch, I note lunch doesn't start for another two hours.

"Why can't you just tell me? And of course."

"Because I want to call Tiff first and tell her. Plus, I might squeal. Loudly."

Christy huffs and slaps her hands down on her desk. The man across the aisle from her peeks up from his computer and gives her a slight head shake, eye roll, and smile. By now, everyone here has probably adjusted to Christy's occasional kookiness. What is funny is that she dishes it right back to him and he goes back to whatever task he was working on.

"I hate waiting." Christy does this odd twitch thing with her neck—a mix of tipping it back, shrinking it down, and bobbing it forward and back. Looks like she's neckless.

Weirdo.

"Yeah, but some things are worth the wait." I rise from the chair and start to leave as I blow her a kiss.

"Bitch," Christy mumbles as she shakes her head.

I curtsy and blow her another kiss. "You still love me, though."

Tiffany ambles through the front door and drops her purse on the floor in the foyer. Seconds later, she's in my arms and I'm spinning her in circles. Musical laughter spills out between her lips. My heart beats faster and faster as we whirl around the room. The more we spin, the dizzier I get. But I don't care—excitement overrides the Tilt-A-Whirl in my head.

"So excited for you," Tiffany says, winded.

"I have you to thank for all of it. You reached out to the schools for me. You did a lot of the heavy lifting."

"Pfft." She waves me off as if her task was menial. "Was nothing. What comes next will be the hard part."

After I told Christy I wanted to have lunch, I went back to my desk and called Tiffany. Even though Tiffany had reached out to the culinary schools, I sat on pins and needles while telling her about the call with Mr. Reed. Once everything was out in the open, she shrieked in my ear. I literally had to pull it away, fearing I might not hear anything for hours after.

Part of me still worries about the financial aspect of it all, seeing how I would need to quit my job in order to attend. But Tiffany says we will sit down after dinner and look at all the numbers. Her certainty of our stability while I attend lightens the pressure currently constricting my chest. Until I see the figures with my own eyes, though, I can't stop the jitters flitting through every molecule in my body. We are financially comfortable. This much I know. But Tiffany and I still have all of our accounts separate, so I have no idea what she has in her savings.

Lowering her feet to the ground, I drop a kiss to the tip of her nose before turning back to the stove to finish dinner. Five minutes later, we sit on fluffy pillows between the coffee table and couch on the floor. I scroll through Hulu in search for something new to watch.

Pausing over *A Handmaid's Tale*, I read the description. Sounds intriguing enough. Plus, several people from work blathered on about how shocking and addicting the show is.

"What about this show?" I ask Tiffany just as she shovels a forkful of salmon and rice in her mouth.

She faces me, tilts her head, and widens her eyes. Rolling her eyes in exasperation, I gape at her squirrel-packed cheeks —which are absolutely adorable—as she tries to chew and answer me.

"Did you do that on purpose?"

"Do what?" I tease with a light chuckle.

"Wait until I have a mouthful of food to ask me a question."

"Swear it was coincidence."

Tiffany squints as her head gently shakes side to side. "Mmhmm. Sure it was. Anyway."

She rolls her eyes again and my heart doubles in size. Love swirls like an energy field from my head to toes, making a continuous circuit. Lost in the billowy sensation floating in my veins, I stare at her moving lips. Lips I love to kiss. Lips I love on every inch of my body. I lick my own and I swear I can taste her.

"Liz," Tiffany snaps. "Did you hear me?"

"Huh?"

She chuckles. "I said we should watch the show. Sounds interesting."

I startle for a beat, remembering we were in the middle of deciding what to watch. "Right. Yeah. Sorry."

Again, she laughs. "No need to apologize. Not going to lie, it was kind of cute watching you space out while staring at my mouth."

This time, I roll my eyes and turn back to face the television as I click the play button on the remote. A quarter of the way through the first episode, we finish dinner. Halfway through, I am thoroughly confused at what we are watching. When the episode ends, a never-ending urge to press play temps me.

But I don't. We will never have our talk tonight if I hit play again.

"That was…" Tiffany trails off.

Yeah, both of us equally confused and mystified by what we just watched.

"I really want to watch the next one, but we should talk first."

Tiffany slowly nods. "Agreed."

Over the next hour, Tiffany and I spill all our financial secrets. And what I learn from it all shocks me. When Tiffany said we were financially stable, she wasn't joking.

While I make decent money—my income rests comfortably on the lower end, but not the bottom, of the mid-range—it is nothing in comparison to what Tiffany brings home. My savings is cushy—two-and-a-half times my monthly salary, which most consider healthy. Tiffany's savings, on the other hand, makes my jaw drop.

Several weeks ago, we started a joint account and added money for the wedding as the opening deposit. We both agreed to keep everything intimate and somewhat small. We were also in agreement on the budget—no more than seven-thousand. Majority of the cost would be our dresses, attire for the bridal party, food, and the venue. We don't plan to go all out, but certain things we want nicer than others.

While checking out our finances, we ignore this account as far as being money on hand if I quit my job. But, at some point, Tiffany added more money to our joint account. Five-thousand more. I won't bring it up now. But I have no intention to ignore it either.

I also can't ignore the fact that Tiffany has over fifty grand in her savings and ten grand in her checking.

But, again, now is not the time to talk about it.

"How about this," Tiffany starts. "Since you're barely into the second quarter at work, finish up these next two months with a bang. When you're locked in for your quarterly bonus, put in your notice."

The idea makes complete sense. Plus, there is no rush. Culinary school will still be there. Not to mention we are planning the wedding and aggressively working on adopting Jensen. If anything, having the extra income and stability a little longer will be good for us, the wedding, and the adoption process.

"It's a good plan. For the first time in..." I trail off, tapping my index finger over my puckered lips "...forever, I'll bust my ass at work and make a bonus worth remembering."

Tiffany laughs. "You do you, Lizzie."

"Plus, I'll spend the time finalizing some of the more tedious wedding plans. Better to get it done now while we the opportunity strikes."

"So it's settled then. You will sign up to start school in a few months." Tiffany takes a deep breath, slowly exhaling as her crystal-clear blues get lost in my hazels. "I am so excited for you." A smile plumps her cheeks and sparkles brighter and brighter as reality sets in.

"Many wonderful things are yet to come for us, Tiff. I feel it deep in my bones."

And it's true. Everything is finally falling into place for us.

The details for the wedding are slowly falling into place. Just yesterday, I secured the venue. An outdoor garden ceremony with an indoor reception. As soon as I landed on the venue images online, I immediately sent a request to book. Within an hour, I received a response and it was done.

Booking the venue happened to be the tipping domino. Shortly after hearing from the venue, my phone pinged with email responses from two of the florists I reached out to. Both offered great deals. Flowers would be simple for the entire day. A bouquet for each of us. Our small bridal party—Sarah beside me, Christy beside Tiffany—would carry smaller versions of our bouquets.

Tiffany and I agreed on one similar component to our bouquets. The darkest, reddest roses available. Other than that, our bouquets would be unique to us. Tiffany adding small blue berry bunches and thistle in her arrangement. And, of course, my bouquet would lean toward my inkling for all things dark. Black lilies and dark filler pieces will be nestled into the tight cluster of roses. I looked up bouquets online and forwarded them to the florist. The owner guaranteed she could make bouquets exactly how we wanted.

With every passing minute, our future became brighter and brighter. Soon, the final obstacle would be out of our way. In less than seventy-two hours, Tiffany would be free. The burden of her past would be history. And we would be able to begin the next phase of our life together without worry.

We were almost there. Almost.

Wednesday ends almost as quickly as it arrives.

Surprisingly, Jensen's parents haven't made another appearance. Part of me is excited at the prospect of them just letting him go. They have already inflicted so much pain and damage, and I pray they don't add more heartache to the equation.

With each passing day, Jensen smiles more. The more positive news we receive regarding his adoption, the happier his demeanor. I love glimpsing his smile. How it lights up the room. Spreads warmth from my epicenter throughout my limbs and fills me with an indescribable joy.

On occasion, I catch his laugh. The laughter isn't often and happens mostly when he is near Samantha, but the low chortle slithers its way into my chest and constricts the thumping organ. Once Jensen is my and Liz's son, I plan to discover all the things that make him smile and laugh.

During our session earlier today, I asked Jensen about his relationship with Samantha. At first, he shied away from the subject. A soft blush pinking his cheeks. Eventually, he told me they were strictly friends but confessed he got nervous when they hung out.

I explained how normal it was for him to develop feelings for her. Feelings which superseded friendship. The duo spent hours together every day. Developing a close bond is natural.

Samantha came to Lewis House a little more than a week

before Jensen. The pair of them close in age, it was inevitable and only a matter of time before they gravitated toward each other. Although different circumstances prompted them to do what brought them to Lewis House, both of them are healing. On their own, and together.

As I walk out the front door of Lewis House, my phone rings somewhere in the depths of my purse. I stop and dive into my bag, digging around and shoving miscellaneous nonsense left and right. Just as it rings the fourth jingle, I locate it and quickly tap the green button.

"Hello?"

"Ms. Page, I'm so glad you answered."

I take a deep breath and calm my erratic pulse. "Is something wrong, Mr. Kelly?" Instantly, my brain conjures up thousands of issues.

Did some snafu come up with Jensen's adoption? Are the Pastor's wreaking havoc? Will they return to Lewis House and attempt to have Jensen discharged again? Shit. Maybe I shouldn't leave for the day yet. Perhaps I should waltz back in and alert the staff of the possible incoming issue.

"Did you hear me, Ms. Page?"

I shake my head and zero in on the call. "Sorry. What did you say?"

"Your husband, he flew into the city today. Originally, he and his attorney were scheduled to arrive tomorrow evening. His attorney contacted me a moment ago and stated he left Florida late this morning."

Every fiber in my body goes rigid as a chill sweeps up my body from head to toe. Immediately, I scan the parking lot. My pupils fully dilated as I scour every bush and tree and car in the lot. Not as if he would be in a familiar car, but his taste is particular. Snobbish. If he picked up a rental, he'd have the most lavish car available. More than likely, it would stick out like a sore thumb amongst the staff's cars.

The cars in the lot easily all match up to one of the staff members. All the shadows hit the ground in the shape of oaks and magnolias and light posts. Not a single person, other than me, stands outside Lewis House. I have never been happier to see a people-free parking lot, and I inhale deeply.

"Thank you for informing me, Mr. Kelly. I'll keep an eye out."

On the other end, my attorney remains silent for a moment. His occasional sigh is the only reason I know the call hasn't dropped. "Ms. Page. Tiffany." He pauses and a rustle echoes through the phone. I imagine him running his free hand over his face. "Please be careful. I may not know all the details, but I'm a smart man. Have seen and heard many stories over the years. And something tells me he is not a good man. Hence why you left the way you did."

I don't respond. As badly as I want to scream the pain of my history to the heavens, I refuse to do so until I know this whole fiasco is over. Once I know he is gone for good. After the divorce finalizes, if he ever comes near me again, I won't hesitate to take legal action. Something I was scared to do in the past because of his reach. More than anything, he will do what it takes to keep his name out of the limelight, especially if it will negatively impact his career. Him and his *precious* career.

"If you need anything at all before our meeting Friday evening, don't hesitate to call me."

"Promise I will," I mumble.

"Take care, Tiffany. See you Friday."

"Friday," I whisper before the line disconnects.

A shiver rolls down my spine and I scan the lot again, checking if anything looks out of place. My eyes graze over the windshields, inspecting them for notes or signs of tampering. Nothing.

I take a deep breath and slowly meander toward my car— eyes darting back and forth, scanning everything in sight the entire time. Halfway to my car, my hand dives into my purse and digs for my key fob, my eyes not veering away from my surroundings.

With each step I take, each passing tick of time I don't find the gosh forsaken fob, a bubbly sensation builds just beneath my diaphragm. The slow-building prickle comparable to a volcano project I assembled once as a kid. The project where I mixed vinegar, baking soda, and a few other minor ingredients, and watched it fizz and erupt down the paper machete mountain I spent weeks creating.

Yeah, that's how my body feels in this very moment. Prone to explosion and mass destruction.

Three strides from the car, my fingertips graze the key fob and I press the unlock button. One last glance around the lot —no one in sight—I hop in my car, mash the lock button, and fire the engine. Once my phone connects to the Bluetooth, I press the button on my steering wheel.

"Call Liz," I command.

"Calling Liz." The robotic sound of my car responding bumps my jitters up another notch and I grip the steering wheel until my knuckles whiten.

Throwing the gearshift into reverse, I check my surroundings and back out of the space. As the third ring wails through the car speakers, I shift the car into drive and zip away. Just as I'm about to disconnect the call to Liz, she answers.

"Hey, Tiff. What's up?"

"Mr. Kelly called." I clutch the steering wheel tighter as I maneuver through the city. Thankfully, the traffic hasn't gotten heavy from all the nine-to-five workers heading home yet. All things considered, the roads are fairly normal right now. If I would have left during rush hour, my anxiety would not survive the trip home.

"And? Don't leave me hanging, baby."

"S-sorry." *Get it together.* "He called to tell me that *he* left Florida early this morning. Probably arrived near lunchtime."

A car two ahead of me slams on its brakes and it's a ripple effect. For a moment, I fear I might smash into the car in front of me or be hit by the person behind me. Thankfully, neither happens, but my heart continues its sprint in my chest.

I need to get off this damn highway.

"Tiff!" Liz shouts and it ricochets off the small interior of my car. "Tiff, are you okay?"

Checking the cars nearby are at a standstill, I take a moment to collect myself. When I let go of the steering wheel, my fingers and hands tremble uncontrollably. I examine them for a beat before returning them back to the steering wheel and clenching until pain shoots through my forearms to the tips of each digit.

"I'm good. Just shaken up. Liz, I need to get home. Now." My voice sounds frail and whiney, even to my own ears.

"I know, baby. Keep me on the phone and let's talk until you make it home. Okay?"

"O-okay."

Over the next twenty minutes, I creep through traffic while Liz tells me about her day and the conversation she and Christy had over lunchtime. Something about a strappy outfit she wore to the club that Rick works at. The way she described it made it seem as if it were a labyrinth on her body. I couldn't help but laugh.

Soon, I turn onto less busy streets and wind my way closer to home. Less than ten minutes later, I park the car and Liz walks out to meet me and walk me inside.

Without another word, Liz draws me close and wraps her arms around me. The world surrounding us pauses as we simply stand next to my car and hold each other. Liz brings her lips to my ear, whispering in soft tones before planting a kiss on my temple. "Let's get inside."

I nod as we slowly inch apart from each other and stroll hand in hand to the front door. With Liz's hand around mine, the world is less chaotic.

Once we step inside the apartment, and the deadbolt has been twisted to the right and the security chain is secure, I breathe a little easier. It amazes me how much solace a couple security measures can deliver.

"I was just ramping myself up to see him on Friday. Now… what if he knows where I work? What if he knows where we live?" The tremors I experienced earlier make a comeback. "No," I whisper in disbelief. "No."

Liz guides us over to the couch and sits me down before taking a seat beside me. She strokes up and down my spine with slow and gentle movements. With each pass, the tremors bouncing around inside me slow their pace. Shifting from tremors to small waves. The more contact I share with Liz, the more secure I feel. As if a weighted blanket lay over me, calming my overactive nerves.

"Baby, I'm here. And as long as I'm here, I promise he won't hurt you."

For the first time since we set foot inside, I face Liz and look square in the swirly depths of her hazel eyes. "How?"

She tilts her head to the side, narrows her eyes, and studies me for three heartbeats. "What do you mean?"

Infinitesimally, I shake my head. "How can you promise such things? How can you promise he won't hurt me? You have no idea what he is capable of." I pause and comb my fingers through my hair. "We don't spend every waking moment together. Tomorrow, we both go separate ways to work. Plus, we both spend part of Friday at work before the meet. So… how?"

One by one, Liz brings her palms to my cheeks and frames my face. "If need be, I'll call off work both days. Follow you to work. Hang out in your office while you work and keep an eye out."

As wonderful as the concept sounds, I don't think it is feasible. All things which sound easy are usually too good to be true. I learned that lesson the hard way.

"I love that you want to do this for me. Love that you will drop everything to stand beside me. Protect me. But it's not sensible."

"Who cares about sensible. Baby, you need to feel safe. And I will do whatever it takes to give you the sense of security you deserve. No person should ever strike fear in you the way this man does. No one."

Her eyes bore into mine. Hold mine with rapt attention and tenderness in equal measure. Inching closer to me, Liz sits taller as she places a hand on my knee. A rush of warmth erupts where her skin meets mine, spreading its way from the single point and filling me. Not just warmth, though. Strength and courage and determination pass from Liz to me. The thumping of my pulse pounds harder beneath my breasts—not from fear, but a new layer of bravery.

When it comes to my own life, I never consider myself as brave. For years, I cowered to a man who hurt me for his own pleasure. When it comes to others, I hold my ground and scour the globe for justice for them. Justice I wish someone would have gotten for me.

But a sense of justice is on the horizon for me. Long overdue, but justice none the less. And when it comes to *him*, there has never been a day since I married him when I thought I would be set free.

Covering Liz's hand with mine, I stare into her swirling pools of ocean and sun. I love how her eyes are more than one color. A golden honey surrounds her pupils in the thinnest layer, followed by a rich ocean blue which is rimmed with a blue so dark it's almost black. Since the day we met, her eyes have always captivated me. Coaxed me closer. Invited me back for more.

Their color wasn't the only component to lure me in. But also the person behind them. Her spunk and tenacity. The way she carries herself—as if she knew I would say yes when she asked for my number or set up our first date. Not as if I lack confidence, but Liz exudes it in all things. Liz is a smidge of class and a whole lot of punk-meets-fiery-meets-closet-romantic.

And she is everything I had been missing in my life.

"You saying that… standing up for me" —I drop my gaze to our joined hands— "no matter how I paint it, my words will never explain how it hits me here." Bringing my free hand to my chest, I pat over my heart. "Thank you and I love you will never be powerful enough, but I promise to say them as much as possible."

The corners of Liz's mouth tip up, a shy, sweet smile perking her lips as she shakes her head. "You still don't get it, do you?"

I tuck my lips inside my mouth and bite them. I replay our conversation and come up blank on what she could be talking about. I replay it all in my mind and nothing sticks out. Obviously, I don't get it. Obviously, I am missing a vital component in her eyes. So, I release my lips—biting the inside of my cheek instead—and shrug.

"In the grand scheme of things, I should be the one constantly saying those things. Thank you for taking the chance on me. Thank you for not completely shutting yourself off from the world. And thank you for letting me love you, and loving me in return. There's no way to fathom how difficult life with him must've been for you."

"With you, love is the easiest part."

Her smile widens. "Please never believe it's a burden for

me to be there for you. If taking a couple extra days off work is what I need to do, I'll take them. Plus, I need to use up some of my PTO before I leave." Liz winks.

"Won't you be bored sitting in my office all day?"

"Nothing a good book or tablet can't fix. I'm chapters away from finishing my current romance read. Plus, I have lots of research to do about school. Believe me, I'll be just fine."

There is no talking Liz out of taking tomorrow and Friday off work. Not after my frantic call and ruffled nature. Surely, the last thing she wants is for me to have another breakdown. Not when I need to be at my strongest for the meeting with *him* on Friday. Heck, I don't want to have another panic attack. I have experienced and handled more than plenty in my lifetime, and I am beyond fortunate to have Liz at my side for support.

I shrug and nod. "If that's what you want." Her face lights up in victory. "But I have one condition."

Liz's face turns serious. "Lay it on me."

"We order takeout tonight. As much as I love your cooking, I'm starving and needed dinner thirty minutes ago."

She tips her head back and laughs, loud and carefree. When her laughter settles, she shakes her head at me. "Yeah, baby, we can order takeout. But I pick where."

"Deal."

And just like that, life feels seemingly lighter again. I only hope it stays this way.

TWENTY-ONE

HARRISON

I HAVE BEEN in this noisy, smelly city for less than half a day, and it already disgusts me. What the hell is the attraction? Is it the fame? Fortune? Oversized homes in the bare mountains? If those are the attractants to this shithole, then the population here hasn't ventured anywhere.

Minus the mountains, I have all those things in Florida.

Not only am I one of the top physicians in the state of Florida, but I was recently recognized as one of the best cosmetic surgeons in the country. If that isn't fame, I'm not sure what is. Along with my obviously stellar career comes a hefty paycheck and a house built for a king. Because I am a motherfucking king.

And my queen lives in a filthy city as plastic as the facelift I performed three days ago.

But not for long. Soon she will be back where she belongs.

Parked across the street in a Starbucks lot, I watch the outside of where she supposedly works. Some psychiatric facility. When I looked up the website and read the mission statement, I almost vomited. *Blah, blah, blah. We help troubled kids. Yada, yada, yada.* What-the-fuck-ever. Figures my wife would turn into her daddy. Probably some convoluted plan to "figure me out."

But I know exactly who I am. Her goddamn husband. And that's all she needs to worry about.

I still don't fully understand why she left me. Why she

packed a handful of things and left town in the middle of the night while I worked the graveyard shift. Like a little fucking coward. A conniving bitch.

Why the hell wouldn't she want to be the queen on my arm? Wearing lavish dresses, countless diamonds, and want for nothing. To be doted upon and envied by every woman who laid eyes on me.

She may be my queen—and I will be returning home with her—but others have fulfilled my needs in her absence. Others have begged for her throne while she has been away. I allow them to please me, but deny them otherwise.

Unlike my queen, every woman with a pulse craves what I delivered to her in our marriage. Plenty of women want my cock between their legs. Plenty of women beg for more. Plead for me to give it harder. To slap them with intention. And I deliver every time.

But I guess poor little Tiffany couldn't handle me. Couldn't handle the fervor of a man with needs. Maybe she needs a reminder of what she has been missing.

Just as I ponder all the possible techniques I can use to refresh her memory, I spot her in the distance a few steps outside the building. God, she hasn't changed a bit. And my stiffening cock agrees.

Her long auburn hair ends at the base of her ribcage, three or four inches longer than I remember. Instantly, I want to wrap the strands around my wrist and grip them firmly. The sunlight glints on her locks, and it is almost as if a fire radiates from her. I remember the spirited fire inside her. The fire I riled up as often as possible. The fire she tried to fight me with, but I controlled.

"Argh," I groan as I adjust my steel-hard cock. God, how I loved it when she fought back.

She halts and starts fumbling in the tote on her shoulder, frustration marring her brows. A moment later, she has the phone to her ear as her body goes rigid. Not a second later, she whips her head side to side as she searches the parking lot. Must be her attorney on the phone, alerting her to the fact I am already in California. Days early.

"I'm not there, darling. But I am close enough to see you."

When she finishes the call, she does another scan of the

cars. Eyes vigilant in their search for any signs of trouble. Satisfied it is safe for her to leave, she bolts for her car with her hand digging through her bag once again.

She gets inside a pewter Nissan Z and slinks into the seat. Perhaps she feels safe behind locked doors. Perhaps she shouldn't be so complacent.

I wonder... does she still have some of the money she withdrew from our accounts the day she left? Did the money buy the sports car she drives? If I hadn't been so concerned about advancing my career while my wife saved home all day, maybe I would have noticed the large cash withdrawal she made thirty minutes before the bank closed.

No worries. I noticed. And for a while, I let her believe she got away. I let her believe I had no clue where she was hiding. But, from day one, I have always known where she is. Known who she is with. Just like the cunt she is supposedly engaged to now.

Did you want my dick to be your one and only, queen?

Yeah, I kept tabs on her every relationship. For years, she never so much as looked at another person. Especially the male population. She went on a few dates with men, but obviously they didn't meet her standards and were ditched quick.

But her current relationship... I never pictured my queen as a lesbian. Never foresaw her being so diverse.

Not to worry, though. Soon, I will remind her what it feels like to be beneath a man. To have his cock thrusting down her throat. Between her thighs.

"Soon enough," I grunt as I fist the painful erection in my dress slacks.

As she drives away, I shift the basic sedan into gear and follow behind her. Normally when I travel, I rent a Mercedes. Sexy and business and classic. She would expect nothing less. So instead, I chose a four-door, American-made, putrid green sedan. The only perk is the pitch-black windows and the hefty backseat—probably intended more for a happy couple with children.

Less than an hour later, I watch her park her car. Her *fiancée* hurries to her side and hugs her close. Too close. Hands in places no one should touch except me. Then they speed walk into the apartment. Once I no longer have a visual of my queen, I throw the car in park and stare at the door. I may not stay here all night, but I'm not quite ready to leave yet. Not quite ready to leave the booming energy which surrounds her like a force field.

So, I sit and wait. I research the closest hotel to her complex and make a reservation. Nowhere near a five-star resort, but at least it's not a roach motel.

Once all the lights extinguish inside the apartment, I put the car in drive and pull away.

She thinks Friday will be the end of what we had. She thinks I'll get thrown out like a sack of garbage.

Perhaps she needs a little reminder. Because she obviously doesn't remember a goddamn thing about her king.

I SPENT all day Thursday in Tiffany's office. When we first stepped into her oversized office, sitting on the plush couch where she conducted some of her therapist-patient sessions sent a shiver up my spine. Although Tiffany's office was a formal and professional space, it was almost as if a million secrets spilled over my skin. Secrets her patients entrusted her with.

After setting my belongings on the small table between the couch and matching chair—which I assume Tiffany sat in during sessions—Tiffany took me on a quick tour of the accessible areas. Most importantly, the breakroom. Where I could satiate my coffee addiction and stash the snacks I brought for the day.

When Tiffany left her office to start her morning meetings and sessions, I cracked open my tablet with a notepad and pen off to the side. Hours breezed by as I read the information Mr. Reed emailed to me. I jotted down countless notes and devised my game plan on how I would conquer culinary school just before our wedding.

Tiffany drove us to a restaurant a few blocks from Lewis House for lunch. Although I had the day off work, a sense of accomplishment flooded my veins in a way that never happened at Hammond Life as I planned out my future. Our future. After lunch, it was much of the same. Tiffany attended more meetings and visited with other patients while I finalized more details for the wedding.

Our wedding was less than a year away, but I wanted everything in place early on. Needed to see all the fine details on paper and ready for the big day. Before long, Tiffany and I left Lewis House for the day. Initially, I thought I'd be bored out of my mind and be restless. Turns out, having the day to tackle activities was exactly what I needed.

So, when Tiffany and I walk into Lewis House this morning, I smile at the prospect of what I will accomplish in my time here today. Although, we won't be here a full day due to tonight's meeting.

As I set my messenger bag on the table near the couch in Tiffany's office, I study her for a moment as she moves around her desk. Jittery. Wired. Her body language mimics someone highly over-caffeinated. Trembling hands. Eyes bouncing from one folder to another on her desk. Vigorously shaking the mouse to wake her computer over and over. Fingers tapping on her desk as she reads something on the screen. Constantly nibbling her lower lip.

"You okay?"

Tiffany pops her head up. Eyes wide. Teeth still fidgeting with her lip. "Fine. Why?"

Every woman with a brain knows the word *fine* is a bullshit excuse for the complete opposite. No doubt her nerves are shot over tonight's meeting. But she needs to remember I will be there, too. For her to lean on and give her strength.

Tiffany picks up a stack of files, holds them upright, and taps the bottoms against the surface of her desk. Once she sets them off to the side, she begins organizing her desk. Picking items up and setting them back in their exact location or an inch off. First, the stapler. Then a cup of pens. Next, she shifts her computer monitor—tilting it left then right then left again —followed by the keyboard and mouse.

Her constant need to be busy, to keep her mind off tonight's meet, is a thousand pinpricks to my heart. If only I could soothe her. Say the right words and ease her anxiety. Hug her tighter than ever before and erase all the ill thoughts stealing her time. Kiss her more passionately and make her forget all the horrible atrocities of her past.

But it isn't so simple.

As much as I wish to wipe away all the horrendous events of Tiffany's past, I am not the person who can. Only Tiffany holds that power. And if she needs to borrow some of my power, some of my strength, some of my fortitude in order to get there, I will happily hand it all to her.

"Tiff," I say, barely above a whisper. "Please don't mask your feelings. Not with me."

Her lips tighten into a straight line before curving up at the corners for a split-second and falling flat. It almost goes unnoticed, but I catch the way her weight shifts from one foot to the next, back and forth for three deep breaths. She chews at the inside of her cheek for a second before opening her mouth and shutting it.

I still have no idea what this asshole did to Tiffany. How he took this beautiful woman and crushed her spirit. Made her cower at the mere idea of being near him. The Tiffany I have grown to love had none of these attributes until I asked her to be mine forever. Until I asked her to make it recognizable to the world.

It is not my fault Tiffany has these demons in her past. But it is my fault they stirred back to life after years of silence. A silence where happiness flourished.

"It's just... I..." she mutters, stumbling over her own words. Walking closer to her desk, I keep my lips sealed and wait for her to continue. Telling me needs to be her choice. Stopping in front of her desk, I get a better view of the dark half-moons under her eyes she painted with concealer before I woke this morning. The bold red veins in her eyes, amplified by the glassy surface. And the slight crinkle around her brows and quiver of her chin.

"You know I'll never hurt you. Right?"

Tiffany has to know I would never do anything to put her in harm's way. Never allow anyone to lay a hand on her or utter cruel words to her. Not in the way which has obviously happened in her past.

Her eyes drop to the desk as she nods. "Yeah, I know." She picks up a paperclip and unbends it. "But what if one day you can't?" As the words leave her mouth, she peers back up at me like a timid child. A single tear slips out and rolls down her cheek.

In four strides, I round her desk and tug her into my arms. "The only way that'll ever happen is if I'm not breathing."

Fisting my shirt, she brings me impossibly closer. "That's what I'm afraid of," she whispers against my neck. Warm wetness hits my shoulder as she buries her face into my skin.

I shift my arms, clutch her harder, and erase any remaining space between us. "Baby, you should know by now. I fight for what's mine. And you are, without a doubt, one-hundred percent mine."

Tiffany creates a small gap between her nose and my skin, sniffling. "But you don't know him. Don't know what he is capable of," she whispers. A shudder ripples throughout her body, head to toe. "What he'll do next."

Tracing the tips of my fingers up and down her spine, Tiffany melts into me slightly. "True. But he doesn't know what I'm capable of either."

At this, Tiffany leans back and studies my expression. Her brows twitch and lips bunch up, shifting side to side. "I love that you want to protect me, but he is a monster. For years, I thought I was free of him. But it was all a façade. He's always known where I am. Hell, he probably paid someone to keep tabs on me." Her eyes widen. "Oh, god." She frees one of her hands and slaps it over her mouth.

"What?" What just clicked in her head and funneled pure fear into her veins?

Her pupils swallow all but a sliver of her icy blue irises. "He knows about you. About us." She sucks in a breath, but doesn't release it for one, two, three... "All this time, he's known and hasn't done anything."

Not quite sure where this all leads. "Okay," I drawl out.

Tiffany breaks out of my hold and takes a step back. "It can't be this easy. Tonight. There is no way he would let me go this easy. Not after the things he did to me. Not after he had someone tail me for almost a decade."

Just as I start to open my mouth in rebuttal, Tiffany snatches her work tablet off her desk and bolts to the door. As she opens the door, she spins around and swipes the tears from her cheeks. "Sorry. I have to go. We'll talk more before dinner." Then she disappears and I'm left standing there, wondering what the hell just happened.

Seeing an ex for the first time in a decade is far from easy. Especially an ex who has done unspeakable things. But I pray Tiffany will not let this man steal the last pieces of her. I pray she digs deep inside herself and locates the ferocious woman I have fallen in love with. And hopefully she harnesses that power and wields it like a sword, slaying the beast torturing her soul.

Most of all, I wish I could do it for her.

My phone pings on the coffee table in Tiffany's office and I pick it up to read the incoming text message.

Tiffany: Meeting still going. Head to the restaurant and I'll meet you there.

After Tiffany's eureka moment earlier, and the fact we haven't finished our conversation, it unhinges me to leave Lewis House without her. Plus, it defeats the purpose of why I'm here in the first place.

Liz: I don't mind waiting so we drive together.
Tiffany: Not sure how much longer. Might have to bolt straight to my car.

I want to tell her I don't mind bolting with her. But I won't. The last thing I need to do is be a helicopter fiancée, hovering over her constantly and telling her what to do. So, I cave. But not before double-checking with her.

Liz: You sure?
Tiffany: Yeah. Sorry ☹
Liz: No need to apologize. I'll take an Uber. See you soon.
Tiffany: Muah.

My stomach twists and grumbles as I pack my tablet and notepad into my messenger bag. With each step I take toward the door, the pain in my gut wrenches more viciously. Before I exit her office, I open the Uber app on my phone and request a driver. Less than a minute passes and a picture of the driver, his car, and tag number pop up on my screen.

This is wrong. All wrong.

Me taking yesterday and today off work had a purpose. A plan. So I could be at Tiffany's side throughout the day and leading up to our meet with her ex. So I could encourage and boost her confidence.

But now… now she wants us to go to the restaurant separately. I refuse to steal her independence, but I won't hide how uncomfortable I feel about leaving without her.

Something about this whole scenario eats me alive inside.

I chat with the woman at the front reception—for the life of me, I cannot remember her name. But it doesn't really matter. The only reason I'm talking to her at all is because I don't want to look like a lost puppy as I stare out the window waiting for the driver to arrive.

"Bye," I say as I walk toward the main doors of Lewis House, waving.

"See you next week," she states.

Not to burst her bubble, but after everything is resolved tonight with Tiffany's ex, I probably won't be at Lewis House anytime soon. Unless coming to visit Jensen before the adoption. But she doesn't need to know the dirty details, so I simply nod and exit.

The drive to the restaurant takes no time and soon I'm at the host podium. I tell the host I'm meeting others, but they haven't arrived.

"Would you like to wait at the bar?"

"Please." The host takes my name and hands me a reservation buzzer, letting me know it will go off when other guests in my party arrive.

Reaching the bar, I slide out a stool and plop down onto the padded wood, hanging the strap of my bag on my knees. A woman slings liquor bottles behind the oak bar top as if she's been mixing and serving drinks all her working life. After she serves a couple to my left, she heads my direction and places a napkin in front of me.

"What's your pleasure?"

Definitely been doing this for some time.

"Martini. Shaken. Extra olives. Extra dirty," I tell her.

"One extra dirty girl coming up."

As I watch the bartender make my drink, the stool to my right scrapes the tile and a man sits down. I throw him a quick smile and return my eyes to the lightning-fast mixologist. Seconds later, she places my martini in front of me. I hand her a bill and tell her to keep the change.

After a wink, she shifts to her left and sets a napkin in front of the man beside me.

"What'll it be, sugar?"

"Jack and Coke. On the rocks."

She walks off to make the man's drink as I sip my martini. *Damn, that woman makes a mean martini. We will definitely return here in the future.*

"Hello?" the man asks.

Setting my drink on the napkin, I twist to see him better in the dimmed lighting. His blond hair short and purposely disheveled. Stubble coats his jawline, ear to ear, and also above his lips. Eyes like warm chocolate. He sits around the same height as me on the stool with a trim frame. Maybe in his late-thirties.

"Sorry. Did you say something?"

The man flashes me a bright, white smile before he drops his eyes to my lips for a quick second, then back up to my eyes. After years of being with the same person, I almost forget what flirting looks like. Almost. Although I don't want to be rude, I maintain my composure and wait for him to respond.

"Asked if you were here alone."

I shoot him a brief smile. "Meeting my fiancée." Just as the words exit my mouth, my phone buzzes in my pocket and I check the notification. "Speak of the angel," I say as my lips curve and stretch tight.

"Such a shame," he says, rising from his stool. He grabs the drink the bartender deposited in front of him seconds before and lays a twenty on the bar before walking off.

As he walks off, the bartender returns. "You good?" she asks.

"Yeah, thanks."

"Sure thing. Always keeping my eyes on the ladies riding solo. Never know what creeps are up to nowadays."

I nod. "Thanks for looking out."

She walks off to check on another patron as Tiffany sidles up beside me. "Hey. Sorry about the meeting. Wasn't sure how long it would run and I didn't want you panicking."

I lean into Tiffany and kiss her. "No worries. Haven't been here too long. Should we see if anyone has arrived?" The host may have given me a pager, but I didn't disclose who I was meeting.

"Mr. Kelly should be here any second. No idea about anyone else."

When we spot Mr. Kelly at the entrance, I slip off the stool, grab my things, and we meet up with him. Greetings are exchanged and we check back in with the host. As we weave our way through the sea of tables and partitions, Tiffany clutches my elbow with fury as she inches closer and closer. I rest my free hand on our connected arms and give a gentle squeeze.

"You got this, baby. Lean on me if you need to."

She doesn't say a word but nods to let me know she heard me.

The host slows as we approach the table. When I take my eyes off Tiffany and peer over to the table, I stop breathing.

Motherfucker.

You have got to be shitting me. Goddamn motherfucking piece of shit.

Staring at us from the opposite side of a large, round table is the same man from the bar. The very same man who practically hit on me. Did he already know who I was? Was he hitting on me because he knew Tiffany and I are together? Was he trying to pull a fast one? Trying to ruin my relationship with her? Or was he playing a game?

I don't know his and Tiffany's history—after all this is over with, I hope she will finally tell me—but from every tremble or flinch or mood flip Tiffany has endured because of him, he is far from a good man.

As we pull out our chairs, his eyes flick to me. A smirk on his lips just long enough for me to notice. Piece of shit—he knew exactly who I was at the bar. Perhaps he wanted to flirt information out of me. Thankfully, his asshole charms didn't, and wouldn't, work on me. He may have known who I was before I did him, but that is where his tricks end.

His lips flatten into a straight line as he shifts his gaze to Tiffany. She stiffens beside me as I observe the silent interaction happening between them. Instantly, the air in the room is cooler. A blanket of tension falls over us and weighs us down. Tiffany holds my elbow in a death grip to rival any. And although she is stiff as a board, a tremor rocks throughout her body and passes to me.

Across the table, his eyes go from warm chocolate to frigid stone. His jaw tics as the muscles in his neck pop and fade. Malevolence radiates off every inch of him and fires daggers at Tiffany.

I guide Tiffany into her seat before I sit on her right and Mr. Kelly sits on her left. Once seated, I lean into her and whisper. "I'm here, baby. Remember, no matter what, I am here. Don't let him steal your spark."

When I pull away, Tiffany turns to face me. We lock eyes for a moment—glacial blue to fiery hazel—and I transfer every ounce of strength I own to her. Passing the torch and lighting the path while she wanders in the dark. Across the table, he growls and I assume it is from the bond Tiffany and I share. But I don't let it hinder our connection. If anything, I hold her more—her gaze, her heart, her soul.

The server steps up to the table and asks for everyone's drink orders. When Tiffany orders, she speaks firm and strong, but keeps her eyes locked on mine. It is not until the server walks off that we break our connection. Everyone peruses the menu and orders their meal after drinks have been divvied.

After the menus are gone and we no longer have the distraction of trying to decide our meals, the table grows eerily quiet. The weighted tension from ten minutes ago returns with a vengeance. Under the linen-covered table, Tiffany takes my hand and grips it with a strength I didn't realize she possessed.

"Mr. Deats," Mr. Kelly says before clearing his throat. "You called for this meeting. What is it you wish to discuss?"

Deats. So Tiffany hadn't taken his last name in their

marriage. This lit a flame of intrigue in my belly. Was it because he didn't want her to have his name? Was it because she planned to become a doctor and wanted to shine in her own light? Or did she once have his name and revert back to her maiden when she left him?

"It's *Doctor* Harrison Deats. *Doctor*. Best you remember." His words a bite to the jugular as he flicks his gaze to Mr. Kelly, then back to Tiffany. "And yes, I did call this meeting. I have the right to see my *wife* before I sign any documents regarding *our* marriage."

Beneath the table, Tiffany fumbles her fingers with mine. Just as I open my mouth to soothe her, to speak up for her, she surprises me and steps up to the plate.

"Harrison, I may legally be your wife, but there hasn't been a marriage since the day after the wedding. Marriages are a fifty-fifty. When people get married, it's because they wanted to lift each other up and help make their partner the best version of themselves. We" —Tiffany gestures between her and Harrison with a finger— "never had any such relationship. Or marriage. Even if I'd ever had the opportunity to leave the house, no amount of makeup would've fixed our marriage."

And there it is. The crux of it all. The nail in the coffin.

Without ever having to ask Tiffany, I now know that Harrison physically abused her. Not to mention, mentally and emotionally scarred her. No wonder she freaked out after I proposed. More than likely, Tiffany associates marriage with abuse.

But I refuse to let her feel such associations going forward. I will do everything in my power to show her marriage is about love and growth and moving forward in life with a partner who adores you.

"Must I remind you, *Tiffany*, how a marriage works. Wives have expectations to meet. Especially wives of prominent doctors. I assumed your mother and father groomed you to know such things. Obviously, I was mistaken."

I squeeze Tiffany's hand, signaling she should keep her wits about her and not cave to his games. Because this is exactly that—a game. He brought her here, asked to meet with her one last time, so he could inflict his wrath on her one last time. He didn't give a shit whether or not attorneys were present. The only thing this *man*, if he was even worthy of such a title, wanted was to watch Tiffany crumble beneath him. To watch her shatter and wither under his malicious behavior.

But he didn't know Tiffany like I do.

Sure, his initial call to her triggered past emotions and stirred up old wounds. But Tiffany ran from him almost ten years ago. Since then, she has rebuilt herself from the ground up. She dug deep and located her strength, her courage, by helping others. She may not realize it herself, but the wounds this man created, she sutured them shut and reinforced them with the strongest force on the planet. Love.

"You were, are, mistaken," Tiffany says as she sits taller in her chair. "As far as marriage goes, you wouldn't know how one works, even if it beat you with a fireplace poker."

My eyes dart back and forth between Tiffany and Harrison. Her reference to a fireplace poker was oddly specific. Too specific. Gooseflesh pricks my skin as visuals I don't want flit through my mind.

And then I see it in his eyes. Hatred. Fury. An unsatiated hunger to hurt Tiffany. Not just with words, but also with force. With his hands. With implements in his hands.

Two servers approach the table and set trays of food on stands. While plates of food are placed in front of the appropriate person, Harrison stares at Tiffany as if he wants nothing more than to wield a fireplace poker and beat the shit out of her in front of everyone here. But she doesn't back down. Tiffany gives just as much as he throws.

Dinner passes without another word spoken. The tension so thick, even a steak knife wouldn't cut a dent in it. Never in my life have I chewed my meal with such precision and intent. Honestly couldn't tell you if it was good or not. Or what I ordered, for that matter.

Once the plates are cleared and bills delivered, Tiffany shoots Harrison with a wicked gleam.

"You got your dinner. Got to see me one last time. I held up my end of the deal. Now it's time you do the same." Tiffany eyes his attorney for the first time, as do I.

A platinum blonde with her hair styled tall and makeup

overdone sits beside Harrison. During the entire evening, she hasn't spoken up once, which is odd. If anything, she should have guided her client to bite his tongue an occasion or two, but never did. Honestly, she seemed rather *proud* of him.

And that's when it all clicks. The blonde may be his attorney, but that isn't her only role in his life. She is so much more. The ostentatious diamond on her left hand a red flag waving high and mighty. This woman sat proud beside Harrison. Tall and powerful. And, somehow, enjoyed the asshole side he displayed with Tiffany. As if it fed an animal inside her too.

The woman bends down and produces a large envelope from beneath the table. She sets it down in front of her and pats her hands on the contents. "Harrison, darling" —she turns her gaze to his and smiles wide— "time to fulfill your end of the bargain." She slides the envelope in his direction and places a pen on top.

Now is when Tiffany opts to freeze.

Is it the fact he is finally signing the divorce papers? Or has she spotted the ginormous rock on his attorney's left hand? Did she catch the term of endearment?

Personally, I don't grasp how this woman wants to marry him. Not after all the horrendous things he has done. But who knows. Maybe she gives as good as she gets. Maybe she gets her jollies helping criminals get away with whatever crime they committed. Maybe she enjoys it. Regardless, she makes me sick.

Harrison makes a show of sliding out the papers, twisting his overpriced pen, flipping to each flagged page and signing with a flourish. After each signature, he lifts his gaze to Tiffany. Although his attorney/fiancée sits beside him, he shoots daggers at Tiffany. As if letting her go is the last thing he wants.

When he reaches the last flagged page, he hovers above the page with the pen. "This is it. You sure you're ready for this to be over?"

Beside me, Tiffany's breaths come and go a little faster. Her palm sweats against mine. But she doesn't let him see it. Tiffany slips on her trained doctor façade, throwing on a smile for good measure.

"I've never been more sure of anything in my life." Her tone firm. Words absolute.

In this moment, I have never been prouder of the woman beside me. Proud of her resilience and poise and relentless determination. Of the courage it takes to stand tall and mighty against someone like Harrison. Proud to call her mine.

With one last flick of his pen, Harrison grants Tiffany the freedom she deserves. With one last flick of his pen, a buzzing builds in my chest and spreads like wildfire as my soon-to-be wife regains a piece of herself once stolen.

TWENTY-THREE

TIFFANY

AM I DEAD? Maybe just dreaming.

Because there is no way in hell I just stood up to Harrison Deats and won the battle. After everything he did to me, after all the pain he inflicted on me, how on earth did he let me go so easily?

Liz and I still sit at the table. Harrison, his attorney—which I believe is also his fiancée, don't even get me started on that string of opinions—and Mr. Kelly left five minutes ago. But I wanted to wait. To ensure a gap of time between their departure and ours.

I am finally free.

Not quite certain the whole notion has sunk in yet. Mr. Kelly immediately took the divorce papers from Harrison after he signed. As he stood to leave, he promised to have the papers filed with the Clerk of the Court first thing Monday morning.

In a matter of minutes, I was ten times lighter. The dark cloud following me since the day I said 'I do' to Harrison is dissipating, making room for the sun to shine. There really is a light at the end of the tunnel.

"We should celebrate," I say. "This weekend. We should call everyone we know and celebrate. It has been far too long since we've had a party."

A sparkle shimmers in Liz's eyes. A light I haven't seen in months, all because of Harrison. But no more. From this day forward, I aim to ignite the fire in Liz's eyes every waking moment.

"Yeah?"

"Definitely. Other than our wedding, what better reason is there to celebrate?" I meant it as a rhetorical question, but Liz will answer me either way.

"Every day with you should be celebrated," she says before leaning in to kiss me.

Her warm lips graze mine—once, twice—before she swipes her tongue over my bottom lip. I part my lips at the slight touch and revel in the feel of her tongue twisting with mine. Hot and wet and a bullet straight to my core. Before our kiss translates into groping, I break away.

"We should leave," I say. My chest heaves as my lungs work to drag in more oxygen. "What I want to do to you… we should be home. In our bed."

Liz bolts upright, shoving her chair backward and hitting the person seated behind us. I cover my mouth with my hand and laugh. She apologizes to the woman behind us before tugging me up from my seat. "Time to go. Now."

In a flash, we exit the restaurant. Liz sticks her hand out and asks for the car keys. I dig through my bag and hand them over. Once we buckle up, Liz starts the car and speeds out of the lot.

Typically, a drive from the restaurant to home would have taken close to thirty minutes. With Liz behind the wheel, and desire coursing through her veins, we make it home in twenty.

I don't remember the walk from the car to the front door. The entire time, Liz and I are lip-locked. Her taste salty and garlicky as she swirls her tongue with mine.

The moment we pass the threshold, the moment the front door closes and the bolt slides into place, it is a passionate battle to see who can disrobe the other first. Buttons and zippers and snaps. My shirt is the first thing to go, followed by hers. As we stumble toward the bedroom, I kick off my heels as she toes out of her shoes.

Still connected at the lips, I fumble with her tight jeans as she undoes my pants and they drop to the floor. I tug at the constricting material on her hips, breaking our kiss to laugh at the stubborn denim. With each tug south, I bellow, "Get. Off. Now." On the last tug, Liz bumps the light switch behind her and accidentally flips on the living room light. Once the material hits the floor, we laugh a moment before our lips magnetize back together.

My hip knocks the corner of the couch as we round the living room for the bedroom. But the pain will have to wait. All I care about is getting Liz to the bedroom. Having her lips on my skin and mine on hers. Rolling her nipples between my thumb and forefinger. Tasting her salty-sweetness on my tongue. Feeling her walls constrict around my fingers as she climaxes from my touch.

As the back of her legs bump the mattress, she rips off her bra before doing the same to mine. Her pert nipples graze mine and all I want is to wrap my lips around them and suck. To nibble on the peaked flesh and listen to her moans.

I push her down onto the mattress and she scoots closer to the headboard. Pressing one knee into the mattress, then the other, I crawl over her body until I hover over the firm peaks on her torso. Licking my lips, I lower myself, keeping my eyes trained on hers, and wrap my lips around her hot flesh.

A rush of adrenaline zips and zings from head to toes as I roll her taut flesh between my teeth and tongue. A light sheen prinks Liz's skin and I taste the saltiness on my tongue. It spikes my hunger for her to a whole new level. I clamp down on her nipple, not enough to break the skin, but enough to cause Liz to bow off the mattress and cry out in pleasure.

I let go of the pert bud and kiss my way across the landscape of her chest. Her chest rises and falls beneath my lips. Silent pleas for more and now and never stopping. Her hands in my hair, gripping fiercely. I latch onto the other nipple and reward it equally as I rake my nails down the sides of her torso.

Her panting echoes in the room as I trail down her midline. Down, down, down. At her navel, I dip my tongue inside and swirl one circuit. Then another. The farther south I go, the more erratic Liz pants beneath me. The more her hips gyrate with need.

When my lips graze the lacy hem of her panties, I nip at the flesh above and mark her from hip to hip with my teeth.

Reaching her midline again, I trail my nose over her mound and stop at the start of her slit. I bury my nose between her thighs and inhale deeply.

"Fuck, Lizzie. Need to taste you. Bad."

Just as I start to peel her panties down her thighs, Liz hooks her hands under my shoulders and hoists me up the bed. Before I rebut her maneuver, she flips me onto my back and pins me to the mattress. Her lips on my collarbone, my neck. Up, up, up until she sucks on my lobe.

"First, let me taste you," she groans.

Releasing my wrists, she dips her tongue between my lips before kissing her way down the front of my throat. All lips and tongue and teeth as Liz marks me as hers. After paying perfect attention to each of my breasts, Liz nips a trail down the side of my torso, stopping when her lips strike the thin elastic band on my hip.

Clamping her teeth around the band, Liz snaps the elastic against my skin. Warm fingers graze my knees and meander up my thighs until my panties are in her grip. Slowly, Liz peels the miniscule scrap of material down my hips and thighs until they hit the floor.

Her nose traces the length of my slit as she teases the tip of her tongue in its wake.

"Oh, god," I moan, rocking my hips into her face.

Her hands slip back down to my knees, spreading them wide. Then her tongue laps at my clit—circling and sucking and flicking. I press my head into the mattress as my back arches up and my breasts stand tall.

I fist my fingers in her hair and throw my legs over her shoulders. White noise buzzes in my ears. My heartbeats blur into one long rhythm. A burn ignites in my lungs as I gasp for more oxygen.

My body lifts higher, higher as Liz feasts on my flesh. Slowly, I ascend the peak to my orgasm. Mewling, I beg for more. "Faster," and "Right there," and "Don't stop," fall from my lips. But when she slips two digits in my slick pussy, I lose all sense of what is happening around me.

Seven pumps between my walls and I detonate.

But she doesn't stop. Not for a second.

Liz continues to pump her fingers in and out of me as she

laps up my juices and drags out my orgasm. "So damn deli-cious," she purrs against my skin.

When she finally slows and I catch my breath, I flip her onto her back and kiss the hell out of her. I groan at the salty taste of my orgasm hot on her tongue.

Breaking our kiss, I straddle her waist, lean over to the nightstand, and open the drawer. Liz has a hand at the junction of my thighs, her thumb circling my clit. As difficult as it is to concentrate, I grab a handful of items and leave the drawer open—just in case.

Once upright over her navel, I wave a toy in each hand. "Ready to play?"

Liz's lips curve up until they can't possibly stretch any wider as she eyes the thick, black dildo in one hand and the much smaller dildo in the other. "Always ready to play with you, baby."

I set the toys on the mattress and shift so both my legs are on Liz's left. "On your hands and knees," I command before pinching her nipples.

"Yes, ma'am."

Liz makes a show of flipping onto her belly and hoisting her ass high. I slap her ass for good measure before leaning forward and biting where my hand reddened her skin. She squeals and I slap her again. "Shh, shh, shh."

With the soft glow of light trickling in from the living room, I spread Liz's ass cheeks wide and savor the sight before me. Her slick core and tight hole scream for my attention. Beg for me to lick and taste and devour. I widen my legs and lower my mouth to the tight bud between her cheeks. Circling the hot skin with my tongue, I relish in the trembles emanating from her body.

After one, two, three circuits of my tongue, I drift lower and taste her arousal for the first time tonight. Sweet and sultry and tangy on my tongue, I lick from her clit up the center of her ass cheeks and relish in the quiver I feel throughout her entire body.

I pick up the bottle of lubricant from the bed and squirt a stream of it just above the tight hole, watching it run a thin stream down her crack. Closing the lid, I toss it back on the bed and pick up the smaller dildo. Swiping it over her arousal and oil, I coat the toy before teasing the tip at her back entrance.

Circle and swipe and tease. I do this over and over, until Liz can't take it any longer and pushes backward into my hand.

"Fuck," she groans. Her head lulls for a beat. "So fucking good." She rocks forward and back again. And again. "Oh, god."

Soon, she sets a rhythm all her own and fucks the dildo with vigor. As she pumps it in and out of her ass, I watch in awe. Reaching down, I swipe up the other dildo and suck it between my lips to lubricate it. Then I bring it between our bodies and trace it over Liz's pussy on her thrust back.

For a split-second, she pauses and peeks over her shoulder at me. "Want the harness?" I nod. "'Kay."

I hop off the bed, snag the harness from the mattress, step into it, and cinch it in place at my hips. I slip the dildo through the ring on the front and climb back up the mattress. Before I line myself up with Liz's slick folds, she stops me. She reaches into the nightstand and retrieves another dildo.

"What's that for?" I ask.

Liz curls her finger at me and I crawl closer. Closing the space between us, Liz kisses me deeply. Then, when I least expect it, she thrusts the dildo between my legs and I gasp. Once fully seated inside me, she snaps two buttons between my thighs before smacking my ass.

"So we both get toy play at the same time," she tells me with a glowing smile on her face. Then she spins away from me, plants her hands on the mattress, and looks over her shoulder at me. "Now, fuck me."

And I do. I fuck her, and myself until we both scream out in pleasure. Over and over and over.

TWENTY-FOUR

LIZ

OVER THE LAST TWO WEEKS, life has returned to normal.

Since the day Harrison finally decided to quit being a royal asshole and sign the divorce papers, Tiffany is a million times happier. Back are the days of her singing in the shower. The nights when we cannot keep our hands off each other. Date nights with friends and the occasional bump and grind in a club.

And the wedding planning… Tiffany is at my side, every night, asking what else needs to be done. Although the wedding is a little more than ten months out, both of us want all our ducks in a row. The sooner, the better.

We also got an update from Mr. Kelly yesterday regarding Jensen's adoption. As of now, everything should be finalized by the end of May. The only part concerning us all is how Jensen's birth parents will react to it all. No doubt, they will lose their shit. But after the way they have behaved towards Jensen, it serves them right. No child—young or old—should have to worry about being sold by their parents. Ever.

Everything in our lives is finally falling into place.

"You almost ready?" I shout from the kitchen.

"Five more minutes," Tiffany yells back at me from the bedroom.

I pop the lid on the storage container of mini spring rolls and slide it next to the batch of satay skewers and dipping sauces I made for tonight. Christy, Rick, Ella, and Thomas asked if they could host an engagement party for us. Originally, I wanted to decline the party. Tiffany and I have been engaged for months now and I thought it silly to have a party for that particular reason. I told them we should just have a party to have a party.

Tiffany strolls out of the bedroom, fumbling with the strap of her tall as sin heels, and steals my breath. These last two weeks, she has slowly crept out of her shell again. And tonight, she looks magnificent.

Her auburn locks frame her heart-shaped face and rest on the tops of her breasts in loose waves. A light dabble of foundation pales her tan, freckled skin slightly while a swipe of rouge highlights her prominent cheekbones. A blend of black and brown highlights her lids, making her icy blue irises a bright contrast. An invitation to be sucked in and never let go. Her perfect lips a few shades bolder than her auburn hair.

But those aren't what lure me closer to her. No. The dress. The dress is what has me stepping forward. What has me itching to press my fingers to her skin.

As Tiffany straightens her posture, she glances down at herself and rights her dress. In three strides, I sidle up against her and trace the back side of my hand down her bicep.

"This dress... when did you get this?"

Her mesmerizing gaze flits to mine. "This week. After work on Wednesday. Do you like it?"

She answers as if the answer were simple and I should have known. As if I should have seen the bag when she walked in the apartment with it. Should have seen the thin scrap of material hanging in the closet every morning since she purchased it.

But I had no clue.

Trailing my fingers back up her arm, I follow the line of the barely-existent strap on her shoulder and down her back. The dress fits her like a glove. Snug in all the right places. The hue reminds me of twilight—a shade of blue not quite black, but just on the cusp. In dim lighting, people will say it is black. In the light of day, you would be able to catch the blue glint.

The two thin straps start at her clavicle, slip over her

shoulders, and merge an inch above the crack of her supple ass. Aside from the skimpy straps, the only material on the backside is the patch covering her ass. My mouth waters at the sight of her backside, so I shift and take in the front. The material up front does nothing to curb my craving for her. Small strips of material cover her breasts—barely—but flaunt her ample cleavage before converging just above her navel.

Honestly, the amount of material covering her breasts reminds me of the same coverage my wedding dress provides. I wonder if she was as turned on when I walked out in my dress as I am gawking at her now.

I swallow. *Fuck.* Am I in trouble tonight or what?

"Yeah, baby. I love the dress. Glad I didn't see you in it before now."

Tiffany tilts her head to the side and narrows her eyes. "Why?"

"We'd never make it to the party. That's why."

She mouths the word *oh* as she presses her thighs together. And just like that, I want to shove the dress up her thighs and lick her clit until she screams and quivers above me.

I close my eyes and moan. "We should go. If we don't leave now, we won't make it at all."

Tiffany flies past me, grabs her purse by the door, and checks her hair in the foyer mirror. "We can't miss the party. We're the guests of honor."

Snatching the bag of appetizers off the kitchen counter, I head toward the front door and step up to Tiffany. "You're lucky we're the guests of honor," I say. "But don't think I won't drag you away at the party and remedy the ache we're both feeling."

The blush on Tiffany's cheekbones darkens, her freckles blending into flush. "Promise," she says, her voice husky and needy.

"Promise." I smack her ass. "Now let's go, before we're late."

My years of throwing parties must have rubbed off on Christy. Everything is on point. From the music to the food to the number of bodies filling the room. She even went as far as to invite Sarah and Jackson, and some of the friends they have made since moving to California.

The bass booms throughout the vast living room and I dance closer to Tiffany. My hands on her hips. Her fingers laced together behind my neck. Our legs between each other's as we grind together and get lost in the music.

When we first arrived, I thought it was going to be one of those boring parties. You know the type you have after you have been adulting a while and get tired early. It appeared to be the case when we walked through the front door and I spotted the immaculate table of hors d'oeuvres, right next to the pristine bar area.

But after we toasted to our engagement, Christy announced it was time for the real party to begin. The quiet music vanished as the dance beats consumed everyone, the lights dimmed, and the vibe morphed to something more intimate.

The song transitions and a sultrier tone fills the air. Inching impossibly closer to Tiffany, a waft of rose and musk and sweat flutters up my nose, and dancing with my girl is no longer enough. I slip my hands down to her ass and drive her into me as I kiss up the column of her neck.

I suck her earlobe between my lips as she pants against my skin. "I need to taste you. Now," I groan against her ear.

Before she responds, I break us apart and drag her off the makeshift dance floor. We weave our way to the back patio, past the pool, and toward a dimly lit sitting area on the back of the lot. Most of the space is masked by plants, shrubs, or trees. An exposed nook, if you will, with a fire pit in the center.

I push Tiffany down onto the cushioned patio chair, drop to my knees, and cinch her dress up her thighs. As soon as the fabric bunches around her hips, I groan at Tiffany's spread legs.

"Good God woman. Are you trying to kill me?"

Tiffany scoots her hips closer to the edge of the chair. Closer to my face. "Quite the opposite, actually." Gleaming in the dim yard lights and the waxing moonlight, Tiffany reaches down and slides a finger between her slick folds before circling her clit. "Wearing panties wastes time."

Fuck. My. Life.

This woman is perfect for me in every way. From her sweet and sassy demeanor to the prim and sometimes not-so-proper appearance. She infiltrates every facet of my heart while quenching every desire in my soul. Never have I met a person so fitting and perfect.

Leaning forward, I lick up her arousal-slicked pussy as I spread her legs wide. The second my tongue laps her flesh, she bucks beneath me and fists my hair. Circle and flick. Circle and flick. My tongue plays with her clit as she rocks her hips beneath me.

I rest her thighs on my shoulders, suck at her clit, and insert two fingers between her folds. Pumping, pumping, pumping in and out of her slick walls. Soft cries break through her lips as she clutches my hair firmer and drives me harder between her thighs. Her body quivers beneath me. Her pussy walls slowly clamping down on my fingers.

"Oh, fuck, Lizzie. Don't fucking stop," she pleas into the darkness.

Flicking my tongue faster against her clit, I insert a third finger and pick up the pace with my thrusts. One, two, three thrusts later and Tiffany cries out as her walls clench around me and cum drips down my palm. I withdraw my fingers and clean her folds with my tongue.

"Best fucking taste in the world is you on my tongue."

After I lick off the evidence of her orgasm, I lift my fingers to my mouth and suck the taste of her off, moaning around my fingers. Tiffany stares at me with fire in her eyes. Popping my fingers from my lips, I lean forward and kiss her deeply. She groans against my tongue as she reaches between us and rubs her palm against my clothed, drenched pussy.

"I should at least return the favor," she says when the kiss breaks. And I don't argue with her.

Switching positions, Tiffany unfastens my pants and watches them fall to the pavers. Our knees will probably have bruises in the morning, but fucking her here and now is well worth it.

Tiffany shoves me down on the chair she just abandoned

and bites her way from the inside of my knee to my apex. Every nip of her teeth has me bucking my hips and dripping for more. When her hot mouth reaches my apex, I arch off the chair and thrust into her touch. Every stroke, lick, and suck has me melting, panting, and begging for it to never end.

Her tongue on my body has me dizzy. Delirious. Floating up, up, up as if I'm having an out-of-body experience.

Lost in the sensation of Tiffany tasting my flesh, it isn't long before my pulse grows wild and my breath becomes non-existent. Heat builds low in my belly, spirals up my spine, and spreads from my breasts up to my cheeks. A tingle ripples through my limbs as I slam my eyes shut and am blinded by the stars. I fist the chair cushion in my hands and cry out as I spill on her tongue.

Every rigid muscle in my body goes limp after a minute. Breaths start to even out as my pulse slows to its normal rhythmic pattern.

"I love watching you come undone beneath me," Tiffany breathes out, breaking the silence. As I open my eyes to meet hers, a shadow moves in the back corner of the yard. I bolt upright and reach for my pants on the ground. Slipping my pants on quickly, I glance down and see Tiffany looking up at me in horror. "Is someone out here?"

As I refasten my pants, I scan the fence line of the yard. The corner where I detected movement is pitch black and hides everything and nothing at the same time. "Not sure. Thought I saw someone. Maybe it was a trick of the moon-light mixed with the shadows of trees. Was probably nothing."

At least I hope it is nothing.

I do one last scan of the blackness before helping Tiffany stand. She resituates her dress in record time and we walk back toward the house. As we reach the back patio to rejoin the party, I take one last glance over my shoulder. The hairs on the back of my neck stand at attention as I scrutinize every inch of the yard and come up with zilch.

We spend the rest of the evening in the house. Dancing. Laughing. Joking with our friends. But when it is time to leave, I can't dismiss the painful twist in my gut. Stronger than earlier in the backyard, the hot piercing penetrates my heart and steals my breath.

But I don't mention a word to Tiffany.

She has done her time. Had her share of pain and misery. For now, I will carry whatever this is and deal with it accordingly.

If only I knew who or what I was up against.

TWENTY-FIVE
HARRISON

Tiffany may not legally be mine anymore, but she is still mine. No law will tell me how to live my life. No law will tell me who belongs and doesn't belong in my life. The law is for imbeciles.

I may have slipped a ring on another woman's finger, but Tiffany is *still mine*. Jewelry is bullshit. A fashion statement. Something flashy stupid bitches like Regina need to flaunt. It's all for show, even if Regina isn't aware.

Tiffany may have acquired a taste for cunt, but she is *still fucking mine*. The faded gleam in her eyes is a clear declaration of how much she misses my cock in her cunt. How much she misses me.

From the day I laid eyes on her, months before her eighteenth birthday, she became mine. Her parents groomed her solely for *me*. Mommy dearest taught her how to be a doctor's wife for *me*. Daddy dearest poisoned her mind with ideas of being more than *my* arm piece. For that, I set him straight. For that, I threatened his life, and the life of everyone precious to him. His bitch of a wife, and his conniving cunt of a daughter. Within seconds, he spilled her secrets all over the floor and begged for his life.

I may have let her slip from my clutches, but I always know where she is. Every second, minute, and hour of the day. Tiffany doesn't speak with her parents often—practically never—but when she does, daddy dearest calls me immediately.

Since I signed the divorce papers, Tiffany is under the false pretense that what we have is over.

Needless to say, Tiffany doesn't know shit. For a smart woman, sometimes she is a fucking idiot.

I will bide my time. Lurk a while longer in the bushes. Jack off at her pussy-on-pussy action. Plan how to punish her accordingly for her wrongdoings.

But soon, I will remind her exactly what her role in this world is. Soon, she will get down on her knees with those weepy, doe eyes and beg for forgiveness like she has countless times in the past.

And if she is lucky. If the stars align perfectly that day. I may show her what forgiveness looks like.

Maybe.

TWENTY-SIX

TIFFANY

Chloe barges into my office five minutes before lunchtime. "You need to come out to the reception area. Now." She spins on her heels and exits as quickly as she entered.

I rise from my chair, speed walk out of my office, shut the door, and follow in Chloe's dust trail. Before I reach the door that leads to reception, a voice booms from the other side.

"Where is she?" he yells. "Where's the bitch trying to kidnap my boy?"

Before I open the bolted door between the hall and reception, I peer through the wired glass and see a very angry, very violent John Pastor. Security has him restrained in their arms as he fights to break free. Eyes bulging. Nostrils flared. Teeth bared. Face as red as a fire engine.

I swipe my badge and complete the scan next to the door. The bolt clicks louder when it unlocks. I turn the handle and step out of the hall into reception. When John Pastor spots me entering the room, he struggles against Zach and Paul's grip trying to get to me. Thankfully, they keep him in check and hold him in place.

Chloe steps up beside me and leans close. "Already called the police. Should be here any second," she whispers.

I nod and take a few steps closer to John. "Mr. Pastor," I say as calmly as possible. "No one is trying to steal your son from you. After some of our sessions, it was deemed appropriate that Jensen not be returned to your custody."

He stops fighting against Zach and Paul. Standing tall, he puffs out his chest as a snide smile pulls at one corner of his mouth. For a moment, he stares at me. As if he has a secret to share, but battles whether or not he should. His solemn appearance sends a shiver down my spine more than his anger.

"Really, lesbo?"

I jerk my head back an inch and hone in on his expression. This man doesn't know me outside these walls. Doesn't know a goddamn thing about me personally, other than my name. Sure, he may have been served documentation regarding Jensen and the adoption, but his assumption of my lifestyle is oddly specific. For all he knew, the names on the legal paperwork could have been me and another doctor from Lewis House. Which would be the case if we deemed a minor's home unsafe.

"Sorry, what was that?" I ask while maintaining my composure.

"You heard me. Lesbo. What? Don't think I know all about you? About you trying to steal my kid while you strip women bare in public and ram your face between their legs?"

Holy shit. My eyes bulge in their sockets. My lungs tighten and burn as I work to drag in air. *This can't be real.* I pinch my eyes tightly as my heart blows strike after strike against my sternum. *This can't be real.*

Liz said she thought she saw someone in Christy and Rick's yard. Had the feeling someone was watching us. Was it John Pastor? If it was him, how the hell did he know where to find me? Did he follow us from home? How the hell does he know where we live?

In my line of work, keeping our personal details hidden is of utmost importance. And all of mine are locked down. I don't have social media accounts, but I do scroll through Liz's from time to time. Anything she posts about us never mentions my identity or shows my face. Not just because of my job, but because of Harrison.

I suck in a deep breath and lock eyes with a menacing John Pastor. He smirks at me as if he knows all my secrets. But I ignore his mission to strike me down. Breathing deep again, I dig deep and retrieve every ounce of courage I need to stand against this piece of shit. This poor excuse of a human.

"Mr. Pastor, no amount of bullying or demeaning will help you right now." I point to a camera mounted on the ceiling to my right, one on my left, and another behind the reception station. "If anything, it will just add to the case built against you and your wife. Jensen will not be returning to your custody due to reasons attributable to your behavior in which you were deemed unfit. As far as the names on his adoption paperwork, take a look around you." I wave my hand around the room, pointing out the dozen or so women in the room. "Any one of these other women could be on the adoption paperwork with me. You aren't the first set of parents, and sadly won't be the last, that we remove parental rights from."

His conspiratorial smile from earlier returns. "This has nothing to do with paperwork. Maybe next time you're in public and you want to hike up your blue dress, maybe you should make certain you're alone."

Before I process a word he just said, the very specific details of my and Liz's time in Christy and Rick's backyard, the police step through the doors. Chloe goes into mother hen/CEO mode and explains the entire situation. Zach and Paul release John Pastor when the police slap handcuffs on his wrists and read him his rights.

But the entire time, John Pastor stares at me with a wicked grin plastered on his face. As the police escort him out the door, he spins in their arms and looks me square in the eyes.

"You think it's over? You think you've won. Well, guess what little girl. The game has only just begun."

The officers yank him out the door and shove him into the back of a patrol car. I stare out the window and watch as the car drives away. Once the car is out of sight, I wait for the solace to hit. The sense of finality. But it never comes. Because his words lurk in the back of my mind. Creep in like a fast-paced fog and blanket every ounce of comfort in my bones, seeping into my marrow.

"You think it's over? You think you've won. Well, guess what little girl. The game has only just begun."

And a part of me believes him, even if it scares me to death.

The rest of my day at Lewis House goes by without a hiccup. After John Pastor was escorted from the premises, I returned to my office and immediately called Liz. She didn't freak-out quite as bad as me, but she was definitely disturbed by the specific details the man had regarding our evening. By the end of our conversation, I asked if we could go out for the evening. Just the two of us. Dinner and maybe a walk in the park. Anything to help tame the wild commotion in my head. Her response was a resounding yes.

Thank god.

I finish my client notes before shutting down the computer for the day. As I sling my purse strap over my shoulder, my phone pings. I fish it out of my purse and read the text message.

Liz: Finishing up some last-minute things at work. Meet you there soon.

I type out a quick response before stuffing my phone back in my bag.

Tiffany: I'll be waiting. See you soon.

Taking my time as I exit Lewis House, I stop at the front reception and chat with them a moment before leaving. It was an eventful morning for all of us here and I just want to be certain everyone is alright after today's episode. After we exchange our thoughts on the whole John Pastor situation, I bid Ron and Greta good night and walk out the door.

The door whooshes shut behind me and I step forward as the cool May air whips my hair across my face. One thing I learned when we moved from Georgia to California, the summer heat isn't quite the same. Does it get hot here? Definitely. But the air is drier and the time in which the heat sticks to you isn't as long—during the day and throughout the year. Slowly, I am adapting to the lesser, drier heat, but every once in a while—like now—I miss the early warmth.

I tug my jacket tighter at the front and head for my car.

Halfway across the lot, a shiver rolls up my spine and I survey the nearby cars. The chill not coming from the occasional sweep of wind, but something familiar. Something I never wish to relive again.

When I spy nothing except cars and the normal plant life in the lot, I start digging for my keys and pick up the pace as I trek to my car. Thirty feet. Twenty feet. Ten feet. Keys in hand. I press the unlock button on my fob. Two feet. I yank the door open, jump inside, and smash the lock button as the door closes.

I take a deep breath. "Paranoid much," I say to the steering wheel as I press the ignition button.

The car sparks to life and I take a few more deep breaths before I shift it into gear and drive to the restaurant. More distance stretches out between me and Lewis House. I breathe deeper and try to shake the gloom lingering in my bones. But no matter how many inhalations I take in, no matter how many mental reassurances I give myself, the feeling never subsides.

A mile from the restaurant, the traffic light I approach shifts from red to green. Without checking, I breeze through the intersection. Midway through the intersection... everything shifts into pain. Metal crunching metal squeals in my ears. Glass shatters and sprays in every direction. My eyes slam shut as I whirl like a tornado. Everything around me flickers in and out. Then, after what seems like hours, the car stops spinning.

Although fully aware of what happened, my mind has trouble grasping at reality.

My driver's side door opens and someone tugs me out onto the pavement. Voices erupt around me.

"Is she alright?" one asks.

"I have 911 on the phone," another says.

Several "Oh my god, is she alive?" are faintly heard.

"Everyone back away," a man says. "She needs air."

With shut eyes, I recognize the shift of bodies as people back away and more light shines down on me. Someone pokes and prods at my head, my neck, my limbs. But I don't move. I don't fight the strangers around me as darkness becomes more prevalent and exhaustion consumes me.

"She's losing consciousness," the man says. "I need to get her to the hospital now."

"The ambulance is on the way," another person shouts.

"Can't wait."

And then I'm up, off the ground, and moving. I try to open my eyes. Try to see the man who has lifted me up and is taking me away from this horrific scene. But they are too heavy and won't budge.

His arms shift beneath me and I land on something cool. Every muscle in my body flexes at the sudden temperature difference and I flinch. I feel the seatbelt on my arm, around my waist, before it clicks and a door shuts.

After I hear another door and feel the shift in weight as he gets in the car, I internally sigh. Until he speaks.

"I've got you, Tiff. Don't worry, I will always take care of you."

A tear rolls down my cheek as my body quivers uncontrollably. *This can't be real. Just one of my nightmares. My subconscious playing tricks on me. Wake up, Tiffany! Wake. The. Hell. Up.*

But instead of waking, the darkness consumes me entirely. The darkness of my past. The darkness of the present. And the impending darkness of my future.

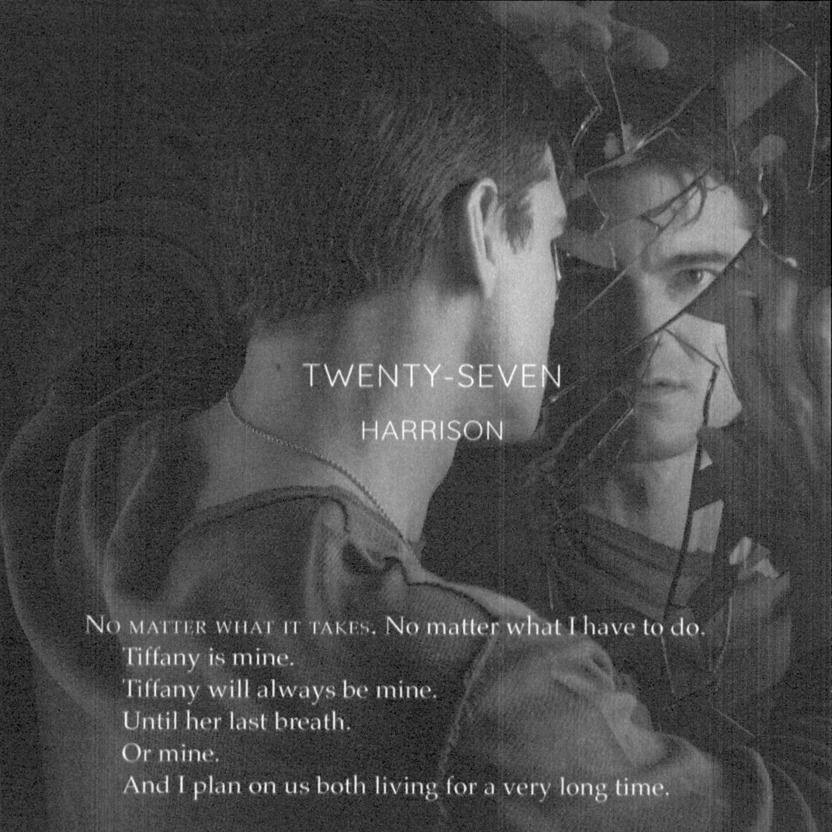

TWENTY-SEVEN

HARRISON

NO MATTER WHAT IT TAKES. No matter what I have to do.
Tiffany is mine.
Tiffany will always be mine.
Until her last breath.
Or mine.
And I plan on us both living for a very long time.

TWENTY-EIGHT

LIZ

I PARK in front of the restaurant and rush inside. My last client kept me on the phone far longer than I expected but purchased a tremendous policy that will fluff my bonus quite nicely. Has been almost an hour since I texted and told Tiffany I was running late. Guilt washes over me and I pray she isn't too upset.

After the couple in front of me is guided by one of the hosts to their table, I amble up to the podium.

"How many in your party?" the young girl asks without peering up from the stand. She continuously wipes a laminated grid of the restaurant's table layout with a dishtowel. *Kids.*

"I'm meeting someone. She should be here already. Tiffany Page."

The young girl sets down the towel and taps the screen in front of her over and over, her eyes bouncing left and right after each tap. After scrolling forever, she says, "No one by that name has checked in with the hosts." Eyes still downcast as she goes for the dish towel again.

How the hell do kids like this keep jobs nowadays? Not through charm.

"Will you please look again? Might be under Dr. Page."

Now is when she pops her head up and opts to make eye contact. Is the magic word doctor? Does she think seating a doctor is going to garner her better tip share for the evening?

Not likely after the whole I-refuse-to-look-up-and-acknowledge-people moment. Honestly, the manager should be informed of her lack of work ethic.

She taps the screen a few more times and scans what I assume are names or reservations. When she reaches the end of the list, she shakes her head, meets my eyes again, and shrugs. "Sorry, don't see a Tiffany Page or Dr. Page on the list."

"Thanks," I mutter and move off to the side. I scan the slightly packed waiting area for a head of auburn hair and come up with nada.

Where is she?

Taking out my phone, I type out a quick text message and wander out the restaurant entrance.

Liz: Sorry I'm so late. Are you here?

Walking back to my car, I unlock the door and get inside, but don't start the engine. I stare at my screen and wait for the speech bubble and floating dots to appear. Five unbearable minutes pass, and I still have no response from Tiffany. *Where the hell is she?* I ask myself again.

A moment of clarity hits and I click on the info button under Tiffany's name in the message app. Early on in our relationship, Tiffany suggested we share our location with each other in case something happened. At the time, I thought nothing of it. Now, I wonder if it was her secret way of keeping herself visible in case something like this happened. In case I couldn't seem to locate her.

It takes a minute for the map to populate, but the map shows her location up the street... over an hour ago. I tap the screen and enlarge the map before hitting refresh in the upper corner. Still no change. I try calling her and it goes straight to voicemail.

"Shit. Tiff, where are you?"

I start the car and drive to the location her phone last mapped her. The closer I get to the map's location, the more prominent a sharp searing pain grows in my side.

When I finally arrive at the intersection, I stop breathing. Tiffany's car has a massive dent in the passenger door. The front bumper is on the ground, surrounded by a mountain of glass shards. A tow truck driver latches a hook under the front of her car, presses a button and loads the car onto a flatbed.

Throwing the car in park, I jump out and sprint over to a nearby police officer. As I approach, he throws his hand in the air to stop me. "Ma'am, you need to step back."

"Where is the driver?" I shout. "She's my fiancée."

The officer walks in my direction. His expression is everything I don't want to see and a million terrible thoughts run through my mind at once. Brows furrowed. Lips in a tight line. Eyes darting back and forth between mine. The closer he gets, the sharper the stab in my side pierces me.

He stops less than a foot away and works to straighten his features. "Sorry to be the one to tell you this." No. *No, no, no, no, no.* "When we arrived at the scene, she was no longer here. A witness informed us she was taken to the hospital by a doctor."

At the mention of a doctor, every molecule in my body shoots to hyper-awareness. Thousands of doctors live in the area. Could be an absolute stranger who was being a good Samaritan. Someone who used their expertise and knew she needed medical attention right then and there, rather than waiting for the paramedics to arrive.

"Do you know who the doctor was? What hospital did he take her to?"

"The closest hospital is five miles from here. I imagine he took her there." The officer said *he,* and the knife twists further. "One of the witnesses got his last name. Let me get it for you." As he flips through a small steno notebook, I beg the gods to not be the single name I do *not* want to hear. "Ah, here we are. Deats. Dr. Harrison Deats."

"No," I whisper as I sway in place.

The officer plants his hands on both my shoulders. "You okay, miss?"

I shake my head, again and again. "Why did she go with him? Why didn't anyone stop her from going with him?" I ramble on like a madwoman. My stomach roils and I slap a hand over my mouth.

There is no possible way Tiffany would have elected to go

with him. The only way she got in a car with Harrison is either by force or she was incoherent. Neither possibility sits well with me.

The officer shakes my shoulders and lowers his gaze to meet mine. "Ma'am. What are you saying? Why should she not have gone with him?" He scrunches his brow as he studies my eyes.

This isn't happening. This. Cannot. Be happening.

I locked eyes with the officer, his jade irises gentle and full of concern. "He's her ex-husband." I swallow hard as a tear rolls down my cheek. "He used to—" *Do I really have to finish this sentence?*

"What? He used to what?"

I slam my eyes shut and hot tears waterfall down the lines of my cheeks. "He used to *hurt* her. Years ago. She just got free of him." My crying morphs into full-on sobbing. "She finally got her freedom."

Like a bolt of lightning, the officer speaks into the radio attached to his shoulder. "All officers, be on the lookout. Caucasian female. Longer auburn hair. Early thirties. Last seen wearing" —he looks at me and I mouth what I remember Tiffany wearing this morning— "a white blouse and black pantsuit. Victim was abducted by one Dr. Harrison Deats. Age unknown. Identified by witnesses as approximately six-feet tall. Blond. Slender build."

As he continues to prattle off details of the last place Tiffany was seen and the vehicle Harrison drove away in, I space out. A buzz overtakes my hearing as my vision fogs. My lungs burn as I hyperventilate, unable to pull adequate oxygen into my lungs. *Bam. Bam. Bam.* I clutch my shirt above my breastbone and tug—harder, harder—as my heart thrashes and viciously punches behind its cage.

I collapse and crack my knees against the concrete, welcoming the pain as it shoots up my legs to my spine. The pain is the only reminder this is actually happening. That this is very real. That Tiffany has been abducted by her deranged ex-husband.

The officer squats down in front of me and speaks. His lips move, but I don't hear a word he says. I wring my shirt tighter in my fists as tears rain down my cheeks. He clutches one of my shoulders and waves someone over with the other hand. His lips continue to move, but darkness coats the edges of my vision. A fireman drops down on his haunches in front of me.

Lifting my chin, the fireman watches my pupils as he shines a light in my eyes. He speaks to me, but sounds miles away. Muffled. Faint. Dropping his hand from my chin, he snaps his fingers beside my ears and I shake my head slightly. He does it again, the clicking more perceptible.

Gradually, all the noises flood back in. Horns honk. Passersby laugh or holler or chat on the sidewalk. Engines rev and brakes squeal. The fireman continues to snap his fingers and speak to me.

"Can you hear me?" the fireman asks.

I nod. "Yes."

"Do you have any health conditions we should be concerned about?"

Squinting, I lift my line of sight to his. "No," I whisper. "Not that I know of." The fireman extends his hand and slowly rises from the ground. I take his hand and stand. "Thank you." I swipe the unrelenting tears from my cheeks.

"Might be a good idea to call family or a friend. You shouldn't be driving right now. Do you have someone you can call?"

Driving might not be in my best interest right now, but there is no chance in hell I'm ignoring the fact my fiancée was abducted. By an abusive lunatic. Although, I have no clue where the hell to start looking for her. Harrison doesn't live in California. Searching every hotel in a ten-mile radius is out of the question. It would take days. And days is far too long.

I dig deep and try to think like a fucked up man. Someone who doesn't live locally, but seems to know his way around the city. A light flicks on in my head and burns like an Olympic torch. "He knows someone here," I mutter.

"What?" The fireman leans in and lowers his ear close to my mouth.

"He knows someone here," I repeat.

He straightens and peers down at me, cocking his head to the side. "The man who took your fiancée?"

I nod. "It's the only logical explanation. How else would

he know where to go? Where to take her? Not a hotel. He has to have a place to take her. A place no one would know about."

The fireman waves the officer back over and repeats what I just said. The officer listens attentively, nodding at where my brainstorm leads. After one last look over, the fireman deems it safe to leave, joins his brethren in the truck and drives away.

"Do you know who Mr. Deats may interact with in the area?" the officer questions.

Tiffany's earlier recount of John Pastor's visit to Lewis House sparks in my memory. "This morning, Tiffany called and told me of an encounter she had at work. Lewis House." He nods and waits for me to continue. "A patient's birth father came into the facility and made threats. He followed the threats with divulging a personal, very private moment Tiffany and I shared recently. In vivid detail. The only way he'd know is if he was following us."

"Or someone else told him," the officer ponders.

Honestly, I had never considered the idea someone else watched us and shared the details. But, at this point, anything is possible, and nothing should be discounted. The officer asks for his name and any additional information I can provide regarding the father. I give him the measly amount of information I have referencing John Pastor and his wife.

As the officer heads to his car to look up John Pastor on his laptop, I stop him. "Wait." I jog over to him and continue walking with him to his car. "Not sure if she is local or from Florida, but when Tiffany and I met up with Mr. Deats two weeks ago, he brought his attorney with him. I can make a call and get her name, too."

"At this point, any and all information helps. When you get a name, let me know."

He opens the car door and sits in the vehicle with the door propped open. I step to the back of the car and call Mr. Kelly, who tells me he'll grab the information and call me back. Then I call Christy and Rick, passing along what happened and ask them if they can pick me up. With every tremble of my hands, my arms, my legs, I agree driving my car is a bad idea.

Fifteen minutes later, I hand over every snippet I learn to the officer. Turns out Harrison's attorney—Regina Tucker—has been practicing in Los Angeles for two years. *One guess where she previously practiced? Mr. Kelly asked me.* I didn't have to guess. It flashed brighter than a neon sign in a porn shop window. Florida. Florida was where she previously practiced law.

The officer put out another BOLO. This time for John and Margot Pastor, and Regina Tucker. As soon as their names hit the radio waves, Christy and Rick pull up. Rick asks for my fob so he can move my car and I hand it over. Without another word, he strides over to my car, starts it up, and steers it into the parking lot of the drugstore I'd loitered in front of for the last however long. Rick goes into the store a moment, then walks back over to us.

"Car will be fine here overnight." I nod. "Catch me up on what's going on."

I recount everything to Rick. Christy had some of the details about Tiffany and Harrison, but I had yet to tell her every piece. At the time, I thought it better to not spew Tiffany's past without her present. Now, I give no fucks. Right now, I will do whatever necessary to rescue her.

Near the officer's car, Christy leans closer and listens to every word muttered across the police radio. Her eyes bug out as she turns to face us. Pointing to Rick's SUV, she mouths *let's go.*

Secure in the SUV, Christy spins from the front passenger seat to face me in the back. She rattles off an address and I stare at her blankly. "It's the attorney's address," she states. "Officers are on their way now. We should head there too."

"Gorgeous, we should let the cops handle this. Not sure if it's a good idea."

On the fence, I understand why Rick says we should steer clear. We don't want to get in the middle of a potential cross-fire. But... I also cannot just sit here and wait. Waiting to hear the outcome. Not when I could be helping. Not when I could save her.

"Rick, please," I beg. "We'll hang back and let them do their part. But there's no way we can sit idle at home and wait for the phone to ring. I'll lose my goddamn mind, if I haven't already."

He looks between me and Christy. After a beat, his eyes soften and he nods. "Yeah, okay. But"— he holds up a finger — "we stay out of the way. We have no idea what's happening inside the house. Until we know it's safe, we don't go in. Agreed?"

"Yes," Christy and I say in unison. Normally, I would laugh at such antics. But now isn't the time.

With our agreement etched in stone, Rick starts the SUV and puts it in gear. Seconds later, we whiz through the streets of Los Angeles faster than safe. I stare out the window as I clench and unclench my fists over and over.

Hang in there, baby. We're coming. Just hang in there.

TWENTY-NINE

TIFFANY

PAIN. Every inch of my body is in pain. Shooting. Stabbing. Searing pain.

I wake and all my awareness focuses on the pain. My head throbs violently as if my pulse encapsulates my brain and suffocates the organ. A spasm lances through my neck and shoots down to my shoulder blades. The length of my spine stretches and stiffens and seizes with each breath I take.

Wherever I am, the space is dark and dank. A pungent odor floats in the air—a strange mix of mildew and bleach and citrus. It invades my nasal cavities, sets up camp, and refuses to leave.

My wrists ache above my head while my ankles burn at my base. Beneath me, the ground is solid and cold, and it feels as if my body is on its side being stretched as far as humanly possible. Attempting to bring my hands to my face, I learn quickly I am unable to move an inch. The ache in my wrists stems from a set of binds. When I tug my legs next, a burn rips up my limbs and meets in my middle. Metal-on-metal echoes in the space as my limbs suddenly stretch farther apart.

"Aaaahhh!" I cry out, my scream echoing back to me.

The screeching metal noise ceases, but the scorching pain throughout my arms and legs continues. I heave for air as the pain consumes me. Minutes or hours pass, all sense of time is lost in the darkness of wherever I happen to be. The pain simmers after a while and I breathe easier. Adjust to the awkward position of my body and try to think.

Until a tongue clucks in the darkness.

I clamp my jaw so tight my molars shoot pain across my face. The amperage of electricity spiderwebs from my teeth to the hinge of my jaw and spreads like wildfire over my eyes and scalp. Although my body is stretched almost to the point of dislocating my shoulders and hips, I tremble on the cold, smelly floor.

"H-hello? Is some—is somebody there?"

The clucking ripples in the darkness again. This time, much closer to where I lay bound and elongated like an elastic hairband. Followed by a low, sinister chuckle.

A new wave of fear pumps adrenaline into my bloodstream. That laugh. Anything but *that* laugh. The sound I hoped to never to hear outside of my nightmares. *The laugh*— the one which has haunted my life and nightmares for more than a decade.

Harrison's laugh.

"Just because I signed a piece of fucking paper," he says before his sinister laugh ricochets in the room again. "That paper doesn't mean shit, princess. You will always belong to me."

Warm wetness pools between my legs as I weep into the darkness. Somewhere, hiding in the blackness, is Harrison Deats. A man who charmed my mother then father with his intelligence and charisma. A man who flaunted every trophy worthy attribute he owned. And a man who could make any woman—or man—swoon at his pristinely groomed stature.

But those aren't the only aspects of Harrison Deats.

After he wooed my parents, then me, and laid his supposed claim to my heart, he morphed into a whole different Harrison. One which made me cower at the mere sound of his voice. Who kept me *in line* with his fists, knees, and feet. And let's not forget the wooden bat or the switchblade. At times, he enjoyed using them more than any person should.

"Harrison," I whimper. "P-please. Can we just talk about this?"

His wicked laughter rings in the darkness and dizzies me. "The time for talking is gone, princess. Maybe you should have asked to talk before you packed a bag, stole half our cash, and bolted. But you did no such thing." His voice grows louder as I assume he steps closer, although I still can't see a damn thing. "No, instead you ran off to Georgia. But don't think for a fucking second I never knew where you were." Heat grazes my cheek and the urge to vomit takes hold. "I have always known exactly where you are, princess. *Always.*"

I slam my eyes shut. Although the room is pitch black, not seeing a damn thing with my eyes open disturbs me more than keeping them shut. Harrison brushes his fingers across my cheekbone and I flinch. The shooting pain of literally being stretched limb to limb jolts through my joints. He traces his fingers down the side of my neck before slowly wrapping each digit around my windpipe.

Slowly, his hand constricts my throat. Tighter. Tighter.

During the four years Harrison and I lived together as a married couple, I learned several things. But three stand out more than the rest.

One—Harrison gets off on torture. No matter what form, he lives to inflict pain on others. Thrives on it. Gets hard from it.

Two—Harrison also gets off on the screams and struggle. The cries of pain. The begging and pleading for him to stop. Anytime I yelped in pain, his eyes would roll back into his head and he would palm his growing erection. The end result had him learning more reasons for me to scream.

Three—Harrison will never change. There is a missing link in his mind. It was never my place to diagnose people close to me, but Harrison is in serious need of it. Couldn't say with one-hundred percent certainty, but Harrison displays the tendencies of a psychopath. Narcissist also fit the bill.

The list is ever-growing. Any person who gets off on beating someone they supposedly love, someone who they vowed to protect, has several issues beneath the surface. Issues I don't care to gain knowledge of.

So, as I lay on the cold concrete and struggle to remain still and silent while my ex-husband fondles and twists my breast in his palm, I pray to the heavens. Pray to anyone who will hear my silent pleas. Ask for someone to rescue me from this hideous excuse for a human being.

I refuse to give in. Refuse to scream or shed a tear or physically struggle. Because if I do any of those things, it will egg him on further. Drive him to inflict harsher punishments. In his eyes, this lesson is exactly what he believes I deserve. Punishment. For disobeying him. For escaping the life we shared. For standing up to him and refusing to back down.

It has been almost ten years since the last time he laid a hand on me, but I remember it as if it were yesterday. The pain Harrison inflicted on me… it never leaves.

But I will not be his punching bag for the rest of my life. Not a fucking chance in hell.

"If you've known where I am, why haven't you come for me? Why wait all this time? Why wait until now?"

His hand clamps over the side of my torso. *Clamp, clamp, clamp.* He squeezes his way down to my hip and I bite the inside of my cheek as I fight the yelp wanting to escape my lips. Inches above me, Harrison chuckles under his breath. And suddenly I wonder if he can see me in the darkness.

"Because you wanted freedom. And I wanted to give you the illusion of said freedom. You never had it, though. Not for a single second." He leans his weight into my hip and pain ricochets throughout my body. "I was always there, watching. If not with my own eyes, I used someone else's." Grabbing the bottom hem of my blouse, he yanks it up and tears near the buttons at my cleavage. The material rips down the center and cool air prickles my skin. "Some of those men you kissed, I paid them to ask you on a date. When they took it farther than I liked, I put them in the ground."

I squeeze my eyelids tighter as I absorb what he just said. Not only did he pay men to ask me out, to take me on dates and probe me with question after question, but he also just admitted to killing them—or having them killed.

Acid churns in my stomach. I take deep, steadying breaths and try to calm the cyclone spinning in my body. But it is no use. Bile rises up my throat. My diaphragm contracts, over and over, and forces the contents of my stomach onto the floor in front of me. My body continues to dry heave as my joints threaten to displace.

"You're lucky I love you," he mumbles under his breath. "I should smear your face in the mess you made. But, lucky for you, I'm in a forgiving mood."

And I snap. His words the final slap. "You wouldn't know love if it ran you over in the form of a semi." I spit in front of me. "Honestly, you're a fucking coward."

"Better watch your fucking mouth, *princess*."

"Why? What are you going to do, *asshole?* Tie me up and torture me? Beat the shit out of me? Newsflash! Been there. Doing that. But I'm not the same woman I was ten years ago. I'm not some frail, helpless girl hiding in the closet from her nut job of a husband."

An overhead light flickers on and temporarily blinds me. I peel my eyelids back slowly, trying to adjust to the dramatic light change. Although my eyes were closed, the shift in light stings my eyes.

"What the fuck, Regina!"

I glance up and take in Harrison above me. He rips a mask off his face—probably how he was able to see me in the dark. Clad in a pair of black dress slacks, his chest is bare. Sweat rolls down his flat, undefined chest as he aims his rage toward the woman standing fifteen or twenty feet from us.

"Cops on the radio said they're heading here. You need to wrap this shit up." She waves a manicured finger at me on the floor. "Don't care what you do with her. Just finish it."

As quickly as the light flipped on, the woman spins on her red-soled heels and exits the room.

"Fuck!" Harrison grunts above me and fists his hair.

I glance around the space while Harrison paces three steps one way, then backtracks. Several feet in front of me, sheets of plywood are nailed against what I assume are windows or doors. When I shift my eyes to the ceiling, I spot three sets of garage door rails. Wide enough apart to be for a two-car-sized garage door.

Slowly, I tip my head back and follow the lines of my arms. When I reach my wrists, I take in the thick, red-stained rope. It stretches a few feet past my wrists and attaches to a post with gears and more rope wrapped in layers near the bottom. Shifting my eyes down in the direction of my feet, I notice a replica of the same.

Has he done this before? Or did Harrison create this medieval-like torture device with me in mind?

Harrison throws the mask across the garage. Glass shatters when it strikes the intended target. He looks down at me and his pupils dilate so wide the brown of his irises is swallowed in black. My confidence from minutes ago hides in the sheltered corner of my mind.

Because this version of Harrison... it terrifies the hell out of me.

And he knows it.

The corners of his lips perk up a millimeter per second. He squats down on his haunches in front of me and plants his palms on the concrete as he invades every ounce of my personal space. He presses his nose to the base of my throat and inhales deeply. Then he licks his way up my neck onto my cheek and over my temple.

"Still so fucking sweet."

He rocks back on his heels. For a moment, I think he is going to get up and leave. Honestly, if he left me here and the cops rescued me, I wouldn't give a damn. At least I would be safe. But Harrison never does what I expect. Today will be no exception.

Instead, he unfastens my slacks and yanks them down my legs. Followed by my panties. The surge of pain in my limbs is the least of my worries and I ignore it as I fight against the binds. He stands and reaches in his back pocket. As soon as the light glimmers off the steel, I scream at the top of my lungs.

Even after four years with Liz, there is a reason why we have sex in the dark more times than not. A reason why I never trim or shave off my pubic hair. The scars. Liz wouldn't judge or say anything derogatory regarding scars on my body. That's not the type of person she is. Yet another reason to love her. But exposing the physical scars of my past still haunts every ounce of me. Bathing suits and tanning and beaches are *not* my friends.

Harrison flips the blade of the knife out. A knife gifted to him by my father on our wedding day. Engraved with our initials and wedding date. It is more than *just a knife*. It is the weapon which has marred my breasts, stomach, and pubic bones. His surgical precision sliced my skin, small enough to give him pleasure, deliver me pain, and ensure no one would easily see the evil lines. Not unless they were specifically searching them out.

"Noooo!" I scream at the top of my lungs.

Harrison sweeps his leg back, and swings forward in full force, connecting with my pelvis. *Crunch.* Pain ripples in my lower abdomen. "Shut the fuck up, you stupid whore!" He rears his fist back and smashes it against my cheek. A crackle pounds in my skull as it smacks against the concrete.

Pain doesn't even remotely describe the horrific sensation ricocheting from every muscle fiber and shattered bone in my body. My consciousness flickers in and out. On the verge of blacking out, Harrison rotates the blade in his hand with an ominous glint in his eyes.

As he brings the blade to my skin—the blade that has *only* sliced my skin—the door flies open. Several sets of feet patter over the concrete before coming to a stop.

"Put the knife down, Mr. Deats," a man screams from somewhere behind me.

Above me, Harrison throws his head back and laughs. The menacing sound bounces off the concrete floor and walls. He glances over his shoulder at the man who screamed at him and shakes his head. Lifting his hands up to the sides of his face in surrender, he still holds the knife in his palm.

"Put the knife down," the man shouts again.

"Sure thing, officer."

Harrison turns back to face me and slowly lowers his hands. When his hands hover a foot above the floor, he locks eyes with me and smirks. Before I realize what he has done, fire blazes beneath my left lung and eats every atom in my body.

Loud pops reverberate in the empty space and hot liquid sprays across my face as Harrison falls to the floor in front of me. His static brown eyes wide open and staring at me. His lips perked up at the corners in pleasure.

Feet clap against the floor nearby. Bodies swarm me and ask question after question. But I don't hear a single word. I don't see a single thing they do.

All I see is darkness. All I hear is white noise. All I feel is an inferno beneath my ribcage before the world disappears from view.

CHRISTY AND RICK stand outside an ostentatious house beside me. Red and blue lights take turns flashing and illuminating the darkened structure.

Ten minutes ago, more than a dozen officers decked out in swat gear stormed the house. Shields raised. Guns cocked and aimed forward. Batons and tasers unlatched and at the ready.

Five minutes ago, a gunshot ripped through the air.

A minute later, two gurneys scurried past us into the house, followed by a forensics team.

Now, I pace back and forth in front of Christy and Rick, biting my nails—a habit I always deemed disgusting but cannot stop with the current events. None of the cops who entered the house has exited yet. I rip my fingers away from my mouth and ball them into fists at my side in an effort to quit biting them.

"What the hell is taking them so long? Would it kill one of them to come out here and update us?"

Rick walks up to me and halts my pacing. He plants his hands on my shoulders and stares at me. "If they don't come out soon, I'll go in there. Okay?"

I lock gazes with him and see the promise etched in his eyes. He hauls me into his chest, and I nod against his warmth. The second he releases me, an EMT wheels a gurney with a zipped black bag out the door.

"Oh, god," I whisper. Rick drags me back to his chest and constricts me in his arms. "No," I garble out. The EMT pushes past us as a chill swallows me whole.

"It's not her," Rick says. "Not her."

A second later, the other gurney rolls out the door with Tiffany laying on the surface. Not in a body bag. Rick drops his arms and I run to her side.

Flat on the stretcher, Tiffany is strapped to a backboard on the padding. Her neck locked in a hard, plastic brace. One of her cheeks is swollen, the skin a light purple. A blanket covers the rest of her body.

"Is she okay?" I ask one of the paramedics. The EMT cocks a brow at me. "She's my fiancée."

She nods and speaks up. "We'll know more once we get to the hospital. As of now, we believe she has a broken pelvis and cheekbone. Not sure about other bones. She also has a stab wound below her ribcage. We've lessened the bleeding, but she has lost a lot of blood."

When they reach the back of the ambulance, the EMT presses something on the legs of the gurney and the legs collapse as it rolls into the miniature, mobile hospital.

"Can I ride with you?"

The paramedic nods and I hop inside. Christy runs up to the doors before they shut them. "We'll follow you." Then the doors slam shut and someone taps on the outside.

Sirens blast around us as the ambulance speeds down the road. I steer clear of the paramedics as they insert an IV in the inside of Tiffany's elbow. The EMT near her head slides the blanket down her chest and slaps sticky electrodes to her bare flesh. Attaching wires to the metal tips of the pads, the EMT taps a button and the sound of Tiffany's heartbeat erupts in the ambulance.

Thump-thump. Thump-thump. Thump-thump.

The rhythm is slow, but I hear every beat. I glance up at the monitor and read the screen. Fifty-four beats per minute. Not great, but not horrible. My eyes flit over to her blood pressure. Eighty-six over sixty. Not so great.

The paramedic notices my locked gaze. "Don't let the numbers worry you. Yes, they're low. But she lost a lot of blood. Her body is in protection mode. As long as her body doesn't reject blood, she should recover."

I reach forward and clasp Tiffany's fingers in my hands. Glancing down at her arm, I spy a thick band of missing skin at her wrist. I lean down and kiss her fingers as a tear escapes my eye and lands on her skin.

"Baby, I'm so sorry this happened to you. Sorry I couldn't get to you sooner. Sorry I ran late." My tears fall harder. "But it's over now. He will never hurt you again. Never."

As I lift my head, the ambulance slows. Steering into the emergency bay of the hospital, the back doors fly open and I scurry out of the way as the paramedics wheel Tiffany inside. I follow behind them and try to keep up, but it's no use. Within seconds, Tiffany vanishes from sight.

A woman in scrubs steps up to me. "Did you just come in with the ambulance?"

"Yes. Tiffany Page."

She wraps an arm around my shoulders and guides me to a waiting area. "Sit here a moment, sweetie. I'll be back as soon as we have more information. What's your name?"

"Liz Warren. Thank you" —I read her hospital badge— "Destiny."

Nurse Destiny walks away and I stare at the white hospital walls. When I finally breathe, the weird hospital odor infiltrates my nostrils. An odd mix of disinfectant and sweat and something metallic has me scrunching up my nose and holding my breath.

Tiffany is here. Safe. And she will recover.

Doctors and nurses zip past the waiting room. Some with tablets, others with gowns or sheets or carts. I zone out as Christy and Rick rush in and sit beside me. Christy hugs me close and tells me Tiffany will be fine. Stroking my hair, Christy whispers how incredibly strong Tiffany is and how this will be her final battle.

In the frigid, sterile walls of the hospital, I close my eyes and melt into my best friend. I believe every word she whispers in my ear. And I pray to every divine power to make my girl whole again. Because there is no way in hell I can survive without her.

"Argh..." A groan stirs me from my sleep. "Lizzie," Tiffany whispers, her voice like sandpaper.

I bolt out of the worn recliner, blanket falling to the floor, and rush to Tiffany's side. "Baby, don't move. Let me get a nurse." I press a kiss to her forehead and grab my phone before heading out to the nurse's station. "We need someone in Tiffany Page's room. She just woke up."

Before the nurse responds, I dash back to her room and send a text to the group message we all formed after Tiffany was admitted. As I walk in the room, Tiffany attempts to scoot herself to an upright position. I run to her side and press the button on the side of her bed to adjust the back. Helping her lean forward, I slip another pillow behind her head.

"Thank you," she says, working to catch her breath.

"Someone will be here in a minute. Are you thirsty?"

She nods, then furrows her brows. I pour her a cup of water and add a straw. As she brings the straw to her lips, a nurse walks in the door.

"Small sips, Ms. Page." He walks to the side of her bed, checks her IV line, then her vitals. "On a scale of one to ten, what is your pain level?" he asks.

Tiffany hands me the cup. She shifts to face him better and winces. "Maybe a seven or eight. But I've been worse."

He gives her a brief, sad smile. "We've paged Dr. Landers. She should be here shortly." Pointing to the cup I set on the rolling table, he reminds us, "Small sips." Then he leaves.

When I face Tiffany, she glances away and stares down at our joined hands. A tear bubbles at the corner of her eyes before it breaks free and spills down the side of her face. She drops her chin and her hair falls forward.

I give her fingers a gentle squeeze. "Hey." She peeks up through her fiery locks. "Look at me, Tiffany." She swipes at her nose and sniffles before meeting my gaze. "Don't hide from me, okay?"

For a beat, she glances off to the side. Outside, street and building lights illuminate the inky sky. "What day is it?"

This was one question I worried over while Tiffany laid unconscious in the hospital. The first few days weren't worrisome. But when it surpassed a week, my feelings on the whole situation changed. The doctors told me the coma would be temporary. Her body needed to heal, and this was the best way. Especially after multiple surgeries.

I don't want to freak her out, but I refuse to lie to her. Lies won't solve anything. She will eventually know, regardless.

"It's Thursday." I pause and take a deep breath, cringing internally. "July thirtieth."

Tiffany jerks back and winces again. She rubs her index fingers over her ears. "Did you just say J-July?"

I press my lips to her forehead, leaving them there for a moment before pulling away. The indigo bruise that painted her cheek for three weeks a distant memory. The swelling no longer visible. A thin, two-inch scar now mars the skin over her left zygomatic arch. Most people would never see it, but we will. Tiffany always will.

Beneath the blanket on her lap and belly, she has three more scars. One the width of the blade that stabbed the flesh beneath her ribcage. The other two on the anterior and posterior of her pelvis near the iliac crest and iliac spine. Thankfully, none of her bones required much other than minor repair. The fact she was unconscious for so long helped aid her recovery.

"Yeah, baby. July."

"Oh my, god. I've been in the hospital for over two months." Tiffany's eyes widen as her chest rises and falls in rapid succession. The heart rate monitor beeps louder beside me. As much as I want to tell her to calm down, I don't. "What about Jensen? Is he okay?"

As I open my mouth to answer her, Dr. Landers walks into the room. "Dr. Page, glad to see you're awake." She glances at the monitor, then eyes us. "Everything okay?"

I nod. "Yeah. Just told her the date."

"Ah, I see. No need to worry, Dr. Page. Your body needed the time to recover. I promise everything has been running like a well-oiled machine while you slept." Dr. Landers glances to me and continues. "Your fiancée is an amazing woman. Not only has she worked from your bedside, she also took care of things for you at Lewis House."

Tiffany shifts her glassy, ice blues to me. I gently cup her cheek. "No tears, baby. We've had more than our share."

She sniffles. "What if they're happy tears?"

I shrug. "Guess happy tears are okay. But you may want to hold off a little longer." Tiffany's forehead bunches. "You'll see."

As Dr. Landers explains her injuries and the surgeries performed to correct them, I zone out. Most of this is common knowledge to me. Information I have deciphered time and again, thanks to Google. Tiffany asks Dr. Landers questions regarding physical therapy and anything she needs to be mindful of going forward. Over the last six weeks, a physical therapy assistant has visited Tiffany's room. She performed a routine with Tiffany's arms and legs to help prevent muscle atrophy and keep her joints mobile.

When Dr. Landers leaves, Tiffany sags into the pillows and sucks in a deep breath. I want to tell her all the things she has missed while she slept, but I don't want to overwhelm her. I don't want to upset or make her feel guilty. Missing so much time has to be disorienting and confusing.

Watching her lay in the bed, out cold, for weeks was beyond challenging for me. The first few days were touch and go. Doctors and nurses came and went so often it was impossible to sleep, even if my mind would let me. After the second week, I managed to coerce Hammond into letting me work from Tiffany's hospital bedside. It was either that or I was quitting.

Culinary school shifted to the back burner, temporarily. When Tiffany is physically and mentally ready to move forward, I will look into it again. But until the day arrives, I won't consider it. Tiffany matters more.

A knock raps against the open doorframe. I glance up and spot Christy. "You up for visitors?"

Tiffany smiles. "Yes." More happy tears well in her eyes.

Christy and Rick step in the room and step up to the opposite side of the bed. Christy winks at me.

"Baby, I'm grabbing a drink. Be right back."

Tiffany nods as Christy rambles on about all the world events that have happened since May. I walk out of the room and round the corner two rooms down. Sitting in the chair in the hall is the smiling face I have been waiting to see. Rising from the chair, we walk back to the room together in silence.

Stopping just before the doorframe, I ask, "You ready?"

"Yeah."

We step inside and walk around the backside of Christy and Rick. Tiffany stops talking the instant her eyes land on Jensen. Her eyes leak uncontrollably as she clutches at her chest. He steps up to the bedside opposite Christy and Rick and bends over, hugging Tiffany tight to his chest.

"Hi, Mom," he whispers in her ear. Tiffany sobs louder and tugs him harder. "So happy you're awake. I missed you."

Until this very moment, I have never witnessed Tiffany this emotional. Over the last four—almost five—years, Tiffany and I have experienced so much together. From our instant attraction to falling in love. Normal days and far-beyond-normal days. Lust and frustration. But with each and every one of those experiences, not a single one of them matches this moment. The moment Jensen truly embraces Tiffany for the first time and calls her Mom.

Tears run torrents down her face and tell me there is more to the story. A story she will tell me in time. When Tiffany is ready, she will share another one of her skeletons. And until said day arrives, I will embrace her wholeheartedly.

My beloved. My life.

THIRTY-ONE

TIFFANY

Two Months Later

A KNOCK RAPS on the door. "Mom, can I come in?"

"Yeah, J. I'm dressed."

Jensen walks into the room and smiles when he sees me. "You're so pretty. Are you nervous?" He steps closer, wraps his arms around me, and hugs me with a level of tenderness I never thought I'd have in my life.

I brush my palms down my thighs and sigh as the supple ridges graze my fingertips. "Thanks, J. Yes and no." Stepping over to the long mirror, I shift my chin left and right, examining my brows and eye shadow. Grabbing the palette and brush on the side table next to the mirror, I neatly paint the deep rouge on my lips. When both lips are done, I press them together and pop my lips apart.

"What do you mean?" Jensen asks.

Setting the makeup back on the table, I step up to him and take both his hands in mine. "J, one day you'll meet someone. A girl, or guy, who makes your heart skip a beat. Makes you breathe faster." I pause and smile as warmth floods my chest. "Who you never want to stop kissing and… more." A blush blooms over Jensen's cheeks and neck. "When you meet this person, you will understand why I'm not nervous about today. The only thing making me nervous is the crowd."

Jensen squeezes my hands. "Well, good thing I'm here then. I'll help with the crowd."

He envelops me in his arms again. "Thanks, J. Go check on Liz, then get ready." Jensen winks and leaves the room.

As soon as I'm alone, I take a deep breath and stare at myself in the mirror. The soft champagne tulle and white lace press gracefully against my curves. The flailing skirt dances a quarter-inch off the floor. Instead of a veil, I opted for a tiara over my minimally styled locks.

The word princess comes to mind when I study myself in the reflective glass.

If someone would have called me princess prior to the finale with Harrison, I would have cringed. Crumpled into a human ball. Now, I embrace the word. Use it as a tool to empower myself. To remember the time when I conquered my demons.

Since awaking from my coma two months ago, a lot has changed.

The first change—and the most challenging—was making peace with my past. Not necessarily with Harrison and the horrible things he did to me. Some deeds can never be forgiven, but I can make peace with them. If not for Harrison and the horrendous way he treated me, I may have never fled Florida. I may have never met Liz.

Everything happens for a reason. The good and the bad. It took several years to discover the good result of being with Harrison, but I did.

Liz is my prize.

The second change was learning how to bare all my skeletons. Change two was more difficult than the first. Because I had to confess a secret not a soul had heard. A secret I kept hidden to protect myself.

Last month, I sat Liz down and spilled it all. After one of my regular counseling sessions, it was time. I told Liz everything. About all the horrible things Harrison did to me. How I used to hide in the bedroom closet with a photo of me and my grandparents, praying for a miracle. And even the miscarriage I had after Harrison beat me to within an inch of my life.

On that specific night, I sat on the toilet and bled into the bowl, tears spilling down my cheeks. If I were in any other relationship, I would have gone to a doctor. Would have sought help. Instead, I sat alone in the bathroom as my unborn child passed away. I cried for the child I would never know. And I cried for the child who would never experience pain and hatred at the hands of Harrison Deats.

After I lost the baby, that was the night I planned my escape. The night I said no more. The night I discovered true strength.

The third change was agreeing to therapy sessions twice per week for the foreseeable future. It won't be forever, but we will play it by ear. For now, we have many topics of discussion. One session is just for me, the other is joint for me and Liz. It was one of the best decisions we have made together. And my heart bears less weight now that she knows every aspect of my life.

Another knock raps on the door. "Come in," I say.

"It's time, baby girl."

"'Kay, Daddy."

My father walks into the room, and a warmth spreads through my chest. After I fled Florida, I lost contact with my parents. Scared to call them, in fear they would tell Harrison where I was, I opted to detach from everyone in my family.

While in my coma, Liz reached out to them. Told them everything which transpired with Harrison. Days after I woke up, we reunited and shared mountains of tears. My parents may have been an odd duo. Prim and proper mom. Somewhat clinical dad. But they love me in their own way. And I love them too. Until they walked into my hospital room, I had no clue how much I truly missed them.

After everything, the most valuable lesson I learned was to not let anything slip out of my reach. To not take life for granted. To live for today. Which brings us to now.

My wedding.

Moving our wedding up six months wasn't as challenging as most would think. We had to pay a little more, but sealing our hearts together forever is worth every penny.

Life is too short. True love only strikes once.

Pushing off our ceremony to the "perfect date" was no longer desirable. Liz and I were more than ready to make everything official. There was no need for all the pomp and circumstance. Everyone we loved is here. Family we haven't seen in years. Friends near and dear to our hearts. Those who matter.

Absolute perfection.

The music shifts and Dad juts his elbow in my direction. I slip my arm in his and the tall double doors swing open. Hundreds of red rose petals litter the pale oak floor and guide us down the carpeted aisle. *Right foot. Left foot. Right foot. Left foot.* We round the wall of family and friends, and I halt with a gasp.

Less than a hundred feet away, Liz stands in front of an archway in her bold, black dress. Her long, black locks curled from the shoulders down. The gorgeous tulle pops against her light brown skin. But, for added effect, she decorated her arms and exposed cleavage in a subtle shimmer.

"One foot in front the other, baby girl," Dad says with a light chuckle.

Each step Dad and I take, everything around me disappears. The only two people in the room are Liz and me. The music fades. Oohs and aahs slip away. Three more steps. I drop Dad's arm and take Liz's hand.

Tears blur my vision, but Liz is still the most magnificent person I have ever seen. Ever known. Her heart and soul resonate with mine. When I can't stand tall, she loops her arm in mine and hoists me higher. She makes me a better version of myself. Shows me how beautiful the world can be as long as we are together.

And because of Liz, I finally know love. Experience it every single day. In her simple touches. The way her lips brush against mine. How she holds me just long enough… and then a little longer.

The minister gives us the opportunity to say our own vows, signaling to Liz first.

Liz slips a small piece of paper out from the tulle near her breast and I laugh. She simply shrugs as she unfolds the paper.

"Tiffany, since the first day I laid eyes on you in that swanky wing shack—" Liz pauses as Sarah and Christy snicker in the crowd "—I knew we were destined to be more than just a fling. Something about the way you looked deep into my eyes lit me on fire. No one has ever made me feel alive the way you do. You make every breath and heartbeat worth it. In five years, you have managed to give me more love than I expected to have in a lifetime. Not just your love, but also Jensen's." Both of us glance over at the young man who has made our world a million times better. "Every part of you makes every part of me glow. Tiffany, you're my North star, lighting my way in the darkness. And I am beyond proud to call you my wife. To tell the world you belong to me. Forever."

Liz folds the paper into quarters and tucks it back in her dress. Laughing, I swipe the tears trailing down my cheeks. Digging into the side of my bouquet, I retrieve my vows and make a face at Liz. She sticks her tongue out and I laugh.

Taking a deep breath, I unfold my paper and drop my gaze. The black ink blurs as tears pool in my eyes. I wave the paper in front of my face. "How am I supposed to read this if I can't see?" I joke.

Liz reaches forward and rests her hand on my forearm. "Just speak from your heart, baby." I nod and take another deep breath.

Locking eyes with the stunning woman in front of me, I tuck the paper back in my flowers. Liz is right. I don't need to read my own scripted words. All I need is to speak my truth.

"Liz, I owe you everything. Giving you my heart seems like an unfair trade. After everything you have given me, I owe you several lifetimes of love. If not for you, my heart wouldn't be as whole as it is right now. Because of you, I have a family again. I am surrounded by love—more than I ever imagined possible. If we hadn't met, I'd probably still be slinging wings in Georgia." Liz laughs and I join in as I wipe tears from my cheeks. "But in all seriousness, no one has given me so many gifts. Jensen. My parents. The rest of my family, who I never thought I'd see again. Liz, you gave them all to me. And I will spend the rest of our lives loving you for that. But most of all, the best gift you gave me was… me. Someone I thought, at one point, I'd never know again. Thank you. For encouraging me. For pushing me to be stronger. For loving me. I love you. Forever."

I reach out and swipe the tears off Liz's cheeks. Honestly,

there hasn't been many occasions where I have witnessed Liz cry. She is a pillar of strength. *My* pillar of strength. If not for this astonishing woman, there is no telling where I would be right now.

Fate is an interesting creature. Through the ugly and astounding, fate weaves us down the path we are meant to travel. For better or worse, our destiny is written in stone. And my destiny stands a foot in front of me, itching to kiss me.

My beloved. I will never take her devotion for granted. And I will love her until my last breath. Forever.

EPILOGUE

LIZ

Three Years Later

"Did you grab the gift?" I shout across the house.

"Already in the car. Get your ass out here," Tiffany throws back at me.

I trade out my shirt for a fresher option, sling it over my head, and walk out to the living room. On the couch, Jensen leans into Samantha and tickles her sides. She swats at him while laughing nonstop. The way they smile at each other reminds me a little of me and Tiffany.

Shortly after Jensen was discharged from Lewis House, he and Samantha started talking more. They had formed a bond in Lewis House and Tiffany didn't want to discourage it. It may not have ever developed into anything more than a friendship, but I had a feeling it would evolve. And it did.

The first year after Jensen and Samantha left Lewis House, they kept in touch as friends. At that point in their life, they each had several battles to conquer. As soon as they won those battles, we knew they would be strong enough to handle a more intensive relationship with each other. And we didn't hide our reasoning from Jensen. We had an open door, full honesty policy in our house. As difficult as it is at times, it just works better in the long run.

After our first year together, Jensen sat down with me and Tiffany and asked for permission to date Samantha. The gesture was one of the sweetest things ever. His blush never subsided as he constantly fumbled over his words.

"You two ready?" I ask, ruffling Jensen's sun-bleached locks. He kept his hair a little longer now. It reminded me of a skater and suited his personality.

"Yeah, Ma. I think Mom is in the kitchen grabbing the cake."

"Shit." Jensen laughs as I make a beeline for the kitchen. I catch Tiffany as she peeks in the reusable tote on the counter. "Hey, get out of there."

"Damnit," Tiffany mutters as she releases the edge of the bag.

A few months after Tiffany and I got married, I officially quit my job at Hammond and started culinary school. The classes were intense and jam-packed with knowledge I never considered in the world of food. I loved every second of school—it drove my passion for being in the kitchen to an all-new high. Shortly after graduation, I tinkered with my own catering business. Needless to say, the tinkering paid off and business is booming. Expansion is currently in the works and we're hiring additional staff as we speak.

"Don't think I don't know your distraction techniques. Grab the gifts and get the kids in the car. Shoo."

Tiffany mumbles as she exits the kitchen. I snatch the cupcakes off the counter and walk out to the living room. We all file out of the house and hop in Tiffany's tank-sized SUV. As we drive through the city, I listen to the whispered laughter in the backseat.

Jensen hasn't mentioned the topic, but I imagine him taking his and Samantha's relationship to the next level soon. A year and a half of friendship, followed by two years of dating. They smile at each other as if no one else exists. For both their hearts' sake, I hope it stays that way. Watching their love bloom is the most beautiful thing. So pure and uplifting.

Half an hour later, we park on the street and meander past the long line of cars to Christy and Rick's house. We walk in the door and exchange hugs with some of our favorite people. Christy, Rick. Ella, and Thomas. Sarah, Jackson, and their three-and-a-half-year-old daughter, Alexandria. Judy and Kenda. Pete and Mark. And Chloe somehow managed to drag her husband, Stanton, as well. Being with everyone here, I feel home.

Music pours through the speakers in the living room as I head to the kitchen with Christy. When I set the bag on the counter, I scan the room and make sure no one else followed us before I take out the cupcakes.

Christy shrieks. "Yes! I knew it."

"Shh." I wave a hand in front of her face. "No one else knows yet. So shut it, bitch."

"Hey, only I get to say that. Bitch." Christy giggles.

We stash the cupcakes and join everyone else in the living room. I mingle throughout the room, eventually chatting with everyone before the big announcement. Christy lowers the music and all eyes flick her way.

"Alright, everyone. Announcement time. Jackson. Sarah. Alexandria. Come sit here." Christy guides them to a trio of chairs she set up in the center of the room. "Don't move. Be right back."

Christy and I scamper off to the kitchen and grab the cupcakes. Walking back to the living room, Christy bounces beside me. She may never have wanted to become a mother, but she loves being an auntie. And she can't wait to become an auntie again.

Sarah sits at one end of the seating. Christy and I sidle up beside her, each of us setting a hand on our best friend's shoulders.

"Thanks for coming today, everyone," Christy says. "This lady right here" —Christy obnoxiously points at Sarah— "has brought every single one of us together. I wouldn't have the friendships I do today, if not for her. And today, we get to celebrate her. Her and Jackson's next family addition. Is everyone ready for the big reveal?"

In the chair beside Jackson, Alexandria bounces up and down with her hands clapping vigorously. "Me, me, me."

We all laugh. I unlock the white, non-transparent lid on the cupcakes and slowly lift it up. Sarah slaps a hand to her mouth and grabs Jackson's arm.

"It's a boy," I announce.

"Baby Anderson," Sarah croons as she rubs her belly. "Anderson William Ember."

I stare at my best friend as everyone crowds around her and Jackson, congratulating them on their upcoming little boy.

Christy is right. Sarah is the reason we all sit here, together, today. If not for my best friend, I wouldn't have this amazing family. Sarah is the bond between us all.

Through our friendship, I met Tiffany. Because of some distorted devotion, she and Jackson moved to California. Soon, Christy and I followed in her wake. Neither of us able to imagine our lives without her nearby. Out here in California, Christy and Rick rediscovered their undying devotion for each other. They also found new love in Ella and Thomas. A commitment which surpasses and triumphs traditional relationships.

And although our journey in California started off a little rocky, Tiffany and I have unearthed the most beloved devotion of them all. A bond which stands the test of time. A love I thank the gods for with each breath I take.

A love which transcends time. I anticipate spending the rest of my life in her heart. Forever and ever.

BELOVED DEVOTION PLAYLIST

Here are some of the songs from the *Beloved Devotion* playlist. You can listen to the entire playlist on Spotify!

Issues | Julia Michaels
Not About Angels | Birdy
Where's My Love | SYML
Like Real People Do | Hozier
You Are My Sunshine | The Civil Wars
I Can't Breathe | Bea Miller
Life Support | Sam Smith
Sorry | Chief.

ACKNOWLEDGMENTS

Thank you to my family and friends who continually encourage me to write. For putting up with my craziness and odd hours and constant busyness. Without your love and support, I wouldn't push myself as hard.

Thank you to Ellie McLove and Rosa Sharon at My Brother's Editor. You ladies always polish my manuscript, fix my irrational punctuation, and enlighten me with your wisdom. Your feedback is invaluable and I cannot express enough thanks for all you do.

Thank you to my author friends and fellow Inkers. For your advice and encouragement and opinions and expertise. I love that we support each other and thrive more when we lift each other up. This journey isn't done alone and I am so thankful to all of you for any nuggets of wisdom and advice you share.

Thank you to every person who picks up this book and reads it. Without readers, there would be no books. I am honored you have taken a chance on me and are reading my words. There are no words to express how deeply moved I am by this. I remain humble and bow to you with gratitude.

THANK YOU

Thank you so much for reading the ***Devotion Series Novels***. If you wouldn't mind taking a moment to leave a review on the retailer site where you made your purchase, Goodreads and/or BookBub, it would mean the world to me.

Reviews help other readers find and enjoy the book as well.

Much love,
 Persephone

CONNECT WITH PERSEPHONE

<u>Connect with Persephone</u>
www.persephoneautumn.com

<u>Subscribe to Persephone's newsletter</u>
www.persephoneautumn.com/newsletter

<u>Join Persephone's reader's group</u>
Persephone's Playground

<u>Follow Persephone online</u>

instagram.com/persephoneautumn

facebook.com/persephoneautumnwrites

tiktok.com/@persephoneautumn

bookbub.com/authors/persephone-autumn

goodreads.com/persephoneautumn

amazon.com/author/persephoneautumn

pinterest.com/persephoneautumn

x.com/PersephoneAutum

MORE BY PERSEPHONE

The Click Duet
High school sweethearts torn apart. When fate gives them a
second chance, one doesn't trust they won't be hurt again.
Through the Lens (Click Duet #1) and Time Exposure (Click
Duet #2) is an angsty, second chance, friends to lovers
romance with all the feels.

The Inked Duet
A man with a broken heart and a woman scared to put herself
out there. Love is never easy. Sometimes love rips you apart.
Fine Line (Inked Duet #1) and Love Buzz (Inked Duet #2) is a
second chance at love, single parent romance with a pinch of
angst and dash of suspense.

The Insomniac Duet
He was her high school bully. She was the outcast that
secretly crushed on him. More than ten years later, he's her
boss, completely oblivious to their shared past, and wants no
one but her. More importantly, he doesn't understand her
animosity toward him.

The Artist Duet
A tortured hero with the biggest heart and a charismatic
heroine with the patience of a saint. Previous heartache has
him fighting his desire to be more than friends with her. But

she is everywhere, and he can't help but give in. The Artist Duet is an angsty, friends to lovers slow burn.

Sweet Tooth

Two people with the same rule. No dating. What happens when they bend the rules? A steamy standalone romance with a trigger warning.

Transcendental

A musician in search of his muse and a woman grieving the loss of her husband. Two weeks at an exclusive retreat and their connection rivals all others. Until she leaves early without notice. But he refuses to give up until he finds her again.

Depths Awakened

A small town romance which captivates you from the start. Mags and Geoff are two broken souls who have sworn off love. Vowed to never lose anyone else. But their undeniable attraction brings them together and refuses to let go.

Ink Veins

Persephone Autumn's debut poetry collection, Ink Veins, explores topics of depression, love, and self-discovery with a raw, unfiltered voice.

Broken Metronome

When the music of the heart dies…
Broken Metronome is an angsty poetry collection full of heartache and the possibility of what may have been.

ABOUT THE AUTHOR

Persephone Autumn lives in Florida with her wife, crazy dog, and two lover-boy cats. A proud mom with a cuckoo grand-pup. An ethnic food enthusiast who has fun discovering ways to veganize her favorite non-vegan foods. If given the opportunity, she would intentionally get lost in nature.

For years, Persephone did some form of writing; mostly journaling or poetry. After pairing her poetry with images and posting them online, she began the journey of writing her first novel.

She mainly writes romance, but on occasion dips her toes in other works. Look for her poetry publications, and a psychological horror under P. Autumn.